I0831435

THE SUMMONING OF MAGES

THE SAINT ELIAS UNIVERSITY SERIES

NADIA TATE

BLUE PROSPECT PRESS

Cover art and design by Chloe Hughes

Map art by Virginia Allyn

Developmental and line edits by Danielle Ellison

Copyedits by Jessica McKelden

Author Photograph by Tarisha Tillery

Published by Blue Prospect Press

Cataloging-in-Publication Data is on file with the Library of Congress

Printed and bound in the United States of America

First Edition

To all the wise, willful, wonderful women in our lives

CONTENT WARNING

This book contains mature themes, including explicit sexual content, strong language, and depictions of violence. It may not be suitable for all audiences. Reader discretion is advised.

Saint Elias
University
Alterion
Incantor
Volare
Belltower
Sybil
Muruari
Circen
Professor's Quarters
Dining
Dorms
Ruzo Field
Arcane
Library
History
Classes
Alchemy
Administration
Cavern Entrance
Fjordhaven Lodge
Sled Dogs
Tunnel Entrance
Town Square
Aviary
Eagles Ridge

CHAPTER 1

Hazel

Hazel sat at the head of the table in her family's log cabin, her brother on one side, her father on the other. The air smelled of buttercream frosting. Light from the flames cast eerie shadows upon their faces as they sang in the dim room. The empty chair in front of her stole the attention from this happy moment, but she willed herself to skim over the hole her mother had left. Four years had passed and Hazel still detected the missing voice from the familiar chorus.

"Blow out the candles, Hazy," said her brother, Forrest.

Hazel took in a deep breath and closed her eyes, focusing on her countless wishes, but they all slipped away like water between her fingers, save one: her mother. She wanted to see her mother, despite her abandoning them. The need for answers outweighed the hurt and anger. So when she opened her eyes, she let the questions of her mother hang there as she blew out the eighteen candles before her.

Instantly, pitch black consumed them.

No longer could she see the cake, her brother, or her father. She used to call out for them, but she'd learned long ago it did no good. She was dreaming—again—and simply had to wait for the dream to continue.

The room brightened slowly, like the coming of dawn, revealing a new room. Soft light spilled over the ornate ebony desk in front of her, casting shadows across the piles of books stacked high atop it. Hazel rose from her seat and walked toward the shelves directly in front of her. She'd explored the strange library many times, but the space never lost its sense of mystery.

Tightly packed shelves towered above her, full of ancient tomes in muted browns, deep forest greens, and wine-dark reds, their colors reminding her of autumn leaves. Centuries of use had cracked and frayed many of the book spines. Faded gold lettering hinted at titles she'd grown to recognize, though she'd never read them. The surrounding air was dense with old magic. Denser than any she'd ever sensed before.

Hazel approached the end of the aisle, and her heart raced. She knew what came next.

Her mother appeared at the end of the third row, her familiar hazel eyes locked on Hazel. Her mother's long, obsidian hair curled slightly at the ends, in a way Hazel had never noticed as a child. She wondered if it would still feel like silk between her fingers. She longed to reach out and touch it once more, but her mother moved down the aisle to another row. Hazel followed, like she always did.

When she turned at the end of the row, the room brightened in the light of floor-to-ceiling stained-glass windows. Her mother's retreating form appeared to glow, resplendent in the greens, yellows, reds, and blues emitted from the colorful panes before her. The windows always gave Hazel pause.

She knew if she walked closer, she'd be able to see armored battalions of magic users locked in battle upon the numerous panes, some warriors with wands raised while others conjured elements with their minds. If she moved close enough to peer out the window, she'd see the hazy outline of a campus built in stone below.

"Hazel."

Tears pricked Hazel's eyes at the sound of her mother's youthful voice. How long had it been since she'd heard it?

"Come, you have important things to learn here at Saint Elias," her mother said as she beckoned with an outstretched hand.

When Hazel drew near, her mother smiled at her, perfectly at ease, as if she hadn't left a gaping hole in Hazel's life. Hazel's knees shook with the warring emotions inside her—fear that her mother would bolt if Hazel ran to her and embraced her like she wanted to, and anger that her mother had ever left in the first place.

Before Hazel could grasp her offered hand, her mother disappeared. Not in a blink, but in windblown smoke.

Hazel jolted upright in her bed at the sound of her alarm. The emptiness of her bedroom overwhelmed her and Hazel blinked back tears she refused to let fall.

Would she ever have the chance to see her mother again? It was one of the three recurring dreams she'd been having since her birthday a few months ago. Eighteen promised freedom, but the absence of her mother and a lack of a SEU summons left her feeling more imprisoned.

But that could all change soon. It was Summoning Day! The thought filled her with adrenaline. Each year, the prestigious Saint Elias University summoned mages from all over the world to take its entrance examination for freshman positions. When her summons inevitably arrived, everything would change.

Hazel dressed quickly and slipped out the back door. Her family's red barn waited in the far corner of the acre their home sat on, right next to the cornfields. She started out by feeding the horses, pigs, and chickens, then moved on to picking the ripe vegetables from their personal garden before collecting eggs from the henhouse. The chores added up quickly, and before she knew it, the sun was high overhead. If she could get the stall mucked, she could spend the afternoon waiting on her summons in peace.

Unfortunately, Garth, her large Emden goose, had other plans.

He insisted on being fed twice the amount the veterinarian had recommended.

The large white goose honked to demand oats from Hazel, but she ignored him and continued to shovel fresh hay into a stall. Onyx wisps of long hair escaped her clip as she worked, sticking to the sweat gleaming on her forehead. Her ivory complexion was usually fair, but was currently a rosy red thanks to the manual labor.

"Ouch," Hazel yelped, grabbing her behind.

Turning about quickly, she swung the rake to fend off her attacker. The goose honked again, wings fluttering as it danced out of reach. If it was possible for a goose to sound smug, this one did.

"Garth, no more oats! You're going to be so big you won't be able to deliver mail, and I'll never hear the end of it from Dad."

The goose honked once more, stepping closer to sniff at her pockets. Hazel sighed in defeat. Never able to deny him anything, she reached for the brace on her nondominant forearm and pulled out a slim redwood wand with a raw emerald handle.

"*Aperta.*" With the flick of her wrist, the lock popped open on the small chest across the barn.

She smiled—magic made everything easier. Her father hated when she used magic at home and sometimes forbade it. Even he only used it when absolutely necessary. But for Hazel, magic was life.

"You better know how much I love you after this."

The goose waddled playfully around her in response.

"*Venire.*"

With the flick of her wand, a small, white cloth bag floated out of the chest toward her and Garth. Snatching the bag out of the air, Hazel offered him a handful of oats. The goose munched furiously out of her hand, as if he hadn't eaten in days instead of literally ten minutes prior. Hazel knew it probably wasn't the best for him, but she loved food too, and understood needing a treat. She'd just give him a little more.

Watching the bird eat, Hazel's mind wandered back to the

thought that had been plaguing her since she'd realized it was Summoning Day. "Ugh. Garth, why hasn't the letter come?"

Garth continued to eat, oblivious to Hazel's inner turmoil. While she'd hoped her chores would distract her, it was impossible to push it from her mind.

"Everyone promised the letter would come a week after graduation. Surely it should have arrived by now."

Garth headbutted the underside of her now empty hand to demand more. She offered another, smaller, handful. Garth ate again with gusto.

"What if I wasn't summoned?" She whispered the question more to herself than to Garth. It was the first time she'd allowed herself to consider the thought.

A deep voice boomed from the double barn doors. "Hazel Thorne, what have I said about overfeeding that bird?"

Hazel flinched, dropping some of the oats to the ground. Garth hissed his annoyance before glaring at Hazel's father for his unwelcome interruption.

Thomas Thorne ignored Garth, his eyes narrowing in on the chest. He was good at that—ignoring things. But only when it suited him. "I thought that chest was locked."

He'd given her an opportunity to deny it. There were two routes —pretend it was open or admit she'd used magic. Pretending would likely get her in more trouble.

Hazel dusted her hands on her jeans to avoid his gaze. "Garth wasn't letting me get much work done. He'd been following me around all morning, so I thought it'd be okay if he had a little extra."

"So you thought it'd be okay if you magicked the lock open?" He crossed his arms.

Hazel gulped. "I didn't think it would hurt anything."

A humorless laugh escaped her father's lips. His dark-brown eyes looked at her with disdain, a frown marring his suntanned face, earned from long days in the fields.

"You sound just like her," her father said.

Hazel recoiled at his words. She knew he meant her mother, his wife, who'd abandoned them. He'd said them to punish her, and the knife landed right in her heart like he'd wanted it to.

"How about my trust, Hazel?" He didn't wait for her to respond. "How am I supposed to trust someone who disregards my rules because magic makes it easy for them to do so?"

Hazel's stomach knotted. He was right; she'd known better. "I'm sorry, Dad."

"If you can't control your temptations, then I will," he said as he stalked over to the chest and pulled out a small, metal circular hoop. Branded symbols covered the sides and the locking mechanism that held it closed. The hoop was no bigger than the size of his wrist and weighed no more than a horseshoe. She'd never seen one so small, but the weight of its meaning hung heavy in the air.

"Dad, that's unnecessary." Keeping the rake in her hands, Hazel stepped in front of Garth, shielding him from view.

Her father waved it in the air. "I promise you, if it happens again, I will put this command collar on him until he learns he isn't in charge."

Garth honked as if he was giving her father the what-for.

Hazel spoke over him. "I've got it under control."

Garth hissed. If she didn't know better, she might think he had a death wish, but Garth didn't understand what this magic-embedded item was, as he'd never worn one before. These collars were usually for sheep, cows, or horses, to prevent livestock from escaping or maiming, and to keep them working. They stripped the free will from the animal completely, requiring them to follow all commands given. Hazel thought they were barbaric. Despite Garth being a pain in her butt, she preferred to never know what he was like without his free will.

Hazel went back to putting hay into the back corners of the last horse stall and said nothing, as she was saving her fighting energy for something more important.

"Any word yet from UCA?" her father asked, referring to the University of Central Arkansas, the university just down the road.

Hazel reached up to wipe her face on her T-shirt to hide her discomfort. "Not yet."

She prayed he believed her as she thought of the stack of acceptance letters hidden in her room under an enchantment to look like a pile of panties.

Unwilling to disappoint her father, Hazel had applied to the expected colleges: University of Central Arkansas, University of Arkansas, and Arkansas State University. When she'd told him she wanted to go to Saint Elias University, the only magical university in North America, he'd given her an emphatic "*No*." And not just to SEU, but to *any* magical university. He'd ended the conversation by forcing Hazel into promising that she wouldn't apply. That promise was easy enough to keep because SEU was not a school one applied for. One had to be summoned.

Her father hadn't attended a school for mages like his children. He'd received a non-magical education and never left the farm he'd grown up on. Magic wasn't as natural to him as it was to her. Hiding magic was a sad necessity to protect the mage community, but her father was more than happy to pretend that magic didn't exist, as he lived as a mundane.

"Is that what's been keeping you up the last few nights?" he asked.

Hazel winced. Her sleepless nights had nothing to do with UCA, but she wasn't about to tell him that.

"Don't worry. You're going to be a Bear like me," her father insisted.

Hazel was thankful he couldn't see her grimace. He had high hopes his daughter would attend his alma mater and help manage the family farm one day with her brother. There were worse things than being like her dad, but in moments like this, Hazel struggled to think of one.

There was no changing him now. Her mom had tried and failed.

She was certain that's why her mom had disappeared from their lives four years ago. Hazel just couldn't comprehend why she'd left her behind, which made the dreams that much harder. She'd do nearly anything to know the truth, but her mother never answered her in her dreams. She only ever said, "Come to Saint Elias." So that was exactly what Hazel intended to do.

Her father pulled Hazel back to reality as he reached for the rake in her hands. "Looks like you're done. You better hurry and clean up before Forrest heads into town without you."

He didn't have to tell her twice. Hazel kicked off her muck boots when she reached the barn doors. She was faster without shoes.

Hazel raced through the lush yard of clover and grass. Her bare feet dodged deftly where she knew the few stickers in the yard grew, having learned them by heart the hard way. She covered the half acre quickly and took the back porch steps two at a time, the oak slats hot under her soles from the summer sun.

As she cut through the spacious living room, Hazel smiled at the newest addition added to the wall. Her graduation photo was now displayed beside her brother's. Five years her senior, Hazel often bemoaned that Forrest beat her to every first, but she hoped she'd be the first of them to get into SEU.

Hazel headed to the study to grab her purse, and she felt a breeze of warm air move through the house. Her father had left the windows open today, which was why she was still sweating despite being inside. As she leaned over to snatch her purse off the desk, a rustle of wings drew her attention to the window.

She was frozen by what she saw. It was a beautiful larger-than-she'd-ever-dreamed, bald eagle.

It tucked its umber wings tightly against its sides, its feathers rustling softly in the breeze. Her heart threatened to stop when its head turned sharply to focus one of its golden eyes upon her. Glued to the door frame, she did not speak or move for what felt like a lifetime as the bird summed her up, their gazes never parting. Finally, it looked away. Without the weight of the magnificent gaze, she was able to take it all in—the glossy feathers, the large talons anchoring him on the wooden window frame. And the envelope attached to its leg.

Her heart beat again, thumping so quickly she thought it might burst.

While delivery fowl often came in all shapes and sizes, there was only one location in the world that used bald eagles.

"It's here," Hazel whispered in disbelief.

Terra, take me, she prayed to the mage goddess. Her palms began to sweat. She needed to sit down, but knew her nerves would never allow it.

The eagle clicked its beak as if to tell her to hurry. She took an eager step forward, and it whipped its gaze upon her again, reminding her it wouldn't be sensible to charge such a creature, no matter how domesticated he might seem. She approached slowly, eyes downcast, and stuck out her hand. The eagle stood still, cocking its head in that inquisitive way all birds did. When it made no sudden moves, she gently pulled at the intertwined string of white and blue tied about its leg, grabbed the letter, and took a few steps back. Only then did she again meet its gaze.

It nodded at her, as if to bid farewell, or perhaps congratulations, before it jumped backwards off the window frame, unfolded its great wingspan, and took flight.

Hazel rushed to the window. "Thank you!"

"What have you done?" a voice demanded behind her.

Hazel jumped at the sound.

She whirled to face her brother, tucking the letter behind her back, into the waistband of her jeans. She plastered on a smile, looking anywhere but his eyes, which were far too similar to their father's.

"Sorry! I was hunting down my purse. Oh, there it is!"

Hazel hoped he wouldn't pinpoint the forced saccharine tone in her voice as she rushed over to pick up the purse. She planned to sail through the door, right past Forrest and to the garage, but his hand wrapped around her forearm, bringing her to an abrupt stop. He stepped in front of her and closed the door.

"Hazel, look at me."

She did the opposite, turning abruptly to put space between them. She didn't want him to hear how hard her heart was beating. Hazel had to keep her calm so Forrest would keep his.

There was no way he could know for sure that it was an eagle from SEU. She could think of something to appease him. Then she just needed to figure out how to convince her father to actually let her go.

She started to tell Forrest it was a letter from a friend from Elkmont, but before she could get a word out, he drew his wand and enchanted *Venire*. Quick hands, her brother.

Retreating, Hazel felt a cold emptiness at her back and let out a yelp. The letter was now hanging over her head, not quite within reach. She stood on her tiptoes to snatch it from the air, but he was again one step ahead, floating it a few inches higher with a flick of his wrist. He gave her a taunting smile and raised a brow, challenging her to come and get it.

She glared at him, imagining shoving his wand somewhere he'd have a hard time flicking it, before giving up and sitting down on the couch. She wouldn't give him the satisfaction of making her work for it.

"It's a federal offense to open someone's mail," Hazel gritted through her teeth.

"Good thing the US government doesn't know a damned thing about mage mail," Forrest retorted.

He sat on the arm of the chair across from her. Their dad would hate that.

"No, but the Brecilian Knights definitely frown on it." Hazel referred to the only form of government and law enforcement honored by all mages on Earth. One of the strictest laws was theft of magical knowledge. The letter contained neither spell nor recipe, but Forrest didn't know that.

"Oh, I'm so scared of the big, bad, old mages," Forrest snarked, but they both knew better. Everyone feared the Knights, the most powerful and knowledgeable group of mages on Earth. Mages had the true innate ability to borrow magic from the earth, and the Brecilian Knights were the most skilled of their kind. If you were ever dumb enough to gain their attention, you deserved whatever punishment you received.

"Reading your little sister's mail is beneath you, Forrest."

Hazel was sticking with her initial inclination. He didn't know what he'd seen.

At this, Forrest belly-laughed because they both knew it was definitely not beneath him. His laugh was rich, vibrating in his chest. Normally, the sound of it made her smile, especially now that Forrest was living off on his own. But she wouldn't let her guard down. She studied her brother, with his brown hair like their father's, different from her own onyx strands that she'd inherited from their mother. He was tall like their father and brown-eyed, while Hazel was tall with hazel-green eyes. The only things they shared beyond their height were their thicker, athletic builds and ivory complexions.

Slowly, he lowered his wand. The letter fluttered down before gently landing in her lap. "I saw the damn eagle, Hazel. You and I both know that's not just any letter."

Of course, he knew. He always knew.

He looked at the envelope as if it might bite him. "It's a death sentence."

Hazel rolled her eyes. Her annoyance with him forced her to admit the truth. "No, it's a summons."

"Yeah, to a funeral." Forrest crossed his arms. "Possibly yours."

"You're being dramatic. The entrance exam death rate is incredibly low." Hazel's voice raised an octave despite herself.

"The exam death rate isn't what I'm talking about and you know it." He didn't wait for her to respond as he continued, "Though it *is* way too high."

"I'd like to point out there's a higher probability I could be killed by an armed shooter at any of the mundane schools you seem so supportive of."

Forrest smirked as if the point in whatever game they were playing had gone to him. "Yes, but we both know you can protect yourself in that sort of situation."

Hazel squinted at him. "Are you implying that I can't protect myself during the entrance exam?"

"No, I'm telling you outright that you're insane to set your heart on Saint Elias. You have an aunt who died there and you're still trying to go. Your head isn't on straight, kid."

Hazel resisted the urge to bite out that she wasn't a kid, knowing that saying it would only make it sound true.

"Aunt Evelyn died of a magically resistant illness. That had nothing to do with SEU."

Forrest lifted a finger. "Yes, but where did she get the cancer?"

Hazel rolled her eyes. He was really reaching. Yes, their mother's sister Evelyn had died there, but their mother had not. She'd been among the best at SEU. Which was why Hazel had spent the last four years of high school fighting to be the best too. She'd started her magical education at fourteen at Elkmont Academy of Magic, one of the three magical high schools in North America, and had been well behind her peers who'd been learning magic since elementary school. No matter what she'd learned or conquered, she'd always wanted more, sure that the next accomplishment would bring her mother back. It never had.

Now, a part of her believed the dreams of her mother were a sign, an omen, that she had to attend. Perhaps, just maybe, her mother was at SEU, along with all the answers to the questions she had. That possibility, however illogical, was enough. She was desperate to go.

"You never wanted to go to college. I've always wanted to go, and I'm dying to go to this one."

Forrest scoffed. "Yes, literally."

He was so annoying. Instead of smacking him, Hazel rested her shaking hands upon her thighs. "Those deaths are tragic, but those students aren't me. I'm better than that. Mom passed and so will I."

The university shrouded the entire examination process in secrecy to prevent cheating, which was why people were so scared of it. However, university officials assured examinees that the mountain of Saint Elias didn't kill purposefully. If a student didn't make it out, it was because they didn't withdraw from the exam when an opportunity was offered, or they lacked integrity and one was never provided. The mountain was a magical source, an entity so old and so powerful, it had developed rules and opinions along the way. If the mountain didn't find you worthy, you weren't getting in, which was another thing that made the exam feel so risky.

"Listen to me and drop this." Forrest swallowed as he nodded to the summons lying in her lap. "Tear it up, flush it, burn it, whatever. Then forget it." He lifted his wand, as if he'd do so himself.

Before he could, though, Hazel drew her wand from its brace on her forearm and incanted, "*Praestringo.*"

Forrest's arms were jerked behind his back with invisible restraints. He wrestled, unable to break loose, before staring back at his sister with disbelief.

Hazel held back a smirk. "I graduated at the top of my class. The best universities in the state accepted me. I applied to Stanford on a dare and got in. I've never failed at anything I've set my mind to, not once." She stared him in the eyes to emphasize her next point. "And I've set my mind on this."

Forrest quirked a brow. "I thought you were wait-listed at Stanford. As a matter of fact, I thought you'd been wait-listed everywhere."

Hazel blanched, the color draining from her face as she realized she'd revealed too much. He thought she'd been wait-listed everywhere because that's what she'd told him and their father to buy herself time for her summons to arrive. Her silence was all Forrest needed for confirmation.

"Dad's going to lose his shit."

His words distracted Hazel just enough to make her drop her focus on the binding spell. With a grunt, Forrest was free. He brought his hands forward and rubbed at his wrists.

Hazel snatched the letter up to keep it safe, grasping it with shaking hands. Her voice cracked as she asked, "How is it so easy for everyone to ask me to give up my dreams?"

Forrest had the decency to look ashamed. Without returning her gaze, he stated, "You'll be happy at UCA, I'm sure of it."

Hazel felt as though steam could start pouring out of her ears. "Don't do that. Don't act like this decision's already been made. That's all I hear. No. No. No." Hazel's voice rose.

Forrest rolled his eyes. "Now who's being dramatic?"

The red of rage seeped into her vision. How dare he sit there and act like he hadn't seen all of her choices and independence being stripped from her until she didn't know where her father ended and she began?

"Add it to the pile of things I have no say in, that I simply have to live with. I'm always expected to give in or give up. I begged to play ruzo in high school. Dad said no, it's too dangerous. I asked to join the magricultural club. Dad said no after-school extracurriculars, I need you home to help on the farm."

Hazel blinked back tears, unable to contain the adrenaline from the fight coursing through her body. She hated conflict, but Terra, did it feel good to get it off her chest.

"The only extracurricular I got to do was wand-fishing because we could participate during free periods. Wand-fishing! You got to be on the broom-racing team!"

Forrest studied the nonexistent dirt under his fingernails. Fueled by his silence, Hazel paced. She'd started and now she couldn't stop. Four years of suppressed opinions, hopes, and dreams fought to break free. All of her disappointments since her mother left were bubbling up inside her like a poison she had to get out. Forrest was its unlucky victim.

"I begged to visit friends outside of school or even just go to a birthday party. Dad said no, people can't be trusted. I begged him to come with me. Dad said no, I have to work." She listed the items on her fingers while she paced. "I begged him to let me have friends over from school. Dad said no, it's too much of a liability when you don't know their parents. I got asked to go to Samhain Ball—by an extremely cute senior, I might add—and Dad said no dating." Each refusal left her more angry and even more isolated. Tears threatened to fall as she continued, eyes locked on her brother. "You got to go off and live your life after you graduated. Better yet, you got to enjoy high school before Mom disappeared, taking all of Dad's sanity with her. I have been stuck here under dad's thumb since you and Mom abandoned me. It's only me. *I'm* the one who always has to bend. I'm so incredibly sick of bending." Her breath caught. "If I bend on this, I'll break."

Forrest finally met her gaze. She hoped to see understanding in her brother's eyes, but the emotion there was unexpected. It looked like frustration. His lack of sympathy made her want to lash out.

"It's been so incredibly lonely for me, but you wouldn't know that because you've only been back for a year," Hazel said.

Forrest's jaw flexed, but Hazel didn't regret her words. They were true, no matter if he hated them or not.

"I came back, didn't I? That should say something to you about what life is like away from here."

"Forrest, you've missed your own point! You chose to leave, and you chose to come back. You had a choice. I deserve a choice too!"

"It's literally dad's job—and mine—to help keep you from making mistakes. You're naïve to believe you should make mistakes just for the sake of making them."

Her blood boiled. Hazel scoffed, "Naïve? How could I not be n*aïve* when he's denied me nearly every opportunity to grow up?"

He ignored her question. "You believe magic is going to give you this great big wonderful life, but you're forgetting how many of the fairy tales Mom read to you that had heroes who died in the end. I promise you, there's always a price. Has it ever occurred to you that Dad and I are trying to keep you safe?"

"Then enlighten me! Tell me what I should be so afraid of at SEU."

Forrest opened his mouth, but closed it quickly. He said nothing as he studied her from his seat on the leather sofa.

Then a thought occurred to her. Perhaps they weren't trying to keep her from SEU—perhaps they were trying to keep her from *someone* at SEU.

"I don't know what it is, but you're hiding something. You want to impart all this sage wisdom to me, but when I ask what happened while you were away, you have nothing to say. You tell me stories about monsters under my bed, but you can't tell me what they look like or what they'll do to me."

Hazel let her words hang in the air, hoping Forrest would fill the silence. He disappointed her yet again.

"Were you with her?" she finally asked.

Forrest's gaze snapped to hers. His jaw clenched.

It was the only answer she would get. Forrest had refused to speak of their mom since he'd returned from wherever the hell he'd been. Hazel wanted to ring his neck for his silence.

"You just expect me to take your word for it, but I'm done doing that. I got summoned. I'm going to Saint Elias University whether you like it or not." Hazel's chest heaved from her tirade, but she didn't feel tired. She felt empowered. The fact that she hadn't even opened the letter yet was irrelevant.

Forrest's eyes filled with pity at her words. He let out a long sigh. "Stomp and yell all you want. He's never going to say you can go."

Hazel was prepared for that. All summer long, she'd been honing her arguments and speech. She was ready to convince him. She only worried about whether he could actually be convinced.

"When he realizes I'm good enough to get the summons, he'll let me go." Or so she hoped. Every magical high school submitted the names of its graduates, regardless if they wanted to be summoned or not. The mountain decided from there, and history proved only the best and brightest were chosen.

Forrest shook his head. Hazel wanted to hit him. Instead, she set her jaw. He'd taken after their father more than he'd ever admit, but she was different. Hazel wanted to know more. She wanted to know it all. UCA couldn't teach her the things she wanted to know. UCA offered no help in finding her magical identity. She needed Saint Elias University for that.

And a shameful, unshareable part of herself wanted to go so she could feel closer to her mother, regardless if she found her there or not.

Forrest opened his mouth to retort when the study door flew open. Their father stood in the hallway.

His monotone voice rang out. "Hazel. Kitchen. *Now*."

CHAPTER 2

Gwen

Gwen chewed her lip as she willed the knife in her hand to steady. Her eyes pinched in concentration as she carved out the intricate design she'd sketched into a five-inch, tapered-cylinder wand made of black walnut attached to raw gemstone. Wood chips littered a large workbench and the surrounding floor.

Charming Carvings, the store where she worked, was quiet today. Her grandfather, the owner, believed in having the weekend off. Gwen had come in this Saturday to keep her mind—and hands—busy. The art of carving always relaxed her.

Rainhart Bishop could embed magic into anything—from clocks to bookcases to brooms. Embedding was a beautiful craft that breathed life into inanimate objects. Masters of the skill were highly sought after, but Gwen's grandfather often reminded her the carvings were as important as the magic itself. Though embedding could be used for nefarious purposes—cursed trinkets, surveillance charms, or worse—her grandfather would never create anything sinister. He believed in the craft's honor and refused to compromise it. Some embedders sold enchanted items to unknowing mundanes for profit or entertainment, but not him. He only sold to mages. A severe punishment was in store for those caught selling on the black market, especially considering the secrecy surrounding the existence of mages. The Brecilian Knights enforced that law with ruthless precision.

Since wands didn't have magic embedded into them, but were simply conduits necessary for mages to cast magic, he'd made her start her training there. She'd worked in the store every summer since her freshman year of high school at Bathurst Institute of Sorcery; her woodworking skills had grown exponentially with time, as well as her fondness for wand-making. Now that she'd graduated, she hoped her grandfather would take her on full time and finally allow her to begin a true apprenticeship.

Gwen heard the metallic slide of the lock, followed by the creak of a floorboard.

"I swear you get louder every single day," she said, never taking her eyes off the carving in front of her.

A laugh sounded behind her. "No point in trying to keep quiet with that supersonic hearing of yours."

"What took you so long?" Gwen asked, rolling her eyes.

Her cousin Klaus moved closer, his tall form looming over her as he inspected her work. She was making adjustments to her own wand this morning, embellishing the wood above the onyx handle with a new method her grandfather had finally shared.

Klaus whistled. "Impressive."

Gwen smiled, hoping for the same response from her grandfather.

"I had to get Manfrit and Ahren in place," Klaus finally answered.

Manfrit and Ahren were Klaus's older brothers. At eighteen, Gwen was the youngest of the four, and she looked up to each of them. They were more like brothers than cousins. Adult responsibilities had slowly reduced her quality time with them, so she was looking forward to seeing them today. She just wished it were to play a game of ruzo, the most popular mage sport.

"Do we have to train?" Gwen whined.

She'd been training all her life. She was tired of training.

"Come on, you know your favorite place to be is in the woods," he reminded her.

He wasn't wrong; she did love being in the woods that backed up to her family's property. It was the only place she felt truly safe to be herself.

"Plus, Manfrit let me borrow this, so hopefully I can keep up this time." Klaus held up a beautiful broom with a freshly polished ebony handle and a tail that had been shaped to a point. Gwen recognized it immediately. Her grandfather had been working on its speed capabilities last week.

"Oh, that broom was for Manfrit?" She grabbed for it, narrowly missing it, as Klaus pulled it out of reach.

Klaus beamed, holding it high above her head, which wasn't hard to do, considering she was only five feet tall. "He made me swear I'd be the only one to ride it, and if I break it, I have to replace it." He made a shooing motion towards her. "You've got to make your own deal with Manfrit if you want to test it out. This is an expensive broom."

A warning never stopped her. Gwen jumped for it. Missing, she stumbled, almost knocking Klaus backwards as he tried to get out of her way. Klaus was not the type to catch her; he'd definitely let her fall on her face.

"Stop it, you big giant," she yelled at him.

Klaus was a giant compared to her at nearly seven feet. Gwen often teased him about his giant-like qualities, though not around the rest of the family. The Bishops didn't want anyone thinking they were anything but ordinary mages—especially because Gwen wasn't.

After a few more attempts, she finally gave up jumping and

reached for her wand. "*Cadere*," she muttered, knocking his legs out from under him.

Klaus crashed to his knees and cried out in pain.

He's so dramatic. She gracefully snatched the broom from his grip and inspected the intricate carvings her grandfather had made.

"What the fuck, Gwendolyn?" Klaus scolded.

She reluctantly set down the broom to help him up. Bright-red specks of blood showed on the knees of his jeans as he stood, and she felt a tinge of remorse. "Sorry."

"And *this* is why you have to train," Klaus berated her. "Your impulse control is terrible. What have you and your dad even been working on these past few years?"

Gwen winced at the mention of her father. He'd been training her her whole life. He was technically the only one qualified, but he was mean and his methods were brutal. When he got too busy last year, Gwen had been relieved. She'd wanted to stop training all together. Unfortunately, Klaus refused to let her quit. He stepped in on his breaks from college, insisting she needed all the help she could get if she wanted to go to Saint Elias University. And she did want to get into Saint Elias, even if she knew it was a fool's errand.

Deep down, she'd always hoped the school would have answers for her. Klaus had said the SEU library held thousands of books. She liked to believe somewhere, buried in all that knowledge, there was something that could help her. So far, the few books he'd had time to read hadn't been much use, but she refused to believe that was all there was.

If nothing else, she'd kill for the chance to read every bit of history and lore about her ancestors. That was why she'd always been drawn to history. It wasn't just about the past. It was about connection. She longed to know the ones who'd come before her, to understand what they had endured, what they'd fought for.

Maybe, if she could understand them, she'd finally understand herself.

"Fine, I'll train," she relented.

"Don't do me any favors," he said, using his wand to remove the bloodstains.

Unlike her, Klaus couldn't heal himself. She needed to keep that in mind when casting against him—not casting was out of the question.

"Okay, give me your bracelet." Klaus ordered.

Gwen slapped her left hand over the gold chain that had adorned her right wrist for the last fifteen years. Five distinct charms hung between the links, each one meticulously chosen: an iridescent blue sphere, a sharp opal fang, a teardrop pearl, a rose quartz claw, and a dark-green stone carved into a curling knot. Strategically placed, the charms weren't decoration—each one was embedded with magic and made up her lifeline, her safety net.

"Why?" Gwen asked him, still protecting it.

As much as the bracelet sometimes felt like a cage, it kept her from exposing who she truly was.

"I want you to go through town with it off today," he said.

Her heart rate increased and her chest tightened. "Why?" Gwen asked again. She always waited until she reached the Northern Maine woods to take off her bracelet. Was he confused or just stupid?

"You need more practice staying in control around people, specifically strangers."

Gwen didn't argue—she knew he was right. A few years ago, while training with her father, a lone hiker had wandered into their territory and she had attacked him. His scent had been unrecognizable to her, and she'd seen him as a threat. Luckily, her father had been there to pull her off, and he'd walked away with only a few scratches down his back.

It was definitely easier for her to stay in control around familiar people, and most of the local townspeople had known Gwen since she was little. However, Britton Place was a bustling town for mages, especially in the summer with its controlled climate and specialty shops. There would be plenty of people whose scent she wouldn't recognize and might see as dangerous.

I'm not giving him my bracelet.

"Let's go," Gwen said, holstering her wand and leading the way out of the shop.

With a tug, Gwen double-checked the tightly locked door before pocketing her gold key.

Klaus drew his wand as they made their way into town. "*Silentia.*"

An invisible bubble formed around them, continuing with them as they walked. The spell contained their conversation inside of it, allowing them to speak freely without others overhearing. It was a spell they used often, being part of a large family like theirs.

Klaus waited for the sounds of the streets to disappear before speaking. "The summons go out today. If you get summoned by Saint Elias University, you'll have to take off your bracelet for the entrance exam, and you'll be around a lot of people you don't know. We've got to focus on improving your control." His voice was strained, full of seriousness.

Gwen stopped dead in her tracks, and Klaus followed suit. She needed to look him in the eyes when she spoke her next words.

"Which is exactly why I'm not going."

"Gwendolyn Grayce Bishop," her cousin scolded.

She crossed her arms. "It's not possible and you know it."

"What I know is you want to go."

Gwen bared her teeth. "Of course I want to go. Who wouldn't? But two years ago, when you said I couldn't use my bracelet in the exam, that dream went up in smoke."

"I told you to prepare you, not discourage you."

"Well, it's all one and the same, Klaus. Maybe if you or my father had been more successful in my training, I wouldn't need it, but—"

"Hey, don't lump me in with him," Klaus interjected.

Gwen looked away sheepishly. She knew that was unfair to Klaus, who'd been working diligently with her this past year. He was nothing like her father.

Her father used to leave her in the woods for days, withholding her bracelet, claiming he'd return it once she learned to overcome her instincts. Which she never did. Every time she went missing, her mother would hunt her father down and force him to return the bracelet. Dolphus Waitz was the scariest man Gwen had ever met. He feared nothing and no one, except Liana Bishop. That might be the only thing Klaus and her father did have in common. Her mother, while short and soft, was a formidable opponent. Neither of them would ever go against her.

"I don't even know why we're talking about it. You're the first in our family to even receive a summons. They aren't going to call on me," Gwen insisted. Klaus opened his mouth to say something, but before he could, she added, "Even if they do, I can't go."

Her shoulders slumped. She was tired of this argument. It never changed, no matter the person—her mother, Klaus, her grandfather. They all said the same thing. She wished for once they'd see it from her perspective, because every time they brought it up, it just reminded her that she couldn't go. She hated it.

Gwen stalked further ahead down the brick road, leaving Klaus behind. The bubble stretched between them as she moved. It would hold until one of them released the spell or someone walked through it.

The road continued through the heart of the town nestled against the towering pines. Timber-framed buildings with thatched roofs covered in wildflowers leaned together, their stained-glass windows glowing as the sunlight bounced off of them. There were no cars on the roads, as mage towns didn't permit vehicles—not that they'd work around magic, anyway. Instead, people either walked or flew their brooms. Cars weren't the only thing that didn't work around magic. They couldn't have telephones, radios, or television either. Gwen felt that was a small sacrifice. Besides, the one time she had visited a mundane town, she'd felt wildly overstimulated.

"Your bracelet?" Klaus called after her.

"Fine. It's your death sentence."

Gwen slowed, waiting for him to catch up, then unclasped her bracelet. Without it, everything sharpened—her sense of smell heightened, her strength and speed surged, and even her vision adjusted to the shifting light. Her hearing would've stretched further, too, if not for the lingering silencing spell. The smell of wildflowers mingled with the woody cologne of Hans, the owner of Paris and Stolls. His scent was stale, which meant he must've gone back inside.

"Here." Gwen handed Klaus her bracelet, and they continued.

The bustling streets required her to brush past shoppers, their polyester rubbing her skin, making it itch when they got too close. Small children raced by on broomsticks, inches above the ground, almost knocking her over.

With most of her senses heightened, the town grated on her nerves. Her breath began to come out in little pants and her heart pounded in her chest. She was going to lose it. Unwilling to let that happen, Gwen sought the familiar—something she'd done many times in training. After a few seconds, she found the bakery and focused all her energy on it until there was nothing else. The nostalgic scent of baked goods was the only thing strong enough to block out the rest of the town. Gwen smelled the cobbler as keenly as if it were right in front of her face rather than three blocks away. Her eyes glazed over and her breathing returned to normal.

I can do this.

"What's the dessert of the day?" Klaus asked. He took a deep inhale despite the fact that he was incapable of smelling the bakery from this distance.

"Blackberry cobbler," she said, resisting the urge to follow the smell down the street and into the bakery.

"Well, if you beat your record today, a slice will be your reward."

She knew Klaus was only trying to make up for forcing her into town, but she'd never pass up Ruby's blackberry cobbler.

"With ice cream?" Gwen quirked a brow, determined to milk the situation for everything it was worth.

Klaus rolled his eyes. "Sure."

"Done and done!"

As Gwen matched Klaus's pace, a shopper walked between them, popping the invisible bubble that surrounded them. The three of them grabbed their ears as the spell disarmed with a ring. The woman threw Klaus and Gwen a dirty look and continued on down the street.

Adrenaline surged through Gwen, and her eyes flashed gold. A low growl rumbled from her throat, but Klaus was fast—he caught her wrist and snapped the bracelet into place. The moment the clasp clicked shut, her eyes faded back to their usual icy blue, and the wild edge inside her settled. All of her heightened senses returned to normal, no better or worse than any mage's.

"I told you I wasn't ready," Gwen hissed.

That woman was lucky Klaus had quick reflexes.

"Maybe not yet," Klaus admitted. "But you will be."

Gwen was frustrated that she'd proved him wrong; she desperately wanted to be ready. "She should have gone around," Gwen mumbled.

"It's not like she could see the spell," he reminded her. The point of the spell was privacy, after all.

They walked the rest of the way through town in silence, not daring to recast the spells. There were too many people on the streets today. Gwen strained as she tried to listen to the conversations happening in the Many Sisters, the local pub. She loved to eavesdrop, but with her bracelet on, she couldn't make out what anyone was saying. Fresh bread floated outside of Ruby Reds and raw pastry dough twisted itself into intricate shapes on the counter. Gwen spotted the blackberry cobbler in the window, and her mouth watered.

I have to break my record today.

As soon as they entered the woods, Gwen relinquished her bracelet back to Klaus. Hundreds of wards surrounded nearly 10,000 acres of her family's property, keeping anyone who wasn't family out as a precaution after the hiker incident.

Wasting no time, Gwen took off at a sprint. She shouted over her shoulder, "Let's see how fast Manfrit's broom really is."

Freedom washed over her as she ran through the woods. Her breath stayed steady, but the exertion sent fresh adrenaline humming through her veins. The panic she'd felt in town vanished. It wasn't the act of removing her bracelet that rattled her—it was doing it in front of people. The real stress came from the risk of exposure. Out here, there was no danger of being seen. She could let go. This was home.

The familiar aroma of Britton Place was replaced by pine and dirt. The scents she picked up without her bracelet were one of her favorite things, second only to her hearing. Squirrels and chipmunks skittered around her as they ran up the trees, their tails brushing along the bark, and she smiled as they chased each other through the branches. Small bugs crawled through the earth below her and birds chirped high above the forest's canopy. Forcing herself to ignore them, she pushed her senses even further out to locate her cousins. She'd already outpaced Klaus on the broom, as he couldn't maneuver through the trees as quickly as she could and had to fly above the tree line. A rank odor wafted toward her: Ahren.

Whew, that all natural deodorant is doing nothing for him.

"Tell Ahren to wear regular deodorant next time," Gwen shouted behind her, her eyes now watering from the smell.

"He won't listen. Thinks it makes him more manly!" Klaus yelled down to her from Manfrit's broom, flying high above.

Gwen laughed at the thought of Ahren trying to be more manly when he was the largest and burliest man she knew. She continued her sprint in his direction. Her feet flew over tree branches and rocks as if she knew exactly where they'd be. She picked up the trail of a buck and began tracking it along with its doe. Veering slightly off her intended trajectory, she followed it until they were right in front of her.

Rushing past them, her breath never faltered. It would be a long while before she tired. She was well-trained, and she was fast. Faster than most of the things in these woods. Even Klaus, who was now a quarter mile back.

When she got close enough to her eldest cousins to hear their heart rates, she slowed her pace and began stalking them through the trees undetected. She opened her mind, letting her natural instincts take over. She crouched in the brush, creeping from tree to tree. Finally, they were in her line of sight. In a small clearing, the young men walked around an upright tree stump where a magically elevated red flag floated freely in the breeze.

Ahren and Manfrit, as well as Klaus, were all carbon copies of one another—unbelievably tall, thick builds, dark-brown hair, and ocean-blue eyes contrasting against their porcelain skin. Gwen had always been thankful she shared at least one family trait with them: her eyes. While her skin was pale, it was near alabaster and her hair was white, traits she'd inherited from her paternal grandmother.

Her cousins looked off into the distance, waiting for her. They had no clue she was there already. The birds that had sung earlier grew quiet. Gwen knew they could sense an animal on the prowl. The silence was enough to give her away.

Her cousins turned, facing her direction, and took aim. Spell after spell flew around her. She dodged the magic as she circled them, the spells hitting the trees right behind her as she moved. So focused on avoiding them, she missed the tree root in front of her and tripped. A hex hit her right shoulder and pain seared through her.

She growled, angry and ready to fight back. Instantly, another spell connected and Gwen's eyes turned gold, her canines sharpening to fangs as her nails extended into claws.

Enough.

This had to end before she lost control. She dashed across the clearing, their incantations barely missing her, and leapt for the bright-red flag they protected. She clenched the silk tightly in her hands before she rolled to a stop and jumped up with a cackle.

"Damn," Ahren swore.

"Next time, use regular deodorant." Gwen waved her hand in front of her nose.

Ahren sniffed himself. "Is it really that bad?"

Manfrit gave Gwen a look that said, *I'm glad someone finally said something*, and they both burst into laughter.

"You both suck," Ahren groaned.

Gwen waved the flag in their faces. "Let's go celebrate my victory."

"After you retract the claws," Ahren said wearily.

Ignoring him, she continued to dance and wave the flag around.

"Do you have to be both a sore loser *and* a sore winner?" Manfrit asked earnestly.

"Yes," she replied as she beamed up at them.

Klaus flew into the clearing from above, setting his feet gently on the ground, before dismounting the broom.

"About time you showed up. Did I beat my time?" Gwen asked.

"Just barely. If you would've ignored the deer, you might have set a new record."

"Can you give her the bracelet?" Ahren asked. "Her teeth are freaking me out!"

"Chicken." Gwen grinned, showing her teeth.

His fingers brushed the scar on his neck—the one she'd given him as a child. Guilt tightened in her chest, and she silently held out her hand for the bracelet. Before Klaus could clasp it on her wrist, though, a scent she'd smelled only once before wafted in on the breeze. The blood drained from her face.

"What is it?" Klaus asked, alarmed, as he studied her face.

Gwen didn't answer. Instead, she backed up to the tree line, searching the skies frantically. The animal tracking her grew closer.

"Shit," Gwen grumbled.

"What?" the three cousins chorused.

"It appears" —she paused for dramatic effect— "I'm being summoned."

"Congratulations!" Manfrit ran to Gwen and wrapped her up in a hug. She did not reciprocate as she stood there, arms at her sides, stiff as a board. "Seriously, this is a big accomplishment!" Manfrit continued. "We're proud of you."

Manfrit and Ahren were among the many family members who had not been summoned. She wondered if they resented her or Klaus for it. She'd never admit it but she'd resented him. While it had faded over time, every once in a while, she'd catch herself daydreaming about being a mage—*just* a mage—like Klaus and what it would be like to go to Saint Elias. Jealousy about how easy he'd had it would rear its ugly head.

As her cousins congratulated her, the feeling overcame her once more because no matter how much she wanted to, she could not join Klaus at Saint Elias University. She forced herself to shove the resentment deep down inside of her, knowing it wasn't fair to Klaus.

Once Manfrit released her, Ahren ran past him to give her a grizzly bear hug too. He shook the flag still in her hand. "So proud! Now put your bracelet on and let's go celebrate—your victory and your summons."

She looked into their happy, hopeful eyes and realized no matter how hard she tried to explain it to them, they'd never understand. They loved her too much. They'd never see the truth of it—that she was a danger to everyone who wasn't family. She was a monster.

As SEU's delivery eagle drew closer, Gwen saw her apprenticeship with her grandfather disappearing. If her family knew she'd been summoned, there was zero chance of them allowing her to reject it and stay in Britton Place. There was only one option: avoid the summons at all costs.

Gwen took off at a dead sprint, leaving her cousins behind with no explanation. They called out to her, but she blocked out their words. She had to move. She had to focus.

There was a cave nearby that Gwen sometimes used for shelter when her father withheld her bracelet. She'd gone there once and warded it against other animals. She only hoped to make it there before the eagle got to her. Gwen could hide out and wait until

Summoning Day had passed. Then she could go back to living her life in peace.

With a hard push, she ran faster than she ever had before, but a glance up through the trees told her the eagle was right above her. Apparently, she was no longer faster than everything in these woods. She extended her speed as far as she could on two legs. Desperate to hide from a future she couldn't have, she did something she'd never done willingly.

Her skin stretched as her bones grew, rearranging themselves into a giant white wolf.

Gwen had been told the shift was painful for all therians the first time, but she had no memory of it. How could she? She'd been born a wolf. As far back as she could remember, the change had always felt no more painful than when your leg fell asleep and you worked to wake it up—uncomfortable, unpleasant, but manageable. The sensation went away as soon as the transformation was complete.

All four paws thudded on the soft green grass of the forest as she picked up speed. The bird screeched at her and beat its wings harder. Gwen just had to make it to the cave. She could see it.

Twenty yards.

Fifteen.

Ten.

Large talons sunk into her back. Blood ran down her white fur as she came to an abrupt stop. Flinging her body left and right, Gwen tried to throw the eagle off, but it held firm. After several minutes, all her energy spent, she finally conceded mere feet from the cave.

The eagle released her flesh and fur to land in front of her. It stared at her, waiting for her to remove the letter from his leg. As gently as she could, she used her teeth to untie the envelope and dropped it in the grass. Before the eagle took flight, it pecked at her nose and she snapped back as it flew out of reach.

I hate eagles, she roared inside her head as the wolf fought her for control. Her back itched as the gashes the eagle left began to heal—a therian perk.

“Well, that was the opposite of control,” Klaus said, landing near her on Manfrit’s broom.

Gwen growled at him.

His brothers came running up behind him moments later. Manfrit must have tripped and injured himself on his way there, as blood was trickling down his arm. Being upset was hard enough, but smelling blood made the predator in her lunge forward. The wolf clawed at her mind. She howled in frustration, attempting to convey that she was barely holding on.

Klaus understood immediately. “Go *now*!” He threw Manfrit his broom.

Manfrit didn’t hesitate, and neither did Gwen. He’d just lifted off the ground when she lunged at him, missing him by inches. The wolf was in full control now. It detected the presence of two others.

Familiar. Familiar people are not to be harmed.

She bared her teeth.

“*Advinere*,” the remaining two men cast.

They vanished before she could attack.

The smells and sounds of the forest told her the threats were gone—no footsteps, no voices, only birdsong and the rustle of leaves remained. Her muscles twitched as the instinct to defend herself faded. The tension in her limbs began to ease, and her breathing slowed. The wolf hesitated, then relinquished its hold. The letter was gone. Klaus had probably taken it.

Gwen hung her head in shame as she began to make the long trek home.

I’ll never be able to control myself or shift out of this stupid wolf form on my own!

She was so angry with herself. This was why she couldn’t go to Saint Elias. Her own family wasn’t even safe around her. The only exception was her father, and that was only because he was a therian too.

No wonder mages hate therians.

As a child, she used to dream of a world where she could

control her shift and was accepted by mages. Her father had squashed that dream immediately. There was a long history of hatred between mages and therians that went back to the Great War, when all the species of magic users fought for control against the siphoners. The war ended with the extinction of siphoners, fae, and elves—while the therian numbers dwindled dangerously low. So low they stayed hidden, letting the mages think they'd all died out too. If the mages knew the spirit-users still existed, they'd be seen as a threat.

"They'll never accept us, Gwendolyn. They'll never accept *you*. They fear our power," her dad would say. "The Brecilian Knights would kill us all if they could."

Gwen feared if she went to Saint Elias University, she'd be the one to expose them. Yet another reason she wouldn't be going.

Unfortunately, her family wouldn't understand. They were all mages. Receiving a summons was a great honor to them. Her only shot was to convince her cousins to lie and say the eagle wasn't for her. She picked up the pace, heading to her house, where she hoped they'd be waiting for her.

She made it to her backyard and padded up the stone path. The light-brown shingles matched beautifully with the ornate wooden doors her grandfather had made. The front and back door both had a bishop chess piece carved into them, for their last name. Each time she looked at those doors, she felt proud to be a Bishop, like her mother.

In addition to the mage doors, her grandfather had also made a "wolf door," that featured a carving of a small cub surrounded by flowers. She used her snout to push on the door, and it swung upward, allowing her to enter the home. Her grandfather had embedded it to recognize her and only her. It wouldn't budge for intruders, no matter the species.

She walked through the kitchen, her steps quick and purposeful, barely registering the scent of brewed coffee and lingering spices from this morning. As she entered the living room, she spotted Klaus sitting on the couch, but she didn't slow. Bypassing him, she headed straight upstairs to her room.

Her bed, tucked into a gable alcove and surrounded by windows on three sides, felt like a small observatory. At night, she could lie back and watch the stars, tracing constellations until sleep finally took her. She plopped down onto the tangled mess of navy-blue sheets, kicking at the matching comforter until it rested at the foot of the bed.

She exhaled, staring up at the ceiling, letting the familiar weight of the mattress beneath her steady her racing thoughts.

"That was incredibly unnecessary!" Klaus shouted as he clomped up the stairs. "You'd have been better off accepting the summons and hiding it."

He entered her room, carrying her precious bracelet. She was both grateful and resentful he'd brought it to her. She had a love-hate relationship with the item. He covered her with her comforter and then fixed the bracelet on her right paw before rushing out of the room. The world quieted once more. Gwen shifted back moments later and dressed quickly, before rushing after Klaus.

She had to convince him to help her keep her letter from SEU a secret. If anyone was more stubborn than Gwen, it was her mother. She'd insist Gwen accept the summons for the exam, and, as today had proven yet again, that wasn't an option without her bracelet.

As she rounded the corner, she skidded to a stop.

Her mother stood next to Klaus in the living room, still wearing her pointed hat, as if she'd just stepped inside. Sunlight from the wide bay window filtered through heavy emerald-green curtains, casting golden streaks across the blue and white parchment in her mother's hands. She was reading the summons.

Fuck. I'm so screwed.

CHAPTER 3

Hazel

This was not how Hazel had imagined it. She was already starting off in a hole when she needed time to soften her father to the idea. How much had he heard? If he'd heard her speak of her mother, her chances of convincing him were lower than zero. That was a truth she could never share with him if she hoped to gain his support in attending SEU. Hazel begged Terra, the goddess of the mages, to sway her father and spare her from his temper.

Her mantra repeated in her mind.

Be happy. Smile. Nothing is wrong.

She entered the kitchen to find her father leaning against the counter while he drank tea from a mason jar. She lifted the envelope up to show him. The blue and white ribbon that wrapped around each edge was sealed beneath a wax stamp at the mouth of the envelope. The SEU crest gleamed in gold foil.

"A bald eagle delivered it a few minutes ago. An actual bald eagle!"

She didn't hide the excitement in her voice. She didn't want to. It was a tactic she'd learned long ago. The more excited she acted, the harder it was for her father to get upset at her for asking.

"Let's get on with it," he said in a monotone voice as he set his glass down.

Be happy. Smile. Nothing is wrong.

She cleared her throat before beginning to read aloud. "*Dear Miss Thorne, You have been summoned to complete the entrance exam for Saint Elias University*... I did it! I've been summoned!"

Hazel practically squealed, letting her joy show outright. She pulled out the big guns and flashed her dimples as she did a little dance in place. An icky feeling overcame her like it always did when she had to pretend like this. It was overkill and she knew it. But this naivety kept her father complacent, and she needed him to be complacent and not angry.

"Alaska! I'm going to Alaska!"

She allowed the rise and fall of her voice to convey first her disbelief, then elation. He couldn't know she'd been hoping for this. Planning on this. Surprise was the key to selling it.

The deafening silence in the room tried to swallow her. Feeling like her heart might fly away, she let herself look at her father. His eyes and mouth remained flat as he watched his thumbs twiddle between his clasped hands. The lack of acknowledgement still pierced her heart, even though she'd expected it.

Be happy. Smile. Nothing is wrong.

The air swelled with a tension unlike any Hazel had ever experienced. Her throat felt tight, her mouth dried, but her mind couldn't connect the dots. Just as Hazel thought she might try to crawl out of her skin from the silence, her father finally spoke.

"That's a great accomplishment, Hazel." His tone did not convey that he thought it was great in any way. He said it as if she'd told him she'd won an award for coloring within the lines.

"Dad, they summoned me!" Hazel said joyfully, trying to get him to continue.

"Of course they did. You're a talented mage." He finally met her eyes, with something like pride lurking in his own, although his expression remained stony.

Crap. Crap. Crap.

That feeling of pride was what she needed to convince him to support her decision, but it had come too quickly, too easily. It was supposed to be a hurdle. Even Forrest had scoffed at her chances of getting this far.

Something was off. She had to be missing something. It was time to move on to her next point.

Be happy. Smile. Nothing is wrong.

"I can pass the exam, I know it," she said, letting earnestness sugarcoat her words.

Her father's eyes shifted back to his hands. He took a deep breath. "I made myself clear last spring. I will not pay for you to go there. The answer is no."

His words set a steel vise around Hazel's heart. While it continued to do its job, it hurt with every beat. But she was one step ahead of him.

"You haven't heard the rest of the letter," Hazel said, coldness seeping into her tone. Lifting the summons, she prepared to read once more.

"There's no need—"

Hazel interrupted her father. "*To allow scholars to focus on their advancement of magical skills, Saint Elias has the privilege of providing tuition, along with full room and board, to all scholars who pass the entrance exam...*"

Hazel looked up from the letter slowly, giving the words time to sink in, not only for her father, but also for herself. She did not need his financial support to go to SEU. She'd done her research. She'd known this, but seeing the words made it feel real. Relief washed over her. She hadn't mentioned SEU would be free and now she was glad she hadn't.

Her father said nothing. Instead, he grabbed a cloth and began to clean the kitchen. He wiped down the countertops, the sink edges, the stove, and then he moved to the cabinets. And she let him. She'd said enough. She was going to SEU and her father needed to come to terms with it.

Be happy. Smile. Nothing is wrong.

As he worked, he didn't seem the least bit surprised by what Hazel had read. His face showed not one ounce of relief at not having to pay for Hazel's tuition. But she knew deep down that was really not his objection at all. It was about losing control of her.

Seconds turned into minutes. In all of her planning and visualizing how this conversation would play out, she'd never guessed how he would react to the news that she didn't need him to go. She'd never pictured such a calm reaction. Rather, she'd imagined he might scream and rage, or even kick her out. She'd mentally prepared for the anger, not this.

Is he hurt?

Guilt started to seep in. Her father had cared for and protected her when her mother had left them both. He was flawed, but he hadn't always been so bad. Her childhood had included so many wonderful memories—camping trips to the Buffalo River as a family, her dad teaching her how to ride a horse that he'd let her name Snow White, and their own silly rendition of "Old MacDonald." Yes, he'd changed. The happy memories were few and far between now, but Hazel knew why he'd changed. She'd been broken too. But despite his heartbreak, he'd never left her. Never stopped taking care of her. Losing him would mean saying goodbye to any hope for new happy memories, and Hazel didn't want that. She wanted SEU *and* her dad's support.

"A full ride! Can you believe it?" she asked, letting warmth back into her voice. She wondered if she sounded manic.

These words had a magic-like effect, though Hazel had cast no spell. Her father's hand stopped and dropped to his side, the rag dangling. He looked up as he remained crouched in front of the rustic bottom cabinets, as if imploring Terra herself for an answer. "Do you see that?" He gestured above his head, beneath the upper cabinet.

Hazel's eyes furrowed. "The cabinets?"

"There, on the bottom."

Hazel realized he was crouching because it provided a better view and approached him, bending over to see the faint ink doodles of a child. She fought to keep the frustration out of her voice. "Dad, that's been there for years. I'm trying to—"

"Do you remember how it got there?" He cut her off calmly, as if she'd never spoken.

Hazel sighed. "Yes, I drew it there when I was little and I wasn't allowed to sit on the countertops anymore."

"You've left out a lot of details. First, the part of the story where your mother stood right here at this sink," he said, gesturing at it a foot away, "ignoring you, a four-year-old on a countertop, while you drew on the bottom of our brand-new oak cabinets."

"I don't understand what this has to do with anything. Accidents happen." Hazel crossed her arms.

Her father sighed as he mirrored her movement. "Astral projecting your psyche to allow yourself to be somewhere else, while your child plays alone in the house, is absolutely not an accident."

Hazel jerked in response to his words. She hadn't known her mother even knew how to astral project, let alone that she'd practiced it in the house. Astral projection was rare, according to the little she'd learned about it at school. It was also dangerous. Faint memories of catching her mother sleeping and taking a long while to be roused pushed to the surface of Hazel's mind.

"The point is, Hazel, that magic is a distraction. And distractions have real consequences," he added.

She rolled her eyes. "I hardly think a little ink on the underside of a cabinet can be called consequences."

Her father tsked. "No, but it certainly could when you fell and cracked your head open on the tile and we had to rush you to the hospital."

Hazel narrowed her eyes. "I don't remember that..."

"You wouldn't. You were four. When I asked your mother what

she'd been doing, she'd said, 'I projected to go visit a friend, and I didn't plan to be gone long,' as if that was a perfectly acceptable explanation." He laughed, though she knew it wasn't because he found it funny. "She said you were napping when she'd left the house, but we'll never know the truth."

"I'm fine now." Hazel tried and failed to keep the exasperation out of her voice. "Dad, I'm trying to talk to you about making one of the biggest decisions of my life, and you're talking about something that happened fourteen years ago."

"For me, it feels like yesterday." He stood to toss the rag in the sink. He took a deep breath before he said, "I wake up every day, afraid of the distraction of magic in your life. Afraid of the temptations it presents. I go to bed every night afraid it was our last good day."

"Temptations?" Hazel scoffed. Then she remembered her dad saying that exact word this morning after comparing Hazel to her mother. "Dad, it's not my fault Mom left and you can't blame magic either. It was Mom's decision!"

"You know nothing about her decision!" her father roared. "Magic has absolutely *everything* to do with it."

Hazel saw red as her frustration bloomed to resentment. She didn't know what she detested more: his belief that magic was an evil presence in their lives despite his use of it, that she was like her mother, or that she couldn't make sound decisions when it came to magic.

"You're such a hypocrite!" Her voice quivered as tears welled in her eyes. She blinked rapidly, refusing to let them fall. "You say magic is a temptation that took her away, that distracted her from us, yet you use it whenever it benefits you."

As she seethed, the kitchen's bay windows darkened behind her. It had just been a sunny midafternoon. A storm must have been brewing. She hoped it would wash her away from here.

"You use it to grow drought-resistant crops. To grow unnaturally large produce. To protect them from weather and pests. Really, in any way that makes you successful. But I can't? I'm not allowed to make my life successful with magic?"

Her father looked out the kitchen windows before turning back to Hazel and eyeing her closely.

He opened his mouth, but Hazel continued, "I will not pay for her sins. I won't limit myself to be a simple mage for the rest of my life, living off the breadcrumbs of a family grimoire when I know I'm capable of so much more."

Thunder punctuated her words overhead. Her father flinched. She felt sharp satisfaction at watching the world reflect the turmoil churning inside her.

Her father's jaw clenched as he looked into her eyes, arms crossed. "You really are just like her..."

Hazel inhaled sharply at this. It was the second time today he'd made such a statement. She knew how much her father loathed her mother, knew what an insult it was.

"I'd rather be like her than anything like *you*!"

Rain began, a hard barrage against the roof, filling the air with noise. Her father glanced at the ceiling, his face turning a deep shade of scarlet.

Of all the things she'd said in this conversation, these words were the first to put a crack in her father's façade. But the hurt flashing in his eyes fueled Hazel. She wanted to hurt him like he was hurting her. Like he'd been hurting her since her mother left.

"Did you ever think that maybe she left because you suffocated her so much that the only way for her to breathe was to leave? That maybe she would've stayed if you hadn't made all these dumb rules about magic?"

Once the words were out, she knew she'd gone too far. They were thoughts she'd had at least a dozen times, but they weren't thoughts she'd ever intended to voice, especially not to her father. He'd just pushed so hard, she'd snapped.

Yet the damage was done. Her father crossed his arms, a familiar steely glint flashing within his eyes. Not a trace of the warmth she'd known as a child was still in them. He'd once only looked at her with the adoration that dads often did with their baby girls, their princesses, who could do no wrong. Now, brows furrowed and mouth downturned, he looked at her as if she was nothing but a disappointment.

"Your mother didn't leave because of me," her father said, bitterness soaking his words as he crossed his arms over his chest. "She left because of you. She saw what you would become, and she wasn't brave enough to stick around and fight it."

A single tear spilled from Hazel's eye. She tried to process his words. Saw what she'd become? She didn't understand. Surely, she would've known if her mother had the Sight. Her mother would've told her.

"You're lying! Mom didn't have the Sight!"

As she screamed the accusation, lightning cracked above, bathing the kitchen in a blue-white light as the lights flickered and then went out. Hazel's attention snapped to the windows. A solid sheet of rain came in sideways against the glass as a deluge of wind rattled the panes.

"She ran off to get answers, while I stayed to save you. After four years, it's fair to say I'm the only parent you have that will fight to keep you from ruining your future. Your mother didn't even have the decency to tell you the truth, then left you to fail." Her father's sharp words cut through her like a blade.

A sob broke free from Hazel's lips as the constant fear she kept inside was used against her. She had no breath for words, so she shook her head in denial, but doubt crept in. If she hadn't known her mother could astral project, what else did she not know? Then Hazel thought of her own dreams.

Do I *have the Sight?*

The thought sent Hazel into a spiral, her heart and logic now coinciding for the first time. Her mom could actually be at SEU. Maybe that's where she'd gone to look for answers. It made sense.

But if that was true, it meant her mom really must have left because of Hazel and what she'd Seen.

Her father's movement caught Hazel off guard. By the time she registered his approach, he was already too close. He was a big man, and in the narrow space, his presence felt overwhelming. She had nowhere to go but back, the counter digging into her hip. He closed in quickly, his large frame filling her vision. Her father lifted Hazel's chin with a calloused finger.

"I know I'm hard on you, but it's because I love you. I want what's best for you."

Hazel's lip quivered. Either the rain had eased on the roof or she'd become numb to the sound because she couldn't hear it anymore. She absentmindedly nodded, her mind still trying to process the revelations about her mother.

Her father slowly wrapped his arms around her. She felt his warmth and leaned into it, desperate for any reassurance in this moment. Remorse for the harsh things she'd said crept in.

Then she felt cold steel sting the skin of her neck.

Surprised, she tried to pull back, but her father's arms held her tight as the familiar metal clink of a lock sang out. She knew that sound. She'd heard it more times than she could count, always when her father was fed up with an unruly animal.

Desperation fueled her as Hazel fought against him, throwing her elbows and pushing at his face. But with the counter behind her and her father in front of her, she had nowhere to go. She'd never physically overpower him. Thinking fast, she slid to her knees, then darted under his arm and around his side. She made it across the room before she realized he wasn't chasing her. She whirled about, yanking at the command collar he'd placed around her neck. One like he'd threatened to place on Garth earlier today.

Eyes wide, she pulled at the cold steel futilely. Her breath quickened and her head felt light. How could he do this to her? Hazel knew her father was backwards in some ways and strict in most, but she'd never thought him capable of something so horrible, so heinous. Magically stripping someone of their free will was a crime.

"This is for the best. At least until you calm down and the exam has passed."

He was planning to keep her in this thing all summer? Hazel felt acid rise in the back of her throat. Thunder boomed above them, matching the pounding in her head.

"This storm is wild..." Forrest froze in the kitchen doorway, his words fading as he looked between his sister and father. His eyes widened. "Dad, what did you do?"

"I did what was necessary. We tried it your way. She left me no other option."

Hazel's breath caught in her throat as she processed her father's words. They'd discussed this? Planned this? All to stop Hazel from following her dreams? A cry escaped her lips as she realized how deep the betrayal truly went.

Forrest shook his head. "Hazel, I swear I didn't—"

But he had. He'd begged and pleaded with her not to go to Saint Elias, feigning big brotherly protectiveness, when in reality, he'd been keeping the truth of their mother's vision from her. Her stomach churned.

Lightning streaked through the sky, filling the kitchen once again. Then they were bathed in darkness.

In the same instant, rage consumed her, burning away her disbelief and the hurt of betrayal. She whirled away from them both and tried to run from the room, but she stopped in the doorway when her father said, "There's no use, Hazel."

Hazel kept her back to him, refusing to let him see the effect his words had on her. How could her own father do this to her?

"Your mom may have given up on you, but I won't. I know we can change the future," her father said behind her.

But Hazel was done listening. Her back still turned, she tugged her wand from its holster and whispered a spell she'd been practicing since the minute she'd learned it existed. *"Ad liberum arbitrium."*

The audible click of metal sounded once more.

"Hazel?" The confusion in her father's voice was apparent.

Hazel spun about, flinging the collar off her neck. It hit the ground with a clang as thunder erupted and lightning cracked across the sky, illuminating his shocked face. Hazel aimed her wand at him.

His eyes were wide with disbelief, as if he'd never imagined she might know stronger magic than him. There was also pain there, and it broke Hazel's heart. The wand shook in her hand as she pointed it at him. What if he was right? What if she was no better than her mother? What if she wasn't good enough to survive SEU?

He raised his arms in alarm, as if she might hurt him. Despite the last four years of isolation he'd put her through, she couldn't do it. She still loved him, even if she hated him. Hazel lowered her wand.

Regardless of her fear of failure and the uncertainty of her future, one thing was certain: Hazel was done following anyone else's rules.

Her voice never wavered as she spoke. "You may not have given up on me, but I've given up on you."

CHAPTER 4

Gwen

"Gwendolyn!" her mother cried, rushing to her and wrapping her in a hug.

With her mother's arms around her, happiness clear in her voice, Gwen's defenses shattered. The weight of her mother's hopes pressed down on her, suffocating her. Gwen was strong and forceful around everyone but her mother. When she was with her mom, she could be weak and vulnerable. Outside of her family, she never let anyone see that side of her. Her father had ingrained in her that she needed to be a warrior. "If you're always on the defense, you'll never be defenseless," he'd said.

Safe in her mother's arms, the emotions of the day crashed over her like a breaking wave. Anxiety, fear, and guilt surged to the surface, breaking free in giant, shuddering sobs against her mother's shoulders. Her mother held her tighter.

"Mom, I'm so sorry. I can't go," Gwen said between sucking breaths. "You should have seen me today. I completely lost it when the eagle came. I even tried to attack Manfrit. Manfrit, Mom!"

Her pitch rose as she spoke, and she felt like she couldn't get enough air as the incident replayed in her mind. She pulled away from her mother and paced around the room while she tried to catch her breath. Gwen hadn't attacked one of her cousins since she was a cub. Ahren still bore the scar she'd given him on his neck.

"It's true, she did," Klaus added with a shrug.

How can he remain so calm? Lives are at stake here! My *life is at stake here.*

Her mother nodded, her expression unreadable at first, but then her eyes softened. She reached out, resting a gentle hand on her arm; it was a silent reassurance that, despite everything, she still loved her. "You're stronger than you think, Gwendolyn." Her mother slid her hand down to Gwen's wrist and thoughtfully thumbed the charms on it. "This doesn't define you."

Her mother had created the bracelet because Gwen had been born a tiny wolf cub, covered in white fur instead of skin. Her mother had been furious that Dolphus had never mentioned this was a possibility. She had begged him to fix her, desperate for a way to turn Gwen human, but he'd ignored her concerns. "I had no way of knowing. There's no record of this happening since the Great War. She'll shift when she hits puberty," he'd told her, as if that was the end of it.

But that hadn't been good enough for Liana Bishop.

She'd torn through his archives until she'd found an obscure passage claiming enchanted gold chains could help control a therian's shift. She'd used her own methods to replicate them and craft a golden bracelet, each charm woven with a different enchantment.

But instead of unlocking Gwen's wolf, the magic suppressed it, binding her to her human form. When Gwen removed it, the wolf eventually returned, uncontrollable.

When her father had first discovered the bracelet wrapped around Gwen's wrist, he had attacked Liana for her betrayal, saying she'd cost Gwen a chance at control. That now Gwen might always be a slave to the wolf.

The scars that ran down her mother's back were a permanent reminder of what therians were capable of. What Gwen was terrified she could become. And the last place she wanted to be if that happened was Saint Elias University.

"You don't understand. I can't wear my bracelet during the exam," Gwen explained to her mother.

"Why can't she wear her bracelet?" her mother asked, her gaze sharp as she crossed her arms and turned to Klaus.

"Because you can't have charms or spells on you," he explained, rubbing the back of his neck. "Barring tattooing glyphs on her skin—"

"Absolutely not!" Gwen roared.

This wasn't the first time he'd suggested it, but no matter how much she feared what her wolf form was capable of, she'd never give it up completely.

Her mother nodded in agreement with Gwen. "How do they ensure no charms or spells are used?"

Gwen straightened. She'd never thought to ask that before. She turned to Klaus, hope flickering in her chest.

He hesitated, then sighed. "I can't tell you. I took an oath."

Great. Another dead end.

Klaus offered an apologetic shrug, his face genuinely regretful.

Her mother was silent. Gwen felt the pressure releasing from her as she assumed her mother was coming to the same conclusion she had years ago: Gwen couldn't answer the summons.

A surprising wave of sadness rose up. This was it. The moment her dream of Saint Elias University truly died—both for herself and for her mother. Gwen thought she'd accepted it a long time ago, but facing it now, the wound felt fresh. Wanting to go and knowing she couldn't somehow existed together in the same space.

SEU might be the only place in the world that held the knowledge she needed to master her shift. She knew from Klaus that the university actually taught students about the Forsaken—the post-Great War term for therians, fae, elves, and siphoners, all believed to have since gone extinct—something no other school would do. Without Saint Elias University, she might never find the answers she so desperately needed. Which made giving it up that much harder.

"What *can* you tell us?" her mother asked Klaus. Apparently, she wasn't giving up so easily.

Gwen clenched her jaw, frustration rising with each passing second. Her mother could be so stubborn, pushing and pushing when there was nothing left to say. This conversation was going nowhere.

If anyone were to find out what I am, it would be earth-shattering, life-altering. I can't risk it! Why don't they understand?

She couldn't take it anymore.

With a sharp breath, Gwen shoved herself up from the couch, the legs accidentally scraping against the floor with her effort. A hard session of training and a full day's work at Charming Carvings always left her starving. Maybe food would help—at the very least, it would give her something to focus on that wasn't this.

"I need a break." She didn't wait for a response before turning on her heel and stalking toward the kitchen.

Walnut cabinets lined the walls, their deep color standing out against the black-and-white tiled floor. She yanked open the fridge, her gaze flicking over the magnets covering the freezer door. They were a patchwork of memories—seaside trinkets, faded amusement park souvenirs, and tiny tokens from the mountain towns she had explored with her mother.

Her fingers drummed against the stainless-steel handle as she scanned for a snack. She needed something to do, something to keep her from storming back into the living room and continuing a conversation that had no solution. Nothing in the fridge looked appetizing. She slammed the door shut and turned toward the kitchen island.

Beyond the island, the sunroom glowed with warm evening light, casting long shadows across the dining table. The scent of dried herbs lingered in the air, a constant presence from the potted plants spilling across the floor. Her mother liked to have them close at hand for cooking and spells. This space had always been a sanctuary, a place of peace. Today, it felt like a prison as she screamed into the void, waiting for someone to hear her.

Her mother and Klaus spoke in hushed tones in the other room, but Gwen did her best to drown out their words. Spotting the fruit trees along the back wall, she decided to make a smoothie. That would be loud enough to block them out.

She moved into the sunroom and picked a peach, along with a handful of strawberries. As she headed back to the island, she heard a familiar tapping. A hawk in a ridiculous black leather vest with a Sons of Chaos patch embroidered on it pecked at the window.

Great, just what I need—another unwelcome delivery fowl.

Her father's bird flew through the window as she opened it and landed on her shoulder.

"Hello, Pan," Gwen said, scratching the top of his head.

This was the first letter she'd had from her father in weeks, and suspicion of the timing made her hesitate, but a snap of Pan's beak told her he wasn't feeling patient.

She removed the letter from Pan's talons carefully. The bird nuzzled his head into her neck in response. Well, he wasn't entirely unwelcome.

Dearest Gwendolyn,

I heard you received your summons today.

"How does he know I got summoned?" Gwen looked outside for eyes in the trees, but saw none. Shaking off the thought of him spying on her, she continued reading.

As you know, we don't go to university. While I'm proud you were summoned by SEU, I expect you to ignore it. In our society, it's important that you surround yourself with your own kind.

Gwen rolled her eyes. He had never cared before. He'd kept her away from the therian community, away from her own grandparents. He called her his secret weapon, but she knew the truth. He was embarrassed by her. Why wouldn't he be? She couldn't even master the most basic therian ability.

For years, he'd tried to undo what her mother had done, forcing Gwen through grueling training sessions, demanding she shift out of her wolf form on her own. Every failure was met with stiff silence or a sharp reprimand, his disappointment settling over her like a weight she could never shake. She felt his anger in the way his grip tightened, in the way his voice dropped into something cold and edged. He was the only one who could help her though. The only one qualified to teach her. If she had any hope of controlling her shift, of proving she belonged, she had to endure it.

She was supposed to be his greatest asset. Instead, she was his biggest failure.

I know it has been a lifelong dream of yours to join the Sons of Chaos. As you know, the Sons don't take daughters.

The Sons of Chaos were her father's pack. He'd always sworn that when he became Alpha, things would change. That the old ways would fall, and women would finally have a place among them. He'd been promoted last year. That was why their training had stopped. Had he done it? Had he kept his promise? Had he convinced the Sons to let women into their ranks?

Maybe she didn't need Saint Elias University after all. Maybe she could find what she was looking for among her own kind. The thought filled her with something unexpected—hope.

No matter how many times he had hurt her, she'd never stopped wanting to earn his love. His approval was always out of reach, doled out in careful, conditional fragments, not freely given like her mother's. And part of her still believed—still *wished*—that if she proved herself, if she became what he wanted, he wouldn't be so cruel. Maybe she'd finally be enough.

But it wasn't just about him. Wolves weren't meant to be alone. She'd spent years trying to understand her kind, scouring every inch of the library for scraps of history, piecing together a world that should have been hers. More than anything—more than even his love—she wanted to belong. To stand among her people and know, without question, that she was one of them.

However, joining her father's pack meant leaving her mother. Leaving the one person who'd fought for her, believed in her, protected her from the worst parts of his world. From him. Gwen had never blamed her mother for making the bracelet. She hadn't wanted to grow up as a wolf and she understood that her mother couldn't allow her father to raise her alone. The only reason Gwen put up with him was because he was her only connection to the therian world.

Her chest tightened. She wasn't sure the cost was worth it.

In an effort to bring you into the fold, I've spoken with the Hellhounds.

Gwen made a face at the mention of her father's rivals. There was a constant power struggle between the two packs. Currently, the Hellhounds sat beneath the Sons of Chaos in the hierarchy. In her world, anything below the top was insignificant. Her father had drilled that into her since birth. Be the best, or be nothing.

"Why would he speak to them?" she asked out loud, seemingly to Pan, but mostly to herself.

Their next Alpha, a fox by the name of Crevan Reid has agreed to an alliance. Your wedding will take place this fall.

He has to be fucking joking!

But she knew he wasn't. Her hands curled into fists and her nails dug into her palms. Rage burned through her. He wasn't just making an alliance—he was using her to cement his power. Like a bargaining chip. Like she was nothing more than a means to his end.

Tears rolled down her cheeks. How could he do this to her?

Therians only had arranged marriages to help strengthen their political power between the packs. The Sons of Chaos had been using this technique for centuries with their daughters, as they didn't allow women to join. They never mated with other therians for that reason. Which was why Dolphus had chosen Liana as his wife. Women had always been thought of as expendable within the therian community, but even after all he had done, she'd never thought her own father would use *her* this way.

His demand for her to ignore the summons wasn't about her. It had never been about her. This arrangement would secure his place as the next Alpha of Alphas, something he'd spent his entire life chasing. And he'd decided she was the price he was willing to pay.

His betrayal felt like a knife through the heart. This was worse than being summoned to Saint Elias University.

A sob tore from her throat as she fled the kitchen, the tears falling faster, unchecked, as she ran to the one person who could make this better.

"Mom!"

"What's the matter now?"

Her mother looked up from the couch as Pan flew into the room behind her. He circled about, searching for a place to perch, finally settling on one of the many bookshelves.

"Great. What has he done now?" she asked, but the second her gaze landed on Gwen, the teasing edge faded. She motioned towards the letter. "Hand it to me."

Gwen relinquished it gladly, wanting to pass the burden into her mother's capable hands. She wiped the remaining tears from her face as her mother read over the contents of the letter. Klaus gave her a sympathetic look.

"He's arranged for you to be married?" Her mother shook her head. "The audacity of this man."

"What am I going to do?" Gwen started pacing around the room. "I can't marry a man I've never met, especially a fox."

I'm going to throw up. How can he do this to me?

"What's wrong with a fox?" Klaus joked, clearly trying to lighten the mood.

"He could be a two-headed snake for all I care. I'm too young to get married!" Gwen's voice raised as she added, "And if you must know, foxes are tiny, for one, and sly, for two, and he's a Hellhound, for three. I want to be a *Son*!"

Her mother sighed, her expression tired. "Gwendolyn, you have to know you'll never be able to join your father's pack. The Sons don't take daughters."

"I'm so sick of that expression!" Gwen snapped.

Her mother flinched but didn't argue. Instead, she let out a slow breath, her fingers absently grazing the scar on the back of her neck, a faded reminder of what therians did to women who overstepped. "I know it's not fair." Her voice was quieter now, raw with something old and bitter. "But women are tools to them. Breeders. Bargaining chips. They obey or they suffer. And those who step out of line—" She exhaled sharply and let her hand fall away from the scar. "Well, you know what happens to them. If I'd have known how they were, I never would've..."

Gwen swallowed hard. She didn't need her to finish. *If I'd known,*

I never would've been with Dolphus. But there was no easy way to say that—no way to rewrite the past without rewriting Gwen herself.

Her mother took a breath and straightened. "Luckily for you, I think Klaus and I have a solution." She held up the summons, her expression expectant.

Gwen blinked, the weight in her chest lifting just enough for curiosity to slip through. "You're kidding. What's the solution?"

Her mother's lips twitched. "Well, first, I have to tell you the problem." She paused, letting the moment hang before finally saying, "You'll have to pass through enchanted water that washes away any spell or charm."

Gwen's fingers immediately went to the charms dangling from her wrist.

"We need to find a way to waterproof your bracelet," her mother said, then quickly added, "Non-magically."

Gwen turned her glare to Klaus, who was sinking further into the armchair like he wished it would swallow him whole. "For Terra's sake, are you saying the solution this whole time was a plastic baggie, Klaus?"

Klaus exhaled sharply, resting his elbow on the armrest and pinching the bridge of his nose. "Obviously not."

Her mother chuckled. "It needs to be impenetrable to magic."

"So glad this is amusing to someone," Gwen muttered, grabbing a throw pillow and tossing it at her mom. She caught it with ease, still looking far too pleased with herself.

Klaus sighed and dragged a hand down his face. "Look, it's not that simple. You'd need something durable, something that won't let water touch the bracelet but also won't trigger any of the enchantment-detection wards."

Her mother nodded. "Exactly. What's something you'd be allowed to have on you but doesn't contain magic?"

Gwen eyed her skeptically, arms crossed. "My clothing? But that's not waterproof. Unless we're talking rain jackets," she added dryly, knowing full well those weren't impenetrable to magic either.

“What else?” her mother asked, eyebrows raised as if she already knew the answer.

Gwen thought about it, then realized what her mom was trying to lead her towards. “My wand?”

The wood wouldn’t be waterproof, but the onyx handle would. It was also impenetrable by magic. If she hollowed it out, she could safely store her bracelet inside. She pulled her wand from its sheath on her thigh, looking it over with new eyes. It was wand-making 101, and the first thing her grandfather had drilled into her—a wand was a conduit for magic that couldn’t be influenced or tainted by outside magic.

“Precisely,” her mother said with a satisfied smile.

Oh shit!

She wavered, caught between hope and disbelief. Had the answer really been in front of her this whole time?

For two years, she'd mourned a future she thought was lost. She’d convinced herself there was no way to set foot on SEU’s campus without risking everything. One mistake, one slip, and the secret she'd spent her life protecting would be exposed. The idea of going had felt so impossible that she'd buried the thought entirely.

If she had just told her mom from the start, she could have spared herself all the disappointment and anger that came with knowing she’d never have the life she desperately wanted.

Then a thought occurred to her. “But what about while the bracelet is still in my wand?” she asked. “What if I can’t control myself long enough to pass the exam without it?”

“Make friends fast and use their scents to ground you,” her mother told her. “So your wolf can recognize them, if it comes to that.”

That could work.

The weight lifted from her chest as the realization hit her—she had a chance. A chance to go to SEU. A chance to escape her father’s control. A chance to avoid the marriage entirely. For the first time today, the future didn’t feel like a cage.

"I have to go hollow this out," Gwen told them.

"Right now?" her mother asked.

"Of course right now!" Gwen kissed her mom on the cheek and rushed upstairs, heart pounding.

She threw open her bedroom door and raced inside. Bookshelves lined the walls, packed with every history book she'd ever found that mentioned therians, no matter how obscure. At the foot of her bed sat a sturdy wooden chest, filled with the things she couldn't part with—birthday cards, letters from both her parents, the family grimoires, and her father's old leather jacket with its Sons of Chaos patch. She'd found it in the shed the day her mother had kicked him out.

A corkboard hung above her desk filled with pictures of her and her friend Jordan at Camp Camelot. Her desk was cluttered with books. She gathered them up and stacked them to the side, clearing enough space to work. She crouched by her leather tool bag on the floor and unzipped it before searching through it until she found the ones she needed. The bag was one of a matching set, its counterpart sitting in her grandfather's shop. Magically linked, they allowed her to access anything stored inside either one. She'd asked for a second set of whittling tools last Christmas, but her grandfather, ever practical, had decided this was better. Embedding tools were rare and expensive—why waste money on duplicates when she could have a direct link?

With a quiet sigh, she pulled out the tools she needed and set them on the desk. Time to get to work.

An hour of cursing and many tears later, Gwen was finished. Snapping the handle off her wand had been emotionally taxing, but now, a small screw lip seamlessly affixed the onyx handle to the shaft. The seal was watertight and secure. From the outside, it looked unchanged, but in her hands, it felt lighter from the hollowed-out handle.

Taking a deep breath and hoping for the best, she unscrewed the handle and slid her bracelet inside, pressing a final piece of onyx on top as a precaution before sealing it shut.

She exhaled slowly, turning the wand over. No visible gaps. No sign of what lay hidden inside. Gwen tightened her grip, surprised by a faint hum of magic beneath her fingertips. Was it her imagination, or was the bracelet really that powerful?

Either way, it comforted her.

The door creaked open behind her, and Klaus's voice broke the silence.

"How's it going?"

Gwen turned to see him leaning against the doorframe, hands in his pockets. His gaze flicked from her face to the wand in her hands.

"It's finished," she said, holding it up.

Klaus pushed off the doorframe and stepped closer, studying it with quiet approval. "Looks solid."

Gwen nodded, relief washing over her now that it was done.

"Did it fit?" he asked.

"Barely, but yeah."

"Okay, one last test," Klaus said, nodding toward the wand. "You need to make sure it's waterproof."

Gwen hesitated, gripping the handle tighter. What if it wasn't? If she had messed this up, she'd have wasted hours and shattered the one real chance she had.

Only one way to find out.

She headed for the sink in the adjoining bathroom. Cold water gushed over the polished onyx, droplets sliding down its surface like tiny glass beads. The seconds stretched, each one pressing heavier on her chest.

Voices drifted up from downstairs—at first, a murmur, but soon, footsteps and laughter followed. Her mother wasn't alone down there; all her family was gathering. They'd want to know if she'd done it, if she had succeeded.

Her pulse quickened. They were waiting for her. Expecting something worth celebrating.

This had to work.

Shutting off the tap, Gwen quickly unscrewed the handle and held her breath as she peered inside.

Dry.

Her bracelet sat exactly as she'd left it, untouched by the water. She had done it. She pulled the bracelet free and slipped it back onto her wrist. The weight of it grounded her, steadying the emotions tumbling through her.

"Looks like you're gonna have to go take the exam after all," Klaus said from the doorway, giving her a shit-eating grin.

Gwen punched him as relief soared through her.

Klaus laughed, rubbing his arm. Gwen was not sorry.

"Let's go tell them," Klaus said.

Her mother, aunt, uncle, cousins, and grandparents filled the small living room, their voices carrying so loudly even Klaus could hear them from upstairs.

Gwen stepped into the crowded space, her breath catching at the sight. Streamers hung crisscrossed from the ceiling, and homemade banners floated around the room, flashing phrases like *Congratulations!* and *You did it!*

The moment they saw her, the room erupted into cheers.

"Hip hip hooray!"

"We couldn't be more proud!"

Laughter and whistles rang in her ears as hands clapped her back and arms wrapped around her. She'd never seen them all this excited —this proud of her.

"Speech!" Ahren called out once she reached the center of the room.

Gwen turned in a slow circle, taking in their beaming faces, their unwavering belief in her. Her chest tightened—not with fear, but with something warmer, something fierce and unshakable. She grinned so hard her cheeks ached. And then she said something she never thought she'd have the chance to say.

"I'm going to Saint Elias University!"

The words felt surreal.

As long as I pass. Oh, Salem, what if I don't?

Fear slithered in. She'd spent years learning how to disappear, how to exist only within the safety of her family. No one outside of them knew what or who she really was. And now, for the first time in her life, she was going out into the world alone. Well, almost alone—at least Klaus would be there.

But before the fear could take hold, it was swallowed by the roar of her family's excitement. Whistles, shouts, and cheers crashed over her, pulling her back to this moment—to them, to their love.

For tonight, she'd let herself celebrate.

CHAPTER 5

Hazel

Hazel stood at the edge of the forest, the evergreen trees towering around her, so different from the ones near her family's farm in Arkansas. Bellflowers blanketed the forest floor. Overhead, a pair of ravens circled before landing on a pine branch, their dark eyes watching.

Rooftops and smoking chimneys peeked above the tree line, marking a town she'd never been to but could guess with ease: Eagles Ridge, the town nearest Mount Saint Elias—the mountain that held all her hopes—and, if she was honest, all her fears. As much as she wanted answers from her mother, she was not naïve enough to believe that they wouldn't hurt. But nothing was worse than not knowing.

A flicker of movement pulled her gaze forward. A woman stood beneath a towering pine, wrapped in a deep-purple velvet cloak. Hazel's breath hitched.

Her mother.

She looked younger than Hazel recalled, but then, it had been so very long since Hazel had last seen her.

"You must be quick to catch me!" her mother called, laughter dancing in her voice.

The gurgling croak of a raven sounded overhead, sending a chill down Hazel's spine.

Mischief gleamed in her mother's eyes, playful and inviting. Laughter and tears threatened Hazel all at once. She had missed that teasing lilt in her mother's voice. Hazel took a step forward, answering the invitation. The moment her foot touched the ground, her mother vanished.

"Not that kind of quick..." her mother's voice taunted behind her.

Hazel turned slowly, unfazed. She knew this game by heart now.

As expected, her mother was waiting, leaning against another pine, tapping her temple with a knowing smile. "Quicker."

Hazel barely had time to register the command before she felt a hand land lightly on her shoulder.

"You're going to shock the world with your quickness," her mother whispered beside her.

A faint hum filled the air as tendrils of purple electricity flickered from her mother's hand, dancing along her skin for a split second before disappearing. Hazel's gaze flicked back toward the pines, where her mother rested against a tree, yet she could feel the warmth of her touch, hear her breath, see her standing right beside her.

There were two of her.

Everything about this moment was the same as it had always been in her dreams, but Hazel was not. Too many words had been spoken, words that shattered illusions and refused to be forgotten. Her fight with her father had torn the blinders from her eyes, forcing her to see what had always been in front of her. What she'd once dismissed as strange and surreal now made perfect sense.

Hazel grabbed her mother's hand. "You're astral projecting."

It wasn't a question, because Hazel now knew without a doubt that's what her mother had been doing all along.

For the first time, the dream shifted. Her mother cupped Hazel's face as she graced her with a proud, brilliant smile. "You're getting quicker."

With a gasp, Hazel sat up in bed and wiped the sleep from her face. She was on the right track. She knew it.

Hazel stared out the bay window of her brother's guest room for a few moments, then reached for the book on the nightstand for the thousandth time since moving in with him three months ago. *The History and Applications of Astral Projection* was worn out—not because of Hazel's misuse, but because it had been published in the fifties and it was the only book on astral projection at the hidden mage library in Little Rock.

Mages hoarded magical knowledge like dragons hoarded gold in mundane stories of old. Only the strongest and bravest got the chance to touch even an ounce of it. Her mother wasn't the only reason she wanted to go to Saint Elias University. It was reported to hold one of the most extensive magical libraries in the world with one-of-a-kind books on magic she'd only ever heard of. Not to mention the fact that she'd get to learn from professors actually trained in these magics.

Hazel flipped through the yellowed pages of the loaned book, tracing her fingers along the familiar words. She crossed her legs before closing her eyes and envisioning her symbol of freedom, as the book instructed. She thought of the willow outside the window in Forrest's backyard, tossing about in the wild abandon of the wind.

Hazel breathed in. "I wish to be without constraint." She breathed out. "I wish to let go of the ties that bind me." She breathed in. "I wish to be free." She breathed out. "So I lay these bonds down." She rushed the next words, afraid of forgetting the most important part of the mindful chant—the part needed to anchor her to her body. "And to pick them up again when I so choose. *Projectura.*"

Hazel felt a tug in her mind and chest. She peeked open an eye and looked down at her body. Lifting her hand and examining both sides, she found herself very much still attached to her physical form.

A sigh tore through her as she collapsed back onto the bed. Hazel rubbed her face with her hands as she stifled a scream of frustration. "Damn it!"

"Language," rumbled Forrest sarcastically next to Hazel as his finger prodded her rib. When he made contact, there was an audible crack and a sharp prickle. Hazel yelped as her eyes flew open—not because it hurt, but because Forrest had startled her. She hadn't heard him come into the room.

Forrest shook his hand out as he looked at her accusingly. "You shocked me!"

Hazel gave him a wicked grin, as if she'd somehow planned to punish him for sneaking up on her. For a moment, they almost felt like their old selves, before their mom had left, before that night in the kitchen. Almost. Hazel was thankful for a place to stay—and Forrest was eager to make up for whatever part he'd played in their father's betrayal—but they were different now. *She* was different and she couldn't bring herself to lower the walls she'd built around her heart that night.

"Still no luck?" Forrest asked, pointing at the book.

She turned her head to look at him. "I can tell something is happening. It's just not enough. My consciousness won't separate from my body. I'm doing everything this damn book says. I've read it a hundred times, envisioned all of my favorite spots, and nothing is working."

Forrest plopped down on the bed, his thick frame jostling it. He half-heartedly reached out to rub her head, but Hazel swatted him away. His immediate frown told her he was saddened by it, by the emotional distance she'd placed between them, but he didn't acknowledge it.

"Come on now, Sis. You're supposed to be the smart one. You don't really think you're going to learn how to do one of the hardest magics in three months, do you? Go easy on yourself." She began to protest, but Forrest continued. "I love that brain of yours, but I can't say I always understand what's going on in there. I don't get this obsession. You've never once shown an interest in it before."

"Do you remember the class at Elkmont where they cover the soft magics?" Hazel said, defensiveness creeping into her tone. Soft magics relied solely on the use and manipulation of the mind.

Forrest nodded. "Sure, the arcane section in Magic Theory. I remember. It creeped me out. I don't like the idea of people running around invisible, watching me."

Hazel slapped the bed. "You can't tell me you didn't always wonder what it would be like to leave your body and explore the world without fear of the things in it."

Forrest shrugged and then rubbed a hand through his sleep-mussed brown hair. "Sure, theoretically. Hypothetically. I never spent weeks with my nose in a book trying to make it happen and I definitely didn't do it after I learned about our mom doing it and then leaving us."

"We don't know if that's why she left." Hazel twisted the comforter between her fingers.

"The point is, you never had any interest in actually pursuing this and now you're trying to make it happen. I guess I don't understand this need to do it."

Hazel suddenly became fascinated with her hands resting in her lap. She looked at them in tense concentration. "Astral projection is *supposed* to be hard. The hardest of the arcane magics, even harder than Sight. I just wondered... if she's good at it, maybe I might be too."

Forrest seared Hazel with a knowing look that told her he knew that wasn't the only reason.

She gave in to the silence. "And maybe I want to know what's so fascinating about it that she'd leave us for it."

"I just want you to be careful. I don't agree with what Dad tried to do, but I get he was worried," Forrest continued. "I've heard people say astral projection is addicting. I can only imagine how freeing it would feel to be in two places at once and to move about while your body rests."

Hazel recoiled from his words and rolled away from him on the bed. She released a sigh and asked, "Did you know what Dad was going to do?"

Forrest shook his head adamantly. "No, I swear, Hazy, I didn't. I never would've let him do that."

She searched his face. Earnest honesty shone in his brown eyes. She believed him. She wished she'd been brave enough to ask him that at the beginning of the summer. Instead, she'd never dared ask lest she find herself completely alone. A weight lifted from her shoulders with the knowledge, but it didn't erase the fact that her brother had not stepped in to defend her.

"Do you—do you really think Mom's need for magic is why she left?"

As Forrest studied Hazel's face, her eyes filled with tears that didn't fall.

Please say yes. Please say she left because she was addicted to magic. Say it wasn't because of me.

When he released a heavy sigh, she realized he'd been holding his breath too. "No."

Tears threatened to roll down her cheeks. She'd been sure he was going to say yes. "Why not?"

"Because Mom loves us more than anything. Every decision she ever made was for us."

Hazel's head dropped in relief. If Forrest was right, their mother hadn't abandoned her out of fear or temptation. She looked at her hands in her lap, avoiding Forrest's gaze. She'd told him most of what had happened that night with her father—everything except that their father had insisted Hazel was the reason their mother left. It wasn't something she could bring herself to say out loud.

Hazel's alarm went off, startling them both. Smacking the off button, Hazel stood to grab her clothes and then wiped the unshed tears from her eyes as she walked to the bathroom.

"Is it time already?" Forrest asked.

"Yep. You know me, always early," she answered from behind the bathroom door.

The entrance exam wasn't until the next morning, but all the invited mages had received a warning about no late entries and a recommendation to arrive the night before. The school incentivized this with a free stay at Fjordhaven Lodge and a free meal at Kodiak Brew. Hazel, who'd never been allowed to go to magical towns before, had decided to make a day of it.

When she exited the bathroom, she found Forrest standing beside her suitcase. He yanked at the handle. "Dang, what do you have in here?"

"Everything." Hazel meant it. She'd left nothing behind at her dad's, refusing to allow him any memories but the ones he'd created.

"Well, Hazy. I guess this is goodbye. Will I see you at Christmas?" Hope filled Forrest's voice.

Hazel thought about lying in order to leave without hurting her brother. Instead, she was honest. "I don't know."

Forrest nodded. He stepped forward and wrapped her in a hug. After a moment, he pulled back enough to look her in the eye, hands bracing her arms. "Is there anything I can say to convince you to stay?"

Hazel considered his words. "I'll stay if you tell me why I shouldn't go. No bullshit reasons. The truth."

"I can't, Hazy." Forrest's eyes turned glassy as he shook his head.

She knew by his tone that he meant it. "Why not?"

Forrest released a tight breath, his gaze never leaving hers. Finally, he shook his head and shrugged, imploring her with nothing more than a look.

Hazel's heart ached at the distance she felt between them and the knowledge that, with her absence, it would only grow wider. But she would no longer tolerate lies or manipulation. She didn't care what his intentions were. "Then I can't stay."

Forrest nodded as he wiped his eye. His voice came out rough when he said, "I want to say one more thing. I want you to remember that magic is enticing, more so than any drink or drug, or even money. Draw a line in the sand that you'll own it, that it'll never own you. If you don't, if you cross that line, you may lose yourself on the other side."

Hazel swallowed, feeling the sincerity of the words but also knowing she was missing something. Was this a warning about her? About what her mother had Seen? The need to ask clawed at her, but she held back. If he was going to tell her, he would've already done so.

"I understand." She didn't, not really. It wasn't nearly enough, but it was something—a warning.

Forrest's intense gaze softened as he released her.

Hazel pulled her wand from her pocket. "Be good," she said.

"Hey that's my li—"

But Hazel was already waving her wand as she incanted, "*Advinere.*"

One moment, she stood in Forrest's guest room surrounded by oak walls and glass windows, the next she stood on cobblestone streets. A gateway made up of limestone in varying shades of yellow and ochre loomed over the road before her. Buildings flanked the gateway on either side, with deep-brown exteriors and two-toned wooden trim encircled by a true iron fence extending as far as the eye could see. A sign that hung over the archway read *Welcome to Eagles Ridge, Alaska.*

A salty breeze blew from the bay behind her, carrying the sounds of gentle waves lapping against the shoreline. The road leading down to the bay wound down to a single pier lined with several small fishing boats and a sailboat that dwarfed them in size. Evergreens of spruce and pine soaked up the sun along the coastlines of the fjord that secluded the little town from passing ships headed to and from Anchorage on the open ocean.

Hazel sighed as she took in the snowcapped mountains looming over the town in the not-so-far distance. It occurred to her that one of those peaks was Mount Saint Elias, and her heart raced with the possibility that this place could be her new home.

She was officially on her own for the first time in her life, and it left her feeling like she'd swallowed a jar of butterflies.

Hazel shook her head, attempting to find her resolve again. *I can do this.*

She snagged her suitcase once more and made for town under the archway.

The road led to a roundabout with a fountain in the middle. A hooded statue stood in the center, offering a tipped pitcher through which water flowed and fell back into the pool of the fountain. As she approached, she noticed a small inscription on it—*The waters here are deep and true. One drop, one sip. Saint Elias will bless you.*

Wooden ladles laid along the edge of the fountain, but she grimaced at the idea of drinking from anything communal.

The faint music she'd heard from the gateway grew louder, drowning out her thoughts. To the left of the fountain, wood-beamed stores with steep, snow-shedding roofs and carved balconies lined the road. In front of them, a street fair spilled onto the cobbled road, colorful market stalls stretching beneath rippling awnings that snapped and shifted in the wind.

The market buzzed with life—people her age greeted each other, laughing like long-lost friends. They were all probably here for the entrance exam too. She wished she already had a friend of her own here. But that would change. Now that her father was no longer holding her back, she was determined to make it happen.

Resenting her suitcase already, Hazel dragged it to a bike rack and pulled a piece of string from the seam inside her coat pocket. She waved her wand. "*Dispando.*" The string grew longer, and she wrapped it around the bike rack and her suitcase. "*Similo Catena.*" The string transformed into a chain. "*Mutare Cursoriam.*"

The suitcase now looked like a bike, but if someone were to ride it, it would move no better or faster than a suitcase with two bidirectional wheels. At least she wouldn't have to worry about lugging it around town now, or someone trying to steal it.

Excited to explore the town, Hazel headed straight for the row of stores next to her. Martella's Wand Shop had striped burgundy and pink curtains that framed the storefront windows. Hazel peered inside and saw a girl with her mother buying a wand with a flower-shaped crystal handle. The sight made Hazel smile as she remembered purchasing her own wand with her mother. They'd waited until her father left for work one morning and then her mother had driven her all the way to Little Rock to make sure Hazel got the proper wand she'd dreamed of. She fought the urge to step inside. Her wand was perfectly fine.

The store next to it was even harder to resist, with every broom Hazel could ever imagine lining the walls. She hovered by the window, trying not to press her nose against the glass. Inside, an attractive dark-haired boy laughed with his friends as they tested out a sleek oak-handled broom. Hazel smiled despite herself.

But reality tugged at her. She didn't even know how to ride a broom yet—and with the tiny amount of pretium, the standard currency for mages, she'd brought with her, there was no way she could afford one.

The scent of freshly brewed coffee wafted towards her as she headed past Crowley Chronicles & Curiosities towards an open window beneath a wooden *Kodiak Brew* sign. The line was short, so she stepped into place, already anticipating the warmth of a cup in her hands.

Hazel spared a glance behind her at the market while she waited in line. Two girls around her age stepped up behind her and smiled at her. Maybe it wouldn't be so hard to make friends after all.

"Thank Terra, we found something to drink that doesn't come

from the community fountain," the girl with ebony-brown skin and black twists with blonde tips said.

"It's a natural spring from Mount Saint Elias, Nova," the other girl with short brown curls, a freckled beige complexion, and teal glasses said. "They encourage people to fill their bottles."

Nova made a gagging sound. "I'll pass. But you go ahead, Elodie."

Hazel stifled a laugh. *Me too.*

Elodie sighed. "The water is enchanted. It's as clean as it gets."

"I know that," Nova sniffed. "That doesn't mean I want to put my lips on ladles everyone else has drank from."

Hazel chimed in. "Sorry to interrupt, but did you say the water is enchanted?"

Elodie nodded. "Yeah, but only for mundanes."

Nova added, "It keeps this place a mystery. They can walk around into mage shops, watch mage sporting events, basically experience the town as we do, without being able to actually use magic. Though I guess they could technically drink mage brews since it doesn't require them to have magic of their own to work. Then when they leave here, their memories of magic are wiped clean. They just remember Eagles Ridge as a cute nature getaway where there are more bald eagles than anywhere in the world and they can watch the northern lights."

Hazel's stomach dropped. Had she done magic in front of a mundane today?

"I heard some never leave, they work in the shops around town, so their memories won't be wiped. I don't blame them though. I don't think I could give up the knowledge that magic exists either," Elodie added.

"Why would they let mundanes come here? I thought this was a mage community?" Hazel asked.

"That's how they fund Saint Elias University. All the tourism money from their stays at Fjordhaven, the town lodge," Nova said, as if that information was common knowledge.

Elodie gave Hazel a reassuring look. "But don't worry, no one actually *has* to drink from the fountain. They pump the spring into the town's water supply. The town bathes in it, drinks it, washes their food in it. Otherwise, they'd risk a mundane leaving town with the knowledge of magic. Instead, mundanes leave with a general feeling about the place. No specific memories."

"But what about the shops? What keeps them from buying something magical and taking it home?" Hazel asked. There seemed to be too many loopholes for Hazel's liking.

Nova laughed. "Good luck to them getting any of it to work without magic."

Elodie nodded. "Even the embedded items sold here require magic to use them. It's a business requirement in Eagles Ridge, enforced by the Brecilian Knights."

Okay, maybe they did think of everything.

Hazel let out a slow breath. "Good to know. Thanks."

Elodie smiled. "No worries."

Before Hazel could ask more, a voice from the counter called, "Next!"

She turned to order. The barista, who was not much older than her, oozed confidence in a green plaid flannel, sleeves rolled up, a pen tucking his long blonde hair behind his ear. His gaze flicked over her dark jeans, plaid jacket, and hiking boots, and she suddenly felt self-conscious under his beautiful blue-eyed gaze. Hazel tucked her hair behind her ear with one hand and tugged at the hem of her top with the other—a nervous habit to cover her belly and hips.

When she didn't answer, the barista asked, "Vacationing or studying?"

Her cheeks warmed. "Studying. Is it that obvious I'm not from around here?"

His eyes warmed. "No offense meant. I just didn't think I'd seen you before. Also, our coffee menu is pretty small, so most people don't need time to think about their order."

Hazel glanced at the three drinks on the menu—black drip coffee, a salmonberry latte, and a cloudberry cold brew. The last two she'd never heard of. She wasn't sure if these were magical or Alaskan ingredients. She wanted to ask but didn't want to sound any more like an out-of-towner.

"A coffee shop that only serves three coffees? Is there another in town?"

He chuckled, shaking his head. "We're actually not a coffee shop. We're a brewery, but the owner likes to take part in the town market and not everyone wants a pint before noon."

"What do you recommend?" Hazel asked.

"I recommend the cloudberry cold brew. It'll wake you up without the jitters."

She raised a brow. "That sounds too good to be true..."

This earned her a small smile. "Magic always does, doesn't it?"

"Is it the cloudberry in it? I haven't heard of it before," Hazel said.

"Yeah, it's not a common ingredient. It grows in an arctic climate. The berry itself has a lot of health properties, but it's the magical brewing that does the jitter trick, or so I'm told," the barista explained.

Something about the way he said that piqued her curiosity. Was he one of the mundanes who had stayed in Eagles Ridge after discovering magic? A soft cough reminded her that people were waiting.

"You've convinced me. I'll take that."

He rang her up, and she grabbed for her wallet, suddenly realizing she wasn't sure what kind of money the shop—or even the town—accepted. Tucked inside was a handful of pretium saved from the birthday gifts her mother had given her every year until she'd disappeared. Hazel had hoarded every last coin, and now she was grateful she had. Her heart pounded with regret at the thought of spending even a single precious pret on coffee, but she looked back at the barista, forcing a smile.

"Pretium or mundane currency accepted," he said.

Relief coursed through her. She had plenty of mundane money earned from working on the farm. She grinned as she paid and gave him her name before stepping aside.

When her name was called a few minutes later, she took a sip and let out a soft sound of satisfaction. The rich, slightly tart flavor was unlike anything she'd had before. She took another drink. She felt her mind clear and perk up instantly. She waited for the usual racing heartbeat and nervous jitters to ruin the moment, but they never came. This drink *was* magic.

The vendors and townsfolk moved around her happily, interacting with one another in a way that felt so familiar to Hazel's own mundane town. She began to feel more at ease as she moved through the market, but there was a layer of anticipation she couldn't shake. What if her mother was here? What if she shopped in the market, or sold wares at one of the booths? Hazel looked at each and every person she passed with no success.

A booth that sold enchanted gems and jewelry caught her eye. Careful not to touch—as indicated by no less than five signs at the booth—Hazel admired the wares—earrings to increase hearing, necklaces to bring luck, and rings to gain attention. There were even some nefarious enchantments, such as bracelets to produce a rash, and hairpins to give dandruff. Hazel tried to commit those items' designs to memory, so she'd be sure to never accept them as gifts.

"They don't actually produce any of these results, just so you know," a woman said.

Hazel tore her eyes from the wares and found herself looking at a beautiful, beige-skinned woman with pin straight blonde hair pulled up into a bun on top of her head. She wore a long-sleeved, form-fitting maxi dress under a long cardigan that accentuated her height. Her dangling earrings almost rested on her shoulders.

"They simply give the appearance of the embedded property. Once they're removed, the spell stops immediately. Imagine it like a projected image. Looks real, but it's not," the woman explained.

"Good to know. I was never allowed embedded objects growing up. Seems a bit silly now," Hazel said.

Someone spoke from behind the woman. "Oh, Mara would be lying if she said embedded objects can't be much more malicious.

But I don't sell those types of things to the public, and I'd caution you to be wary of anyone who does."

Mara rolled her eyes. "Don't let Jude scare you. They can't help but turn everything into a teaching moment."

Jude stepped beside Mara and slid their arm around her waist. They had wavy, chin-length dark hair; porcelain skin; piercings along both ears; and spider bites along their right lower lip. Dark-blue tattoos peeked above a black crewneck sweater, but Hazel wasn't able to make out the images without staring.

"Got it! Thank you," Hazel replied. After a beat of silence, Hazel added, "You do beautiful work, by the way. I wish I could afford a piece right now, but I'd be happy to spread the word about your designs."

"Thanks. I'm Jude. I don't have a card, but I'm opening up a brick and mortar shop soon, Incanted to Meet You. Tell your friends about me, or better yet, bring them."

"Nice to meet you. I don't think I've ever met an embedder before. Today's a lot of firsts for me, actually. First time in Alaska, first time to avoid drinking from a communal fountain, first time to try cloudberries." The need to be liked was making Hazel ultra chatty today. "Sorry, I'm rambling. You don't need to know that about me."

Jude smiled. "I find it endearing. Not everyone feels comfortable rambling around me. It's refreshing."

"Why? Because you're an embedder?" Hazel asked.

"No, it's my not-so-sunny disposition," Jude said neutrally.

"Jude puts it on," Mara explained.

"I tend not to like most people," Jude said, as if that were reason enough.

Hazel couldn't help herself. Her nervous laughter bubbled up, loud and rhythmic. She'd never met someone so matter-of-fact. She admired Jude.

The town's clock tower chimed, making Hazel's laughter die down. "I better be on my way. It was nice to..."

As Hazel spoke, she caught sight of a mage in a purple velvet cloak wandering through the market—a cloak like the one her mother had worn in her dream last night. Hazel's heart threatened to fly out of her mouth. This had to be it. All she had to do was reach out.

She extended her hand, but then the mage turned. A young blonde man beneath the hooded cloak nodded toward the three of them before moving on. Her heart dropped. She needed to calm her expectations.

Hazel looked back to find both Jude and Mara watching her, so she flashed a smile. "Sorry, I thought I saw someone I knew. Well, I should be going."

"What was your name, sweetie?" Mara asked.

"Hazel."

Jude nodded, then added, "Good luck on your entrance exam tomorrow, Hazel."

"Thanks," she replied. She was going to need it.

CHAPTER 6

Gwen

The lodge's deep-green exterior blended so seamlessly with the forest that Gwen almost missed it. The vivid moss clung to the old wooden beams, softening the edges of the three-story building. She slowed her steps, taking in the wide wraparound porch, with its sturdy railings carved with glyphs that shimmered faintly in the dim evening light. Damp cedar and rich earth permeated the air, and it reminded her of home. She let out a slow breath.

After a grueling summer of training, she had finally arrived.

Per the summons, Gwen had arrived at the lodge five minutes before seven p.m.—the cutoff time for check-in. She was excited and hopeful for the exam, but saying goodbye had been even harder than she'd imagined. Still, it was worth it now that she was actually here.

Gwen looked around the grounds and veranda, hoping to recognize someone from Bathurst. A few students lounged on the porch in rocking chairs, their shoes propped up on the rails as they chatted. On the grass, a group of girls sat cross-legged with a deck of enchanted cards floating in front of them. In the far corner of the porch, two boys pointed their wands at a small floating orb, tossing it back and forth. Gwen didn't recognize any of them.

I wish Klaus were here.

She pushed open the heavy wooden doors and the warmth of the lobby enveloped her. Its large windows soaked up the last of the Alaskan sun while keeping away the brisk breeze from Tan Fjord on the shore of Eagles Ridge. The interior of Fjordhaven Lodge was a blend of old-world craftsmanship and rugged mountain charm. Polished wooden walls gleamed beneath the soft glow of iron chandeliers. Plush green carpets that matched the mossy exterior muffled the steady hum of conversations, and stone fireplaces anchored each wall, their mantles carved with fjords, forests, and mountains. Students filled the space, their voices low and familiar, laughter rising in bursts from the plush armchairs and well-worn sofas flanking the hearths.

Gwen's gaze settled on the *SEU PROSPECTS CHECK-IN HERE* sign at the far end of the room. A wall of brass hooks lined the space behind it, each holding an ornate key etched with a different number. Two young women sat behind the desk, conversing in quiet tones.

Gwen approached the desk, and the redheaded young woman stood. Gwen flashed her eyes toward the girl's name tag. *Resident Advisor: Victoria.*

"Welcome! Are you here for your entrance exams?"

Gwen leaned away from her, affronted by her volume. "Yeah."

"Perfect!" Victoria said with such a hard final consonant that Gwen cringed.

Wow, you're annoying.

"Name?" she asked, her ringlets bouncing.

Gwen opened her mouth to answer, but Victoria cut her off. "Wait, let me guess. I have a knack for these sorts of things." Victoria picked up the clipboard on the table and ran her alabaster finger along the edge. She licked her finger to turn the page.

"I can just tell you—" Gwen started.

“No, I have it!” The RA tapped the page. “You definitely look like a Samantha. Samantha Titsworth?”

Gwen shook her head, not caring to hide the grimace on her face. Glancing down at her small chest, she knew that wasn’t meant as a compliment.

This bitch.

“Okay, one more guess!”

The blonde RA, still seated, snapped her book closed, startling them all. “Salem burn us, Victoria. Let the girl tell you her name,” the RA, whose name tag read Serena, said. Serena’s tone was deep and smoky for someone so small.

Gwen sagged in relief, thankful she’d spared her from losing her temper five minutes after her arrival.

Victoria pouted. “Serena, I’m just trying to have a little bit of fun.”

Serena leaned back in her chair and crossed her arms. “We need to work on your definition of fun, Victoria.”

Victoria looked like she was going to give a retort, but Gwen couldn't take any more of this or she might attack someone on purpose.

“My name is Gwendolyn Bishop,” Gwen snapped.

Victoria humphed before flipping a few more pages and locating Gwen’s key number. “I definitely would’ve guessed that.” She handed Gwen a stack of papers before lifting her wand. Gwen’s room key floated to her from the other side of the wall behind the host’s desk. Victoria held the key in one hand as she studied the clipboard in the other, her brows creased. “It looks like your roommate, Catherine Thorne, has already arrived. “

“Roommate?” Gwen demanded. She hadn’t known they’d have to share rooms in the lodge. *Damn it, Klaus.* Why hadn’t he warned her? She’d never had to share a room with anyone. Camp Camelot had cabins with individual rooms. She hated the thought of having someone watching her or questioning her. *Salem, what if she snores?*

“I’d rather rub my face in Merlin’s sweaty balls than share a room,” Gwen swore.

Serena snorted as Victoria’s eyes grew to the size of tea saucers. While they might think her response was a tad dramatic, Gwen was serious.

Victoria stared, horrified, at Gwen. “We don’t use that phrase here.”

“*You* don’t use that phrase,” Serena mumbled under her breath.

There was definitely no love lost between these two mages.

“I’d like a private room.” Gwen crossed her arms; she wasn’t going to back down. Her safety depended on it.

“Sorry, no can do,” Victoria said.

“There are no private rooms?” Gwen questioned her.

“No, sorry—”

Gwen cut her off. “You keep saying that, but I don’t think you are.”

Victoria’s eyes narrowed.

Serena set down her book and stood, taking the clipboard from Victoria’s hands. “She’s right. We don’t have any private rooms.”

Gwen fought back a groan, and Serena shrugged as she handed her the key. Reluctantly, she grabbed her bag and headed for the large mahogany staircase beside the check-in desk, its steps covered in a rich yellow runner worn soft from years of passing shoes.

The second-floor hallway stretched ahead, lined with wooden doors, each fitted with a brass handle and an intricately etched number. She walked past them, scanning until she found the one that matched the number on her key.

The moment she stepped inside, she found a black-haired girl unpacking a suitcase in a wooden chest of drawers; probably Catherine. Seeing her there, already settling in, made the reality of sharing the space sink in fast. At least the bed closest to the door was Gwen’s —an easy escape if she needed it. More importantly, in case her wolf needed it.

Her mother’s voice echoed in her head. *Make friends fast.*

"Hi, I'm Gwen," she said cheerfully.

"Hazel," the girl replied in a Southern accent, sticking out her hand.

"Oh, I must have the wrong room," Gwen said. She backed out of the room to look at the door. The number was right. "I was told my roommate was Catherine."

"That's me. Hazel is my middle name."

Gwen smiled before walking back into the room and shaking Hazel's outstretched hand. The charms on her bracelet clinked together with the movement, and Hazel's eyes slid to it.

"Cute bracelet."

Gwen thanked her as she tucked it discreetly into her sleeve and Hazel returned to placing her clothing inside the chest neatly.

What a waste of time. They wouldn't be there more than a night.

The room was dimly lit by two wrought-iron lanterns hanging from the ceiling. The twin beds sat beneath them, positioned on either side of the room with barely enough space for one person to walk between them. It was going to be a tight fit. Thick yellow quilts draped across each bed were paired with cream-colored sheets and matching embroidered pillows. At least they looked comfortable. She'd need a good night's sleep with what was coming tomorrow.

Behind the beds, a large window framed by deep-navy velvet curtains overlooked the mountains beyond. Gwen resisted the urge to stick her head out for a better look. Opening the window would let in the cold breeze, and Hazel might not like that. The room was drafty enough as it was.

She tossed her bag onto the chest at the foot of her bed, dug through it, and pulled out her Bathurst sweatshirt before plopping down onto the mattress. Her wand clinked softly as she set it on the shared nightstand, next to a small oil lamp. She absently pulled open the drawer and found a folded map of Eagles Ridge tucked inside. She left it there as she shut the drawer and laid her head on the pillow, staring up at the ceiling.

Tomorrow, everything would change. She would either become a freshman at SEU or start the fight of her life against her father.

After a few minutes of laying there, Gwen's stomach rumbled. She should have eaten before she left home.

"Hungry?" Hazel asked.

Gwen sat up to see Hazel sitting cross-legged on her own bed, staring at her. "Starved."

"There's a pub in town called Kodiak Brew," Hazel said slowly.

Gwen perked up. She needed to eat and wasn't against going into town.

"The one the school is covering?" Gwen asked.

"That's the one," Hazel said, nodding. "Want to head over there for dinner?"

"Sure."

Hazel stood, and Gwen followed her out of the room, stopping only to holster her wand and then lock the door.

"Where are you from?" Hazel asked as they walked down the hallway towards the stairs. Gwen felt short standing next to her, but that wasn't unusual.

"I grew up in Britton Place, with my mom. It's a mage community in Maine. I went to Bathurst Institute of Sorcery in Canada," she answered, pointing to her sweatshirt.

Gwen didn't recognize her from Bathurst. While there was only one university in North America, there were three mage high schools Hazel could have gone to.

"What about you?" Gwen asked.

"I lived near Conway with my dad."

"Conway?" Gwen's brows creased as she tried to place the town name.

Hazel fidgeted under Gwen's gaze. "Conway, Arkansas. It's a mundane town."

Interesting. Gwen had never met anyone who didn't live in a mage town.

Taking a right down the hall, they began descending the stairway to the lobby.

"Did you go to a mundane high school?" Gwen asked.

How did this girl get a summons? Does she even know any magic?

Hazel laughed. "No, I went to Elkmont Academy of Magic. Have you heard of it?"

Gwen knew a few people from camp who'd gone to Elkmont. The school had nearly two thousand students, so odds were Hazel wouldn't know them.

She nodded. "My friend said it was beautiful there."

"Yeah, it's in the Smoky Mountains," Hazel confirmed.

"I bet the ruzo games were insane, with the smoke rolling in," Gwen said as she pushed open the front door and walked onto the wraparound porch.

Hazel swallowed and then asked, "Who's your friend that went there?"

"Jordan Foster. Cool guy. He was basically my only friend at camp."

As soon as the words were out of her mouth, Gwen suppressed a groan. *Why did I tell her that?*

"Aw, I'm your only friend?" a masculine voice taunted from below.

Gwen looked over the railing to see a tall young man with tawny-brown skin beaming at her from the bottom porch steps. His bright-green eyes pierced through her as he smiled.

Jordan.

Oh Terra, he's never going to let me live that down. Embarrassment washed over her, but she tried to play it cool. "I can't believe you actually got summoned."

His long legs took the steps two at a time. He'd grown a lot since last summer. He was closer to Klaus's height than her own now.

When she was within arm's reach, Jordan lifted her off the ground as he embraced her. He ignored her quip and repeated in her ear, "I can't believe I'm your only friend."

When she let go of him, he set her back down, and she smacked him on the arm. He had more muscle than she remembered, though he was still quite lean.

"I said *at camp*," she reminded him.

"Maybe I'm your only friend because you're so mean," he teased. "And your cousins don't count."

She glared at him until another young man to his right coughed, diverting their attention.

"Gwen, this is Rafael De La Vega. He went to Elkmont with me. Rafe, this is Gwendolyn Bishop. She's cool despite her desperate need to put her hands on me." Jordan winked.

Gwen stuck out her tongue at him, resisting the urge to smack him again. Then she nodded hello to Rafe. His short hair was a warm, dark brown that matched his eyes. His skin was a terra cotta brown, hinting at a latino heritage. Rafe was a little shorter than Jordan, but not by much. His shirt curved around each massive muscle in his arms, and she resisted the urge to touch them. He could be a ruzo player for sure.

Remembering Hazel, Gwen looked away from Rafe and introduced her. "This is my new friend, Hazel."

Friend was definitely a strong term for what they were, but who knew, maybe they *would* be friends. Hazel seemed nice and had respected her space so far, which was important to Gwen.

Gwen flashed Jordan an obscene gesture. "Sorry to disappoint. You aren't my only friend anymore."

If Hazel minded, she didn't let on.

"You went to Elkmont, didn't you?" Rafe said to Hazel.

"Yeah, I think we had a few classes together," Hazel answered warmly with a small smile.

"Oh, yeah!" Jordan pointed at her. "You were valedictorian!"

Hazel blushed as she nodded.

Okay, maybe she's not as behind as I thought.

"We are about to go eat at Kodiak Brew. Want to join us?" Gwen asked.

"Hex yeah! I'm starved," Jordan said as he wrapped his arm around Gwen's shoulder and led the way into town.

CHAPTER 7

Hazel

The smell of hops, barley, and coffee washed over Hazel as the group stepped through the doors of Kodiak Brew. The brewery looked almost mundane, with its wooden tables, metal chairs, and bookshelves full of party games. What made it magical were the brooms that lined the front wall and candles that floated above each table.

Hazel had never seen magic so openly used and displayed in public.

"Oi! Watch out!" a thick British accent called out as they weaved through the tables, looking for a spot to sit.

Hazel felt a tug from behind just before she bumped into Rafe.

What the heck? Hazel thought, her cheeks flushing as she looked over her shoulder to find Rafe's warm brown eyes.

"Sorry, the drinks were coming through," Rafe said. He pointed above where Hazel had been standing. A mug with turquoise bubbles teetering along its rim floated through the air. A few moments later, a blonde young man snatched it from the air, promptly took a drink, and belched.

“Oh, thanks!” Hazel said.

Rafe flashed her a beautiful white smile. “Of course.”

The brewery was packed, probably because of the free voucher given to all the summoned mages.

“It doesn’t look like there's anywhere to sit. We may have to wait a while,” Hazel told Gwen over her shoulder.

Gwen focused intently across the room. Hazel followed her gaze to a guy sitting in a booth near the bar who appeared to be drinking alone and reading a book. His five o’clock shadow made him look older, while his glasses and book made him look studious. Hazel understood why he’d caught Gwen’s attention.

“You have good taste,” Hazel told her.

“What?” Gwen said, snapping her attention back to Hazel.

“I said he’s cute.”

“Oh, look, I see a spot open near the bar. Let’s grab it before someone else does,” Gwen said, changing the subject.

Jordan raced towards it before anyone else even moved.

Hazel looked back at Gwen, barely catching her resheathing her wand in her thigh holster. Gwen smiled up at Hazel suspiciously. Hazel wondered if that table had really been empty or if Gwen had magicked their good fortune.

Jordan hovered over the booth until they caught up. He let Gwen slide in on his side first before sitting next to her.

That left Hazel to sit with Rafe. She didn’t know why, but it made her a little nervous. She’d known of Rafe for years, but he was still a virtual stranger to her. They’d spoken a few times; he’d always been nice but had never seemed to have a spare second between ruzo, his friends, and the girls that liked to follow him around. It felt more comfortable to lean into a new person than build a connection with someone she’d walked past in the halls hundreds of times. Deep down, she knew a kernel of rejection was part of it. He’d had years to befriend her, yet hadn’t.

Rafe looked at her for a moment. When Hazel hesitated, he slid into the booth first. Hazel sat down next to him. His elbow grazed hers, sending a tingling jolt down to her fingertips, and she fought the urge to jerk away.

"Sorry, I shocked you," Rafe said sheepishly. He readjusted his body into the corner of the booth to give her more room. His warm brown complexion contrasted beautifully with his white teeth as he flashed her a smile.

Hazel snapped her gaze toward the table, realizing she'd been staring.

Smooth, Hazel. Get it together.

She couldn't afford to be distracted right now. She needed to keep her focus on the thing that mattered most: the entrance exam.

Maybe I should have stayed in the lodge and studied.

The thought was fleeting; there was no material to study. The entrance exam was an enigma. Skipping dinner wouldn't help her keep up her endurance tomorrow.

Rafe handed her a menu from where they rested on the side of the table.

"Salmon and rice sound good," Hazel said after browsing the options.

In response to her words, the food appeared on the table.

Surprised, Hazel exclaimed, "Hey, what if I change my mind?"

The food disappeared as soon as the words left her mouth.

"Haven't you ever been to a magical restaurant?" Jordan asked her.

"No, not outside of the cafeteria at Elkmont," Hazel admitted. "I grew up in a mundane town."

She studied their faces, looking for judgment. More than a few people had treated her like she was less than for not growing up in a magical community. Her shoulders relaxed when no one looked fazed by the news.

"Elkmont definitely wasn't this advanced," Rafe reassured her with a bump of his shoulder that sent a wave of heat down her arm and blood straight to her cheeks. "When you know what you want, you just say it and it'll appear at the table."

Magic really is incredible.

Chewing her lip, Hazel considered the options. She wanted to test the limits of the magic. What could she order, exactly?

"I'll take a beer?"

The table erupted with laughter.

Hazel's cheeks burned, not understanding her faux pas.

"Nice try," Gwen told her. "Those you have to get at the bar so you can show your ID, but I admire your tenacity."

A comfortable silence descended upon the group as they ate. Hazel chewed slowly, dragging out dinner, not wanting the night to end. When she finished, their empty plates disappeared as suddenly as they'd come.

"Truth or Dare?" Jordan beamed at Gwen.

"Not a chance," Gwen answered.

Hazel sensed by their tone this was something they did often together and she was instantly envious. To have such a fun, lighthearted friendship was something Hazel had always dreamed about.

"Come on. It was your favorite game at camp," Jordan pressured.

"It was not. It was always *your* favorite game, and I only played it because *you* wanted to," Gwen said.

Jordan grabbed at his chest and let his full bottom lip pout dramatically. "Such a good friend."

"I know." Gwen patted herself on the back.

"So then, if you're such a good friend, you'll play with me now."

Gwen groaned. "I walked right into that one, didn't I?"

Jordan grinned ear to ear, his blue-green eyes flashing in his tawny-brown face. He was so adorably charming, Hazel wondered if he was ever told no.

"What if Rafe and Hazel don't want to play?"

"I'll play," Rafe said.

"Sorry, Gwen. It sounds fun." Hazel gave her a sympathetic look.

She hadn't had many opportunities to spend time with friends growing up. She wouldn't miss out on it now.

Gwen was outnumbered. "Fine, but *you're* explaining the rules."

"It's Truth or Dare. We all know the rules," Rafe said.

"We have a slight variation to the normal rules," Jordan said. "You can switch from truth to dare or dare to truth after you've heard what it is, but you can't switch back. The person who does the truth or dare gets to go next. I always go first."

No one argued with Jordan's rules.

"Gwendolyn, truth or dare?"

Hazel suspected Gwen would choose a dare.

"Dare," Gwen answered, rolling her eyes.

Jordan clapped his hands and rubbed them together. "Kiss someone in this bar—"

Before he could even finish, Gwen leaned over and grabbed his face before he could pull away, holding him in place as she smacked her lips on Jordan's cheek. After about two seconds, she released him.

He leaned back from her, wiping his cheek with the back of his hand. "Damn it, Gwen. I wasn't finished with the parameters of the dare!"

Gwen smiled devilishly at Jordan and shrugged. This new friend of hers was trouble. "Truth or dare, Rafe?" Gwen asked.

"Truth," Rafe said cautiously.

"Boo, you're no fun," Gwen grumped. "Who's the prettiest girl in this bar?"

Rafe made a show of looking around. His eyes landed briefly on Hazel, and the warmth of a blush fought to the surface as she held her breath. She didn't know if she wanted him to say her name or not, and that concerned her.

"Easy. Jordan," Rafe answered.

Gwen and Hazel laughed at the unexpected answer.

Jordan flipped his imaginary hair. "Obviously."

"Truth or dare, Hazel?" Rafe asked as he turned toward her.

"Truth," Hazel said without a moment's hesitation. She didn't know these people, let alone trust them well enough to do a dare yet.

"Do you have a boyfriend?" Rafe asked quickly.

Hazel looked up into his dark-brown eyes. She saw warmth and curiosity, and the nervousness she felt sitting next to his muscular frame dissipated. "Not yet," Hazel said coyly.

It was nice to think a guy wanted her for a change. Once word had gotten out that her father wouldn't let her date, no one had bothered to ask. At least she hoped that was the reason for his question. Then it was her turn.

"Jordan, truth or dare?"

"Dare," Jordan said quickly.

Shit.

Hazel should have come up with a dare before asking the question. Mulling it over for a minute, she finally dared Jordan to ask a stranger for a drink.

"Pfft, Hazel, that's too easy," Jordan said, shaking his head.

Hazel flashed him a mischievous grin. "I mean a sip. From *their* drink."

Rafe hooted with laughter, while Jordan looked repulsed.

"That is un-fucking-sanitary, Hazel Thorne," Jordan declared, wide-eyed, before adding, "I love it. If we'd have known you could get up to this kind of mischief at Elkmont, we'd have been friends long before now."

Hazel smiled at Jordan's compliment, but squirmed in her seat. She tried not to let the implication that somehow she wasn't mischievous enough for them to be friends at Elkmont hurt her feelings. Knowing her thoughts were visible on her face, she forced a smile.

"What Jordan means to say is that we were in way too much trouble for someone top of our class to mess around with. You were better off killing it in the classroom, but we obviously missed out," Rafe explained. Hazel sensed he may have read between the lines of Jordan's comment as well. "Right, J?" he added.

Jordan slapped the table dramatically, startling both Rafe and Hazel. "Speaking of mischief, I heard a rumor about you—"

Rafe kicked him under the table.

"Hey! It was a good rumor," Jordan insisted.

Hazel's heart sped up. She could only imagine what anyone in Rafe and Jordan's circles could have said about her. They'd run with the "in" crowd, from what she remembered about them. Jordan was an infamous class clown, constantly being reprimanded for pranks and jokes, as well as popular with girls. Hazel understood why, even with her limited view of a gray Henley and black jeans hugging his lean frame. He was fit, clean-shaven, and had an easy grin. But in Hazel's first impressions today, it was his laugh, freely given, that made him so endearing.

"Honestly, Rafe. You've got to cool it with bodily injury. Not all of us are ruzo players," Jordan half-joked. "Between you and Gwen, I'm going to be covered in bruises."

Rafe only shrugged, clearly not remorseful. Hazel knew less about Rafe. Well, less about his personality. He had been known all over Elkmont for his ruzo skills. Even Forrest had heard about him, not that Hazel had ever seen him play.

Rafe was nearly double Jordan's size, with a thick barrel chest and biceps that stretched his Elkmont T-shirt at the seams. Come to think of it, Rafe had probably received a lot of offers to play ruzo at other universities with typical application processes, yet he was rolling the dice on passing the entrance exam at Saint Elias. Rafe's priorities were obviously about more than just being good at sports.

"You're not going to say you've heard a rumor about me and then not elaborate, right?" Hazel probed when Jordan didn't offer the information himself. "That's not what friends do, Jordan." She attempted to sound lighthearted and teasing as she reached across to smack him on his sleeve, but feared that they could see straight through her façade of nonchalance.

"Yeah, Jordan," Gwen teased him too.

"What'll you give me for it? The information, I mean," Jordan asked, wiggling his eyebrows.

"I'll let you out of your dare and take the dare myself?" Hazel offered.

Jordan didn't hesitate. "Deal, but I get to choose the dare!"

Hazel nodded.

"The rumor I heard was that you hexed Dane Bellamy's fly closed, and that they had to cut him out of his pants before the last ruzo game of the season."

Rafe took a drink from his water, and Gwen's mouth fell open. All eyes were now focused on Hazel.

She didn't even try to suppress the grin that spread across her face or her treacherous dimples as she remembered one of the most rebellious moments of her life. "People say the craziest things, don't they?" Hazel said. What she didn't mention was that Dane had deserved it. He'd spelled her locker full of horse manure and she'd had to rewrite three assignments, nearly costing her the valedictorianship. In retrospect, it probably wasn't the smartest or most mature way of getting back at him, but he'd pushed her too far and she'd been desperate to get even.

Jordan, Gwen, and Hazel erupted with laughter. Rafe choked on his water. It pleased Hazel to entertain them, maybe even shock them. It wasn't something she did often; she was a good girl, steady, predictable. She was glad to prove to them, and to herself, that she could be more than that.

"Okay, time to cash in on my dare," Jordan said as the laughter died down.

Hazel groaned audibly, regretting her earlier decision. "You're welcome to save it," she offered, hoping he'd eventually forget all about it.

"Ha! I wish I had that kind of patience. Unfortunately for you, I don't."

"Let's hear it then."

Jordan leaned over and whispered into Gwen's ear.

Gwen's eyes narrowed. "I don't think she'll do it."

"Do what?" Hazel demanded, both scared of what it might be and offended that Gwen doubted her bravery.

Jordan pointed toward the bar. "I dare you to go over to the bar and get us some drinks, by any means necessary."

Hazel's face fell. She had a baby face. There was no chance they'd sell her alcohol.

"Vodka, preferably," Gwen added with a wicked smile.

"Y'all, I'm *not* going to steal from the bar! That's not a dare. That's petty larceny."

"I mean, there are other ways," Gwen said, making her eyebrows dance suggestively.

Hazel's eyes grew wide.

Gwen taunted, "I told you she wouldn't do it."

Her words struck a chord. Hazel had spent her whole life doing the safe thing. She'd promised herself she'd start taking some chances, hadn't she?

Hazel waited a heartbeat before sliding out of the booth. "I'll be back."

No one would consider Hazel a goody-two-shoes coward here. She'd missed out on shenanigans and memories throughout her time at Elkmont because of her dad. But her dad was not with her in Alaska. There was no reason for him ever to learn about what she was up to, given the simple fact that he'd made it clear he wanted nothing to do with her. She would no longer be giving up on experiences for the sake of a man who could only love her if she were perfect—if she obeyed.

These thoughts steeled Hazel's resolve. As she approached the bar, she recognized the coffee barista from this morning, smoothly pouring a tray of shots without spilling a drop. Maybe she was in luck. She just needed a plan. He'd seemed friendly enough earlier today. Maybe if she told him the situation, he'd help her out. The worst he could do was say no. Stealing it would be an absolute last resort. The idea of doing something so blatantly wrong burned in her stomach. She hoped it didn't come to that.

Hazel sidled up to the bar and sat on a barstool directly behind the barista who had turned to pass shots to a customer.

"I'm not surprised Alec kept you on for your gap year. He needs you to bring in all the college girls for karaoke night," the customer joked with a wink before paying his tab.

Hazel had to admit they weren't wrong. The bartender *was* pretty.

He finally turned to her. "Hey, Hazel."

His memory of her name sent a wave of shock through her. "Hey, y-yourself."

Smooth one, she thought.

"Tristan," he chuckled, introducing himself. "What can I get for you?"

"I was wondering if I could get four shots of vodka?" Hazel asked.

"Vodka?" Tristan raised his eyebrows. "I'll need to see your ID, along with your companions', to confirm you're all over the age of twenty-one."

"Oh." Hazel looked away, trying to hide her fear that she'd fail this dare.

"If you aren't twenty-one or over, I could get you a mage's brew instead," Tristan offered.

She breathed a sigh of relief. Technically, all Jordan had dared her to do was get drinks. In her eyes, this counted.

"What's in a mage's brew?" Hazel leaned against the counter, eyeing the mixtures.

"I'm not exactly sure. The drinks are pre-mixed." Then he pointed to the rest of the bar. "Several mages are partaking tonight."

Hazel scanned the room. A group of mages were belching fire, two of them putting out the flames on the table. Another table of mages had bubbles floating out of their mouths every time they spoke, and a third group had grown wings. The wings weren't strong enough for suspended flight, but the mages were elevating up and down in their seats for a few seconds at a time.

How the hell did I miss that?

"I'll take four mage elixirs, please," Hazel said.

"What kind would you like?" Tristan asked with a smile.

"Surprise me." As Tristan poured the drinks, Hazel asked, "How long do these enchantments last?"

"They'll wear off at the stroke of midnight."

That sounded reasonable.

Hazel was pulling her wallet out of her back pocket when a deep, rough voice surprised her. "It's on the house."

Hazel looked up to see a man with shoulder-length dirty-blonde hair and ivory skin who looked to be in his late thirties. He wore a green Kodiak Brew long-sleeve shirt and a pair of dark-wash jeans. He was taller than Tristan, making him a few inches over six feet, if Hazel had to guess. The most notable thing about the man was his eyes—they were the color of amber, unlike anything Hazel had ever seen. Well, on a person. Hazel had seen cats with similar eyes around her farm.

She realized she'd stared for too long and gave a little nervous cough. "Oh, are you sure? We don't mind paying."

Tristan laid a finger over his own lips and gave a small shake of his head. "Hazel, when the owner offers to pay, you let him. I'll send the drinks over when I'm done."

Hazel nodded and smiled at the owner, but he didn't smile or nod back. He simply studied Hazel, his eyes searching hers with a question on his face that he never asked. It was odd, but she wasn't going to pass up free drinks. Hazel thanked them both and walked back to their booth.

A few moments later, the drinks floated over to their table on a round wooden tray with carvings of bears and pine trees etched around the rim. Jordan reached up, taking the drinks off the tray hovering above them, and set them in the middle of the table before the tray flew back to the bar. The vials were pure silver, disguising what was inside. Hazel was happy to see the liquid was clear and smelled a lot like alcohol when she peered over the top of the glass. Maybe Tristan had snuck them something stronger after all?

"Damn, girl! We're besties now," Jordan told her.

Hazel smiled at Jordan's easy familiarity.

The four of them lifted their shots in unison.

"May the best of our past," Jordan shouted.

"Be the worst of our future," Gwen finished. They clinked their shots together and then downed them.

The liquid gave off a disturbing simultaneous sensation of hot and cold, the flame and ice alternating down her throat until it hit her stomach with a gurgle.

"Hazel, what in the Salem Trials did you give us?" Gwen all but growled at her.

Hazel looked across the table, but all she could see were the clothes Gwen and Jordan were wearing. *Oh no.* She looked down at her own hands—they were missing. Next to her, Rafe's Elkmont T-shirt appeared to float in thin air, although the form of his muscles still pulled at the seams.

They were all invisible.

"I'm so sorry, I forgot to tell y'all. The bartender wouldn't sell me any alcohol, so I got us mage brews instead."

"And you picked the invisibility elixir?" Jordan asked.

"No, I asked him to surprise us. But don't worry, it'll wear off at midnight." Hazel didn't know if her words brought them any relief, since she couldn't see their faces.

A moment passed, and the three of them laughed. Okay, so they weren't mad. She breathed a sigh of relief.

"We might as well hang here until it wears off," Rafe said.

"Hazel, I believe it's your turn. I think you should pick Gwen," Jordan added.

"Jordan!" Gwen objected. Gwen was wearing a leather jacket, so Hazel saw as her arm lifted towards Jordan. She couldn't see Gwen's hand smack him, but she heard it.

"Gwen, truth or dare?"

"Ugh," Gwen groaned. "Fine. Truth."

Hazel wanted Gwen to like her, so she decided on an easy one. "What do the charms on your bracelet do?" Hazel asked.

"Dare."

"Is it some kind of glamour charm?" Hazel tried to push back. Gwen was really pretty. Maybe she had some enhancements in her charms.

"I want to switch to dare," Gwen said in return, a bite to her words.

Hazel dropped it. She hadn't meant to upset her. She could see now that a glamour charm might be embarrassing to admit to. If she wanted others to think it was natural, she might not want Hazel outing her.

"Make the dare worse," Jordan told Hazel. "She can't switch back now."

"Oh, it'll be worse." Hazel looked around the room, her body turning this way and that. Then she grabbed the straw from her drink and pointed across the room at the gorgeous guy Gwen had been checking out earlier. He still occupied a booth alone with his book in one hand, a beer in the other. Hazel guessed he was an upperclassman; there had been a few around the lodge helping mages with check-in and questions.

"I dare you to go over to the guy in the booth and flirt with him."

"Easy," Gwen laughed.

"I wasn't finished. *Naked*!"

Silence took over the table. Maybe she'd gone too far?

Then Rafe and Jordan burst into laughter.

"*Naked*?" Gwen finally said when the boys' laughter dulled enough for her to be heard.

"Yes, that way he won't see you coming."

"I wouldn't have thought you had it in you to come up with something so devious," Gwen said, sounding half put out and half impressed.

"I bet you'll never underestimate me again," Hazel chuckled, proud of surprising Gwen a second time tonight.

Gwen

To the boys' dismay, Gwen refused to undress right there at the booth. She crawled over Jordan's lap and headed to the ladies' room.

Gwen would have to take her bracelet off to be completely invisible. She'd been practicing going into town without it all summer and had managed to go hours without shifting by the time she had to come to Alaska, but this time, she didn't have Klaus to put her bracelet back on if things went sideways.

Taking a deep breath, she slid the bracelet into her wand for protection. She could do this.

She stalked toward the door but turned on her heel once more to pace the room as she built courage. Nakedness didn't embarrass her as a shifter, so what was the holdup?

The handsome mage's face flashed before her mind.

Ah, fuck it! She pushed out of the bathroom, clothes in hand. The scent of hops practically punched her in the face as she passed the storeroom on her way back to the table.

Sips of foam and slurps of beer grated on her nerves as she took in the room with her therian hearing for the first time. The air was cool on her bare skin as she sped up to get back to her friends. A few people noticed the floating clothes in her hands, allowing them to track her movements through the bar with curious looks on their faces. She had to pass them off before people realized what was going on.

She leaned over the booth and tapped Hazel on the shoulder. Hazel's clothes shifted in her seat and then turned back around once more.

“Hey!” Gwen exclaimed in hushed tones. “Naked girl here! Being ignored isn't good for my self-esteem, invisible or not!”

“Sorry, I couldn’t see you,” Hazel said as she looked back once more.

Gwen tossed her balled-up clothes to her over the back of the booth. “You better not run off with my clothes,” Gwen told her. “I know where you’re staying and I’m not afraid to hex you.”

“I would never!” Hazel promised.

Gwen snorted. “You told me not to underestimate you again. Now here.” Gwen extended her wand, which held her most prized possession. “Lose this and you’ll wish I’d hexed you when I’m through with you. See you all in a minute,” Gwen said as she walked away.

To block the smell of the vomit now emitting from the men’s restroom and the sounds of the fight breaking out near the bar, she concentrated on her small group of friends. Their laughter steadied her. Time to put her training to the test. She stretched her sense of smell to find one as strong as blackberry cobbler. Jordan smelled like fresh-cut grass. Clean, crisp—but not strong enough. Rafe smelled like pine, his scent tangled with the cedar tables, aggravating her nose. Not what she needed. Then Hazel’s honeyed scent wrapped around her, rich and warm, sinking into her like the comfort of home. It was always the sweet scents that grounded her most. That was why she always focused on the bakery back home. She anchored herself to Hazel’s scent and let everything else around her fade away.

What was she even going to say when she reached him?

An oncoming group headed straight for her as they made for the exit. Hoping to avoid being touched, she maneuvered between them, and made it to the table without incident but still hadn’t come up with a way to flirt with this man, so she stood there, watching him read. She studied the way his jaw clenched when he read a specific line, and how his deep brown hair moved when he ran his hand through it. The idea of using the book title to strike up conversation occurred to her, and Gwen leaned over the table to get a better view.

The guy's dark brown eyes met hers, wide and beautiful against his ivory skin, but he immediately looked away. Gwen glanced behind her to see if someone else was there, but the space was empty. When she returned her gaze to him, his eyes were downcast and his hand was outstretched, holding a navy-blue suit jacket.

"I can see you."

Gwen's stomach fell into her ass. *You've got to be fucking kidding me.*

"How?" was all she could say. If her friends were watching, she didn't know. All she could do was stand there. "How can you see me?" she repeated, voice cracking the second time.

Eyes still averted, he tapped his glasses with his free hand. She noticed a small carving etched into the frames.

They're enchanted! She cursed herself for not noticing right away. Her grandpa would be disappointed she'd overlooked such a thing. What were the etchings? She didn't recognize them.

She was going to kill Hazel.

Gwen hastily grabbed the man's jacket to cover herself, mortification burning her cheeks. The jacket was so oversized on her, it covered her butt. But it was now blatantly obvious that an invisible person was standing there wearing only a suit jacket—and she was growing increasingly aware of the fact that she didn't know what time it was and how much longer this elixir would last.

"Please, sit."

She sat down next to him immediately, hoping to hide herself from the rest of the bar, only there wasn't much room on the bench and her leg was almost on top of his.

"I meant over there," he chuckled. He pointed to the empty seat across from him.

She moved to stand, but he placed a firm hand on her knee, rooting her in place as he slid over to make more room. The warmth of his touch eased her tension. Then he locked eyes with her, as if searching for something not seen on the surface. The longer his hand rested on her knee, the more her embarrassment faded away. She could only think about him, what he was looking for, the feeling of his skin on hers. Soon, the embarrassment was gone altogether. All she felt now was a powerful attraction towards him.

She leaned in towards him. Almost as if he could sense her need, the yearning between her legs, he removed his hand. Embarrassment flowed through her once more and her heart rate picked up pace as her anxiety increased. She needed to get out of here.

Before she could leave, he extended his hand to her. "I'm Harland."

"Gwendolyn Grayce Bishop, but everyone calls me Gwen. You can call me whatever. I mean, whatever you want." *Great, I'm rambling. Why did I give him my full name?*

She took his hand to shake it, and the feelings from a moment ago resurfaced. The embarrassment was gone in two shakes of his hand, replaced by the urge to leap across the booth and straddle him. She no longer cared that she was naked in front of him and began to remove the jacket he'd given her.

"I'm a gentleman, Miss Bishop, but I'm still a man. I can only endure a beautiful, naked woman for so long. Please keep the jacket on," he told her as he released her hand.

Gwen covered herself immediately.

"I think it best you go back to your friends."

The absence of his touch was stronger this time. It felt like someone had stolen the warmth of a blanket from her. She wanted it back. Embarrassment crept back in. She didn't want to return to her friends; she wanted to stay right here, but she knew she was being dismissed. Her cheeks warmed with the rejection.

She swayed when she stood, and he jumped up to catch her. Squaring her shoulders with his hands, he steadied her.

"Are you alright?" he asked, his arms dropping to his sides.

"Yeah, sorry, I got a little woozy."

She grabbed her forehead, and the suit jacket rose. Noticing his eyes move down her body, she froze, hoping to entice him to change his mind. His eyes lingered, and she moved closer to him. Licking her lips, her mouth silently begged for him to kiss her. Their bodies now less than an inch apart, she unbuttoned the jacket, her arm grazing his chest as she did. The jacket hung slightly open now, and he moved his arm inside it, resting it on her waist.

As he leaned forward, his lips touched her ear. "You're a hard woman to resist, Miss Bishop."

Before she could blink, his hand was gone, and he was back in his seat. His jacket was buttoned up again. The lack of his presence left an ache inside of her, an ache she hated. He made her feel weak and yet she yearned to be near him again.

What is this guy doing to me?

She'd never felt this way about the other guys she'd met before.

It was time to get back to her friends—before she did something she couldn't take back. She turned to leave, but stopped, remembering the jacket wasn't hers, and started to remove it again.

"Keep it." The man winked, then turned his eyes back to his book.

Gwen sighed in relief and finally moved toward her friends. The further she got from him, the more embarrassed she felt. By the time she returned to the group, she thought she might die from it. Her cheeks were on fire at the realization of what had just taken place, and she was thankful they couldn't see her face.

"What happened?" the three of them chorused.

"He could see me," she hissed.

They all gasped collectively.

"What do you mean, he could see you?" Hazel asked.

"He's wearing enchanted glasses!"

"I'm so sorry," Hazel half-whispered in horror.

Jordan looked past her. "He's totally staring at your ass right now."

Then Jordan bent forward at the waist as if to look for himself. Gwen smacked him. He straightened back in his seat, laughing. When Gwen turned around to look at the booth she'd just left, Harland was still reading his book, but she noted a grin on his face.

She yanked her clothes off the table where Hazel had put them and grabbed her wand before storming to the bathroom.

As Gwen returned to the table fully dressed, she looked across the bar at the now-empty booth and tucked the jacket under her arm. Crawling over Jordan, she sat down next to him. He put a consoling arm around her and she buried her head into his shoulder. His familiar embrace made her feel safe, which Gwen desperately needed.

"I'm so, so sorry," Hazel said again.

Gwen lifted her head. "It's fine. You didn't know." She looked at the empty table where Harland had been. "Besides, it wasn't that bad."

CHAPTER 8

Hazel

Gwen had fallen asleep around three a.m., but an hour later, Hazel still laid there, sleep impossible as thoughts of the exam consumed her. She'd thought the summer of waiting was long, but these last few hours felt like a small eternity. To distract her brain, she started counting sheep. As she counted, they morphed into geese.

Great, now I miss Garth. If she'd been brave enough to steal him away with her, he could be snuggling up to her right now. That always helped her sleep at home.

A light staccato of taps sounded on the window next to her bed.

It can't be! She rushed to open it. Instead of her sweet, cantankerous bird, a menacing-looking hawk wearing a vest met her. The bird snapped its beak as it flew past Hazel's face and landed on Gwen's head.

"What the—" Gwen said groggily as she sat up in her bed. She took one look at the bird and threw herself back down on the bed with a groan. "Damn it, Pan, do you have a tracker on me?"

"Sorry, he flew in before I could ask if he was yours," Hazel explained.

The bird, apparently named Pan, hopped to Gwen's hand. Gwen reached for the letter, ripped it from the bird's grasp, and threw it toward the trash can in the corner of the room. Pan pecked at her hand and she tried shooing him away, but he was persistent.

"I'm not reading it. Nothing good can come from it," Gwen said.

The sight of the demanding bird stirred something in Hazel, a familiar ache she refused to dwell on.

"Whose side are you on, anyway?" Gwen growled at the bird.

Pan immediately started pecking at his vest. He was clearly showing he was on the side of whoever the Sons of Chaos were.

"Is this your bird?" Hazel asked.

"No," Gwen spat out. "And if he doesn't stop pecking me, he's going to be a dead bird."

Hazel's eyes widened as the bird dive-bombed Gwen. What in Salem was happening?

"Fine, I'm reading it, but it changes nothing! I'm taking the entrance exam tomorrow," Gwen swore to the bird. She lunged out of bed and snatched the letter off the floor. Pan perched calmly on the nightstand as Gwen tore open the envelope.

What on earth is in that letter?

Hazel waited, not sure what to say. The room was silent. Then Gwen stuffed the letter in the trash and threw herself back on the bed, pulled a pillow over her face, and let out a muffled scream.

"Is everything okay?" Hazel asked.

"No, everything is *not* okay," came Gwen's muffled reply.

"Do you want to talk about it?" Hazel suspected the answer was no, but she was dying to know what was in that letter.

"You live with your dad, right?" Gwen asked.

"I did," Hazel answered hesitantly.

"Is he a giant piece of shit?" Gwen asked as she sat back up. Her words were in response to Hazel's answer, but her gaze slanted at Pan, who was still sitting quietly on the nightstand.

Hazel let out a nervous laugh as Gwen had hit entirely too close to the truth for Hazel's comfort. She had never shared the truth about her dad with anyone, but this was a new start. *Why act like he's something he isn't?* She'd pretended for years, and she didn't want to anymore.

"Actually, yeah. He is."

Gwen finally looked at Hazel. "Well, that's what's in the letter."

"Your dad wrote you to tell you he's a giant piece of shit?" Hazel asked, more intrigued than ever.

"More or less." Getting information out of her was like pulling teeth, so Gwen surprised Hazel when she volunteered, "He wants me to skip the entrance exam."

Hazel's eyes widened.

Well, that's a weird coincidence.

"He's arranged for me to marry a man I've never met, so he's demanding I leave tonight," Gwen confessed.

Maybe they were less similar than she'd thought. Hazel's mind flooded with questions: What kind of culture was Gwen from that arranged such marriages? Was he cute? Was he kind?

"I'm sorry," Hazel said instead. And she was.

A prison—a different kind than the one my father tried to use, but still. Are all men the same? Hazel seethed for herself and her new friend. They weren't possessions to collect or trade. Shouldn't their own fathers see that?

"I have to get into Saint Elias," Gwen explained. "I should've known he'd track me here, but he won't be able to get to me, not once I'm inside the mountain."

Pan moved to Gwen's side and nuzzled her neck. The bird might have been her father's, but he seemed genuinely sorry for hurting Gwen. The compassion he showed her made Hazel miss Garth that much more.

"My father put a cattle collar on me to keep me from coming here," Hazel admitted, looking away at the last moment. Shame bubbled in her gut, but she pushed it aside, reassuring herself she'd done nothing wrong—*he* had.

Gwen sat up, Pan resting on her shoulder, both staring at Hazel across the dark room lit only by the moon. Hazel could've sworn a flash of rage filled Gwen's eyes. The darkness must've been playing tricks on her.

"He didn't want me to come here. He said it was for my own good. I have to get into Saint Elias too. If I don't, I have nowhere else to go," Hazel added. She realized then that Forrest wasn't an option anymore for her. If he couldn't tell her the truth, he couldn't be in her life.

Gwen said nothing for what felt like forever.

Did I share too much? Hazel's hand slid to her neck as memories of what she hadn't shared with Gwen pushed in: the weight of the cold metal against her skin and the triumphant anger in father's eyes as he looked at it wrapped around her throat.

"Hazel, I promise you never have to go back there." Gwen's voice was rough when she spoke.

Tears welled in Hazel's eyes. She never wanted to go back. What happened to her wasn't okay. It wasn't normal. It definitely wasn't something she had to forgive and forget.

When tears fell down Hazel's cheeks, Gwen moved across the room and sat next to her, wrapping her arm around Hazel's shoulders. Hazel had no money, no resources. She'd pinned everything on getting into Saint Elias. Forrest would let her stay with him, but that was the second to last place she wanted to be. She needed to be free of them both after everything that had happened.

Hazel squeezed Gwen's hand in silent solidarity. It made it easier knowing she wasn't alone.

They both had to pass the exam tomorrow.

Gwen

Mount Saint Elias loomed overhead, beautiful lavender and peach hues coating the mountain's white-capped peak in the dawn. There it was—her only hope of escaping her father's demented plans and possibly finding a cure for her lack of control. Just looking at it made Gwen want to throw up. Sure, it was stunning, but it held Gwen's future. The mountain was freedom. It would decide if she was worthy.

What if I'm not worthy? What if I fail...

She couldn't think about it. She wanted this so badly. One wrong step, one unforeseen obstacle, and everything would shatter.

She glanced back over her shoulder toward the hundreds of mages trailing behind her. The sight sent a jolt of panic through her veins. This wasn't just risky; it felt like a descent into madness. Her pulse hammered a frantic rhythm against her ribs as she looked back at Jordan and Rafe. She wasn't just concerned for her own place at Saint Elias, but also theirs. What if they didn't all make it? She stole a glance at Hazel walking beside her.

Hazel met her gaze with a reassuring smile and whispered, "We've got this."

It helped, but only a little.

The mages in front of them bottlenecked at the opening into the mountain, and Jordan slammed into her, clearly not paying attention. She growled at him in warning.

"Sorry!" Jordan said.

A few minutes later, their group reached the cave entrance. The sign overhead read: *Abandoned Mine Shaft: Cave-In and Carbon Monoxide. DO NOT ENTER!*

The scent of old magic resembling aged parchment and incense wafted towards her.

Serena, the RA with blonde hair and porcelain skin from yesterday, greeted them at the entrance. She was wearing a pair of blue jeans and a navy Saint Elias University sweatshirt. Gwen was in a long-sleeve shirt, but the cool air coming from the tunnel made her wish she'd worn a sweatshirt as well.

"Enter the mine shaft," Serena instructed as she moved through the crowd. "Fill each cart!"

Bodies pressed in on her as everyone shuffled into the mine; upperclassmen stood along the side, shoving mages into the carts. Some mages tried to postpone their impending fates by lingering back, while others rushed to the front, pushing people out of the way. The grating sound of carts on metal echoed in her ears. She heard every crunch of gravel under hundreds of pairs of feet. The scent of their nervous sweat was too much for her. Gwen searched for Hazel's honey scent to ground her, but it wasn't there. Gwen looked to her left, but Hazel and her other friends were gone.

I'm alone.

Her breathing quickened. She reached for the handle of her wand, now holstered on her thigh, and rubbed the onyx stone. The hope that just an ounce of magic from the bracelet hidden inside might make it to her died quickly, but simply knowing it was there—only a twist and clasp away—helped.

Gwen blinked slowly, pushing her wolf back down, relaxing as her fingers kneaded the smooth crystal. She searched the crowd until she spotted Rafe's head over the sea of bodies. Gwen pushed through the crowd of mages, hoping to make it to him.

She elbowed mages out of her way until someone caught her by the shoulder.

"Gwen!" Jordan said from behind.

She whirled and grabbed his hand firmly, holding on like it was a lifeline. He squeezed her hand before continuing forward. As they walked, Gwen tried to search for Hazel's scent; it was so much sweeter and therefore stronger than Jordan's, but the rest of the mages overwhelmed her senses. Forced to abandon her search, she did her best to focus on Jordan's familiar grassy scent as they waited for a cart. But the push and pull of bodies, the noise of the metal, the voices bouncing off the walls, and the unfamiliar smells made it impossible.

Hex me.

Her heart pounded. The surrounding mages suffocated her. This was harder than anything she'd done during her training. Her town was so familiar and small. Nothing could've prepared her for the onslaught, wreaking havoc on her nerves now. Taking deep breaths, she tried to lock down her senses. She could not shift here. She'd kill someone. Then they'd kill her.

I have to get out of here.

Gwen pulled Jordan through the line of mages clamoring for carts and raced toward the first two open seats she saw. She released him as she climbed into the moving cart, exhaling as she settled into her seat. The tension coiled in her chest loosened a little as Jordan sat next to her. At least she'd made it this far without a disaster. But as she glanced up and spotted her cart companions, she let out an audible groan. Victoria and Serena sat across from her. Serena watched her with amusement as Victoria sniffed in derision.

The tracks of the mine cart carried them quickly from the shaft opening. Dim light from the entrance was visible, soaking the walls in a warm yellow glow. After a sharp curve in the track behind a jagged shaft wall, they entered total darkness.

A scream tore through the air.

"Was that—" Jordan began.

Another scream sounded. And another a few moments later.

Gwen's night vision was uninhibited, but the tunnel was too narrow, the track too straight, and the carts too dense for her to determine what lay ahead.

The mages in the cart in front of them screamed, and Gwen felt Jordan's hand clamp around her shoulder. She leaned into him.

Then the floor fell out from under them. They fell.

Gwen's stomach sank, and she held her breath to keep from screaming like everyone else. She refused to make a peep as they plummeted downward, choosing to abandon focusing on Jordan's increasingly rapid heart rate for Serena's steady one.

Another moment and the world righted itself.

It was just a steep decline.

Gwen let out a sigh of relief.

The screams from behind her grew fainter and fainter as their cart hurtled along the bottom of the mountain. After a few minutes, a faint glow illuminated the tunnel ahead, and as they rounded a bend, the track took them into an enormous cavern filled with the blue-green light of bioluminescent mushrooms. The mushrooms ranged in size, some as small as thimbles, while others were bigger than table lamps. The blue-green glow rippled out from the tracks in mesmerizing waves.

Jordan stuck his hand out as if to touch one.

Serena's voice cut through the air. "I wouldn't do that."

Jordan snatched his hand back quickly, and Gwen furrowed her brow.

"Why not?" she asked.

Serena studied her before answering. "These mushrooms feed on magic. So unless you have some to spare, I wouldn't offer so willingly."

Gwen had never heard of such a plant before, but the idea of something stealing her magic sent a prick of unease down her spine. She tucked her hands firmly inside the cart. Today was not the day to risk losing any magic.

Moments later, the cart slowed as it arrived at an enlargement in the tunnel where fire sconces lined the walls. Like at the entrance, the carts did not stop. Gwen hopped out of their moving cart first. Before Jordan could exit, the swarm of mages who'd arrived before them pushed past, sweeping her away.

Shit.

Tension thickened the air, pressing in on her, and she fought the instinct to run. Instead, she listened to her father's voice in her head telling her to put a wall at her back. Unable to push against the tide of bodies, she veered sideways, cutting through the crowd towards the cave wall.

She brushed against one student after another, the crush of bodies pressing in from all sides. The stench of sweat and more than one case of bad breath assaulted her senses, aggravating both her and her wolf. When a group of mages ahead slowed to a crawl, blocking her path, her patience snapped. She started swinging her elbows to rush them along.

"Hey!" a short male mage yelped, holding his arm gingerly where Gwen had gotten a good connection in.

Better than my teeth.

The desire to snap back at him, at his throat, racked Gwen. She knew the signs, knew she needed to distance herself. She'd expected the urge, but would not give in. Instead, she sped up to put distance between herself and this stranger who did not know who—or what—he was dealing with.

Desperate to escape, Gwen's awareness of her surroundings diminished. Her foot hit a stalagmite. One moment, her eyes were on the wall a few feet from her, and the next, her face was inches from the ground. Before she touched the dirt, a pair of muscular hands grabbed her waist. Turning in her savior's grasp, Gwen gazed up into the all-too-familiar deep-brown eyes of the man she'd met last night.

Harland smiled. "We meet again, Miss Bishop."

The way he said her surname, the subtle inflection in his voice, sent a shiver down Gwen's spine. A strange warmth bloomed in her chest. She felt eerily calm in his arms. The pressure of the exam ebbed away as he held her. His touch was magic, and she wished she could stay with him for the rest of the exam. But he was clearly an upperclassman here to facilitate the test.

A flicker of something dangerous and exciting ignited within her. The familiar heat flared low in her belly, an echo of the previous night's untamed desires and, along with it, the almost overwhelming urge to shed every layer of clothing and throw herself at him. She didn't know what it was about this guy that turned her on so much, but if she got in, she was determined to find out.

His right hand moved to settle possessively on her nape while his left pressed firmly against her waist, pulling her close. “Are you alright?” he asked, his voice a low rumble vibrating against her ear.

Gwen’s breath hitched. The world narrowed to the feel of his touch as the scent of leather and oak filled her senses. “I am now,” she whispered.

Harland laughed as he set her upright, but he didn’t release her. His gaze lingered on her, the intensity of it making her heart race. The urge to be closer to him overcame her, and she closed the small space between them. Her body brushed against his and her breath became shallow. All thoughts of the exam escaped her. She longed for his lips to be on hers, but the fantasy shattered as he stepped away, releasing her from his grasp.

The sudden absence of his touch was a stark coldness, and a wave of mortification washed over her, staining her cheeks crimson. Disoriented in the swirling mass of students, she froze, suddenly uncertain.

Harland’s gaze softened, a hint of something unreadable flickering in his eyes. “I think your friend is waiting for you,” he said, gesturing towards the dark tunnel entrance.

She looked up to see Hazel waving her arms a few yards away before the masses swallowed her. The sight of her new friend lifted a weight off her shoulders.

Gwen looked back to thank Harland, but he was gone.

Without him near, the calming sensation she’d felt was gone and all the anxiety she felt before rushed back, clawing up her chest. It was too loud, too busy, and the urge to shift was too strong.

Hazel. Get to Hazel.

Gwen’s focus sharpened, following the scent of honey through the cavern. When she reached her, Hazel pulled Gwen into a quick hug. Normally, Gwen was not a hugger, but these weren't normal circumstances. The tension in her chest eased, her wolf settling into a quiet slumber, no longer clawing at her mind as it labeled Hazel a friend.

“I got separated from Rafe. What happened to Jordan?” Hazel asked.

“I lost him at the jump,” Gwen explained, looking around hopefully as she said the words.

Hazel linked her arm through hers, and Gwen released a breath. Nothing would separate them again until the exam.

As the girls stepped into a narrow tunnel, Gwen glanced up. The ceiling pressed low overhead, the jagged rock uneven and looming. She figured it was high enough for most to pass through comfortably, but Klaus probably had to duck.

Bodies pressed in around her in the cramped space. Gwen forced herself to focus on Hazel’s honey scent, on the light dancing on the walls from an unseen source, on the crunch of loose limestone beneath their shoes.

Hazel leaned in closer to Gwen as they walked. “I saw you with that guy from the bar last night. He’s so hot!”

Gwen felt eyes on her. She looked over her shoulder and met Harland’s gaze from only four feet away. He flashed her a smirk as he walked in sync with a mix of mages. Gwen turned back abruptly.

Is he following me?

They emerged into the largest cavern yet, with ceilings that stretched impossibly high, swallowed in darkness despite the sconces lining the circular chamber. Ribbons of gold permeated the walls like veins dancing in the firelight. At the far end of the room, a waterfall cascaded from the darkness above and disappeared into an unseen opening behind an outcropping of rocks.

More students trickled in, their hushed murmurs of awe filling the space. Gwen forced herself to stay steady, resisting the instinct to tense as the crowd swelled around her. Thankfully, by the time the last of them had filed in, there was still plenty of room to breathe.

A group of mages climbed onto the stone outcropping, using it as a platform, with Victoria and Serena among them. Gwen suppressed a groan.

Of course, she’d be involved in this.

A glint of glass flashed in Victoria's hand as she lifted a small vial to her lips. "Attention!" Victoria called out, her magically amplified voice reverberated against the cavern walls grating Gwen's nerves.

Conversations hushed, and bodies shifted as students turned their attention forward.

A woman in all black—tailored trousers, turtleneck, and a long blazer—stepped forward with effortless authority. Her age was hard to pin down; her deep taupe skin was smooth, yet the subtle gray streaks in her curly brown hair hinted at experience. Regardless, her presence alone commanded the respect of someone much older. She also lifted a vial to her lips before she spoke.

"Good morning, potential scholars. Welcome to the Saint Elias entrance exams. I am Chancellor Pascale Lucas, the head of the university. The exam will start as soon as I am finished."

Thank Terra. I'm ready to get this over with.

"Those who pass the entrance exam will earn a place at one of the most prestigious institutions on the continent. If you fail the exam, you will leave knowing you gave it your best effort... hopefully."

Gwen would not fail. She was here; she was giving it her all.

"She means hopefully we tried, right? Not hopefully we will leave?" Hazel whispered.

Gwen chuckled. "My cousin made it; we'll be fine."

Please let everything be fine.

Hazel said, "That's not what I ask—"

"Do not take this opportunity lightly. Roughly fifteen hundred mages around the globe received a summons this year and less than half are expected to pass."

Hazel leaned into Gwen. "That's five percent. Five percent of high school graduates will pass."

Chancellor Lucas continued, "I know motivations and emotions are quite high, and with those, desperation as well. Consider this a warning: the decisions you make in the mountain matter. Choose wrong and you may never leave it."

A murmur rippled through the tense silence.

Damn, maybe Hazel's right to worry.

The chancellor motioned to the three tunnels behind her, and instantly, water cascaded over each of them. Once obscured, a bright light appeared within the tunnel in the center. The right tunnel was now dimly lit, while the left tunnel remained pitch black within.

"The tunnel you choose determines the tests you face, and could mean the difference between success and failure. You will enter the tunnels alone and you will be alone for the remainder of the test. The mountain likes to play tricks, so beware."

Gwen swallowed as she studied the walls of the cavern. She knew it was supposed to be sentient, but tricks?

The chancellor pointed to the waterfalls. "Last, the water is hexed. It will wash away all enchantments you have."

This received a few groans from the mages hoping to have a leg up, but Gwen smiled to herself. When she made it through this, she'd owe Klaus big time.

"The hex will remain dormant unless an examinee attempts to cheat, collude, or divulge school secrets. You have likely heard it referred to as 'the oath.' This is because it would trigger the hex to discuss it. Your check-in documents included a list of secrecy topics. I hope you study it. Should you trigger it, your magic will be stripped for one full year."

A whole year? Damn. Gwen swallowed.

Beside her, Hazel's face went pale as the gravity of the situation crashed down on them. Instinctively, Gwen hand gripped her wand. Without her bracelet, she truly couldn't attend SEU. Klaus had risked a whole year without magic for her. If he had said the wrong thing... Gwen had never been more grateful for him.

Please, let this plan work!

"If you wish to withdraw from the exam now, please find an RA among those positioned along the cavern walls. They will help you do so, though the hex will still be required in order to receive safe passage from this mountain. This is not our rule, but the mountain's. There will be no negotiations."

Gwen listened and heard only a few footsteps rush out of the crowd toward the walls. *Cowards.*

"Choose a tunnel. You have twelve hours to complete your examination." The chancellor pulled a pocket watch from her cloak and twisted the dials before tucking it safely back into her pocket. "Your time starts now."

Bodies crowded and rushed against one another as they fought to reach the tunnels. Gwen and Hazel waited at the back of the cavern and studied them all. Like moths to a flame, most students lined up in front of the middle, well-lit tunnel. Gwen was sure that choosing a tunnel was just one of many tests they would face, and her animalistic instincts told her the middle one was the wrong choice. Something about the tunnel felt wrong.

A smaller, but still considerable number of the thousand summoned mages, lined up before the dimly lit tunnel. Gwen felt like this option was better than the middle tunnel, but still not right.

One by one, students passed through the waterfalls that flowed over the mouths of the tunnel entrances. The first two lines were so long that the wait was going to waste precious minutes for those at the back of the line to enter the exam. Those minutes could make or break their chance of attending Saint Elias University.

Only a handful of students approached the pitch-black tunnel. Two had already cleared the waterfall. Gwen knew there was no time to waste, and she wasn't afraid of the dark. She'd have no problem with it, given her night vision. Hazel wouldn't have that same advantage.

Gwen just had to worry about staying in her human form, not hurting anyone, and keeping her therian half a secret from the mages. *No biggie.*

"What will you do?" Hazel asked Gwen, pulling her thoughts from what the sorcerers would do if they discovered what she truly was.

"We can't test together, but they didn't say we can't decide together," Gwen replied.

She didn't want to persuade Hazel either way and be wrong, be responsible for Hazel not getting in, but she also wasn't ready to part from her yet.

"What if we want different tunnels?" Concern laced Hazel's words.

Gwen thought for a minute. "We'll both walk towards the tunnel we want. If we pull in the opposite direction, we let go. If not, we follow each other and enter the belly of the mountain together."

They both began walking towards the dark tunnel, behind the two other applicants yet to pass under the waterfall. Gwen felt Hazel's pulse pounding in her palm and knew it matched the pace of her own.

"Together then," Hazel whispered, her voice scratchy.

As soon as they approached the waterfall, the professor at the mouth of the entrance stepped forward, lifting a hand. "One at a time."

"Good luck," Hazel said as she took a step forward.

Gwen tugged on Hazel's hand to stop her before she slipped through the water. "We don't need luck. We have all the motivation we need to nail this fucking test."

Please, let me not be completely full of shit.

Hazel's eyes sparked at Gwen's words. "Never going back."

Gwen nodded as she squeezed Hazel's hand. "Never going back."

CHAPTER 9

Hazel

Hazel slid her hand along the cool limestone wall, using it to guide her through the tunnel. She spared one last look backward, but nothing was visible beyond the waterfall. Each step further into the mountain brought cooler, damper air, and the light from the mine beyond bled away. Her heart quickened as darkness swallowed her whole.

I'm not afraid.

Step after silent step, she moved forward. Her fingertips grew raw from clutching the rough tunnel walls, grounding herself with every scrape. The rhythm of her movements became hypnotic—until doubt gnawed at her. *How long have I been walking? What if I'm running out of time?*

The thought jolted her into a run. Her pulse roared—not just from exertion, but from the terror that she'd missed a turn. Her feet throbbed with every step. There should've been something by now. A sign. A sound. *Maybe I missed it in the dark.*

Tears pricked her eyes. *Do I turn back? Did I miss something vital in the blackness behind me?*

She stumbled as the solid wall vanished beneath her hand. An opening! *This has to be it!*

Moving more slowly now, Hazel continued until she noticed a faint glow illuminating an empty path ahead. Sweat slicked her neck as she drew closer to it. Her hair felt damp as she smoothed it back. *Maybe I've been pushing too hard.* Her hands trembled as she wiped the sweat onto her pants. *Or maybe it's my nerves.* Her tongue felt thick and dry. *Water...* The thought caused a physical ache.

The tunnel grew steadily warmer, each step hotter than the last. The hazy light at the end pulsed with an unnatural heat. Even the soles of her feet felt damp with sweat.

This isn't from exercise; this is actual heat.

The tunnel curved, then abruptly opened into a violently bright cavern. Hazel threw up an arm to shield her eyes from the searing white light, and then she *saw* it. Not a glow, but a churning, licking wall of fire that filled the far end of the cavern. Orange and red tendrils writhed and danced, casting a suffocating heat that slammed into her like a physical blow. The air shimmered and distorted above the inferno, and the roar of the flames was a hungry beast devouring the silence.

Hazel whirled, desperate to escape back the way she'd come, back to the relative coolness and the darkness, but her outstretched hands slammed into solid, unyielding rock. The passage was gone, and the wall of fire was her only way forward.

"Think, Hazel, think! This is obviously a test. How can you get past the wall of fire?"

She turned back again to observe the cavern. The firelight danced along the walls. There were three rows of flames between her and the other side of the cavern, each running parallel and roughly ten feet apart. Hazel couldn't see beyond the last row. as it was too tall, too bright, and too far to see over. No, she definitely wasn't going *over* that one.

Hazel took a deep breath to steady her nerves and then stepped over the first fire, landing in the space between it and the next. She was pretty sure she could jump over the second row. She began jumping up and down, trying to see how high she could get. Her head pounded and swirled after the second jump. Hazel couldn't be sure she'd clear the next row of flames. The last thing she needed was to fall and burn to death.

Hazel put her hands on her knees and tried to focus on breathing. Below her, the ground was solid stone. Fire required fuel to burn, so this had to be magic. That meant there had to be a magical way to get through it.

She freed her wand from her arm holster and cast, "*Fame.*"

It was a spell she'd used a dozen times on the farm to starve a wildfire by removing the fuel it used to burn, which was usually dead brush or debris.

Hazel held her breath, hoping for a delayed reaction, but the flames continued. Determination fueled her. This was the hardest exam in the world. Of course, it wouldn't be that easy, but that was okay. She'd prove she was good enough. She had to.

Hazel blew air onto her forehead, desperate for any type of reprieve from the oppressive heat as she considered her next options. Perhaps she could try manipulating or herding it, like the Arkansas firefighters she'd seen.

"*Contineo.*"

A wall of air shot through the middle of the fire. This time, the fire reacted, but instead of parting it to leave room for her to cross, the fire rose high to the ceiling, burning brighter and hotter. After a few seconds, it died back down.

"Damn it!"

Sweat and heat stung at Hazel's eyes. She groaned as she wiped her dripping face with the hem of her shirt. This was her first true task, and she was failing miserably.

What if I can't do this?

As soon as the thought crossed her mind, she pushed it away. The heat was getting to her.

She jumped back over the smallest row and moved to the front of the room, away from the flames and their heat. It was barely any cooler, but it was better than nothing.

"If I can't starve it and I can't contain it, I need to smother it."

She needed water for the fire and for herself. If she didn't get some soon, she was going to dehydrate.

"How can I get water out of thin air when I'm underground?" Hazel asked herself.

Water, like the other elements, could only be manipulated, not conjured from nothing, as that magic had disappeared long ago. There was nothing she wouldn't give to find that information right about now.

That was it! There was no water in this part of the mountain, but she knew there was somewhere. She'd seen the waterfall herself. All she needed was to find it.

Hazel sighed, upset with herself for not considering it before.

She aimed her wand at the floor this time, instead of the fire, as she cast, "*Fodere*."

The ground shook as her magic tunneled through the cave floor in search of water. She'd never tried this spell underground before, but knew it worked. Her father used this spell to irrigate his crops during droughts when water restrictions were highest. It had never failed him. She hoped it didn't fail her now. What would he say if he knew she was using a spell from his family grimoire to pass this test? She could picture the disappointment and rage on his face and the spittle on his lips as he screamed she had no right. But she'd proven she had every right.

Water bubbled up through the hole.

"Yes!" Hazel cried. It wasn't much, but it would have to do.

Hazel focused on the water. "*Intendere*."

The water gathered into a large wobbly sphere. It took all of Hazel's strength to maintain its form, as water manipulation wasn't easy for even the most experienced mages. She attempted to levitate it, praying the sphere held as Hazel pushed with her mind.

It shot over the first row toward the second. Hazel tried to ignore her throbbing temples, as a drop of sweat rolled into her eyes and broke her focus.

The bubble burst and the water splattered on the ground as she rubbed her eye. Hazel had to try again.

Blinking away the burning sensation, she called up the water once more and turned it into another sphere. This time, she didn't lift it. Instead, she aimed the sphere at the wall of fires in front of her and sent it rolling with the flick of her wand. It rolled past the first row, leaving a path for her to walk through. The sphere continued on, and the fire did not rekindle. It moved through the second row without a hitch. Then her legs began to shake with exertion.

Every ounce of power she had went into maintaining the sphere long enough for it to pass through the third wall. The sphere slowed and quivered as if it might give way and return to a puddle on the floor. Sweat blurred her vision, and she relied on sheer will alone until, inch by inch, it passed through the third wall, leaving her a neat path to walk through the fire.

An exit tunnel appeared on the other side.

Her knees sagged with relief. She'd done it. She was good enough. The floor called to her—she needed to rest—but Hazel didn't dare sit. This exam wasn't over and she wouldn't stop until she was a student at SEU.

Hazel trudged as far and fast from the cavern as her feet could manage, never slowing until she reached the tunnel. She sagged against the wall, catching her breath, wishing the heat would dissipate. She didn't have the energy to even blink when the tunnel sealed behind her with a slam, granting her wish.

She took a few quick minutes to rest and then moved down the tunnel. This one was much shorter and she could see the fuzzy outline of whatever lay ahead. She rubbed her eyes, convinced the sweat had blurred her vision.

At the end of the tunnel, a cornfield greeted her, alight with a soft, silvery glow, like moonlight. She walked down the first row of corn and was immediately overcome by a wave of déjà vu.

It was impossible, but she knew she'd been here and walked down these well-worn paths more than once. In the near-dark, it took her a moment to recognize the structure in the far corner of the cavern—an old barn with a dull light glowing through the open door. Despite the darkness, she knew the barn was red, even from such a distance. She also knew the door creaked from age and that there was an old, locked chest inside, containing oats. She knew because it was hers.

No, not hers anymore. Her father's.

Why would the test show me this? Bring me here?

Hazel's heart raced as she continued down the rows, peering intently into the distance.

Is he here? Oh, Salem—is he the test?

A wave of lightheadedness overcame her. Stumbling, she knocked into a stalk. When she righted herself, she watched as the stalk withered before her eyes.

Then the next and the next. The entire row and those on either side of it began dying at a rapid rate.

Hazel ran.

She scanned the rows as she moved, trying to decide where to hide from whatever was killing the plants, when a face appeared a few rows away. The face was thin, with dark circles beneath unreadable eyes. She screamed, then tripped from surprise. She scrambled to her feet to find a dozen more faces rising from the fields, all staring at her.

Hazel ran as fast as she could to the barn. The couple who owned a farm a few miles down the road from her father's appeared in her path. She smiled in greeting, but then she saw their faces were gaunt, as if they were withering away like the fields. She stopped when they brandished pitchforks in their hands.

The man opened his mouth, and a raspy voice, on breath that smelled of death, said, "We need rain or the whole town will perish."

"Help us, Hazel," the woman begged.

This poor couple was so sick, but Hazel couldn't help them, not without magic, and that was forbidden. The Knights would come for her if they knew she'd exposed magic to mundanes.

Hazel paused. Was this part of the exam? To see if she'd reveal her mage identity?

Hazel backed away from them. "I—I don't know how I can help you."

A different woman appeared behind her, pitchfork in hand. "Help us, Hazel."

Hazel froze, realizing that she knew her too. She knew all of them. These were her neighbors, people from her town, her family's friends. People she'd spent her whole life lying to and hiding her true identity from.

She swallowed, searching for the right thing to say. "I'm sorry, I don't know how," she lied.

"Rain," Stephen, her mailman, croaked out a few rows over.

Hazel shook her head. "I don't know how to make it rain."

"You're a witch! We know you are!" cried the gentleman who owned the gas station on their edge of town.

"I'm not a witch," Hazel said quietly. That wasn't a lie. A witch had no more power than a regular mundane, but she knew they wouldn't care. To mundanes, it was all the same.

As the townspeople crowded around her, she noticed her father and brother standing amongst them. The shame of letting them see her so desperate, proving them right, nearly rivaled her desperation. Yes, she'd let them down, but surely they still loved her enough to help her.

"Tell them!" she begged her family. "Tell them I'm not a witch!"

Forrest and her father said nothing as they stood there in silence, watching the townspeople grow impatient. Her father lifted his arm out to the side. Hazel held her breath, hoping he'd step in, when a raven landed on his arm. It cocked its head to the side and stared at her.

"Help us or die." The voice was from a young child.

The surrounding voices echoed him. "Help us or die! Help us or die!" As their chants grew louder, the pitchforks they were carrying lit up with flames.

Hazel stumbled backwards, barely remaining upright.

The raven took flight and transformed into Hazel's mother, landing in front of Hazel close enough to block the townspeople from view. Her long black hair shone in the moonlight, her eyes like mirrors of Hazel's own but glowing from within. Stunned, Hazel reached for her mom. This was why she'd come.

"Mom, help me."

"You are a raven. You do not belong here. Leave this place and fly east."

Before Hazel could ask her what she meant, her mother transformed back into a raven and flew through the tunnel behind her, leaving the cave.

"Wait!" Hazel cried.

She didn't understand. Her mother had been calling her to this very place in her dreams all summer. Why now, when she was so close, would she tell her to leave? Hazel ran after her mother to find out, but more townspeople appeared in front of her, blocking her way.

"Kill the witch!" the townspeople shouted.

"I'm not a witch!" she yelled back.

They charged her at once.

She accepted then that her family would not help her. Her mother had abandoned her, while her father and brother had joined the hunt. Hurt and rage filled the empty cracks in her heart and her mind. These people were supposed to protect her, yet they had disappointed her again and again.

Hazel ran into the dying fields, toward the barn. She could hear the footsteps thudding behind her, but she did not risk a look back.

Her legs grew weak and a stitch in her side ached. She couldn't outrun them forever. They'd be on her in seconds and she'd be at their mercy if her family wouldn't help her. If they wanted to kill her, she would have to save herself.

She pulled out her wand, but hesitated, not sure what spell she could use to protect herself—she didn't want to hurt these people, just escape them—but she was so tired and so scared, her mind could only think of one thing: run. Then she felt a raindrop hit her face. Then another, and another, as dark clouds rolled in and the sky began to cry.

The ground grew muddy within seconds, and she slid to her knees. When she rose, she found herself surrounded once more by the townspeople, hatred in their eyes. They would kill her, their own neighbor.

Lightning cracked directly above.

"You got your rain. Now leave!" Hazel yelled as she stood.

The townspeople stepped toward her in unison. They would kill her for being different? For being something she couldn't change? Fear and anger seared through Hazel.

Lightning struck the ground in front of her, the force so strong that those closest to her went flying backward. Fire caught on the stalks next to the strike zone and spread quickly. The townspeople turned and ran, screaming in panic. Hazel sank into the mud and cried as she watched the people she'd known her whole life turn their backs on her.

"It's not real. It's not real. It's not real," she told herself, because for a few moments, when her family rejected her and she had run for her life, she'd forgotten it wasn't real—that it was just the exam. The rain poured overhead, cleansing her, the fires, and the fields.

The cavern lightened, the pinks and oranges of an early dawn filling the room, although there was no horizon. Hazel rose to find the diseased field had come back to life, the rows green and tall once more. Regardless of its restored beauty, she could only see the rot that had taken hold in the night. She could stand the cavern no longer and ran to a passageway on her left.

The light from the cavern behind her disappeared and Hazel knew without looking that the tunnel had sealed behind her once more. The light from ahead remained just bright enough to allow Hazel to navigate the path to a fork in the tunnel.

She had a decision to make. Go right or go left.

Now was not the time to let her indecision kick in, so she veered right. She continued down the curving tunnel, deeper and deeper into the mountain, not running into any more turnoffs or openings, until she heard the familiar sound of rushing water. Rounding a curve, she saw a waterfall flowing over the path in front of her.

Am I back at the start?

Hazel was unsure if this meant failure or success, but she'd seen no other paths to take. She prepared for the worst and passed through the water.

Gwen

Gwen maneuvered carefully between the stalagmites that littered her path within the dark cave using her night vision. The stalagmites as tall as her hip were easy to see as her eyes adjusted, but the smaller ones were nearly undetectable, even to her.

Roughly ten feet ahead, a forked tunnel grew visible.

Thank Terra. Time to get the hell out of here.

Gwen took the first turnoff on her right.

A large black pool of water stretched before her, spanning the entire cavern, aside from a small landing on the other side that appeared to lead to an exit. Gwen studied the water and the walls to see if there was a way around or across that didn't involve her submerging herself. She angled her body to get closer to investigate, and, in response, the water rippled across the pool.

Ah, hell no, there's something in there.

Gwen turned to go back, but found the opening was gone, a solid wall in its place.

"Shit," she swore, facing the water as another ripple rose to the surface.

The water was so dark, Gwen couldn't tell what was down there, but she was sure she'd find out if she got in. Gwen lamented she hadn't been born a shark or a bird. The room was empty save for her and the water ahead. The walls along the edges were smooth with nothing to grip on to. A shiver ran down her spine. There was no way out of this. She was going to have to swim.

I'm so fucked.

If Klaus was here, he'd have told her that negativity would get her nowhere. And then she'd flip him the bird. She still wished he was here, if nothing else, but to act as bait. She chuckled at the thought.

"This is fine. I can totally do this," she said aloud. *I can totally* not *do this.*

She weighed her options as she paced along the small landing.

I could sit here and die in this cave, or I can swim across and die in the water.

Well, she'd never been one to back down from a fight.

She stretched her arms and cracked her neck.

Her wolf form was a much faster swimmer, but she wouldn't be able to use her wand for whatever lay beneath the water should she need it. Not to mention there was no way for her to shift back, no one to attach her bracelet on her wrist. It wasn't a chance she was willing to take. These tests were supposed to be made for mages. Mages used wands. She could do it. And even in her human form, she was faster than most without her bracelet. She just had to jump in and swim like her life depended on it.

Which it did.

Her foot touched nothing as she cautiously dipped it into the pool of surprisingly warm water. An immediate drop-off was likely.

Yanking her foot back out, she stared at the water again. If she dove as far as she could, she might make it to the middle. Then she'd only have half of the space left to cover. It wasn't a brilliant plan, but it was all she had.

While being a wolf wasn't a smart choice right now, being a mage who mimicked animals to enhance themselves was. Gwen didn't have the knowledge of full transmutation yet—that was something one had to go to college for—but she knew the spell all teenage girls with annoying-as-hell cousins knew.

She pulled out her wand. "*Contego.*"

A faint shimmer enveloped her. If anything brushed up against her—on purpose or by accident—the hex would sting it. It wasn't enough to truly hurt an enemy, but it might be enough to scare one off. If she couldn't be a shark, she could at least pretend to be a jellyfish. Plenty of things feared those little bastards. Unfortunately, the spell was only good for one use, so she'd have to be careful not to bump into anything non-threatening in the water.

Gwen put her wand away and dove into the pool. She remained submerged and kicked her feet as hard as she could, allowing the momentum to take her as far as possible. After a dozen kicks, her lungs burned for oxygen. While Gwen was in great shape, training to hold your breath during physical exertion was something she'd never done before. She swam to the top while continuing her forward progression to find that she'd already made it halfway across.

Almost there.

She put her head down and swam hard and fast. The urge to open her eyes and scan her surroundings underwater called to her, but she refused, fearing what she might see. A few seconds longer and her hand slapped a solid slab of stone. Exhausted, Gwen placed her hands on the edge of the pool and used momentum, her legs, and sheer strength to lift herself up. As her waist passed the waterline, she felt slippery flesh wrap around her left leg.

A jolt of magic warmed her body. The *contego* hex had worked and her leg was free once again. Her knees scraped along the bank as she scrambled to get out of the water. She took a deep, shaky breath as she lay on the ground.

She made it. She was out.

There was a splashing sound, and she turned her head just in time to see a large black tentacle emerge from the water.

Fuck!

Gwen scrambled backwards, but the tentacle snaked itself around her leg before she could get away. Needles of pain shot through her and the scent of iron filled her nostrils. Blood. She was bleeding.

It fucking bit me!

Gwen pulled out her wand, preparing to fight, when it yanked her back to the edge. With no time for anything other than a deep breath, Gwen sucked all the air she could into her lungs and waved her wand. "*Sectam aere!*"

A bubble formed around her, molding to her body as she slid beneath the surface of the water. It would allow her to breathe for an hour under ordinary circumstances. With physical exertion and stress, she'd be lucky to get ten minutes.

The tentacle pulled her deeper, the pressure making it hard to breathe even with the bubble spell. Panic bloomed in her chest. She needed to hurry. She looked within the murky depths of the water, but saw nothing except the tentacle wrapped around her leg, which was now climbing further up her body.

She used some of the bubble spell's precious reserve and pointed at the tentacle wrapped around her leg as she cast, "*Vulnus.*"

A multitude of red gashes appeared across the tentacle. Immediately, it released her and a thunderous roar pulsed through the water. Gwen swam as fast as she could toward the surface. She was still too far from the top when she used up the last of the air in the bubble, and the spell released with a pop. She was on her own. She'd have to hold her breath.

With only a little further to go, Gwen kept swimming upward until her head burst out of the water and she gasped for air. She lunged toward the bank, the water receding as she swam. When she made it to the ledge, the tips of her fingers were all that could reach. She dug her nails into the stone and crawled her way up the side until she was on land again. Gwen did not stop until she hit the back wall, dragging her feet as far from the edge as she could manage. Dark blood spread outwards in the water. She knew she had injured it, but she didn't think it was that bad. If the creature hadn't attacked her, she'd almost feel sorry for it.

Bubbles formed along the surface. Maybe it wasn't dead. She waited with her shaky wand hand outstretched, but nothing appeared above the water's surface.

Gwen waved her wand. "*Sicco.*"

She was instantly dried.

After allowing herself a few minutes to catch her breath, Gwen slowly made her way through the next tunnel. It was wider than the last one, with smooth terrain and no stalagmites, and she could see a bright light shining like a beacon at the end. Could that be it? Had she made it to SEU?

No, it couldn't be that easy.

Klaus had warned her the mountain would push her to the brink. One test wouldn't be the only thing she faced today.

Moving slowly at first, she walked for several minutes, but the light at the end of the tunnel seemed just as far as it had been when she'd started. She paused and turned to look back the way she'd come.

That's odd.

Hadn't the tunnel been wider at the end? It looked much smaller now. Gwen felt a tingle at the back of her neck. Turning to look in the opposite direction once more, she noticed the light at the end of the tunnel grew smaller as each second passed—smaller, not further away.

The walls were closing in.

Gwen bolted into a full sprint. Her feet pounded against the limestone, but the exit remained too far away.

Push, Gwen, push!

Her legs moved as hard and fast as they'd ever carried her. In a matter of moments, the walls were so close she could feel them bump against her shoulders and elbows as she ran. It wasn't enough. The walls were going to crush her to death if she didn't get out of there soon. She needed to be faster. She'd have to shift.

There was no time to question it. She let her wolf out and shifted mid-sprint, bounding forward on four padded paws. The light was so close now. She was almost there. The walls moved closer and scraped against her fur. She had to hunch lower to the ground and move slower as the wall reduced her range of motion, but she saw the cavern at the end of the tunnel.

The walls scraped her hips as she squeezed through the gap. She turned just in time to see the wall the seal shut behind her.

I made it! But at what cost?

Gwen couldn't shift back on her own. She'd finish the exam as a wolf. Her stomach churned, sick with dread and frustration. She should have never come. The minute she finished the exam, they'd learn her secret. If only her family had listened. She needed to find a way out and a place to hide.

She turned to find herself in a wooded area with trees towering high, the bright sky overhead. A sigh of relief escaped her. Maybe she'd get out of this easily. She padded through the green grass, the blades nearly as soft as feathers, unlike anything she'd walked on in Maine.

It was eerily silent.

As Gwen explored the trees, she picked up an unfamiliar scent—one she'd never smelled in the woods. She followed the irregular trail and the scent quickly grew stronger. She was being followed—stalked.

She turned sharply, planning to backtrack, when a leopard leapt from the trees and landed a few feet in front of her.

First, a sea monster. Now, a leopard. What's next, a dinosaur?

The jungle cat was large, but not nearly as large as Gwen. It crouched in the attack position, bared its fangs, and hissed. It stared her in the eyes, showing no fear or respect for Gwen's wolf form. Gwen made a slow, wide circle, making it shift its weight out of its defensive stance, just like her father had taught her. Its movements mirrored hers as they sized each other up.

The leopard lunged at Gwen, but she darted swiftly out of the way. It slammed face-first into a tree.

Gwen hurtled toward the leopard, sinking her canines into its neck. It fought for a second until blood filled her mouth. The leopard went limp with a whine.

She spit out the blood, hating the metallic taste. Her father had always taught her a swift kill was a mercy, but that never assuaged the guilt. It was still a living thing. Why did the leopard have to attack her?

After wiping her mouth on the grass to remove some of the blood, she lifted her head to see the leopard's fur melting away to reveal a lifeless woman, no older than Gwen, her blonde hair soaked in blood. She approached the body cautiously, knees shaking and fur raised. This couldn't be real. She sniffed—the scent of skin, blood, and death certainly smelled real. Gwen nudged the body with her nose. It was human.

No. No. No!

Gwen licked the girl's face, desperately trying to rouse her, but Gwen knew she was gone. She'd learned the killing blow from her father when she was twelve and never missed. Not once.

Gwen sat down protectively beside the girl, a howl tearing from her throat. Then another and another, until her voice was raw.

I'm a monster.

Gwen laid down in the grass, exhausted. She would stay here forever with the girl. She didn't deserve to go on.

Something touched her head. Gwen jolted up and found her mother staring back at her as she pet her fur, comforting her. Her mother had come to save her and Gwen had never been more grateful.

Her mother knelt down, her vanilla scent washing over Gwen. She pulled Gwen's wand from the pocket of her dress, removed the bracelet from the handle, and attached it to Gwen's front right paw.

Gwen shifted back and her mother handed her the same clothing she'd been wearing earlier. Gwen accepted it and dressed quickly, her brain fogged with confusion and grief. *How did she get my wand and my clothes?* They were spelled to return to her bags. None of this made any sense, but Gwen was too consumed with guilt to question it further.

"Thank you," Gwen muttered between sobs as she ran back to the girl. Gathering her in her arms, she cried at the unnecessary loss of life. "She came at me, Mom. I had no choice." She looked up at her mother with tear-filled eyes. "I had no choice."

"We have to go to the authorities," her mom told her.

"What?" Gwen set the girl back down, shaking in fear. "You said —you said you'd always protect me. You said you'd keep me safe!"

"Gwendolyn, this was no accident. It was a clean-conscience kill."

Her mother looked at the girl with no marks other than her shredded neck that jutted to the side, broken. The horrified look on her face told Gwen everything she needed to know—her mother was afraid of her.

"Mom!" Gwen raised her voice. *This can't be happening.* "She attacked *me*! What was I supposed to do? Lay down and die? I didn't know she was a therian."

Her mother said nothing as she stepped away from Gwen.

"Mom, please, you can't tell anyone!" She desperately reached for her mother, who recoiled at her touch. The motion landed like a knife in Gwen's heart.

Wrapping her arms around herself, she sobbed harder.

"Mom, you know what will happen," Gwen begged.

Gwen didn't say what they both knew. *The Knights will come for me. They'll cage me like a dog.*

"Come with me, my cub. I'll hide you. I'll protect you," a voice said behind her.

Gwen whirled to find her father standing beside the girl. His blue eyes, usually so mischievous, were somber as they connected with her own. His thick, wavy grey hair and powerful jaw hadn't changed since she'd last seen him, but he had more fine lines around his eyes and mouth than before.

Why was he here? Why were they both here?

"We can give her a therian burial, send her off into the stars," he said. He took off his Sons of Chaos leather jacket and covered the girl's body.

Gwen's mouth hung open as her father lifted the girl into his arms. He was being so soft, so tender. Gwen didn't think her dad possessed such qualities.

Her mother put a hand on her shoulder, turning her around to face her once more. Gwen's eyes welled with tears at her mother's touch.

"Gwendolyn, this isn't right. What if that were you?"

Frustrated that her own mother would rather protect this stranger over her own daughter, Gwen stepped backwards toward her father.

"Gwendolyn, don't do this. Her family deserves to know," her mother protested.

"What about me? What do I deserve?"

Maybe she deserved to be caged for what she'd done, but it was an accident, an act of self-defense. Did her mother truly think she deserved to be punished?

When her mother said nothing, she added, "Will you tell them I'm a therian?"

"I meant it when I said I'd always protect you. We'll tell them it was an accident, that it happened in the test, but we won't tell them the details." Her mother moved towards her, holding her head in her hands. “I know you didn’t mean to do this. You’re not a monster. I'll be there with you every step of the way.”

But Gwen still remembered how her mother had recoiled from her. The horrified look on her face. She desperately wanted her to never look at her like that again. If she went with her mother, maybe she'd forgive her. Maybe over time she'd forgive herself. She knew she never would if she went with her father.

As much as she hated to admit it, her mother was right. She wouldn’t be able to live with herself or the lie. She’d have to hope and pray everyone believed her when she told them it was in self-defense.

“I’m sorry,” she said to her father. As tempted as she was to hide her mistakes, that would make her like him, and that was something she could never stomach.

At her words, he looked at Gwen with sadness in his eyes, then he disappeared, the young girl with him.

She spun around to find her mother, too, was gone without a trace.

Gwen sagged with relief. It wasn’t real. It was the exam. Just the exam.

She fell to the ground and cried into her hands. It was then she realized the bracelet her mother had given her was still on her wrist. She studied it until she was sure it was hers. She wouldn’t have been able to shift back without it. Quickly, she tested her senses, and found only her mage abilities and none of her therian. Her wolf was locked back up.

Gwen wandered through the woods until she found another tunnel. Entering slowly, she watched over her shoulder as the woods behind her vanished and the wall sealed.

CHAPTER 10

Gwen

The sound of rushing water greeted her. Gwen grinned as she turned the corner to see a waterfall in her path.

"I made it," she half-whispered in disbelief. "I actually fucking passed."

The waterfall was a risk she couldn't take, so she unclasped the bracelet and stuffed it back into the handle of her wand. The smell of sulfur overwhelmed her as soon as the bracelet's clasp was released. How deep had she gone in the mountain? It looked like the beginning of the exam, but she knew by the smell it couldn't be. If Saint Elias's campus smelled like this, it was going to be a long year. She wrinkled her nose as she stepped through the waterfall.

On the other side, Gwen found herself on the ledge of a large magma chamber aglow from the streams of magma bubbling hundreds of feet below. A slim stone walkway bridged from her ledge to the other side of the chamber.

Fuck this.

She began to turn back when movement across the chamber

caught her eye. It was Hazel. She was on the other side. Excitement filled Gwen, quickly followed by confusion. How was this possible? The number one rule of the exam was that they couldn't work together.

Hazel waved her arms in the air. Gwen waved back, her eyebrows pinched. Was this a trap? A test? Was Hazel even real?

Hazel cupped her hands to her mouth as if to shout. Gwen strained but heard nothing, even with her bracelet off. Which reminded her—she needed to put it back on. She placed her hands behind her back and slipped the bracelet on once more.

Gwen deliberated on whether to trust the friend before her. Ultimately the desire not to be alone any longer won out over her suspicions.

She picked up a small stone and tossed it onto the pathway in front of her. The pathway didn't quiver or move. She cast a spell at it next, but that didn't trigger any type of hex that she could see. Gwen stepped gingerly onto the path. She half expected her shoes to warm from being suspended over the molten rock, but she felt no heat from the stone.

The air around her churned, carrying a powerful stench of sulfur that burned her nose. Gwen walked slowly, unsure of how steady this pathway truly was. She wanted to remain alert enough to backtrack, should it give way. It felt like no time before she'd made it a quarter of the way across.

A loud screech reverberated through the chamber. Gwen's gaze immediately landed on Hazel, afraid she might have fallen and cried out in fear. Hazel was still on her ledge, staring at the ceiling, a look of awe on her face. Gwen followed her gaze, and the air in her lungs evaporated.

Four winged creatures with clawed feet and scaled bodies breathed flames a hundred yards overhead. The beings above were supposed to be extinct, things of fairy tales and nightmares.

Impossible!

The beast with garnet scales dove at her. She ran as fast as her human shape would let her. Almost halfway across the pathway, she tore her eyes away from the dragon to see Hazel running toward her.

"Go back!" she yelled at Hazel.

But Hazel kept coming, and she was screaming too. Gwen couldn't hear her, but she read her lips clear as day.

DRAGON!

Gwen looked past her to see the ledge Hazel had stood on moments ago was now occupied by a large amber dragon. Razor-sharp claws dug into the rock as it opened its maw, throwing its wings wide. The dragon's jaws quivered as saliva sprayed, and Gwen knew it roared then, though she couldn't hear it.

Forward was no longer an option. Gwen looked over her shoulder to find her own ledge empty. She turned back, but only made it two steps before the garnet dragon landed on the bridge between her and the ledge. The whole bridge shook with the force of its landing, and Gwen stumbled, thrown off balance, nearly falling off the edge.

The only thing left to do was get to Hazel. They'd have to fight them together.

They reached the middle of the stone bridge at the same time, running smack into an invisible wall. Gwen screamed in surprise and saw Hazel's mouth widen, but no sounds crossed the barrier. The girls drew their wands simultaneously, each casting spells at the wall, but it held.

"What kind of fucking test is this?" Gwen screamed.

Gwen felt searing heat at her back and turned to see the dragon's flames miss her by inches. Holstering her wand, she threw her fists into the barrier, desperate to get away.

Nothing.

Hazel banged, too, with no better luck.

Gwen could see the amber dragon only feet from Hazel now. A burst of wind coated her back from behind, and Gwen knew the garnet dragon was right behind her as well. Gwen's knees shook from the adrenaline and fear coursing through her.

She turned her back to Hazel and faced the garnet dragon. Its golden eyes locked onto hers, unblinking. A jagged scar cut down its left eye, sending a chill through her. This dragon had survived battles—and won them. She had no idea how she was going to win against it. *I don't have to win,* she reminded herself. *I just have to survive.*

Hazel

Hazel watched Gwen and knew their time to run had passed. Her whole body quivered with fear, but she couldn't give up. She'd come too far to give up. She had no choice but to face the amber dragon breathing down her back.

She inhaled.

This is just a test. This isn't real.

The amber dragon's massive face was inches from her own as she turned.

The heat of its breath drenched Hazel in a fresh layer of sweat. Its golden-orange scales glowed in the magma's light from below, making it look as if it was made of magma itself. How could something so beautiful be so terrifying? Its amber eyes studied her.

Hazel drew her wand. The dragon blew a plume of smoke from its nostrils as if to caution her against using it. As Hazel lowered her wand, a voice, like a crackling bonfire, filled the chamber.

"What spell would you have used?"

Hazel jolted at the sound of the voice. Rough and masculine, it slid across her mind like jagged glass, and her skin broke out in goosebumps despite the heat. Dragons could speak?

It blew another plume of smoke. Feeling as though her life might depend on the answer, Hazel swallowed nervously before responding, "A sleep spell."

The dragon narrowed its eyes with a gleam. It laughed, a deep huffing sound that sent hot air washing over her. Hazel's shirt clung to the sweat on her back as she impulsively stepped back against the barrier.

"Using a spell like that means you are either weak or merciful. We shall see." As the dragon spoke, its lips didn't move.

Hazel glanced back at Gwen. A garnet dragon loomed over her, as well, and Gwen appeared to be talking to it, though its mouth didn't move either. The dragons were communicating in their minds.

Hazel's heart threatened to pound right out of her chest.

It's not real. It's just a test!

Her shoes should be puddles of rubber and her skin nothing more than ash given the heat emanating from the magma below, yet she was fine. This had to be part of the exam. She needed to figure out the problem so she could find the solution.

Hazel looked around. She could scale the walls with magic. A look upwards made her swallow. Two more dragons roosted at the top of the cavern, hundreds of yards above. That wasn't an option. Going through the barrier wasn't possible, and neither was heading back past the dragon. That only left one direction—down.

Hazel took a step towards the edge of the stone path. That must be it, the way to SEU. She had to overcome and embrace this last level, this ultimate fear: death. It had to be the final test.

The dragon narrowed its eyes. "What are you doing?"

"Ending this and going to Saint Elias University," Hazel said. She continued towards the edge. Two more steps and this damned exam would be over.

"No such luck, little bird," the amber dragon growled.

Hazel groaned with effort as she tried to take another step, but her feet didn't budge. She cast a spell at her feet to release herself, then another. Nothing happened. When that didn't work, she looked at the dragon. It studied her, amber eyes slit into near lines, as if it knew her thoughts.

Hazel thought about what to do. She could attack the creature, but something in her gut held her back. Instead, she aimed her wand at the cavern walls.

A large chunk of rock fell from the wall and landed with a loud splash in the magma below.

Yes! Something finally worked!

She doubled her efforts, but aimed higher, hoping a chunk of rock might break the pathway and send her into the magma. She sent down another rock. Another. The ground shook and the molten rock roiled below, but no rocks had come close to collapsing the pathway.

Hazel fumed. *What's the point of this test?*

"Who says this is a test?"

It had read her mind. If the dragon knew her thoughts, *maybe*... Hazel pushed back to see if she could know its thoughts as well, and if it would reveal the test's answer.

Hazel felt a steel door slam down in her mind. The dragon had driven her out. It clicked its tongue at her as if to chastise her for trying, though it smiled.

Her fascination with the dragon almost rivaled her fear. Almost. It didn't matter that it wasn't real. It felt real, and that was enough.

"Clever bird! Someone has been reading you too many fairy tales, but not enough of the ones where the heroes die."

The dragon's words echoed in Hazel's mind and déjà vu hit her once more. She'd heard those words. Not the same, but similar. So similar. During her conversation with Forrest in their father's study. He'd pointed out that there were fairy tales in which the heroes died. Something scratched at the back of her mind, trying to fall into place, but the dragon interrupted.

"I think I like you, so I'll let you decide."

"Decide what?" She tried to sound brave, but the quiver in her voice betrayed her.

"You may leave here on one condition."

"What's the condition?" she asked.

Hazel glanced back at Gwen. Would they give her an opportunity to leave too? She hoped so. Unless it meant selling each other out.

Surely the mountain wouldn't ask that. She couldn't do that to Gwen. She hoped Gwen wouldn't do that to her.

"If you leave, you fail the exam and you will not be admitted to Saint Elias," the dragon purred, showing perfect awareness of what a wretched offer that was.

Hazel's eyes widened. She'd fought so hard, given up so much, to get to this point. This was all she'd ever wanted. She couldn't—*wouldn't*—walk away so easily.

"What's my other option?"

"Stand here with another, face the wrath of our fire, and hope to be reborn together."

Burn in fire? Panicked bloomed in her mind, and she panted as she fought to free her legs from the magic holding her in place. Somehow, diving to her own death was easier to stomach than sitting here, leaving her fate up to this monster.

"Ah, there she is—the scared little girl beneath the brave mask."

The truth of his words sliced into her. She *was* scared. Scared she was wrong, scared her father had been right.

A loud crack caught her attention. The seiche she'd caused in the magma below grew. The vibrations up the cavern walls caused rocks to crash down into the river of fire beneath them. One large slab landed upon the stone pathway not a dozen feet from where she stood. Hazel cried out as shards ricocheted from the impact and embedded in her arms and neck. Pain seared her skin, and the growl of the dragon reverberated through her.

"Choose," the dragon demanded.

Its wings beat faster, betraying its own heightened emotions.

Doubt crept in. What if this wasn't an illusion? What if she actually died here alone in this cavern with no one to mourn her? What if she never saw her mother again or learned about her abilities?

The dragon growled as the walls fell down around them. It wasn't real, but she was really bleeding.

"If you stay, I can promise you will never be the same; you will be more powerful than you ever dreamed of. You will find the answers you seek about your mother and your powers."

Hazel's breath caught in her throat. He was offering her the exact things she'd come for.

She hadn't told the dragon or Gwen or anyone.

This had to be it, what Forrest meant when he said there was always a price. Would this one be too high to pay? Perhaps this was the exact thing her father had tried to keep her from. Perhaps she was supposed to walk away.

The dragon spoke again. "There's a catch. If either of you decide to leave, you both fail."

Great. Hazel's future at Saint Elias lay in Gwen's hands.

Gwen

"What's the catch?" Gwen demanded.

No way in Salem were these fire-breathing bastards going to just let them walk out.

Gwen's cool composure slipped when she glanced at Hazel. Hazel held her wand, unaimed, her shoulders stiff. She wondered what kind of deal the amber dragon was offering Hazel.

The dragon's gravelly voice sounded in her mind. "The catch is that you will fail the entrance exam and will not be accepted into Saint Elias. So will Hazel."

Gwen didn't want to be the reason Hazel failed. She'd promised her she'd never have to go back to her father. But she wasn't willing to die in this chamber. Certain she could convince her mom to let Hazel stay with them, she gave the dragon her answer.

"Great. No sweat off my back. Where's the exit?" Gwen stepped to the side, but the dragon stood firmly in her way.

"I thought you might say that. Let me offer you one last piece of information before you decide."

Gwen let out a deep breath as if to say, "get on with it." It was hot. She'd been through hell and back during this exam, and she was tired.

"If you stay, the help you desperately seek awaits you at Saint Elias. Should you pass this ultimate test, you will never be the same."

Gwen said nothing, did nothing. The words rooted her in place. How could this dragon possibly know what she needed?

The mountain likes to play tricks. That had been the chancellor's warning.

Of course, the mountain had already figured out her secret in the last test.

"The answer to mastering your fera condition awaits within Saint Elias," the dragon said.

Her wolf growled within her. She hated that term, it made her sound like some kind of rabid animal. *How does he know I'm a fera?*

"The whole point of mastering my instincts is to keep the world from learning about me. Why should I agree to move forward where others might find out the truth and expose me?"

The dragon smirked. "The *whole* point?"

The image of the young woman lying dead on the ground flashed in her mind. Gwen sighed. She wasn't used to having her thoughts on display.

"Tell me," Gwen demanded. "Was it real?"

She needed to know if she'd actually killed that girl. She couldn't live with the question clawing at the back of her mind.

The dragon tilted its head, eyes gleaming. "Does it matter? You saw what you're capable of."

His vague response made her swallow hard. It wasn't real—none of it was. Not even this conversation, not even the dragon before her. But he was right. She'd seen what she was capable of. And real or not, she never wanted to feel the fear and shame she'd felt today ever again.

Gwen turned to the side, hoping to catch Hazel's eye. They couldn't speak, but she'd try to encourage her any way she could.

The amber dragon towered above Hazel, its great maw widening as it looked down on her.

Not needing any more information, she steeled her voice with conviction. "I'll do whatever I have to do to make it to Saint Elias."

Before Gwen could even tap on the barrier, the garnet dragon, in tandem with the amber dragon, shot molten hot fire from its mouth. It enveloped her in a pain she'd never known. A scream ripped from her as she fell to her knees.

Then she became nothing.

CHAPTER 11

Hazel

Hazel's scream froze in her throat until it was singed away, along with every cell in her body. She could no longer see the fire or the dragon. Or anything. She had no sense of time or self. She was purely pain and consciousness adrift.

While the other tests had been terrifying and painful in their own ways, she'd been able to reason or magic her way out of the situation. Now there was no logic left, just the same chain of thoughts repeating over the soundtrack of agony in her mind—was this the future her mother had seen? Had her father and brother been right? Was this how she died?

Suspended in anguish for a moment or an eternity, she didn't know.

Suddenly, a new sensation occurred. Or rather, a lack thereof. The pain dulled. Hazel's bones solidified against a hard surface and her eyes flew open just in time to lift her hands and save herself from landing face-first on the ground. Hazel looked down to see she'd braced herself upon a grassy meadow.

Dragons!

She frantically scoured the meadow in front of her and the air above her, wincing against the bright light. She shielded her eyes before looking again. No dragons were to be found. She checked her clothes and her body for injury, but she was fine, completely intact.

Solid stone walls surrounded her. She was still inside the mountain, standing before a single line of trees with several pathways leading between them like spokes on a wheel. At the end of the central path was an unfamiliar building, tall and solemn. Its gray stone facade appeared smooth, probably worn down by age. The narrow arched windows aligned perfectly beneath the crouching gargoyles clinging to the edge of the steep roof, their hollow eyes fixed in silent observation. The structure's centerpiece drew her gaze—a glass dome rising from the heart of the third story. Its delicate ironwork was woven together like vines and curling branches.

A sound of rustling grass behind her sent Hazel scrambling forward. She turned to find Gwen directly at her back in a similar position.

"Gwen!" Hazel wrapped her arms around her friend. "You're okay!"

Gwen stiffened. "Thank Terra."

Hazel released her quickly, her happiness fading as questions crept in. *If Gwen had really been in the exam, what else had been real?*

Before Hazel could bring up her concern, a voice spoke from the path on the far right. "Peculiar."

The sound brushed against Hazel's eardrums as if it was said right against her ear. A shiver ran down her spine.

Gwen stood abruptly, goosebumps visible along her skin. Hazel's own skin pebbled too. A middle-aged woman with golden bronze skin stood within the tree line wearing a pencil skirt and high heels, her dark, wavy hair flowing over one shoulder. Hazel recognized her as one of the mages on the stage in the cavern.

"What's peculiar?" Gwen asked.

Hazel winced. Gwen's voice somehow sounded even closer, like it was in her ear. *Why was everything so loud?*

"That you both arrived at the same time," the woman informed them. As she spoke, her voice went from unbearably loud to tolerable, and finally normal. Perhaps her ears had needed time to adjust from the caverns.

The woman studied Hazel and then Gwen for a long moment. It took everything Hazel had not to fidget under her probing gaze. She'd done nothing wrong. It wasn't her fault the test had thrown her and Gwen together.

Surely we won't be disqualified.

The woman opened a scroll and left it to float in the air as she made two quick, long strokes with her short acorn and quartz wand, as if to scratch out their names.

Hazel spared a glance at Gwen, hoping for some support or even clarity about what had happened. *Did we pass? Did we fail?* Salem, this was scarier than the dragons. This was everything she'd fought for. She had to make it in.

The woman cleared her throat, jolting Hazel back to the present. "I'm the dean of admissions. You may refer to me as Sorcerer Maduro."

Hazel gulped—she had never met a sorcerer before. Becoming a sorcerer was the highest level of magic, and Hazel hoped to earn the title one day.

Sorcerer Maduro's gaze landed on Hazel, and she wrinkled her nose.

Hazel grimaced as she looked down at her clothes to see them stiff with sweat and covered in ash. This wasn't the first impression she'd hoped to make. A second glance at Gwen reassured her that at least she wasn't alone in her messy appearance.

"This is Miss Amelia Johnson. Please follow her."

Right on cue, a young woman stepped around Sorcerer Maduro to stand beside her. Amelia Johnson looked like she was in her twenties—an upperclassman, if Hazel could guess. She wore jeans and a white button-up shirt with a thick pearl-studded headband in her short brunette bob, which contrasted nicely with her fawn skin. She smiled at Hazel and Gwen encouragingly.

The dean didn't wait for any other acknowledgment before she turned abruptly and began to head back up the path on the right side of the clearing.

Is that all she's going to say?

"So does that mean we passed the exams?" Hazel called out after her.

Sorcerer Maduro turned around. With a twinkle in her eye, she replied, "It does indeed. Congratulations to you both, Miss Bishop and Miss Thorne."

Hazel's heart soared. She let out a tiny squeal, unable to suppress the flood of joy that overcame her. She slapped a hand over her mouth as Gwen let out a squeal of her own. The girls looked at one another before they burst into a round of laughter. Hazel did a happy dance, and, to her surprise, Gwen joined in.

"We made it!" they chorused together.

Another throat clearing sobered them up quickly. Sorcerer Maduro watched them with vague amusement in the half-smirk on her ruby-red lips. She pointed at Amelia, who was now walking back up the center path. "*Now*, if you will."

Hazel immediately straightened, nodding her understanding.

When they caught up, Amelia began rattling information off as if she'd been doing this tour all her life. She waved her hands like blades when she gestured, the way Hazel had seen flight attendants do in movies. "This is the administration building, and where most professors hold their office hours. You won't come here too often, just to pass through on your way to and from town. And for your advisor meetings." Amelia gestured to the rectangular structure Hazel had noted earlier. "The greenhouse on top is for professors' use only."

Hazel frowned. She loved spending time in the greenhouses on her family's farm. She hoped there was another on campus.

"Don't worry, there are two student greenhouses on campus. Located on the north and south oval," Amelia said as if reading her mind, and Hazel shivered as she thought of the dragon doing it. Amelia wasted no time before continuing. "The dog sled housing is inside the woods, right outside of town. You passed it on your way to the mine. The sleds stop around midnight. If you want to go to Eagles Ridge when they're not running, take the brooms. I'll warn you that those brooms tend to go missing and can't be relied on, which leaves you on foot. The walk is forty minutes unaided."

What would an aided walk entail? A performance-enhancing potion, perhaps? She imagined power-walking like the Olympians on TV and suppressed a laugh.

As Hazel climbed the six gray steps leading to the administration building, she realized they weren't actually entering the building, but passing underneath it, through an extended gateway. They made their way down the exit steps on the posterior side of the building.

Hazel's eyes widened as the campus unfolded before her. It was breathtaking. She stumbled into Gwen, too enchanted to watch where she was going. "Sorry," she said as her gaze continued to dart from one towering structure to the next.

They walked along the left curve of the massive oval lawn, its grass an impossibly lush green for being inside a mountain.

"These buildings will be where you go for classes. They are divided by area of study."

Every building shared the same deep-stone hue and Gothic architecture, but no two were the same. Some stretched skyward with multiple spires, while others crouched low and wide. Gargoyles clung to every ledge, and stained-glass windows shimmered with pictures of the past. The sight made her feel as if she'd traveled back in time. Then she realized the buildings weren't lining the cavern walls—they were *carved* into them. Her breath caught.

Amelia gestured to the enormous glass building in the center of the oval. "And here is one of the student greenhouses."

The bottom half was stone, while the upper half was glass that came to an ornate point at the top, running its entire length. The panes blazed with the dusky hues of the enchanted sky above, like the administration greenhouse did behind them. Hazel sucked in a breath at the impressive beauty. *I bet they have plants I've never seen before.* But to Hazel's dismay, Amelia walked right past the entrance.

"The ruzo field is over there on the left."

Hazel looked down the turnoff but all she could see was the entrance to the field and the stands floating above it. She couldn't wait to go to a game.

I can't believe this is my new home. She'd dreamed of this place for nearly four years, yet it still surpassed all of her wildest expectations. Pride washed over her; all the hard work and every sacrifice had been worth it. Her father wouldn't agree. But her mother had walked these same steps. If Hazel was right, and she really possessed Sight, her mother was somewhere nearby.

It took everything she had not to run to the library and look for her mother right then.

Amelia stopped abruptly, causing Hazel to crash into Gwen and bring her thoughts back to the tour. They were standing in front of a squared-off section of grass between the two ovals with several towering oaks creating pockets of shade on the ground from the setting sun.

"This is the quad. It's always packed on sunny days. As I'm sure you've noticed, the ceiling is enchanted to look like a sky. The elementalists on campus could make every day sunny, but they choose to force us to go through the seasons."

The quad was empty. There definitely weren't any leisure activities taking place this evening.

"Where is everyone?" Gwen asked.

"Most are getting settled into their dorms. Also, upperclassmen that aren't helping with the summons won't arrive until tomorrow. It will be much busier then."

Gwen nodded, and Hazel realized she likely knew because of her cousin. How nice it must be for her to ask questions to someone who knew firsthand.

"The north oval is identical to the south," Amelia continued.

"There's more?" Hazel asked in amazement.

Amelia simply grinned and led the way down the cobblestone path. In the north oval, the buildings were as grand, Gothic, and gray as those on the south oval.

"As you can see, in the center of the oval is the second student greenhouse. Both are open to students for coursework only."

Hazel nodded eagerly, committing the information to memory but wishing she had a notebook to write the information down.

Amelia pointed as she spun slowly in a circle, naming buildings as she went. "The dining hall, freshman and sophomore dorms, the library, and the arcane college."

The dorms were impressive in size and design, but the true star of the north oval was the library. While most of the buildings had stained-glass windows, none were as intricate as these. It would take Hazel hours to truly note them all. The sight of it set butterflies loose in her stomach, but they had nothing to do with the beauty and everything to do with her dreams—her visions.

"A word of caution while on campus: SEU is haunted, and while the spirits are generally harmless, they do get restless and bored."

The words made Hazel smile, but it quickly faded as she took in Amelia's very serious expression. Elkmont had had rumors of ghosts, but she'd never actually seen one. Ghosts were real, but sightings were rare. Something in Amelia's eyes told Hazel the girl wasn't exaggerating.

Gwen's stomach grumbled, and she asked, "What time is it?"

Amelia turned, as if searching for something. She pointed to the clock tower on the other side of the library that read eight o'clock. They'd been in the test for almost twelve hours? How was that possible? Hazel's stomach churned. They'd come so close to missing the deadline. Her cheeks flamed with the embarrassment that she'd been the last. She could almost hear her father telling her she'd gotten lucky, that she had no business being here. Maybe he was right, but she'd made it, nonetheless.

Amelia pointed to the houses that sat behind the dorms, oblivious to Hazel's inner turmoil. "That's Coven Row, and the faculty housing is in the opposite corner, behind the dining hall."

Hazel rushed to take in the sights as Amelia sped up her rehearsed speech and her steps.

"As you were the last two to pass the exam, you'll room together. You'll have a double room that's attached to a suite. Your stuff should already be there," Amelia said, coming to a stop at the end of the oval. "Well, here we are. This is the dining hall. I know you must be starving."

As if on cue, Gwen's stomach rumbled again. Hazel laughed at the timing. She was hungry too.

"Here are your orientation pamphlets. You'll need to be on the ruzo field by eight a.m. to sign up for classes tomorrow." Amelia pulled out two folded pages from her clipboard and offered them.

Hazel took hers quickly. She didn't miss the smirk on Gwen's face as she did so.

So I'm a nerd for pamphlets. Sue me.

"Questions?" Amelia asked.

At least half a dozen came to Hazel's mind, but she could tell by Amelia's tight smile and glassy eyes that she was ready to be done with this task. Hazel said nothing as she shook her head. Gwen didn't ask anything, either.

"Great! I'm off. Welcome to SEU!" Amelia said, and then left.

Amelia was less than ten feet away when Gwen broke the silence. "I'm starving."

"Me too," Hazel said. "I really think it was a crime to ask us to remember all of that on an empty stomach."

"No kidding!" Gwen agreed.

The girls walked into the dining hall to find it a quarter full, but the students were the least interesting thing in the room. Candle chandeliers hung from the high vaulted ceilings. The walls were lined with oak, etched with elaborate carvings of magical ingredients, which reminded Hazel of the log cabin walls she'd grown up within, though they truly had nothing in common but a sense of warmth and welcome. The odd familiarity comforted her.

Hazel and Gwen headed straight to the white marble counter. Hazel picked up a tray, white with a floral border hand-painted in blue. In the center, a hydra was being attacked by a knight with a long sword. It was a shame she had to cover it up with the plain white plate. At least they had pretty scalloped edges. The gold silverware had a manticore, the school's mascot, etched on the handle.

They each grabbed enough food to feed a small army. Gwen piled several slices of deep dish pizza onto her plate and bypassed the rest. Hazel scooped salad, chicken, and green beans on her plate, then she heaped a mountain of bread on top. Life was about balance.

"Better late than never, I guess. Huh, Hazel?"

A chill ran down Hazel's spine. She'd know his Scottish lilt anywhere. He was so close she could feel the warmth of his breath against her cheek and the tickle of his black wavy hair against her ear. There was only one person in the world who enjoyed getting a rise out of her—her constant tormentor throughout high school. She'd never dreamed he would have the integrity to make it through the test. As a matter of fact, Hazel had hoped the mountain would eat him up.

"Get hexed, Dane."

Hazel heard Gwen cough, but it sounded suspiciously like it was covering a laugh.

"Always a disappointment, Hateful," Dane said, using the nickname she despised. "What took you so long, anyway?"

Irritated by his words, both the moniker and the implication that he'd beat her, Hazel whirled on him. He stepped back quickly, his deep-green eyes widening on his alabaster face ever so slightly. She'd surprised him. His provocation didn't typically elicit such a fast reaction from her, but she was exhausted. While this was easily the happiest day of her life, it had somehow also held some of the very worst things she'd ever experienced. Hazel was feeling a lot of emotions right now and if Dane Bellamy wanted to offer himself up as a target, by Terra, she'd let him.

"As if I'd ever tell you," Hazel bit out before walking off. Maybe it was her overactive imagination, but she would've sworn she felt him stare a hole into her retreating back. She refused to look back at him, and a full minute passed before the burn of his gaze went away.

Booths lined the walls beneath the decorative carvings, while long tables filled the middle of the dining hall. Hazel grabbed the first booth available, under a window by the door. As soon as her butt touched the cushioned bench, her body melted into it, relaxing for the first time since she'd woken that morning.

"What an ass. Too bad his attitude doesn't match his smokin' good looks," Gwen said as she plopped down across from Hazel.

Hazel made a retching sound. "Please, I'm trying to eat."

Gwen smirked, then yawned. Hazel yawned too.

"I didn't realize how tired I was until I sat down," Hazel said. The only thing keeping her eyes open was the delicious-smelling food in front of her. And the dessert she planned to get when she finished it.

"I'm exhausted. I can't believe we were down there for so long," Gwen replied.

"Me either. I wonder if Jordan and Rafe made it?" Hazel asked.

They both glanced around the cafeteria, but it was nearly empty. Neither of them were here. Hazel hoped they were already in the dorms, getting settled like Amelia had said. She wondered what their exams had been like, then chewed on her lip as she contemplated her own.

"What?" Gwen asked.

Hazel looked around them to make sure no one was listening. The closest students sat several booths away. "I can't help but wonder why we were so much later and why the mountain put us—"

Gwen threw up her hand, stopping Hazel mid-sentence, then she lifted her wand. "*Silentia*."

Of course. They couldn't afford for people to know the truth or to question the validity of their exam.

I should've known better.

Hazel was exhausted and obviously not thinking straight.

"Keep going," Gwen instructed.

"Why did the mountain put us through a shared test? Why were we allowed to see each other at the end?"

Gwen took a big bite of her pepperoni pizza, pinching off the stringy cheese as she chewed.

"Maybe it was the test itself? Maybe we needed to feel it was more real, like more was on the line?" Hazel proposed.

"What do you mean?"

"I mean, I guessed immediately that my other tests were an illusion or whatever you want to call them—although there were a few times in my second test I found myself forgetting," Hazel explained. "Did you think your tests were an illusion?"

Gwen nodded, her mouth full.

Hazel continued, "When did you realize?"

She seems so unbothered by this. Am I overreacting?

Gwen swallowed. "Not until after my second test. I watched my test evaporate when I had passed it. I knew it had to be a play on my fears. But I don't get what that has to do with letting us see one another."

"This reminds me of something I learned in school last year. I took a psychology class my senior year through concurrent enrollment at a local mundane college to get a head start on my gen eds in case I didn't get into SEU."

Gwen looked at Hazel like she had a bug on her face.

"What is it?" Hazel asked, alarmed.

"Wow, you *are* a big nerd, aren't you?"

Hazel's cheeks warmed as she ignored the question. If Gwen truly understood how desperate Hazel had been to have any reason to stay busy back home, she wouldn't be asking that question.

"One lesson discussed how psychological tests can be invalidated, or results can be biased, if the subjects know *why* they're being tested, or sometimes even simply *if* they know they're being tested. It's called the Hawthorne Effect," Hazel continued with her line of thought.

Gwen's brows raised. "Connect the dots, please."

"Maybe because the mountain knew we had figured out the entrance exam, it had to find more authentic means to test us. Maybe mental illusions weren't enough, so it added a real person to the equation."

Gwen nodded, snapping her fingers. "I saw you at the edge. Were you going to jump?"

Hazel felt the blood drain from her face, a mixture of embarrassment and fear. She'd come so close to dying today. She would've, if it hadn't been for the dragon keeping her from jumping to her death.

"At that point, I didn't think it was real. I thought fear of death was my last test. That I had to face it and then I'd be let into Saint Elias."

"What made you stop?" Gwen asked.

Hazel shuddered with the memory. "The dragon stopped me. He told me 'Today is not that day.' I didn't register what that even meant. I didn't think it was real until the walls started crumbling and he became..." she paused, "nervous, I think?"

"How did that convince you I was real?"

"I don't mean just you. I mean all of it. Everything. The cavern, the magma," Hazel said, hesitating before adding, "The dragons."

I can't believe I admitted that out loud. I sound insane.

Gwen looked at Hazel, wide-eyed at this omission, before throwing her head back and laughing. "You had me there for a second."

"I'm not joking," Hazel insisted softly. Maybe she shouldn't have said anything.

"I'm telling you, the only thing in that exam that was real was us," Gwen insisted so strongly her words almost sounded like she was trying to convince herself.

Hazel paused, still not sure.

"I know you *think* it was real, but there is absolutely *no way* this mountain has dragons living in its belly that interfere in the entrance exams of freshmen and then let them *go*."

Hazel gave a small smile. *Okay, she has a point.* "That would be pretty wild," Hazel said.

"Exactly. I think that's a little far-fetched, even for Saint Elias," Gwen said.

Hazel gave a halfhearted laugh. She couldn't shake what her gut was telling her, what her senses had told her in that cavern. It was real. Somehow, they'd seen dragons.

"Yeah, you're probably right."

Hazel's appetite was gone. The unanswered question of why they'd been allowed to see each other left her feeling too uneasy to eat. They were missing something.

The girls trudged up the front steps and through the large wooden door of the dormitory. A common area of dark wood and deep-green walls greeted them. A brass chandelier with small crystal adornments hung overhead, casting spectacular shadows upon the floor.

A large fire crackled in the hearth. As they walked closer, Hazel noted there was no heat coming from the fire. Aesthetic lighting, she guessed. Floor-to-ceiling bookshelves lined the walls on either side of it. She could see herself curling up in one of the many wingback chairs for an evening of studying. She loved this place already.

The girls collected their room keys from Serena, the RA they'd met at Fjordhaven. Had it only been a day since then? Hazel felt like so much time had passed.

"Welcome to Poe Hall. Feel free to make your rooms your own as long as it's a temporary spell, otherwise you'll be charged for damages at the end of the year," Serena said as she handed them a list of housing rules and regulations.

The girls' dorm room was on the second floor. They followed the stairs up, took a left, and made their way down the long hall to room 215.

"Home sweet home," Hazel said, opening the door.

It was a tiny space, and every single surface in the living area was white. The room was screaming for her to add color. But Hazel didn't care for now. It was hers. It was freedom.

"Reminds me of an asylum," Gwen said with a grimace.

"Don't say that. That's creepy. I need to sleep at night, not worry if they're coming to put straitjackets on us," Hazel whined.

"We'll make it our own tomorrow. Tonight, they can put me in a straitjacket. I'm too tired to care."

They had a small shared living space with a kitchenette in the back. A short hall contained three doors. Gwen found her luggage in the room on the left and went to unpack.

Hazel opened the door to the right to find her suitcase at the edge of a twin bed. The room was just as sterile as the rest of the dorm, and so cramped the desk barely fit next to the bed.

She pulled out her sheets, along with a maroon quilt her grandmother had handcrafted. Or so Hazel's mother had said. She'd never met her grandmother. The quilt was the only piece of evidence she had of her. Every time she looked at it, she wondered about the woman who'd so painstakingly stitched the Nordic rune-type symbols.

Hazel unpacked the few picture frames she had, tucking away the one of her whole family into the bottom of the chest of drawers. The rest she placed on top.

"Hazel, come here," Gwen called from the other room.

Hazel followed Gwen's voice to the bathroom. A shower, toilet, and two sinks filled the tiny space, leaving barely enough room for Gwen to lay on the floor and peek under the connecting door.

"Note to self, put a towel under my door while living with Gwen," Hazel joked.

"Spoilsport," Gwen said. Laughing, she hopped back up and

grabbed her toothbrush off the sink. "Must be suitemates," Gwen guessed.

"Oof. One shower for four girls isn't going to be fun for anyone."

"I hope they're cool. Nothing worse than getting stuck with a pair of witches."

As if on cue, the door opened. Hazel and Gwen froze.

A short young woman with ebony-brown skin and beautiful black twists stuck her head into the bathroom. Hazel recognized her instantly from Eagles Ridge.

"Hi. We could hear you, so we thought we might as well make it awkward for all of us."

Hazel laughed because it *was* awkward. She was glad someone else had said it.

The mage's eyes grew wide as she studied Hazel. "Hey, we've met! Outside Kodiak Brew."

Hazel nodded. "Nova?"

The door swung all the way open to reveal Nova's friend Elodie, the young woman with short, brown curly hair and beige skin with a smattering of freckles and cute teal glasses.

"Hazel, right?"

She grinned, pleased they'd remembered her. Reintroductions were the worst. "Yes. And this is my roommate, Gwen."

Gwen waved with one hand and popped her toothbrush in her mouth.

"I'm Nova. This is Elodie."

Elodie smiled. "We're both nice, we swear."

"We are too. Well, I am." Hazel elbowed Gwen.

"Hey!" Gwen protested with a mouth full of toothpaste, smacking Hazel in the arm.

Hazel smiled in response. "I'm kidding. Gwen's great."

"You went to Bathurst didn't you, Gwen? I think we took spell-casting together," Elodie said.

"Yeah, I think so," Gwen said, offering no more.

The room grew quiet. Hazel felt uncomfortable.

"Well, we were fixing to call it a night. The entrance exams took their toll on us," Hazel said, unable to stand the silence any longer.

Elodie nodded. "Us too. We're beat.".

"Good night." Nova punctuated her words with a yawn.

"Good night," Hazel echoed.

Nova and Elodie closed the door, and Hazel left Gwen to finish her nighttime routine.

"They seemed nice," Hazel whispered when Gwen came out of the bathroom.

"Yeah, they did," Gwen agreed. She stretched and released a big yawn. "Good night, Hazel."

"Good night," Hazel replied before they split up into their respective rooms.

As Hazel closed the door to her room, reality set in. She'd earned what she'd fought tooth and nail for. What she'd sacrificed her relationship with her father for. She was on her own, charging a new path for herself with no one to answer to and nothing standing in her way of finding her mother and practicing magic. It was thrilling yet terrifying.

She couldn't wait.

CHAPTER 12

Hazel

The ruzo field was a madhouse as students rushed to sign up for their classes the next morning; the most coveted courses only had a few slots. Hazel had just finished putting down her and Gwen's names on the sign-up sheet for Demi-Human Diplomacy and Politics. She was currently standing off to the side, trying to make herself small as she waited for Gwen, who was signing them up for Glyph Decryption. It didn't stop several students from brushing up against her in the crowd.

A girl ran straight towards Hazel, holding her nose. Blood dripped onto her white shirt and Hazel ducked out of the way, not wanting to get any on her own clothing. Moments later, Gwen strolled up casually to Hazel with a wide grin on her face.

"You?" Hazel asked, pointing toward the bleeding girl.

Gwen smirked. "All you need to know is you're now signed up for Glyph Decryption."

It was the last class they needed, after successfully snagging spots in Demi-Human Diplomacy and Politics, Alchemy 101, Study of the Arcane for Hazel, and Spell-writing 101 for Gwen.

Hazel had forced Gwen to make a game plan for orientation at breakfast. Picking the right classes mattered, even if Gwen pretended otherwise. They'd agreed to divide and conquer, maximizing their chances of getting their top choices. Hazel had expected Gwen to go along with it begrudgingly, but to her surprise, once the scramble started, she actually seemed to enjoy the challenge.

"We should head over to the coven tents next," Hazel said.

"Why? I wanted to go get lunch," Gwen whined. "Besides, they don't even select freshmen."

"It's not even eleven," Hazel said as she shook her head.

Right on cue, a champagne-pink and light-tan striped food cart rolled by, its wheels gliding smoothly over the grass without leaving a trace. The sign above it read *Viola's Coffee and Toffee*, and the air filled with the comforting fragrance of warm spices and sugar. When it came to a stop, Gwen pulled Hazel with her up to the counter.

The vendor, a small woman with gray hair, flicked her wand, sending silver trays of floating toffee, pastries, and steaming mugs into the air in front of her. A menu appeared next to the cart, listing teas Hazel didn't recognize—lavender lumen, and dreamleaf chai, alongside coffees like midnight roast and spellshot macchiato. When her gaze reached the bottom of the list, her lips curved into a smile.

"Ooh, they have the cloudberry cold brew," Hazel said, brightening. "It's seriously the best thing I've ever tasted."

"That one is good!" Gwen nodded, not taking her eyes off the pastries.

Gwen's hand hovered over the raspberry muffins indecisively, and the stripes on the cart shifted colors—turning a soft pale red. When her hand moved toward the custard buns, they changed again, this time to a rich golden hue. They pulsed purple when she paused over a plum donut, then finally settled into a dark royal blue the moment she selected the berry tart—a flaky round pastry filled with blueberries and a cream cheese center.

“I’ll take two, and two cloudberry cold brews,” Gwen said.

Hazel opened her mouth to protest, but her stomach betrayed her with a well-timed grumble.

Gwen smiled—either at the sound or the look on Hazel’s face—and handed a few coins to the vendor without a word. Hazel accepted her coffee and tart with a quiet, “Thanks.”

“Alright, let’s check out the covens,” Gwen said before popping a piece of her tart into her mouth.

They passed several colorful booths that different university clubs had set up to gain new members. The Alchemy Club’s booth featured rows of bubbling vials. Enchanted quills floated in midair, scrawling incantations onto parchment before rolling themselves up into scrolls at the Spell-Writing Club’s booth.

The broom-racing team had designed a miniature track where several students lined up to ride brooms through the air in a loop. The Wand-Fishing Club drew an even larger crowd. Students stood around a deep basin filled with water that rippled unnaturally as they cast magical lines into its depths. Gwen snorted as she watched a student yelp in surprise, struggling to reel in a fish that seemed determined to pull them into the basin.

“I can’t believe people actually take this seriously,” Gwen murmured.

Hazel blushed and took a sip of her cold brew.

Gwen’s eyes widened. “Not you too!”

“Wand-fishing wasn’t that bad,” she said. Hazel honestly meant it, and sometimes it was even fun. There was something oddly soothing about casting a line and waiting for the familiar tug of something beneath the surface.

Hazel slowed her steps as they approached the Wilderness Watch table. Unlike the others, this one had no glowing enchantments, no interactive displays, and, most noticeably, no eager students clamoring to sign up. A gruff-looking man with a faded brown bomber jacket sat behind the table. Despite the early hour, a five o’clock shadow darkened his sepia-brown face. His straight dark brown hair was shiny, but unstyled as if he couldn't be bothered.

Hazel hesitated, feeling a pang of sympathy. He looked so bored. "Come on," she urged, nudging Gwen's arm.

"Why?" Gwen asked.

"Because it's empty, and that's sad."

Hazel dragged Gwen forward, ignoring her groan.

The man barely glanced up as they approached, only acknowledging them when Hazel cleared her throat.

"So, what does this club do?" she asked.

The man shut his book with a soft thump and leaned forward, steepling his fingers. His lips curled into something that might have been a smile—if it weren't for the sharpness in his eyes.

"SEU feeds you precious babies with the funds provided by tourism, aka the mundanes who visit Eagles Ridge and stay at the lodge," he said. His voice matched his appearance—rough and edged with gravel, a tone that made it seem like he'd seen too much and cared too little. "We get to graciously accept that money with the promise that we'll help protect and locate mundanes in order to keep our little magical community here a secret. After all, we can't have mundanes going missing and then their families turning up looking for them with a news crew, now can we?"

Hazel blinked. Well, that was an answer. She forced a tight smile. "Thanks for the information." She grabbed a pamphlet from the edge of the table, not bothering to read it, and took a step back. "We'll think about it," she added hastily, before turning on her heel and scurrying off, Gwen right beside her.

Gwen tossed her empty cup into a nearby bin, and Hazel followed, downing the last of hers before doing the same. Then, without a second glance, Gwen plucked the pamphlet from Hazel's hands and tossed it in after. "There's no way we're looking for mundanes dumb enough to get lost in Alaska."

Hazel laughed in agreement; she definitely wouldn't be joining that club. But as they neared the end of the booths, a steady thrum of nerves replaced her amusement. Her heart pounded as the four coven tents came into view.

Getting into a coven was everything. It was the only way to stay at Saint Elias for all four years, the only path to the future she wanted. Without a coven, she'd have to graduate with a two-year degree and join a workers' guild to learn any additional magic.

Today wasn't just about looking—this was their first chance to make an impression, to prove they belonged. And Gwen's actions would reflect on her, whether or not she liked it.

As they made their way to the end of the booths, Hazel studied the four tents in front of them. Each was a different color, with the coven's sigil flag flying high on top. The first tent's canvas was made of white silk. Its sigil was the silhouette of a green kelpie on a white backdrop that matched the canvas. The way the silk reflected in the faux sunlight reminded Hazel of an opal. Its shimmer contrasted with the heavily tattooed coven members lingering outside in long white cloaks—which set them apart from the other students in plain clothing.

A spark of anticipation flickered in Hazel's chest. This was her chance. *Their* chance. She had to make sure they didn't mess it up.

Hazel and Gwen joined the small group of people congregating in the front of the tent. One of the white-cloaked members silently handed Hazel a pamphlet before retreating to rejoin their friends.

Incantor, Hazel read on the top of the pamphlet.

A coven member cleared their throat to draw everyone's attention. "Welcome to the Incantor coven's exhibit. As you can see from the pamphlet, our coven honors the imbuing practices of the fae. Although the fae have been extinct since the Great War, our exhibit today reflects one of their most common practices that has survived the past millennium—magically embedded tattoos. We hope you enjoy your experience today. If you have questions, please seek out a member. We'll be the ones with the white cloaks and neck tattoos."

The joke earned a few laughs as two Incantor members pulled back the tent flaps.

Hazel elbowed Gwen. "Did you know the covens were made in memoriam?"

"Yeah, but only because of my cousin," Gwen whispered.

"But why?" Hazel asked. It didn't make sense; the Forsaken were long dead and thought of as the mages' mortal enemies. They'd been vanquished for a reason—betrayal of the mages during the Great War. What was the point of honoring them?

"So that their practices never die and to strengthen mage knowledge," Gwen said with a shrug, as if she was guessing.

"And people are good with it? Even the Brecilian Knights?" Hazel asked.

Before Gwen could answer, the Incantor member holding the flap back snickered. "The mountain is outside the Brecilian Knights' domain. They couldn't stop it even if they wanted to."

Hazel's eyes grew large as she looked at Gwen. Gwen nodded in confirmation. The realization sent a ripple of unease through her—so much of mage society bent to the Knights' will, but here, in Saint Elias, apparently their reach stopped at the mountain's edge. She barely had time to process that before stepping forward—only to freeze.

Sitting in the tattoo chair at the center of the tent, looking as smug as ever, was Dane Bellamy.

"Not this tent." Hazel grabbed Gwen's arm and spun them both around before Gwen could step inside.

"What? Why?" Gwen tried to peek past her, but Hazel pulled her out of the tent.

"Just trust me."

The next tent was a beautiful, deep royal purple, its velvet fabric shimmering with an almost ethereal sheen under the sun. Silver and white stars were embroidered across its surface, twinkling faintly as if capturing a real night sky. Constellations were woven in intricate patterns along the edges. As Hazel stared at the star pattern of Aries, it shifted into the familiar shape of Leo.

Above them, the coven's flag billowed gently, bearing the sigil of a Hydra. The three-headed serpent, embroidered in silver thread, gleamed ominously against the dark fabric, its eyes seeming to follow them as they approached.

"Wow, this tent is gorgeous," Gwen said.

"Agreed. But let's not judge a book by its cover," Hazel murmured, still sour about the near miss with Dane at Incantor. She hoped to avoid him as much as possible.

As they entered through the pulled-back flaps of the Sybil tent, the scent of aged parchment and incense wafted towards them. Unlike the structured elegance of Incantor's exhibit, Sybil's space felt much more intimate. Layers of eclectic fabric draped from the ceiling in soft waves, casting shifting patterns of pinks, purples, and whites as candlelight flickered against them.

A much more enthusiastic coven member than in Incantor passed them a purple pamphlet. "Hi, I'm Jiana," she said as she tugged at the sleeve of her purple cloak. "Welcome to the Sibyl exhibit—"

"What Forsaken does Sybil honor?" Hazel blurted.

Jiana looked at her with wide eyes. "I was getting there. We honor elven magical practices, most often referred to as the arcane—which is why our selection process is so stringent."

Hazel shared an impressed look with Gwen.

"The only other coven on campus with as tough a selection is Alterion."

"You're getting off topic again," a guy in a purple cloak called through the tent. "We aren't Alterion." He sounded like he'd been reminding her of this all morning.

"Right, sorry," Jiana shouted back, blushing. She turned back to the girls with an apologetic smile. "Where was I?" She glanced at her notes. "Oh, right." The poor girl was nervous—her hands fidgeted at the hem of her sleeve again, twisting the purple fabric between her fingers. Her gaze darted between the coven members watching her, never settling for too long, and when she finally spoke again, her voice was thin, like she was afraid of saying the wrong thing. "While Sybil coven is based mostly in arcane magicks, we do sometimes accept mages with different aptitudes—but it's rare. The arcane is a hard discipline, rooted in the unseen and intangible. It revolves around four core pillars: shadowsong, telekinesis, astral projection, and foresight. If either of you has a knack for any of those, you should definitely check us out when you're eligible to join."

At the mention of astral projection, a jolt shot through Hazel. Had her mother been part of this coven during her time at SEU? Her mind raced with the possibilities, and the answers Sybil might hold. Without hesitation, she moved it to the top of her list. She glanced at Gwen, hoping she felt the same. If they were going to join a coven, Hazel wanted it to be together.

Jiana led them further into the tent. Delicate strands of beads hung from the tent's supports, chiming softly as Hazel and Gwen passed beneath them. They stopped in front of three round antique tables that stood in the middle of the space on a richly woven rug. Embroidered silk cloths and decks of cards partially obscured the dark wood surfaces.

"We've arranged a tarot reading opportunity for those of you talented enough to pull and brave enough to know." Jiana looked at them hopefully.

Tarot was one of the hardest of the arcane magics. It required a natural aptitude, and Hazel didn't know anyone who'd successfully done it.

She sat down at the table on the left. A small sigh escaped her as she sunk into the soft cushion. An elegant, loopy script adorned a small sign at the table.

Learn what your past, present, and future hold.

"Yeah, I'll pass," Gwen snarked.

Hazel studied her. "You don't believe in tarot?"

"Most of this arcane stuff is impossible. I've never seen anyone actually read tarot. Have you?" Gwen asked from the other side of the table.

Hazel opened her mouth but was interrupted by a Sybil member walking by.

"Just because *you* don't possess the talent doesn't mean it doesn't exist," the young man said.

"Okay, whatever. Let's draw for each other," Gwen said.

Hazel peered down at the cards. The deck was beautiful, expensive-looking and old. Gold-foiled ravens shone in the candlelight flickering above the table, the writing around the edges faint, barely visible. The sight of the ravens sent a ripple of unease through her. They reminded her too much of the ones from her dreams—circling, watching. For a second, she felt the weight of that connection pressing in on her. She forced the thought aside and focused on the cards in front of her.

"How do I make sure I'm reading for you and not me?" Hazel asked.

Jiana called from across the room, "Have your friend shuffle and then cut the deck, then make sure your internal intent is for her when you pull the card."

Grateful for the instruction, Hazel placed the deck closer to Gwen. She watched as Gwen slid the cards left and right, their worn edges gliding smoothly against one another before stacking them back together. Gwen cut the deck about a third of the way down and tucked the section beneath the pile. Hazel accepted it back, feeling the weight of the cards in her hands. She carefully spread them out in a straight, fanned line across the table.

"What do you want to know?" Hazel asked.

"There's only one way to tell if it's real. Start with my present," Gwen told her.

Hazel ran her finger along the gold-foiled card edges before pulling one from the middle and flipping it over to reveal the image. Two cups poured into one another, each with a snake coiled around its handle, their tails intertwined. A manticore loomed at the top of the card, its piercing gaze watching over the design, while intricate filigree framed the edges. The Two of Cups.

It's beautiful.

Hazel had never seen artwork like this before. There was something about it—something significant.

"Well, it got the manticore right. I'm at Saint Elias, but I haven't intertwined with anyone since I've been here," Gwen said.

"What about Harland?" Hazel chuckled.

Gwen blinked. "Who?"

"The guy from the bar," Hazel reminded her. Gwen was playing dumb. She'd told Hazel the juicy details from their conversation last night.

"Oh, is that his name?" Gwen smirked, tossing the card back onto the table. "If you think that's intertwining, we have very different ideas on the term." She winked.

Hazel blushed. She had no thoughts on intertwining.

"That's not what that card means," the man from before said. He wandered back to their table as he studied Hazel. "You may have the gift, but you should think about training for interpretation."

"By all means, tell us then," Gwen said, gesturing dramatically at the table with a sweeping motion.

He looked at the card closely, the light overhead bouncing off the skin of his receding hairline. "The Two of Cups represents partnership and compatibility. Despite common misconceptions, that can apply to platonic or professional relationships as well as romantic."

"Okay, my turn," Gwen said. She was clearly ignoring the coven member. Hazel shuffled the deck carefully, and cut it in two before handing it back to Gwen. "I'm going to do your present too," Gwen said, her tone hopeful as she plucked a card from the middle of the spread. She glanced at it—and her face fell. With a frustrated huff, Gwen laid the card face-up on the table to show Hazel.

The card was completely blank.

"Great," Gwen muttered.

"I'm not surprised. You don't have the gift," the balding coven member said dismissively, barely sparing Gwen a glance. "Try again."

Gwen grabbed another card, flipped it over, and scowled. Another blank. Gwen shot the mage a look.

The mage rolled his eyes. "Not you—your friend." He turned to Hazel, his gaze expectant. "Draw a card, but this time, set the intent for yourself."

Hazel stiffened. She hadn't expected to be pulled into this, but the way he said it made her feel like she had no choice. Slowly, she reached for the deck and drew another card. When she laid it down, the artwork was identical to the card she'd drawn for Gwen.

"Hmm. Seems you can only pull that one card. Maybe you don't have the gift after all." The young man shrugged before walking off.

Hazel barely registered his departure. She stared down at the card, her brows drawn in concentration. Something about it unsettled her, though she couldn't say why. It felt like there was something she was missing—something she *should* be seeing.

She didn't look up, even when Gwen shifted beside her. After a few moments of silence, Gwen waved a hand over the card. "Hellooooo."

Hazel blinked, shaking her head as if clearing away cobwebs. "Sorry, zoned out for a second."

"Want to draw for our futures now?" Gwen asked.

Hazel shook her head immediately. "No. Sorry."

Gwen frowned. "Why not?"

Hazel hesitated, glancing down at the card once more before flipping it face down. "That kind of creeped me out."

Gwen

As they stepped out of the Sybil tent, Gwen immediately noticed the shift in Hazel's mood. The tension that had settled over her during the reading seemed to lift as they made their way toward the next coven tent—if you could even call it that. It was more of a hut. A thick layer of moss and tiny wildflowers covered the surface. The structure looked as if it had been there for centuries rather than set up today for orientation.

Gwen couldn't help herself. As they approached, she reached out and touched it. The moment her skin made contact, a sharp tingle shot up her arm. She jerked her hand back. "What the hell?"

"What?" Hazel's eyes widened in confusion.

"Nothing, it's..." She hesitated, searching for the right words. "It feels alive."

Hazel reached out as if to touch it, too, but before she could, a coven member approached, and she pulled her hand back.

The man had umber skin, short black curls, and sharp brown eyes that flicked between them before he handed each of them a pamphlet. "We're Circen, and we excel in alchemy and potion-making, also known as the mage specialties," he said as he shoved his hands into the pockets of his deep-green cloak.

As they approached the entrance, a familiar pair emerged. Gwen's eyes settled on Rafe and Jordan, who smiled widely. His green eyes practically glittered as they met hers. She was happy to see neither of them looked hurt after their exams.

"Salem, burn me! I can't believe you got in. We waited up in the dorm commons until dark. We thought for sure you both bombed the exam," Jordan crowed.

"We looked for you all day and couldn't find you," she lied. She didn't want to admit they'd finished dead last. Or that the twelve-hour test had exhausted her so much she could only wonder about him. "We thought for sure the mountain ate you up and shit you out."

Hazel and Rafe both laughed. Jordan rolled his eyes as he wrapped an arm around Gwen's shoulders.

"I'm glad to see you both made it," Rafe said as he looked at Hazel.

"You too," Hazel replied.

"This tent is boring," Jordan said. "They only have mage elixirs inside and they're tame compared to the shit Hazel dosed us with the other night."

"I didn't mean to!" Hazel protested.

"Everyone watch out!" Jordan yelled. "This one is a wild one!"

Hazel's cheeks turned bright pink.

Jordan wrapped his free arm around her as he laughed. "Come on, let's go see what Alterion's got to offer."

Gwen nodded excitedly. She was ready to see Klaus and finally get a close-up look at the coven that honored therians.

Jordan steered the girls to the last tent as Rafe followed.

The Alterion tent was made of black leather, its surface worn and weathered. Through the flaps, Gwen glimpsed the interior—thick brown fur lined the walls, its coarse texture uneven in places. She wrinkled her nose but didn't let herself dwell on it.

At least they used all of the kill.

Before they could enter, a coven member with sun-bleached hair and sun-kissed beige skin stepped forward, arms crossed, blocking their path. He wore a black cloak, though it wasn't closed. Without a word, he handed them a pamphlet, his expression unreadable. "Two at a time," the mage said.

Jordan released the girls and smacked Rafe on the shoulder. "See you on the other side, ladies!"

As the guys stepped inside, Gwen glanced down at the pamphlet in her hands, her eyes scanning the bold lettering. *Alterion*—the coven designed in memoriam of the therians, which was almost laughable to Gwen. Therians were still alive and well, but, like mages hid from mundanes, therians hid from mages, who were stupid and prideful enough to believe they'd wiped therians from the earth.

Her pulse quickened. Maybe they'd have answers—real ones. It was one of the few places Klaus had yet to scour, since the covens didn't let freshmen and sophomores wander through their houses. This was her first glimpse of what Saint Elias University offered her in the way of finding out who and what she was.

She swallowed back the excitement threatening to creep onto her face and looked up. The Alterion member stood before them, staring above their heads as if they didn't exist. As they waited for their turn to enter, Gwen's thoughts were interrupted by a noise she knew all too well—the unmistakable crack of fists connecting with flesh and bone. Growing up with boy cousins had given her a unique insight into that particular sound.

"What's going on in there?" Hazel asked, standing on her tiptoes to see over the coven member.

I hope Rafe and Jordan are okay.

A few moments later, another Alterion student wearing a black cloak with the hood up to cover their face poked their head out and whispered something into the guard's ear. The hooded mage vanished back into the tent and the guard waved Gwen and Hazel inside.

The tent was empty of people except for the Alterion student who'd stuck their head out earlier. A fireplace sat at the far end of the space with a portrait above it and two bookcases on either side.

The hooded student spoke in a deep, ominous tone. "Password?"

Gwen and Hazel looked at each other, eyes wide. Had someone given them a password? Gwen was sure they hadn't.

"Can you give us a hint?" Hazel asked sweetly.

The Alterion member gave no response.

"Rafe and Jordan made it through. There must be a clue somewhere in here," Hazel said.

The girls spread out, taking in the room. Gwen kept her gaze moving, careful not to linger too long on the portrait above the fireplace. She'd recognized him instantly. The man in the painting was a therian—one of the many faces erased from history that her father had drilled into her memory. It startled her to see him here. Whoever hung that image had to know he was a therian. It was far too deliberate to be a coincidence.

"I think this is a founder of Saint Elias University," Hazel said. "Maybe he's the password?"

And the last Alpha of Alphas.

Gwen shrugged, unwilling to reveal any knowledge about the man.

Hazel snapped her fingers. "Bertold Alger," she said, whirling to look at the Alterion member.

They said nothing.

"Well crap," Hazel grumbled.

Gwen went back to studying the bookshelf in front of her. She noticed a small brass figure, half bull, half man. She knew from Klaus that this was Alterion's mascot. Picking it up, she studied it for clues. Inscribed on the bottom was the word *password.*

Gwen snorted. *Too easy.*

"Minotaur."

The mage took out their wand and cast a spell. The fire guttered out in seconds, revealing an opening to a spiral staircase which descended into the earth. Gwen didn't hesitate and practically skipped to the stairs with Hazel hot on her heels.

"Thank you!" Hazel called out as they descended.

At the bottom, they found a smoke-filled cigar lounge with its own bar. Students filled the room, lounging on leather chairs, sitting at the bar on stools, and standing around a large boxing ring. Gwen spotted Jordan and Rafe at the bar.

"There they are!" Gwen yelled above the noise and led Hazel toward them.

"We got you some drinks," Rafe said as they approached.

"And look who we found," Jordan added, pointing to Klaus behind the bar.

"Oh, thank Terra!" Klaus said, jumping over the bar and wrapping Gwen up into a giant bear hug.

"You're squishing me."

He hung on another second before finally setting her back on her feet, and she grinned up at him. Seeing her cousin felt like a small piece of home, familiar and grounding. It had only been a day—barely enough time to miss anyone—but she was happy to see him, to show him she was safe and here.

"You did it. You got in," Klaus said.

"Do you mean Saint Elias or this?" She motioned around the room.

"Saint Elias! I knew you could get in here, no sweat!" Klaus replied before glancing past her. "Who's your new friend?"

Gwen turned slightly, her excitement shifting into something warm and steady. "This is Hazel," she said, nudging her toward him. "We survived the exam together."

"Nice to meet you." Hazel stuck out her hand to shake his.

Klaus grinned as he shook it. "Nice to meet you too. I'm Klaus—since my cousin sucks at introductions." He shot Gwen a playful look before adding, "Glad you're making friends, so Jordan and I don't have to babysit you all year."

Gwen flipped Klaus off as he moved behind the bar and began mixing more drinks.

A loud metal clang filled the room—a match was beginning. Students abandoned their stools and pushed in toward the ring to get a better view.

"Let's go watch the fight," Jordan said, taking off and pulling Gwen behind him.

"I'll see you later," she promised Klaus.

"Alright. Be good and scry your mom or send her a letter. She worries," Klaus shouted after her.

Gwen ignored him, following her friends over to the ring.

Bodies pressed together in anticipation as they prepared to watch the fight. Normally, crowded spaces made Gwen's skin crawl, but the room was filled with an animalistic tension that made her feel at home.

A stocky man stood in one corner of the square ring, looking to be in his early twenties. His crooked nose indicated this was not his first fight. He had buzzed brown hair and wore skintight shorts. Gwen knew from time spent with her father that this was to keep opponents from gaining the upper hand. The guy reached into the crowd, grabbing an offered potion. He tossed it back in one gulp. Within seconds, his height grew by a foot and his muscles doubled.

Glamour. Lame.

A glamour wouldn't actually help him in a fight unless he was already a good fighter.

Across from him, a man pulled his shoulder-length, golden-blonde hair into a tight bun. His chest muscles rippled as he removed his shirt, his skin a tanned ivory. He didn't drink a potion or cast a spell; instead he pulled off his grey sweats to reveal his own skintight black shorts.

Gwen swallowed hard. *Well, damn.*

She hadn't been expecting a show, but she wasn't about to complain. The guy was ridiculously hot—broad shoulders and a sculpted chest, the definition suggesting he didn't rely on magic to keep himself strong. Not that she was looking too hard. Okay, maybe she was.

"Our last fight of the day is the one you've all been waiting for!" a deep voice echoed around the room. "In the left corner, we have Peter Stump! Don't let the name fool you, ladies. Peter's packing a log!"

The crowd cheered.

Peter looked unamused as his jaw clenched, his gaze never wavering from his opponent.

"In the right corner, we have Logan Wilder. Wild Her? I barely know her!"

So the hot one's name is Logan.

Gwen threw Hazel a knowing smile, and Hazel wiggled her eyebrows in response.

The room erupted into a deafening roar as Logan ignored the announcer. His thick thighs flexed as he bounced on his toes, jabbing his fists twice into the air in front of him.

Gwen couldn't help herself. Excitement bubbled up in her chest, and before she knew it, she was shouting along with the crowd.

"You know the rules: leave your teeth and claws at home! Everything else is fair game!"

The fighters moved to the center of the ring, knocking knuckles once before stepping back.

The metal bell tolled once again.

Peter swung first, lightning fast. His fist connected with Logan's jaw. The crowd gasped, shocked by the quick delivery, but Logan didn't pull away. Hell, he didn't even flinch.

It wasn't a sucker punch, but it somehow felt dirty. Logan reached up and touched two fingers to the red cheekbone Peter had hit. Where calm focus had been before, death now filled Logan's eyes as he narrowed them on Peter.

A hot surge of adrenaline rushed through Gwen. She had the sudden, almost overwhelming urge to leap into the ring and knock Peter out herself. But Logan didn't need her help—he was clearly a trained fighter.

Just not as well as me.

She smirked, certain she could take both of them if it came down to it. The fight tugged at something buried deep inside her, something animalistic almost feral. Even with her bracelet on, she felt the instinct rise, and she fought to clamp it down.

Peter's face gave away no fear, but his feet danced backwards. When Logan didn't follow, Peter skirted around the right side of the ring. Logan stayed light on his toes, keeping his hips squared up to Peter and his fists raised to protect his face.

Peter invaded Logan's space once more. He jabbed at his ribs with his right hook. Logan didn't fall for it, keeping his hands in place, so when Peter swung at his face again, Logan deflected it easily with a jab of his own.

There was a crack as Logan's gloved fist landed on Peter's chin. A vacant expression filled his eyes as the crowd whooped with excitement.

"Get 'em!" Rafe yelled next to her.

She didn't know who he was cheering for. Several other shouts filled the air as the crowd thirsted for violence.

Peter skittered away when Logan's second jab came close. He obviously didn't want another taste of Logan's full strength. Shaking his head, Peter bounced on the balls of his feet for a few moments. When he appeared to regain his wits, he charged forward and swung at Logan's ribs, left, then right, then left again.

Gwen had seen enough fights with her father at The Hideout, his bar, to know Peter wasn't trying to provoke Logan. He was trying to get even. Anger had taken over, which meant illogical decisions were imminent.

He barreled into Logan, lowering his head and wrapping him up into a vicious hug. He rained punches on Logan's ribs, leaving his head exposed from above.

His inexperience was showing, and she wasn't the only person who noticed. Logan's eyes lit up as he lifted a fist and brought it down on Peter's head. Normally, the angle and proximity would limit the force of such a strike, but Peter's knees buckled. That had been no ordinary hit.

Logan stepped back, slipping out of Peter's slack grip. With nothing to hold him, not even consciousness, Peter smacked into the floor face-first.

The room went wild as deafening screams tore through the air, some ordering Peter to get up and others calling Logan a god.

The announcer rushed to Peter's side and began slamming his hand down on the mat as he counted out, "One. Two. Three."

The magically enhanced vocals were barely audible above the insanity of the crowd. Peter did not stir. When he reached ten, the announcer stood and raised Logan's fist into the air. "Logan Wilder is the victor!" the announcer boomed, and the room rattled with the force.

When the students exploded into cheers, Hazel leaned over and yelled, "Let's get another drink."

Gwen still had some left, but she didn't mind going along to chat with Klaus. She moved out from under Jordan's arm to follow Hazel. She only made it a step when she ran into a brick wall—a sweaty and muscular brick wall. Her drink shattered on impact.

"Oh fuck!" Gwen yelped. She looked up to see it was Logan, the victor, standing before her, completely drenched in her drink. Not only were his abs tinged blue from the beverage, but glass shards stuck out of his skin.

He emitted a low growl, his jaw flexing so hard it was a wonder his teeth didn't crack. "Move, freshman," he seethed.

"I'm so sorry." Gwen scrambled to pull her wand out to dry him off and clean up the glass, but he yanked it out of her hands.

"Hey, tha—" Gwen's objection died as Logan snapped her wand in half, tossed it to the ground, and shoved past her without a word.

She blinked, stunned, fury bubbling up so fast it left her breathless. Rage told her to chase after him—to make him regret it. He was *so* lucky she was wearing her bracelet. If she wasn't, she would've shifted right then and there. Whatever guilt she'd felt before evaporated.

Screw him. I hope he gets a thousand more drinks spilled on him today.

Hazel picked up the pieces of Gwen's wand and handed them to her. She accepted them, staring down at her ruined work. Countless hours of whittling, carving, and polishing down the drain. *I'll fucking kill him.*

"Are you okay?" Hazel asked as they moved away from the scene.

"Fine," Gwen said through gritted teeth.

"Is it fixable?"

Gwen inspected her wand more closely. Logan had snapped it far up enough on the wooden shaft that it hadn't revealed the attachment threads of the onyx handle or her secret compartment. A small mercy.

Luckily it was fixable and she'd had the foresight to bring her woodworking tool bag with her.

Not that it made her any less pissed.

Maybe I have the Sight after all. Take that, Sybil.

"I think I can salvage it," Gwen answered.

As the crowd dispersed, the group moved to a seating area near the ring. There were limited chairs, so Gwen sat between Jordan's legs on the ground, allowing Hazel to have the last remaining seat.

"How am I ever supposed to get a girl with you sitting like this?" Jordan asked her.

Gwen scoffed. "You don't need a girl. Every time you get one, you abandon our friendship."

"That's not fair. That was one time," he reminded her.

She rolled her eyes. He wasn't wrong; it *was* only one time. Maybe it wasn't fair for her to hold it against him, but she couldn't help it. Her instincts made her possessive of the people she cared about. That was simply her nature. She already felt that pull towards Hazel and Rafe, and she'd only known them for two days. With Jordan, it was worse. She'd known him for nine years. He'd always been hers—her best friend, her pack. And whether or not it was rational, the idea of being pushed aside again made her tense.

"Nova! Elodie! Come meet the guys," Hazel said, waving at their suitemates across the room.

The two girls strolled over, casual and confident. Hazel made quick introductions. Jordan attempted to push Gwen away, but she refused to budge, acting as if she didn't notice Nova's gaze lingering on her and Jordan.

Let her wonder.

"We were about to grab a drink," Elodie said sweetly.

Nova's eyes drifted to the bar. "The bartender is so hot."

Gwen gagged. "Gross. That's my cousin."

"Oh. Good genes," Elodie winked at Gwen.

Gwen smiled at the compliment.

"Well, if you like drinks, we're heading to Kodiak Brew tonight if you want to come. First round's on me," Jordan said, gesturing to the group.

Hazel and Gwen exchanged a confused glance.

"Trying to bribe us with drinks?" Nova raised an eyebrow.

"Is it working?" Jordan flashed a grin.

"Definitely," Nova said without consulting Elodie. "See you tonight."

The girls turned and headed toward the bar, and Gwen watched as Nova leaned across the counter to talk to Klaus, who smiled in response and touched her arm. Jordan stiffened in his seat behind her.

Gwen liked Nova—she seemed cool and funny—but Gwen couldn't help the brief twinge she felt seeing Nova charm her way into the group. She didn't enjoy sharing. Not her cousin. Not her best friend. Not the spotlight. It wasn't jealousy, exactly, but growing up an only child had made her territorial by default—as well as the wolf inside her. Still, if Nova had to pick someone, Klaus wouldn't be the worst. Gwen could use another girl in the family. Plus, it would leave Jordan all to Gwen.

She bumped Jordan with her shoulder. "You ready to get into some trouble?"

"You know it," Jordan said with a smirk as he rubbed his palms together.

CHAPTER 13

Hazel

A squeal tore through the air. "Oh my gosh! Look at them!"

Hazel winced at Elodie's high-pitched reaction to the sled dogs sitting before them. Looking at their fluffy fur, pointy ears, and lolling tongues, Hazel had to admit they were quite squeal-worthy. It was the decibel she took offense with. She knew they were working dogs, but that didn't stop her from wanting to take each and every one of them back to her dorm. Surely she could convince Gwen.

"They're so cute!" Nova gushed before rushing forward to pet the fluffiest one. Her hands sunk into the Alaskan malamute's fur so deeply they disappeared from sight altogether. It reminded Hazel of a polar bear cub. "And soft!"

"What if *I* want Gracie?" Jordan asked, eyeing the dog tag in Nova's hand.

Nova's face faltered, and Hazel glanced over at Gwen, who rolled her eyes.

"I'm kidding," Jordan told her, but Hazel noticed the subtle glance he gave Nova before he went to find another dog.

Is that his idea of flirting? He's terrible at it.

Hazel looked toward Rafe, who met her eyes with a knowing look. They both stifled a laugh. Then he crossed the space between them and joined her beside a beautiful husky with mismatched eyes. The dog's tag read *Atlas*. Atlas gave an excited hop, tail wagging furiously as he pawed at them.

"He looks like a good one," Rafe said.

"Yeah, he seems hyper, though, like he'll need a strong lead," Hazel replied, grinning. "You can have him."

Rafe smiled at her words, and she caught it out of the corner of her eye. "So you think I'm strong?" he asked, light and teasing—but something in his tone made her pulse skip.

Hazel quickly looked away. "Well," she said, trying for nonchalance, "you're used to handling Jordan. Hyper, unpredictable, hard to manage..."

"Hey!" Jordan called from a few feet away, clearly having caught that. "Don't start a war you can't finish," he added with mock seriousness.

Gwen laughed, securing her dog's lead. "Don't worry about Hazel. She has backup. Right, Rafe?"

"Definitely," Rafe said without hesitation.

Jordan huffed. "Fine. I have Elodie and Nova."

The two girls flanking him exchanged a look before chiming in together, "Sorry. Suitemate code. We side with Hazel."

Laughter rippled through the group, the sexual tension with Rafe dissolving into something lighter—but Hazel's heart still thudded harder than usual.

Everyone else had chosen their dogs, but only Gwen was already hooked up to the sled—and judging by the others' tangled leads and uncooperative pups, Hazel still had a little time.

She stepped away from Rafe and headed towards a white Samoyed whose whole body wagged from its head to the tip of its curled, fluffy tail. It approached her with a walk which was more like a silly little dance. It was not unlike her dear Garth's waddle. The thought of her cantankerous but lovable bird sent a pang of sadness through her. She hoped he was okay without her.

After passing the Samoyed's sniff test, Hazel ran her fingers through its thick coat. The dog leaned into her touch, pressing all its weight into her. Hazel had to adjust her stance not to lose her balance.

Why did I wear heels?

Hazel felt ridiculously dressed for the Alaskan climate in a deep-crimson wrap dress and heels, but Nova and Elodie had insisted she'd only be cold for a little bit; the tunnel was weather controlled and the walk to the bar would be short. She wouldn't have gone through with it if Gwen hadn't also opted for a dress. Gwen wore a short dark-green dress, Nova a burgundy maxi with a thigh slit, and Elodie a shiny navy satin slip dress.

The sled dog gazed up at her with a mix of affection and curiosity as she searched for its tag.

"Snowbell. What a perfect name for a perfect girl."

A big, wet, slobbery kiss landed on her cheek. She groaned as she wiped her face gently, sure the dog had taken off half of her makeup, but she couldn't be mad at Snowbell for it.

Gwen had already steered her sled to the tunnel entrance—Hazel needed to hurry. She quickly hooked Snowbell to her sled. She knew it was magically enhanced to pull quadruple their weight, but she still felt a twinge of guilt as she stepped onto it. Nova had claimed the space next to Gwen, the two of them joking about something Hazel couldn't quite hear. Jordan and Elodie had already taken their places behind them, leaving only one space—next to Rafe. Hazel guided her sled into place next to his. Her pulse picked up as she glanced over at him. His olive shirt wrapped tightly around his muscles as he held a firm grip on Atlas's lead.

"Ready?" Gwen shouted from the front.

"Ready!" the group chorused.

Gwen and Nova took off, and the rest of the group followed behind.

The dogs were faster than Hazel expected, and the wind hit her full force, snapping her dress around her legs. She yelped, fumbling to keep it down as it flew open entirely.

A flush of embarrassment crept up her neck. *Please tell me Rafe didn't just see my panties.* She wasn't wearing anything particularly alluring—just plain black boy shorts. It wasn't exactly the impression she wanted to make. Not that she was thinking about him seeing her underwear. Not really.

Determined to salvage what dignity she had left, she yanked her wand from the thigh holster hidden beneath her dress and cast a wind shield charm. A shimmering barrier settled around her—and then, with a flick of her wrist, she extended it to cover Rafe too.

He glanced over, clearly surprised, and said, "Thanks." With the wind gone, she could hear him clearly—like he was riding in her sled instead of his own.

"Don't mention it," she replied with a smile.

Silence settled between them again, but not uncomfortably.

The tunnel curved gently ahead, the path opening wider as they picked up speed. Hazel loosened her grip on the sled handles and, with a grin, lifted her arms into the air. The air rushed around her shield as Snowbell picked up her pace, the torches along the cavern walls blurring as they flew by, and the sled glided smoothly beneath her—it was like a rollercoaster, and she resisted the urge to take down her shield to experience the whole thing.

Then she saw them. A jagged line of stalactites hung low from the ceiling ahead. Hazel yanked her arms down and ducked with a sharp gasp, narrowly avoiding them. Her heart pounded, but laughter bubbled up in place of her fear.

When she glanced sideways, she caught Rafe watching her—no, not watching, staring. There was something like awe in his expression, like he was seeing her for the first time.

He blinked, as if realizing he'd been caught, and quickly looked forward. "Don't you think this is kind of weird?" he asked. "I mean...

this is a university for magic. You'd think they could find a more efficient way to get out of the mountain."

"I don't think it's because they lack the means," Hazel said.

"What do you mean?" he asked.

"The chancellor said it during the commencement. The mountain decides who stays and who leaves. I think the answer is pretty clear. We dog sled because it's what the mountain permits."

"So you're saying the mountain is old school," Rafe joked.

"Something like that," Hazel replied.

She'd read countless books on Saint Elias before coming here. Almost all the legends stated the mountain was a living, sentient thing, with its own rules not governed by any outside source. Since being here, she felt like she could sense it somehow, but that was probably just her imagination.

Rafe didn't object to her theory as they exited the tunnel. And for that, she was grateful—maybe he believed her.

The group bade farewell to their new furry friends at the dog kennel outside the tunnel. Gwen kissed hers on the head before departing.

Hmm, maybe Gwen is secretly a big ol' softie.

The town was aglow with streetlamps, but the moon was cloud-covered tonight, giving it a darker feel than their last visit. Water covered the cobblestone streets, and a shiver went down Hazel's spine as a crisp wind blew between the buildings. Autumn was on its way.

The group walked the last few blocks to Kodiak Brew, enjoying the crackle and pop of music filtering through the air. Warmth washed over them as they entered the brewery, which was filled to the brim with college students and townspeople. A vintage jukebox played in the front window as a few patrons danced nearby.

Hazel scanned the crowd for an open table.

"There's a booth open over on the back wall," Rafe called from behind them.

It was the same booth they'd sat in two nights ago and Hazel wondered about the coincidence.

Elodie and Nova slid into the booth on the left while Gwen and Hazel took the right side. Rafe slid in beside Hazel when Jordan rushed to sit next to Nova. Jordan had been all over Gwen the other night, but it looked like he was ditching her for their suitemate. Hazel wasn't sure what their deal was. Gwen stiffened, but her face remained neutral—if she cared, she was doing a decent job of hiding it.

"We should play a game," Nova suggested. Hazel was learning quickly that Nova liked to be the life of the party. "Maybe Truth or Dare?"

Hazel suppressed a snort. She wasn't sure any of them could stomach another round of Truth or Dare so soon.

Elodie excitedly clapped her hands together. "Oh, love it!"

"How about a drinking game?" Jordan offered instead. "I overheard someone ordering a round of roulette."

"What's that?" Elodie asked.

"It's a roulette wheel of mage elixirs. You spin it, and whatever you land on, you drink."

Hazel and Gwen shared wary looks. The magic brews had burned them before. Once was enough.

"Sounds risky," Gwen said.

"We both know I'm going to get you to play, so just give in now," Jordan said.

Gwen rolled her eyes, but she smiled at the playful banter. Her shoulders eased as she said, "Fine."

"Great. Rafe, will you help me?" Jordan asked.

Rafe followed Jordan to the bar.

"Fair warning, one elixir can turn you invisible," Hazel cautioned them.

"Seriously?" Elodie asked, shocked.

"Yeah, well, it's not a big deal unless Hazel here dares you to approach people naked," Gwen joked.

Nova's eyes widened. "You didn't."

The table erupted with laughter as Jordan and Rafe returned, carrying a round wooden tray with a strange wheel and several colorful vials—red, clear, blue, pink and two greens. Jordan set it down in the center of the table.

"There are six elixirs." He tapped the center, where two additional orange vials sat under a glass cloche. "These are the antidotes. The cloche is on a time release. When it vanishes, the fastest two people to grab one get it."

"What do they each do?" Nova asked nervously.

"Where would the fun be in that?" he answered, then spun the wheel.

Soft movement beside her drew Hazel's attention. She watched as Gwen discreetly pulled out her wand from her thigh sheath and gave it a small flick. The wheel slowed as the clear vial moved in front of her, but it didn't stop. It continued going until the two green vials landed in front of Gwen and Hazel.

Thank Terra. I can't do another night of invisibility.

Hazel scanned the table, but no one seemed to notice Gwen's interference. The colorful vials held everyone's attention, anticipation running high. She wasn't sure what green meant, but if she was going down, she was glad Gwen was coming with her.

Gwen and Hazel each reached for their green vials. Jordan took the red one without hesitation, and Rafe groaned reluctantly, grabbing the pink vial.

"Oh no, is this the invisibility one?" Elodie asked, holding up the clear vial with a skeptical look.

Hazel almost felt sorry for her... but not sorry enough to give up her green one. "You'll be fine," she said with a grin.

Nova picked up her blue vial, raising it with a playful smile.

They all clinked their shots together.

"May the best of our past!" Jordan shouted.

"Be the worst of our future!" Gwen, Hazel, and Rafe chorused back, and then they downed them.

The liquid tasted how Hazel imagined pus to taste, and she had to slap a hand over her mouth not to gag. As she did, she discovered large, angry, white-headed and red-ringed boils covering her hands.

Oh no. No, no, no. I can't be stuck like this all night!

Panicked, Hazel turned to Gwen to find she'd been dealt the same hand.

"Fuck!" Gwen cried out.

Across the table, bubbles came out of Nova's mouth as she let out a burst of laughter. Following her line of sight, Hazel turned to see Rafe's hair had turned pink, and tiny white butterflies circled him. He looked absolutely precious, which made Hazel sink back into the booth out of his view.

Jordan's face was red, and every time he spoke, steam blew out of his ears. Meanwhile, Elodie had not turned invisible. Instead, she had an iridescent glow that shimmered along her skin.

Gwen beat on the cloche. A boil burst on the back of her hand, sending pus flying.

Elodie screamed as the pus landed on the table in front of her.

Hazel slapped a hand over her mouth, fighting a gag.

The cloche finally vanished into thin air. Gwen's and Jordan's hands dove for the vials, but Gwen was already in position. Desperate, Hazel was right behind her. But it was no use, both of the antidotes were gone.

"Gwen, you can't have both!" Jordan held out his hand, eyes locked on the second antidote vial. "Come on—I'm your best friend."

How am I supposed to compete with that?

Hazel gave Gwen her most pleading look as more itchy boils bloomed across her arms. "*I'll* be your best friend if you give me the vial," Hazel whispered dramatically.

Gwen sighed like she was making the hardest decision of her life. Then, with a smirk, she turned and handed the vial to Hazel. She turned back to Jordan. "Sorry, you got a demotion."

Hazel snatched it like it was life itself. "Thank Terra!" She threw her head back and tossed the antidote down her throat. She felt a rush of cool relief where her skin had been hot and angry moments ago. She watched her skin closely as the boils disappeared as instantly as they had appeared.

Gwen wiped her mouth with the back of her perfectly smooth hand. "No, thank *me*, bitch," she said.

Steam continued to billow out of Jordan's ears, adding true menace to his scowl.

Nova reached over and laid a hand on his forearm. "Aw, Jordan. I think you look cute."

More steam blew from his ears. Was he blushing? Hazel could've sworn his cheeks got even redder.

"Oh, this is my favorite song!" Elodie squealed.

"Let's go dance," Jordan said, standing to let Nova and Elodie out. Rafe stood to join them, and Gwen followed.

"Aren't you coming?" Nova asked as she slid out of the booth.

Hazel hesitated. She'd never danced in front of anyone—ever.

"Yes," she finally said, climbing out of the booth and heading toward the dance floor.

The music pulsed through the room, fast and energetic.

Gwen grabbed Hazel's hand as they reached the edge of the crowd. "Come on, it's not scary if we all look ridiculous together."

Elodie joined in, looping her arm through Hazel's. The three of them stepped into the rhythm as a unit, laughing and spinning like they'd done this a hundred times. Nova and Jordan twirled nearby, already lost in their own world, and Rafe danced with a girl Hazel didn't know nearby.

Hazel's nerves faded with each beat. She wasn't great—her movements were a little awkward, her timing off—but it didn't matter. Gwen was swinging her arms like a lunatic, Elodie had somehow turned interpretive dance into a performance, and Hazel felt... free.

The high-energy beat faded into something slow and sweet. The crowd shifted almost instinctively, couples drawing close as the lights dimmed and the song pulled them into something quieter, more intimate.

Hazel stepped back instinctively, unsure. She glanced toward the booth, thinking she could slip away before anyone noticed—but Rafe turned.

"Dance with me?" His voice was gentle, his gaze steady. Not demanding. Not teasing. Sure.

Hazel's breath caught. She nodded, unable to form actual words as he reached for her hand. His fingers were warm and certain around hers.

He guided her in—not too fast—and his hand settled at her waist like it had always belonged there. Her other hand found his shoulder, and she tilted her head up, eyes meeting his. Her heart beat hard beneath her ribs as they swayed back and forth. The world around them faded—Gwen's laughter, Jordan's showboating, even the pulsing lights. All she could focus on was the way Rafe's thumb traced slow circles against her waist, and the steady rhythm of his breath.

"You're a good dancer," he murmured.

"You're a good liar," she said, her mouth tilting upward into a smile.

She laughed, soft and breathy, her forehead brushing the edge of his collarbone.

She was dancing. In front of everyone. With him. And she didn't want it to end.

Gwen

Gwen turned slowly in Elodie's arms, her grin wide from the last song's chaos. They hadn't planned to pair up, but when the music slowed, the rest of their friends had coupled off.

“See anyone cute?” Gwen asked as she scanned the room, looking for Harland.

Elodie looked around the room.“No.” She seemed bummed, but then her rhythm faltered as her eyes flicked over Gwen’s shoulder.

Gwen turned her head to follow her gaze and immediately spotted the reason: a cute girl wearing a black bomber jacket stood at the edge of the dance floor. Amelia. The same girl who’d given them the campus tour.

“Want to change your answer?” Gwen smirked.

Elodie blushed, and Gwen glanced back over her shoulder. Amelia was watching Elodie now, a lazy smile on her lips as she strolled forward.

Elodie froze. “Oh no.”

“Oh yes,” Gwen said, amused.

Amelia reached them, stopping with a glint in her eye. “Mind if I cut in?”

Elodie looked like she might pass out.

Gwen smiled and stepped back, letting go of her hand. “She’s all yours.”

Amelia took Elodie’s hand without hesitation, and the two moved together as if they’d already danced a dozen times before. Gwen backed away from the floor, her heart warm and buzzing with secondhand joy.

She slid into the empty booth and watched her friends dance. It sucked to be the odd one out. She was going to have to spell the DJ so he’d only play fast songs the rest of the night. But before she could move to cast, Klaus slid into the booth across from her, carrying a beer.

“Not dancing tonight?” Gwen asked.

“You know me. I have to have the right partner.”

Gwen glanced around the room. “Where are all your friends?”

“Getting drinks at the bar.” He took a swig of his beer.

She reached out to grab his glass, but he smacked her hand away.

“Looks like you have a suitor.” Klaus nodded to the guy looking their way, and she dropped her outstretched hand. The blonde-haired man was staring, stirring his drink with a straw. He flashed Gwen a smile, and she smirked back. Then he stood up—and Gwen groaned.

Too short. Strike one.

The guy walked toward their table, and Gwen averted her gaze. Klaus snickered beside her. Then the guy was there, at the edge of their booth. He leaned down so his face was right by hers.

Personal boundaries, buddy. Strike two.

“Want to dance?” His hot breath smelled like garlic, and Gwen barely kept her food down.

Strike three.

“Sorry, I’m taken.” She pointed at Klaus, then reached over for his hand. He didn’t give it to her, so she kicked him under the table. The guy’s eyes widened at Klaus—who took her hand with a forced smile and looked up at the guy. He practically bolted from the table.

“I hate when you do that,” Klaus mumbled.

Gwen shrugged her shoulders. So she was picky. At least she had the decency to lie and not hurt his feelings. She watched as the guy made his way to a table of five girls. Whatever he said made them laugh. He seemed to have much better luck with them than he did with her.

She glanced back at the dance floor, this time happy to find that Rafe and Hazel were locked in each other’s arms, swaying to another slow dance. His hands sat on her hips as Hazel looked into his eyes.

A pair of brown leather cowboy boots walked into her line of sight, stealing her attention, and headed straight for her.

Now that I can get behind. She loved cowboys, and growing up in Maine, there were next to none.

When she looked up, she saw none other than Logan Wilder, the asshole who’d broken her wand.

Fuck.

Immediately she stood, unwilling to let him have the upper hand, and crossed her arms as she waited for him.

“Gwen,” Klaus warned. “Please don’t start. He’s my covenmate and precepts.”

Gwen knew from Klaus that precepts were coven leaders elected to serve out a school year. *How did this asshole get elected?*

She pushed the question aside. Gwen couldn’t give two shits.

Logan stopped inches in front of her and matched her stance. His muscles bulged through his long-sleeve shirt and she hated how it made her stomach clench. She’d vowed to hate him forever in the Alterion tent. She shouldn’t be drooling over him.

“I came over here to apologize for breaking your wand,” Logan said.

She waited for the actual apology, but it never came. Instead, they stood there glaring at one another. He towered over her even when standing, forcing her gaze upward. She hated it.

“Aw, it’s okay, Logan. Gwen is a pro at fixing those types of things,” Klaus said. He still sat in the booth, which was probably best, given the tension flowing around them right now.

Gwen flashed a look that could kill over her shoulder. “Stay out of this, Klaus.”

Klaus threw his hands up and leaned back in the booth.

“Well?” Logan finally asked, breaking his silence.

“Well, what?” Gwen arched a brow at him. He couldn’t possibly be expecting her to apologize to him.

“Do you accept my apology?”

“You haven’t apologized yet, only made a statement of intent,” Gwen pointed out.

Logan let out a low growl. It ignited a flicker of excitement in her stomach.

Stop that! We hate him! Gwen tried to lean away, but the table at her back stopped her.

“I’m sorry for breaking your wand. I’d like to offer to buy you a new one.” His tone became very formal, emotionless, as he uncrossed his arms.

"No, thank you," she said, mimicking his monotone voice and stance.

"Don't be stubborn," he snapped, all formality evaporating.

"Get hexed, Logan."

His jaw clenched, then he took a deep breath through his nose. "Just let me replace your wand, Gwendolyn."

He knew her name. She hated how pleased that made her. So he'd asked about her? That didn't mean anything. Maybe he hadn't asked about her, only overheard her name in passing.

Focus. He broke your wand.

Her beautiful wand.

Bastard.

Gwen rolled her eyes. "Like I'd ever let you buy me some crappy, plywood wand to replace the walnut one I handcrafted and intricately carved myself before spending days searching for the perfect onyx handle and then grinding it to fit my grip." She drew her freshly repaired wand from its sheath and held it in a defensive position, but Logan showed no sign of fear. "I don't need you *or* your version of a shitty apology."

Klaus failed to stifle a groan behind him.

"You're an embedder?" Logan asked as he looked her up and down with a level of distaste she'd not seen from him before.

"Yes," she spat back, slitting her eyes at him. "What's wrong with being an embedder?

"Nothing. I just thought you were..." he paused, "something else."

What the fuck does that mean?

"Well, I'm not!"

"Fine. Do you accept my apology or not?"

He seemed angry with her, but she couldn't figure out why. There was nothing wrong with her being an embedder. Plus, he should have been kissing her feet, knowing he didn't have to buy her an incredibly expensive wand replacement—because, of course, she'd have picked an expensive one.

"Yes, I accept your poorly delivered apology."

Not.

He nodded to her and Klaus, then turned on his heel and left.

Ugh, his butt looks so good in those jeans.

"Gwen, you can't go picking fights before school has even started," Klaus said once Logan was out of earshot.

"Get hexed, Klaus! *I* didn't pick that one!"

"Just try to keep your temper under control, please." He searched her gaze earnestly.

He was right. The last thing she needed to do was start making enemies for her wolf to hate if she ever shifted again at school.

Gwen nodded, and that was all she was going to give Klaus on the matter. "I need a drink."

Klaus shook his head. "This bar's not like Many Sisters in Britton Place. They'll easily spot a fake."

"I have my ways." She waved him off.

The brewery was nearly full by the time Gwen sidled up to the bar. She listened as two old men next to her moaned about their missing livestock.

"I've had five chickens disappear since the university started back up. I'm down to ten."

"You think that's bad? I had a pig go missing last night! Found it dead the next morning in the woods behind my house."

I wonder what's hunting them. Before she could give it much thought, the bartender approached.

"Hey, beautiful," the bartender said. He wore a plaid flannel button-up with a black tee and a pair of black jeans.

"Hi, handsome. What's your name?" She twirled her hair in her fingers.

She wasn't above flirting to get a stiff drink. Salem, she wasn't above doing more than that either.

He smiled at her. "Tristan."

"I need something strong, Tristan." Gwen grinned at him, then added, "That doesn't make me invisible."

"On it, boss." He saluted.

Gwen looked around the bar as she waited. A few coven members in purple sweatshirts—Sybil—played roulette at a table nearby. The dance floor had become so packed she could no longer see her friends. The smell of sweat competed with the scents of beer and magic. She turned to inspect the back half of the brewery when she spotted Harland standing only a few feet away, surrounded by a group of girls.

He smiled at them tightly as he tried to turn towards the bar, but each time, the girls shuffled with him and he grimaced slightly. The poor guy was clearly in distress.

Gwen moved over to him and whispered, "Looks like you have an entourage."

"I've tried everything. They won't go away." He grimaced as he shook his head.

"Everything?" She cocked her eyebrow, taking it as a challenge. Gwen was sure she could get them to go away.

He gave her a weary glance, but before he could say anything, she slid her arm around his waist and began laughing.

"You're so funny!" She pitched her voice high and bubbly, very unlike herself, but sure to grab attention.

"What are you doing?" he whispered in her ear.

She ignored him. "Harland, stop."

His cheeks flushed, but he finally caught on, putting his arm around her and pulling her into him.

He smells so good.

His free hand slid under her chin as he held it, staring into her eyes. Gwen's mouth went dry with the look and she stood on her tiptoes to bridge the gap between them until their lips were inches from each other. She held her breath and waited for him to make a move, but it never came. He simply held her there, and they stood still in time while everything around them moved.

She noticed the girls glaring at her from over his shoulders. Glancing away from them, she looked him in the eyes and leaned forward to kiss him, but he dropped his arm immediately and put a few inches between them.

Damn. Maybe she'd misread the signals.

"Here's your check, Harland." Tristan's voice saved her from having to address the awkwardness.

Gwen took advantage of the distraction to scoot over and give him the space he clearly wanted. Her cheeks burned, and she spent several seconds studying the opposite wall of the brewery to let her embarrassment pass.

Tristan set down a clear drink with a lemon twist. Gwen sipped it, pleasantly surprised to find it was a gin and tonic. She drained half the glass while Harland paid his check.

"Thank you for the help. Have a good night," Harland said. His voice was colder than she'd have liked.

"You're welcome," she replied before taking a drink. At least she had something to do with her hands, so she didn't foolishly try to wrap them back around Harland.

Gwen felt an uncomfortable emptiness once he was gone. It wasn't as strong as last time but something about him called to her. It was unexplainable—she'd never felt anything like it. She craved his presence and had half a mind to follow him out, but thought better of it. Stalker wasn't a good look. If he liked that kind of attention, those other girls would've gotten further with him. She'd have to continue to play the long game.

She took another drink before sulking all the way back to the booth in defeat. None of the other guys in the bar tonight interested her. Logan had also left, not that he was worth her attention.

"Have any luck?" Klaus asked.

"With what?"

His eyebrow raised in question. "The drink?"

"Oh, that." Gwen held up the nearly empty glass with a smile. "Gin and tonic."

Klaus shook his head. "How—"

“We have to leave,” Hazel said, rushing up to the booth. She yanked on Gwen’s arm so hard Gwen knew she meant business.

“What’s going on?” Gwen glanced past Hazel for any signs of trouble.

Hazel looked over her shoulder, back at Rafe. Gwen followed her gaze. “I don’t want to talk about it. Please.”

“Fine. It’s not like there are any cute guys here, anyway.”

Hazel made a face at her. “You seemed to do fine at the bar.”

Klaus peeked over the booth, trying to get a look at who they were talking about, but Harland had already left. *Thank Terra!* Klaus knew enough of her business.

“Here.” Gwen handed Klaus the rest of her drink. “Go make some friends.”

“I *have* friends,” he said as he stood. “I only came over here so *you* wouldn’t be alone.”

“Aw, that’s so sweet,” Hazel said.

“Barf. Let’s go.”

CHAPTER 14

Gwen

The cool autumn air hit them as soon as they stepped outside, making Gwen slide her arms into her leather jacket. A few people lingered near the entrance of the brewery, smoking and chatting in small clusters. The smoke drifted into their path as they walked, making her wrinkle her nose as they passed through it.

"What was that about?" Gwen asked once they were clear of the crowd.

"I was dancing with Rafe and things started to..."

Gwen raised a brow when Hazel paused. "Started to what?"

"Heat up," Hazel said, looking at her feet.

Gwen snorted. "How so?"

Hazel chewed on her lip, then whispered, "We were dancing and his hands were on my hips. I thought it was harmless, but when a slower song came on, I could... It felt like he might want to kiss me."

"Isn't that a good thing?" Gwen asked, a huge smile forming on her face. It was obvious Hazel wasn't experienced with guys, but Rafe seemed like a good one.

"I—I don't know!"

"Hazel, do you like him?"

Hazel nodded.

"Then what's the big deal?"

"I've never kissed anyone before," Hazel whispered. "I didn't want the first time to be in a bar."

"So you *do* want to kiss him!" Gwen teased.

Sweet Hazel is so innocent. Gwen had lost her innocence long ago.

Hazel grinned as her cheeks turned pink.

Gwen chuckled, grabbing Hazel's arm and linking it through her own. The gin and tonic was making her affectionate. "Come on, nerd."

She wondered if this was the type of friendship all girls had. Had she been missing out on this the whole time? Or was this comfortability rarer? Something you had to hunt for? It felt rare to Gwen, and she was thankful for the hundredth time that she was rooming with Hazel. She might have been joking about demoting Jordan, but Hazel was rapidly becoming one of her best friends.

"You should—"

When they reached the forest, a shift in the wind carried a familiar scent. It tugged at Gwen's memory, but with her bracelet on, everything was dulled and she couldn't quite place it. Something felt off, though, wrong even.

"Everything okay?" Hazel asked.

"I'm not sure." She was pretty tipsy. It could just be her imagination.

There was only one way to know for sure. Gwen slipped her bracelet into her pocket and immediately sobered as the wolf burned through the alcohol. The wind swept up again and the metallic scent hit her all at once. Now she knew where she recognized it from—Manfrit's nose bleeds, fights at The Hideout, and countless kills she'd made as a cub in the woods behind her house. The hair on the back of her neck raised as her therian senses came to the forefront, alerting her to danger.

She tried to listen to see if there was something in the tree line, but she couldn't hear anything except the crunch of the leaves under their shoes.

Wrong. Something was very wrong.

Her brain fought to find the thing that was missing. What should it sound like? There were no homes in this area, nothing but the forest and the kennels. Gwen's breath hitched. The dogs. There were no sounds of playful nipping, panting, or even the jingle of collars or leashes. If Gwen noticed something was off, the dogs should have sensed it, too, but there was no noise.

Gwen pulled Hazel to a stop. It was too dark and too far for Hazel to see. They needed to be careful.

"You're freaking me out," Hazel said.

Gwen hesitated, unsure how to explain what she was feeling without revealing what she was. Hazel seemed trustworthy, but she couldn't risk being wrong. It was impossible to give up a lifetime of fear in a moment.

"Something feels wrong."

Hazel nodded, as if sensing it too.

They cautiously moved ahead once again. Gwen kept Hazel tightly by her side while she inhaled slowly, drawing in the scents without making it obvious she was actively tracking with her therian senses. It was unlikely Hazel would put two and two together, but she also didn't want Hazel to think she was crazy.

Hazel shivered beside her. Gwen hoped it was from the cold, and not fear. She needed Hazel to keep a cool head while she figured this out.

They covered another five yards before the dark silhouette of the kennels sharpened against the tree line. A few more steps and the tangy smell tickling Gwen's nose grew pungent. It was animal blood.

She didn't think before she dropped Hazel's arm and sprinted, her heart a frantic drum against her ribs—not from running, but from chilling fear. The two men talking about their livestock flashed in her mind, and she silently begged Terra for her instincts to be wrong.

"Gwen!"

Despite the smell of Hazel's fear and the sound of her heels pounding on the pavement behind her, Gwen didn't falter. She couldn't. She had to know.

She reached the kennel first. The chain-link gate hung wide open. She'd been right. There was blood. So much blood.

Gwen sank to her knees next to the first sled dog. Its tan fur was nearly black with dark blood.

Behind her, she heard rustling before Hazel uttered, "*Lux.*"

Underneath the light of Hazel's wand, the brutality was much worse. Each and every dog had been slaughtered.

The savagery and senselessness of what laid before them was truly haunting. Blood slicked the dirt in dark, congealing pools. Tufts of fur clung to the trees and fence. Bones jutted from mangled flesh like splintered wood, and entrails curled upon the ground like discarded rope. The body count was indistinguishable; none of the dogs remained in one piece.

Hazel gasped as she took in the scene and fell on her knees next to Gwen. "Terra, save us."

A sob tore from Gwen's throat, a raw sound she couldn't suppress. She reached for the dog in front of her, pulling it into her lap, and found that the blood was still warm. Fresh.

If only we'd been here sooner...

With a trembling hand, she gingerly turned over the dog tag lying beside the dismembered body—clearly ripped from its neck when the dog was slain. Gwen wiped the bloody tag on her dress, not caring that she was becoming covered in blood. The name read *Midas.*

It was the dog who she'd established a connection with earlier. Tears welled in Gwen's eyes as she looked up at Hazel. She set him down and pulled her bracelet from her pocket, slipping it onto her wrist. The blood was getting to her—she couldn't risk shifting.

"What the hell happened here?" Hazel asked, face pale and eyes wide.

Before Gwen could answer, movement in the trees caught her eye. A shadow darted back into the forest.

Without a second thought, Gwen was on her feet and sprinting into the trees. Whatever did this would not get away.

I'll kill you.

"Gwen, don't! You don't know what kind of monster did this!"

But Gwen didn't stop—because she knew the real monster in the forest was *her*.

Hazel

The cold air burned in Hazel's chest as she raced to catch up with Gwen.

Ahead, Gwen dropped to her knees once more. A few seconds later, Hazel found Gwen wrapped around another slaughtered dog. Hazel fought off the urge to cry and wretch as she stood back to keep watch. Whatever had done this could be nearby. A shiver went down Hazel's back with the thought.

She wanted to give Gwen time to grieve, but they couldn't stay out here like sitting ducks. They needed to get help. They needed to get to safety.

Abruptly, Gwen stood and walked around in a wide circle.

Hazel was terrified she'd take off into the forest again. "Gwen, we need to go tell someone. We're not equipped to hunt down a predator in the dark." She gestured at Gwen's dress to emphasize her point.

Hazel winced when Gwen finally turned to face her. She was a scary sight to behold. Her hands were covered in blood, the green dress she wore was ruined, and crimson streaks ran down her face.

Gwen was looking at her, but her gaze was vacant. It was like she didn't even see her.

Hazel walked to her and put her arm around her friend. "Let's go back and get you cleaned up and ask for help."

Gwen said nothing as Hazel led her toward the tunnel. She wondered if she was in shock, but then considered that this might be Gwen's version of grief.

As they approached the tunnel entrance, Gwen pulled them both to a stop.

"What is it?" Hazel asked.

Gwen looked over her shoulder, and Hazel followed her gaze. There were shadows in the distance, heading toward them from town.

"We should warn them," Hazel said. She wouldn't wish that discovery on anyone. Not even Dane.

Gwen squeezed Hazel's arm. "No," she said firmly, shaking her head. "We have to go!"

"What? Why?" Hazel asked. Maybe these people could help them.

"We just ran into the forest chasing a shadow that probably killed those poor dogs. Our footprints are the only ones out there—and I'm covered in blood."

Hazel jerked to look back in the direction they'd come, her heart trying to jump out of her throat. "You saw a shadow?"

She chased after a shadow? Is she nuts?

"Don't you get it, Hazel? They're going to think *we're* the thing in the forest."

Hazel shook her head as her stomach clenched. "Surely if we explain—"

"No," Gwen cut her off.

"Gwen, I honestly think it'll be—"

"Hazel, I'm begging you." Gwen squeezed her arms so hard Hazel nearly cried out. "Please, let's go. We have to move fast."

Hazel chewed her lip as she considered. Gwen's jaw was set, but her eyes were wide with fear. She realized this was the first time she'd seen it on Gwen's face tonight. If Gwen was right, they could be expelled for something they didn't do.

"How do we get out of here?" Hazel asked.

"The brooms." Gwen released Hazel and rushed for the tunnel.

Hazel sighed as the blood flow returned to her biceps. "Salem, take me," she muttered as she trudged behind Gwen.

Could this night get any worse?

They stood in front of a *FOR EMERGENCY USE* sign where five brooms hung. Hazel begrudgingly accepted the broom Gwen handed her.

She studied the straw broom and its smooth wooden handle as if it were a snake about to bite her. Five feet long and dangerous, it might as well have been a snake. The last thing she wanted to do was take her head off on the cave ceiling, trying to fly a broom in a dark, unfamiliar tunnel. If they weren't careful, the people coming in behind them would find *their* dismembered bodies.

Gwen swung a leg over her broom and mounted it. It immediately rose into the air, close enough for her to reach up and touch the ceiling.

Hazel attempted to do the same—except she hung on for dear life as she wobbled three feet above the ground.

"Why does it look like you've never flown a broom before?" Gwen asked.

Hazel laughed awkwardly, but said nothing. *Probably because I haven't!* Her knuckles were white with tension as she slowly urged the broom forward next to Gwen.

"You've never been on a broom before?" Gwen demanded.

Hazel's cheeks warmed. She hated being bad at things.

"I grew up in a mundane community. I couldn't exactly fly a broom around without being seen."

"What about Elkmont?" Gwen asked, the judgment thick in her voice.

“My dad refused to sign the permission slip,” Hazel mumbled, as she focused on staying upright. It was harder than it looked.

“Salem burn me,” Gwen said before taking off.

Hazel willed her broom forward with a slight downward press of her hands. It shot off like a bullet, and she nearly flew over Gwen. When she tilted the broom handle up to stop, she jerked too hard and almost ended up on the tunnel floor.

“This broom is so touchy!”

“Quit using your hands and shift your weight! It’s not a stick shift, it’s like a horse!” Gwen shouted from ahead.

Hazel knew about horses. That analogy could work. Taking a deep breath, she focused on her core. She leaned forward slowly, and the broom sped up. She leaned back slowly, and the broom braked gently. Well, more gently. She was tense and the broom could sense it, but it was better than her first attempt. Leaning forward again, she flew to Gwen.

The journey back was taking twice as long as it had on their way in. Hazel knew it was her fault. While she was good at many things, broom flying was not one of them.

Yet.

The wind whipped past, and Hazel didn’t bother shielding herself. Her hair, makeup, and this night were already ruined. Every time Gwen tried to speed up, Hazel refused to match her, which forced Gwen to slow back down to a steady pace. Hazel almost felt bad, but her self-preservation instincts were stronger than her people-pleasing tendencies in this instance.

If it weren’t for her fear of crashing into a stalactite or being wrongfully expelled, Hazel might actually enjoy riding a broom. Instead, she thought she might die of a heart attack before they made it back to SEU; she’d have given up her family and passed the entrance exams for nothing.

The ache in her chest eased when she finally spied a bright light at the end of the tunnel. Hazel quickly realized that mounting had been easy, but dismounting would be another story.

How am I supposed to get off?

Gwen lowered her broom until her feet touched the ground. Hazel attempted to do the same, but as she leaned forward, her broom tilted down and she crashed into the dirt.

"Smooth," Gwen said.

Hazel rolled her eyes as she picked herself up. One of her heels had broken during her fall. She'd have to carry them back. It was just as well—the idea of walking another second in them was intolerable.

Gwen snagged Hazel's broom off the ground and propped it against the cavern wall with her own. After glancing around the administration building that blocked the campus from view, she drew her wand. "*Cinis*."

The brooms disintegrated to ash in seconds.

Hazel gasped. "You just destroyed school property!"

"I just got rid of the only evidence linking us to the sled dog massacre. You're welcome." Gwen slid her wand back into its holster.

Hazel didn't respond. They'd done nothing wrong up until this point, but now they had, and guilt churned in her belly as questions swirled in her mind. Was all of this subterfuge really necessary? And why was Gwen so good at it?

Gwen zipped up her jacket and shoved her hands into her pockets. "What do you think the odds of making it back to the dorms unseen are?"

Hazel scrunched her nose. "About as good as this night turning itself around."

"Yeah, I thought so." Gwen sighed. "We'll have to go through the trees. It's our best option."

Hazel nodded.

They kept to the tree line, avoiding the north and south oval, until they made it to the grouping of pines behind the library. Hazel noted Gwen was very good at remaining hidden, as her feet made no sound and she somehow always found a shadow to walk in. How had she learned that skill?

Hazel pushed the thought away. Now was not the time to ask.

The back door of the dorm was unlocked, but they'd forgotten one thing: the RA on duty.

Gwen stopped abruptly right outside the door, and Hazel ran smack into her.

"Ow!"

"Shh!" Gwen said, whirling about. "I can't go in there looking like this. You need to get her out of there so I can get up to the room."

Hazel looked over Gwen's shoulder and grimaced. "Of course it's Victoria."

The obnoxious RA sat behind a desk near the front entrance reading a large textbook, but the rest of the common area was empty and dark as the firelight dwindled with the late hour.

The need to get this over won out. Hazel took a deep breath to steel her nerves and moved around Gwen to make her way to the desk. "Hey, Victoria?"

The curly-haired redhead looked up from her book. "Yes, Miss Thorne?"

Hazel forced a smile. She would *not* be calling Victoria by whatever her last name was. "Is the cafeteria still open? I saw some students inside, but I thought it closed at midnight. I'm hungry so I wanted to double-check. I'd love to go grab something."

Victoria snapped her book shut in alarm. "Absolutely not. Are you sure you saw someone in there? It's locked this time of night."

It was well past midnight, which was exactly why she'd used that excuse.

Hazel nodded slowly. "Yes, I'm pretty sure I saw wand light."

Apparently, those were the magic words to get Victoria to move. She stood abruptly, bid Hazel good night, and took off out the front of the dormitory.

Hazel let out a shaky laugh as the doors closed. Evidently, people who were not her dad were easy to convince.

Gwen immediately entered through the back door. She grinned

at Hazel and held up her hand for a high-five, which Hazel reciprocated proudly. Then, they took off to their dorm room in total silence.

The door hadn't yet closed when Gwen said, "I'm going to take a shower."

As dirty as Hazel felt, she knew Gwen needed it more. How would Gwen feel when she finally looked in the mirror? She wished she could comfort her, but Gwen was already closing the bathroom door before Hazel thought of anything. She wasn't good at these sorts of things.

The sound of the shower filled the air as she stripped her clothes off and tossed them into her hamper. Hazel perched on the end of her bed in her underwear, waiting for the shower to free up. When sobs sounded from the bathroom, she raced to the door and knocked. The sobbing continued, but Gwen didn't answer. Hazel chewed her lip. Should she go in?

"Are you okay?" Hazel finally asked through the door.

She heard Gwen take a shuddering breath before she answered. "I will be."

Hazel slid down the other side of the door and sat on the cold floor. How had such a great night gone so wrong?

The words her father had spewed about her cursed future rolled through her mind. Was this an omen?

"Are you okay?" Gwen called over the sound of the water.

A tear slid down Hazel's cheek as she thought about how those poor animals didn't have a future anymore. Shame and grief washed over her. How selfish she was to complain about her ruined night.

"I will be," Hazel echoed back to Gwen.

CHAPTER 15

Gwen

A grumble sounded from Gwen's stomach as she and Hazel rounded the bottom of the south oval to enter the building for Glyph Decryption. Neither of them had slept much. Instead of going to their own rooms, they'd spent the night talking, trying—and failing—to scrub the images of those poor, mutilated dogs from their minds. They'd fallen asleep on the couch and overslept, missing breakfast entirely. That was a cardinal sin in Gwen's world. She *never* skipped breakfast. This was going to be a long morning.

Following the room numbers, they found their classroom with ease. The space was square, with a massive chalkboard stretching across the far wall. A few students were already seated, voices low but animated.

"...surrounded by Knights," one girl whispered, eyes wide.

"My friend Julia said when she got back from Kodiak Brew, the whole kennel was taped off," another girl added. "She didn't see much—just a lot of blood—before they put up a visual shield spell."

Gwen and Hazel exchanged a glance as they continued down the aisle. Gwen was relieved Julia hadn't seen the full horror of it, but the mention of the Knights sent a ripple of unease down her spine. That was the last thing she needed—them poking around nearby.

Hazel led them to a pair of seats at the front of the class. The smooth, gray slate tables had drawers beneath containing a variety of erasers and colorful chalk. It was to be a hands-on class. Hazel sorted her chalk colors while Gwen doodled on the table as more students filed in.

At the strike of nine, the clock tower on campus chimed, commencing their first class. A lean, black-haired man in his thirties entered from a door at the front of the room and approached the chalkboard wall. He glided from the door on roller skates. Gwen wanted to laugh. He looked ridiculous in a buttoned vest, light-blue bow tie, and rainbow roller skates. As he approached his desk, he struggled to stick the landing and almost ended up on the floor. Snickers echoed through the class as he righted himself. The professor grinned outwardly, his fawn complexion ruddy with a blush, and straightened his glasses.

"I'm Sorcerer Miggins. I'm the glyph specialist here on campus, and I teach Glyph Decryption 1 through 4. I enjoy the unexpected, as I think it helps us to continue to think outside of the box. And that's what I'm going to challenge you to do in this class." He paused, his expression becoming more somber. "Before I continue with today's lesson," the professor began, "Chancellor Lucas asked me to address the unfortunate incident that occurred last night. For those of you who haven't heard, the school's sled dogs were slaughtered. It appears to have been an animal attack, but footprints leading away from the scene have drawn the attention of the Knights."

Gwen and Hazel exchanged weary looks.

"While I'm sure it was nothing more than a heinous encounter with a wild creature, a full investigation is underway. You'll get updates as more information becomes available."

Despite Sorcerer Miggins's reassurance, a rock settled in the pit of her stomach. Gwen knew it wasn't just an animal attack. She also knew those footprints in the forest belonged to them. They should've covered their tracks. Literally.

How could I have been so stupid? At least she'd been smart enough to burn the brooms. And Hazel's diversion had worked—no one had seen them covered in blood. That, at least, they'd done right.

"With that uncomfortable conversation behind us, let's proceed." He cleared his throat. "Glyphs were created by the fae who walked this earth long ago, with their own struggles and joys. What we may deem usual or typical should not be projected upon those who existed before us."

Gwen straightened. Miggins seemed downright sympathetic to the fae.

What are his feelings about therians?

"When interpreting glyphs, it's important to keep an open mind. Although the fae haven't walked the earth in a millennium, we still use this type of magic today. It's the root of the embedding magic on our buildings, in our wards, and even on our bodies."

Gwen thought of the tattooing tent at orientation.

"Aside from historical relevance, Glyph Decryption will also make sure you don't enlarge the wrong head, like Kennedy Joplin did five years ago." He paused when the class laughed, including Gwen and Hazel. When the class finally quieted, he continued. "Glyphs must be precise, as they can be the difference between life and death, which is where the chalk tables in front of you come in. We'll practice writing glyphs, along with deciphering them."

Gwen already knew how important glyph work was, thanks to her grandfather. The risks were precisely why he'd started her out on wands. She was excited to try more advanced work.

Sorcerer Miggins continued, "Of course, glyphs can often be a very dry subject, so I try to bring levity when I can. While I wish I could say I wore these skates to entertain you, that would be a lie. I wear them because I enjoy skating and because they allow me to dash around the room during lessons. So buckle up for the ride, students." He did a twirl on his skates, demonstrating agility none of the students would've guessed he possessed after his entrance. "Or don't," he added with a wink.

This class was going to be entertaining, if nothing else.

The girls had Alchemy 101 with Sorcerer Maduro following Glyph Decryption. She seemed like a tough yet fair teacher and Gwen was looking forward to learning more about elixirs, but she'd struggled to focus on anything but the hunger gnawing at her stomach.

Gwen was relieved to find they were some of the first in line for lunch. They grabbed their food quickly before scanning the room for a place to sit.

"Oh, there's Elodie and Nova." Hazel nodded in their direction.

Gwen smiled at their suitemates as they headed to their table. She'd had a lot of fun with them last night before the evening turned sour. She couldn't wait to ask Elodie about Amelia.

"Is anyone sitting here?" Hazel asked.

Mouth full of food, Nova simply shook her head while Elodie said, "Yes, you!"

Hazel joined Nova on her side of the table while Gwen sat next toElodie. The contrast between the two girls was obvious. Elodie radiated warmth, her sweet nature wrapping around them like sunlight. Nova reminded Gwen a bit of herself—observant and harder to read.

"So, how was last night?" Gwen elbowed Elodie playfully.

Elodie looked up, eyes brimming with tears. *Oh no.* "It was awful," she whispered. "Did you hear about the dogs? You're so lucky you left when you did and didn't have to see it. Did you get your dogs back in time?" Elodie's tears spilled over now, sliding down her cheeks.

Across the table, Hazel's eyes filled with tears, too, but Gwen didn't cry. Her father had taught her long ago how to keep the hurt hidden.

"Oh, Elodie, I'm so sorry." Gwen's stomach twisted as she thought up a lie. How could she have been so careless? "No, our dogs..." She swallowed hard, trying to keep her voice steady. "They were among the dead. We got there right after the Knights showed up." She hoped Elodie wouldn't catch the lie.

Elodie simply nodded, wiping her cheeks with the sleeve of her shirt.

Gwen let out a slow breath. "On a lighter note," she said, trying to shift the mood, "how did things go with Amelia?"

At the mention of her name, Elodie's face lit up. "Good." She sniffled. "I think she likes me."

"Do you like her?" Hazel asked.

"Of course! *And* she's an upperclassman," she added, like that fact alone made her cooler by default.

Nova, Hazel, and Gwen laughed, and just like that, the weight at the table lifted, although thoughts of the dogs still loomed in the back of Gwen's mind, and if she closed her eyes for too long, she could picture the scene clearly as if she was still there.

"What class do you have next?" Hazel asked Nova and Elodie.

"Demi-Human Diplomacy and Politics with Sorcerer Thacker. They say he's tough in class but nice to look at." Nova wiggled her eyebrows.

"That's who we have next too," Gwen said. She hoped he was as cute as Nova said. She didn't care if the class was hard or not, as history was one of the few subjects she actually enjoyed.

"I'm excited about trying to figure out what I want to do with the rest of my life," Elodie said.

"I'm going to be an embedder," Gwen said.

She'd always wanted to be an embedder, like her grandfather. Coming to Saint Elias wouldn't change that.

"What are you leaning towards, Nova?" Hazel asked.

Nova played with the food on her plate. "Maybe something in alchemy, or maybe enviro-mysticism. What about you?"

"I was thinking of going into elementalism. Fire, water, wind, and earth. The whole ordeal," Hazel said proudly.

Elodie and Nova looked like they'd swallowed a bug.

"You sure didn't come here to have fun, did you?" Elodie joked.

An uncomfortable laugh burst from Hazel. "No. I mean, yes. But ultimately I came here for an education I can't receive anywhere else."

Nova leaned forward, brow arching. "They say only five percent of students graduate with that degree. And only ten percent of *those* students master all four elements. It's a hard major."

Gwen could see the doubt creeping in on Hazel's face. *Absolutely not.*

"You were valedictorian at Elkmont," Gwen reminded her. "You'll definitely be in that five percent."

Hazel smiled back at her and straightened her shoulders.

"Wow, you were valedictorian? Gwen's right. I'm sure you have nothing to worry about." Elodie chimed in.

Hazel blushed, her smile widening at Elodie's compliment. "Well, I guess it's time for us to head to class. Gwen refuses to sit in the front for any more classes and that will be all that's left if we show up late."

"You'll want to be front and center for Sorcerer Thacker," Nova informed Gwen. "And something tells me those seats go first in his class."

Gwen gave a devilish grin. "Race ya."

Nova and Gwen looked each other in the eye before standing from the table and taking off for the door, each playfully shoving the other as they grappled to put their backpacks on.

Gwen and Nova walked-slash-ran into the amphitheater-style classroom for Demi-Human Diplomacy and Politics. Students were still trickling in. Given that this history class was a mandatory course for freshmen, nearly 500 students would fill this room shortly.

There were very few history professors at SEU. The skeptic in Gwen wondered if it was perhaps to control the narrative. She knew from the mages' history record of therians that their version of events was incredibly flawed at best and an outright lie at worst. She couldn't be the only one who knew that, and SEU couldn't have just anyone spilling the truth. Assuming they taught the truth here at all. For all she knew, they continued to spread the same misinformation she'd learned at Bathurst.

Gwen started down an empty row in the middle of the room.

"Absolutely not. I won't be able to see Sorcerer Thacker's jawline from back here," Nova said. She snagged Gwen by the wrist. "This way."

Moving to the front of the room, Gwen noticed several familiar faces from Bathurst. She did her best to avoid eye contact. None of them had been her friends, and she hated small talk.

The girls made their way to a grouping of four seats in the third row. Gwen lifted her backpack to save the seat next to her for Hazel, but a tall young man with a beautiful dark-brown complexion got there first. He had a sweet smile with perfect teeth. She'd eat him up. Normally, Gwen would've relished the chance to exchange accidental elbow grazes and knowing glances with such a good-looking guy for an hour, but Hazel needed a seat.

"Sorry, this seat's taken," Gwen said.

The guy moved down to the first row and sat in the last empty seat. It was for the best. She only had her sights on one guy—Harland. She'd searched for him all day, but he wasn't in any of her classes. The campus wasn't that big; they'd cross paths eventually. When they did, she was determined to end the interaction with her pride intact.

Gwen and Nova exchanged childhood stories while they waited for Hazel and Elodie—though Gwen fibbed more than told the truth. As the room filled, several students eyed the empty seats beside them, but Nova was quick to send them packing. Gwen simply pretended not to notice.

A loud thump sounded from the far end of the row.

Gwen and Nova both turned abruptly to find Rafe rubbing his forehead as Jordan kicked an invisible wall at the end of the aisle. The boys glared across the room, and Gwen followed their gaze. Hazel and Elodie were entering the row from the other side. Hazel's wand was aimed at the end of the row, where Jordan and Rafe now cast spells at the transparent shield blocking their way. Gwen surmised that they'd both been racing for the empty seats. The guys were much closer to the seats than the girls. If they got the shield down, they could still beat Elodie and Hazel, who were slowly scooting ass-to-face in front of the students already seated. Elodie cast a tidying spell, neatly sending everyone's bags and belongings under the students' chairs before plopping hastily in the seat next to Nova. Hazel stuck her tongue out at the boys as she sat next to Gwen.

Rafe's cheeks darkened and Jordan rolled his eyes. They picked up their backpacks from the floor and headed to the back of the auditorium. Other students in their row laughed and clapped.

Gwen took in Hazel's satisfied grin. Maybe she wasn't as nice as everyone thought after all. She couldn't wait to find out.

"I'm coming thirty minutes early next time," Elodie groused.

"What made you guys sit so close?" Hazel asked.

Gwen opened her mouth to respond, but Nova popped forward in her chair to look at Hazel with wide eyes. "I *told you* this man is delicious. I enjoy my snacks up close."

Hazel giggled, shaking her head at Nova's dramatics.

Gwen rolled her eyes. "Nova, this guy had the longest syllabus out of all our classes. Good looks can't make up for neurosis."

The organized syllabus, with its *five* attached rubrics for the upcoming reports and group project, told Gwen a couple of things about their professor, Sorcerer Thacker. First, that he was thorough. Second, that he was a sadist.

"Just wait," Nova promised.

The clock tower chimed. After a single toll, the lights in the auditorium dimmed, highlighting the small stage at the bottom of the amphitheater that had a podium with a book and a small brown vial perched atop. The last of the stragglers took their seats. Everyone quieted.

A minute passed, then another handful of minutes.

Hazel squirmed in her seat while the class hummed in small talk at the delay. Gwen leaned back in her chair, closing her eyes. She felt Nova's knees bounce on the edge of her seat while she heard the scrape of Elodie's pen across her notebook.

An echo sounded out from the stage and then another, a cadence indicating strides across the floor. The sound caused the room to quiet once more. Gwen kept her eyes closed, basking in the silence after a day full of so many people. That was, until Hazel let out a gasp before sending an elbow into Gwen's rib cage.

Gwen lurched upright. "Ow!" she strangled out, eyes now open and slitted at Hazel in exasperation.

Turning in her seat towards Gwen, Hazel tilted her head towards the stage.

Had she lost her mind?

"He hasn't even started talking yet," Gwen whispered.

Hazel tilted her head again, less subtly this time.

Is Hazel really that uptight? Gwen rolled her eyes as she looked over at the stage. Her eyes widened at the man—Sorcerer Thacker—who stood at a podium. Her heart raced at the sight of his white button-up and navy pants. Gwen knew there was a matching jacket, even though he wasn't wearing it. He was a walking contradiction with his five o'clock shadow contrasting against his professional attire. Objectively speaking, he was handsome. He looked like he'd stepped out of a magazine advertisement. But it was the glasses—those damned bewitched, gold-wired spectacles—that had Gwen sucking in a breath of pure shock. She'd never forget them, or the mortification they'd caused her.

Before he spoke, he picked up the brown vial that sat upon the podium. He removed the cork, lifted the vial to his lips, and threw his head back quickly. His throat worked swiftly to swallow the contents.

Gwen swallowed involuntarily. Watching his throat, she remembered what it looked like when he laughed. How his Adam's apple bobbed. How she'd thought about kissing it in the dark lighting of Kodiak Brew the night before the entrance exam, and then again last night. Her heart slammed in her ribs.

This cannot *be happening!*

"I'm Sorcerer Harland Thacker. I'll be teaching this course, Demi-Human Diplomacy and Politics. This is a course required by the university. As such, many of your predecessors mistook it as a fluff class. I'm standing here to tell you that this course is incredibly important."

Gwen bit back a groan. Dropping the class had just been ruled out.

"Specifically, the performance you achieve in this course will inform what electives you're permitted to take in your coming years at Saint Elias. That is, if you prove yourself a valuable addition to the university and a coven inducts you."

Gwen's eyes narrowed as she processed his words. She hated being intimidated, and that's what this speech was. But damn it, it was working. She was starting to sweat.

Never in a million years would she have guessed he was a professor—let alone her history professor. History teachers were supposed to be rotund, graying men who enjoyed smoking cigars and saying, "back in those times." She couldn't believe someone so young had made it onto the faculty of a university. This had to be a sick joke.

Then another thought occurred to her—she was clearly visible, directly in his line of sight.

Fucking Nova.

She sunk low into her seat.

The sensation of being watched pricked her senses and Gwen turned to meet Hazel's probing stare. Hazel took one look at her eyes and a small laugh escaped her lips. She slapped a hand over her mouth as she hung her head low to hide her face as her body shook with silent laughter. Gwen looked quickly back at Harland on stage, thankful to see it hadn't drawn his attention.

Gwen would kill Hazel later. She hoped to Terra that someone was taking notes because she didn't have a clue what he was saying.

Hazel continued to laugh silently, her shoulders shaking with the effort of holding it in. It was Gwen's turn to elbow Hazel in the ribs. Hazel squeaked out a sound of pain behind the hand still covering her mouth and Gwen instantly regretted her actions—not because she'd hurt Hazel, but because she was worried Harland might've heard her.

After a few moments, he still hadn't looked at her and the tension in Gwen's chest loosened—only to be replaced by something far worse: hysterical amusement. This was ridiculous. Absolutely ridiculous. *He was her teacher. He'd seen her naked. She'd tried to kiss him.*

Gwen doubled forward, pretending to rummage through her bag as a laugh bubbled up in her throat. Her eyes watered, and she scrubbed at them quickly, trying to pull herself together. She had to calm down. If she didn't, she was going to lose it completely—and draw his attention for all the wrong reasons.

Hazel leaned forward, too, and unzipped her bag. She sucked in deep breaths as she whispered, "We'll be sitting in the back from here on out," then threw something at Gwen, landing at her feet.

Gwen lifted it to find a beige baseball cap. "Thank you," she whispered.

At this, Hazel sat back, took in a deep breath, and let it out slowly once. Twice. After the third time, she grabbed her notebook and started taking notes.

Gwen put on the cap before sitting up. She kept her eyes downcast, looking at her shoes, nails, pants, anywhere but the stage.

Only minutes had passed, but Gwen hoped she hadn't missed anything important.

"In this course, we're going to be discussing the cultures, abilities, and practices of each demi-human population, beginning with their appearance and finally ending on their interactions prior to the Great War."

"Merlin's balls," Nova whispered to them. "Is he kidding?"

Gwen closed her mouth as she processed the words. At Bathurst, they'd spent one *day* discussing the Forsaken. One day! Now she was going to get an entire semester's worth of information. This was unreal.

"Your expressions tell me you're surprised to hear that this course will cover the Forsaken. Rest assured, it will, yet it will not all be thrilling. Some of it's going to make you question history as you know it. Some of it's going to make you uncomfortable."

Gwen realized he'd also be talking about therians—about her. What if he hated therians? Gwen wouldn't be able to listen to lies and slander every day—but she couldn't drop a mandatory class.

"There are texts within the walls of this university that provide rare historical accounts, information that is unavailable anywhere else in the world. The ever-present question is 'why?' Where did the texts and information go?"

Her father would say the Brecilian Knights destroyed them, just like everything else. Maybe they hadn't destroyed them all. She needed to get to the library.

"I can't answer that for you, but I can tell you there is a reason that Saint Elias University's admittance is so highly sought after and why people risk life and limb for it. This mountain holds answers that have been safeguarded for a millennium, and while speaking about the Forsaken outside of bedtime stories might be taboo, this mountain yields only to the truth. Whether you're ready or not, you'll learn it while you're here or you'll leave."

His speech was met with complete silence.

"Let's begin, shall we?" He flashed a smile, then used his wand to summon a piece of chalk and directed it to the giant chalkboard behind him. "The players," he said as the chalk wrote his words.

"Elves, therians, fae, and siphoners—each magical powerhouses in their own right. Elves were masters of the arcane, or intuitive magics, while therians were their counterparts with control of the physical form. Fae were masters of physical elements, while siphoners magically manipulated the mind."

A shiver went down Gwen's spine at the thought of being mentally manipulated. As sorry as she felt for the exterminated species, part of her was thankful *that* magic was no longer around.

"Because elves and therians rely purely on spirit magic generated from the mind or soul, people often pair them together. It also means they cast magic without a wand. While fae are capable of both spirit and earth magic, they have the ability to cast with *or* without a wand. As earth magic users, siphoners and mages both require wands to use their magic."

Luckily I'm half-mage, half-therian, so I have both, like the fae.

"In this class, we will not be using the term *Forsaken*."

Gwen arched a brow. *Where is he going with this?*

"The victors write history, and in this class, we're discussing prewar, pre-negative connotative concepts. The only title aside from their species name that will be used is demi-human, as it is the term coined to separate us all from our magic-less counterparts, homo sapiens."

The class snickered. It looked like Harland was too good to use the term mundane as well.

"Please read the first five chapters of your textbook before the next class."

Harland as her professor and five chapters in two days? This class was quickly becoming Gwen's least favorite. There was no way she was going to get through all this homework, and she couldn't exactly sleep with him now that he was her professor. Or could she?

No, I can't. Can I? Ugh, I have to get out of here!

Sorcerer Thacker spoke for a few more minutes about the expectations within the course, then dismissed them early to give them time to find their next class.

Gwen and Hazel were stuck in the middle of the aisle as 500 students bottlenecked towards the exit. They both did their best to keep their backs to the stage while the auditorium emptied. When they finally reached the end of the row, a familiar, deep timbre called out from the stage once more.

"Miss Bishop, please meet me on stage."

Gwen's blood froze in her veins. She was almost free. Could she act like she hadn't heard, or that she'd already left the room? Yes, she could.

At the end of the aisle, Gwen turned towards the door, but before she could take a step, he called, "The stage is this way."

Her spine tingled. He knew *exactly* where she was in the auditorium. Had he known the whole time?

She ducked her head in embarrassment as she turned in his direction.

Hazel grabbed her wrist and squeezed. "I'll meet you out front."

"Don't you dare leave me," Gwen demanded, but Hazel was already going.

Gwen wanted the ground to open up and swallow her. She didn't want to face this man in the light of day, especially not here, on a stage for the entire freshman class to watch. Every time she got near him, she acted like a complete fool.

She glanced around as she walked. The room wasn't full anymore —nearly empty, in fact. Regardless, it was the principle of the matter. They could have this conversation in a less crowded place, for Salem's sake.

I can't believe he didn't tell me he was a professor. My professor!

Frustration fueled her courage, and she lifted her head. She'd dealt with meaner, deadlier men than him her whole life. She refused to be intimidated. Her pride had taken a hit, but he was the one who should be embarrassed.

Straightening her shoulders and letting her hips sway, she walked up the small set of stairs to reach the stage. She planted her feet in a haughty stance on the top step and let herself meet his gaze.

He watched her with an expression she couldn't read, arms crossed and a glint in his eyes. "Over here, Miss Bishop."

She clenched her teeth as she reluctantly moved forward. Her eyes trained on him. She couldn't resist taking him in, from his professional attire to his jawline covered in shadow. She imagined what it would be like to unbutton his shirt and run her hands up his chest.

Inappropriate, Gwen.

The chip on her shoulder lightened as she stopped before him.

"Congratulations on passing the entrance exam, Miss Bishop."

A bit of pride surged through Gwen at the compliment, but then she remembered he wasn't just some cute guy she'd sat next to naked in a bar, or flirted with to scare off a bunch of girls. He was her professor.

"I can't believe you didn't tell me!" she tried to whisper, but failed.

He glanced around. "This isn't the best time nor place for this."

Gwen took a deep breath, bringing the boil of anger down to a simmer of annoyance. "You are my *professor*. You should have told me."

"I think we should discuss this during my office hours."

She scoffed before putting a hand on her hip. He was trying her patience and underestimating how over this moment she was.

"If that's not what you want to discuss, why did you call me up here?"

"The administration has assigned me as your faculty advisor. We'll be working closely together these next two years. Four, if you're chosen by a coven."

No. Fucking. Way. His words slammed into Gwen like a physical blow. She couldn't spend the next four years spending one-on-one time with him.

Not when her body betrayed her every time she was around him. The last few days, she hadn't been able to think of anything *but* him.

What it would feel like to close the space between them. What his hands might do if he ever let them linger.

It hurt more than she cared to admit, wanting someone who'd never given her any reason to believe he wanted her back—except for that one moment. That one stupid moment when his arm had wrapped around her waist like it belonged there. Her thoughts spiraled, latching on to that memory like it meant something.

CHAPTER 16

Gwen

"What do you mean, you're my advisor? Isn't that the role of someone in admissions?" Gwen blurted out.

"Unfortunately, the university doesn't have enough staff to have one set advisor. The chancellor assigns all incoming students to faculty members to help guide them depending on their skill set." Sorcerer Thacker rested his arm on the podium with infuriating composure.

Gwen was spiraling. *This has to be some kind of cruel joke.* Of all the professors, of course, it had to be the infuriatingly attractive man she'd practically offered herself to. The man she wanted to offer herself to *now*. How in the hell was Gwen supposed to maintain any semblance of professionalism after their previous encounters?

"How long have you known?" Gwen demanded, her voice trembling slightly.

"Known what?" His brow furrowed in what she suspected was a practiced display of innocence.

"That you're my advisor? Did you know the other night at the bar?" Gwen's cheeks burned as she scanned the lingering students. "When I helped you with those girls?"

His face reddened. A flicker of something—amusement? Guilt?—danced in his eyes.

He knew! The smug bastard knew!

He'd stood there, letting her dig herself deeper into a pit of awkwardness. He'd had countless opportunities to tell her, and he'd remained silent. Had he been internally laughing as she'd made a fool of herself? He'd let her flirt shamelessly, let her try to kiss him, without a single word of warning.

Then a dangerous thought coiled in her mind.

What if that *was why he'd pulled away? What if he actually* wanted *me to kiss him but stopped himself because he's my professor and my advisor?*

The heat of that possibility flared briefly before Gwen reluctantly extinguished it.

No! Absolutely not! Get that delusional fantasy out of your head.

He was her professor. End of story.

A wave of nausea washed over her. She desperately wanted to rewind time, to wake up from this bizarre, humiliating nightmare. What were the actual statistical chances of having him assigned as her advisor? Surely incredibly low. A cold, creeping suspicion took root. *Did he orchestrate this? Did he request to be assigned to me?*

A tingle shot down her spine, a mix of dread and a forbidden flicker of something else.

"Why were you paired with me?"

Harland—no, *Sorcerer Thacker*—studied her with an unnerving intensity. "You're a talented and promising scholar according to your transcripts." His tone suggested he was still reserving judgment. Gwen's scowl deepened. "The pairings are made after the exam based on a student's demonstrated strengths and areas for growth. The chancellor believes your aptitude in advanced historical concepts would benefit from a more tailored guidance."

Gwen's internal alarm bells were screaming. *Tailored guidance?*

Or tailored supervision of the student who almost jumped his bones? She wasn't buying it.

"This assignment was completely random? It has nothing to do with our previous interactions?" she pressed, needing a firm, unequivocal denial.

"I assure you, Miss Bishop, I had absolutely no say in the decision," he said. His arms were now crossed over his chest, a subtle barrier between them.

The truth rang in his words, and that stung more than she wanted it to. It was the appropriate answer. He shouldn't have requested her, but a foolish part of her had briefly hoped he'd wanted to be closer to her.

This whole situation was a colossal mess.

She sighed. "Now what?"

"We'll meet once a month to go over your courses and discuss how things are going. I'm here to guide you through your studies." His professional demeanor was a stark contrast to their previous encounters.

Harland studied her. For the briefest, most agonizing second, his gaze drifted downwards towards her lips, and Gwen's breath hitched. Imagined or not, her pulse hammered against her ribs. She felt an urge to step closer, to touch him one more time, to get the kiss she wanted. Maybe he wanted the same thing.

No, stop it.

Gwen pushed the thought away. She had to put up walls—they both did.

"I'll see you during my office hours next week for our first meeting," he said in a clipped and direct tone, then turned back to the podium, shuffling the papers there with an air of finality.

Clearly dismissed, and desperate to put physical distance between them, Gwen turned her back on him and made her way off the stage and down the aisle to the exit. The entire time, the hairs on her neck stood on end and she was sure he watched her, but she refused to allow herself to look back. When she walked out of the door, she breathed a sigh of relief at being out of his line of sight.

Hazel was nowhere to be found in the halls, but Gwen found her quickly on the steps outside. She was speaking with a mage with chin-length dark hair and at least a dozen visible piercings who Gwen didn't recognize. Not caring that she was interrupting, Gwen marched up to Hazel, pulled her by the wrist, and said, "We need to talk."

"Good to see you again! Talk to you later, Sorcerer Roth!" Hazel said quickly over her shoulder as Gwen dragged her toward the building exit. "You're flushed. What did he want?" Hazel asked, concern lacing her words.

Gwen debated on what to say. What would Hazel think? She knew their history. Knew Gwen liked him. Would she think she wanted this? *Did* she want this?

"He wanted to tell me he's my advisor," Gwen said as they walked away from the history building.

Hazel's mouth popped open. "Oh."

Gwen stopped short. "What?"

"That mage I was speaking with is Sorcerer Jude Roth. They teach Practical Curses. They're going to be my faculty advisor."

Gwen groaned, sliding a hand down her face as they walked across the oval. "Why the fuck couldn't they have been *my* faculty advisor?"

"I'm sure you could switch if you talked to the chancellor," Hazel said.

Hazel was right—she *should* switch. Not only had Harland hidden the important information from her, letting her make a huge fool of herself, but he was her professor and advisor. And yet... she didn't want to switch. As infuriating as this entire situation was, the thought of giving up the chance to spend one-on-one time with him left a hollow ache in her chest. It was reckless. It was a terrible idea. But the truth settled in her gut like a weight: she didn't care. She wanted to be near him. Even if it made everything worse.

When Gwen didn't answer right away, Hazel tilted her head. "You don't want to switch, do you?"

"Come on, let's go home," Gwen said.

"I wouldn't want to switch either." Hazel smiled at her. "Oh, Nova is going to die! Please let me tell her."

Gwen laughed, feeling a bit of joy this time. "Not a chance. It's my one bright spot in all of this."

Hazel twirled in the enchanted sunlight that had been hidden behind clouds earlier in the day with her arms held out. Gwen laughed as students walked around Hazel in the grass so they didn't get smacked in the face with her outstretched hands.

"How are you not enjoying this?" Hazel asked, walking backwards to look at Gwen.

"I hate the heat. You better learn elementalism fast and turn the thermostat back down in this mountain," Gwen griped.

"Never," Hazel countered, still basking in the sun.

When they got to their room, Hazel quickly fell asleep on the couch while Gwen read her course book for Demi-Human Diplomacy and Politics. She was determined to be the top student in Harland's class.

By the time Hazel woke from her nap, it was time for dinner. They didn't spot any familiar faces in the overcrowded dining hall, but luckily, their usual booth was empty, and they sat right away. Well, it wasn't luck. Gwen had hexed it, but she wasn't going to tell Hazel that. She'd probably make her remove it, and honestly, Gwen needed a few comforts in life that no one made her feel guilty about.

The girls ate and chatted about their day, keeping their voices low when they circled back to Harland.

"Did you call your mom yet?"

Gwen jerked at the familiar voice, praying internally that he hadn't heard their conversation. "Klaus!" The last thing she needed was a lecture from him. She stood and hugged her cousin. "No, but I sent a letter to her yesterday. You know she hates scrying."

Klaus shooed her back into the booth and then sat next to her. "Well, your mom's driving everyone nuts at home. Being an empty nester doesn't suit her."

Gwen didn't appreciate the guilt trip and elbowed him in the ribs to let him know. "I tried to stay home, remember? You all forced me out."

Ignoring her comment, Klaus said, "How was your first day?"

Gwen grimaced dramatically. She didn't want to talk about today—specifically about one singular professor or his class—and knowing Klaus, he'd ferret out information she did not want him to have. "It was fine. You remember my friend Hazel?"

"Yes, of course. Good to see you again. I know she's a handful, but please keep my cousin out of trouble," Klaus said, as he turned to look at Hazel.

Hazel opened her mouth to respond, but a booming voice cut her off.

"Klaus, we've got a meeting in ten minutes."

Gwen looked up to see Logan. The content smile slid from her face. She'd almost forgotten the two men were in the same coven. Now she'd have to share her only link to home with this asshole standing before her.

Klaus flashed a proud smile. "Logan, you know my—"

"*Now*, Klaus," Logan said, locking eyes with Gwen.

"See you later," Klaus said to Gwen, then added, "Bye Hazel." Klaus got up from the table, but stopped short as Logan cleared his throat, clearly displeased with Klaus's pace. "I almost forgot to tell you—the first ruzo game of the season is on Saturday. Alterion plays and we're the best, so you don't want to miss it."

Hazel nodded profusely.

"Yeah, we'll be there," Gwen said.

"Great! I'll see you both later." Klaus knocked the wood with his fist as he backed away from the table.

Logan still stood at the foot of the table, staring at Gwen. In the therian world, making eye contact was a way to assert dominance. No way was she letting this mage have any semblance of dominance over her. He'd broken eye contact first yesterday, and she'd make sure he did again today.

Logan stepped in closer after another moment, and Gwen knew he was trying to intimidate her with his size. What Logan didn't know was that Gwen grew up playing these sorts of games with actual alphas, and not just young men who wished they were.

Instead of cowering, Gwen leaned forward. She could see death in Logan's eyes and knew she'd truly pressed a button. *What's this guy's problem?* With the way he was acting, you'd think *she'd* broken his wand.

Gwen held firm, knowing Logan had a meeting in ten minutes and he'd need to leave soon. She'd win by default.

Hazel let out a very polite dry cough.

Logan blinked, then flashed a sharp threat of teeth and left the dining hall. Had his teeth been that pointed before?

"That was weird." Hazel broke through Gwen's thoughts. "That Logan guy doesn't seem to be over the *accident*. Your cousin is nice, though. You're lucky to have him here."

Gwen blinked rapidly, clearing her mind of the standoff before looking at Hazel. "Klaus? Yeah, I am. I just wonder if he'll have much time for me being in a coven."

"There you are!" Jordan called as he approached. Slamming his dinner tray down next to Gwen, he shot Hazel a dramatically scathing look. "We need to talk about your behavior today during history. You're supposed to use your powers for good, not evil!"

Rafe sat his tray down beside Hazel. "He's just mad he didn't think of it first."

Hazel blushed slightly, but she looked pleased at the compliment as she continued eating.

Gwen took another bite of her pizza. A gong sounded in her mind and she nearly gagged on a pepperoni. Her head reverberated from the inside out. The feeling was wholly unnatural, overwhelmingly uncomfortable. Gwen pushed on her temples, afraid they might explode. Hazel whimpered, and Gwen could barely manage opening her eyes under the pressure of the sound.

"What the fuck?" Jordan cried out, voice laced in pain.

Then it stopped.

Gwen opened her eyes to see everyone at her table clutching their heads, their faces twisted in discomfort. Every student in the room seemed to feel the same as they lowered their hands and looked around cautiously.

At the front of the dining hall, Chancellor Lucas stood with her hands crossed at her waist, waiting expectantly. "Please lend me your full attention, scholars."

"She could've asked first before making our brains bleed out of our ears," Jordan whispered.

Gwen glowered at the chancellor. There were a million ways to gain attention that had to be better than that. As effective? Probably not, but definitely less likely to cause a mutiny. Gwen had no idea what kind of spell the chancellor had used, but she doubted it had ever been used on her or she wouldn't be going around performing it on unsuspecting students.

The room was completely silent. Not a scrape of utensil nor a smack of food could be heard as the chancellor eyed them.

"By now, you have all heard about the sled dog incident on Saturday night. As a result, we are implementing a curfew to ensure the safety of staff and scholars while we seek out the truth and deal with the perpetrators." As the chancellor said "truth," her eyes landed on Hazel, then slid slowly to Gwen.

She can't know, right? No, there's no way. No one saw us.

Gwen clenched her hands, thankful Chancellor Lucas couldn't see them under the table as she continued.

"Weeknight curfew is ten p.m., and weekend curfew is midnight. All we ask is that you be back within the mountain by then. We find these to be very reasonable curfews that simply allow us to rest knowing all mages are safe and accounted for once we lay down at night."

Gwen rolled her eyes. She didn't need a curfew, and she definitely didn't need to be babysat. She wasn't afraid of whatever had done this—it should be afraid of her. The image of the dogs' broken bodies flashed in her mind, and something deep in her chest twisted. They hadn't deserved that. They were just animals, trusting and defenseless. The rage that rose up in her was sharp and blinding. If she ever crossed paths with the thing that killed those dogs, she'd make it pay. Part of her hoped she ran into it.

"Any scholars who break this curfew will be rendered a severe punishment befitting of their negligence." The chancellor gave the crowd one last sweeping glance. "That is all. Good night." She tipped her head and then left.

When the door closed behind her, the hall erupted into complaints and curses.

"This has to be a joke!" someone shouted from the table behind them. Several others nearby said, "Yeah!"

Another person said, "We're mages. Nothing out in those woods is dangerous enough to stop us." Some students nodded, while others didn't look so sure.

Gwen knew the ones speaking up hadn't been there that night, hadn't seen the blood, bones, and fur in lifeless piles upon the ground, otherwise they wouldn't be speaking so confidently—so ignorantly.

If only she could tell them they all needed to be afraid—unless they could turn into a merciless predator like her. But she couldn't tell them. Hazel and Gwen couldn't let *anyone* know what they'd seen. They had to take that heartbreaking secret with them to the grave.

Jordan slapped his hands on the table. "Well, that blows. I was planning on opening a male strip club in town, but I guess that idea's a wash now."

CHAPTER 17

Hazel

"When you said you wanted to explore today, this isn't what I thought you had in mind," Gwen whined.

Hazel readjusted her bag, avoiding the fact that she'd intentionally left out the details of her planned adventure. The second she'd arrived on campus, she'd been too busy with this new life to think about the unsettling questions surrounding her mother's abilities. But last night, she'd dreamt of the library again and had woken up feeling guilty. She was closer to answers than ever before, yet she hadn't visited the library. What if her mother was waiting for her and she'd just been out partying all this time?

Students were given Fridays off for their studies, but with it being the first week of the semester, there wasn't much—aside from reading—to be done yet. The open day in her schedule had given Hazel the perfect opportunity to let the question consume her once more: Were her dreams simply dreams, or did she have the Sight?

There was only one way to know for sure, and it was to find those exact locations and see if she'd truly Seen things here in Alaska. The alternative—that she just had an overactive imagination—was entirely possible, but Hazel needed to know.

Which was why she and Gwen were now trudging up the steps of the library. Now was as good a time as any to look around for the aisle and window that Hazel could recognize in her sleep—literally—before the library was flooded with students later in the semester.

They entered under the characteristic pointed archway that adorned each building at SEU. The ceilings above were vaulted with intricate ribbing somehow more complex than any of the other buildings they'd seen on campus so far. Dark mahogany panels, shelves, chairs, and tables filled the space. The woodwork was nearly as detailed as the ceilings.

Despite it being the first week, each table they approached was occupied, which was fine because Hazel had yet to see the window from her dream and was happy to have a reason to keep searching. They made their way to the second floor.

"Looks like this is the one," Gwen said, pointing to an empty table partially secluded in the corner.

Hazel nodded in agreement, and the girls sat their belongings on the table. Then came the tricky part. Nervousness overcame Hazel as she looked about, pulling at her shirt as she tried to think of a way to ditch Gwen politely to go in search of her aisle. Luckily, Gwen did the hard work for her.

"I'm going to go look for the history section. I'll meet you back here in a bit." Gwen moved toward the information desk as she spoke.

The knot in Hazel's chest loosened. She smiled as she said, "Sounds good."

Hazel took off down an unfamiliar aisle before Gwen could change her mind. She made good time covering the sections of the second floor since she knew exactly what to look for. Walking down the center of the third floor past couches and lounge chairs, she spotted stained-glass windows and her heart beat against her ribs, but the aisles weren't right, and neither were the images in the panes.

Or maybe it's me that's not right.

Doubt sliced through her. Perhaps it hadn't been a vision at all. Perhaps she just had good deductive skills about what this university would look like. Had she blown up her life, her family, for a silly dream?

Fear of being wrong overwhelmed her, but she pushed through and continued her search.

When she reached the fourth floor, a familiar glow emanated from the aisles on her right. She approached the first and saw there was a stained-glass window, but the aisle wasn't familiar. The books were brightly colored, nothing like the muted autumn tones she'd seen in her dreams. She walked past three more aisles, and then she saw it—a dark-blue bound tome with silver foiling upon its spine. She approached it slowly, holding her breath. Was this it?

Hazel reached out a trembling hand and traced the raised lettering. *Conquering the Arcane.* If her dreams were truly visions, she'd find a water stain on the back cover. Letting out a shaky sigh, she tugged at the book, pulling it to the very edge of the shelf. A gasp tore from her lips and she nearly dropped the book when she saw the dark-edged spot.

"Terra take me." The words tumbled from her lips as her knees shook with the weight of what she was seeing. The tiny spot flipped her entire world on its axis, but still, part of her refused to believe just yet—she needed more evidence.

She glanced toward the window at the end of the aisle as she returned the book to the shelf. The stained glass depicted an unnamed battle on its vivid, colorful panes. Rain poured from dark skies at the top of the window, streaking downward in jagged lines of gray and blue. On either side of the window frame, magic users cast spells at each other. In the center, swords clashed in midair, their blades ablaze with fire that refused to die—unfazed by the storm pouring down around them.

Hazel walked towards the stained glass and tested herself along the way, naming title after title upon the shelves before their spines were actually legible to her. Each time, she held her breath until the title came into view, then let out a burst of air when she'd predicted the words correctly.

This shouldn't be possible.

Unless I have the Sight.

It sounded absurd. Who would believe her? So few people in the world possessed the skill of foresight that many people scoffed at it. Even Gwen, who'd grown up in a mage community, didn't believe in tarot reading. The chance of finding a truly gifted mage was slim to none.

As she reached the end of the aisle, Hazel closed her eyes and willed her heart to calm. There was one final test: to look out the window and see if the view matched the one from her dreams.

Hazel stopped when she reached the short light beams that reflected the colors of the stained-glass window on the floor.

What if it doesn't?

Part of her worried about how silly she would feel, how regretful she might be if she'd been fooling herself this whole time.

But what if it does?

She didn't know if she was ready for that reality either, but the not knowing was killing her slowly.

Just do it.

The window was too opaque to see through clearly thanks to the staining and melting processes, but when she approached the glass and peered through a light-colored spot, Hazel could see it—that same hazy outline of the campus below from her dreams. It was identical—except now she knew the markers. Poe Hall across the oval. The tall trees of the quad casting shade. The entrance to the ruzo field in the far corner.

I have the Sight.

She hadn't been dreaming all these months. She'd been Seeing, a power so rare that her teachers at Elkmont had insisted they'd never met anyone who could do it. The idea sent a surge of exhilaration through her, followed by a wave of panic.

If she had the Sight, then maybe her father had been telling the truth. Her mom had it too—and she'd seen something so horrible about Hazel that she'd left.

Mom.

Her mother had been in each of her visions. Surely that meant her mother would be here soon.

This was it. This was where she was going to see her mother.

But doubt crept in once more. Who knew how long she'd have to wait to see her mother here? Days? Weeks? An eternity?

Hazel sagged to the ground in front of the window. The questions and information flooding her mind were too much. She and her mother had the Sight, and her mother had Seen *something.* What was in the vision that made her leave? What was Hazel going to do now?

She didn't know how long she stayed in that spot, allowing reality to cascade over her, the questions crushing her under their weight and stealing her breath. The Sight. Was it a gift or a curse?

The whisper of paper against a metal shelf jolted Hazel. She wasn't alone anymore. Or maybe she never had been, simply too consumed by her search and overwhelmed by the truth. Hazel stood and pulled herself away from the window.

A thunderous *thwack* of a book slamming shut sounded from the next aisle over.

Hazel's heart leapt into her throat. She spun, every nerve ending now on high alert. She stepped slowly to look down the aisle. "Hello?"

No answer.

A low, familiar hum crept through the air, too quiet for Hazel to locate, but she recognized it as the tune of a familiar lullaby.

The edge of a deep-purple cloak fluttered in the air as a mage with long black hair slipped around the shelf at the far end of the aisle.

Hazel knew that cloak, and the hair that was identical to hers.

"Wait!" She ran the length of the aisle, her heart pounding so hard it began to beat in her ears. She emerged in the center of the floor, but she stood alone.

A chill went down her spine.

"Mom?" Hazel asked tentatively, her voice cracking over the word as if she'd forgotten how to utter it.

Silence.

Hazel took off once again, sure of what she'd seen: her mother. She raced past the aisles, turning to look down each of them. Disappointment hit her again and again with every vacant aisle she discovered. Hazel paused at the last aisle. There were no doors, nor stairwells on this side of the floor. Where had she gone?

Maybe she went the other way.

Hazel spun on her heel and covered the entire floor once more.

A form appeared in the shaded alcove of the stairwell.

This was it. She was going to see her mother.

But the woman who emerged from the stairs had mahogany hair pulled back in a loose bun while her light-russet skin was blotchy with anger. The beautifully polished woman stood with her fists on her hips in a cowl skirt that complemented her tall curves nicely. She was definitely not Hazel's mother.

"Miss, you're certainly old enough to know there is no running in a library!"

"Yes, I'm so sorry. I thought I saw someone—"

The librarian scowled. "I can assure you, you did not. We have capacity spells on each floor of the library. No one has been on this floor for the last two hours but you."

The woman's words felt like a knife to Hazel's stomach.

Hazel shook her head. "That can't be right. I saw someone." She paused as she fought to find an explanation. "Perhaps it was another librarian?"

The librarian was shaking her head before Hazel had finished the utterance. "I'm the only librarian on duty today."

Hazel felt like she was losing her mind. She'd seen someone. *Didn't I?*

"Are there any librarians here named Cora?" she asked, grasping at straws, at anything that might mean she wasn't going insane.

The librarian studied her face. Whatever she saw there made the woman's posture soften. "No, dear, I'm afraid not."

"What about a professor, or support staff?" Hazel asked, though it sounded more like a plea.

The librarian shook her head.

A rock settled into Hazel's stomach as tears sprang to her eyes. Had she imagined it?

"O-okay. Thank you," Hazel said, looking at the librarian's name tag, "Sorcerer Girard. I'm sorry for running. It won't happen again."

Sorcerer Girard gave Hazel a soft smile and nodded before heading back down the stairwell.

Great, now the librarian thinks I'm crazy.

Maybe I am *crazy.*

Hazel spared one more glance around the floor, but no one was there. She could take the silence and the stillness no longer, so she left to search for Gwen. She found her on the third floor, sitting in the middle of an aisle with books strewn about her. Hazel moved to join her when Sorcerer Girard came into view from behind Gwen. She loomed over Gwen, the same annoyed expression on her face.

Hazel paused at the end of the aisle and pretended to look at a book—she didn't need another run-in with the librarian so soon.

"Miss, this is not your dorm room. Such a mess is unacceptable and, furthermore, a danger to our books," Sorcerer Girard scolded.

Gwen didn't bother to look up. "These books are enchanted, ma'am. The floor isn't going to hurt them. I could light one on fire and it wouldn't leave a mark."

Why did it sound like she'd tried?

Sorcerer Girard huffed.

Gwen flashed her an impossibly sweet smile that Hazel knew was fake. "I promise to clean up."

“I expect them all to be put back in their proper places,” Sorcerer Girard said as she stalked off.

“You didn’t have anything useful anyway,” Gwen remarked.

As the librarian walked past Hazel, Gwen finally looked up, her gaze locking onto Hazel’s. Her eyes widened and her face went white. “Hazel,” Gwen said, in a tone that suggested she’d forgotten Hazel had come to the library with her.

“Wow, you’ve been busy. Let me help you clean these up,” Hazel said, ignoring her friend’s odd behavior.

She bent to help Gwen clean up, but before her fingers could even brush the spines, Gwen drew her wand. She levitated the books out of Hazel’s reach.

“No, thanks. I have a system.” Gwen stood, her body now positioned to obscure the scattered books completely. She took a step closer to Hazel, then another, effectively backing Hazel out of the narrow aisle. Gwen offered a tight, insincere smile that didn’t reach her eyes. “I’ve got it covered. I’ll meet you back at the table.”

Hazel’s brows furrowed in confusion. “I don’t—”

“No, thanks.” Gwen’s clipped words brooked no argument.

Hazel nodded slowly, a prickle of unease settling in. Gwen clearly did not want her help. More accurately, she did not want Hazel to see the books. Every instinct in Hazel screamed to peek over Gwen’s shoulder, to catch a glimpse of the titles, but Gwen’s tense posture and the stubborn set of her jaw told Hazel that wouldn’t go over well.

Hazel desperately wanted to share what she’d learned, what she’d seen, but the tension on Gwen’s face kept her silent, and perhaps the fear that she really was losing her mind. If she was going crazy, she needed to know, but part of her wanted to hold on to the possibility of seeing her mother, or being as special as she’d always hoped to be a little longer. Her memory of Gwen’s open disbelief of foresight during orientation sealed her decision, and she said nothing, deciding to keep her secret close to her chest until she had more answers.

"Okay. I'll see you back at the table then." Hazel gave an awkward little wave, glancing up and memorizing the aisle number as she walked away.

Gwen

Blood pounded in Gwen's ears. Had Hazel seen the books? Gwen was positive she'd tried looking, but she was only a mage. Her eyes weren't like Gwen's, so surely she hadn't been able to actually read any of the titles before Gwen had stopped her.

Annoyance buzzed in Gwen's veins. Hazel was too nosy for her own good, but in reality, it was Gwen's fault. She'd had no business making such a mess looking for information on her specific therian condition in public. She'd have to be more discreet in the future.

Actually, it was that damn librarian's fault for drawing attention to Gwen in the first place.

Gwen bit back a growl as she twisted her wand and returned the books to their correct homes. She'd pulled nearly twenty books, all with very telling titles, such as *Therianism*, *The History of Shifting*, and more that seemed promising. Feras had been in the index of each, but they'd all said the same old bullshit.

...Feras are uncontrollable menaces to society...

...Feras are best kept in captivity...

...The fera condition is irreversible...

Blah fucking blah. What did they know? From what Gwen could tell, none of them had even tried. *They're fucking cowards, not experts.*

Gwen needed proof—solid information about failed attempts, experiments, and case studies, but the books only vaguely alluded to such things. However, that was enough to tell her the information had to exist.

Where the fuck is it?

The frustration with lack of information had finally overcome her when the librarian had found her. It was unfortunate that Hazel had stumbled upon them, but Gwen could deal with it. Hazel wouldn't push the clear boundary Gwen had set, and if she did, Gwen would just place another.

As the last book finally slid into place, Gwen sighed. Maybe she'd been looking in the wrong section. Maybe feras were considered an ailment or condition rather than part of therian lore. The librarian would be the perfect person to ask, but she'd pissed Gwen off with her bullshit about hurting the books, so that option was out. Plus, she couldn't risk her asking why she wanted that information.

Gwen found Hazel at a table, head down and reading. She plopped into the chair across from her and opened her book bag to go over the list of books she'd checked once more. She propped it up so Hazel couldn't read the words upside down.

Hazel didn't look up from the book she read, or even acknowledge Gwen. Tension seeded the air and Gwen wondered if it was her words or what Hazel had seen of the books that kept her quiet.

The question gnawed at Gwen over the next minute, to the point that she had to test the waters to determine the source of this discomfort so she could do damage control. If it was because of her sharp words, she'd fix it quickly. If it was because Hazel had seen more than she should have, well, Gwen didn't know what she'd do. Play it off somehow?

Gwen cleared her throat, and Hazel's eyes lifted slowly.

Yeah, she's definitely bothered.

"Find anything interesting?" Gwen asked.

Hazel's eyes went back to the book as she nodded. "Yes, more than I thought possible."

Gwen squinted at her. *Was that a dig? Is she alluding to the books I had?*

Silence blanketed the table once more.

Gwen sorted through options of how to bring up the books, to explain them away, but it was Hazel who broke the silence first.

"I think I saw my mom."

Gwen's mouth popped open in surprise. That was the last thing Gwen had expected her to say. "What?" Gwen knew Hazel's mother had run off years ago. Had she been hiding at SEU this whole time?

Hazel set down her book before continuing, "I saw someone upstairs watching me in the stacks, and I think it was her."

Gwen's brows drew together. "Why wouldn't she say something?"

Hazel sighed. "I don't know. Maybe she didn't expect to see me. Or maybe she got scared."

It sounded like Hazel was grasping at straws, and Gwen wanted to put her friend at ease, but none of this made any sense.

"What did she do when you saw her?"

Hazel looked down and away, pink tinging her cheeks. "She ran."

Gwen leaned forward. "That's fucked up. Surely it wasn't her."

The wet gleam in Hazel's eyes conveyed she knew just how fucked up it was. She sucked in a breath and shrugged. "Maybe."

If it had been her mother, she was grade-A fucking bitch in Gwen's opinion. Hazel had told her about her family's situation. At the time, Gwen had thought Hazel's mom was a victim, but now she wasn't so sure.

Hazel opened the book in front of her once more and studied the pages again. Gwen took it as a sign to drop the subject, which was fine with her.

The knot of tension in her chest loosened as she accepted that Hazel had bigger things on her mind than the books Gwen had been looking at.

CHAPTER 18

Hazel

Anticipation buzzed in the evening air and the stadium smelled faintly of hot dogs and kettle corn. The crowd's excited chatter echoed through the stands as Hazel and Gwen weaved through the throng of students, scanning for familiar faces. They were late. Really late. Hazel didn't want to miss the start of her very first ruzo game. Her excitement edged into urgency as she picked up the pace, grabbing Gwen's wrist and tugging her along.

They'd spent the entire afternoon getting ready—painting black A's on their cheeks and layering on their team pride in the form of sleek black jerseys with *ALTERION* and the number *40* stitched in silver across the back. Gwen had insisted they show up supporting her cousin properly, which apparently meant full glam. Hazel hadn't argued; she was happy to have a distraction from her mother. She'd gone to the library again this morning and found nothing.

Gwen had styled her own hair in two high space buns and braided Hazel's into matching pigtails. Between the eyeliner, glitter, outfit debates, and last-minute touch-ups, the pre-game prep had practically turned into its own event. Now the game was minutes from starting, and they were still hustling up the stadium steps, eyes peeled for Rafe and Jordan.

Hazel spotted them about halfway up the stands—Jordan waving frantically, Rafe leaning on the railing with a lazy grin that made her heart skip a beat.

"There they are!" Hazel said, pulling Gwen toward the seats they'd saved.

As they climbed, Hazel noticed Rafe and Jordan were decked out in Circen colors—deep-emerald jerseys with gold accents. Jordan even sported a foam hoof on one hand like it was a badge of honor. Hazel glanced at Gwen, suddenly nervous.

Is this going to start a fight?

Gwen came to a halt in the row, her eyes narrowing as she took in their outfits. Jordan slid aside to let them pass, but Gwen didn't move. Hazel held her breath.

"You traitors," Gwen said flatly.

Rafe's grin widened. "Of course you're wearing Alterion colors—and you even dragged Hazel into it. Poor thing doesn't know she's backing the wrong team."

Hazel felt a challenge stir inside of her, cementing her loyalty to Alterion. Rafe was going to eat his words.

Gwen scoffed as she slid into the seat beside Jordan. "Please. I didn't drag her anywhere. Hazel has taste. Unlike some people."

Hazel smiled at Gwen's comment as she eased into the open seat next to Rafe.

Yeah, I have taste!

"Circen's defense is top of their league," Rafe said, resting his arms behind his head.

"Yeah, well, Alterion's offense *is* the league." Gwen smirked.

Hazel exchanged a glance with Jordan, both of them wisely staying quiet. This was clearly not their moment.

"You want to bet on it?" Rafe asked, cocking a brow.

"Obviously," Gwen countered.

They shook on it before settling back into their seats, the spark of competition still flickering between them.

"Count us in too, right, Hazel?" Jordan said, nudging her arm.

"Sure," Hazel said automatically, then blinked. "Wait, what are we betting on?" She tried to sound casual, but a tiny knot of worry twisted in her stomach. She didn't have any money, mundane or magical, to spare.

Rafe and Jordan shared a devilish grin.

"Losers have to sing at next week's karaoke night at Kodiak Brew," Rafe said.

"In costume," Jordan added, grinning wider.

Hazel groaned, but she couldn't help laughing. "You're evil."

"Do you want to back out?" Jordan shot back.

Hazel and Gwen both shook their heads no. The boys were going down.

With the bet made and the playful banter fading into the background, Hazel finally turned her attention to the field. It was unlike anything she'd ever seen. Laid out in four quadrants like a giant chessboard, the field alternated between deep forest-green and bright-emerald turf. The two lighter quadrants sat diagonally across from each other, each with a wide end zone at the far edge painted boldly in Circen green, flanked by silver alicorns in flight. The darker quadrants belonged to Alterion, the name scrawled in jagged black lettering across each end zone, flanked by snorting, red-eyed minotaurs. Players jogged laps on the field to warm up while the stands filled rapidly with excited students in team colors.

The energy in the air was electric—laughing fans, thudding footsteps, and the low rumble of music pulsing from the speakers. Hazel's legs were still buzzing from the sprint through the stands and maybe from sitting so close to Rafe, but the rest of her settled into the moment.

A vendor to their left shouted over the music, selling glittering headbands adorned with a single centered, white horn or twin curved black horns. Another peddled small vials of shimmering elixirs in house colors. One student tossed back a black-glass vial, and Hazel watched in awe as a pair of obsidian horns sprouted from his forehead, followed by a pronounced snout.

Wow! A transmutation elixir. Hazel had never seen such a realistic one before. Students at Elkmont weren't advanced enough; their transmutations were typically too small or misshapen.

Before Hazel could get a better look, a Circen fan in emerald green elbowed past the Alterion fan and snatched a glowing green elixir from the vendor's tray. He downed it in one go. Right before their eyes, a pointed white horn erupted from his skull, spiraling upward at least a foot from his forehead.

Hazel blinked in amazement. "Impressive."

Images of her dad and brother's reactions to such a sight surfaced for a brief moment, uninvited, but she shoved them away. She didn't want to think about either of them today—not while she was experiencing something they'd both tried to keep from her.

A shout of anger snapped Hazel out of her thoughts just in time to see the Alterion fan square up. Within seconds, the students were nose to nose—literally. Horns clashed as they locked onto each other, pushing and grunting, their feet scraping against the stone stadium. The surrounding crowd erupted into cheers and chants, egging them on. She barely had time to register what was happening before the vendor clapped his hands and muttered something under his breath. A burst of shimmering green and black smoke exploded between the two students, forcing them apart like repelling magnets.

"Enough!" the vendor barked, eyes narrowed. "Buy the potions. Don't *be* the potions."

The crowd groaned in disappointment, but the students backed off, laughing as they retreated.

"Wow, does this happen at every game?" Hazel asked.

Rafe leaned forward, eyeing Hazel. "Wait a second. Is this your first ruzo game?"

Hazel hesitated, then gave a small, sheepish nod. "Technically yes."

“You’ve never been to a game?” Rafe practically yelled for the world to hear.

“What?” Gwen and Jordan demanded at the same time.

They all stared at her wide-eyed.

Hazel felt the eyes of the nearby crowd on her and lowered her head. Everyone was staring.

Great. Now they all know what a sheltered freak I was.

She shrugged, doing her best to act like it wasn’t an oddity that’d she’d missed out on one of high school’s most traditional experiences. Besides, she wasn’t totally clueless. While her dad had forbidden her from going to a game, he’d never said she couldn’t learn about it. She’d read articles in the Elkmont student newspaper and in the *Casting Quarterly* when she was able to talk her dad into purchasing it.

Rafe’s hand brushed her arm gently, grounding her. His voice dropped a little. “Honestly, it’s cool we get to experience your first game with you.”

Hazel nodded, grateful her friends weren’t teasing her. Still, her smile wavered. The relief was real, but so was the awkwardness creeping in around the edges. Rafe must have noticed.

“Do you know how it works?” he asked. His tone was softer now, like he didn’t want to embarrass her further.

Hazel nodded quickly. “I’ve read about it.” She didn’t add that it had only been a handful of times or that her dad had scoffed every time she asked for a new issue.

“You’re going to love it. Trust me.”

Hazel smiled and glanced across the field, spotting Klaus, already lined up with the rest of his team. The number forty stretched across his back, but his name was nowhere to be found.

“Why aren’t there any names on the jerseys?” she asked, leaning into Rafe so she could hear his answer. Her shoulder grazed his and butterflies took flight in her stomach when neither of them pulled away.

“Players only wear numbers,” Rafe explained. “It’s meant to keep their magical abilities a secret. Not everyone wants the world knowing they can brew an elixir powerful enough to turn themselves into a beast or lift a boulder with one hand."

That makes sense.

He leaned in a little. "It also helps protect them off the field. If someone gets seriously hurt during a game, there's no easy way to track the player down and retaliate."

"What about a roster?" Hazel asked.

Rafe shook his head. "Top secret, only the umpires and the team get to see it."

Hazel nodded, still processing everything he'd said, when something on the field caught her eye. A few players standing near the side box had faces that looked wrong. Not masked exactly, but blurred—as if someone had smudged their features with a paintbrush.

She squinted. "Why do some of them look like that? Their faces are all blank."

"Ah—casters," Rafe said, following her gaze. "They bewitch their features to appear as blank slates during the game. It's another layer of protection. No one wants to be held accountable for the curses and hexes they sling from the side box."

Hazel nodded slowly, but her eyes drifted back toward Klaus. His face was fully visible as he stood in position, a picture of confidence in his black jersey. She and Gwen wore his number proudly on their backs. She hadn't thought much about it earlier, but now it felt a little like announcing his identity to the whole stadium. Still, it wasn't like his face was hidden. And from the way Klaus carried himself, he didn't seem like the type to worry about being recognized.

"Of course, rumors still fly, and people figure out who's who anyway," he added with a smirk. "Unless they're casters or can transmutate."

Before Hazel's next question could leave her lips, the crowd shot to their feet, erupting in a deafening roar. The stadium shook beneath their seats as if the earth was opening up to swallow them whole. Hazel lurched upright, fight-or-flight flaring—but when she glanced at Rafe, Gwen, and Jordan, their faces weren't alarmed. Just excited. Then she felt it—the rhythm. The tremors weren't chaotic; they pulsed in patterns through her sneakers, steady and powerful. Not an earthquake. *Reverb.*

She scanned the stadium. Across the field, a wave of students in green and black stomped in perfect unison, shouting low and deep from their chests, but the words were too guttural to make out. On the opposite side, students in green clapped their hands and chanted back, creating a thundering call-and-response.

Rafe leaned in, cupping his hand over his mouth to be heard. "Here's where the real fun of ruzo comes in. The transmutated players are coming out now." His breath brushed her ear, sending goosebumps down her arms.

Did he notice?

She forced herself not to look and kept her focus on the field instead.

From the mouth of the Circen runout tunnel, a mountain lion sprang onto the field, muscles rippling beneath golden fur. The crowd erupted in fresh cheers. Hazel's breath caught, but only for a second. She'd seen one once, growing up in Arkansas. This one was close, but not quite right. The head was too large, the nose too long. The gait lacked the effortless grace she remembered. It was easy to spot the inconsistencies between the player and a real mountain lion. Disappointment tugged at her. She'd expected better. Transmutation spells of that complexity were difficult. They required years of training, precision, and focus. She'd assumed a SEU coven member would be capable of mastering it. Apparently not.

When the mountain lion reached the closest light-green square belonging to Circen, the crowd erupted. Pausing, he looked back over a shoulder and snapped his jaw toward a group of students covered in green body paint. People in the crowd laughed as the mountain lion returned his attention to the field and made his way to the mutual zone. Within the mutual zone, four umpires stood in bright yellow. The big cat kept its distance, sitting just inside the circle's border.

After the mountain lion sat, the noise of the crowd reached deafening levels. Hazel searched for the cause of the noise, wondering what had come out of the locker room that could produce a more visceral response than a man modified into a mountain lion. She saw nothing outside of the Circen tunnel, so she panned to the tunnel with the Alterion sign across the field.

A cheetah slipped silently from the Alterion tunnel, low to the ground and fluid in its movements. It was enormous—easily standing as high as a tall man's hip—and like the mountain lion before it, something about it wasn't quite right. The only thing they seemed to get right was the fur. Orange and yellow hues gleamed between the black rosettes covering its pelt. Ignoring the crowd, its eyes stayed trained on the center of the field. Instead of picking up the pace on its way to the mutual zone, it slowed, crouching lower and lower to the ground. Eventually, it halted behind a huddled group of players, shoulders bunching in tension. It was oblivious to the Alterion players around it, and they ignored it, too, as if they knew better than to draw attention to themselves.

What's it doing?

Just when Hazel felt she couldn't take the anticipation any longer, the crowd sucked in a collective breath as the cheetah sprang forward across the dark-green rectangle, taking one, two, three strides before it reached the center of the mutual zone, landing inches from the mountain lion.

Hazel's hand shot out, grabbing Rafe's arm without thinking. The mountain lion let out a snarling hiss, and she instinctively dug her fingers into his skin, too focused to let go. Then the cheetah sat—calm and unbothered—lowering into a perfect sphinx position before casually licking one of its front paws, as if the other cat didn't exist.

Laughter rippled through the stands and heat rushed to Hazel's face as she noticed her fingers still gripping Rafe's arm. Feeling self-conscious, she let go and brushed her hands against her thighs.

Circen fans in green began to sit. The reverb, which had died down after the initial introduction of the transmutated players, returned with force. Alterion fans began to stomp in unison once more as they focused on the locker room tunnel.

Stomp. Stomp. Stomp.

Stomp. Stomp. Stomp.

Stomp. Stomp. Stomp

Other students without coven allegiance began to join in. The deep-chest chant from earlier began once again, but this time, Hazel could hear it. In sync with the rhythm of the stomping, they called,

"Bring. The grizzly. Out!"

"Bring. The grizzly. Out!"

"Bring. The grizzly. Out!"

Hazel's eyes widened. She and Gwen shared a curious look. Grizzlies were massive. It would take twice the magic to transmute into one than it had for the cheetah and mountain lion. Was there really someone at SEU who could pull it off?

Rafe, along with Jordan, stomped and cheered. The chant was infectious.

A loud, incredulous laugh erupted from Hazel's chest, seeing her friends feel so excited and free. *This* was what her father said was dangerous? She didn't know whether to scream with the overload of her senses, the pure adrenaline of excitement, or the sadness that she'd missed out on this for so long for no real reason. Gwen grabbed her hand and squeezed it twice before releasing. It was truly incredible to feel part of something so big.

In that moment, Hazel swore to herself she wouldn't be deprived of the things that made life fun ever again.

She threw her head back and lifted her foot, bringing it down against the metal floor. "Bring." The force of the contact zinged up her leg. "The grizzly." Her voice broke with the force of her scream. "Out!"

A deafening roar swept across the stadium, making the chant die in their throats. Another roar rang out from the locker room tunnel before a bear charged out. Hazel's breath hitched at the sight of it.

While the coloration, formation, and pelt were exact replicas, this bear was larger than even the famed grizzlies of Alaska preparing for hibernation. But the size alone wasn't what left the stadium speechless. It moved like lightning, quicker than any animal that size should be able to move. Most bears in pursuit still appeared to be ambling about, the bulkiness of them large and cumbersome, while this bear finessed its way across the field, by and around the players, moving so quickly they didn't even have time to try to move out of the way. When it reached the mutual zone, the bear approached the cheetah before standing on its hind legs and emitting another deafening roar. It killed Hazel that she might never know who they were.

Hazel was addicted. She couldn't look away. The grizzly walked towards the umpires, along with the other modifiers. She watched its movement and mannerisms in awe as it passed the tests of sanity performed by the umpires done to ensure the players' and crowd's safety.

"That was insane!" Jordan said as he reached over Hazel's head to high-five Rafe. "I've never wanted to rip my shirt off out of excitement before," he joked. "I still might."

"Rip. The shirt. Off," Gwen chanted while stomping her feet in time.

Jordan made his eyebrows dance saucily while Hazel and Rafe laughed.

The umpires lifted their wands together, each emitting a shrill whistle from the tip to signify it was time to start. The stadium *erupted.* Cheers, stomps, and magical noisemakers burst into life all around Hazel, the stands pulsing with excitement as the players jogged, or in some cases bounded, to their respective sidelines.

A ranger from each team stepped into the mutual zone on opposite sides of the central circle. Hazel watched closely. According to

Rafe, rangers were responsible for catching and running the ball and typically served as team captains. Alterion's prime ranger was Klaus. Tall and broad-shouldered, he moved with easy confidence, his dark curls falling loosely in his face and his black jersey clinging to his frame. Hazel couldn't help but feel a flicker of pride seeing him out there, representing Alterion.

"Come on, Klaus!" Gwen shouted beside her, cupping her hands around her mouth.

Hazel grinned and let out a loud whistle in support.

Circen's prime ranger stood opposite him: a beige-skinned young man with a shaved head and a spattering of acne across his cheeks. He was slightly shorter than Klaus, but thicker-built, especially around the quads and biceps.

Hazel chewed her lip in anticipation as one of the umpires placed the ruzo ball directly in the center of the mutual zone. He walked away backwards, hand in the air, palm facing out. When he reached the out-of-bounds line, just beyond the caster side box, he lowered his raised hand and flicked his wand, releasing a sharp, piercing whistle into the air. The moment the sound hit, both rangers sprang forward. Klaus was a blur. He reached the ball first—easily—snatching it up and launching it to a teammate in one fluid motion, all before the Circen ranger even closed half the distance. Hazel's eyes widened. He made it look effortless.

Hazel grinned, turning to Rafe. "Oh, you're *so* going to lose."

"Not a chance," Rafe shot back, but there was a flicker of something behind his smirk—nerves. Hazel caught it, but didn't say a word. She just sat back and smiled wider.

Gwen

"Did you see that? That bear just put the mountain lion's entire head in its mouth!" Hazel exclaimed.

The entire Alterion side of the stadium erupted as their team scored again, the stands shaking with cheers.

"I saw," Gwen replied once the noise had died down, her eyes never leaving the field.

Of course she had. She'd been laser-focused on that grizzly since the game started. Normally, she loathed transmutation, as most therians did. It stung to watch inferior magic be celebrated for mimicking something she had to spend her life hiding. Mages paraded around in beastly forms, pretending to be something they weren't, and the world applauded. But when a real predator had walked among them, they had called them dangerous.

The truth was the Brecilian Knights feared therians because therians were better—stronger and faster than them. Even with their elixirs and enhancements, those animals they conjured would never heal the way she could. Never smell scents from miles away or see clearly in total darkness.

Transmutated beasts were barely more than illusions—convincing at first glance but hollow. Still, she couldn't deny how well the bear transmutation had been done. Its size, its weight, the way it moved—it looked and acted like the real thing. It was the kind of spell work she usually rolled her eyes at, but not today. Today, it was impressive. The mountain lion, though? A disgrace.

Gwen's stomach gave a loud, protesting growl. One of the downsides of being a therian—aside from living in constant fear of discovery—was constantly being hungry. Her metabolism burned through food like wildfire, and sitting still this long had made it worse. As if the universe wanted to taunt her, a student walked by balancing a tray of cheesy fries and a buttered broomstick roll. Gwen's mouth watered. She raised her wand slightly, considering a casual summoning charm.

"Don't even think about it," Hazel said without looking away from the field.

Gwen laughed. "Fine. I'm going to the concession stand like a law-abiding mage." She stood and dusted off her jersey. "Anyone want anything?"

"Me!" Hazel said quickly. "I can go with you—"

"This is the first foul shot," Rafe cut in, eyes glued to the aerials now rising into position on their brooms.

Hazel hesitated, torn, and Gwen caught the shift in her face.

"I can bring you something back," Gwen offered, nudging Hazel's shoulder lightly.

Hazel looked relieved. "That would be great—if you really don't mind."

"I don't mind at all. Be right back," Gwen promised.

Hazel was already focused again, her gaze tracking the players as they lined up midair.

As Gwen started to step away, she glanced back at Jordan. "Aren't you going to offer to help me?"

He raised an eyebrow. "Sorry. Chivalry is dead, my friend."

"Apparently," she muttered, rolling her eyes.

"Bring me back a drink?" he added with a grin.

"You're lucky I'm feeling generous. Rafe?" Gwen asked, glancing over her shoulder.

"I'll take a drink if you're offering," he replied, eyes still on the field.

With a dramatic sigh, Gwen turned and made her way down the steps, weaving through the rows of students. She disappeared under the stadium, heading toward the glowing signs of the concession stands. The hum of the crowd above dulled to a distant rumble as she moved through the cool tunnel beneath the bleachers, the scent of buttered bread and something fried growing stronger with each step.

A sudden shout from the stadium made Gwen whip her head around, instinctively turning back for a glimpse of the field as she rounded a corner, and slammed straight into someone.

"Sor—"

She froze as she looked up, heart thudding. He was already

staring down at her, that familiar smirk tugging at the corner of his mouth.

"Are you alright?" Harland asked. His voice felt like a caress against her ear, and she fought off a shiver.

His hands rested on her shoulders, steadying her. Desire flooded her veins with his touch. His dark-brown eyes looked deeply into hers, warming her from the inside out. A small smile tilted up the corner of his lip and she thought her knees might melt. It had been almost a week since they'd been so close and it still wasn't enough for her. She wanted him to pull her closer. She wanted to touch him.

All her annoyance with him hiding the fact that he was her teacher and advisor was gone. She liked him, even when she knew she shouldn't. She did not understand how this man had such a hold on her, yet she felt it in her bones.

"I'm fine!" she said too quickly, then just stared at him like an idiot.

"Enjoy the game, Miss Bishop." He winked at her as he released her and then headed to the men's room behind her.

The moment his touch left her skin, she longed for him, needed him. She didn't know why he had such a hold on her, but he did. The desire to follow him overcame her and she headed straight into the men's room. The bathroom was empty except for the two of them. She opened her mouth and then closed it unsure of what to even say. He was approaching the urinal when he realized she was there.

"Gwendolyn?" His eyes were wide as he turned back to her. The look of shock on his face brought her back to reality.

Oh goddess, what am I doing?

"I—I thought," Gwen started, but all words and excuses fled her. What could she say that wouldn't sound insane? When another second passed and nothing came to her, she ran out of the men's restroom. The burn of embarrassment stung her face. Why did she keep doing everything wrong around him?

Salem burn me! Please don't follow me. Please don't follow me.

"Miss Bishop, wait!" His voice was so close, he was clearly following her.

Fuck!

Gwen stopped. Running was going to make her look even crazier. At least these few seconds had given her time to think of a plan.

Lie. Lie. Lie.

Gwen turned around and flashed him a small, stiff smile. "Sorry, I thought it was the women's restroom," she said with a laugh.

Could he tell how fake it was? Gwen hoped not.

His brow furrowed as he searched her eyes. "You thought I went into the women's restroom?"

Damn it, why can't he just let me have this?

Harland stared at her, waiting for a response that she couldn't give him. She had no idea what had come over her. This man was turning her into a fool.

She shrugged, spun on her heel, and prepared to flee again. Maybe she could find a hole to crawl into and die.

I can't believe I did that! What's wrong with me?

She didn't get far. He grabbed her arm, pulling her back to face him. All her desire for him came rushing back.

"You've got to stop doing that!" Gwen whined as she looked at the floor, too ashamed to look him in the eyes.

"What?" Harland asked, his voice deep and low as he took a step closer.

"Touching me."

He dropped her arm. Cold loneliness filled her from the loss of his warmth.

"Is that what you really want?" His voice came out rougher than she'd ever heard it.

She looked up at him. In his eyes, she saw a feeling she knew all too well. There was only one word to describe it: ravenous. But he blinked, and the look was gone. Calm interest had taken its place.

Had it even been there? Did I imagine it?

She wanted to rip her hair out. Of course, she didn't want him to stop touching her. But she couldn't keep wanting him unless she knew for certain he wanted her too.

"What do *you* want?" Gwen asked.

"I—"

Before he could answer, a familiar voice echoed toward them.

"Sorcerer Thacker, Miss Bishop! How lovely it is to run into you today!" Sorcerer Miggins said.

Thank Terra! She was spared from having to explain her spontaneous insanity.

"Sorcerer Miggins," Harland said curtly, looking away from Gwen and taking a small step back.

"How are you enjoying the game?" Miggins looked in Gwen's direction. He wore a black button-up shirt and a green tie. He'd obviously decided not to pick sides for today's game.

Are all men so damn indecisive?

"It's been a formidable match," Gwen said, flashing him a polite smile.

She looked back at Harland for any hints of an answer to her previous question, but his expression was unreadable as he avoided her gaze. How could he turn it off so easily? She'd been so stupid. There was no way he felt the same way about her.

"I should actually get back to my friends," Gwen added. "Enjoy the rest of the game." She refused to look back at Harland, even when she felt his gaze on her once more.

"Yes, you too, Miss Bishop," Sorcerer Miggins chirped happily, completely unaware of what he'd interrupted.

"See you on Monday, Miss Bishop," Harland said.

The promise in his words sent a chill down her spine as she walked away.

CHAPTER 19

Hazel

The crowd cheered. Rafe's strong arms wrapped around Hazel, and her feet started to lift off the floor. *What if he can't lift me?* The thought barely formed before he hoisted her into the air effortlessly. His biceps flexed as he spun her around, and Hazel laughed, breathless. When he finally set her down, his cheeks were flushed—but his breathing was steady as he joined the chant with the rest of the crowd. Her heart raced, not from the win of the game but from him. She should have kissed him that night at the bar. Maybe tonight he'd try again.

"Alterion!" he shouted with a grin.

They had won with mere seconds to spare. What a game. Hazel still couldn't believe Rafe had switched sides at halftime, shrugging and saying, "You both are too intense. I might as well cheer with the loudest team."

She was glad he had. Having him chant along beside her had made it even more exciting, and she was glad Rafe was there to explain the plays. Gwen had been zero help. She hadn't paid any attention after coming back from getting snacks. As the chanting faded and the stands began to empty, students shuffled toward the exits, bodies pressed together like sardines.

Hazel nudged Rafe with her elbow and gave him a cheeky smile. "You know, even though you switched sides, you still lost the bet, right?"

Rafe groaned but grinned. "Yeah, yeah."

"I can't wait to see you pay up next week," she teased.

A faint blush crept into his cheeks. "Just don't make the costume too terrible."

"I promise nothing," she said sweetly, already plotting.

He laughed, then reached out and took her hand, gently tugging her through the crowd. "Hold on to me."

Hazel's heart did a little stutter. His hand was warm, steady—and she liked the way it felt way too much.

I wonder what they'd feel like on my skin. Excitement fluttered in her chest, mixed with something that made her a little breathless. She didn't let go until they arrived outside the archway to Coventry, the area where the coven houses sat on campus. As they stood beneath the entrance, the group slowed to make a plan for the evening.

"Alright," Rafe said, glancing at each of them. "Which house are we hitting first?"

"Alterion," Gwen offered immediately. "We're already wearing the jerseys."

Hazel nodded in agreement.

Jordan made a face. "Ugh, let's skip Circen. No one wants to go to a loser party."

Gwen raised a brow. "Says the loser."

"I didn't lose, you got lucky." Jordan pointed accusingly at Gwen, though there wasn't much heat behind it.

Hazel rolled her eyes. "It's our only shot to see inside Circen and Alterion this year. We're going to both—at least for a bit."

Once per semester, following the first and last ruzo games, two covens opened their doors for non-members. Although all non-members were welcome, it was mainly used as a recruitment tool for freshmen.

“We can start with Circen,” Rafe offered, always the diplomat, “and if it sucks, we bail and hit Alterion. Deal?”

Hazel appreciated that Rafe had stepped in to help the group come to an agreement. Gwen sighed dramatically, but she didn’t argue.

The atmosphere changed immediately as they stepped under the archway and walked deeper into Coventry. The dark-gray stones of the arch and the houses beyond looked older, more primitive than the rest of campus. The stones beneath Hazel’s feet were uneven, worn smooth by generations. Dust clung to the cracks, and lichen crept up the walls, swallowing the edges of the structures. The coven houses flanked the road ahead, which were less grand than the towering halls behind them but distinctive in their peculiar designs. These weren’t uniform structures. Each home bore layers of additions, mismatched and uneven, as if the architects had gone from mastering Gothic design to merely imitating it over time.

Hazel glanced from one house to the next, taking in the chimneys, spires, and pointed gables that jutted out at strange angles. A tall astronomy tower pierced the sky from the center of the house on the right. Across from it, a miniature castle stood with its low defensive wall repeating in intervals along the top, a fortress tucked among the dwellings. But nothing caught her attention quite like the house ahead.

Rafe slowed beside her, eyes narrowing. “What happened there?”

The house’s windows were black, hollow. Even in the darkness, its crumbling form was easy to make out, bathed in an eerie glow. Bioluminescent mushrooms spilled from the shattered window panes and open doorways, creeping over the roofline and suffocating the overgrown flower beds below. The mushrooms were identical to the ones Hazel had seen on their journey through the mines. The yard was a field of glowing spores, their tendrils stretching toward the neighboring houses. Though most of the other homes had only a few on their lawns, the spread had begun.

"It must be the coven that closed. Mutari, I think," Hazel said.

"Why did they close?" Rafe asked.

"I don't know," Hazel answered. "That wasn't in the pamphlet."

"Mutari was the coven that memorialized siphoner magic. Apparently, there were rumors that siphoning magic had resurfaced during the Salem Trials, and even 700 years couldn't get rid of their fear after the Great War."

They all stared at Gwen. Hazel hadn't expected to get a history lesson from her this evening, but she was here for it.

"What?" Gwen shrugged. "Klaus told me last Christmas. He knows how much I love history."

Hazel frowned as she observed the house, all of its memories wiped out. The story made her think of her own lack of information about the abilities she'd possibly inherited from her mother. She would give anything for answers.

"You're bumming me out, Gwendolyn," Jordan complained.

Hazel agreed this conversation was putting a damper on her post-game bliss, but it was fascinating to learn the lore SEU kept locked up tight.

Gwen rolled her eyes. "You asked, I answered. If the truth bums you out, that's on you."

"Technically, these two asked," Jordan said, knocking both Hazel and Rafe in the head.

Hazel led the group past the abandoned house, toward Circen in the back right corner. Her memorization of the school map was going to come in handy tonight.

"This party is going to be more depressing than Gwen's story," Jordan whined.

"It wasn't a story, Jordan. It's history," Gwen said defensively.

"Yeah, yeah," Jordan replied, brushing her off. As they approached the house, he said, "At least the drinks will be flowing while everyone drowns their sorrows."

There was so much glee in his voice, it made Hazel snort.

Circen's yard overflowed with plant life, leading up to a three-story house of weathered stone with steep gables and arched windows. Hazel stopped and leaned forward to smell a blossom on the rose bushes lining the walkway, but she was quickly pulled away when Gwen grabbed her arm and led her towards the front porch.

Ivy clung to the exterior walls, its twisting vines creeping toward the glass greenhouse attached to the right side of the house, where the faint glow of lanterns illuminated the tangle of plants inside. Hazel could stay out in this yard for hours, studying the plants.

Maybe this *is the coven for me.*

Laughter and music spilled from the open doorway. Jordan couldn't have been more wrong; there was nothing depressing about this party. Inside the doorway, two students stood behind a small table, passing out drinks with easy smiles.

"Specialty cocktail or a shot?" one asked, holding out a tray filled with tiny glass cauldrons, each one a different color.

Gwen immediately plucked a larger, deep-purple one off the tray, which Hazel guessed was a specialty cocktail. Hazel's eyes lingered over the tray before she selected a large, soft rose-pink cauldron. It was cool and delicate in her hand, and as she brought it closer, a familiar sweet and floral scent hit her. The fragrance instantly transported her to summers back home, plucking honeysuckles from the vine.

"Is there alcohol in this?" Hazel asked. She'd never actually had any before, despite her attempt to get some at Kodiak Brew. Would it be better or worse than the mage elixirs she'd already had?

"It's better," Jordan promised, draping his arm around Hazel's neck. "It's bumble juice."

Hazel had no idea what that was, but before she could ask, Jordan plucked a tiny green shot from the tray and raised it in the air.

Rafe lifted his own small red cauldron with a grin. "May the best of our past!" Rafe called out.

"Be the worst of our futures!" they all chorused back before clinking their glasses together and tipping back their drinks.

Hazel's body hummed as soon as the liquid touched her tongue. The smile on Gwen's face told her she'd liked it just as much. The guys reached for second shots while the girls sipped more on their drinks.

After a few more sips, Hazel started to feel warm and fuzzy, and her body began to vibrate on the inside. She needed to move, to let it out.

Music pulsed in the room as Hazel grabbed Gwen's arm and pulled her to the makeshift dance floor in the center. The girls danced to lilting notes that were anything but mainstream, yet somehow dove deep into Hazel's bones. With each drink she took, she felt increasingly light. She never wanted to leave.

With her head thrown back in laughter, Hazel noticed the guys chatting up some girls on the side of the room. She felt a ping of jealousy towards the girl Rafe was talking to. After last Saturday at Kodiak Brew, she knew what Rafe's hands felt like on her hips as they danced and how his muscles felt pressed against her back. While she'd caved into her anxiety and backed away, Hazel highly doubted these girls would. And she hated that knowledge.

She'd told herself that waiting was the right decision, yet here, with the elixir flowing through her, she started to wonder if she'd made the right choice.

"They should serve this at Kodiak Brew," Gwen said, bringing Hazel's attention back to the dance floor. Gwen pointed at her nearly empty cup.

"Another one!" Hazel yelled over the music, then tipped her head back, draining the last bit.

Gwen nodded, eyes wide in agreement.

Hazel led the way to the bar at the back of the first floor.

"Can we get another of the house specialty?" Hazel hiccuped as she smiled at the green-cloaked young woman serving drinks behind the bar.

The bartender eyed Hazel and then Gwen as she swung Hazel's hand back and forth like a child. "How many have you had?"

"Just one." Hazel didn't mention just that one had left her feeling like she was dancing on clouds.

The mage arched a brow as she looked at Gwen. "And your friend?"

Hazel looked beside her to find Gwen studying the ceiling, smiling like a loon. Gwen seemed to be feeling the elixir a bit more than herself.

Hazel elbowed her.

"Ow," Gwen pouted.

"She's only had one too."

Hazel knew, from a faraway place in her brain, that Gwen was acting very out of character, but the music was too good and the elixir too strong for her to worry. Yes, Hazel should definitely try to join Circen next year.

The mage hesitated after pouring them a second drink. "Maybe take your time with these."

Hazel and Gwen nodded profusely as they joyfully accepted the cups.

The girls went back to the packed dance floor and continued their fun. It wasn't long before two guys joined them. One came up and wrapped his arm around Gwen, while the other gave Hazel a little spin, which left her facing him. A giggle escaped her as she placed her hands on his shoulders for balance.

College is fun.

She closed her eyes and lost herself to the music and the elixir's effects.

Then a sharp burst of pain shot through the top of her foot.

"Ow!" Hazel yelped.

She opened her eyes to find a man looming over her. Hazel instantly recognized the green eyes and loose black curls, frame that was somewhere north of six feet four inches, and peekaboo neck tattoos—Dane Bellamy.

His eyes filled with hatred as he stared at Hazel. "Sorry about that, *Hateful.* Didn't see you there."

Why didn't she believe him? Oh yeah, he was a dick.

"With your nose so high up in the air, I'm sure you didn't," Hazel answered.

Gwen snorted next to her. Subtly, Hazel shifted her weight to her left foot, so he wouldn't see how badly he'd hurt her.

Dane leaned in closer to her, stopping just shy of touching her before he whispered, "This place is filthy. You can't blame me for confusing you with a piece of trash." He gave Hazel a cruel smile and then turned his back, walking to the other side of the room.

"We'll see who's trash," she mumbled under her breath as she grabbed her wand. Dane had picked the wrong night to mess with her.

With a flick of her wrist, she aimed at the back of Dane's head as he walked away and cast, "*Foetor*."

A collective repulsed gasp rang out from those around Dane as they inhaled the foul odor Hazel had hexed upon him. Partygoers held their noses and some covered them with their shirts. Another second passed, and Gwen did the same. The ripe smell of animal excrement and day-old food permeated the air.

Gwen looked at Hazel wide-eyed, then threw her head back and laughed. Hazel smirked back at her. Dane Bellamy needed to be brought down a peg.

"Hazel Thorne!" Gwen said. "I am so proud."

Hazel grinned. Without the elixir, she knew she wouldn't have done such a thing so publicly. Oh well, she'd worry about it tomorrow. She wasn't going to let Dane harsh her buzz.

"How long before he notices?" Gwen asked.

Dane whirled around, rage painted across his features.

"I'd say he just did," Hazel snickered.

Gwen yanked Hazel to the right, and they disappeared behind a large group of upperclassmen. He'd have to be an idiot to take the chance on trying to cast back at them in this crowd. Dane was hotheaded, not dumb.

Hazel clenched Gwen's hand once in silent reassurance. Turning back, she found Dane looking for them in the crowd. They wouldn't be able to stay concealed forever.

"We should probably get out of here," Hazel said. She had no regrets about the spell, but she was sad to say goodbye to her drink as she set the remainder down on a table nearby.

"The boys can catch up later." Gwen said, before she tossed back the rest of her drink and set the empty cup next to Hazel's.

Hazel didn't argue about finding the boys. She couldn't risk running into Dane while trying to look for them.

Once outside, she let the satisfaction with what she'd done sink in. She was nice, but it didn't mean she had to let people treat her badly.

"What spell did you cast?" Gwen asked.

"It's a family spell. We use it to manipulate livestock and pests on the farm. The smell can last up to twenty-four hours, but Dane will have it off in two, talented bastard that he is."

As much as Hazel loathed to admit it, Dane was a very gifted mage. He always managed to find a counterspell quicker than Hazel would like.

Gwen looked down at Hazel's foot. "Are you okay?"

"Yeah, it didn't hurt that bad. I honestly don't think he meant to do it." Hazel was sure if he'd meant to hurt her, the damage would be much worse. "Have you ever had a Dane? Ya know, a bully?"

Gwen was silent for a moment. "No. Well, not at school. My dad was always tough on me. He was obsessed with magic. He used to make me do drills when I was younger. It could last anywhere from hours to days."

"Wow. My dad never taught me *anything* about magic," Hazel said softly.

"I can see how it would seem cool at this moment, but I can assure you, it wasn't."

I guess magic doesn't make a difference. Dads will be dicks no matter what.

"I'm sorry he put you through that," Hazel added. She was glad Gwen had told her. Secrets like that couldn't be easy to bear.

When Gwen said nothing, Hazel changed the subject.

"Dane's been a jerk to me since ninth grade. I wish I knew what I'd done to make him hate me so much," Hazel confessed.

"Hazel—" Gwen started.

"Were you really going to leave without us?" Jordan shouted from behind them, as he and Rafe ran to catch up.

"Sorry, we had to make a quick exit," Hazel explained.

The four of them started down the cobblestone road once more. They'd only gone a few more steps when Rafe pointed across the road. "What's that?"

Hazel squinted, trying to see such a far distance in the dark. A large arch overgrown with vines sat across from Circen's own walkway. While Circen's gates were barred and thrown open, these were solid wood and closed.

"I don't know. It's not on the map," Hazel said. She changed course to approach the gate and the others followed suit.

How odd. There was no mention of it in the pamphlet she got at the start of school.

"It's not another closed coven house?" Rafe asked.

Hazel inspected the solid wooden gate and wished she could see what was on the otherside. Two golden dragons adorned the handles. Seeing them made Hazel think of the exam. Was there any connection?

"I'm not sure. I only know of the one." Gwen touched one of the dragon's tails.

"Boo!" Jordan yelled.

Both girls jumped, and Hazel let out a startled squeak.

Gwen spun around and punched Jordan in the arm. "You ass!" Gwen said. "Let's go, Hazel!"

Hazel suppressed a snort. *Note to self: don't scare Gwen.*

Gwen grabbed Hazel's arm and took off at a fast pace. Hazel's buzz was completely gone now, but she was still having fun. This was what it was like to have friends, to go to parties. She'd been missing out.

"Aw, don't be mad, Gwendolyn," Jordan called, trailing behind them.

"Hey, guys, I think the gate is op—"

"Not going to work, Rafe!" Gwen cut him off, pulling Hazel along with her towards Alterion.

Gwen

The Alterion house reminded Gwen of a medieval castle, which she loved. The gargoyles, on the other hand, were creeping her out. She felt a call to this house, probably since it was the coven that memorialized her ancestors. She desperately wanted to feel a connection with them. It was the same reason she was so obsessed with history. If she knew more about therians, she'd know more about herself.

She was also excited to see Klaus. He'd be happy after their win, and she hoped that joy was contagious to the rest of his coven members. Specifically Logan.

The group entered through the large wooden doors to find more students dancing.

"Let's go dance!" Jordan shouted over the music.

Rafe took Hazel's hand and led her towards the dance floor. Gwen met her eyes and gave her a huge smile, and Hazel blushed. They made a cute couple.

Nova appeared in the crowd. "We've been looking everywhere for you guys!" she said as Elodie walked up beside her. They were wearing Alterion colors, as well, and Gwen was pleased to see they'd rooted for the same team at the game.

“Hazel made us go to Circen first,” Jordan said, rolling his eyes. He made his way over to Nova and pulled her towards him to dance.

Elodie reached for Gwen, but she shook her head. “Amelia is right over there.” Gwen pointed a few feet away, where Amelia was dancing with her friends. When she saw Elodie, she waved her over.

“What about you?” Elodie asked hesitantly.

“I’m going to go find Klaus.”

She did want to find her cousin, but she also wanted to explore. Alone. Tonight was the only chance she’d have to look around this year.

“Want me to go with you?” Hazel asked, as Rafe spun her in a circle.

“No, I’ll be right back.”

Gwen walked away from the dance floor and moved through the packed room. It was hard to get between people and she was feeling impatient without Circen’s elixir in her veins. If she didn’t get across this room quickly, she was going to start using elbows. As she approached the far side of the space, she felt a shove in the back and fell face-first into a large light-bronze bear statue.

“Fucking ow!” Gwen yelped as she whirled about to see who’d shoved her.

No one met her gaze.

Coward.

She turned back to the statue to see if there were any therian references, but the plaque simply read *American Grizzly*. The bear itself stood on its hind legs, front paws stretched forward and mouth open in a roar. It reminded her of the grizzly from the ruzo game.

Could the bear have actually been a therian?

She glanced around the room, wondering who the bear had been, but none of the students screamed, “Hey, look at me! I’m a bear!” She’d ask Klaus who it was when she found him.

A few students were coming and going from a hallway to the left, and she headed for it, hoping she wouldn’t look suspicious. She made her way down the hall, discreetly testing door handles along the way. The first one she opened was clearly an Alterion member's room—a boy's from the looks of it. No decor, just clothes on the floor. She shut it and continued further down. Moaning sounded behind the next door, and she resisted a peek.

This must be the sleeping quarters.

The next hall was long and empty, so she veered down it. The first door she came across had the head of a mountain lion carved into a gold handle. She turned it slowly. When she entered, the ceiling candelabras lit up, revealing a small library with a fireplace and a reading area. The fireplace was gray stone, and it, too, looked like the mouth of a mountain lion. A painting of a family in a gold frame hung above it.

I bet these are the original mountain lion therians.

She wondered if there was another room identical to this one, with a wolf's head as the doorknob, and a painting of her ancestors hanging above the fireplace.

If only it were that easy.

Shelves upon shelves of books lined the walls. Therian artifacts adorned the empty spaces, including a chain of large golden links with precise but weathered and unfamiliar glyphs. Some books were made of cloth, their titles embossed with gold foil, while others were nameless altogether. She wanted to run her fingers over the spines, but remarkably resisted, unsure if these books had the same protections as the ones in the library. *Cultura et Opiniones Leoninae. Pumas Throughout History. Malsano de la Animo. The Historical Ancestry of the Therian Wolves.*

The last one made her pause.

Her willpower evaporated in an instant, and she pulled it off the shelf.

The door slammed loudly, causing Gwen to jump before she'd even cracked the pages. She fumbled the book, barely holding on to it, and spun around to find Logan standing inches from her face, a vein in his neck pulsing.

Anger burned in his eyes with a golden sheen. "How did you get in here?" he asked through gritted teeth.

"The door was unlocked." Something about his pissed-off face steeled her spine.

Fuck him.

"That's impossible. This room is warded."

"I was looking for a quiet place to step away from the party and this room was unlocked, I swear." So it was a half lie.

His brow furrowed as he looked back at the door. "That doesn't make any sense." His words were less harsh this time.

"I'm telling you, it was open."

His facial expression changed again, but this time, she couldn't read it. He was infuriating.

"I'll leave. I really didn't mean to intrude." Her heart beat against her ribs as she gripped the book and attempted to take it with her, but Logan held out a hand. Gwen eyed it before reluctantly handing it over to him.

He glanced at the title, then placed it back on the shelf. "You're drunk. I'll take you back to your friends." He wrapped his hand around her arm like a prison guard.

She wasn't drunk, he just wanted to make sure she left.

As they headed back down the empty hall, she looked up at him. "Why are you such a dick?"

His eyes flashed gold. It was so quick she wasn't sure it actually happened. Looking back up at them now, they were their normal green color.

"I'm not a dick. You just don't belong here."

Logan was wrong. This might be the only place she *did* belong.

He steered her through the party, but instead of leading her to her friends, he led her right to Klaus, who was flirting with some upperclassman.

Logan's face twisted with disdain as he practically threw her at Klaus. "You need to keep a better eye on your girlfriend."

Gwen and Klaus turned on Logan simultaneously and both shouted, "*Girlfriend*?"

"Dude, this is my cousin," Klaus said, disgust in his voice.

Logan looked back and forth between them, then boomed with laughter as he walked away.

"Great, he scared off my date," Klaus complained. The girl he'd been flirting with had bolted the second the word *girlfriend* had left Logan's mouth.

"Sorry," Gwen said.

"What happened?" Klaus looked between Logan and Gwen once. Twice. "You didn't..."

"Ew, he's not my type!" she said.

"Really? Logan Wilder seems to be *everyone's* type," he informed her.

"*Anyway*..." Gwen glared at Klaus. "I'm glad I found you." She discreetly pulled out her wand and cast, "*Silentia.*"

As the silencing bubble formed, the room went silent, although the party was still in full swing around them.

"I thought you said there weren't any useful books on therians here!" Gwen accused.

"There aren't. I've scoured the place," Klaus insisted.

"Well, I just found a book about the ancestry of therian wolves. It's not exactly what I'm looking for but I still want to read it."

"I've never seen that book in my life," Klaus said. "Where did you find it?"

"In the mountain lion library," Gwen said. "I need you to get it for me. I can't get caught again."

Gwen looked over her shoulder to see Logan watching her. She definitely wouldn't make it back in there tonight.

"The what? Wait, who caught you?"

"The library with the mountain lion knobs and fireplace. And Logan. I think the wolf book was misplaced since everything else was about mountain lions. Logan may move it. You'll need to check for a wolf library."

"Gwen, neither of those libraries exist in this house."

Okay, maybe the wolf one was a stretch, but I'm sure the mountain lion one does! I stood in it.

Was he joking with her? His confused look told her no. Klaus had said he'd scoured the place, and she believed him. He wanted to help her more than anyone. Why, then, had he never seen a library that she'd found in mere minutes of being here?

Wards. Logan had mentioned wards. Why would he ward it against his own coven members?

Then it hit her. *Shit.* Wards, teeth, golden eyes.

"Klaus, who's the grizzly bear?" she blurted out.

"Gwen, I can't tell you that. Coven rules." Klaus squirmed like he knew she was about to crack him like a walnut.

"Is it Logan?"

He said nothing, but his face gave him away. "Why do you care?"

"I think he's like me," she whispered, even though the spell was still intact. It made perfect sense. It explained why the grizzly seemed so lifelike compared to the other animals in the game. Why Logan and Gwen could see the library, but not Klaus. Why he growled in his throat when he was angry.

She looked over her shoulder at Logan. She was surprised to see Victoria glued to his side. They certainly didn't seem like each other's type.

Klaus's eyes widened. "I thought therians wouldn't come here."

"So my dad says," Gwen said with a pointed look. Therians would never risk being discovered, according to her father. Which made her wonder, if Logan were a therian, why did *he* risk it? Was he running from an arranged marriage too?

"What are you going to do?" Klaus looked at Logan like he was seeing him for the first time.

"Find out if I'm right."

She'd never met a therian outside of immediate family. The idea was thrilling.

Before she could talk herself out of it, Gwen unclasped her

bracelet. Beer and body odor stung her nose. The unfamiliar pheromones of the surrounding students roused her wolf immediately. She forced herself to take a deep breath and find a familiar scent. The faint smell of clove wafted over her. Klaus reminded her of a spice jar left open on a hot day, warm and familiar, but it made her want to sneeze. Instead, she stretched her senses further until she found Hazel's familiar honey tones and focused fully on them.

Klaus reached for her wrist. "No, Gwen, don't. It's too dangerous."

"Too late," she said. *Shit, I don't have pockets.* She threw her bracelet at him before walking out of the bubble. Klaus doubled over in auditory pain, and she did her best to ignore the ringing in her ears from bursting her own bubble.

Once the ringing stopped, the sounds of the room hit her like a punch. Her wolf reacted, lunging to the forefront of her mind to take control, but Gwen refocused on the honey scent and blocked out everything else.

She eyed Logan, who was now facing her as he danced with the curly-haired redhead. With a renewed sense of self, she headed straight for him. He watched over his dance partner's head as Gwen approached him, never taking his eyes off her.

"Mind if I cut in?" Gwen asked, never breaking eye contact. She wouldn't let a little thing like Victoria get in the way of her answers.

He eyed her suspiciously before nodding. "Excuse me, Vicky," Logan said.

Victoria's mouth gaped open in disbelief as he moved from her to Gwen. "It's Victoria," she whispered.

Gwen almost laughed out loud at the look on her face.

"To what do I owe this pleasure, Gwendolyn?" Logan asked as he placed his hands on her hips. They were warm and firm as they pulled her forward to close the space between them, leaving only a few inches.

As Gwen placed her hands on his muscular shoulders, she inhaled slowly to find the scent of pine and earth clinging to the air around Logan. He smelled like her after a long day in the forest. But that was insubstantial evidence at best.

Gwen rolled her eyes. Nobody called her Gwendolyn except her mother when she was in trouble and Jordan when he was being cheeky. "She irks me."

It wasn't necessarily a lie, but it wasn't the whole truth either. Gwen glanced at Victoria, now skulking against the wall next to Serena, who chatted closely with an Alterion member.

"I wanted to show her I could take what she wanted," Gwen added.

"Even by force?"

"By whatever means necessary," Gwen said.

His fingers squeezed her hips as he digested her words, but he avoided her gaze. She needed him to let his guard down.

"So you thought I was dating Klaus?" Gwen asked, trying to get him talking again.

"I overheard you say he was your boyfriend at Kodiak Brew. I realize now that was a ruse."

"And now that you know I'm single?" Gwen bit her lip playfully.

He smiled and his eyes flashed gold. This time, in her heightened state, there was no mistaking it. He was like her.

Gwen gave him a wolfish grin. He had no idea he'd just let her in on his secret as he let his hands answer her question. His palms moved lower and his fingers made small soothing strokes that nearly made Gwen forget the reason she was dancing with him. She ran her hands over his shoulders, down his biceps. He was built unlike any guy she'd been with before, hard and unrelenting. She wanted to touch more of him, and when he encouraged her with a small smile, she moved her hands lower. Her fingers brushed over a scar on his forearm. She looked down to see a small double *H* branded into his skin, long healed.

The heat that had been rising inside her iced over. How had she missed it before?

He was a Hellhound.

"I've arranged for you to marry a Hellhound."

Her father wanted her to marry a member of his pack to strengthen his alliance with them.

Her wolf snarled in her mind with the memory, vehemently against any type of forced arrangement. She was not a pet to be gifted. Her canines grew with the thought.

Logan's smile faded. A hand loosened around her.

He knew she was like him.

His eyes flashed gold once more, this time in a predatory response, and her wolf threw itself against the cage she kept it safely inside.

It's not him. He's a grizzly, not a fox.

Without her bracelet, her wolf was not easily persuaded. It fought against her defenses, scratching and clawing to be set free. Gwen felt her fingernails lengthen.

"Control yourself," Logan growled, dominance soaking his words.

Her wolf hated that—so did Gwen. Who did he think he was, trying to command her? She could see the panic in his eyes that she'd expose them both, but also fear in the realization that his Alpha voice had no effect on her.

"Gwendolyn." He tried a more calming tone, but her wolf didn't care. Her wolf resented the patronizing tone and wanted to punish him for being such an asshole in each of their encounters. She wanted to teach him a lesson. Images of fangs sinking into Logan's flesh flashed through her mind.

Fuck, I have to get out of here.

"I can't. Tell Klaus I'll be in the woods," Gwen blurted out as she pulled from his arms and ran toward the front door, pushing others out of her way. She fought to keep her wolf from scratching and biting at the ones who didn't move fast enough.

"Gwen!" Logan yelled, but she was already at the door.

She ran from the house—away from Logan and his grizzly and away from people. Innocents. Gwen fought her wolf back as she walked through Coventry, recoiling in her own body. She felt herself splitting in two as she began to shake uncontrollably.

Please, Terra, don't let my friends follow me.

She made it past the arch. Now she just needed to make it to the trees.

You're almost there. You're almost there.

"Miss Bishop, are you alright?"

Fuck!

Gwen stopped dead in her tracks. She didn't need to look up to know who'd spoken. She could've picked his voice out of a crowd.

Harland.

Gwen looked down at the sidewalk, trying to hide her eyes, but the wolf was sick of hiding, sick of not getting to run freely, being denied. And here Harland was, just one more thing she wasn't allowed to have. And it. Pissed. Her. Off.

The wolf took its claws to the exhausted barricades of her mind.

"No," she managed.

Gwen fought to keep up her mental boundaries, the effort blackening her vision. Harland grabbed her as she convulsed. She'd never fought against her wolf this hard. Normally, she would've given in by now, but she couldn't shift, not here. She had to hold on, no matter how hard it was. If she didn't, the entire school would be in danger, and so would she. Her future depended on her ability to stay in control.

"Gwen, stay with me. I've got you. You're going to be okay," she heard Harland say as he picked her up and held her tight to his body.

As he walked with her in his arms, Gwen kept her eyes closed, trying to block the world out. She felt herself calming after a few steps. The warmth of his body, the steadiness of his stride, and the rhythm of his heartbeat lulled her to a state of ease. Her wolf was silent as the anxiety drained from her body at a rapid pace.

Gwen slipped further and further into darkness until there was nothing else.

Gwen felt groggy as she woke. Next to her, a clock glowed in the dark. It was five a.m. She wiped her eyes and took in the unfamiliar bedroom.

Where am I?

Gwen looked up at the nightstand and noticed a photo of Harland hiking on a mountain.

She gasped.

This was Harland's bedroom.

She rolled over, nearly too afraid to look, but he was nowhere to be found. Moving as quickly as she dared, she found her shoes by the bedroom door and slid them on quietly. When she opened the door, she heard the familiar sound of a crackling fire and saw Harland on the couch. His soft, even breath reached her ears and she knew he was sound asleep.

He looked so peaceful there, so reachable, unlike in the classroom or on campus. Here, there were no societal pedestals in sight. The desire to join him there was nearly irresistible, but she had to go. She needed her bracelet.

How did he calm my wolf? Is his presence that strong?

Whatever the answer, she would be forever grateful that he was the one she'd run into last night.

Gwen tiptoed out of the room. The floorboards creaked beneath her foot, and she froze. A glance told her Harland was still sleeping, so she continued, slower this time. Her heart pounded as she tried what she hoped was the front door.

She stepped outside to find herself in the professors' quarters. Gwen prayed no one saw her as she closed the door quietly behind her, and then slipped out the front gate.

When she reached the north oval, a student was walking across the lawn in her direction. She kept her head down to avoid being recognized.

Steps sounded behind her just before a hand wrapped around her arm.

"Not a word," Logan practically hissed as he yanked her to a stop.

Surprisingly, her wolf stayed silent. As a matter of fact, Gwen hadn't heard a peep from her wolf since she'd woken up. *Strange.*

"Back at ya," she bit out, not needing her wolf to be annoyed with Logan. It would be her luck that he'd be the first therian she'd meet outside of her family. It was mutually beneficial for them both to keep their secrets, but she wasn't sure she could trust him outside of that. He was a Hellhound, after all—her father's pack's rival. Not to mention, he reported to Crevan Reid, the man her father had arranged for her to marry.

Of course the only other therian at school is him. It couldn't be someone I could confide in and ask all the questions my dad refuses to answer.

"Gwen!" Klaus ran up to her, wrapping her in a hug. "We've been looking for you for hours."

Gwen looked around, but there was no one here besides Logan. *By "we," does he mean him and Logan?*

"I'm sorry. I needed to clear my head," Gwen said, unsure of what Klaus and Logan had disclosed to one another, but she didn't need to know right now. This was awkward enough. She just wanted to go to her room.

She wordlessly held out her hand, and he quickly clasped the bracelet around her wrist.

"Never do that again," he whispered.

She nodded. *No fucking shit.* "I won't."

"Thanks for helping," Klaus said, as he turned to Logan.

Logan looked between Klaus and Gwen's wrist. "Sure. Glad you're alright," he said as he finally looked Gwen in the eye. "See you later."

Logan's message was clear. He would be watching her.

CHAPTER 20

Hazel

"When is Gwen going to quit being a baby and drag her ass out of bed?" Jordan asked.

Rafe, Jordan, and Hazel walked quickly toward the Alchemy building. They were running late and had to skip breakfast. Partly because of Gwen.

Hazel fidgeted with the straps on her backpack as she worried about her friend for the thousandth time this week. It was only Tuesday. "I tried to get her to come to class today, but she swears she's not feeling well."

Something was off.

It had been since Sunday morning—well, afternoon—when Gwen had finally gotten out of bed. She'd been dodgy when Hazel had asked for details about her time in Alterion and had become a locked vault when Hazel had asked for details about her time after Alterion. Gwen insisted she'd felt unwell and had gone back to their dorm to rest. But Hazel knew that wasn't true. She'd heard her come in just before six that morning.

What could be so bad that she'd want to hide it from me?

"I haven't seen her sick a single day since we were ten. I smell bullshit," Jordan said.

Me, too, Jordan. Me too.

They entered the building and headed downstairs to the lower floor for Alchemy Lab. Hazel stopped short when she spied a glass globe-like machine on the lower landing. She'd paid no attention to it last week with so many things to take in at once.

"Terra was looking out!" Rafe told them as he approached the vintage gumball machine.

Miniature snacks and treats filled the tiny glass balls instead of gum. A peanut butter cupcake inside one called Hazel's name.

Rafe dug into his pocket and pulled out some pretium. He stuffed in his coins and twisted the knob. A glass ball rolled to the bottom with a *clink*. He took it into both hands and tapped it on the metal point atop the machine. A crack splintered up the sides of the glass like an egg, while the inside was filled with steam. He pried the top loose, and the steam escaped. Blowing on his fingers, Rafe plucked out a tiny muffin. The group watched it grow to normal size before their eyes.

The smell wafted throughout the hall, and as the scent hit Hazel's nose, her stomach ached in response.

Jordan got lucky with a cream cheese bagel.

"We better head to class. We're going to be late," Hazel said.

"Wait." Rafe's words were barely audible through his muffin. "You don't want anything?"

Hazel shook her head. Of course she did, but her money wasn't for frivolous moments like this. "I left my money in the room."

"I can spot you," Rafe offered.

"No, I shouldn't be spending what little I have on food, since I can eat for free." Hazel turned to head to class with Jordan, but stopped when she realized Rafe wasn't following them. "You coming?" she asked.

"I'll be right there."

Hazel nodded and took off. She'd definitely have to start getting up early enough for breakfast.

Arriving in the room, she was immediately distracted from her thoughts of food. Vials, cauldrons, stirrers, and ingredients lined the walls. Most of it had a thin layer of dust on top and she wondered how much of it she'd use in this class.

Rows of lab tables filled the space, two chairs to a table. Dane was sitting in the back, alone. She cursed Gwen for the hundredth time this morning.

No way I'm sitting next to him.

The room was filling up quickly with students. She needed to act fast. A table in the middle row was unoccupied, so Hazel made her way there. Jordan sat at the table next to her and saved a seat for Rafe.

Moments later, Rafe joined them. He slid a blueberry muffin and a carton of apple juice in front of Hazel. She tried to look at him, to tell him thanks but no thanks, but he refused to return her gaze.

Emotion overcame her as she stared down at the food in front of her. She was grateful for Rafe's kindness, but that wasn't what pricked her eyes. It was the thought that a person she knew so little of would use his money to help Hazel when her own father wouldn't. She was thankful that Rafe was focused on his own juice and not on her as she fought back tears.

"Good morning, scholars. I hope your first week went beautifully," Serena, their TA for the lab, said from her table at the front of the room. Her eyes landed on Hazel as she spoke, and Hazel's stomach knotted. When Serena's eyes slid to the back of the room where Dane sat, Hazel thought she was going to be sick. "Today, we'll work in pairs. Dane, please join Hazel at her table."

Hazel hung her head. *Salem burn me.* When she heard no movement, a tiny part of her hoped he'd refuse, but the loud screech of metal against tile made her jump and the hope died.

The sound of his boots against the floor hit like a countdown as he drew closer and closer. How was she going to survive this?

I will never forgive Gwen for this.

He reached the table and yanked the chair next to her out so suddenly Hazel jumped again. He pulled it to the corner of the table, as far away from Hazel as possible.

What a dick.

"Great. Now, please set out the supplies I instructed you to gather last week. Some of you may have guessed it already from your Alchemy 101 lecture yesterday, but we're going to be focusing on the transmutation of spark to burning flame." Serena lifted her wand and wrote ingredients in the air, the glow similar to a dull sparkler, but never fading.

Dane's jaw clenched as he stared forward, refusing to look at Hazel.

She rolled her eyes. This was going to be a fun class.

"As you all know, the art of conjuring the elements—air, fire, water, and earth—were lost when the fae disappeared. However, we can still control and expand the elements that are already within our environment. For today's assignment, you'll need a fire starter, whether it's flint, steel, or matches," Serena finished, tucking her wand away.

Dane's lip curled as she said *matches*, as they were typically used only by mundanes, clearly displaying his disdain of the idea.

"Be sure to clear your work bench of any flammable materials. One partner will spark while the other works to control and then expand it to flame," Serena explained.

"You're sparking first," Dane said, still avoiding her gaze.

Hazel shook her head. "Not a chance. I like my eyebrows how they are."

A loud laugh escaped Dane before he could stop himself. Hazel stared at him wide-eyed. He immediately frowned and looked away.

I actually made Dane Bellamy laugh. It was official—the world was ending.

Hazel pulled out her jasper stones, while Dane pulled out two jagged little pieces of quartzite. They were so tiny, Hazel wondered if they'd even work.

Without preamble, Dane struck the two pieces together, generating a spark on the first try.

Okay, so he's good at this. The fact annoyed Hazel more than it impressed her. She hadn't been expecting it and the spark came and went before she could cast the transmutation spell.

Dane's eyes narrowed at her. "You're supposed to cast at the spark, Hateful."

Hazel's cheeks burned. "Go again."

Dane arched a brow.

"Please," Hazel added.

He struck the stones once more, but this time, Hazel was ready.

She cast, "*Teneo.*"

The spark froze midair. It was such a tiny thing, but dangerous nonetheless.

Hazel imagined the spark growing to the size of a baseball—it was important to place parameters according to their lecture with Maduro yesterday—and then she cast, "*Excresco.*"

The spark grew instantly to a ball of flame, and Hazel felt its warmth all the way across the table. *I did it!*

But her joy evaporated when she noticed Dane's look of hatred as the light of the fireball danced in his eyes.

After escaping Alchemy Lab with all her hair intact, Hazel said goodbye to Rafe and Jordan and made her way towards the Arcane building on the north oval.

While all the buildings on campus were of Gothic design, the Arcane college took it a step further. It was the tallest on campus, only bested by the administration building and the clock tower. Four towers loomed above, representing the four branches of arcana: foresight, shadowsong, astral projection, telekinesis.

The rose-colored window that adorned the tallest steeple glowed from within, even in daylight, and the niches were countless, filled with gargoyles on the backs of griffins, as if guarding what lay inside from the dangers of the outside world.

The hair on the back of Hazel's neck stood on end as she entered the building. She'd felt this same sensation last week, and while it was cool inside, it was no colder than any other building. The dimly lit halls were now familiar enough for her to find her way without having to look at the directional etchings. Like last week, Hazel didn't encounter any other students as she took the winding staircase, nor did she see any when she reached the landing. Her shoes sounded against the floor, echoing along the hall.

She slipped inside the classroom and chose the desk on the edge of the row that she'd sat in for each class so far. She opened up her backpack and pulled out her syllabus, reading over the class description for the fifth time.

Study of the Arcane was an introduction to concepts course, touching on the four branches. The principles of the psychometrical portions of the brain were abstract at best and convoluted at worst. Hazel had been told it was a weed-out course because not all scholars could grasp these metaphysical concepts with mastery.

The class was a year long, with this quarter's focus on foresight. Hazel would've preferred to cover astral projection, but she was happy to focus on something else her mother had been able to do. Something that Hazel herself might be able to do given they apparently shared the ability of Sight. Regardless, she was just ready to learn *something* about the arcane.

Movement to her left caught her attention, and she looked up to see Nova standing beside her.

"Hey!" she said as she sat next to Hazel. Nova dug through her bag and pulled out her books, setting them on the desk in front of her. "The reading last week was brutal. I barely got through it all."

"I'm glad it wasn't just me. I think I only understood seventy-five percent," Hazel admitted.

"Better than me. I think I only understood thirty."

They both laughed but quickly quieted as Sorcerer Oswald walked past them on the stairs. Today, he wore purple paisley robes that suited his porcelain complexion and made his short white hair and long matching beard pop. Sorcerer Oswald was simply missing Merlin's pointy wizard hat to be his doppelgänger. He glided down the stairs to the sunken middle and then turned in a slow circle to address the students.

He smoothed his beard and then his robes. The professor didn't bother with a vocal magnification potion as he began speaking. "Scholars, foresight isn't for the faint of heart, nor is it for the fanciful."

Perfect. Turns out I'm neither.

"Seeing into the future is disconcerting, to say the least. Like the rest of the branches, it has driven more than one mage mad. Now—"

Hazel's hand flew into the air.

Sorcerer Oswald did not look up while he paced across the stage. "Yes, Miss Thorne?"

"H–How, Sorcerer Oswald?" Hazel stumbled on her words, unsure how he even saw her with his back turned to the other half of the room.

"How foresight works is kind of the point of this lesson," Sorcerer Oswald said as he turned to her, a teasing smirk on his face.

"I meant, how do they go mad?" Hazel flushed.

Great, he thinks I'm an idiot.

Sorcerer Oswald nodded at her wording. "Imagine being able to see your future, your father's, your best friend's. Like a child with presents to open on Christmas morning, it becomes incredibly hard to resist the temptation to take a peek. First, you tell yourself there's no harm, and then you're spending more time in the future than the present."

Goosebumps covered Hazel's skin. His words implied that she could have visions at will, but Hazel only ever saw them when she slept and had never made them happen on command. Was that possible?

Could she find a way to see more of her mother?

“Of course, no one living today can change the future. That power was lost with the elven species.”

Hazel still couldn’t get over how openly sorcerers spoke about the Forsaken within SEU. Finding information about them was next to impossible. The professors at Elkmont had only briefly taught about the Forsakens’ powers and their transgressions, and even those lessons were vague and shrouded in mystery.

“Seeing the future and knowing you can’t change it is one thing. Accepting it is entirely another.” Sorcerer Oswald narrowed his gaze at her. “That’s typically where the madness takes root, as the future will inevitably reveal a path you cannot willingly accept yet have no hope of changing.” He waved his wand and the floor came to a stop. She wondered how he didn’t get motion sickness. Silence filled the air. He aimed his crooked, wooden-tipped wand with a deep-blue lapis handle at the ceiling. Light erupted from it and filled the space above him, forming outlines of numerous mages.

The first outline sat at a table, shuffling, cutting, and then spreading a tarot deck on a loop.

The second outline drank continuously, poured from a teapot, drained the teacup, and then peered into the cup for several seconds.

One outline held the palm of another and studied it closely while the outline next to it gazed into a sphere that lit up with images from within.

A miniature universe bloomed above another mage, who pointed to the constellations.

The final projection was not only an outline. It started as the shape of a person and zoomed in on the brain, the space within filled with vivid imagery.

Visions.

That projection was depicting the visions Hazel was experiencing in her dreams. She was sure of it.

So many types of foresight: tarot, tea leaves, palmistry, crystal gazing, astrology, and visions. Hazel breathed a sigh of relief. With so many options, surely she could master at least one method.

"Above you are the primary methods of foresight. Most mages will never accomplish this skill even once in their life, and only a fraction of those that do will actually master the ability with any type of consistency. Fractions of that fraction will use more than one method."

At least half a dozen hands shot into the air.

Sorcerer Oswald chuckled and gestured at the nearest student as he resumed the floor's rotation with the flick of his wand.

"Have you ever met anyone who had foresight?" the student asked.

"The funny thing about foresight is that because it can be very hard to interpret, it also makes it very hard to prove."

His words fed into Hazel's own fear that no one would believe her—that they'd think she was crazy.

"Some visions are literal, while some are metaphorical or representational, which means it's impossible to standardize any type of testing protocol. However, some abilities are so strong, a perfect test isn't needed." Sorcerer Oswald stroked his beard as he continued, "In my long life, I have only met a few dozen people who I believed truly possessed the Sight, some with the method of tasseography or palmistry and others with cartomancy."

"And visions?" another student asked, not waiting to be called on.

"I have met three people," he paused briefly, before continuing, "who had visions in front of my own eyes, although there have been rumors of others. Only one of them was a student of mine."

Only three mages in at least seventy years. Was her mother one of the three?

Will I be the fourth?

Hazel threw her hand up. She asked the question no one had yet dared. "Can *you* perform any of these types of foresight?"

Sorcerer Oswald smiled, teeth flashing in the light of his spell overhead. "I am adept at one method, Miss Thorne."

"Have you ever had a vision?" Hazel asked.

Sorcerer Oswald shook his head as he studied her. Hazel resisted the urge to squirm. Had it been impertinent to ask?

"To my utmost regret, I'm just a simple mage. Visions remain out of my reach."

Hazel chewed her lip. *Out of his reach?*

But she didn't have time to dwell on it, as Sorcerer Oswald continued on with his lesson. "For the next five weeks, we'll cover theory for each method of foresight."

Hazel's heart raced at his words. She wanted to control her visions, to See more, See the exact moment she'd speak to her mother again for the first time. She wanted it so badly she could taste it, and here the information was, being presented to her by a sorcerer on a silver platter.

Was this her life? She could hardly believe it.

"While each branch of the arcane is entirely different from the others, they're rooted in two pillars: mindfulness and natural talent."

Hazel had already achieved one of those prerequisites through no work of her own. She was confident she possessed natural talent, thanks to her mother. The only thing standing in her way now was mindfulness, and she'd stop at nothing to get it right, like her mother.

Hazel's hand flew into the air. Beside her, Nova sighed.

"Yes, Miss Thorne?"

"How do you achieve mindfulness?"

"Ah, you're jumping ahead. Mindfulness is on the agenda for next week. But to satisfy your curiosity, in the most basic sense, it is clearing the mind of all distractions and focusing on the present moment, accepting your emotions and thoughts but letting them pass around you like water around a stone."

At the end of class, Hazel and Nova walked out together.

"Well, that was intense," Nova murmured.

Hazel studied her face. It was clear Nova was not feeling the same adrenaline pumping through her veins at the mention of that kind of power.

"Yeah, I'm interested to see how this class will go," Hazel said. She was more than interested, but after all her questions today, she didn't want to come off any weirder than she already had.

"I have a feeling we may regret it in the end," Nova groused.

Hazel hoped to Terra that Nova didn't possess any powers of foresight, just a pessimistic attitude.

The girls parted ways at the front of the building because Hazel needed to go meet with Sorcerer Roth for their monthly advisory appointment.

For the first time since arriving at SEU, Hazel headed for the administration building with the purpose of going inside. Jude had told her their office was in the left wing, the last door on the left. The inside was fort-like, with portcullis grooves along the stone walls. There were actual holes in the south walls to allow spells to be fired from within towards outside enemies.

Hazel took her time inspecting the paintings and tapestries that lined the walls, as she was the only one in the hallway. No doors were open, but she figured it was because it was late afternoon and the professors were likely teaching.

She continued down the hall until she found Sorcerer Roth's office. The door was closed, but a deep voice carried out to her.

"I'm telling you, Jude, she has more power than anything I've ever felt."

Hazel's eyes narrowed. She recognized that voice. It was Sorcerer Thacker.

Who is he talking about?

"I'm dying to get a new baseline, but I haven't seen her since Saturday night."

Saturday night?

Her gut had a guess because her brain knew who he definitely hadn't seen all week: Gwen. But had he seen her Saturday night? Was that where she'd been? It would make sense why Gwen would want to hide that from her.

Hazel shook her head. Nothing good would come from jumping to wild conclusions. She needed to ask Gwen to know for sure.

Harland spoke again, but this time, his words were so low Hazel couldn't make them out. Instinctually, she stepped closer toward the door to listen. As she leaned in, the plastic clip on her backpack strap rubbed against the door.

Hazel winced at the small sound and prayed to Terra they hadn't heard it.

"Just a moment," Jude said. Hazel held her breath as she heard the roll of a chair. "I think I heard something."

Hazel stepped back quickly before the door opened. She came face to face with Jude, their eyes wide.

"Hazel. Stopping by for your check-in?"

"Yes, I didn't want to wait too long." Hazel flashed a big smile. She was good at playing innocent.

Jude nodded and turned back to Sorcerer Thacker. "Thanks for stopping by, Harland. I have a check-in, so I'll have to catch up with you another time."

Sorcerer Thacker studied Hazel as he stood to leave. She kept her plastic smile in place and tried not to let him know she'd heard anything.

"Of course. Have a good day." He nodded to them both.

Hazel watched him walk down the long hallway, but he never looked back. Something inside her urged her not to trust him, although his friendship with Jude made her want to do so.

"Come on in, Hazel. Have a seat." Jude gestured to the empty chairs in front of their ebony desk. "How is your second week starting off?"

"It's been a whirlwind. I've been meaning to come check in with you, but I haven't had the time," Hazel said. She glanced down, hoping Jude didn't know she'd been busy partying and hanging out with friends. Guilt crept up once again that she'd been spending precious time with her friends instead of looking for her mother more.

"Well, I suppose that's my fault for not giving you a day and time. Why don't we meet in my office on the first Friday of the month at two moving forward?"

"Not a problem." Hazel smiled.

"If anything comes up before then and you need me, you'll reach out, yeah?" Jude said.

"Of course." Hazel felt seen. She didn't like asking for help; she didn't enjoy being trouble for anyone, and reaching out to bother someone with her problems was the least likely thing she'd do. Yet Jude had been in here talking with Harland. Could she trust them?

Jude surprised Hazel when they laughed. "I mean it, Hazel. Otherwise, I'll see you next month."

Hazel rushed home to tell Gwen about what she'd heard and find out where she'd been on Saturday. But when she opened the door, she was sure she'd stepped into the wrong dorm.

Inside was a spacious living room, now furnished with a five-person sectional, instead of the old loveseat, positioned in front of the newly added fireplace. The full-sized kitchen featured a large refrigerator and a gas stove.

What in Salem is going on?

Hazel stepped back into the hallway and closed the door to check the room number. 215. It was the right room.

She opened the door once more and stuck her head in before she half-whispered, "Gwen?"

Gwen came out of her room, sparing Hazel a look as she plopped down on the plush, dark-green couch.

Hazel entered the room cautiously, pulling the door shut behind her. "What happened?"

Gwen flipped open a leather-bound book with wolves embossed on the cover. "I redecorated."

That's one hell of an understatement!

"Gwen, this is three times bigger than our dorm room! This can't have been on the permitted spells list."

Gwen winced. "Okay, so to be completely honest, the spells I used weren't exactly on the approved list, but they aren't illegal, so it's fine."

"This is most definitely *not* fine. We went from living in a tin can to a 1,000-square foot condo."

"You don't like your room?" Gwen shut her book and crossed her arms.

"My room?" Hazel's rule-abiding ways twisted her stomach with unease. There was more?

Hazel dropped her book bag by the door and made for her room. It had nearly doubled in size. A cream-colored, queen-size four-poster bed now stood where her old twin had been. The stark-white walls had transformed into a deep forest green, and trailing vines now wove through the trellised ceiling. The space felt warm, alive, and inviting. For the first time, Hazel could actually imagine spending her free time here. She couldn't even pretend to be upset.

How on earth did she pull this off?

"It took me all day to weave them. I thought you'd be more grateful," Gwen said as she leaned against the doorframe.

"Where did you learn this?" Hazel insisted, her curiosity overruling her better judgement.

Gwen paused before answering, "My dad. On top of being a colossal ass, he's also a creative spell-writer."

Hazel was impressed. Creative spell-writers were rare. If you wrote the incantation wrong, it could be terrible. Very few had the talent for it, so most mages kept to the standard spells.

Gwen held up the book she was reading. "He gave me my own

copy of his family grimoire a few Christmases ago with all his spells added."

Hazel resisted reaching for the book. She was curious what other spells Gwen's dad had written. Her family grimoire contained mostly fungicide spells.

Damn, it did look good in here. Hazel didn't want to go back to living in the asylum-like boxes they'd been assigned, but she still wasn't sure this was a good idea. She needed to know more about the spells Gwen used.

Hazel paced back out into the living room. "How did you get the extra space?"

Gwen shrugged as she went back to sit on the couch. "I took a few inches here and there. But not enough that anyone will notice."

While the decor was likely reversible and the furniture could be removed, the space was literal theft. It belonged to everyone else. There was no way the university would be okay with this.

We're going to get expelled!

"Breathe, Hazel," Gwen said, clearly unfazed by the severity of the situation.

She took a deep breath, then another and another, until her breathing returned to normal. "Thanks," Hazel finally said.

"For the room, or...?" Gwen asked, smiling.

Hazel cut her a sharp look.

Once her breathing returned to normal, she started walking through the space again, this time taking everything in. She noticed the hardwood floors with the large ornate rug and the L-shaped sectional framing it. Across from the sofa was the fireplace, which gave off calming vibes along with a small amount of heat. Next to it was a set of shelves filled with books.

"Where are the books from?" Hazel asked, continuing her interrogation.

"Borrowed," Gwen offered.

Hazel arched a brow at her.

"The library. It's on a loop, so the books will go back and new ones will appear, all checked out under my name. On the up and up, I swear." Gwen crossed her heart.

"The couch?" Hazel asked.

"Conjured it and the back door. That's a spell I learned in school, and it's perfectly allowed." Gwen smiled proudly.

"Back door?" Hazel looked toward the kitchen. Sure enough, there was a door nestled next to the fridge.

"It will lead us to the woods behind the library. It will be great for sneaking in and out," Gwen explained.

"Why would we need to sneak in and out?" Hazel asked. Why did it seem like Gwen made a habit of hiding things?

"I figured after the dogs..." Gwen's eyes were downcast. "Well, I just figured it couldn't hurt."

Hazel understood.

"How do we get back in?" she asked cautiously.

"There's a matching door in the trees, but it's not very well hidden," Gwen explained, frustration lacing her words.

Great. Someone was going to find that door and they'd be busted for sure. Hazel was going to have to convince Gwen to get rid of it if she wanted to keep the rest of the room.

"Won't that look a little conspicuous if someone stumbles upon it?"

"I put it deep in the trees."

"Right. No students go into the trees," Hazel countered. "This is already out of hand, and how are we supposed to have people over?"

"Probably best if we don't," Gwen said gently.

"If we have to hide it, then we shouldn't have it. You have to change it back," Hazel huffed, although part of her hated the idea.

Still, no matter how much Hazel loved the homey space Gwen had created, it wasn't worth the fines they would certainly pay if Gwen couldn't put it back, especially since Hazel had no way to pay her share. Or the expulsion they might face.

Plus, I want to have friends over!

"I mean, technically, we can have people over that we trust.

Jordan and Rafe will for sure keep their mouths shut. Though Jordan will probably make me spell their room too."

Hazel was certain Jordan would insist on it.

"I'm telling you, none of it's on the forbidden spell list. The door in the woods is a problem, I'll admit," Gwen added.

"The door isn't the only problem. None of these spells are on the pre-approved list."

"Some of the spells are." Gwen paused. "But most of them aren't."

"And the only reason they aren't on the don't-use list is because your dad invented them and the dorm advisors don't know them?"

"Maybe, but I think it's a great technicality."

Hazel chewed on her lip. There was a loophole there, and it was enough to get her on board. "Fine, it can stay—"

"Yes!" Gwen whooped.

Hazel held up a hand. "It can stay *if* you tell me why you keep skipping classes."

Gwen sobered quickly. "I told you I'm sick."

Hazel looked around the room dramatically. "Yes, so sick."

Gwen threw a decorative pillow at Hazel, then sighed. "I just needed some time."

"What happened on Saturday? The truth this time," Hazel insisted.

Gwen said nothing.

"Does it have something to do with Sorcerer Thacker?"

"How did you know?" Gwen's eyes widened.

"Call it a hunch."

Gwen finally broke down. "Klaus wasn't lying. I headed back to the dorms, but on my way, I ran into Harland. He invited me back to his place."

This time, Hazel's eyes widened. That was definitely *not* what she'd thought Gwen would say. She did her best to keep her jaw off the floor. She knew Gwen had a crush, but that she would go so far as to spend time at his house was an entirely different story.

"Nothing happened! But I guess I was more tired than I thought and I fell asleep on his couch. When I woke up, he was asleep on the recliner. I didn't know what to do, so I left, and now everything's all messed up and confusing and I really don't want to see him."

"Why did you lie to me?" Hazel asked.

Is she still lying? Hazel didn't want to think so, but Gwen was being awfully forthcoming and Hazel knew that trick. She'd used it with her dad all too well.

"I don't know. I guess I felt stupid," Gwen mumbled.

Her words struck a chord in Hazel. She understood the fear of making mistakes.

"We're friends. Friends don't lie to each other. There's nothing you can't tell me," Hazel said softly.

"You won't give me the whole 'he's your professor' speech?"

Hazel laughed. "Oh, I'm definitely giving you that speech."

Gwen cracked a small smile—the first since Saturday. "I'm sorry. I won't lie again," she promised.

"Are you sure you can trust him?" Hazel asked.

"He's never given me a reason not to."

Hazel debated whether to tell Gwen what she'd heard, but she wasn't even sure it was about her friend. For now, she'd keep it to herself. She wasn't hiding it from Gwen, she just needed to gather more information.

"Okay, great. Now that you've had time to lick your wounds, it's time to go back to class."

Gwen paused, then said, "Okay, fine, but promise me we can sit in the back of Harland's class?"

"I promise." If it would get her friend back in class, Hazel would suck it up. She also wasn't sure she wanted to be sitting in Thacker's line of sight anymore, anyway.

With Gwen's promise to return to class in hand and feeling better about the dorm changes already, Hazel sat on the couch. Its velvety softness melted her worries down to nothing.

"You'll have to teach me these spells," Hazel said with a smile. "Ya know, I actually might know a spell that can help us."

"I'm all ears," Gwen said.

"If we use an illusion spell, we can make the room appear like our original dorm room when we open any doors to potential onlookers, like when we're going to class, if someone knocks, or when we're using the shared bathroom. I can use it on the door in the woods too. We don't want just anyone peeking in here!"

"Now we're talking!" Gwen sat up on her knees, excitement lighting her eyes.

"But it'll break if they step through the threshold," Hazel warned.

"Okay, so we won't let them step through."

Easier said than done.

CHAPTER 21

Hazel

"Move your ass, Gwen!" Jordan shouted, adjusting the sparkling-pink unicorn horn on his forehead with a dramatic scowl. "I want to get this over with!"

"You wear glitter surprisingly well. Laughter laced Hazel's words as she took in the rainbow tail swishing behind him.

Rafe chuckled beside her, the fuzzy round ears of his teddy bear costume flopping slightly as he walked. The soft brown onesie was clearly designed for someone half his size, but somehow, he made it look cute instead of ridiculous. Probably because Hazel had picked it.

Jordan shot a glare at Gwen as she caught up to them near the tunnel exit to Eagles Ridge. "Seriously, why am I the one in full public-humiliation mode when Rafe made the original bet?"

Gwen grinned. "Not my fault Hazel went easy on Rafe."

Rafe shot Hazel a quick smile, and her cheeks flamed. She glanced down at her feet, fiddling with the hem of her sweater.

Jordan groaned. "You're a sadist, and I swear you're walking slower to prolong my humiliation."

"I'm not—*that's* just a bonus," Gwen said. She'd insisted on stopping by the school aviary before they met up tonight and she was running late because of it. "You know if I don't write to my mom, she gets worried. It's been two days since my last letter."

Guilt washed over Hazel. A part of her knew she should be exploring the library or trying to find the location of her dream, rather than going on yet another outing with her friends, but after three unsuccessful attempts this week, she needed a break from the disappointment.

Each mage grabbed a broom, now the primary method of coming and going through the tunnel. SEU administration wouldn't be replacing the dogs until the beast responsible for their slaughter was apprehended or killed.

They stopped in front of the curfew posting listed at the tunnel exit: *All students will be back on campus no later than 10pm on week nights and midnight on weekends until further notice. Any student caught breaking curfew will be met with the harshest of punishments.*

"This is stupid!" Jordan groaned.

Hazel and Gwen exchanged a knowing look. If Jordan had seen what they'd seen he wouldn't be complaining.

"Look on the bright side, we only have to be in these costumes for two hours." Rafe told him.

They made it to Eagles Ridge in record time and stashed the brooms at the end of the tunnel. Gwen spelled them to be invisible to others—just as she had their table in the dining hall and the one in the library. She thought Hazel didn't know, but she wasn't stupid. Hazel just had bigger secrets to worry about—like her own visions and Gwen's odd behavior at the library.

As they approached Kodiak Brew, the sun was beginning to set, making the town and the fjord behind it awash with bright pinks and purples. Rafe opened the door to the brewery and Hazel winced at the sound of someone butchering Taylor Swift's "Bejeweled."

A noise overhead drew her attention from the caterwauling. A shiver went down her spine as she looked up to find two birds flying overhead. Oil-slick feathers gleamed iridescent in the setting sun, their wedge-shaped tails giving them away as ravens. A sense of déjà vu settled over Hazel as she watched them circle over the pines on the edge of town. She'd seen them before—in her dreams.

Hazel froze in the doorway as her heart raced and everything inside her screamed to follow the birds.

"Hazel, you coming?" Rafe asked, still holding the door open.

Hazel's gaze darted from the trees to Rafe, then to Gwen, and back to the birds that were diving low, preparing to land. She swallowed. "No, I just remembered I didn't get my mindfulness practice in today."

Liar.

She'd already done the meditation that morning—up at six, like Sorcerer Oswald had said was necessary for mastering arcane magic. But this wasn't about that. It was about the ravens. Would she find the same wooded area she'd dreamed of? Would she see her mother? She wouldn't know unless she followed through on her dream.

No, not dream. Vision.

Gwen groaned. "Surely you can miss a day. Sorcerer Oswald will never know."

"But *I'll* know," Hazel said, watching the birds closely once again as they lowered to land. She was going to lose them. "I should go before the sun fully sets. I'll meet y'all back here at 9:30."

"Do you want me to go with you?" Rafe asked.

Hazel gave him a soft smile. It was sweet that he'd offered. "The point of mindfulness is to be alone in one's thoughts."

Rafe nodded, his brown cheeks pinking. "Got it."

Gwen opened her mouth to argue, but Hazel took off down the cobblestone street towards the pines. Hope filled her for the first time in days. Her confidence had taken a hit every time she went to the library, only to leave without a sighting of her mother, but now that she'd possibly found the location of another dream, her optimism flared to life once more.

"Don't be late. We have curfew!" Gwen yelled after Hazel.

A chilly breeze blew in from the fjord and Hazel pulled her jacket tighter as she searched the sky and trees for the ravens. She followed them down to the end of the road. The strike of her soles against the cobblestones changed to the crunch of pine needles and dirt underfoot.

The subtle noises from town faded and she could no longer hear the hum of music as she entered the forest. She hadn't seen the ravens land, only the direction they'd headed, so she walked forward on a hunch. The pines shielded what little light remained as the sun dipped below the horizon. The rhythmic sound of her pace against the ground soon grew eerie. Each scratch and crack of the woods set her on edge, and she strained to listen for any unexpected sounds.

The snap of a branch made her jump. Hazel whirled to look behind her, toward the sound. She peered through the trees, but saw nothing. Steeling her spine, she trekked on once more.

It's just your imagination, Hazel.

But the truth was, she knew firsthand that there were dangerous things lurking in these woods—things that could kill a kennel full of dogs and were quick enough to not get caught or be seen. The thought almost made her turn back, but she was *so close*. The chance of seeing her mother was too enticing.

The dogs were attacked late at night. It's still early. I'll head back as soon as I check.

Hazel tried to clear her mind as she hiked through the forest. She allowed herself to focus internally, on the cool air coming in and the warm air exhaling out of her nose. The idea of being followed washed over her as if it were water and she was stone. Thoughts of her friends, the hope of her mother, came and drifted away. There wasn't room for it in her mind. She focused on the sound of the ravens, the wind through the trees, and the sensation of her own breath until she was calm and almost lost in it.

Which was why it took her a second to notice when she'd reached a small clearing. All around her, bellflowers blanketed the forest floor, and she knew she was in the right place. Déjà vu tugged at the back of her mind, urging her to turn around.

She took a deep breath and attempted to hold on to the mindfulness she'd cultivated as she turned. The rooftop outline of Eagles Ridge peeked above the trees in the distance, and she gasped. It was a sight she'd seen many times before. Just ahead, between the trees, was where her mother liked to play a game of cat and mouse with her.

A gurgling croak from above made her heart race. It was all the same. Except it wasn't. The sun never set in her dreams. And her mother wasn't here.

The snap of another twig sounded behind her, this time much closer. Hazel's heart threatened to pound itself right out of her chest. The timing wasn't right. It couldn't be...

Hazel pulled her wand from its brace. "*Lux.*" The tip of her wand glowed with a small ball of light. Then she turned slowly, taking a deep breath to calm her nerves. Fear flooded her veins and air caught in her lungs when the light from her wand washed over the clearing. Hazel was not alone. A set of glowing orangey-red eyes reflected off her wand light from across the clearing, and the outline of an enormous creature took shape in the shadows.

Immediately, the memory of the dragons surfaced in her mind, but she pushed it aside. Impossible. *Impossible.* The dragons had been so large, their hulking forms would've reached over the tree canopy.

Blood pounded in Hazel's ears as the animal took a step forward, the snap of twigs and pine needles beneath its foot echoing through the clearing.

What is it?

Hazel held still as she recalled the research she'd done on the Alaskan wilderness. It was either a moose or a bear based on height alone. Both were incredibly dangerous, but if she had to choose, she'd take the bear. Well, depending on the bear. Alaska had more than one type, and although they didn't have grizzlies in Arkansas, they had black bears, and she knew enough about bear safety to survive. She knew next to nothing about moose.

"Hey there," Hazel announced herself.

She chose her next steps carefully. All the nature guidebooks said to make yourself look bigger, so she lifted her arms high and waved calmly to increase her size, hoping to scare it away.

A roar tore through the air, and goosebumps erupted over Hazel's skin.

Not a moose!

Instinctively, Hazel took a step back, and then froze. If she ran, she was dead, as any bear could outrun her.

The bear moved forward a few steps on all four legs and into Hazel's wand light before halting. It threw its head back to let out another roar. Hazel's knees shook at the sound.

The bear was black with thinning patches, some spots bald altogether. Its head hung low, swinging rhythmically as it watched her. Drool dripped from its slack jaw as its fire-glazed stare cut straight through her.

Something was wrong with it; it looked sick. The sight of it turned Hazel's stomach and made her heart ache at the same time. *Poor animal.*

Within seconds, the last vestiges of sunlight disappeared and the only thing standing between Hazel and utter darkness was her wand.

How am I going to aim in the dark? Once she cast another spell, the light would snuff out.

All at once, the bear charged and Hazel screamed—breaking her spell and plunging the clearing into total darkness.

Gwen

"Where the fuck is she?"

It was nearly time for them to head back, and from the look of the windows at Kodiak Brew, it was well past sunset. Hazel should've been back long before now.

A mage she didn't recognize was singing about a love spell on the tiny stage in the back corner, the crowd hanging on to every sultry note the girl hit. If Gwen wasn't so frustrated with Hazel's absence, she might've been just as enraptured. Instead, she found herself riddled with anxiety as she twisted the charms on her bracelet.

I never should have let her go alone. Images of the dogs, bloody and broken on the ground, surfaced in her mind.

"Should we go look for her?" Rafe shouted across the table.

If Hazel was in trouble, Gwen didn't need anyone else getting in her way or getting themselves hurt.

"No, you guys pay the tab and get back to school. I'm gonna go find her," Gwen said, sliding out of her side of the booth.

Jordan nodded. "Be safe."

"I don't think you should go alone. It's dark out and the thing that attacked those dogs is still out there," Rafe said, brows furrowed.

Gwen smirked. "I'm good." It was sweet of him to worry, but she was more than capable of handling herself.

Rafe looked like he was about to argue, but Gwen took off before he could. One day, he'd learn what Jordan already had: Gwen was no damsel in distress. She wished she could assure Rafe that she was the scariest thing out there, but that wasn't an option.

When Kodiak Brew's door banged shut behind her, Gwen took off at a trot down the cobblestone street in the direction that Hazel had headed, but when she hit the edge of town and took off into the trees, she stopped. She had no clue which way Hazel had gone from here. Removing her bracelet was an option, but not one she wanted to resort to in the woods, where her wolf would be desperate to be in control. Instead, she lit her wand and looked for signs to follow.

Thanks to all her training with her father and Klaus, she knew what to look for when her wolf wasn't free. Gwen easily spotted the fresh tracks Hazel had left in the dirt.

Gwen followed the shoe prints into the woods about a dozen yards, when another began to overlap. Large, square-shaped pads brought her to a stop. Then she noted the long, deep gouges at the tips.

Bear tracks.

Gwen's stomach dropped, and she sprinted. She had to get to Hazel. *Now.*

A high-pitched scream tore through the air.

Hazel!

She sounded far away, but Gwen headed in that direction.

Lightning cracked across the sky as thunder exploded, drowning out any other sounds Hazel might've made. In seconds, ominous clouds bloomed in the clear twilight sky and pitch black descended over the forest.

Where in Salem did this storm come from?

Gwen gritted her teeth with annoyance at the bracelet that she knew slowed her down and impaired her vision. She considered taking it off, but pushed the thought away. Regret still filled her from the last time she'd taken it off. She wouldn't be making that decision again so soon. Gwen kept her lit wand high overhead as she put her head down to watch for roots while she followed the tracks.

She increased her speed as fast as she could go, and soon, she could hear the chuffing of an angry animal.

"*Somnus!*" She heard Hazel invoke in the near distance.

Gwen was getting close. Thunder boomed once more, and she prayed that the rain would wait. The water could wash away her only reliable way to track Hazel.

Gwen made it to the edge of a clearing in time to see Hazel trip over a root and crash to the ground. Her arm remained outstretched, her wand aimed high at the bear that stood on its hind legs in front of her. Gwen watched as magic burst from Hazel's wand, hitting the bear in the face. The bear's mouth sealed shut.

Gwen drew her own wand and aimed, but she was too far away and she couldn't risk hitting Hazel. She had to get closer. Keeping to the tree line, she moved quickly, cutting a path straight toward the bear—and Hazel.

"Gwen!" Hazel's scream split the clearing the moment she caught sight of her.

"I'm coming! Hold on!" Gwen shouted back, not slowing her pace.

Hazel nodded and raised her wand again. Her next spell struck the bear, and he slid backwards, away from her a few inches. It was enough so that Hazel could get to her feet. But the moment she stood, it roared again, louder this time.

How is that possible?

The sealing spell should've lasted minutes, not seconds.

"Hey!" Gwen yelled in an effort to draw the bear's attention.

It didn't even glance over, its attention fully locked on its prey.

Hazel backed up slowly as she cast the invisible wall she'd used to prevent Rafe and Jordan from beating her to the empty seats in history class.

The bear charged, hitting the wall and rebounding a few feet.

Gwen was finally close enough. With a flick of her wrist, she spoke the spell her father had taught her to break the legs of an advancing opponent. "*Crus confractus.*"

Loud twin cracks pierced the air. Gwen had hit her target.

The bear let out another roar that shook her eardrums. She waited for it to fall to the ground in pain, but it didn't.

Gwen's blood turned cold.

It ran again, slamming into the transparent wall once more, completely unfazed by the spell that should have incapacitated it. Gwen's stomach turned. If magic couldn't stop it, what would?

A boom echoed across the clearing as the transparent force field fell and the bear growled.

"Hazel, run to me!" Gwen screamed as she continued her sprint to her.

Hazel tried, but it was no use. She was pinned between the bear and a tree.

As if the sky itself was invested in the fight, blinding-white lightning lanced the tree behind Hazel, which burst into flames as a loud crack of splintering wood echoed around them.

Unfazed by the chaos around them, the bear stood on its hind legs, towering over Hazel.

Fuck.

Panic slammed into Gwen. She couldn't let Hazel die, but the bear wouldn't respond to her magic. She had to do something.

Hazel screamed as the bear advanced again, and Gwen lost all thought for anything but saving her friend's life.

Gwen ripped off her charm bracelet and shifted into a giant white wolf. She bounded across the clearing and howled, pulling the bear's attention from Hazel.

Now that it was right in front of her, she could see its sunken orange-red eyes and its emaciated body. It looked as though it hadn't eaten in weeks; skin sagged from its bones and fur was missing in patches, revealing ragged flesh. It stunk of pungent fish and death.

Was it sick?

The bear growled and lunged to bite Gwen in the neck, but she anticipated its movement, the growl giving her enough time to sidestep him and make a move of her own.

She lurched to the right and then corrected straight on, taking a bite out of its neck. Her teeth ripped away rancid flesh as rotten blood filled her mouth. Gwen gagged as she spit it on the ground.

What the fuck is wrong with this thing?

She wiped her snout on the grass, trying to get the scent and taste off, but the bear leapt at her, tackling her into the grass.

Shit.

Gwen leveraged the bear's weight against it, flipping him off with her back paws. It hit a nearby tree trunk with a crack. Gwen darted past it, luring it further into the forest with hope that the trees would provide her coverage.

The bear stood up and charged again. This wasn't a fair fight. No physical pain fazed it. Gwen wasn't sure how long she could keep it at bay, but she hoped it would be long enough for Hazel to make it back to town.

The bear came at her again, this time managing to sink its teeth into her side. She let out a howl of pain. When it opened its jaw, she slipped from its grip as quickly as possible.

A chorus of howls echoed back to her from varying distances in the woods. She exhaled as she realized she might not have to deal with him alone. A pack definitely stood a better chance. Gwen tipped her head back and let a deep howl rip from her throat.

The bear swiped its paw across her face, knocking her to the ground. Pain lanced through her skull as her vision swam for a moment. The pause cost her precious seconds, and the bear was on top of her again. She thrashed under his weight, attempting to free herself, but remained trapped.

If she didn't get it off of her, he could smash her skull in a single blow. The thought made Gwen fight back with everything she had.

Suddenly, the bear moved off of her and looked up.

Hazel was flying—no, standing—right above them now. She'd climbed a tree.

What the fuck are you doing? You were supposed to run! Gwen screamed in her mind, wishing for the thousandth time she could speak to people in her wolf form.

A giant rock hit the bear square in the face. It growled and stood on its hind legs, swatting the branches above it, forcing Hazel to go higher. Lightning lit the sky once more.

Hazel, get out of that tree!

Gwen slammed into the bear's side, knocking it over, this time careful not to bite into its flesh. She never wanted to taste anything like that again.

When they both stood again, the bear faced her several feet away.

Gwen growled. *Give the fuck up already, you son of a bitch!*

She wasn't sure how she could kill it if ripping out its throat didn't work.

They stared at each other for a few moments before the bear began sprinting towards her once again. She sidestepped the attack, and this time, when she did, two wolves appeared through the forest on her left side. They growled in unison as the bear ran at them. Two more wolves emerged from the trees behind them and ran to the bear's flanks, taking pieces out of its side before spitting them out like Gwen had.

The bear turned, knocking the wolf on its right to the ground. The other wolves howled. A chill went down Gwen's spine when an echo answered. No, not an echo—more wolves. An entire pack—at least twelve wolves, not including herself—soon surrounded the clearing. Gwen's knees wobbled as she took in the predators before her.

The bear growled and stood on its hind legs, but instead of fleeing, it charged toward the tree Hazel was in. Its claws sank into the bark as it climbed up the trunk. It was trying to get to Hazel.

Before it could reach the first branch, a warning rumble filled the air, and a white-hot bolt hit the tree right above its head. The bear fell back to the ground with a roar as a crack rent the air. Hazel screamed as the branch beneath her feet gave way and she fell to the ground.

Gwen ran to try to catch her friend, but in her wolf form, the best she'd be able to do was soften the fall. She watched helplessly as Hazel cast a spell that slowed her descent only seconds from impact. Her body hit the ground with a thud next to the bear.

Please be okay, please be okay.

Beside them, the bear stood, shaking its head. It spotted Hazel and lunged.

But Gwen was already there. She bit the bear by the paw and

pulled with all her might, dragging it away from her friend, inch by inch.

Its teeth snapped then Hazel screamed.

Gwen lost her grip as her own razor-sharp teeth shredded through the bear's fur and skin like butter. As she released the bear to get a better hold, a lightning bolt streaked down and hit the bear squarely in the back. It collapsed to the ground.

Gwen sniffed it cautiously, afraid that even lightning couldn't stop the beast. It reeked of death mixed with the nauseating scent of burned flesh.

Damn, we just got so lucky.

Before Gwen could do anything else, the pack attacked the immobilized bear. Teeth flashed and fur flew as roars of rage rent the air, along with sounds of cracking bone and cartilage.

Gwen ran around the pack and huffed in relief when she saw that the bear was finished. The wolves paid her no attention as they finished off their prey.

It was time to go while they were preoccupied with the kill. Before they realized the meat wasn't edible.

Gwen trotted to the edge of the clearing, away from the wolves, and Hazel followed, slowly backing away from the pack.

Smart girl.

A thunk brought Gwen's attention back to the pack in time for her to see the bear's severed head fall to the ground. The world went quiet as a wolf broke away, inspecting it with a sniff. Gwen was positive the bear wouldn't rise again.

Once Hazel reached her, Gwen wanted to yell at her friend to run. That she wasn't safe here with these wolves. With Gwen.

"Gwen?" Hazel whispered.

But there was no whispering when wolves were present.

At the sound, the wolves began to move once more, but this time, toward the girls. Low growls rumbled through the pack.

Hazel looked at Gwen and then back at the wolves. Gwen practically saw the light bulb go on in Hazel's head that they were growling at them. Hazel stepped closer to Gwen, one hand touching her fur. Hazel's other hand shook as she aimed her wand once more.

A gray wolf took a half-step forward, and Gwen's head snapped up as she growled in warning. But the wolf didn't back up. Two more stepped forward, and three others circled the perimeter.

"Uh, Gwen—" Hazel started.

Gwen already knew. They couldn't eat their first kill. The pack would have to hunt again. She couldn't fight them all off, even if Hazel's magic worked on them. There were too many—but Gwen was faster than a normal wolf.

We have to run.

Gwen let out a small whine as she turned to the side, lowered her front legs, and looked at Hazel. Gwen would rather die than offer this to literally anyone. But these were dire circumstances.

"You want me to get on?"

Gwen nodded. The wolves were moving closer. They didn't have much time.

Hazel let out a burst of laughter. "No, just change back."

A growl answered Hazel, but it wasn't from Gwen.

"Fuck," Hazel said.

Yes, fuck!

Hazel didn't hesitate. She climbed onto Gwen's back. Her friend's scent washed over her, calming the wolf with its familiarity. For now.

Not bothering to glance back, Gwen turned and ran. Hazel hung on for dear life, nearly yanking out a handful of her fur. A snarl grew in Gwen's throat, but she swallowed it down, hoping to keep herself and her friend calm.

She ran hard back the way she'd come, letting Hazel's old trail lead their way. Sounds of paws over dirt told her the pack pursued them. They followed Gwen and Hazel all the way to the edge of town before giving up. Civilization was apparently their hard line.

"Slow down!" Hazel yelled in her ear, but Gwen maintained her speed as they skirted town, only slowing when they reached the trees outside the tunnel. The adrenaline flooding her system made her feel like she had wings, and she was going to use it to their advantage by getting them to safety as soon as possible.

When Gwen came to a stop, Hazel slid from her back.

"That was... I don't even know how to say what that was," Hazel said, throwing her hands wildly in the air. Her words all mushed together as she paced in a tight circle in front of Gwen. "Insane. Intense. Unreal."

Intense was right. Gwen panted from the exertion of carrying Hazel for so long. Therians never let people ride them, so she wasn't used to having cargo.

She scented the air nervously, ensuring the wolves weren't closing in from the other side. She didn't smell them nearby, but the sensation of being watched closely gnawed at her.

Hazel inspected Gwen up close for the first time. Gwen knew what she saw: her wolf form was larger than any natural wolf. Her fur was white, and looked eerily similar to Gwen's hair.

Gwen could see the conflict on Hazel's face as she digested the information before her and tried to make sense of it. She heard Hazel's already fast-beating heart speed up.

Does she know what I am? Will she hate me?

Another even scarier thought loomed in the back of her mind.

Will she tell?

"This is the best transmutation I think I've ever seen," Hazel said finally.

Please keep telling yourself that.

"I think it's safe now." Hazel looked around. "You can change back."

Fuck! My bracelet. She'd never spelled her bracelet to return to her room like she had her wand and clothes because she was usually handing it off to Klaus who was always right beside her to reattach it. She was so screwed.

Panic slammed into her, sharp and suffocating. How could she have been so stupid? It wasn't just lost—it was back there, in the open, unprotected. There was no way to go back for it tonight while the wolves were still on the hunt. She'd barely made it out alive, and going back now would be a death sentence. Her breath came too fast, ears ringing as her mind spun, scrambling for a solution.

Klaus. He could hide her—he had to. But how the hell was she supposed to find him like this? She couldn't shift back without her bracelet.

Her heart hammered so hard she thought she might be sick. She took a deep breath, the smells of the forest attempting to push her wolf over the edge, but she locked her senses down like her father had trained her to do. She had to stay in control.

"Let's head back to school. We're already late enough as it is," Hazel stressed.

Gwen whined. Not being able to speak to her friend really fucking sucked. She was trapped, and there was no way to tell her or to ask for help.

Hazel knew animals; she had grown up on a farm. Maybe she'd understand body language.

Here's hoping.

Gwen laid down on the ground and covered her snout with her paw. She let out a long whine.

Hazel's gaze met hers, and Gwen poured every ounce of distress into her irises she could muster. She pinned back her ears, trying to sell it.

Hazel's eyes widened. "You can't change back, can you?"

It was the next-to-last thing Gwen wanted Hazel to know, but there was no way around it. She needed Hazel's help.

Gwen huffed in confirmation, her panic bubbling higher, pressing against her throat. Hazel—hell, the whole school—was so close to learning her secret. If the Brecilian Knights didn't kill her, her dad would.

Her wolf snarled as it fought against its constraints in her mind. It told her to run, to hide. But Gwen took a deep breath. Then another. Its snarls faded to low growls.

"Oh, shit!" Hazel shook her hands. "Where are we going to get a reversal elixir at this time of night?"

Gwen whined once more, and Hazel stepped forward as if she might try to pet her. Gwen stepped back, barely suppressing a growl. She was not a pet.

Hazel, thankfully, got the message and lowered her hand. Gwen was reminded yet again why Hazel was such a good friend to have, especially as a wolf. She could read the tiniest changes in Gwen's demeanor.

She just hoped Hazel would still want to be her friend after this.

Hazel chewed her lip in thought. "Let's get back to campus and find someone who has a reversal elixir."

Gwen's shoulders relaxed the tiniest amount.

She still thinks this is transmutation.

At least for now, Hazel wasn't questioning. For now, Gwen had a chance to fix this mess.

As they approached the tunnel, Gwen cautiously slowed to sniff the air, and the familiar faint scents of Rafe and Jordan filled her nose. But they were at least an hour old, fading like the others. The curfew must have emptied out the tunnel.

Salem burn us—the curfew! If anyone caught them, things were going to go from bad to worse.

For the first time since coming to SEU, Gwen and Hazel walked through the tunnel to campus. It took forever, and Hazel having to clutch on to her fur for guidance in the dark didn't help speed it along.

Thankfully, they saw no one, and Gwen kept a tight lid on her anxiety, refusing to let ill-fated scenarios play out in her head. Instead, she repeated the steps they would take on a loop in her mind.

I'll lead Hazel around the tree line to the back of Alterion. I'll whine until she understands that I need Klaus. Klaus will hide me until it's safe to go get my bracelet.

She didn't allow herself to poke holes in the plan—that would defeat the purpose of the exercise.

As they exited the tunnel and headed for the tree line that edged campus, a loud, shrill sound emitted from the administration building.

The tunnel must've been warded for the curfew.

You've got to be fucking kidding me!

"Run!" Hazel yelled over the blaring alarm.

CHAPTER 22

Gwen

Gwen didn't think—she bolted. Fear slammed into her chest as her instincts took over, driving her forward. The shrill wail of the curfew alarm ripped through the air, clawing at her ears, drowning out everything else. The trees on the edge of campus loomed ahead, dark and safe, and she pushed herself harder. Faster. She tore across the open ground, legs pumping, heart hammering, lungs burning. All that mattered was getting away. The fear of getting caught in her wolf form wrapped around her like a noose. She struggled to breathe from the weight of it and her vision began to swim.

If the school found out, she'd only lose her place at SEU if she was lucky, but she'd lose her life—whether by death or imprisonment—if the Knights were told.

She couldn't afford the first. She wouldn't survive the second.

She reached the tree line but did not slow, branches slashing at her legs as she plunged into the shadows.

The alarm stopped as Gwen flew behind a tree. Only then did it hit her—Hazel. She'd abandoned her. Gwen hadn't waited. Hadn't even looked back.

The knowledge lodged in her chest, sharp and cold. The uncomfortable truth was that Gwen wouldn't change her choice. She couldn't afford to be caught, and going back could lead her straight into a faculty member.

Hazel will be fine.

Gwen pushed deeper into the forest, panting from exertion, her muscles coiling with tension. Every crack of a branch, every whisper of wind through the trees, sent a fresh wave of panic crawling down her spine. She wasn't safe here. She needed cover now.

A massive tree with thick, low-hanging branches caught her eye, and she darted under it, pressing herself into the shadows. Her breath came fast and ragged as she curled up behind the trunk, tucking her conspicuous white fur out of sight.

I just have to stay hidden until Klaus leaves Alterion for classes.

Her ears strained for movement, but all she could hear was the wild hammering of her own pulse.

Then she heard the sound of a stick cracking underfoot.

"Miss Bishop," a familiar voice called.

Harland.

Fuck!

Gwen's hackles stood on end, her wolf ready to quit hiding, preferring to fight back or run. She squeezed her eyes shut and fought the urge to bolt. She wouldn't make it very far. She was exhausted and needed sleep or food to restore her energy.

"Gwendolyn, please come out."

His voice was too calm, his heartbeat too steady. She didn't trust calm. She didn't trust steady. Her father's lessons echoed in her mind, sharp and unforgiving. *Never trust outsiders. Never let your guard down. Never show weakness.* It was bad enough she'd exposed herself to Logan, another therian, and to Hazel. Now, she was cornered. She had no backup, no bracelet, no control over her condition. She had no choice.

He needed to leave.

A low growl rumbled through her as she bared her teeth and stepped into the open—not in surrender, but in warning.

Harland didn't even flinch. He simply stared at her, eyes wide with piqued interest. Her wolf was insulted and growled at him.

Ignoring her he squatted, resting his forearms on his knees as he studied her at eye level. "A wolf. Impressive."

Surprise rippled through her. She'd expected anger and reproach, not the note of admiration that rang in his voice.

This idiot has no idea what he's dealing with—he thinks it's just another transmutation spell, like Hazel.

Harland took a step forward and Gwen saw red. She lunged, snapping her teeth. If he came any closer, she'd attack.

Harland held up his hands. "Easy, Lassie. It's time to change back," Harland said with a smile.

Gwen's ears flattened, and she emitted a sharp huff.

How fucking dare he compare me to a dog?

"Oh." His smile wavered as his gaze flicked over her stance. "You can't, can you?"

She growled in answer, backing up as she kept her head low and ears pinned back. As much as she needed help, she couldn't accept it from him. He was too close to the truth already. He'd seen her spiraling once and saved her, but this was different. This was a clear piece to the puzzle that Gwen couldn't afford to give.

"I thought therians could shift at will."

His words landed like a physical blow and Gwen jerked as shock coursed through her.

How did he know? Her claws dug into the dirt.

No. No. No.

This wasn't happening. Her wolf told her she should run right now.

"I have a potion that'll help you shift back," he said carefully. "Unfortunately, I don't have it on me. I'll be right back."

Gwen stiffened as he pulled out his wand. She lowered her head, readying for attack.

"*Advinere.*" In an instant, he was gone.

Every muscle in her body coiled tight. She could leave. But then what? She'd have to stay hidden from him until she could get to Klaus, which could be hours from now. She needed help.

But what if he's not getting help? What if he's calling the Knights?

On high alert, her wolf listened to every sound, every movement. Panic threatened to drown her as she waited for the telling crunch of dirt or rustle of leaves. After another minute, she could bear it no more. She needed to move.

Gwen turned to leave, but Harland finally returned, black backpack in tow. She watched him cautiously from a distance as he unzipped it. The scent of leather and oak permeated the air. When he pulled out a small vial and a stack of clothing, she suppressed a groan.

My professor is going to see me naked. Well, I guess it won't be the first time.

Gwen had wanted it to happen again, but not like this.

"I should've brought a bowl," he said with a sardonic half-smirk. The sight of his beautiful teeth and the sound of his joking voice put her at ease, but her wolf couldn't care less.

Gwen growled.

"Sorry, bad joke. I can pour it into your mouth if you like?"

That idea was even worse. She didn't want him anywhere near her when she took it—she had no idea what it was going to do to her.

Gwen took a step back as she considered that maybe the potion wouldn't help her. How could it? Her father, a therian himself, had certainly never shared such a thing.

That doesn't mean much, liar that he is.

There was a high probability whatever was in that vial wasn't going to help her—and it might even hurt her.

"Gwendolyn, you're only dragging this out." He sounded annoyed for the first time tonight.

Gwen flashed her teeth at him.

"I helped you before, didn't I?" Harland said, his voice still and sure.

Yes. He *had* helped her, and he'd not said a word about it. Better yet, the Knights hadn't come knocking at her door.

She let out a guttural sigh before slinking toward him, her head still down as she bared her canines in warning. If he was thinking of doing something stupid like drugging her, he was in for a rude awakening about a therian's fast metabolism.

Her wolf fought for control—it still wanted to run—but Gwen took deep breaths, focusing on logic to keep it at bay. She had to admit it felt stupid, trusting this man after his deception about being her professor, but she had no other choices right now.

Reluctantly, she sat down. He reached for her neck, and she let out a small growl. He pulled back.

Good. He needs to be afraid.

Tilting her head back, she allowed him to steady her neck with his hand. This close, Gwen's therian's senses picked up on the scent of his breath. Peppermint.

He held the vial to her mouth, and she drained every drop. It tasted like grass and dish soap. It didn't matter. She'd drink it even if it tasted like vomit if it meant turning her back into her mage form.

Gwen instantly shifted back, fully naked. Her wounds from the evening were completely healed but her head spun as he released her from his grip. She didn't feel right. She needed to get away, get home. To Hazel.

Her legs threatened to give out as she tried to stand.

Harland swallowed as he averted his gaze. "You're probably feeling a little muddled from the potion. That'll pass quickly."

That's an understatement.

The ever-present hum of her therian instincts faded. Her heightened senses dulled, the quiet awareness of movement around her disappeared, and the pulse of life in the forest slipped away. All of it was gone.

It was worse than the bracelet. The bracelet locked her shift, but at least she still felt like herself when she wore it. Now, she felt completely empty. The familiar warmth of her magic was buried so deep she feared it was gone entirely.

A lump formed in her throat. Would she even be able to cast? Her fingers twitched at her sides, instinct begging her to reach for her wand, but she didn't want him to know how vulnerable she might be. So instead, she swallowed hard and neutralized her emotions, even as unease crawled beneath her skin.

"Clothes, please."

Harland handed them over quickly, eyes downcast. Gwen put on the grey sweatsuit that smelled like leather and oak. Even though she knew she should be wary of him, afraid of how much he knew about her, she couldn't help but feel a small prick of satisfaction, knowing she now had another article of clothing from him.

"Thanks. I'm decent now."

He turned around with a tight smile. "Now for the bad news. I have to take you to Chancellor Lucas's office for being out past curfew."

"Seriously?" Gwen couldn't believe he'd actually hold her to that.

"Seriously." He motioned for her to fall in step beside him. "Hazel is there now."

Shit. Hazel had been caught. Surely she'd explained it wasn't their fault they didn't make curfew.

"They never even saw me."

Putting his hand over his heart, he said, "Unfortunately, that doesn't matter. The curfew spell included an identification charm."

"Of course it did," Gwen muttered. Nothing about this damned night had gone her way, and somehow it was going from bad to worse.

If the spell had already identified her, it was only a matter of time before people started asking questions. Questions she couldn't answer.

Her gaze snapped to Harland. He knew. He could answer those questions whether she wanted him to or not.

She took a step closer as they walked towards the administration building, her voice low and sharp. "You can't tell anyone what you saw tonight." Harland arched a brow, but before he could respond, she pressed on. "Swear to me, Harland. You won't tell." Her throat bobbed as she said, "The Knights will kill me."

His expression flickered with amusement, then became something unreadable. But Gwen wasn't in the mood for games. Everything was on the line. If word got out, if anyone learned the truth, she wasn't the only one at risk. Gwen's heart threatened to beat out of her chest as she studied him closely, waiting for him to answer.

"I swear it," he said, his voice steady.

Gwen narrowed her eyes. That was too easy. She knew from experience with her dad most people didn't do things out of the kindness of their heart. He had to want something.

"And what exactly are you going to tell people?"

Harland let out a slow breath, like he'd already considered this. "That I found you in the woods. You were injured, so I healed you before bringing you back."

Gwen's stomach twisted. It was too neat, too perfect.

"Hazel already had scratches on her," he added, as if reading her thoughts. "No one will question it." He smirked. "You're just lucky I'm such a good liar."

Gwen narrowed her eyes at him. "Why are you so willing to keep my secret?"

"Because I don't like the Brecilian Knights any more than you do."

What did *he* have against the Knights? She'd never heard anyone openly dislike them—except her father. His words felt too good to be true. Still, a small, annoying part of her wanted to believe him.

They walked in awkward silence until Harland opened the door of the administration building, motioning Gwen inside. "This is where I leave you."

"Thanks again," Gwen said.

"Oh, by the way, this potion will wear off after about twenty-four hours, give or take. Find me tomorrow for another dose if you need it."

Gwen shook her head. "I won't."

She'd find her bracelet tomorrow *before* this dose wore off. She never wanted to take that potion again.

Gwen entered Chancellor Lucas's office to find her sitting behind a dark-stained oak desk centered in the back of the space, the walls behind her lined top to bottom with textbooks, some older than any Gwen had ever seen. Her wingback leather chair bobbed ever so slightly, like a boat on water.

"Miss Bishop," Chancellor Lucas greeted her with a slow nod.

Hazel looked up at her sheepishly from one of the wingback chairs across from the chancellor. Gwen was relieved, and a bit surprised, not to see anger or betrayal on her friend's face. Guilt tugged at Gwen for leaving her behind.

"I'm glad you could join us. Miss Thorne was just telling me how you were out for a hike and got lost in the forest."

Oh shit, she lied! Relief blanketed Gwen as she looked at her friend. *Why did she lie?*

She'd worry about it later. Right now she had to help sell it.

Chancellor Lucas studied her face for a reaction, but Gwen was a good liar too. She'd been doing it all her life.

"Yeah, we're so sorry. The woods got so dark so fast, it was hard to find our way back."

The chancellor sat back in her leather chair and studied Gwen over steepled fingers. "While accidents happen, rules are rules."

Gwen looked at her wide-eyed, her stomach twisting. This was it. Chancellor Lucas was going to tell them to pack their bags and go home.

“I’ve already explained to Miss Thorne that you will both be joining the Wilderness Watch.”

“What?” Gwen said. Of all the forms of punishments, this made the least sense.

“The school’s rescue team, Miss Bishop.”

“Sorry, Chancellor, what I meant to say is ‘what the hell’?”

Hazel’s mouth popped open as she stared wide-eyed at Gwen.

Chancellor Lucas pressed her lips into a tight line and Gwen instantly regretted her words. Now was not the time to be pushing the chancellor’s boundaries.

“The Watch is a mutually beneficial alliance between SEU and Eagles Ridge. Fortunately for you, they didn’t have enough students sign up this year and are in need of helping hands.” Chancellor Lucas reached into the top right drawer of her desk and pulled out two silver discs. She slid one toward Hazel and the other to Gwen. “Here are your compacts. They will notify you when someone goes missing. If you’re alerted while you’re in class, you will ignore it. We don’t want you to abandon your studies. Any other time, you will report to Captain Jackson here in the administration building. Do you have any questions?”

Hazel plucked hers from the table immediately, but Gwen stared at it like a snake poised to bite her.

“For how long?” Gwen asked. This punishment seemed too light. She’d been expecting suspension at the least; there had to be a catch.

“Until the end of the year. Unless you are caught out past curfew again and then I will be forced to revise your punishment. Consider yourselves on probation.”

The chancellor didn’t elaborate on what probation entailed, and Gwen prayed Hazel wouldn’t ask. It was better to ask for forgiveness than permission. Besides, it didn’t matter—Gwen was going to be on her best behavior moving forward. She’d exposed herself to too many people. Her bracelet was going to stay firmly on her wrist for the rest of the semester.

Hex it, my bracelet!

Gwen bit back a groan. She'd now have to retrieve her bracelet while under the watchful eye of the chancellor. Maybe she'd need a second dose from Harland after all.

"You are both dismissed."

Hazel and Gwen exited the administration building in silence.

Once outside, Hazel opened her mouth, but Gwen held up her hand. "Not here."

Hazel's mouth snapped closed. After a beat she said, "Fine. Our room. Now."

Okay, so maybe she is *pissed.*

"What the hell was that?" Hazel's voice had reached an intensity Gwen had never heard from her before. With her arms flung open and eyes wide, Gwen knew Hazel was worked up.

"Yeah, that bear was insane," Gwen deflected, making it sound like they'd been through something completely uninteresting as she walked towards her room. "I'm wondering if it was what attacked the sled dogs."

Hazel scoffed. "Not as insane as you turning into a giant wolf and attacking it."

"Well, it was trying to kill you. I didn't have much of a choice, did I?" Gwen regretted her words as soon as she'd snapped them. This conversation needed to end.

Hazel threw up her hands in exasperation. "How the fuck did you turn into a wolf? You just carry a transmutation potion on you at all times? I don't believe it."

Shit, she's piecing things together.

Her transmutation argument wouldn't hold up much longer if Hazel didn't drop this. Gwen considered telling her right then. She was so sick of lying to the people she loved. And hell, Harland knew and he was fine with it. Hazel was a good friend—she'd stuck by her time and time again, through the exam, after the sled dogs. Even tonight. But what if this secret was the last straw? What if Hazel learned the truth and walked away—or worse—told?

"Gwen, say something!" Hazel stomped her foot. Her frustration squashed any hope that Hazel would react well.

"When did you start cursing so much?" Gwen asked, changing the subject again.

"Gwen," Hazel demanded as she began to pace the living room.

Gwen looked at Hazel like she was crazy. "What's wrong with you? I know how to use a transmutation spell. It's not a big deal."

"There's no way you used transmutation magic! It's insanely hard and you're only a freshman," Hazel insisted as she studied Gwen's face intently.

Damn it, Hazel!

Her friend was too smart to miss the glaring holes in her initial transmutation theory. A rock settled in Gwen's stomach. Hazel was too close to the truth.

Gwen rolled her eyes, revealing nothing of the fear she felt inside.

"I'm not crazy, Gwen. I saw you transform. You didn't use a potion or anything. You took off your bracelet and shifted."

Gwen tried to hide her look of alarm that Hazel had noticed the bracelet. She couldn't know.

"Hazel, I'm tired. It's been a long night and we have lab early in the morning."

"If you don't tell me what's going on right now—"

"You'll what?" Gwen interrupted.

She was not going to let Hazel threaten her into giving up her secret. Hazel needed to drop this.

"Gwen, please tell me what's going on," Hazel pleaded, eyes wide and chin quivering. She looked so hurt and desperate. But Gwen couldn't tell her.

"I'm going to bed." Gwen shut her bedroom door and turned the lock.

With the solid wood at her back, Gwen cried, getting out the guilt and shame and fear she'd been keeping bottled up most of the night.

Somehow, she felt like in her effort to keep Hazel from running away screaming from the truth, she'd pushed her away anyway.

CHAPTER 23

Hazel

A stabbing ache in Hazel's back roused her from sleep. Her bed felt hard as a rock tonight. Eyes still heavy with exhaustion, she reached underneath herself and pulled out a small stone.

What the hell?

Hazel rubbed her eyes to make sure they weren't deceiving her. Sure enough, a small lava stone with rough, porous edges sat in her hands. She scrambled to sit up, and the scrape of skin against stone startled her. There was no bed beneath her; she sat upon solid rock in a hot, dark room that stank of sulfur.

Hazel's heart pounded at waking in a different place than where she'd gone to bed. She retraced her memory, making sure she wasn't forgetting something. But no, she'd gone to sleep in her bed, tired, scratched, and bruised from her encounter with the bear. It had taken her forever to feel relaxed enough to sleep after Gwen had brushed her off and even longer to silence the questions racing through her mind.

A chilling thought sank into Hazel's gut. Had she been hit in the head? Suffered a concussion when she fell from the tree?

"Oh Terra, where am I?" she whispered.

Hazel rose shakily, her knees protesting at the same time a wave of lightheadedness washed over her.

The sound of steps, sharp and distinct on stone, echoed in the darkness behind her.

She whirled, straining her eyes in the pitch black. "Hello? Is anyone there?" Her voice shook with terror.

A sudden splash echoed, followed immediately by an explosion of light. Hazel gasped. The light danced along the walls of the colossal cavern where she and Gwen had found one another during the exam. A knot tightened in her stomach. Technically, it was also where *they* had been found—by the dragons.

Hazel glanced upwards to search above her for the winged beasts.

Please don't be there. Please don't be there.

The air froze in her lungs as she spied four colossal shapes perched on an outcropping above, horned heads and shimmering scales reflecting the magma's glow.

Hazel's eyes locked on the amber dragon and memories of its all-consuming fire filled her with terror.

They're not real. They're not real.

But Hazel wasn't truly convinced of that. She hadn't been since they'd completed the exam. Sure, she'd gone about her life and went along with Gwen's theory that they were just part of the test, but it didn't stop the small voice in the back of her mind that questioned it.

And now here they were above her, certainly not in any test.

Had they seen her yet? She didn't know, and she wasn't going to take the time to find out.

She crawled towards the opening she'd come through nearly two months ago. Her breath shortened as she moved as fast as she could, desperately ignoring the stabs of pain beneath her hands, knees, and toes as they landed on random rocks.

Hazel made it halfway down the walkway, the entrance growing clearer every second, when the air was filled with the familiar sound of beating wings. Her racing heart lodged in her throat as she launched herself to her feet and then sprinted as fast as her legs would carry her. The urge to look back at the beautiful creatures warred within her, but she knew that seconds were precious and she couldn't afford to fall off the thin walkway. A rock sliced through the sole of her left foot and she cried out in pain.

Within seconds, the amber dragon landed before her, its weight reverberating through the rock and up through Hazel's bones, making her teeth clatter. She skidded to a stop feet from the hulking creature.

The dragon leaned down to place its face directly before hers; she saw her own terrified reflection there in its eyes. It took a deep breath and released it, hot air covering her like a blanket. A sweat broke out on her forehead.

"You're taking too long," his deep, gravely voice spoke into her mind. It sounded exactly as Hazel remembered.

"I—I don't know what you're talking about," Hazel stammered, fear riding her every thought.

"You have to be quicker." The dragon's eyes flashed with emphasis.

The familiar words sent a shiver down Hazel's spine. Her mother liked to say those same words in her visions.

"How do you know about that?" Hazel squeaked. Those words couldn't be a coincidence.

The dragon didn't answer as he spread his wings wide and launched into the air.

"Wait!" Hazel yelled.

The dragon plunged beneath the walkway and surged up on the other side, flying at least a hundred yards away. She looked at the exit, then back at the dragon, torn between the need for answers and the desperation to get the hell out of the cavern.

The dragon turned, a monstrous arrow of scales and fury, and flew straight down the walkway, belly skimming along the stone, directly at her. No slowing, no hesitation. Its jaws gaped, revealing a fiery spark at the back of his throat. Her knees shook with the memory of seeing it the day of the exam. She knew how it burned, knew there was no escape—she was too far from the exit, with no wand and a chasm of deadly magma below.

At least she had survived the flames before. She'd stand her ground and try to do so again.

As the dragon approached, Hazel lifted her hands, an instinctive act—to brace for impact, to hold him off, to fight him off. She didn't know.

When the dragon's flames swelled, a single, fierce thought ignited in Hazel's mind: *If I burn, you burn too.*

A searing white-blue heat erupted from her palms and spiked across the distance to hit the dragon square in the face.

The dragon roared, rolling sideways and then disappearing over the edge of the walkway. Hazel stared at her hands, at a loss for what just happened. Her shaking fingers and palms looked normal, the heat within them gone with no trace. She'd used a magic she'd never seen before, and without a wand

How did I do that?

Hazel pushed the thought aside. However she'd done it, she might have to do it again. She cautiously approached the edge and looked below. The dragon was nowhere to be seen. Had he fallen into the magma?

She shook her head. No, she'd have heard it.

The dragon suddenly appeared at the edge, flying up and over Hazel so quickly she fell back on her ass. It landed beside her once more as she scrambled backwards.

"Now you're getting it," the dragon purred, before its mouth pulled back to expose its lethal teeth in the most terrifying grin.

This is it. It's finally going to kill me.

Hazel woke shaking in her bed, pajamas and sheets drenched in a cold sweat.

Hazel stifled a yawn as she set her book bag down on her favorite table on the second floor of the library. She'd slept terribly last night, afraid to go back to sleep after waking from her nightmare. That's what she was calling it. Anything else, even the possibility of it being a vision, was too unsettling. She never wanted to encounter a dragon again as long as she lived.

But the deeper, truer reason she denied the possibility of a vision, was her reluctance to accept her actions in the dream. If it was a vision, then it meant she possessed yet another special magic: electricity.

While that would've been easy enough to write off as a dream—since no one on earth could conjure electricity—Hazel knew without a doubt that the lightning had struck the bear last night after she'd begged it to.

Gwen seemed to think the bear was the dogs' attacker, and she was inclined to agree. The pieces fit. On the plus side, she was no longer worried about the predator anymore—and most of the campus had already moved on. But lying last night meant the curfew was still in place. Fortunately, most of the students had adjusted to this as the new normal so Hazel didn't feel too guilty.

She'd lied to the chancellor last night because she couldn't explain the truth—that she'd been out after curfew chasing visions, or that she might've killed the bear with lightning.

And she also couldn't explain what she'd seen Gwen do. At first, she was convinced it was a transmutation spell or potion. But now? She wasn't so sure.

Which was why she was about to look for something other than her mother in the library for the first time since arriving at SEU. After last night, she was going to be searching for information on animal transmutation—for Gwen—and electricity or lightning—for herself. Good thing she loved research.

The tall arched windows bathed Hazel in golden morning light as she looked for the aisle she'd memorized two weeks ago. She was surprised she remembered where it was with all the new information she was having to make room for in her head. Something had been so strange that day when she'd found Gwen surrounded by an avalanche of books on the library floor. As she thought back on it now, it made sense. There were many things about Gwen that didn't add up.

Aside from her deranged hunt through the books themselves, Gwen had been aggressive in keeping Hazel from looking at them. And then there was how secretive she seemed at times, like when she'd disappeared from the Alterion party and tried to hide the reason. Of course, the fact that she'd changed into a wolf without a transmutation elixir was technically impossible. But the most interesting of all the things was her bracelet. She was constantly touching it, and then last night, she'd taken it off before she'd changed into the wolf.

Yes, Gwen is definitely hiding something.

The shelves were packed tight, not a scintilla of space between the ancient tomes bound in cracked leather. She'd need to look at them all to determine a pattern, so Hazel started at the beginning. She ran her finger along the first faded title. *A Therian's History of the Great War.*

Hazel froze, confusion creasing her brow. She'd expected books on transmutation. Not history.

They have to be here somewhere.

But they weren't. Next to the first were other books about therian history, culture, and folklore, and then some about their political interactions with the other Forsaken—elves, fae, and siphoners.

Hazel banged her forehead against the edge of the shelf.

Great. Another dead end.

That was all she was finding lately—no answers about her mother, now no answers about Gwen. What the hell was this library good for? Tears stung her eyes as frustration crept in and Hazel reached up quickly to wipe them away. As she did, her eyes landed on a book on the bottom shelf. She recognized it—Gwen had been reading it that day when Hazel had found her getting scolded by the librarian.

Hazel plucked the book from the shelf and ran her finger over the title on the front cover. *Magical Empires: Pre-Great War*. As she cracked the book open, the smell of old parchment filled her nose. The print inside was faded, but thankfully still legible.

Unfortunately there was nothing in there about transmutation, or lightning or electricity, so she moved on to the next book. The next she picked at random, a red tome with gold foiling. The first page told her the book had been written before the Great War. It was over a thousand years old. Hazel immediately lightened her hold on the book. *Unlocking the Secrets of Therian Magic.*

Hazel flipped gingerly through the delicate pages. Her brow furrowed as the words "spirit magic" caught her eye.

Unlike mages and siphoners, who solely pull their magic from the earth, therians, like elves and fae, possess an internal source of power, one that comes from within. Their magic does not rely on the natural world. Even if earth magic was to be depleted, a therian would still be able to wield their abilities.

Hazel stilled as she thought about how Gwen had shifted without a wand or an elixir.

A therian's magic is directly tied to their physical energy. Instead of replenishing through ley lines or lunar cycles, they simply need to eat, sleep, or rest to restore their power. The stronger they are physically and mentally, the stronger their magic.

Hazel snorted. That would certainly explain Gwen's appetite and incredible figure, despite never working out.

Of all demi-humans, therians are known to have increased senses, strength, and speed. Above all, they can heal at an incredible rate, making them nearly invincible.

A chill slid down Hazel's spine as she stumbled backwards, barely holding on to the book. She thought back to their close encounters with death, but couldn't come up with a single time she'd seen Gwen with a scrape, or even a bruise.

There were so many parallels, so many coincidences, that they couldn't *be* coincidences, could they?

Hazel shook her head.

This is insane. Therians have been extinct since the end of the Great War. There's no way.

"Hey, Hazel. What are you up to?"

Hazel snapped the book closed in surprise. She looked to the end of the aisle to find Elodie. "Hi!" she squeaked, slipping the book behind her back.

"Find anything interesting?" Elodie asked, a smile on her sweet freckled face.

"Oh, ah, no. I'm just browsing," Hazel said.

If she'd been holding a book about lightning magic, she wouldn't want Elodie to see it. She didn't really know what to believe yet, but as much as Hazel wanted to know the truth about Gwen—*deserved* to know, given she was living with the girl—it was not her truth to share.

Elodie nodded, and when Hazel said nothing more, she bid her farewell.

As soon as she was out of sight, Hazel began tearing any books related to therians from the shelves.

She checked out of the library as quickly as possible and headed back to the dorms. She had as much as she could carry discreetly in her book bag; she'd look for information about lightning or electricity another day.

When she finally pushed through the dormitory door, her mind was in a tailspin. Thankfully, Gwen wasn't home. Hazel dropped the books onto the coffee table and kneeled before them to come up with a plan of research. The weight of all these books and the possibility of answers loomed over her.

What if she didn't like what she learned?

Hazel's gaze drifted to the bookshelf beside the fireplace. Could she tuck the ones she wasn't using there? As she leaned forward, a blue-foiled book snagged her attention, and she leaned in closer to inspect the titles. Her breath hitched. Here, in Gwen's collection of books, lay a treasure trove of information that she hadn't anticipated: books on therians.

Hazel pulled one down, then another and another. The bookshelf was nearly empty by the time she'd removed them all. As she stared at the books, her heart pounded in her ears. It had been right here this whole time. How had she missed it?

This evidence was damning. There was only one doubt in Hazel's mind whether Gwen was a therian or not—they were supposed to be extinct. But Hazel didn't think that was enough to disprove her theory at this point. She was positive: Gwen was a therian.

But did that change anything? Gwen was still Gwen—Hazel's friend and roommate. Right? Being different didn't make her bad. If that were true, then Hazel wasn't good herself. She was keeping her own secrets.

Thoughts of her visions crossed her mind. What would Gwen think about those visions? About her ability to have them? Hazel pushed the thoughts away, instead opening the closest book. This one centered around the therians' historical involvement in the Great War. An unfamiliar term stood out—feras. Hazel skimmed through the passage, her eyes narrowing.

Feras are the most animalistic of the therian kind, often living their lives as outcasts, although they were used gladly during the Great War against the siphoners. Feras were therians born in their animal form, with the majority unable to shift into their human form without assistance, most commonly Omega chains. They were stronger, faster, and far more animalistic than typical therians, their instincts heavily governing every decision.

Her stomach tightened. It sounded like a very sad and horrible existence. It was now obvious to Hazel, Gwen hadn't been able to shift back on her own last night or she'd have done so before coming back to campus. But she'd shifted back in the end, so maybe Gwen wasn't a fera. Gwen had grown up as a kid, not an animal; she'd even gone to camp with Jordan. But Hazel couldn't be sure. Not without asking Gwen.

The truth was, she knew next to nothing about therians. They were things of myth and legend, gone from the earth for over a millennium, and so little history remained outside SEU.

Hazel took a deep breath, picked another book at random, and opened it. She was going to learn everything she could about them because she was pretty sure her roommate was one.

Gwen

Last night had been a disaster, and today hadn't been much better. Gwen had woken up at the crack of dawn to go look for her bracelet but Chancellor Lucas had been at the tunnel entrance. Gwen had felt like she was being watched. She'd wanted to go hide out with Klaus, but the second he found out she'd lost her bracelet, she'd be dead. So she'd gone to see Jordan instead, and spent the morning dreading coming back home and lying straight to Hazel's face again.

Hazel sat studying on the couch when Gwen got home, surrounded by piles of books. Gwen averted her gaze, hoping to get to her room without an argument sidetracking her. She needed to come up with a plan for the bracelet. Or go see Harland again.

As she moved toward her room, a book on the couch caught her eye. It looked familiar, with its brown cover and embossed images. Gwen slowed as she looked closer. Not just any images—wolves.

Shock and fear welled up inside her as she looked to the next book. And the next. She knew them all. She'd looked at these very books the first time she'd gone to the library with Hazel. They all held facts and lore about therians.

No. No. No.

Behind Hazel, the bookshelf was half barren. Gwen's stomach dropped as she realized the evidence she'd left for Hazel to find. Her trickery of spelling books on therians from the library to appear there had finally come to bite her in the ass. She'd always counted on Hazel's boundaries to keep her from snooping. Gwen grimaced. What a mistake.

No, this wasn't her fault. It was Hazel's. She had no right to look through her things.

"You just couldn't let it go?" Gwen snapped, throwing her bag to the floor with a loud bang that made Hazel jump.

Hazel looked up at her, startled. The look of fear there hit Gwen like a knife to the heart. Her friend was afraid of her.

Her father's words haunted her. *"People will never accept you, Gwendolyn. If they don't run from you, they'll hunt you."*

Gwen fought back a mixture of angry and fearful tears as she saw everything slipping away from her: her freedom, her friend. Hazel was going to abandon her, or worse tell someone what she was. She was a rule-follower, and Gwen knew it would be hard for Hazel to keep this secret. She still wasn't entirely sure why Harland did. Logan's own secret aligned with hers and that was the only reason she didn't fear retribution from him.

She'd been right about not coming to Saint Elias. She'd exposed herself to too many people, and it was only the second month of school.

"Gwen, I'm sorry, but—"

Frustration bloomed in Gwen's chest. Hazel couldn't possibly be sorry or she wouldn't have snooped.

"No 'but,' Hazel. This was *my* secret. *Mine!* And it was my decision whether or not to share it with you!"

"Why didn't you?" Hazel asked. Tears started to form around her eyes.

"Why? You can't be serious. The Brecilian Knights would kill me if they knew."

"The Knights?" Hazel asked, confusion written across her face. "The Knights know therians still exist?"

"Yes. And that's why I couldn't tell you. You aren't supposed to know. No one is. That's what keeps me safe."

"You think I'd tell?" Hazel said, clutching her chest. "Do you really think so little of me?"

Gwen felt like shit, but said nothing.

"I lied for you in the chancellor's office last night," Hazel said. She sniffed before continuing, "I let you have your completely illegal dorm spells. Hell, Gwen, I faced down dragon fire for you in the exam! I think I have more than proven myself as trustworthy." Hazel snapped the book in her lap closed and threw it on the coffee table before standing and marching toward her room.

Gwen's heart ached with the pain she saw in Hazel's hunched shoulders, heard in her broken voice. Her friend was right. The evidence was there. Hazel had her back. So why was it so hard to tell her?

"That's not the reason I didn't tell you," Gwen blurted out.

Hazel stopped and turned to look at her. "Then what is?"

"I didn't want you to be afraid of me. I didn't want to lose my best friend," Gwen confessed.

There it was. The truth.

"Gwen, I'm not afraid of you," Hazel said earnestly as she held out her hands, palms up, as if inviting Gwen in.

"You're not?"

It couldn't be this easy, but Hazel's voice, her eyes, her words all said the same thing: truth. Still, Gwen kept her walls up.

"You literally saved my life." Hazel let out an awkward laugh. "And also—this is cool as hell."

Gwen blinked at her, uncertain she'd heard right. No one, not even her family, had ever called being a therian *cool.* Dangerous maybe. Useful sometimes. But never cool.

"You think this is cool?" she asked, trying to sound casual, but the question came out softer than she meant.

"Yes! Do you really have heightened smell, sight, night vision, super strength—"

"Whoa. Slow down." Gwen smiled faintly, afraid to let her guard down, but she felt emboldened by Hazel's excitement. "And yes, I do."

Hazel scooped up a book from the coffee table and flipped through the pages as she said, "This is amazing. The only thing I couldn't find is why couldn't you shift back. There's nothing about it in these books." Hazel moved closer as she spoke. Clearly, she wasn't afraid.

Gwen blinked. Then she laughed.

That's what Hazel was worried about? Not that she was a therian, not that she'd been hiding a history-defying secret, but that Gwen was broken. How was it that her secret had been revealed three times since she'd arrived at SEU, and not a single reaction had been what she'd expected? Her father's words played in her head once more. Was there any truth to them at all?

"I was born a wolf," she admitted. "My mom didn't want to wait until puberty to have me shift, so she made my bracelet. Without it, I'm screwed."

Hazel gaped. Then she swallowed. "You're a fera therian?"

Gwen's amusement died instantly. Her jaw clenched. She didn't like being called that. Feras weren't well thought of and the last thing she wanted was people knowing she was one. Hazel must have caught the look on her face because she quickly added, "I mean—no wonder you're so impulsive. But honestly, you don't act as bad as the books describe."

Gwen huffed. She'd read half of the book Hazel was holding but didn't find anything helpful about feras, so she'd stopped reading. The library books were too basic—none of them would help her.

Hazel's brow furrowed. "Your mom was right not to wait until puberty to help you shift. Only twenty percent can shift out of their animal form at puberty. Most never do."

Gwen stilled. "What?"

That can't possibly be right.

Hazel tapped the last page of the book. "You would've always needed help. You were never going to do it alone."

Gwen's stomach turned. Her dad had lied. He had been counting on twenty percent, but she might have never shifted out. He'd blamed her mom all these years, but it wasn't her fault. Hatred for her father flared in her veins. He was a shitty excuse for a father. There was no telling what else he'd lied about.

Anger flooded her, and Gwen ran her tongue over her canines to make sure they hadn't grown—then she remembered the potion and how it had silenced her wolf.

She snatched the book out of Hazel's hands, scanning the section. Her pulse kicked up.

To overcome the limitations of a fera, refer to Malsano de la Animo—

Her blood ran cold. She recognized that title. It was one of the books in the Alterion library Logan had caught her in. She needed to get back in there. She'd have to come up with a plan with Klaus.

"We've got to find your bracelet," Hazel insisted. "Wait, how did you shift out last night?"

"I already tried this morning. The chancellor is watching the tunnel. But don't worry, I had some help," Gwen admitted.

Hazel gave Gwen a suspicious look. What the hell—Hazel already knew her biggest secret. She might as well tell her about last night too.

After she told Hazel about Harland's potion, she waited for a lecture about being cautious, but it didn't come. She was grateful her friend was taking this all so well. Gwen still felt like she'd trusted him too easily.

"Maybe she's gone by now. It's still early enough that we can make it back," Hazel offered.

"Okay, let's go."

As the girls headed out of the dorms, an incessant beeping began to sound from both of their jacket pockets.

"Shit. Wilderness Watch," Gwen groaned.

Gwen had forgotten all about the damned compact since she'd put it in her pocket this morning—she had other things to worry about right now. There was no way they could go check in for Wilderness Watch *and* get her bracelet before curfew. She was going to need Harland again after all.

The problem with *that* wasn't that she needed to trust him. It's that part of her wanted to.

Gwen popped open the compact to find a double mirror, one in each half. Across one side, etchings appeared. *Missing hiker. Report to WW room in AB.*

As soon as Gwen finished reading, the words disappeared, the glass perfectly smooth once more.

Hazel chewed her lip. "Maybe we can get out of it?"

"Remember what the chancellor said? We're already on thin ice. We can get my bracelet tomorrow," Gwen said, and they headed toward the admin building.

Gwen felt Hazel tense beside her when they walked through the door. The room was packed with people and Gwen scanned the room, looking for the source of Hazel's anxiety. She spied the six-foot-four, devilishly handsome, tattooed problem in the far corner.

Of course. Dane Bellamy.

He was the only one who had that effect on Hazel.

Logan was standing next to him, his arms crossed as he glared at her from the other side of the room. A few more people in the back that Gwen didn't recognize wore Alterion shirts. The seats in the middle were filled, and Gwen spied Serena and Victoria in the center.

Why are they here?

A few more girls surrounded them, sporting Circen and Sybil shirts. Incantor students lined the left wall. There were about twenty students total. The professors lined the right side of the room. Harland stood next to Sorcerer Maduro, Jude, and Captain Jackson. Good. She could ask him for another dose when this was over.

"Welcome! You're right on time. I'm Captain Jackson, the faculty advisor for Wilderness Watch. Please take a seat and we can begin," Captain Jackson said before he stepped into the middle of the room to address Hazel and Gwen. "I had hoped to give you a formal introduction but life happens." He picked up two backpacks off of a chair nearby and handed one to each of them. "Here are your packs. They have the basic necessities," he said as he unzipped his own pack and gestured at the items, "including some med elixirs, a magicked stretcher..." He reached inside to fish something out. "And a fire starter."

Gwen and Hazel shared a look.

Why would we need a fire starter?

Captain Jackson added, "Trust me, you'll need it. We don't need our volunteers getting mauled by wild animals or dying of hypothermia while trying to find people. We've had a few more lost hikers in recent weeks than normal, but thankfully, we've had a 100 percent recovery rate so far."

Gwen threw a look at Hazel. How none of them had encountered the bear was beyond her.

Captain Jackson zipped up his pack and stepped away from them. He raised his voice to address the room. "Attention!"

The chatter around them died down immediately.

"The missing hiker is Isobel Crane; female, Black, five-five, brown hair. She is from Quebec and speaks French primarily. We'll work on eight-hour rotations. If we don't find her within the first forty-eight hours, we'll call in the Brecilian Knights. Luckily, we haven't had to do that yet."

His words made the hairs on the back of Gwen's neck stand up. The Knights being called in was the very last thing she needed. She'd hunt morning, noon, and night by herself if it meant keeping them from being called.

Harland, Jude, and Maduro moved about the room, passing out bright-orange uniforms.

"Now suit up! Make a plan with your partner. We head out in ten." Captain Jackson paused, waiting for someone to raise their hand. Victoria started to, but Serena grabbed her arm, holding it down.

Bless you, Serena.

Captain Jackson stepped forward to address Gwen and Hazel once more. "Because you're rookies, you'll be paired—"

Dozens of shrill chirps trilled around the room.

Captain Jackson pulled his compact from his pocket. "Hiker has been found unharmed. Mission aborted!" he shouted.

Gwen's shoulders relaxed. The idea of being out in the woods for who knew how long was starting to worry her. She'd felt her wolf rousing the last few hours, her normal well of magic refilling slowly, and while that was a relief—to begin to feel normal again—she also knew it meant the fight for control would soon consume her. She needed to see Harland before those twenty-four hours he'd promised her were up.

Hazel and Gwen slung their packs on their backs and headed out as the other students began to remove their orange coveralls. As soon as they were outside, Gwen stopped Hazel and cast, "*Silentia.*"

"I need to wait here for Harland. Do you mind waiting with me so it doesn't look so suspicious?"

"Not at all," Hazel said.

Gwen dropped the spell, and the two leaned against the building wall, waiting for Harland. A few minutes later, he exited alone, but was followed closely by a group of students. Now was Gwen's chance.

"See you later," Hazel whispered.

Gwen walked at a safe distance until they were halfway across campus. When they reached the quad and no students were nearby, she quickly caught up to Harland's long strides. He looked over and down at her, a small smile playing on the corner of his mouth as if he was pleasantly surprised to see her. The sight of it filled her with warmth.

"Sorcerer Thacker."

He raised a skeptical brow; she never called him that unless other people were around.

"I was wrong last night. I do need more help."

He gazed into her eyes for a breath as if considering.

What if he says no? A rock settled in Gwen's gut. Somehow, she hadn't even considered that possibility. He'd already helped a therian once; maybe he wouldn't want to take the risk again.

"Understood. I have some free time now," he said.

Gwen immediately breathed easier. He wasn't going to abandon her.

"If you'd like, we could go over the assignment at my place?"

At his place. Butterflies flew in her stomach. She'd been there before, but this time felt different. First, she wasn't waking up alone and sneaking away in the early dawn. Second, he was inviting her instead of carrying her unconscious body to safety. Something about this moment felt big. Like they were about to cross a line.

"Now would be fine," she said, trying to maintain an air of professionalism she didn't feel. She discreetly cast *Silentia* as she and Harland walked towards the professors' quarters. "What if someone sees us sneaking into your house?"

"I'd hardly call this sneaking, Miss Bishop."

"Do you do this a lot?" she asked. Her gaze lingered on him a second too long as they walked under the archway that demarcated the professors' quarters.

"This?" he asked. His eyes met hers and locked there. Gwen's breath hitched. Did he mean for that to sound like there was something between them, or did she just want there to be?

"No, but I do tutor students in my home when the need arises."

She looked down, disappointed. She liked the idea that she was special, that maybe she was the only student who'd gotten to see such an intimate space.

"I can tell that's not the answer you were looking for," he observed, a hint of amusement playing on his lips. He turned at the first house, which Gwen knew was his.

"No, it's not that. I mean, it's good no one will bat an eye about me being here," she lied smoothly, a nervous flutter in her stomach. "I may need more than this dose. Maybe for a few days—unless you can make it last more than twenty-four hours."

The question hung in the air between them as he opened the front door.

"I cannot." His gaze held hers a beat too long, then he gestured for her to go inside.

Excitement filled her. This meant she'd have the opportunity to spend more time with him until she found her bracelet.

He led her into the kitchen and began mixing dried ingredients into a large copper cauldron. Gwen sat in a chair at a small oak table and tried to spy their labels, but they were too small to read from there. The clinking of glass against metal amplified the quiet tension.

“Why do you need this all of a sudden? What’s changed?” His voice, though casual, held a note of focused attention that made her skin prickle.

He didn’t need to know about the bracelet. He’d learned enough of her secrets for now.

“It’s a long story,” she hedged.

The muscles in Harland’s forearms flexed as they stirred, and Gwen’s mouth went dry. He looked so at ease, as if in another life he might’ve been an alchemist.

“This will take a while to simmer,” he said. His eyes caught hers again. “We have time.”

Gwen considered what she could share that wouldn’t put her at risk. He knew her biggest secret, and as long as she didn’t mention her bracelet, she couldn’t see any harm in it.

“We were attacked by a bear.”

He continued stirring, but his gaze immediately whipped to her. “Surely you and Miss Thorne can take on a bear.”

Gwen rolled her eyes. “This bear wasn’t normal. It was…” She paused. Did she want to tell him this? Would he think she was insane?

“Continue, Miss Bishop.” His jaw flexed.

Gwen crossed her arms. Taking orders went against the grain for her.

Harland sighed. “If this… situation is going to work, Gwendolyn, we’re going to have to trust each other. You’re hiding things from me, and I need to know if I feel safe continuing this arrangement.”

The thought that Harland might stop helping her made her heart slow. Until she retrieved her bracelet, she needed him.

“It was impervious to magic.”

For the first time, he stopped stirring. He studied her face, looking for what, Gwen didn’t know. Maybe he thought she was joking, but she didn’t care. She’d been honest, and he could believe her or not.

"Start from the beginning," he said finally, then began stirring again.

Because she couldn't afford to lose his help, Gwen did. As she spoke, his face tensed until he stopped stirring altogether and began to pace. His jaw clenched, his movements mirroring the restrained fury in his eyes. It thrilled her, to see him so worked up about *her*. Once the story was done, he came to kneel before her. His gaze swept over her with an unnerving thoroughness, lingering on her neck, the curve of her arms, and the length of her legs. His gaze was like a drug, and with every glance, Gwen soared higher under his attention.

If this isn't caring, I don't know what it is. It was hard for her to believe this man would betray her when he looked after her so carefully, so sweetly.

Then he took her hands, letting his strong fingers run slowly up the insides of her arms to check for injury. The contact was electric, it sent a jolt of shivers down her spine.

"Did he hurt you?" His thumbs brushed against the sensitive skin of her inner wrist. The warmth seeped into her veins, igniting a fire deep inside her. She wanted his hands all over her, in more hidden places.

"Who?" The question was a breathy whisper. She'd lost all train of thought as her mind plummeted into visions of them together. Of him picking her up and setting her on the table as he pressed his weight on her, between her thighs. She didn't dare move beneath his touch, afraid the moment would end.

"The bear," he demanded.

"No. Well, yes, but... therian perks," she managed, her voice husky.

"Right. Therian healing."

Harland's gaze remained fixed on her for another beat, then he shook his head. He released her and returned to the cauldron. His absence left her feeling raw and bare, a warm blanket ripped away.

Had he withdrawn because of the reminder of what she really was—a therian?

She longed to go to him, but her stubborn pride kept her rooted in the chair. She drew her legs into herself and wrapped her arms around them.

Being around him is too hard. Maybe I should leave and go find my bracelet first thing tomorrow.

Knowing she couldn't make it through the night without shifting kept her where she was.

The silence stretched, thick and heavy, punctuated only by the gentle boil of the potion. Gwen's skin pricked with unspoken desires, an almost unbearable itch beneath its surface. She didn't want to be made a fool, but that was exactly how she felt. Harland didn't want her. That much was clear.

When the potion was complete, Harland used metal clamps to lower a vial into the steaming cauldron. The rapid *glug-glug* told her it filled quickly. He wiped the vial clean with a towel, then carried it over to her. She unwrapped her legs, placing her feet gently on the floor. She held out her hand for the potion, but he didn't give it to her. Instead, he stared at her with a sadness in his eyes she didn't understand. He was infuriatingly hard to read. Hot one minute, cold the next. She just wanted to know what he was thinking.

"Harland," she breathed, barely audible, but it was enough.

He shook his head as he knelt down between her legs, handing her the vial. His hands rested lightly on her knees, the contact sending warmth arcing up her thighs and deep into her core.

"I'd hate to see you hurt," he confessed, his voice low and rough.

"Harland, I'm fine, I swear." Her words were thick with unspoken yearning. She barely recognized her own voice, but that's what he did to her.

He nodded, yet he didn't move away. Her heart stuttered under his possessive touch.

Gwen lifted the vial, the dark liquid swirling within, but hesitated. She didn't want to feel the emptiness she knew it promised.

The memory alone made her shiver, but she didn't have a choice until she found her bracelet.

The potion went down smoothly, the familiar coolness spreading through her body. This time, she felt lightheaded but not nearly as hollow. Perhaps the side effects would get easier with time. When she handed him the empty vial, their fingers brushed, sending a fleeting spark through her. He searched her gaze, and an impulsive urge to reach out, to touch the dark brown strands of his hair, bloomed within her.

"Gwen." His voice was a low warning as she reached for him.

Her hands moved on their own, her fingertips brushing the rough prickle on his jaw. Harland's eyes widened, then he was on his feet and across the room in a second.

Fuck. She hadn't meant to do that. Why did being around him make her brain fall out of her head?

She stood, as a desperate need to escape before she embarrassed herself further propelled her towards the door. It had become clear that she wasn't able to be near him without losing her mind and her dignity.

But he caught her arm before she could rush out of his house.

"Gwen." His words were low and rough.

When she refused to turn, he gently but firmly pulled her around to face him.

"If you weren't my student, things would be different," he admitted, letting out a shaky breath.

"But I am," Gwen whispered.

"You are." Yet his arm kept her in place as he looked into her eyes. His own were full of conflicting emotions he refused to express, but she saw it there—an undeniable heat mirroring her own. She wasn't crazy. She knew he felt this thing between them.

She reached up, her fingers brushing his jawline again. He closed his eyes as he exhaled slowly, but he did not run.

"You have to stop doing that, Miss Bishop." His voice was strained.

Gwen reached for his free hand, weaving her fingers between his. "Don't," she pleaded. "Don't call me Miss Bishop. Don't try to make me feel like I'm making this all up in my head." He was doing it to put up walls between them, she was sure of it. "I'm not crazy. I know you feel it too." When he didn't deny it, she stepped closer to him, leaving only inches between their bodies. "You want this as much as I do." She moved her lips close to his, then angled her head, letting her lips tease the skin of his ear. "Just because you're too scared to go for what you want, doesn't mean you get to make me feel ashamed I'm not."

A minute passed, and he didn't move, didn't speak.

Gwen stepped out of his grasp and made for the door again. She wasn't going to play games.

Her hand was on the door when he said her name again. Despite herself, she turned.

Harland was right there. He pulled her close, their bodies colliding, every inch of her suddenly aware of the hard planes of his chest. His gaze locked onto hers, then drifted down, a slow, deliberate exploration of her face, landing at last on her lips.

Of all the emotions he'd shown her today, she was most sure of the one she saw right then: raw desire.

Gwen wet her lips, a silent invitation to kiss her. And then, like magic, he did.

He cupped her chin, tilting her head up as his soft lips crashed against hers. The taste of expensive bourbon and the lingering scent of leather filled her senses. She melted into him, her arms wrapping around his neck, her fingers tangling in the silky strands of his hair. It was better than anything she'd imagined.

Instead of intensifying, the kiss softened, becoming sweet, tender. But Gwen wanted him to devour her. She leaned into him, wanting him to feel the same fire that was growing within her. He lost himself in it for a moment, in her. One of his hands tugged at her hair, while the other slipped from her waist to her ass, pressing her against the hard length in his pants. He kissed her so deeply Gwen lost track of all time and space.

Harland stepped back, breaking the kiss. His hands settled on her shoulders and kept her at arm's length. "You're not crazy, Gwen," he whispered as he gazed into her eyes.

Gwen reached for his face again, but he quickly wrapped her in his arms, tucking her head under his chin.

"You need to take some time and think about this. We both do. This could have repercussions for each of us."

Gwen *had* been thinking about it. It was all she'd thought about for two months. She'd already decided. Harland Thacker was worth the risk.

Ignoring his words, she stood on her tiptoes and pressed a light kiss to his lips.

"You're going to be the death of me, Gwendolyn Bishop," he murmured, his arms tightening around her. Then he kissed her softly on top of the head.

Gwen sighed, perfectly content. For now.

A wicked smile played on her lips as she left his house, the lingering scent of him clinging to her clothes. A dangerous, exhilarating thought took root as she walked back to the dorms: *Maybe I'll never find my bracelet.*

CHAPTER 24

Hazel

Sorcerer Oswald was teaching a key lesson on telekinesis, but Hazel wasn't hearing a word.

Her best friend was a therian.

They were supposed to be extinct. All of the Forsaken—elves, fae, siphoners, and therians—were supposed to have been wiped out a thousand years ago. That's what they were taught in school, told in bedtime stories. But she'd seen Gwen shift into a wolf without a wand or elixir with her own eyes.

And yet, that wasn't what was keeping her from focusing. What truly terrified her was the possibility Gwen might not be the only Forsaken at Saint Elias University. Lightning magic was unheard of, let alone taught or practiced. But she was certain she had willed the lightning to strike the bear. The questions gnawed at her: had lighting magic ever existed or had Hazel stumbled upon something new altogether? Or was this yet another thing believed to be lost with the Forsaken, and, if so, did that mean she could be one?

No, I'm not special.

Each train of thought led to the same question: if therians weren't extinct, were there any other Forsaken still alive?

"Please be sure to do your reading before next class," Sorcerer Oswald said. "That's all for today."

His words brought her back to reality. She'd missed the whole lecture, consumed by questions of her new abilities. But she had a feeling the one person who could answer her questions was right in front of her.

She packed up her bag as her classmates filed out, then approached the platform where Sorcerer Oswald stood. "Excuse me."

"Yes, Miss Thorne." Oswald looked up from a stack of papers at the podium. "Do you have a question about the reading?"

"Not exactly. I was just wondering if you could tell me what category of magic lightning might fall under. Would it be elemental or arcane in nature?"

Sorcerer Oswald paused at her question, searching her eyes intently. "I'm happy to answer your question, if you don't mind answering one for me first."

Hazel nodded earnestly. Her mind buzzed with the possibility of answers.

"Is your mother Cora Vindiel?"

Hazel's heart stuttered in her chest before it threatened to fly away, right out of her mouth. "Yes, Sorcerer. Do you know her?"

Her heart filled with hope—hope that Sorcerer Oswald knew her mother, that he might know where she was. She'd looked all over campus, but she hadn't seen a glimpse of her again.

Oswald smiled softly. "Yes, I taught her. Though I haven't seen her in years."

Her heart plummeted like a rock. Was it possible her mother wasn't at SEU? Hazel shook away the thought. No. Her visions were too accurate to be anything but real. So how had Hazel seen her mother in the library?

There was only one other way, and according to her father, her mother possessed the ability to do it: astral projection.

Of course! I've been thinking about this all wrong.

"Actually, I taught both of the Vindiel girls—Cora and Evelyn," he said while packing his bag.

Hazel's eyes widened. Information about her mother and aunt tempted her, but she needed to focus on the important things happening right now, not the past. She suppressed the urge to push for more.

"As for your earlier question, the category depends." He motioned for Hazel to follow him up the stairs, talking as they walked. "Lightning can be manipulated with a wand, since it's technically like fire, but timing a lightning strike is quite hard and often tiresome."

Hazel frowned. Had that been what she'd done? Had she simply manipulated the lightning storm going on around them that night? But she didn't remember even looking at the sky. She'd been so focused on the bear, wishing for it to be struck, and then it had. She definitely hadn't used her wand. Then she remembered her dream, of striking the dragon with electricity that certainly hadn't come from a lightning storm or her wand.

"What about the ability to conjure lightning or electricity? To call it forth?" Her light curious tone gave away none of the desperation coursing through her. She needed to know if she'd actually done something that was possible, or if she was losing her mind.

"The ability to conjure lightning and electricity magic are referred to as fulgurkinesis, which technically falls under the arcane sciences."

That made sense. The only branch of magic mages could do without a wand was arcane magic, because it came from fate, not the earth.

"But the practice has long been lost," he finished.

Another thing that was supposed to be lost but was really just hidden. His words knotted her stomach.

"How was it lost, Sorcerer?"

He arched a brow at her as he pushed open the doors of the classroom, but Hazel didn't understand the look. "That secret disappeared with the elves, Miss Thorne."

The words swirled in Hazel's mind. Elves. The same species also had a penchant for the arcane, including astral projection and foresight. Just. Like. Her.

"Are you saying no mage has ever conjured electricity?" Hazel's voice sounded hollow even to herself.

"There's no record of a mage ever having mastered the power," he informed her as they continued down the hall, towards the front doors of the building.

"Oh, okay. Thank you for your time, Sorcerer. I'll see you next week," she said, bidding him farewell and practically running out the doors of the Arcane building.

Hazel digested his words, true bewilderment filling her. Her blood rushed in her ears. The words, *that secret disappeared with the elves,* played on a loop in her mind. She had to get as far away from Oswald as possible before he saw her react and wondered why she'd asked.

How stupid she'd been to believe she'd rediscovered a type of magic. As if magic was that easy.

She exited the building, relieved to find the sidewalk empty, because there was no stopping the tears that flowed. She leaned against the stone wall and tried to collect herself, but the tears kept coming.

Her mother had left her alone to figure this out. Alone to learn she'd inherited abilities and powers no one else on earth was supposed to have. Instead, she'd had to learn about them from a stranger. A man who cared nothing for her. In all her months at SEU searching for her mother with no luck, this was the first day she'd felt true anger towards her.

She left me alone and in the dark.

No, not alone. She'd left her with her father, who'd tried to lock her up rather than tell her the truth. The words from her last conversation with Thomas Thorne floated up through the mental trap door she kept her summer locked behind.

"Your mother didn't even have the decency to tell you the truth, then left you to fail."

He'd known all along and kept it hidden from her. If it wasn't for Forrest, she'd be in Arkansas, completely ignorant to the powers within her. But even he had tried to get her to stay.

"I'll stay if you tell me why I shouldn't go. No bullshit reasons. The truth."

"I can't, Hazy."

The memory of the words landed like a knife. He'd known and he had refused to tell her. Hazel's breath hitched. What could have possibly been so bad her own family couldn't be honest with her? Were these powers dangerous? Was *she* dangerous?

A sob ripped from Hazel's throat as she sagged against the wall outside of the building, drowning in a sea of unanswered questions. Her own personal hell.

"Miss Thorne?" Sorcerer Oswald called out from behind her.

Hazel immediately straightened and wiped at her face, knowing he'd see her tearstained face. "Yes, Sorcerer?"

Sorcerer Oswald closed the front door slowly behind him. "You can find more information on the topic at the library. I'd like to suggest you look at *Spellcraft and Scholarship*."

Hazel swallowed. She knew the book title, knew where it was down to the floor, aisle, and shelf. She also knew it had a green cloth wrap with gold-foiled lettering. Like so many others, her fingers had traced its spine in dreams of her mother—visions filled with endless rows of books, none more important than the next. Until now.

Hazel threw Sorcerer Oswald a shaky smile over her shoulder. "Thank you again, Sorcerer."

He gave her a soft smile in return and nodded. "Knowledge is a wonderful but fickle thing. Sometimes we learn things we wish we didn't know. Other times, we learn things no one else should know," he said, his tone full of quiet gravity as his gaze met hers.

Hazel's heart raced as she interpreted his warning.

Did he know what she was? Whether he did or not, the message was clear to her. Until she fully understood what all of this meant, she wouldn't be telling anyone.

Gwen

Gwen strode across the quad toward Klaus, who lay stretched out on the grass with his hands behind his head, looking far too relaxed. She rolled her eyes and gave his shin a light kick.

"Ow!" Klaus yelped dramatically.

What a baby.

"My bad," Gwen said, not at all sorry. "Get up. I need to talk to you."

"Hello to you too, Gwendolyn," Klaus said as he stood and brushed off a few blades of grass.

Some mages wearing black shirts embroidered with the Alterion minotaur mascot waved to him as they walked by. The group laughed as one of them said something Gwen couldn't hear. Harland's potion dampened her abilities more than her bracelet ever had; it was the only downside to her nightly visits. She'd been visiting him for the past week and although their relationship hadn't progressed much since that first kiss, she hoped if she kept seeing him, that would change.

"*Silentia*," Klaus cast, and the world quieted around them. "What's up?"

The book, *Malsano de la Animo,* hadn't left Gwen's mind since Hazel had found it buried in the citations. The missing piece was gnawing at her. If answers about feras were inside, then she had to get her hands on it.

"I need your help breaking into Alterion," she said, keeping her voice low.

Klaus blinked, then let out a short laugh. "Are you insane? No way!"

"There's a book in the Alterion house library. It was cited in another text I found, and I think it might help me figure out how to control my shift."

She omitted the part about Hazel finding the citation. She wasn't ready to tell Klaus she'd screwed up and let her secret out.

Klaus's expression sharpened. He studied her for a moment, as if weighing how much trouble this could get them into. Then, to her surprise, he sighed and shoved his hands into his pockets. "Figures. You always did have a thing for bad ideas."

Gwen tensed, ready to defend herself, but then he smirked.

"Relax. I'll help."

"You will?" She hadn't expected it to be this easy.

Klaus rolled his eyes. "Obviously. The whole reason you're here is to gain control."

Gwen sighed with relief. For once, something was going *her* way.

"Well, not the *whole* reason," she said, giving him a quick, satisfied smack on the shoulder. "I also want an education."

Klaus barely reacted to the hit, but his eyes flicked downward as her sleeve shifted up. His easy demeanor changed in an instant. Before Gwen could pull her arm back, his fingers clamped around her wrist. "Where the hell is your bracelet?" His voice was sharp, more concerned than angry.

Gwen tensed. *Damn it.* She should have been prepared for this.

"I—I—"

"No," Klaus cut her off, his grip tightening enough to make a point. "The truth, Gwen."

Gwen's stomach dropped.

She forced herself to hold his gaze, already calculating what to say. Telling him everything was *not* an option. If he knew she'd shifted in front of Hazel, he'd be running to use a memory hex on her friend this second.

“It’s in the forest,” she said carefully. “I lost it while hiking with Hazel.”

But Klaus didn’t let go. His sharp blue eyes flicked over her face, trying to see if she was lying.

She kept going. “I’ve been using a potion in the meantime. Found the recipe in one of the books I was using to research.”

Klaus’s grip finally loosened. “A potion?” His voice was quiet, but laced with disbelief. “That’s your fix? What happens if you screw up the ingredients? Miss a dose?”

Gwen clamped her mouth shut. She didn’t need to justify herself—especially not to *him*. And this was one of the reasons she hadn’t told him, aside from not wanting to lie about Hazel finding out and Harland being the one who was actually making the potions. Klaus was like a big brother to her, and that came with every ounce of the overprotectiveness. She didn’t need him flipping out and telling their family, or lecturing her. She knew what a mess she was in, and Klaus knowing was just going to make her feel more miserable about it.

Klaus ran a hand through his hair, already pacing. “Do you even realize how *stupid* this is? If our moms find out—”

“They won’t.”

“They *will* if you shift in the middle of campus!”

Gwen pressed her lips together, folding her arms over her chest as he continued his frustrated pacing. Even with the silencing spell, Klaus was making a scene. His sharp gestures and increasingly agitated body language had already caught the attention of a few passing students. She forced herself to stand still, resisting the urge to shrink under their curious glances.

Klaus suddenly stopped. “Why didn’t you just go get it?”

She huffed. “With classes, homework, curfew, and Wilderness Watch, I haven’t exactly had the time.”

Klaus narrowed his eyes. “You joined *Wilderness Watch*?”

Damn. She’d revealed too much. Klaus didn’t need to know all of her business, especially anything that would get him worked up.

“Hazel made me,” she said quickly. *What’s one more lie?*

Klaus let out a slow, irritated breath, then pinched the bridge of his nose. "You want my help with Alterion? Fine. But first, we're getting your bracelet back."

Gwen sighed, hating it when Klaus put his foot down. She was supposed to be the stubborn one.

"Fine," she muttered. "Let's go get it."

But Gwen hid a secret smile. She'd said she'd go get it, not that she'd wear it.

Guilt fluttered in her stomach, but she pushed it away. She'd only promised Hazel she wouldn't lie to her; everyone else was fair game. Harland didn't need to know. The potion *was* working sufficiently whether Klaus trusted it or not. And Gwen wasn't ready to give up her excuse to see Harland every night.

As Gwen and Klaus flew above the clearing on brooms, she found that it somehow looked even worse in the daylight. The storm had done more damage than she'd realized. Several trees were nothing more than blackened husks, their bark splintered and peeling. The ground below was littered with fallen branches, and the usual hum of wildlife was missing. There was no rustling in the underbrush. No distant hoots of owls. Nothing. She didn't like it.

Unbelievably, the bear's body was nowhere to be found, not even the bones. The carrion birds must have gotten to it quickly, or another scavenger. Nothing else would've touched the foul thing, Gwen was sure. Bellflowers still littered the forest floor, growing up between the dead branches in stark contrast.

As soon as they touched down, Klaus tucked his broom under his arm and gave the area a slow, assessing look. She leaned hers up against a tree and picked a flower as if the scene around her were completely ordinary. His expression had been shifting between irritation and suspicion since they'd left campus, and she braced herself for the inevitable.

"This is where you lost it?"

Gwen plucked the petals off the flower. "Yeah."

He crouched down, sifting through the debris. "You were hiking?"

"Yes."

"With Hazel?" His voice was full of doubt.

"Yes."

"You're lying," Klaus scoffed.

Gwen's stomach tightened. She hesitated, but there was no point in dodging it anymore. "I didn't *lie*," she muttered. "I just... left out some details."

Klaus shot her a hard look. "Like?"

Gwen's eyes darted away. "A bear attacked us."

There was a quick inhale, then silence. When she finally glanced at him, Klaus had gone completely rigid, his eyes wide in shock.

"A *bear*?" His voice was full of disbelief. "And you weren't going to tell me that?"

She rolled her eyes, trying to defuse the weight of it. "Because I knew you'd act like this."

"Like what?" His words came out defensive.

"Like I'm helpless, when I'm clearly not."

I'm a wolf, for Terra's sake.

"Did you shift?" Klaus asked, ignoring her last remark.

Gwen kicked at a leaf, avoiding his gaze. "I—"

Klaus began pacing in a tight circle. "Great! Does Hazel know?"

Gwen said nothing.

"Gwendolyn!" Klaus threw his hands up in exasperation.

She crossed her arms, standing her ground. "She *saved* me, Klaus. She could've screamed and ran. Instead, she helped. And after, she didn't look at me like I was a monster."

"She could change her mind at any time," he said flatly. "She could tell someone."

"She *won't*."

"You don't *know* that," he said.

Gwen clenched her jaw, suddenly furious. "So what, you want to wipe her memory?"

"If it means keeping you safe, then yeah."

Her stomach twisted. "No."

Klaus exhaled sharply. "Gwen, you're being naïve—"

"No," she snapped, stepping closer. "Those spells are dangerous, Klaus. You could erase *more* than just this memory."

He hesitated.

"And besides," she added, quieter now, "I *like* that she knows. I hate hiding who I am. And she's my best friend."

His lips pressed into a tight line, but he didn't argue. "How did you shift back?" Klaus asked as he started to search the clearing once more.

She'd known he would ask, yet her stomach still twisted as she scrambled for an answer.

"Hazel made me a potion," she lied. He might keep quiet about her telling Hazel, but there was no way in Salem he'd keep his mouth shut about Harland.

Klaus stopped in his tracks. His eyes locked on to her like he was putting the pieces together. "How did she know to make this potion we've never heard of?"

"She's smart and reads more than either of us combined," Gwen said. She knew it was a stretch, but she couldn't tell him about Harland, for more than one reason. If he knew she'd kissed a teacher, he'd probably wipe her own memory and send her home.

Klaus muttered something under his breath and started pacing again.

Gwen said nothing.

Klaus shook his head. "And let me guess, that's what you've been taking instead of actually wearing your bracelet?"

Gwen bristled. "It works."

She didn't need him to list all the ways she'd screwed up. Her decision was made. She was going to keep taking the potion to see Harland—bracelet or not.

Klaus motioned toward the ground. "Just find the damn bracelet."

He didn't have to tell her twice. She was ready to get the hell out of there and stop having this conversation.

"*Invensio,*" Gwen cast with her wand while her other hand was outstretched, palm up.

Nothing happened.

Gwen's heart sped up. There was a glyph etched into one of the charms linking it to her, but she couldn't call on it from more than a mile away.

Fuck, where is it?

Then, from beneath a pile of fallen branches, something glinted in the fading light. The gold band shot free, sailing toward her outstretched hand. She caught it easily, the familiar weight grounding her as she fastened it back onto her wrist.

"Got it," she said.

Klaus didn't waste a second. "Good. Let's get the hell out of here. This place gives me the creeps." He softened his words with a small smile.

Hopefully this meant he wouldn't be mad at her for much longer. She still needed his help, after all.

They mounted their brooms, pushing off into the sky. As Gwen rose above the trees, she glanced back one last time.

The deadened trees stretched below like bones jutting from the earth, the shadows between them deeper than they should have been. The whole place felt *wrong*. Thankfully, she had her bracelet now and she never had to come back here.

As they flew back towards the tunnel, Gwen said, "Alright. Now help me get into Alterion."

Klaus sighed, rubbing a hand over his face like he'd been expecting this. "Not today."

Gwen scowled. "What? *Why?*"

"Because there are too many coven members at the house. We'd never get in unnoticed."

"Or is this just about you being pissed at me?" Gwen huffed.

Klaus's brow furrowed. "What?"

She narrowed her eyes. "For losing my bracelet. For letting Hazel find out. For all of it."

Klaus studied her, then shook his head. "I'm not mad at you, Gwen." His voice was quieter, but still firm. "I'm *worried.*"

Something about that made her shoulders relax.

He let out a long breath. "We need to be strategic—which you clearly haven't been."

Gwen opened her mouth to argue, but Klaus held up a hand. "First, you shift in front of someone outside of the family. Then you lose your bracelet. And now you want to barge into Alterion with zero planning?" He let out a short, humorless laugh. "Yeah, sounds like a *great* idea."

Gwen clenched her jaw. He wasn't wrong, but she didn't appreciate the way he'd said it.

"I'll let you know when the coast is clear," Klaus said, already flying away. "Until then, try not to do anything reckless."

He zoomed ahead to get to a coven meeting, and she was happy to be done with the conversation.

Gwen grew quiet as she flew through the tunnel on her own. Klaus was right—about needing to be careful and thinking things through—but that didn't mean she had to like it.

She sighed, glancing down at the gold band around her wrist. The weight of it felt heavier than usual, like a chain instead of a lifeline.

Slowly, she unfastened the bracelet and slipped it into her jeans pocket. She wasn't giving it up. Not completely. But it was almost time to meet Harland.

She entered Harland's house to find him sitting on his couch, a book open in his lap and a glass of brandy nearly empty on the table beside him. He looked perfectly content in the warm, dimly lit space, the air thick with the scent of herbs and spices. At the sight of her, he stood, a smile tugging at the corner of his lips. Relief coursed through her. She'd worried that coming in without knocking would feel weird, even though he'd insisted upon it the day before.

He wiped all doubt from her mind as he stood and said, "I've missed you."

"It's only been a day," she reminded him as she walked to join him, but she couldn't help but blush at his words. She loved that he missed her. She'd missed him too.

When she stood next to him, he pulled her into him, wrapping his arm around her waist. Warmth coursed through her as she studied his lips. Damn, he was handsome.

"Yes, but I miss you the second you're gone," he said, tucking a strand of her white hair behind her ear.

She playfully smacked his chest. Ignoring her, he lifted her chin and kissed her. She sunk into it as his hands roamed down her sides. When he finally pulled away, they were both breathless as he asked, "Are you sure this is still what you want?"

Gwen nodded. "If you keep asking though, I may change my mind."

Harland laughed, tickling her sides and making Gwen laugh. "I won't ask again then."

His fingers stopped their teasing as he pulled her to him, reaching up to caress the sides of her face as he brought his lips gently down on hers. When he pulled back, Gwen almost protested, until he kissed her sweetly on the forehead.

"Let me get your potion."

The moment he stepped away from her, she longed for him as if he was across an ocean instead of in the next room. Any distance was too much distance for Gwen's taste. When he brought the potion back to her, he sat on the couch, pulling her down next to him. She settled into his arms and felt at peace again. He held her hand as he placed the bottle to her lips and she drank.

When she finished he did not release her. "How have your therian abilities been with the potions?"

"The side effects are definitely lessening," she said, thankful that none of the doses had been as bad as the first.

"I've been altering the potion slightly each night, trying to make them easier on you," Harland said as he drew small circles on her back.

Gwen smiled at him, wishing his fingers would go somewhere lower.

As if he'd read her mind, they stopped. "When are you going to tell me why you needed more of the elixir?"

She tried to deflect by kissing him again but he pulled away. He studied her gaze, and Gwen wondered what he was looking for.

"How can I prove to you that you can trust me?" he asked.

Gwen swallowed, hesitating before squeezing his hand. "Stay."

No guy had ever stuck around long enough to get past the physical connection and into an emotional one. All she wanted was for him to be different. In so many ways he already was—he wasn't afraid of her and he kept her secret.

"I'm not going anywhere." He pulled her onto his lap and kissed the top of her head.

CHAPTER 25

Hazel

Hazel was going to have to give Gwen the slip. She'd planned on coming to the library to look for the book Sorcerer Oswald had mentioned, but Gwen had insisted on joining. The problem was, Hazel hadn't told Gwen about the book. Or the fulgurkinesis.

In truth, she wasn't even sure there was anything to tell. She was convinced she'd commanded the lightning that day, but since then, she hadn't even been able to summon so much as a spark. Maybe the storm had simply been on her side. Maybe she hadn't controlled anything at all. She was starting to feel silly. What were the chances two descendants of the Forsaken would end up at SEU at the same time? Rooming together, no less! The thought was ludicrous to Hazel each time she broke it down. When she imagined telling Gwen without solid proof, her friend's blasé attitude about the dragons and the tarot reading played through her mind.

No, Hazel definitely wasn't ready to tell Gwen yet. Not until she had more to go on.

"Can you do me a favor?" Hazel asked, praying to Terra that Gwen couldn't detect the nervousness in her tone.

"Sure," Gwen answered as she dug through her backpack in the chair next to her at their usual table.

"I was wondering if you wouldn't mind going to grab me a few books on glyph decryption. I still don't know what to write my book analysis on and I need to finish looking for a book for my Study of the Arcane class."

None of it was a lie, but Hazel was definitely capable of completing this task herself—and that's where the guilt took root.

Gwen stood from the table without hesitating. "Any special requests?"

Hazel shook her head, relieved that it had been so simple.

Once Gwen headed down the stairs, Hazel snuck up to the fourth floor. The book was on the third row to the right, on the bottom right shelf. It would only take a second to get in and get out. She'd made the journey at least a dozen times by now while trying to look for her mother.

Her mother.

Each time she came to the library, she wondered if that day would be the day. But today, she hesitated when she reached the floor. For the first time since arriving at SEU, she *didn't* want to see her mother. Hazel was upset—no, furious—that her mother had abandoned her with no answers. The angry wound cut deeper when she thought about how her mother might have been astral projecting to SEU but hadn't sought Hazel out.

If anything, she's outright avoided me.

No, Hazel did not want to see her mother today. Maybe ever.

She slowed as she approached the aisles, desperate not to spook her mother if she was there, but a peek around the shelves revealed the aisle was empty. The overwhelming disappointment she usually felt when her mother was nowhere to be seen was replaced with relief.

As she walked down the row, she bent over to grab the book, but the familiar green cloth-covered book was not there. An empty hole where it usually sat glared back at her.

Maybe I missed it.

She confidently reversed and scanned the bottom row of shelves. While there were some green books, none were the right shade.

An uneasy feeling settled in Hazel's stomach. None of these books were ever checked out—at least not that she'd seen in all her visits.

Maybe it got misshelved.

But it had already been several minutes and Gwen would be returning soon. There was no time to stay and look. She'd have to come back another day.

When she turned to make her way back up the stairs, she heard a giggle. Hazel whirled around, but the floor was empty.

She shook her head. The laugh had sounded much too young to belong to her mother.

Frustration and fear of having to answer questions fueled her speed as she ran down the stairs. Gwen was nowhere in sight when she approached their table. Hazel let out a sigh of relief and pretended to work.

"Someone's in trouble."

Hazel jumped at Gwen's words, not realizing her friend had returned.

Is she so quiet because she's a therian? She didn't ask, feeling truly repentant about her nosy ways now that she had her own secret.

"Trouble? What do you mean?" Hazel swallowed as her heart hammered in her chest.

Oh, Salem. Did she follow me?

Gwen set down a stack of books with a small envelope on top in front of Hazel, then took her seat across from her. *Ms. Thorne* was scrawled across it in black, loopy script.

"Sorcerer Roth sent a messenger to deliver this. They found me first. Apparently, someone is past due for their advisor check-in," Gwen said in a smug, singsong voice. She was clearly proud that she wasn't the one shirking her duties for once. Hazel resisted the urge to point out Gwen never missed her check-ins because she had the hots for her professor.

Hazel hadn't met with Jude since the first time in September and it was now nearly Samhain. Part of it was due to how busy Hazel had been with class, homework, looking for answers about herself and Gwen, but also spending time with new friends. Another part was because she was dreading the conversation she needed to have with Jude about her classes for next semester. Hazel no longer wanted to do spell-writing coursework. She planned to use all her elective credits on classes in the arcane college, which meant she wouldn't be taking any classes with Jude like she'd promised.

Honestly, it was curious that Jude hadn't already come to seek Hazel out, since these advisor visits were scheduled for the first of the month. Perhaps Jude wasn't worried about Hazel or perhaps they were incredibly busy themselves.

The letter said that Jude was in town today, working in their shop, but they'd like Hazel to come there for their check-in.

"It's a Saturday. A trip into town will be nice before it gets too miserably cold outside the mountain. Wanna join?" Hazel asked.

Gwen smiled, setting down the drawing pad and charcoal pencils she'd just picked back up. Hazel probably shouldn't have asked her, knowing she was behind on her glyph decryption homework thanks to all her visits to Sorcerer Thacker the past few weeks. Even though she'd insisted nothing more had happened between them, Hazel knew she was lying. She continued to see him despite having her bracelet back, which meant there was only one reason she was going over there.

"Why, Hazel Thorne. Are *you* giving me a reason to procrastinate?" Gwen teased.

Hazel rolled her eyes. "Don't make me regret it."

Gwen popped up from her seat and began packing her backpack. "I wasn't doing homework anyway. I've been doodling my mask ideas for Samhain."

"Gwen—" Hazel began to chastise, but Gwen cut her off.

"Better get going!"

The girls made their way into Eagles Ridge. The last time they'd been in town was the night they'd been attacked by the rabid bear. Hazel pulled her coat tighter around herself as the late October air rushed over her. Or she at least told herself it was the cold air and not the horrific memory. Gwen seemed unaffected as she walked down the cobblestone street with an extra pep in her step, and Hazel wondered if it was growing up in Maine or a therian quality that kept her so unbothered by the frigid temps.

"Mmmm, do you smell that?" Gwen asked.

Hazel inhaled deeply. Her mouth salivated at the scent of roasted coffee beans. "Ah, the sweet smell of cloudberry coffee is somehow even better in the cold."

"Let's go get a cup and some scones." Gwen pulled at Hazel's arm.

Her friend was highly motivated by food and Hazel wondered for the millionth time if it was because she was a therian. Honestly, at this point, she was blaming therian instincts for everything short of her taste in music, which Hazel would never admit she actually liked.

"We can get a cup after," Hazel promised.

Gwen pouted, but continued on towards Jude's shop. The newly painted sign was easy to spot on Main Street. While all of the businesses took pride in their storefront presentations, this store's white sign was a bit brighter and the black lettering a bit glossier than all the others. The sign sported a black quill-tipped pen with a single drop dangling over the I in the phrase, Incanted to Meet You.

Hazel smiled at the cheesy pun of a name. The large bay window frames were also painted black, which was a stark contrast to the mint green and pastel yellow of the neighboring businesses. Nothing could be seen through the windows, as there was brown butcher paper lining them from top to bottom. Jude's shop was set to open next week.

As they entered the shop, they were greeted by a jingle from a bell overhead and the smell of fresh paint with an underlying layer of spice Hazel couldn't place. Boxes upon boxes were stacked along the walls and covered all of the available surfaces, including bookshelves, tables, and what looked to be the register counter. The only other thing in the room was an old-fashioned till.

A bodiless voice greeted the girls from somewhere in the back of the room. "Hello, how can I help you?"

Hazel recognized the voice as Jude, but was unable to locate them amongst the stacks of boxes. "Good afternoon, Sorcerer Roth. Where, um, where are you?"

"Here and call me Jude."

Looking over and above, she tried to follow the voice. Gwen pointed to a stack of boxes in the back right far corner. Of course Gwen could locate them—even without therian hearing she was a trained hunter.

Gwen waited at the entrance as Hazel went around the stack to find Jude sitting crossed-legged in front of the white wall with a paintbrush in hand. They leaned in closely to the corner, making small, precise strokes, their tongue sticking out a bit in concentration. Beside them was a small can of glossy white paint.

"Doing touch-ups?" Hazel asked.

"No, I'm warding the shop." They did not take their eyes off the wall.

Hazel took a step closer to discern the designs. While she didn't have a lot of knowledge about wards, she was still intrigued about what they might look like. The faint glossy symbols on the flat white walls made her eyes hurt when she tried to make them out from this distance.

"White on white?"

"Wards are particularly tricky. I use gloss finish for the wards over a flat white base because it's nearly indiscernible to anyone not looking for it, and hardly discernible for anyone who might be. They would have to stop and study quite hard to learn what wards I have in place."

"Which would make it easy for you to see who might be trying to look hard enough to figure that out. Intentionally visible, intentionally hard to see. Genius," Hazel said.

"Precisely." Jude touched up the paint with one last brushstroke before straightening and looking around the boxes to nod at Gwen. "Hello, Miss Bishop."

"Hi, Sorcerer Roth. Good to see you," Gwen replied from the front of the store.

Jude turned and smiled at Hazel, finally giving her their full attention. "I'm quite glad you made the trip to see me. I'm sorry we missed our last visit."

Hazel's cheeks warmed from the compliment. "Me too."

"So tell me, how are classes?"

"History is interesting. Glyph Decryption is entertaining," Hazel said, referring to Sorcerer Miggins's theatrical tendencies and roller-skating preferences.

With a nod, Jude encouraged her to continue.

"I'm learning so much from Maduro."

"Have you moved past the flame manipulation portion?" Jude asked.

Hazel nodded. "Yes, we finished that up and now we've moved on to water."

"Okay, so let's talk about what you've been saving for last," Jude said, walking to set their paintbrush on the front desk.

Hazel followed, finding that Gwen had cleared a space on a chair for herself by the front door. "Arcane is definitely the hardest thing I've ever studied. Sorcerer Oswald is so brilliant and he tries so many different approaches and techniques to help us achieve clinical application," she said, her voice picking up speed as she spoke. Now was the moment she was going to have to break the news to Jude.

Jude smiled at her. "You're loving it."

It was true, she was. She was also becoming scared of it, of what giant secret she might learn about herself every time she stepped into the room. But she couldn't get enough.

Jude sighed as they leaned against the counter. "I'm going to lose you to Oswald, aren't I?"

Jude's words made Hazel feel special.

Shaking her head profusely, Hazel promised, "Never. I just think my electives will be in the arcane."

Hazel watched Gwen's head jerk to the door.

"Did you hear that?" Gwen asked.

Hazel paused and listened. A muffled noise came from outside, then a deep voice yelled, but she couldn't make out the words. A chill crept down her spine. Whoever it was sounded upset.

"What are they saying?" Jude asked, moving towards the door. They pulled it open and the words became clear at once.

"Help! Someone help!"

Jude sprinted out the door, and Gwen and Hazel immediately followed.

The voice continued to call out from the left of the store, but there was no one on the sidewalk. Jude turned down the alley and froze. "Mara!" they cried before bolting down the alleyway.

The girls shared a concerned look, then ran after them. Hazel turned the corner to find Alec, the owner of Kodiak Brew, kneeling on the ground doing chest compressions on Mara at the end of the alleyway. Jude knelt by their partner's head, tears sliding down their face as they squeezed Mara's limp hand.

"Mara!" Jude shook their partner's shoulder gently. "Baby, can you hear me?"

She did not answer as Alec continued to work, pressing into Mara's chest at a steady pace.

Hazel was surprised to see Alec knew CPR.

Maybe he's a mundane?

Outwardly, there was no way to tell, and she'd only talked to the owner once to thank him for the free drinks. In Eagles Ridge, it was entirely possible he was mundane. They were allowed to vacation here and according to rumors some had even decided to stay. They only forgot about magic if they left and she could see why they might not want that to happen.

After another round of chest compressions, sweat dripped from Alec's face. It seemed he'd been working for a while. He couldn't do this forever.

Suddenly, Jude stood and drew their wand. "Stand back," they instructed.

Alec leaned back on his heels and removed his hands.

Jude cast, "*Exsuscito.*"

It was a basic awakening spell that usually brought individuals back to consciousness. But Mara's still body and closed eyes told them all it hadn't worked.

"*Vivicar,*" Jude cast, their brow furrowed in determination and eyes full of fear.

It was a mid-level med spell that Hazel's dad had used once or twice on the farm to revive injured animals. It always worked. But not today. Mara's body remained motionless.

Jude's knees wobbled as they sagged to the ground. They scrambled forward and pushed the hair out of Mara's face, whispering things to her that Hazel couldn't hear.

"I tried those already," Alec huffed.

Hazel's hands clenched as she watched Jude cry while Alec returned to doing chest compressions. Those spells should have worked, unless something terrible had happened to Mara, but she didn't look *that* bad. Hazel thought she almost looked peaceful with her eyes closed as she laid on the ground. But then she registered her pallid lips, her usually beige skin now sallow. Mara's nice mustard-yellow dress was marred by dark stains down the front of her bodice, but there were no visible wounds.

"Any other ideas?" Alec asked. His gaze connected with Hazel's.

Why is he looking at me?

Hazel shook her head. She hadn't even completed her first semester in college. All she knew were basic first aid spells.

"We need a medic," Jude whispered.

Mage communities didn't have hospitals, only local medics. Medics trained for years and were experts in their fields, their magic so advanced there were few things it couldn't fix. When that happened, they turned to mundane medicine as a last resort.

When no one moved, Jude looked at Gwen. "Can you go to the office on Alameda Street and bring the medic?"

Gwen nodded as she backed away.

"Quickly!" Jude choked out, voice thick with concern.

Gwen subtly reached for the bracelet on her wrist and removed it. Hazel watched as it disappeared from sight and into her pocket before she sprinted back down the alley.

Gwen would make it in record time with her therian speed, but at what cost? She'd risked everything to help Mara, and Hazel had to do the same. She couldn't just stand by and do nothing while they waited. She had to help.

Hazel turned back to the group and wracked her brain for anything she might have inadvertently learned back in Arkansas or at Elkmont. The only thing that stood out to her was the medical TV show her mundane neighbors had been obsessed with, but she didn't think that could be a trusted source of information.

She knelt beside Alec, careful not to crowd him as he worked. "How can I help?" she asked, wringing her hands as she took in Mara's condition up close.

What if she's already dead?

Hazel dismissed the thought. Now was not the time to think like that. She needed to have faith for Mara, and for Jude. They'd been nothing but welcoming and supportive since her first day in Eagles Ridge.

Alec spoke in rhythm with the compressions. "We need an AED."

What on earth is that?

Hazel nodded anyway. "Where can I find one?"

Jude's face sagged at the question as Alec answered, "In Anchorage."

Terra help us. She'd have to run outside of town, advinere into Anchorage without being seen, find an AED, and then come back. It felt like a long shot—an impossible shot—but there were no other options. If the medic couldn't help, then the AED might be their last hope.

Hazel pushed onto her knees to stand, but Alec stopped compressions and grabbed her wrist, stopping her.

"You'll never make it back in time." Alec shook his head. "The longer she goes without proper oxygen, the worse the long-term effects will be." He glanced at Jude briefly. "If she even survives."

Alec reached down to Mara's neck, and angled it to open her airway before Jude provided mouth to mouth. Mara looked so weak, so lifeless, next to Jude's warmth.

Hazel fought back a wave of doubt as she asked, "Are we sure we've tried everything?"

"Yes," Alec said definitively.

Jude simply nodded as tears fell down their cheeks, never taking their eyes off their partner when Alec resumed compressions.

After a beat of silence, Hazel asked, "What does an AED do? Can we mimic it with something else?"

Alec's eyes flashed as they landed on Hazel once more. "It shocks the heart. Can you mimic that?"

Hazel swallowed. Can *I mimic that?*

"Maybe," she said.

He stared at her expectantly, but despite her suspicions, Hazel hadn't been able to draw out the power again. She could try, but there was every chance it wouldn't work. Hazel's stomach lurched at the thought of using her power in front of others, but if Gwen could put herself at risk, so could Hazel.

Jude breathed for Mara once more, their tears falling on Mara's face.

She could not watch Mara die without at least trying to help.

Hazel pulled out her wand, before remembering she hadn't used her wand to call the lightning. Still, it was for the best. Perhaps whatever she managed would look like a spell. She twisted her wrists out of anxiety as she thought about when she'd called lightning down on the bear. She couldn't do it the same way. A bolt of lightning would likely kill Mara, or at least make matters definitively worse.

Okay, so not lightning.

She considered her surroundings. There was very little in the alleyway aside from two trash bins, and a couple of empty boxes from Jude's store. Near the street, a light post hung high above. Maybe she could conduct the electricity from the light post into her body somehow? Hazel shook her head to no one but herself. That sounded like a good way to get hurt.

I need to quit thinking like a mage and start thinking like an elf, she commanded herself. *If I really am one, I should be able to conjure the lightning from nothing.*

Alec studied her closely while Jude breathed for Mara again. Hazel noted the rapid rise and fall of Alec's chest as he breathed in through his nose and out through his mouth in order to catch his own breath.

Hazel closed her eyes and focused on the charge in the air around her, the way it crackled at the edges of her awareness. As if in answer, something deep within her stirred. Her own body began to hum, subtly at first, then in sync with the rhythm around her.

That was it! Her own electricity! How many times had Hazel accidentally shocked the hell out of her brother, her dad, her friends? She was the poster child of static cling—which made so much sense now that she thought about it.

The second she opened her eyes, she felt the hum dissipate, but knew she could call on it again.

"I have an idea."

At that moment, Alec reached the count of thirty and stopped compressions. Jude leaned forward once again to give mouth to mouth.

Alec looked over at Hazel, his eyes determined as they searched hers. "*Finally*."

Hazel jerked, taken aback at his response. Surely he wasn't directing that at *her*. But the look in his eyes said otherwise.

Worry about it later.

The soft pad of shoes drew their attention to the front of the alleyway. Gwen ran at full speed, only slowing once she'd reached them.

Hazel's shoulders sagged with relief. *Oh, thank Terra! The medic will be here soon.*

"Where is the medic?" Jude asked, breath hitching.

Surely, minutes behind because they couldn't possibly keep up with Gwen.

"They weren't there. There was a sign on the door that said they'd be back in one hour. I left a note and told the shops next to it that when the medic returns, we need help," Gwen answered, frustration clear in her voice. "I'm sorry. It was the best I could do."

Hazel's stomach clenched.

"Now or never, Hazel," Alec said as he compressed Mara's chest.

Their last option had just disappeared. This was all on her.

She closed her eyes again and called on her body to respond as it had before. At first, nothing—no spark, no hum. She took a steadying breath, and this time, she imagined the electricity around her, the current that stretched between herself and Alec beside her.

And then she felt it—soft at first, like a brush of warmth through her veins, then fuller, deeper, spreading with a quiet certainty. It came to her quicker this time, like it had been there all along, tucked away in some quiet corner of herself, waiting for her to reach for it.

How had she missed this? This steady, pulsing well of power felt more like coming home than any spell she'd ever cast. It welcomed her like an old friend, humming through every part of her, making her wonder how she'd ever lived without it.

A gasp came from Jude across from her. When Alec's counting faltered, she almost opened her eyes, but kept them closed with sheer will, not wanting to lose her concentration.

Should she send it straight into Mara's body? No, she couldn't. What if it was too much? Her heart pounded as she considered how much was truly on the line. It could be *her* that ended up killing Mara.

"Alec, I think I have what we need, but I don't—I don't know what to do with it." If he could tell her how an AED worked, then maybe she could mimic it.

"Of course not," Alec mumbled, but not so quietly that Hazel couldn't hear. The eye roll she imagined paired with the words was nearly audible itself.

What the hell was his problem? At least she was trying to help!

Her frustration warmed her electrical second skin, and it buzzed with anger as if it wanted to be set loose. Set loose on *him*.

Alec stopped counting, but continued to compress, based on the sounds Hazel could hear and the exhale of his breath. "Keep it together," he hissed.

"Hey, asshole. Watch your fucking tone," Gwen growled.

Hazel said nothing, but shook her head to warn her friend off.

He was right. Hazel was crazy. *This* was crazy. And stupid. If she didn't calm down, she was going to unleash this pent-up energy on the wrong person. What had she been thinking, to try and attempt fulgurkinesis around others—*on* others? The energy thrashed angrily around her, matching her internal battle. She was doing this all wrong!

The sound of ripping of cloth barely penetrated her internal dialogue of self-doubt. "Open your eyes, Hazel," Alec instructed.

The way he'd said her name left no room for argument. Strong and demanding, as if saying no wasn't even an option. Part of her wanted to tell him to shove it. The other part desperately wanted to lean in to his confidence because she sure as hell wasn't feeling any right then.

His surety allowed her to return to reality for a moment, which was all she needed. She yanked the electricity back to her and took a deep breath. Then another. The electricity remained warm, but the incessant buzz calmed.

Hazel opened her eyes slowly and met his gaze, which held an eerie glow. A glance down showed her that the ripping had been Alec baring Mara's chest, leaving only her bralette to shield her from the crowd.

"I need you to direct it here," he said, circling a spot on the left center of Mara's chest with his finger. "And here," he added as he circled a spot on Mara's left upper rib cage while Jude breathed into Mara's mouth.

Hazel's eyes widened in fear. "I don't know what I'm doing. I don't know what I was thinking. I can't do this."

She scooted back on her knees, and Alec started to reach for her but stopped himself. She understood why as she looked down at his outreached hand. She was glowing, a subtle, soft white-blue hue emanated from her skin. It was the electricity.

"I can do CPR all day on Mara, but without an AED, she'lll most likely die," Alec said, his voice firm but kind.

Hazel shook her head. "Then let's get an AED!"

Movement behind her caught Hazel's attention.

Gwen crouched down beside her, but did not touch her. "If you don't do it, Mara is going to die."

"Hazel, she could die if you shock her," Jude said. Hazel met their gaze, filled with tears. "But she could also *live.*"

Hazel knew then she was being selfish. She was afraid of failure more than she was afraid of letting Mara die, and that was simply unacceptable. She'd promised herself when she set out for Saint Elias that she was no longer going to let fear of magic hold her back. Now was the time to take action.

"How much?" Alec's brows creased, so Hazel clarified, "I mean, how much electricity."

"We'll start small and work our way up if we need to. The important thing here is to send quick jolts. Don't prolong it or you could burn her."

Hazel nodded.

"We need to do it now," Alec said.

Taking a deep breath to steady herself, Hazel raised both hands, one with a wand and one without. She called the smallest amount of energy from her skin to the tip of her wand and the tip of her finger.

"Jude, back up. Make sure you're not touching Mara," Alec directed.

Hazel's hands hovered over the spots Alec had shown her. She took a deep breath to clear her mind, and smelled a strong floral scent of roses coming from Mara at this proximity. Hazel pushed all thoughts to the side and imagined the tiny balls of energy that surrounded her darting through Mara's skin at the speed of a light switch that was flipped on and immediately back off.

The electricity flowed through her into Mara.

Mara didn't move.

I failed.

Mara was going to die and it was all Hazel's fault.

"Congratulations! You didn't fry her!" Alec exclaimed. "We're going again, but this time, I want you to give her a hair more."

Hazel let out an incredulous laugh. *"A hair?"*

"Yes."

Hazel looked at Jude for permission.

Jude nodded, their eyes shining, full of resolve.

"Thank you for being so specific," Hazel muttered to Alec as she leaned forward once more. She collected what she felt was the same amount of electricity at the tip of her hand and her wand again, or at least as best she could tell. Then she called on what she thought was *a hair* more. Unsure if this was the right amount, but sure that she needed to act quickly, she turned the switch on and off once more.

Mara jolted slightly. As they waited, Mara's chest rose and fell. Once. Twice.

"She's breathing!" Jude cried. They placed their hands gently on

Mara's head and leaned close to whisper in her ear in between planting soft kisses on her brow.

Hazel sat back on her heels and released a deep sigh of relief. Gwen looked like she couldn't believe what she'd just seen, her eyes so wide they reflected the soft glow still emanating from Hazel's body.

A man with short black curls and bistre-brown skin wearing scrubs rushed past her with a floating stretcher. "I was told you needed a medic. I'm sorry. I came as fast as I could."

"That's okay, Zaire." Jude smiled at Hazel. "We had all the help we needed."

Alec and Jude helped Zaire get Mara on the stretcher.

"I'm glad to see you're awake," the medic told Mara. "I'll take you back to my office to run some tests, make sure everything is okay."

As they walked past Hazel, their eyes remained trained on her while giving her a wide berth. She didn't blame them. She was basically an exposed wire until she discharged the electricity she'd accumulated. It probably didn't help that she continued to glow.

Jude looked at Hazel with eyes full of gratitude. "Thank you so much, Hazel."

Hazel blushed in response under the attention. "You don't need to thank me," she answered.

Once they were all gone, Hazel released the rest of her electricity into a nearby metal trash can, cutting a hole clean through both sides. Gwen's eyes widened as she met Hazel's gaze, but Hazel looked away quickly.

In a matter of seconds, the cold of the electricity's absence filled her and she shivered. The glow was gone, but even though she looked like her usual, old self, she knew she'd never be the same again.

"That was the most insane thing I've ever fucking seen," Gwen said, hot on Hazel's heels.

Not as insane as seeing you shift into a giant white wolf.

Hazel let out a tired half-laugh as she made it to the street. They were an odd pair, but she wouldn't have it any other way.

As they headed back to campus, she thought about how she'd helped save a person's life tonight. Mara was going to go home with her partner and have a chance at another day, and it was, in part, because of her. She'd conquered her fears and trusted herself in a way she'd never been able to before. There was nothing she couldn't accomplish now.

"How the fuck did you do that?" Gwen asked as they walked down the cobblestone street towards the tunnel.

Hazel's stomach twisted with the truth of it. She was an elf. The facts were there. She had Sight and now the power of fulgurkinesis, two powers fully attributed to the elven species, and even if Sight could be taught, fulgurkinesis could not. It wasn't all in Hazel's head. Mara's very life was now proof.

But that sounded so insane. Elves were supposed to be extinct, wiped from this earth a millennium ago.

But if there was one person who might believe Hazel, it was Gwen. Regardless of how Gwen felt about Sight, she'd witnessed the fulgurkinesis for herself. Hazel now had the proof she needed to tell her friend the truth.

"I think I'm an elf."

"*Silentia,*" Gwen cast. "Are you crazy? You can't say shit like that, especially in town. Someone could hear you and think you're being serious." Gwen glanced around the people in town suspiciously. "You're lucky there are no Knights around."

"I *am* being serious, Gwen," Hazel said defensively. She'd spent enough time questioning her sanity and she didn't need anyone else doing it for her.

"Hazel," Gwen said more seriously. "You are *not* an elf."

"You conjure electricity then!"

Gwen's brow furrowed, and Hazel suspected she was trying.

Hazel laughed at the look of effort on her friend's face. "Stop. You look constipated."

"Fine! How did you do it?"

"I did it..." Hazel paused for emphasis, "by being an elf."

Despite her fears that her friend truly wouldn't believe her, Hazel cracked another smile. It felt good saying it out loud.

"Hazel, I'm going to hold your hand while I say this," Gwen said without actually reaching for her hand. "Just because I'm a Forsaken, doesn't mean we're *all* Forsaken."

"Gwen, I'm really going to hold your hand while I say this." She reached for Gwen's hand. The second their skin touched, Hazel sent the tiniest spark into her friend's palm.

"*Ow!*" Gwen yelled, yanking her hand away and shaking it. "How are you doing that?"

"I think my mom's an elf," Hazel explained. "Right before I left home, my dad said she had the Sight and could astral project."

"That's not possible. The elves are extinct."

"So are you," Hazel reminded her.

Gwen's eyes widened, as if she was hearing Hazel for the first time.

"And Sorcerer Oswald told me fulgurkinesis—or lightning magic—was only ever practiced by elves. That mages never mastered it."

Gwen swallowed as she reached for Hazel's hand. "Hazel, if this is true, you can't tell anyone. The Knights will come for you and your mom."

The blood in Hazel's veins ran cold. Gwen was right. She needed to be more careful. Had she already put herself at risk, performing the magic in front of Alec and Jude? She'd saved Mara's life. Hopefully that was enough to buy their silence if they had any suspicions.

CHAPTER 26

Hazel

Hazel drew in a deep breath, finding the crisp autumn air laced with bonfire smoke and the sharpness of magic. The night sky stretched starless overhead, but the ruzo field was ablaze with the flickering glow of hundreds of enchanted lanterns. Each paper lantern was cut with the distinctive shape of a magical creature or glyph, which cast eerie shadows upon the ground as the flames danced in the breeze.

It was unlike anything Hazel had ever seen before, and it was the perfect break from classes, homework, and scouring the library looking for information about fulgurkinesis. Luckily, no one at the school had found out about her using it on Mara, but she couldn't shake the quiet dread that the secret would come out. She hoped tonight would be a good distraction.

Everywhere she looked, there were cloaked and masked students, some standing around the large central bonfire, while others lined up for festival activities. Many of them wore coven colors, but Hazel could see freshmen and sophomores milling about in other colors as well. It was the masks that truly stood out, as they gleamed in the light of the flickering bonfire, some wooden, others polished metal, or embroidered cloth.

"Terra, I love Samhain," Rafe said with a huge grin.

This was Hazel's very first Samhain festival, and her body buzzed with curiosity that she tried to hide. Her father had always forbidden them from attending holiday festivals. Everyone else around her was familiar with the practices of Samhain, leaving her feeling inadequate, like she was on the outside of a secret.

This year, she was going to experience everything the holiday had to offer.

Rafe had talked non-stop about the hunt for will-o'-the-wisps, traditionally held in a corn maze, but SEU did their hunt campus-wide, and the winner was actually granted a prize.

Gwen was obsessed with masks, which was why Hazel was lucky enough to be wearing a stunning one of gold and starlight. Its smooth, polished surface looked like real metal, which she'd overlaid with shifting constellations that flickered like a real night sky. She and Gwen had worked on it for days. It fit perfectly around her eyes and forehead, enchanted to stay in place without a tie. She felt like a celestial princess.

Gwen's mask, on the other hand, was a monstrous visage of ashen black. Its uneven surface reminded her of charred bone. Jagged teeth were carved into the mouth, and its hollow eyes were so deep and dark that they swallowed the light, making it impossible to tell where she was truly looking. Hazel did not understand the vision and had tried to talk Gwen out of the horrific piece, but her mind had already been made up.

In stark contrast, Rafe's plain black mask was bent and slightly lopsided, while Jordan's looked like he'd made it out of cardboard this morning.

"I told you to let us help with your masks," Gwen snarked.

Hazel chuckled, knowing their lackluster masks bothered Gwen way more than it bothered them.

Rafe scoffed. "I didn't have time. All this homework is killing me."

"I didn't care," Jordan said as he adjusted his midnight-blue robe, then added, "Where should we start?"

While Gwen and Rafe had excitedly shared their Samhain stories with her, Jordan had contributed nothing. As a matter of fact, she was pretty sure Jordan had been dreading Samhain. But Rafe and Gwen had never addressed it, so Hazel hadn't pried.

"The line for the wisp hunt looks long. I say we start with a drink," Gwen suggested. She didn't wait for an answer as she strode forward, her dark-green cloak floating in the air behind her as if a magic wind carried it for her.

Their group moved through the thrumming heartbeat of the festival, weaving through masked students, tents lined with festival games, and booths with floating food and drinks. Gwen joined a line in front of a giant cauldron. Bubbles and steam rose from its depths, making it look like a Halloween decoration.

Hazel raised a skeptical brow.

"Trust me. You've never had anything like it!" Gwen pointed to a sign on an easel next to the cauldron, where *Speak to Spirits* was written in elegant script.

Hazel looked at Rafe.

Does he buy into this?

Rafe grinned and winked at her as he bounced on his toes, clearly excited. Beside him, Jordan rolled his eyes.

"I'm gonna go look for some food," Jordan said, not waiting for a response before he wandered away. He was usually the jokester, the life of the party. This type of elixir was exactly the type of thing he'd enjoy. Hazel had to be missing something.

"What's up with Jordan?" Hazel asked quietly.

Rafe and Gwen shared a knowing look.

Rafe shrugged. "Probably best to tell her."

Hazel's brows creased. *I'm clearly out of the loop.*

Stepping closer to Hazel, Gwen quietly said, "Jordan has a hard time on Samhain, but he doesn't like for us to acknowledge it. He wants us to go on with the holiday normally."

"Okay," Hazel said, nodding. "But why doesn't he like Samhain?"

This holiday seemed like the pure embodiment of magic. She'd never felt this kind of irresistible magical joy before.

"It's the holiday for the dead," Rafe said, nodding as if willing her to put the dots together.

"Oh!" Hazel said. Jordan had lost someone. Now it made sense. Of course a holiday centered around spirits and ancestors would be hard for him. "Who did he lose?"

"His younger brother," Gwen said, looking down.

Poor Jordan.

Hazel thought of Forrest, and a wave of sadness went through her. It had been hard enough saying goodbye to him before coming to SEU. She couldn't imagine a goodbye that would last forever, even if she'd only written to him once since starting school. Despite his lack of response, she thought of him often. The problem was, each time she did, thoughts of her father were close behind. It was easier to think of neither of them and the secrets they kept from her.

"How long ago?" Hazel asked.

"It was right before Jordan started high school. He had a long battle with a type of cancer even magic couldn't touch," Rafe explained.

Hazel's heart ached. Such an illness was so rare, that the only other person she knew of personally who'd died of it was her aunt, Evelyn. Magic could cure a lot of things, but cancer was one thing that was still trial and error.

"I had no idea. He always seems so..." Hazel sought for the right word, "lighthearted."

"That's Jordan's coping mechanism. He was the biggest prankster at Camp Camelot. It took me years before I learned his brother was even sick," Gwen said.

Rafe nodded. "You know he was *the* class clown at Elkmont. It's just how Jordan gets through it."

Hazel thought about all the pretending Jordan must have done and felt a new level of understanding for him. She knew how exhausting it was to pretend. The least she could do was not make him do it alone.

"Thanks for telling me. I'll do my best to act like nothing's wrong," Hazel promised.

Gwen turned to grab an elixir. Hazel grabbed hers next, and Rafe followed. The drink smelled of cinnamon and something sharp she couldn't put her finger on. They moved to the side of the line, and Gwen lifted her cup in a toast.

"May the best of our past," Gwen started.

"Be the worst of our futures," Hazel and Rafe finished in unison.

They clinked their cups together, then each took a sip. Power zinged through Hazel the second the liquid touched her tongue. It settled in her belly, twisting and curling like an animal.

Hazel gagged and then grimaced, the sensation in her stomach making her want to wretch. "What in Salem did we drink?"

Rafe and Gwen laughed.

"I brought pastries," Jordan said, surprising them all as he approached and extended out his parchment-wrapped gifts. Gwen snagged a baked apple filled with spiced cream and Rafe opted for the chocolate croissant. Hazel grabbed one with a flaky crust that smelled of caramelized sugar. The pastry practically melted in her mouth. She was in heaven.

"Alright, it's time for Hazel to try her hand at Trickster's Alley," Rafe said.

"This isn't another trick is it?" Hazel asked. "I still don't know what the last one is going to do to me."

Rafe bumped her shoulder, his hand grazing against hers. "Well, it *is* called Trickster's Alley."

Hazel's cheeks warmed, and she was thankful he couldn't see her blush under her mask.

The group approached a table where a deck of enchanted cards shuffled themselves in midair. They sat to enjoy their food and Hazel was asked to guess the correct sequence. She failed—twice—but won a small enchanted pinky ring covered in daisies.

A loud burst of magic drew their attention to a square, raised platform where two mages dueled. The young woman held her wand out, feet angled to the side in an attack stance, as she watched the young man pick himself up off the floor.

"I concede," the young man groaned in defeat.

The crowd surrounding the platform cheered.

"Jordan, let's go duel!" Rafe asked.

Jordan shook his head. "No thanks."

Rafe opened his mouth to press, "Come—"

"Hazel, Gwen! There you are," Nova said as she approached, beaming.

Nova and Elodie slid into the two empty seats next to Hazel and Rafe. They each looked lovely, with Nova in a deep burnt orange and Elodie in a leaf print-patterned cloak. They'd worked alongside Gwen and Hazel on their masks, which had turned out beautifully, matching their cloaks with autumnal accents of leaves, wheat, and pine cone detailing.

"What's the plan for tonight?" Elodie asked.

Hazel looked through the crowd in search of their next activity. The festival around her dimmed, the lights and laughter fading to a dull hum as Hazel's gaze locked on a familiar figure in a purple cloak drifting through the procession.

Her mother.

Hazel's breath caught.

It was impossible.

Yet, there she was, with no mask—onyx hair, her familiar jaw and upturned nose shining beneath the flickering glow of lantern light. She moved through the sea of cloaked and masked figures, slipping between them like a shadow. There one second, gone the next, never looking back.

Hazel's pulse pounded in her ears.

She didn't think, she just moved.

Hazel elbowed Gwen, eyes still focused on her mother. "I'll be right back."

She didn't give Gwen a chance to ask questions.

Hazel turned, slipping into the crowd before anyone could notice.

Her heartbeat hammered in her chest as she followed her mother's path, weaving through the swirling festival, her mind screaming this wasn't possible.

But she pushed forward anyway. She knew what she'd seen.

After pushing through the first grouping of students, she spied her mother's cloak and black hair once more.

Yes! There she is!

Hazel followed her deeper and deeper into the crowd until they made it out on the other side. Her mother approached one of the four large bonfires in the corners of the field. She was so quick, Hazel started to run to catch up to her. But when her mother reached the bonfire, she didn't slow. She walked straight into it, her image blurring away to nothingness within the fire.

Hazel gasped. *Impossible*. But then she reminded herself that her mother wasn't actually here—she'd been astral projecting. Still, that didn't explain why she'd gone into the fire.

She peered into the flame, but saw nothing of her mother. Perhaps the fire was enchanted. Perhaps she could go through it too.

Slowly, Hazel extended her hand toward the fire. The warmth increased to an uncomfortable level as the flames threatened to touch her skin, but Hazel had been burned before and survived. Entranced by the blue, orange, yellow, and red of the flames, she was convinced she could do it again.

She stretched out her hand, but another appeared, clamping down on her wrist, yanking her arm down and turning her away from the fire. Startled, Hazel jolted—Literally.

All of her energy rebelled against the foreign touch and worked to remove it. The shock was so potent, it produced a visible spark where their skin connected. Hazel gasped, and the hand jerked away quickly.

"Fecking hell!"

"What the hell are you doing?" she yelled, turning to see a silver and black masked figure, looming over her. They had no idea, but she could have hurt them.

"What the hell are *you* doing?" the deep, angry voice with a Scottish lilt demanded.

She knew that voice. The heat from the flames at her back evaporated. She felt as though she'd been doused with cold water.

Dane Bellamy.

She glanced back at the fire. What *was* she doing? It was like she'd been in a trance, now broken.

Dane shook his head and threw a piece of parchment in the fire before walking off.

Hazel looked around until she found where he'd gotten the parchment. Off to the side of the fire, a young blonde man sat behind a small table covered in slips of paper.

"Excuse me, what is this?" Hazel asked as she approached.

"It's the Pyre of the Dead," the blonde said as he scribbled on a piece of paper. Hazel thought she recognized him from one of the coven parties, but couldn't be sure.

"The what?"

"The Pyre of the Dead," the student repeated as if Hazel were stupid. "Ya know, one of the Quadrivium."

Hazel had never heard the term, but she knew Latin. Quadrivium meant "four ways." She looked around at the giant pyre in each corner of the ruzo field.

The guy spoke again, drawing her attention back to the table. "You write a letter to your dead ancestors, and on the night of Samhain, you burn it in the pyre. It's said that some receive an answer."

Hazel swallowed. *What in Salem do the other three do?*

"You're welcome to some parchment if you'd like," the student offered.

She shook her head no as she backed away slowly, and a rock settled in her stomach as she went to find Gwen. The magic of the evening dimmed as questions consumed her. Why had her mother astral projected here tonight? Why was she always running from her? And why had she led her to the Pyre of the Dead?

Gwen

Gwen sat at the edge of the table, absentmindedly picking at what was left of her food, while the others clustered nearby at a stall, deep in a round of Hexed Hands. Their laughter and fake outrage drifted back to her in bursts. She scanned the crowds again, searching for any sign of Hazel, but she was nowhere to be found. Everyone had agreed it was time to start the will-o'-the-wisps hunt, but Gwen had dug in her heels and insisted they wait for Hazel.

Where did she run off to? And why isn't she back yet? I'm gonna kick her ass for leaving me.

Finally, Gwen pushed her plate aside and stood to search for her. Before she could take a step, Klaus appeared beside her. He was fully masked as well; his was shaped like a traditional court jester, with the exception of the odd facial expression he'd decided to paint on it. One of the eyeholes was round and wide, while the other was a sharp slit, making his face look permanently skeptical and amused. The mouth was pulled into a grin that stretched across his cheeks in a manic frozen smile that creeped her out.

"It's time." His voice was low and urgent as he looked around to see if anyone was watching.

Gwen blinked. "Now? You've got to be kidding me. It's Samhain."

"It's the only time all the coven members are out of the house," Klaus pressed. "Do you want to break into Alterion or not?"

Gwen hesitated. She glanced over her shoulder for Hazel but she was still gone. Her other friends were still playing their game. No one would notice her absence.

She sighed, resigned. "Fine."

Maybe if they hurried, she could make it back in time to find Hazel for the main event.

Alterion stood before them, its dark stone tower jutting out high above into the moonlit sky. The arched windows and iron sconces gave it its imposing elegance. Gwen had felt drawn to this place ever since her first night in Coventry. Almost as if it belonged to her in some way. Not in the literal sense, but through blood, through history. Information about feras was hidden somewhere inside these walls and she intended to find it tonight.

The gargoyles lining the highest points of the coven were shaped like animals, Gwen recognized them as therians though some were extinct. They sat motionless under the glow of the floating lanterns above. Gwen wasn't sure if it was the play of shadows or something more, but she could have sworn their hollowed eyes followed her every step. As she and Klaus moved toward the entrance, the ground beneath them pulsed with faint blue light. At first, she thought it was some hidden enchantment, but then she spotted the source—small clusters of bioluminescent mushrooms, their glow casting strange, flickering shadows against the castle's foundation. She recalled what Serena had said about them during the trip through the mine and a shiver went up her spine. She didn't want anything feeding off of her or her magic.

Klaus walked beside her, but he remained silent. The weight of what they were doing was enough to keep even him from cracking a joke. He could probably get into a lot of trouble for sneaking her in and she was grateful he was taking the risk.

Gwen reached for the massive wooden doors, running her fingers over the aged iron handles before pushing them open. The air inside Alterion was thick with an unnatural silence. This place was supposed to be full of life, but tonight, it sat unguarded and barren. The dim glow from the sconces barely touched the deep shadows that stretched through the halls, making everything feel too still.

"Watch the door," Gwen murmured.

Klaus gave a curt nod, staying near the entrance as Gwen moved deeper into the twisting corridors, her boots soundless against the stone floors. She'd walked these halls before, but it had been over two months ago and nothing looked familiar.

She passed a door with plain, unmarked wood, the grain worn smooth over time.

Not this one.

Another had iron handles and thick metal reinforcements, looking more suited for a storeroom or vault than anything else.

Not this one either.

Further down, she passed an arched doorway, its threshold yawning open into pitch-black emptiness. Something about it made her skin crawl.

Definitely not it.

Her frustration built, curling tight in her chest, as she turned to go down deeper into the house.

Where is it?

Then she saw a door with the familiar mountain lion head engraved into the handle. Her pulse quickened. This was it.

"Klaus!" Gwen's voice echoed through the darkened halls of Alterion.

She waited for her cousin, listening, but heard nothing. Her stomach tightened. He was still at the entrance. If she left to go find him, she might not make it back to this door.

Gwen pulled her wand from its holster with a smooth flick of her wrist, then quietly murmured, "*Lux.*"

A small orb of light flickered to life at the tip of her wand. It pulsed faintly, hovering in midair, waiting for her command. She focused, picturing Klaus waiting near the entrance, then flicked her wand. The glowing orb shot down the hallway, weaving through the twists and turns of Alterion's corridors, casting long, shifting shadows along the stone walls as it went. Gwen held her breath, watching it disappear around the bend.

Seconds ticked by. Then she heard footsteps, fast and determined. A shape emerged from the darkness, the glow of the light illuminating Klaus's face as he followed the orb.

"I found it," Gwen said excitedly.

Klaus looked over her shoulder, then blinked. "Uh... Gwen?" He tilted his head. "You're just standing in front of a wall."

So he really couldn't see it. A thrilling unease curled through her as she reached for the mountain lion's head, fingers wrapping around the cool, polished metal.

"Just trust me," she murmured.

She twisted the handle, and with a soft, almost imperceptible click, the door swung open. She grabbed Klaus's wrist and yanked him inside. The door snapped shut behind them.

"What the hell is this place?" Klaus asked, wide-eyed, as he spun in a circle, taking in the room.

Gwen looked around, wondering the same thing. Even more so, she wanted to know why it had hidden itself from Klaus. Logan had said at the party—he had warded it. She'd assumed it was just for non-coven members but apparently not.

Bastard.

Suddenly, the fire roared to life on its own.

They both jumped, grabbing for one another. After realizing they were still alone, Gwen snorted.

"Let's hurry," Klaus said as he released her and went to pace in front of the door.

Gwen nodded in agreement, though she felt no rush to leave. She headed to the book-lined shelf containing the golden chains she'd seen the other day. They gleamed brilliantly in the firelight, their golden links undeniably beautiful.

Curious if they were as heavy as they looked, she let her fingers graze over them. As soon as her skin touched the cold metal, warmth spread from her bracelet across her wrist and up her forearm. She dropped the chains, and the bracelet returned to its normal temperature.

What in Salem?

Gwen went to reach for them again, but Klaus's words stopped her.

"Gwen, those don't look like a book. Get moving!"

The chains intrigued her, but he was right, and she forced herself to focus. Somewhere in this room was the book she needed and she couldn't let old artifacts distract her from that.

Her fingers trailed over the worn spines of ancient tomes as she moved through the space, scanning each shelf, each shadowed corner for something that stood out.

She considered pulling out her wand and trying a summoning spell, but if this was the last time she was going to be in this room—at least for this year—she wanted to see everything she could.

She climbed onto the library's rolling ladder to look at the top shelves. As she reached up to the tallest shelf to pull the rolling ladder forward, her fingertips grazed something small and metal. She took another step up the ladder and found a ring.

The band was gold, but not bright, as if it was aged, softened by time. At its center sat an opal, its surface shifting with a kaleidoscope of colors—flashes of blue, green, and fiery orange flickering like trapped lightning beneath its milky sheen.

Unable to resist, she snatched it up. As her fingers touched it, a pulse of warmth shot through her. Not heat. Not pain. Just recognition. A pull, deep and undeniable. A whisper brushed the edges of her thoughts, quiet, familiar.

It's yours, a voice told her.

She looked over at Klaus, who was scanning a different shelf, but she knew the words hadn't come from him. The voice that had spoken had been feminine.

Gwen's mind fought to rationalize it—maybe it had belonged to one of her ancestors. It was Samhain, after all, when the dead were able to communicate with the living. She waited for the voice to say something else, but no words came, so she slipped the ring onto her finger to see if that might produce a response.

Immediately, her bracelet reacted. The gold chain on her wrist gave a sudden jerk, surging away from the ring as if repelled, only stopping when it was fully around her forearm and could go no further.

She frowned, moving it from finger to finger, but the bracelet continued to move, the metal twisting away from the ring, almost writhing. A shudder crawled up her spine.

Slowly, she moved it to her other hand, and watched as the bracelet settled back into place. Her gaze dropped back to the ring. *What are you?*

Shaking herself, Gwen forced her focus back to the shelves.

And then she found the book. Its leather binding was cracked with age, the corners softened, the faintest traces of gold lettering still visible along the spine. This was it. This was what she'd come for.

As she held it in her shaking hands, she couldn't squash the feeling this night had just changed everything.

The door burst open, slamming against the stone wall with enough force to rattle the shelves. Gwen's heart leapt into her throat. Her grip on the book faltered, the leather slipping from her fingers—but at the last second, she caught it, pulling it tight against her chest. A figure stood in the doorway, clad in black robes, his presence like a shadow swallowing the dim light. But it was the mask that sent a shiver down her spine. It was bone-white, smooth and expressionless except for the sharp, jagged carvings that ran like fractures across its surface, as if it had been shattered and pieced back together. The eye sockets were hollow, pure darkness within, save for the faint glow of golden eyes staring out from behind it.

For a single, frozen moment, no one moved. Then, the man lifted his mask. Gwen and Klaus exhaled at the same time, their bodies relaxing as Logan's face appeared beneath it.

"Are you kidding me?" Logan's voice cut through the room, sharp and irritated. "I thought I told you last time, you aren't allowed in here."

Gwen ignored him. Instead, she tilted her head, her expression curious. "Why did you ward the room to keep out non-therians?"

Logan's eyes snapped to her, narrowing slightly—then flickered to Klaus. A shadow of realization passed over his face. Perhaps she could've dropped that bomb more gently, but she was done pretending Klaus didn't know.

Gwen saw the muscle in Logan's jaw tighten, but she just smiled.

Finally, Logan sighed, raking a hand through his hair. "*I* didn't ward it to keep out non-therains. That was done long before I got here." His golden eyes pierced into hers. "I warded it so I'd know when someone broke in."

Gwen smirked. "Well, if it's a library for therians, I'm technically not breaking in."

Logan's expression darkened. "You're a freshman, Gwen. You don't get access to coven magic unless you're admitted into one." His tone dropped, a quiet warning wrapped in authority. "This isn't some school library. You don't get to take whatever you want."

"Yeah, yeah," she muttered, rolling her eyes.

Logan's gaze cut to Klaus. With his dark robes and furious expression, he looked like the harbinger of death. "And you," he said coldly, pointing at Klaus. "You should've known better. Family or not, you don't get to break coven rules to let her in."

"Look, Logan, you don't understand," Klaus said, lifting his hands in defense. "She *needs* that book."

Logan's scowl deepened as he took a step towards Klaus.

They needed to get out of here before the situation escalated.

Gwen slid the book beneath her cloak, letting the fabric hide it against her body. "Fine," she said, turning toward the door. "I'll leave then."

She'd barely taken two steps before Logan moved. He was in front of her in an instant, towering over her. The movement was subtle but commanding, and her heart raced as he leaned in close, so close she could feel the warmth of his breath against her cheek.

"Give me the book," he ordered.

The words carried his Alpha voice, thick with dominance, rolling over her like a command that couldn't be ignored. Except it didn't work, just like at the party.

Gwen's lips curled into a slow, defiant smile. She still had no idea what was going on, but she was sure as hell enjoying it.

For the first time, Logan hesitated. The briefest flicker of something uncertain crossed his face before he buried it beneath his usual facade of irritation. She studied him, her mind racing with questions.

Is he weak? Can betas use Alpha voice?

Alpha voice belonged only to the strongest male therians, or so her dad had said. When her dad used his, it was nearly impossible for Gwen to deny an order.

Or... am I stronger than I realized?

Before she could test that thought, Logan moved. Fast. He grabbed her by the front of her cloak and shoved her back against the bookshelf, the impact rattling the wooden structure behind her. Her shoulder blades and spine protested against the pressure, but Gwen gritted her teeth, refusing to flinch.

"You think this is a game?" Logan growled.

"Hey, man, what do you think you're doing?" Klaus shouted at Logan.

Logan turned his Alpha command on Klaus. "Don't move."

Klaus's body went rigid. He stood there, completely still, his expression frozen in a frustrated grimace. While only therians had the ability to use Alpha voice and sense it, mages were also affected by the commands unknowingly.

Gwen's heart pounded. Logan definitely wasn't weak. His grip tightened, pressing her harder against the bookshelf as he leaned in closer. His chest brushed against hers as his hand slipped beneath her cloak. Gwen's mouth watered as he slid his hand around her waist. Before she had time to think about why, his hand was gone, along with the book. Logan's knuckles were white as they held the tome, his expression unreadable as he stepped back.

Damn it.

"Now you'll be leaving," he said flatly.

Gwen clenched her fists. Fine. She'd just break back in and steal it again. But before she could even think about how, Logan turned to Klaus.

"If you ever let her in here again," his voice was low, edged with finality, "you'll be exiled."

Gwen's stomach dropped.

Shit.

There went that plan.

CHAPTER 27

Hazel

The tree line surrounding campus wasn't what Hazel would call the perfect place to practice fulgurkinesis, but it was the best they had. While Hazel and Gwen both thought it was likely the rabid bear had been responsible for the death of the sled dogs, especially since no other attacks had been reported since they'd killed the bear, their luck outside the mountain hadn't been great. Staying safely inside Mount Saint Elias was the right choice, even if it wasn't the most private.

Soft grass cushioned Hazel's feet as she paced, wringing her hands as she tried to call the electricity in the air without glowing. She closed her eyes and sought out the warm atoms around herself and Gwen, then beckoned only the very closest to wrap around her.

She peeked through one eye to look at her hand. It emitted a soft, electric blue.

"Hex it!" Hazel said, throwing her hands up. "I'm never going to get this right!"

“Hazel, it’s going to take time. But it’s important you keep trying. You need to gain control.”

“Like you have?” Hazel bit out. But as soon as the words were out of her mouth, she knew it wasn’t fair. Gwen had been trying. She’d found the book at Alterion, but when the coven member had come home, she’d been forced to abandon it. Her friend was now resigned to wait until the culling to get answers. In the meantime, she’d seemed to make it her mission to help Hazel gain control. And Hazel was grateful for the help. But they’d been at this for six weeks and nothing was working.

Gwen ignored her quip and instead offered her encouragement. “You can do this.”

Hazel walked roughly twenty feet away and pointed her finger down at the ground—afraid to aim in the air lest she catch the trees on fire. She directed the electricity where to go, and almost instantly, it shot into the grass exactly where she had gestured a dozen feet away. With a small mental push, the warmth swirled around her, then shot down her arm and out of her fingertip. A shiver ran through her as her body tingled with the discharge.

The power still hummed around her, although she was no longer emanating a blue glow.

Hazel shot three more times, pushing the energy away with all her might. When she was done, the target zone was a black, charred hole, at least three feet deep.

So much for channeling just a little.

Failing was not something Hazel had ever been good at, so she’d rarely ever let it happen, but it felt like that was all she was doing lately. Weeks of being unable to call anything between a spark and a lightning strike had left her feeling incompetent and dangerous.

Hazel wiped tears from her cheeks as she turned back to look at Gwen.

Gwen said nothing about her red nose and eyes as she walked up to the hole and hid it with a spell.

Her friend had been nothing but supportive since finding out about Hazel's powers. They'd researched lightning and elves, and while there was plenty of information about the latter, there was hardly anything mentioned about the former.

Gwen turned back to her and paused. "Now you're just showing off," she said as she looked at Hazel from head to toe.

What was she talking about? Hazel looked down and, where moments ago she'd looked normal, she now glowed a faint electric blue.

Hazel swallowed. She'd stopped channeling it. So why was she still absorbing it?

Her heart hammered in her chest. "I—I wasn't calling it."

Gwen approached her slowly. "It's okay. It's a new skill. They take time to master."

Hazel nodded, wanting so badly to believe her friend that this was normal. But she hadn't been reaching for it anymore and it had still come.

"Okay, I'm going to teach you a trick I use when I start to feel out of control," Gwen said. "Close your eyes."

Hazel did as Gwen instructed. She'd take any advice that might help.

"I want you to imagine a steel door in your mind. It's dense and heavy, so heavy. And it's magic. It can't be lifted without your express consent."

Hazel envisioned the door clearly in her mind, making sure to seal off every nook and cranny.

"Do you have it?" Gwen asked next to her.

Hazel nodded. "Yeah."

"Now, in a second, I want you to open your eyes and discharge the energy, but this time, you're going to close that steel door and lock it in place once it leaves you."

Hazel did as Gwen instructed. Once all the energy was gone, she slammed the steel door closed, locking out all the energy that tried to rush in and fill the emptiness. The energy bounced off of her, and the ricochet echoed in the corners of her mind.

The girls waited, watching Hazel's skin closely to see if the blue returned. After a few moments, nothing changed, and a smile broke across Hazel's face.

"It worked!"

Gwen grinned back. "Good. Just remember to shut it when the electricity becomes too much."

Hazel nodded, feeling the tension leave her shoulders immediately. It would be nice to have a safety net, for when the energy came without her permission.

Gwen reached for Hazel, wrapping an arm around her shoulder. The second her hand touched the skin on Hazel's arm, a burst of energy snapped between them. Gwen jerked her arm away and shook it.

Guilt swallowed Hazel. She'd been shocking everyone so much lately, and while that wasn't technically new, she now felt responsible. Hurting her friends was the last thing she wanted.

"It's still a win!" Gwen said emphatically. "You aren't glowing."

Hazel's head hung. How was she ever going to gain enough control to not hurt those around her? A deep exhaustion settled in her at the thought.

"I'm tired. I think I need a nap."

"Your spirit magic has been dormant for so long. The more you use it, the stronger it'll get," Gwen said. "Naps are good for recharging, but food is better."

As they walked toward the dining hall, a bald eagle swooped down towards Hazel.

Oh great. What now?

At the last possible second, she flung out her arm, and it landed on it gently. A letter addressed to her was tied to its leg. The second she removed it, the bird took back to the sky.

Hazel studied the handwriting on the letter. It wasn't her father's or her brother's handwriting, she knew—they both had the same chicken scratch she did. She also hadn't heard from either of them all semester, and she didn't expect to now.

"Who's it from?" Gwen asked, stepping next to Hazel to look at the letter.

The letter was sealed with black wax, just a blob, no image. It popped off easily as Hazel pried her fingers underneath the edges. Scanning the pages quickly, Hazel explained, "It's from Jude. They want us to come into town today for dinner."

Gwen arched her brow. "With them?"

Hazel nodded. "And Mara. Apparently, it's a 'thank you' meal."

"I can't go. I have to see Harland." Gwen frowned.

Gwen didn't *need* to go to Sorcerer Thacker's now that she had her bracelet, and Hazel fought the urge to remind her of that. Gwen was getting inappropriately close to him, but every time Hazel mentioned that fact, Gwen got defensive. Hazel used to respect their professor, but ever since Gwen had admitted they'd kissed, she found it harder and harder to do so. She kept waiting for her friend to see the light, but Sorcerer Thacker had a spell on her Gwen couldn't seem to break.

"That sucks. I guess I'm gonna go ahead and head into town. You did say food was the best form of recovery." Hazel smiled at Gwen. She tried to seem lighthearted about the situation even though she didn't feel it; Gwen was crossing lines with Thacker that Hazel was worried she couldn't come back from.

"Meet up later?" Gwen asked.

"Yes," Hazel answered, then turned to make her way into Eagles Ridge.

The directions in the letter led Hazel to a neighborhood within Eagles Ridge that she hadn't visited before. The houses there were Bavarian style, but with their own personal touches of magicked flower beds, intricate sidewalk designs, and herbs drying out on the porch. As she weaved her way between the houses, she approached one with sage and cream accents. The address matched the one within the letter.

"There you are." Jude stood from a porch swing and gave her a small wave. "Where is Gwen?"

"She couldn't make it," Hazel said as she unlatched a gate within the little white fence that surrounded the house and made her way to the porch. "Your home is so cute!"

"Thank you so much," Jude said, making eye contact with Hazel.

Hazel put up a hand to wave off the gratitude. "It's true!"

Jude smiled for a moment before explaining, "I meant thank you so much for Mara."

Hazel's cheeks warmed. "Jude, you don't need to thank me. I did what anyone would've done."

They looked at Hazel with a knowing look, a vulnerable one that Hazel had never seen on their always-sure face. "We both know that's not true."

Hazel swallowed. Was Jude saying they knew what she was? What she'd actually done? Hazel was too afraid to ask.

I'm just being paranoid.

"Wait here. I'll go get Mara." Jude grabbed their leather jacket and slipped it on. "I have to go around back to the greenhouse. I haven't been able to get her out of there since the incident. It's been her version of therapy, I suppose." Jude shrugged.

Hazel smiled and nodded, glad Mara had some type of outlet.

The porch included a swing with plush cushions and room enough for two, while wind chimes made of seashells and driftwood danced in the breeze. Stained-glass mushrooms and hummingbirds hung in the open windows.

A few minutes later, Mara came around the house with Jude following close behind. There were no signs of soreness or fatigue. Hazel would even say she was showing a little pep in her step. She wore a smile on her ethereal face as she carried a small bouquet of red roses in her fist. "Hazel, it's so good to see you!"

Hazel grinned. "You too!"

Mara threw her arms around Hazel. There was no hesitation as Hazel hugged her back, moisture pooling in her eyes. She hadn't been hugged like this since coming to SEU, and no matter how happy the school made her, part of her would always miss her family.

Pulling back, Mara offered the flowers to Hazel. "These are for you."

"Thank you," Hazel said.

Mara's eyes sparkled. "No, Hazel, thank you."

Taking the bouquet, Hazel said, "Let's call it even?"

A flicker of emotion crossed Mara's face. "Not a chance."

Hazel inhaled the fragrance of the bouquet. The scent made her recall that Mara had smelled of roses on the day of the incident. "Now I know why you smelled of roses last month."

Mara's brow creased at Hazel's words, then she turned to Jude, all happiness vanishing from her face. "I told you I smelled them. I'm not crazy."

Hazel fidgeted, unsure of what can of worms she'd accidentally opened.

Jude lifted their hand in surrender. "I never thought you were, my love."

Something passed between the couple, a tension Hazel couldn't put her finger on, before Mara turned back to her. "I woke up drowning in the smell of them. The scent has been scratching at my brain every day. Jude insisted they couldn't smell it, but I needed confirmation that the scent was roses, so they grew them for me as a test." Mara's face relaxed as she said the next part. "Now I know I was right. It *was* roses."

Hazel looked at Jude. "So you've never grown these before?"

Jude shook her head.

"No, never," Mara replied, her gaze fixed on the flowers.

"Well, I would never have guessed that. They're stunning."

A small, content smile returned to Mara's lips. "Let's go eat," she said. "I'm starving!" She hooked an arm through Hazel's, the other through Jude's, and led them back the way Hazel had come. "I made a reservation at El Encanto Oaxaqueño."

Mara made small talk on the way and Hazel was happy to oblige her, so pleased to see her well and not so shaken, as Jude had implied. They arrived at El Encanto Oaxaqueño quickly. Its exterior matched the town's Bavarian theme, but once inside, Hazel felt as though they'd stepped into a restaurant in the heart of Mexico. Patinated walls of copper, deep blues, and oranges gave it an aged appearance while tables and chairs of warm, light woods made it feel homey. The group was sat in a corner and enjoyed a delightful meal of tamales de oaxaqueños, mole negro, and tlayuda.

The various flavors of spice and sweet corn blew Hazel's mind. Tex Mex and Olive Garden were the closest things Hazel got to experiencing international cuisine in Conway, Arkansas. It was a meal she'd remember forever, though not for the food, but the company.

It was lovely to see Mara and Jude laugh, joke, and sip on their mezcals while they all waited for their nicuatole, which Hazel had learned was a custard-like treat made of corn dough, sugar, milk, and cinnamon.

When their waiter came by to ask for refills, Hazel asked for a top off on her sweet tea and Mara asked for another mezcal.

As the waiter walked away, Jude arched a brow. "Are you sure a second one is a good idea?"

Mara crossed her arms and sniffed. "I survived a near-death experience. If I've learned anything, it's to drink the damn drink and eat the damn dessert because another opportunity may not come again."

Silence settled over the table, but Jude couldn't help themselves. "That's my point, Mara. You just had a near-death experience from blood loss. Perhaps more alcohol isn't the best choice right now."

Hazel startled at Jude's words. "Blood loss?"

Jude's hand came up to squeeze Mara's on the table. "The test the medic ran indicated blood loss and..." they paused, "fear."

"How did you lose so much blood?"

Mara dropped the death glare she'd been shooting at Jude and shrugged. "That's the thing. I have no idea."

"Are you sure the medic's tests were right?" Hazel asked.

Jude nodded. "We're sure. We found blood on her dress."

Hazel's thoughts went back to the day of the incident. She didn't remember seeing any blood. Then it hit her—the dark stain on Mara's dress. But surely that wasn't enough blood to cause cardiac arrest.

"A little bit of blood caused that?"

Mara sighed. "That's the million-dollar question, but we don't know. The last thing I remember was kissing Jude on the cheek before heading home."

"You don't remember anything about walking out the door or seeing anyone?"

"No, nothing," Mara said, frowning.

"You know what's odd?" Jude asked rhetorically. "Two other people in town have said they've had some memory issues in the last few weeks too."

"Are you sure that's not from old age?" Mara joked.

Jude smiled. "The thought did cross my mind, but it's too much of a coincidence. Both men said they'd lost some time in the middle of their day. Will Anderson said he was taking a stroll in the woods out behind his shop and lost five minutes. His worker came and found him out back, confused. Samuel Gracey said he lost about ten minutes a few days after that while taking out the trash. His wife found him in the backyard, and when she asked what he was doing, he couldn't tell her."

"How long were you gone, Mara?" Hazel asked.

"Jude said I was gone for almost fifteen minutes, and Alec said he found me a minute before yelling for help."

"Did Alec see anything?"

"Alec said he found Mara alone," Jude said. They sounded as though they believed him. First a few minutes with Will, then nearly ten minutes with Samuel, and lastly fifteen minutes with Mara. All moments of memory loss but different amounts of time. Something about this didn't sit right with Hazel. Was there any other way these things might be connected outside of the memory loss? They'd all been found by someone, but they'd been in different places. First the woods, next a backyard, and then an alleyway.

Then a light bulb went off in Hazel's mind. How did those things differ? The woods were secluded, while a backyard under the shield of darkness was somewhat more open, but an alleyway had the potential to be very public. Yes, they were different, but they were still connected. They were an escalation. Just like the amounts of time. Whatever was happening was getting worse. Or perhaps getting bolder.

"Don't forget the weirdest part," Mara said, nudging Jude's hand on the table.

Jude studied Mara for a moment before they said, "We noticed that all of them are mundane."

Hazel's eyes widened. "Mara, you're mundane?" Hazel had no idea.

Mara laughed. "Shocking right?"

"Kind of." Hazel grinned sheepishly. "I feel silly that I didn't realize." Thinking back now, Hazel couldn't recall ever seeing Mara with a wand. Hazel had thought nothing of it before—many mages used holsters.

"Don't worry about it," Mara said. The desserts arrived, but the sweet pineapple of the nicuatole couldn't completely mask the unease that settled over the table. The lost time, the unexplained blood loss, the stranger in the alleyway—they felt like pieces of an incomplete puzzle with unsettling implications.

A booming laugh from the opposite side of the room pulled Hazel's attention from her plate, which was a feat in itself because she was pretty sure she was in love with her dessert. Across the restaurant, a large man in height and stature hit his open palm against his table as a smile split his face to show twin dimples and pearly white teeth against his terra cotta brown skin. Recognition flooded Hazel, though she'd never met this man before. He was familiar to her on a deep level, from the way he smiled to how his laugh sounded. The sound of it made her grin.

"Do you know him?" Jude nodded toward the man.

Hazel shook her head. "No, but he's quite memorable, isn't he?"

"Yes, Knight De La Vega definitely stands out in a crowd," Jude answered.

Hazel's eyes snapped to Jude's. "He's a Brecilian Knight?"

Jude nodded before taking another bite.

She'd never seen a Brecilian Knight before. The closest things mages had to policemen, they were the boogiemen of stories told to misbehaving young mages. Use your magic wisely, or they'd come and take it from you. Now, after Gwen's warnings, Hazel's stomach twisted knowing one was in the room.

"What's he doing in Eagles Ridge?" Hazel asked. Her understanding was they spent their time on the fringes of the mundane worlds, keeping mages in line.

Are they here for me or Gwen? Her stomach sank.

"I'm assuming it has to do with the sled dogs. We've found no new evidence or leads in months, but the Knights aren't ones to give up quickly," Jude explained.

The mention of the dogs brought back memories of the night she and Gwen had found them, of bloodstained hands and the thing Gwen chased into the forest—the bear. Maybe they should have told the chancellor the truth so the Knights wouldn't have been called.

"Of course, Knight De La Vega probably volunteered to take the case so he could come see his son, Rafael."

"Rafe?" Hazel asked, connecting the dots.

She understood then why the man felt so familiar to her—he was the exact picture of what Rafe would look like in twenty-five years, with deepened smile lines and salt-and-pepper hair. Before she could look away, Rafe appeared into view as he shifted on the other side of his father. His gaze met hers from across the room and he smiled.

Hazel wondered if she should go say "hi," but her nerves about meeting a Brecilian Knight kept her in her seat. Still, she couldn't help but try to catch glimpses of the two men until the bill came.

They enjoyed the rest of their meal with light conversation and laughter. Mara finished her drink while Jude paid.

"Thank you both for such a wonderful meal," Hazel said.

"Please don't thank us," Jude said sincerely.

Mara wrapped Hazel in a tight hug once more as they headed toward the door. Hazel squeezed her back softly before they stepped outside the door into the chilly air.

"Can we walk you to the tunnel?" Mara asked.

Before she could answer, a deep voice spoke from behind Hazel. "I actually came to offer the same thing."

Hazel turned to see Rafe rubbing the back of his neck, looking at her with a bashful smile.

Hazel beamed at him. "Yes, please."

"And who's this?" Rafe's father asked, stepping outside behind his son.

"Papa, this is Hazel. My friend from Elkmont I told you about." Rafe's eyes never left Hazel's face as he spoke.

What had he told his dad about her? Rafe didn't know her secrets, but the thought still made butterflies dance in her stomach that he'd told his father about her.

Knight De La Vega extended his hand to Hazel. She squashed down her nerves as she shook it back. "Encantado. I'm Estaban."

"El gusto es mío," Hazel answered back.

Rafe's father's eyes glittered in response. He didn't seem so scary up close. Perhaps it was because he was an older version of Rafe and Hazel felt the opposite of scared with him. She felt safe with Rafe.

"¿Su habla español?"

Hazel shook her head. "Not much, Señor, but enough to be polite."

Knight De La Vega smiled. "You were right about what you said about Señorita Hazel, Rafa."

Hazel searched Rafe's face and found a faint blush on his light-brown cheeks. He looked down, avoiding her gaze. Hazel bit her lip, hoping whatever he'd said had been good.

"I heard you saved Mara's life, Hazel," Estaban said, eyes searching Hazel's with something that looked like curiosity.

Hazel stumbled over her words. "I did what anyone else would've done."

"From what I hear, that's not true." The gleam in Estaban's eye shifted and his curiosity grew to something harder as he held her gaze. She felt like a deer caught in headlights. His words implied he knew exactly what she'd done—and it was not something just anyone could do.

Hazel swallowed, fear seeping in. Gwen had warned her what being Forsaken meant to the Knights. Did Knight De La Vega suspect she was an elf?

"Well, it's time for us to be heading back," Rafe said. Hazel could've kissed him right then for the change of subject.

Estaban turned to wrap his son in a hug, and the absence of his gaze allowed Hazel to breathe normally, although her heart still raced in her chest.

She'd done nothing wrong, but his questions and demeanor made her feel otherwise.

The group exchanged goodbyes with Mara and Jude, who headed home, while Estaban made for Fjordhaven.

Hazel and Rafe walked in silence. His warm heat inches away calmed her and she wanted to get closer. Every few steps, his hand would gently brush against hers in passing and she guessed maybe he wanted to be closer too. She was relieved Gwen's training was paying off and she wasn't shocking him each time they touched.

Rafe's gaze fell on her like a blanket that she couldn't resist basking in. "What's on your mind?"

Hazel grinned at him warmly. She debated on whether or not to be honest, but figured she'd go with a version of the truth. "I was just wondering why you didn't tell me your father was a Brecilian Knight?"

Rafe's eyes went wide. *Had he wanted my thoughts to be about him?* "Oh. Well, to be honest, it weirds most people out. They treat me differently when they find out, ya know. No one wants to say too much around a Brecilian Knight's kid."

Hazel nodded. "Does Jordan know?"

"Yes, but he's the only one I've ever told. Some people have figured it out through their parents, but it's rare."

"I won't tell anyone," Hazel promised.

Rafe snorted. "Except Gwen, you mean."

Hazel laughed. "Well, obviously. That's roommate code but I'll swear her to secrecy."

Despite the tailspin this information could put Gwen in, Hazel couldn't risk hiding it from her. Gwen needed to be extra cautious with a Knight in town.

He grinned down at her, his eyes shining at her confession. "It's fine. You can tell her. I trust your judgment."

A warmth spread down her spine at his words. How good it felt to have people to trust and be trusted by. There really was no feeling like it.

They turned around the bend, passing a few more shops and houses as they headed toward the forest tunnel. Students headed in both directions, everyone bundled in their thickest winter coats and tall boots despite the clear skies. Winter had arrived in Alaska.

Hazel was enjoying the glimmer, one of those moments of pure perfection, when she felt a tingle along her neck. Microscopic and brief, a warm essence swept down her spine. Not unpleasant but entirely unfamiliar, the sensation made Hazel jerk to a stop. Rafe looked at her in confusion.

She checked her own energy field and felt a slightly elevated amount of electricity circulating around her. While it wasn't much, she decided to slam the mental steel door down just in case. Rafe's field was considerably less charged. It wasn't either of them that had set off that feeling. She looked up and down the path, but saw nothing suspicious. Perhaps it was all in her mind.

"What's up?" Rafe asked.

"Sorry, I'm being weird. Just one of those moments where you feel like someone's watching you."

Rafe nodded reassuringly as he searched the street as well. "I get it. Talking about the Knights gives a lot of people the heebie-jeebies."

Hazel's laugh sounded hollow even to her own ears. "That's not it," she said, although she wasn't completely sure. Meeting a Knight had shaken her more than she'd ever imagined. Although she'd never imagined she was a Forsaken before, which changed things more than she cared to admit. She didn't know how Gwen did it, and for a fleeting moment, she was glad she hadn't had to hide it all her life.

They made it to the edge of the neighborhood and passed Jacob Menendez, a mage both Hazel and Rafe shared classes with. He smiled at them, then looked past them as they walked forward.

"Hey there, Alec," Jacob said.

Both Rafe and Hazel turned, her eyes connecting with Alec's. He was standing right behind them. How had they not heard him?

Alec quickly averted his gaze, nodding at Jacob before pushing between Rafe and Hazel and rounding the corner. The man's body heat washed over them as he passed.

Well that was rude! She hadn't seen him since the day they'd worked to save Mara. Surely a hello would have been appropriate.

"Hello to you too," Hazel murmured, but Alec did not look back.

Rafe immediately closed the space between them, their bodies like magnets, and her shoulders relaxed.

"Do you know him?" Rafe asked her.

"Sort of. He owns Kodiak Brew. He gave us free drinks on our first night here," Hazel said.

She hadn't lied but she had omitted they'd saved Mara's life together a few weeks ago. While she trusted Rafe, learning his dad was a Brecilian Knight made her a bit more cautious with her information. Telling him about Mara would lead to questions she didn't feel safe to answer and she didn't want to lie to Rafe.

She watched Alec closely until he cut down the path that would lead him toward Fjordhaven. Perhaps he suspected how she'd been able to use the lightning—that she was an elf—and took issue with it. If he did, she was glad he was keeping quiet.

Rafe and Hazel finally reached the edge of town and made their way to the forest tunnel. Hazel glanced over her shoulder every few steps, paranoia overcoming her.

"Slumming it, are we, Rafe?" Dane's arrogant voice echoed through the tunnel.

Rafe stiffened beside her as he peered into the dark opening, but he kept walking. There was a small beat of silence before they heard the crunch of boots and Dane emerged from the tunnel.

"Bellamy, watch your mouth," Rafe said, his eyes narrowing in a way Hazel had never seen before. His arm wrapped around Hazel's protectively and his hand touched her waist where her shirt and pants met. His fingers slid underneath the hem and grazed softly over her skin. Hazel's breath hitched.

Dane cleared his throat and Hazel wanted to hex him. Of course he was ruining this moment.

Hazel had learned a long time ago Dane would keep digging if he didn't get a reaction. She looked sweetly up at Rafe and cocked her head to the side.

Rafe swallowed hard, his eyes focusing on her smile.

"Do you hear something?" Hazel asked. "I thought all the pests had died by this time of year."

Rafe's lips turned up at the corner. She'd been successful at cheering him up slightly.

After a few seconds of silence, Dane sauntered past, the weight of his gaze on her face, but she kept her own on Rafe's grin. She held her breath, waiting to see if he'd retaliate for the hex she'd used on him at the party all those months ago. It was unlike him to take so long, but Hazel knew better than to believe he'd let it go.

She sighed when he was finally out of earshot. "Sorry about that."

Rafe shrugged his shoulders, but maintained his grip on her. "I can't blame the guy."

Hazel's eyes grew wide in indignation. "What?" She smacked Rafe on the chest.

He caught her hand and held it there against him. The action was intimate and entirely new for Hazel. It made her mouth go dry.

"Come on, Hazel, it's pretty obvious." His gaze captured hers, searching for something—she didn't know what.

"What's obvious?" There was no demand in her words as she got lost in the rich deep brown of his eyes.

Rafe raised a brow. "Dane is obviously hung up on you."

His words brought her back to earth. Hazel felt like she was being pranked. Surely this was a joke. "You're sorely mistaken. Dane Bellamy hates me. Always has, always will."

Rafe shook his head. "You're misunderstanding me. Lust and hate aren't mutually exclusive things, Hazel." His gaze dipped from her eyes to her mouth.

The glance seared her to the core. No guy had ever looked at her the way Rafe did. She felt wanted, and for the first time in her life, she felt a desire she couldn't put into words even if she dared to. It was nothing like what she felt for Dane. She wanted Dane to walk into traffic, while she wanted Rafe to kiss her senseless. *Yes, the two are definitely mutually exclusive.*

"Trust me. In this instance, they very much are," Hazel insisted. She needed Rafe to understand she and Dane were nothing to each other. "I know you've heard the stories. He's been at my throat for over four years."

Since the very first time they'd met, during their first week at Elkmont. She'd been walking down the hall with her arms full of books, late to class because she'd spent too long chatting with her Basic Spells teacher. She'd turned a corner and run smack into the solid, unforgiving wall of Dane Bellamy. She'd practically bounced off of him, landing on the floor with her books on top of her.

"I'm so sorry!" she'd said without looking up, scrambling to collect her books and loose papers.

"Dinnae worry yerself, lass," a masculine voice with a Scottish burr had answered. "Let me give ye a hand."

Hazel had finally looked up, ready to tell the boy no thank you, when her eyes connected with his. A gaze the color of spring leaves met hers and all words emptied from her head. He was the most handsome boy she'd ever laid eyes on. Shiny black hair with a boyish wave had hung shaggy across his forehead, and he had a strong jaw, even though he looked to be about her age.

He had smiled, and Hazel had felt sure that if she'd still been standing, she would've fallen. He'd extended a hand to her, and she'd stared at it for a moment before accepting it. As her hand slid into his, a warmth spread through her palm, up her arm, straight to her heart. She'd never felt anything like it. Hazel had gasped. But Dane had dropped her hand as if it burned him. Without a word, Dane had spun on his heel and walked the other way.

From that day on, Dane had made Hazel's life a living hell.

Thinking back on it now, she considered the possibility she'd shocked him—but even that wasn't grounds for his behavior over the years. Whatever had happened, Dane Bellamy hated her for it.

Rafe leaned in close, pulling her from the memory. "For someone to hate you, you'd have to give them a reason." His signature pine scent teased her senses. "And I know you." He tucked a stray wisp of hair behind Hazel's ear. "You're the most unhateable person I've ever met." He paused and looked down at Hazel's mouth again, a gleam in them indicating he was lost in thought.

Is he going to kiss me? She looked down at his full lips and imagined them pressed against hers. The fantasy lit a fire inside her. *Terra, please let him kiss me.* Compulsively, Hazel wet her lips.

Rafe blinked and stepped away, then moved for the tunnel once more.

Hazel felt the absence of his proximity immediately. The desire inside her was smothered with rejection.

Maybe she'd gotten it all wrong. If Rafe didn't want to kiss her now, maybe he hadn't wanted to kiss her in Kodiak Brew that night either. Maybe she'd gotten a little bit of male attention for the first time in her life and it had all gone to her head, filling it with fantasies.

"You coming?" Rafe asked from the mouth of the tunnel.

Hazel pushed down the humiliation growing inside her and joined him. There was no point in ruining their friendship over this. If Rafe just wanted to be friends, then she could live with that. No one was better at hiding their true feelings than Hazel.

Gwen

Gwen opened the door of Harland's home as casually as she opened her own. She'd grown quite familiar with it over the last month. Harland stood at the stove, stirring ingredients in a low-simmering cauldron with practiced ease, his sleeves rolled to his elbows, forearms flexing with each motion.

Without a word, she crossed the room and slid her arms around him from behind, pressing into the heat of his back. Her hands flattened over his chest for a second and he stilled. Then he turned to face her, slowly, like he'd been waiting all day for this exact moment.

"You know, you make it incredibly hard for me to focus in class when you dress like this."

"I know." Gwen smiled up at him. She'd hiked her mini skirt up a little higher than usual and picked a top that enhanced her small chest, just enough to make him look twice. And he had. His eyes had lingered on her more than usual in class today and she'd known then it had worked.

She was ready to take their relationship to the next level and hoped he was too.

"What was with asking me the therian question in class today?" she asked, taking a step back from him.

His arm snaked around her waist and pulled her back against him. "It would've been just as suspicious if I didn't ask you as if I did."

She supposed that was true, so she dropped it.

When he leaned down to kiss her, his lips were so soft, she couldn't help the sigh that escaped her. All of her doubts and frustration melted away. He lifted her effortlessly, and she wrapped her legs around him. One of his hands slid beneath the hem of her skirt to steady her. His palm was hot against her skin, leaving a trail of warmth as it slid further up. Her breath hitched, but she leaned into him without hesitation, wanting more—wanting all of him.

"Are you sure you want this?" he murmured against her ear, the warmth of his breath making her shiver.

"You know I do." She ran her fingers through his hair, slow and deliberate, letting the strands slip between her fingers like silk.

His jaw tightened, just enough for her to know he liked it. Her gaze locked with his dark-brown eyes that always held back just enough to drive her mad, always hinting at something he refused to say.

"Touch me." Gwen's whisper landed between them like a heavy stone.

"Gwendolyn." Her name was a warning, thick with restraint, but his hands never left her.

"Harland," she breathed, leaning in until their foreheads almost touched. "Your hand is already there and kissing is fun, but I want to feel you inside of me."

He almost dropped her. His grip slipped for a heartbeat, and she gasped—but he caught her, arms tightening around her, his hands now firmly grasping her ass.

"Damn, that mouth of yours is going to get both of us in trouble," he groaned.

Gwen smirked. "You know you like it."

His chest rose hard against hers, their bodies pressed so close she could feel the tension vibrating through him. "I like everything about you."

The room went still, save for the sound of his tightly held breaths and the echo of desire pounding through her chest. This was the first time he'd admitted it and the words fueled her desire.

She leaned in, lips brushing against his ear, and whispered, "Don't you want to feel how wet you make me?"

Without a word, he led her to the couch, the potion forgotten. When he sat down with her still in his arms, she shifted to straddle him, her skirt rising around her thighs. His hands slid up her back, fingers threading into her hair as he pulled her mouth to his. She kissed him like she was daring him to break.

Grabbing one of his hands, she guided it down the curve of her waist to the bare skin of her thigh. He let it rest there, warm and still, but didn't move an inch.

She waited. And waited.

But of course, he wouldn't make the first move. *Always the good guy*. She resisted the urge to roll her eyes. It was driving her insane. If he didn't want her, she'd find someone who did. She started to lift herself off his lap, jaw tight with frustration, but his hands clamped down, holding her in place.

"Look," she said, voice sharp, "if you're not into this, just say so."

He looked down at the obvious bulge beneath the seam of his pants. "You know I'm into you, Gwendolyn. It's not..."

She shifted to move off him again, fed up with half measures, but his hands caught her hips and held her firmly in place. She could feel him rock hard between her legs, straining against her.

His fingers dug into her hips. "I'm begging you," he said, voice low and wrecked. "Please stop moving."

The desperation in his tone made something click. She was

driving him wild and he was barely holding it together. For once, she held the power. But she didn't want to be the only one reaching. She didn't want someone who stayed frozen, always waiting for her to make the first move.

"Then give me a reason not to," she said, her voice dripping with defiance.

His hand slid towards her inner thigh, slow as sin, fingers trailing heat as they inched higher. When they finally grazed her clit through her panties, she gasped—it felt so damn good. Her hips shifted before she could stop herself.

"I said don't move." His other hand clamped down on her thigh, anchoring her in place.

There he is.

His fingers began to glide over her with maddening precision, each stroke winding her tighter. And every time she got close—too close—he eased back, slowing just enough to keep her aching for more. He knew exactly what he was doing, and he was doing it on purpose.

"Please," she whispered, voice soft and raw, letting her lower lip pout without shame. He leaned in and caught it between his teeth, biting down just enough to make her moan. Terra, this man made her crazy. And she didn't care—she wanted more.

Ignoring her plea, he abandoned her clit and slid her panties to the side. Cool air kissed her exposed skin, before his fingers slid inside her, stealing the breath from her lungs. She panted, every muscle tense with restraint, trying not to move as he slid his fingers in and out, each thrust slow, deliberate, consuming. His fingers, slick with her arousal, found her clit once more, circling, teasing, never giving her quite enough. Again he pushed her to the brink, then stopped.

She held her breath, strung tight, desperate for release.

"Beg for me," he murmured in her ear. His breath was warm against her skin, sending a shiver down her spine.

"Please, Harland," Gwen whimpered.

The sound of his name on her lips broke whatever control he had left. His fingers moved faster, circling over her, wave after wave driving her towards the edge until she shattered around him. Warmth pulsed from her core, spreading through every inch of her body until her limbs gave out. She collapsed in his arms, breathless, her heart pounding in her chest. He wrapped his arms around her waist, holding her steady as she tangled her fingers in his hair and kissed him again—slow, happy, still dazed.

"Now can I finish making the potion?" he teased.

"What about you?" Gwen asked, her voice softer now. She wanted him to feel what he'd made her feel.

But he only shook his head then gently set her back on the couch, careful with her, as always. "That *was* for me." He leaned down, lifted her chin, and kissed her.

Instead of going to the large cauldron on the stove, he walked toward a small entry table, opening the drawer. "Here," he said, returning to her with something in his outstretched hand.

An intricate golden key glinted in his palm. Gwen took it carefully, inspecting its delicate curves. It looked like any other vintage key.

"What's that for?" Gwen asked, eyes narrowed.

"Winter break starts tomorrow. You'll need a daily dose."

Gwen blinked. Shit, she hadn't even thought of that. She had her bracelet to get her through Christmas, but Harland didn't know that. He was thinking ahead. Thinking of her. She'd been steeling herself for weeks of distance, for the ache of being without him. Despite her best efforts, Gwen had grown attached to him beyond the physical.

Warmth bloomed in her chest—the kind that unraveled knots she didn't even realize she'd woven. She fought back a grin, one that threatened to stretch too wide, too revealing, like a Cheshire cat. *I won't have to be without him after all.*

"I thought transport keys wouldn't work in Saint Elias?" Gwen asked.

"They don't," he answered. "This key will take you to my home, my real home."

Gwen couldn't help the smile that tugged at her lips. Their relationship was extending beyond the bounds of school. Maybe this had potential after all.

Harland walked back to the stove and poured the potion into a small glass vial. When he returned, he handed it to her with one hand and pulled her into his arms with the other. The potion was cool and bitter on her tongue, its chill spreading fast through her veins. But it couldn't compete with the warmth of his arms around her.

And as her fingers curled around the key still clutched in her palm, the cold didn't feel quite so sharp.

CHAPTER 28

Hazel

A soft glow seeped through the curtains of Gwen's childhood bedroom. The cold grey light of early winter cast faint shadows across the warm blankets, making Hazel burrow deeper in the warmth. For a brief, sleepy second, she thought she was waking up in her own bedroom back in Arkansas, but the frosted windows reminded her that this would be her first Christmas outside of the South.

Instead of the scent of cinnamon and apples drifting from the kitchen, chocolate and peppermint permeated the air. Rather than the off-key hum of her father's favorite Christmas carols, she only heard strange chirps from unfamiliar birds outside the window.

Her heart ached for her old traditions, but that life was gone. She'd burned it to the ground when she'd left for SEU. The weight of that realization settled deep in her chest. Despite herself, she wondered what her father and Forrest were doing this morning, if Forrest had waited to open the package she'd mailed or if he'd opened it the second he'd gotten it. Did they miss her?

Suddenly, the mattress lurched beneath her and Hazel yelped as Gwen hauled herself onto the top bunk in a way no normal person would've managed, landing beside her with a dramatic bounce. Hazel groaned, throwing an arm over her eyes as Gwen giggled, shaking her shoulders. "Wake up, Hazel! It's Christmas morning!"

"How are you so awake?" Hazel mumbled, voice thick with sleep. Gwen's steel door technique had been working well for Hazel when she couldn't keep the electricity at bay, but it often left her exhausted after using it. She didn't know how Gwen did it so effortlessly.

Oh, yeah. She's been training her whole life.

"I've been up since five a.m. and it's eight now. My patience has run dry. Get your ass out of bed," Gwen said as she slapped Hazel on the butt.

Hazel laughed, rubbing the sleep from her eyes as Gwen scrambled down from the bed and all but sprinted for the stairs.

Hazel hesitated as she listened to her friend's animated voice drift up from the living room. Christmas morning felt so different here. There was still warmth, still excitement—but the familiar ache of homesickness crept into the edges of her thoughts. The thrill she usually felt was dimmed; in fact it felt nonexistent next to Gwen's glee, but she wouldn't let that show. She'd been having the best time with Gwen and her family all week. She was beyond grateful to them for giving her a home for the holiday. There was no way she was going to dampen their Christmas spirits.

So, instead of lying back down and wallowing in the emptiness she felt, she forced a smile and followed Gwen.

The scent of something warm and buttery filled the air as Hazel stepped into the kitchen. Gwen's mother flipped pancakes on a cast-iron skillet. Her brunette hair was swept up into a loose bun while her cheeks were flushed from the heat of the stovetop. It was clear she'd been cooking all morning.

"Merry Christmas, girls!" Liana greeted, turning with a bright smile.

She pulled Gwen into a quick hug before wrapping Hazel up in one too—tight, warm, unwaveringly genuine. Hazel wasn't used to this, but she leaned into it. After several seconds, she felt something break loose, and she let out a contented sigh in Liana's motherly embrace as tears filled her eyes.

She snagged a croissant to soothe her wistfulness and followed Gwen to the kitchen island. Gwen sat on a stool, nibbling on her own.

"Mom, these are so damn good!"

"Language, Gwendolyn!"

Gwen rolled her eyes and grinned cheekily. After finishing her pastry, she clapped her hands together. "Okay, now let's open presents!"

Liana didn't even look up from the stove. "After breakfast."

Gwen groaned dramatically. "Please! Don't make me wait until after breakfast."

Hazel bit back a laugh as Gwen's mom shot her a knowing look. It was odd seeing Gwen this way, more childlike and less guarded, but Hazel enjoyed it immensely. It was a side of her best friend she rarely got to see.

"Gwendolyn, you do this every year," Liana said matter-of-factly.

"Which makes it a tradition," Gwen huffed, stomping over to the stove to steal a bite of crispy bacon.

Her mother swatted her hand away, but Liana smiled as she moved the platters of pancakes, eggs, and bacon to the table.

Hazel watched the easy, familiar back-and-forth between them. The warmth, the lighthearted teasing—the unconditional love woven into it all.

Gwen was lucky.

When breakfast ended, they all moved to the living room. The Christmas tree was even more magical this morning. Twinkling lights wrapped around the branches, illuminating ornaments collected over generations—faded paper snowflakes, tiny handprints pressed into clay, a wonky-looking star Gwen admitted to making when she was six. This morning, someone had added antique golden candle holders that held tiny lit candles, each floating around the tree as an added layer of decoration.

Below the tree, a pile of gifts filled the previously empty space. Hazel's eyes bulged as she took in the presents wrapped in colorful paper and curly ribbons that overflowed past the tree skirt. This was so very different from her own family Christmas, which typically consisted of two or three presents per person. There were ten times that amount under the tree, but then again, Gwen *did* have a large extended family.

Gwen settled onto the floor, grinning ear to ear, and began passing out gifts. She handed Hazel a brightly wrapped package, and Hazel accepted it with a smile.

Then Gwen tossed her another one. And another.

"Wait. Are all these for me?" Hazel asked, wide-eyed.

"Duh," Gwen answered as if it was completely normal for Hazel to be getting so many gifts from a family that wasn't her own.

By the time the last gift was passed out, Hazel's stack was as tall as Gwen's.

Hazel blinked hard, overwhelmed by the sheer thoughtfulness behind it all. For the first time in years, she felt something stir in her chest—a kind of warmth that had nothing to do with the fire crackling in the nearby hearth.

Hazel quickly retrieved Gwen and Liana's gifts, and a wave of worry washed over her. She'd only gotten Gwen and her mother one thing each.

I hope they're not disappointed.

She added them to the piles of presents.

"Okay, let's begin!" Liana said.

Gwen and Liana dug into their presents with reckless abandon. Hazel watched them with fascination as they tore through the wrapping to open their first gifts. Gwen revealed a mismatched pair of socks and let out a cackle, while Liana unwrapped a pointed hat, immediately trying it on.

"Hazel, what did you get?" Gwen asked as she picked up her next present.

"Oh, um, let me see," Hazel said as she looked at her pile to pick one. Deciding starting at the top was best, she picked a small box and unwrapped it to find a tiny glass snow globe. Looking inside, she found the town of Britton Place, covered in snow. To her fascination, snow continued to fall within the globe although she held it still.

"It's enchanted to change with the season, in spring it will rain," Gwen said happily.

Hazel grinned. "It's adorable. Thank you!"

By the time the unwrapping was finished, Gwen had acquired a new leather journal, a box of enchanted hot cocoa that would change flavors depending on her mood, and a golden book charm from Hazel.

"For your bracelet," Hazel explained. It wasn't enchanted, but Hazel decided to keep that to herself in front of Liana—she didn't know what Gwen had shared with her mother.

Gwen immediately held out her wrist, insisting Hazel put it on her.

As far as Hazel's haul, she'd received a hand-knit scarf in SEU's colors, a set of tarot cards from Liana, and a book of spells from Gwen with notes.

Hazel ran her fingers over the deck of tarot cards before slipping open the top and sliding them into her hands. Each card was beautifully gold-foiled, and she dreaded the idea of tarnishing them.

Gwen nudged her. "Do you like them?"

Hazel swallowed the lump in her throat, managing a smile. "I love them."

While her heart was overwhelmed with the thoughtfulness of their gifts, it only made her realize how out of touch her own family was with her interests. Last Christmas, her father had gotten her an Arkansas keychain with her name on it and a stuffed teddy bear.

A knock on the door pulled Hazel from her thoughts.

"Come in!" Liana called. She grabbed the remaining presents beneath the tree as the door swung open.

Klaus entered first, nodding at Gwen before flashing Hazel a full smile. "Merry Christmas, ladies," Klaus said. His loose waves flopped on his forehead as he took off his jacket.

Hazel's eyes widened as she took in the men who entered after him. She'd thought Klaus was tall, but his brothers were even taller. They all had similar features, height, and the same blue eyes. Each of them were good-looking, fit young men, and Hazel wondered how she was going to keep them straight.

"Hazel, these two ugly ghouls are my brothers. Manfrit," Klaus said, pointing to the guy next to him as Manfrit slipped on his glasses, and then the guy closest to the door, "and Ahren."

Manfrit and Ahren both gave Hazel a nice smile before moving out of the doorway to make room for the others. Gwen's grandparents, younger cousin, and aunts and uncles greeted them with hugs and warm exclamations of *"Merry Christmas!"*

Hazel felt stiff in their unfamiliar arms, but she kept the smile plastered on her face, thankful to each of them for including her so wholeheartedly in their day.

Once everyone had found a seat, more presents were passed out. Hazel had barely recovered from the shock of the morning gifts, so when her name was called again, she just stared for a moment.

"Me?"

Gwen's Aunt Alda grinned. "Of course, you! You're family now, aren't you?"

Hazel swallowed hard. She didn't trust her voice enough to respond.

The package Alda extended was oddly shaped and ill-wrapped, making it overtly obvious what was inside: a broom.

Hazel shook her head, sticking her hands out to decline. "Oh, no. I couldn't possibly accept that. That's entirely too much."

Hazel looked to Gwen, beseeching her silently for help, but Gwen only rolled her eyes before grabbing the package from Alda and tossing it at Hazel.

Hazel brought it to her chest. She blinked down at the wrapped broom in her hands, her chest so full it hurt. Brooms were so very expensive; the idea that this beautiful family had gotten her one was too much. It was more than she'd ever expected.

Gwen's grandfather cleared his throat. "I made that broom myself, so if you don't take it and use it, the only thing that's wasted is my time and effort," Rainhart said with a cheeky smile.

The family laughed at his joke, and Hazel gave him a small smile.

"Go on. Open it. It won't bite, dear," Bettina, Gwen's grandmother, encouraged her.

Gwen's family watched expectantly, patient smiles on each of their faces, and Hazel realized not opening it would be rude. So she tore into the paper carefully. The smooth broom handle was made of cherry wood, while the golden straw bristles were refined to a sleek point.

It was stunning.

Tears filled Hazel's eyes as she took it in. "Thank you so much. This is the most incredible gift."

Gwen clapped her hands. "Alright let's go!"

"Go where?" Hazel asked, confused.

"Riding, of course," Gwen answered.

Klaus, Manfrit, and Ahren stood instantly as they raced to put on their coats and head outside. Gwen looped her arm through Hazel's and dragged her behind them. Out on the porch, the boys grabbed their brooms lined up along the railing before jumping off the top steps and launching into flight. One broom remained on the porch, for Gwen.

Hazel turned to Gwen, still feeling somewhat dumbfounded. "Why didn't you bring your broom to SEU?"

"The letter said we didn't need them," Gwen said. "But trust me, I won't be making that mistake again." Then Gwen took Hazel's broom and pointed at a small glyph in the handle. "This will link the broom to you, so you can call upon it when you need it, but it'll only work for up to about a mile away. I carved it myself," she said, clearly proud of her work.

Hazel threw her arms around Gwen. It was the best gift she'd ever gotten. When she released her, Gwen mounted her broom and launched into the air.

"You coming?" Gwen asked Hazel over her shoulder.

Hazel grinned. "Of course."

The cold air bit at Hazel's cheeks as she pushed off from the ground and away from the protection of the porch, but the sheer exhilaration of soaring through the sky made up for it. It turned out she enjoyed flying much more when she wasn't inside a mountain tunnel.

Klaus circled overhead, laughing as he looped in the air around Ahren, while Manfrit tried—and failed—to knock Gwen off course. Hazel's heart pounded in excitement as she pushed forward, her broom responding smoothly to her movements. Compared to the rough, jerky motions of the brooms at SEU, this one felt as though it glided like butter through the air.

For a while, they forgot everything else—just five friends racing through the winter sky, the world below covered in a blanket of fresh snow.

By the time Hazel and Gwen made it back home, Hazel was exhausted—but in the best way possible.

They said their good nights to Liana, and Hazel retreated to Gwen's room, feeling a strange mix of contentment and disbelief. While she had dreaded the holiday without her family, it had truly been the most beautiful day.

As she sat on her bed, Gwen flopped down beside her, grinning.

"I have another gift for you," Gwen declared, bouncing on the mattress.

Hazel scoffed. "Absolutely not. I've received more than I deserve. I don't want anything else."

Gwen shoved a small, red box at her. "Shut up and take it."

With a sigh, Hazel unwrapped the tiny package. Inside, she found a small wolf figurine, carved from obsidian, its eyes flickering with faint golden light.

"Aw! It's you," Hazel said, holding it in her palm.

Gwen snorted. "No! It's enchanted. It'll help with your electricity issue—kind of like a grounding charm. Just push the electricity in here and it will store it for you until you're ready to use it."

Hazel ran her fingers over it, feeling a faint hum of energy. "This is incredible."

"Well, I'm pretty thoughtful." Gwen smirked. "But to be honest, this is a hand-me-down. Before my bracelet was perfected a few years ago, this little guy used to help me take the edge off."

Hazel dropped the steel door Gwen had taught her to build in her mind and the familiar warm buzz flooded in. She'd gotten better at using Gwen's technique, though it wasn't completely foolproof. It required immense focus to hold, which was why it always left her exhausted. She clutched the wolf in her palms and wondered if this might be easier.

Closing her eyes, she imagined the energy slowly flowing from herself into the wolf figurine. In seconds, the buzz quieted and the warmth faded. But unlike the steel door, there was no strain on her mentally. While Hazel felt somewhat empty, she also felt in control, and she was thankful. When she opened her eyes, the wolf stared back at her, eyes glowing the brightest blue.

It worked!

The wolf was holding the energy. And for the first time, she didn't feel like she was barely holding it together. She felt steady.

Another incredibly thoughtful, touching gift. Hazel said nothing as tears and emotion clogged her throat. She looked at Gwen and smiled, not bothering to hide the moisture gathering in her eyes.

Gwen stuck out her tongue quickly. "You're welcome. Just remember, you have to be touching it for it to work. Otherwise it's just a pretty paperweight."

As they settled in, Hazel idly shuffled through her tarot deck. The cards felt cool and smooth, their weight oddly comforting in her hands.

"Wanna try them out?" Gwen asked her.

Hazel hesitated, looking at the instructions. "I don't actually know how."

"We have time before I go to Harland's. Find out how to pull my present again. Maybe that card you pulled at Sybil was right after all." Gwen winked.

Hazel resisted pointing out that Gwen didn't have to go to Harland's. Her friend had it bad, constantly finding excuses to go see him even after finding her bracelet, which was why Hazel hadn't bothered to try to convince Gwen to give him up. A part of her was afraid Gwen would choose him over her.

Hazel reviewed the basic steps of tarot and how to see someone's present. Then, after shuffling the cards, she let Gwen cut the deck and place them on the table. Hazel turned over the first card.

Two of Cups.

The image was of two cloaked figures facing one another, each holding an extended goblet. Hazel remembered this card meant partnership and compatibility from her reading at the Sybil tent during orientation.

She flipped the second card. Two of Cups.

Then the third.

Two of Cups.

Her vision blurred, her fingers trembling as she flipped the next card—

Two of Cups.

Again.

And again.

And again.

The world tilted as a strange haze clouded Hazel's thoughts. A soft ringing noise filled her ears, and for a moment, she felt disconnected from reality—like she was drifting somewhere else entirely.

Then, suddenly, she snapped back to the present, gasping as the room came into sharp focus.

Gwen was staring at her, pale as a sheet. "Are you okay?" she demanded.

Hazel did an internal check before nodding. "Yeah, I think so."

"That was so weird," Gwen breathed.

Hazel blinked, looking down. Every card in front of her was the Two of Cups.

"Is that normal?" Hazel asked, chewing on her lip. She felt like she knew the answer.

Gwen swallowed, glancing at the identical cards scattered before them. "Hazel, that doesn't happen. Even enchanted decks don't repeat like that." She pushed the cards away. "Must be an elven thing."

Hazel's eyes widened. "You think so?"

Gwen stood abruptly, shaking her head. "I don't know. But don't play with them again until I get back from Harland's."

"Don't worry I'm never touching them again." Hazel reassured her.

Gwen grabbed her coat, flashing her a final, uneasy look. "You're sure you're okay?" she asked.

Hazel nodded.

Gwen turned the key in the lock and headed out the door to Harland's. Hazel stayed behind, staring at the deck.

The Two of Cups still gleamed up at her.

Something about it felt unshakably significant.

But she had no idea why.

Gwen

Gwen hoped to start the new year with a bang—literally. She looked in the full-length dressing mirror in the corner of her room. Nothing had changed from the last ten times she'd checked her appearance, yet she still smoothed her perfectly curled, white-blonde strands before sticking a heeled foot forward to check the height of her little black dress's slit. It hit her right on the upper thigh, just low enough to keep her covered as she walked.

"You're going to give him a heart attack," Hazel joked behind her as she got dressed in her own pair of cute jeans and a thick sweater.

"That's the point," Gwen said. She flashed Hazel a wicked grin in the mirror as she reached for the perfume on her vanity. Made of vanilla extract and orchid, the scent was made especially for her and her wolf senses, since most manufactured smells left her with a headache and itchy nose. She only wore it for special occasions, and tonight was exactly that.

Her first New Year's Eve with Harland.

A knock sounded on the front door and Hazel hopped on one foot towards the hall as she worked to get on her winter boot.

"Coming!" she yelled downstairs.

Gwen whirled, completely serious now as she said to her friend, "Remember, when they ask where I am, just say I'm sick."

Hazel snorted as she finished adjusting the boot laces. "Yeah, love sick."

Gwen rolled her eyes, but she didn't deny it. The truth was, she didn't know if she was in love, but she did know that she'd never felt this way—this need—for anyone else before.

"Have fun with the guys tonight," Gwen said.

Her friend's face lit up at the mention of Gwen's cousins. "Klaus promised me this is going to be the best New Year's Eve of my life, but I wish you were going to be with us."

Gwen looked away from Hazel, a tiny seed of guilt threatening to take root for abandoning her friend on her first New Year's Eve away from her family. But she was in great hands with Klaus, Ahren, and Manfrit. They'd all become fast friends, as Gwen knew they would.

"You better get going before he decides to come up and check on me," Gwen said.

"Have fun." Hazel chewed her lip. "Be safe."

"What's the fun in that?" Gwen joked.

Hazel ran across the room and threw her arms around Gwen. Gwen shifted uncomfortably, unsure where this emotional outburst was coming from.

"You were the best thing to happen to me this year," Hazel said with a squeeze.

Unable to deny her friend, Gwen hugged her back fiercely. "Ditto," she said, truly meaning it.

The girls parted, smiles on each of their faces as Hazel slipped out of the room. Gwen listened to her boots echo down the stairs, her cousin's greetings, and then the front door closing quietly behind them.

Sure that she would not be followed, Gwen plucked the key from its hidden spot on her desk and put it in the key hole of her closet door. She took a deep breath, steadying her building nerves as her hand settled on the knob.

Get yourself together. It's now or never, bitch.

They were due back to SEU tomorrow, and Gwen knew that the bubble of winter break would burst. This was her last chance, and she wasn't going to miss it.

Gwen turned the knob and opened the door, anticipation thrumming in her veins. She stepped across the threshold into his house, dimly lit and smelling faintly of herbs and something distinctly Harland. It was a beautiful house with old-world decor, dark woods, and muted deep-green paint. There were more history books than Gwen could get through in a lifetime, although she'd done her best to snoop when Harland allowed it—which was almost never.

The sound of stirring drew her into the kitchen, where Harland was already waiting. He leaned back against the kitchen countertop in a white oxford button-up with the sleeves rolled up past his crossed forearms. His charcoal-grey trousers fit him snugly and Gwen was pretty sure there was a visible outline of the part of him she'd been dying to see. A matching suit jacket thrown over one of the kitchen chairs caught her eye and she realized he was dressed for an occasion, though she wasn't sure if he was coming or going.

Whatever his plans were, Gwen was going to ruin them.

"You look lovely," Harland said, his stoic expression giving nothing away per usual, but the rough gravel in his voice revealed his true feelings. He was turned on.

That knowledge was all the fuel she needed. Gwen sauntered to him, hips swaying deliberately, the click of her heels echoing with purpose. His gaze followed her, slow and unashamed, trailing the curve of her calves to the slit in her dress. When it reached her waist where the fabric clung to her, his eyes darkened. But it was when his gaze landed on her breasts, perfectly framed by the deep V of her neckline, that she felt the air shift. She had his full attention now.

"Are you going somewhere?" she asked innocently.

"I got an invitation to an event this evening," he said flippantly as he reached behind him to grab the elixir. "What about you?"

Gwen remained silent as she grabbed for the dose. As her fingers wrapped around the vial, he snatched it to his chest and her with it, wrapping his strong arm around her waist and pulling her flush against his body. He stared into her eyes as Gwen fought to calm her racing heart.

He held the vial to her lips, and she hid her wince as the numbness swept across her tongue, but this time, it was mild, like a phantom breeze, there and gone in the next instance. Maybe she was getting used to it.

He took the empty vial from her and set it on the counter, but he didn't release her. Instead, he positioned her back against the island countertop and reached up to cup the sides of her face.

"Where are you off to dressed like this, Gwendolyn?" he whispered in her ear, and then inhaled. "Salem, you smell incredible."

"Dressed like what?" Gwen asked with feigned innocence.

He dropped his hand to her exposed thigh and ran it up the length of her slit, stopping at the top. A delicious chill swept through her, and his pupils dilated as he watched her nipples pebble, clearly visible without a bra underneath the thin satin material of her dress.

He groaned. "What are you trying to do to me?"

Gwen bit her lip, releasing it as he studied her. "Whatever you'll let me."

Harland snapped. He sealed his lips over Gwen's, stealing her breath away. Good. She didn't want it. She wanted *him*. Only him.

His hair felt like silk in her hands as she tugged him even closer to her, pressing her breasts and body against his hard length. His hands gripped her hips tightly as his tongue swept across hers. She let out a moan as he picked her up and sat her on the island countertop without breaking the kiss. He stepped between her thighs, and anticipation coiled inside her as he started to kiss and suck a line down her neck.

Closer. She needed him closer.

She wrapped her legs around his back, pulling his hips directly into the warmth of her own. He was hard, the seam of his pants rubbing against her clit, making her cry out. A smile tugged at his lips then he laid her down on the counter. He lifted her ankle and nipped at it before placing it on his shoulder. Gwen watched with bated breath as he kissed his way up the inside of her calf, then her knee, and her thigh, until he reached the top of her slit. Then he paused.

"Please don't stop," Gwen nearly panted, growing wild under his touch.

"I like it when you beg."

His words sent a wave of heat through her core. Before she could reply, he hoisted her other ankle onto his shoulder and pushed her dress up to the bottom of her ass, fully exposing her red, lace thong.

“And who the fuck were you wearing this for?” Harland said, a trace of anger in his voice as he reached up to the waistband and traced the scalloped edge with his fingers. As his touch approached the center of her heat, Gwen squirmed, but he put a hand on her belly, silently telling her to stay put.

“Gwendolyn, answer the question,” he demanded, “or this stops.”

“You, Harland. I wore it for you,” Gwen said softly. This man was turning her into a fool, but as long as he kept touching her, she didn’t care.

A satisfied smirk tugged at the corner of his mouth, but it vanished when he dropped to his knees. He hooked his fingers into her panties and slid them down, slowly, then leaned in and kissed the inside of her thigh, so close she could barely breathe. Her core clenched as his mouth hovered over her, his breath warm against her slick skin. And then—Terra—his tongue pressed against her purposefully. They’d never made it this far and it was better than she’d ever imagined.

When he finally pulled back, his lips were wet and there was a fire in his eyes she hadn’t seen before.

“You taste so fucking good,” he murmured, voice wrecked with hunger as he looked up at her like she was the only thing that mattered. If she wasn’t laying on the counter, she was certain her knees would have given out at the raw, reverent way he said it. Like she was something sacred.

He methodically kissed his way up her breasts, and by the time he reached her mouth, she was grabbing for him. Their lips met, hungry and full of promise. His hands found her hips, pulling her up with him in one fluid motion as he deepened the kiss. One hand slid to the button of his pants, working it loose with practiced ease, never breaking contact with her mouth.

Gwen pulled back enough to watch him as he freed himself. Her breath hitched at the sight, desire sparking hot and fast. Before he could move, she leaned forward and wrapped her hand around him, claiming him for herself.

He was huge, big in girth and length. Her fingers barely touched as she wrapped them around him. Definitely the biggest she'd ever been with. Smiling mischievously, she pumped his length before letting her thumb run over his head.

Harland let out a hiss and grabbed her chin, kissing her hard once again. Gwen hummed against his lips, perfectly pleased with his reaction, and stroked him again. Harland took her hands and maneuvered her onto her back on the counter before pinning both her hands above her head with one of his. Then he worked his way back down her body, kissing the swell of her breasts and biting her nipples through the satin.

"I can't wait to see all of you," Harland said against her stomach. "But right now, I need to be inside you."

Gwen's walls clenched in anticipation, and if she could come from words alone, she'd have done it just then.

Harland grabbed her by the hip with his free hand and pulled her ass halfway off the counter. Surprised, Gwen gasped, and then Harland thrust inside her and she moaned. He held her by the hip as he drove into her, hitting the most sensitive spots at this angle while his weight pressed deliciously against her clit each time he fully entered her.

A wave built within Gwen and she chased it, lifting her hips to meet his with each thrust. He felt so good. Better than she'd ever dreamed.

"Come for me, Gwendolyn," Harland gritted out. He was barely in control. Seeing him like this, so lost in her, so hungry for her, sent her over the edge. She saw stars as she orgasmed. He thrust again and again while she rode out the waves of bliss until he cried out, "Gwen!" and then thrust one last time before leaning into her.

The weight and warmth of him was better than anything she'd ever experienced. All of it had been.

Eventually, Harland stood up and pulled Gwen up after him. He gently lowered her dress and hugged her close. Then he kissed her forehead before tucking her head under his chin. "You're amazing," he said softly against her hair as he traced invisible patterns on the skin of her back.

Things between them were growing beyond the physical and there was no way either of them could ignore it anymore.

CHAPTER 29

Gwen

In the morning, Gwen struggled to get out of her cozy bed despite Hazel's encouragement.

"Someone had a late night," Hazel teased as she safely tucked her Christmas presents in her bag.

Gwen flashed her a mischievous grin. "You have no idea."

Hazel flushed as she gave Gwen a knowing look. She knew Hazel didn't approve, but she appreciated her friend keeping her thoughts to herself. She didn't want anything to ruin the good mood she was in after last night.

Hazel stepped on the bottom bunk, careful not to touch Gwen as she stripped the sheets on the top.

"How was your night?" Gwen asked, curling up snugly under her blanket, not even remotely swayed to crawl from her safe space yet.

"We had a great time. Or at least I did," Hazel said as she tossed the sheets into the hamper in the corner. "But I have to admit, I'm ready to get back to school. I miss Rafe," Hazel said, and then added quickly, "and Jordan."

Gwen rolled her eyes. Rafe and Hazel weren't fooling anyone. They were clearly into one another; the question was, who would make the first move. Hazel's words reminded Gwen of who else waited at SEU: Harland.

Thoughts of his touch, his lips on hers—on other parts—filtered through her mind. Motivation surged through her and she threw back her sheets and began to get ready. She missed him though she'd been with him just hours ago and she wanted to see him again, to remind him of how great their night had been. Suddenly, she wasn't so bummed to be going back to school.

"Well, that was a quick turnaround," Hazel said.

A knock at the door saved Gwen from responding. "Girls, I have breakfast ready."

Her mother was a saint.

"Thank you, Mom," Gwen said. She changed quickly into her day clothes—a pair of black jeans and a green cable-knit sweater.

Hazel went downstairs, bag in tow, leaving Gwen to pack in a whirlwind. Shoving clothes and presents wherever they'd fit. Her bag was much bulkier than when she'd arrived, so she cast an anti-gravity spell on it. When it tried to float to the ceiling, she reduced the spell slightly before slinging it onto her shoulders with ease.

Her mother and Hazel sat at the kitchen table, laughing together, when Gwen joined them. Their fast connection brought Gwen so much joy. She let them chat while she grabbed one of the croissant and ham sandwiches her mother had made.

"Thanks, Mom," Gwen said, giving her mother a kiss on the cheek before taking a bite. It was warm and buttery, just as she knew it would be. The food in the cafeteria was good, but nothing beat her mom's cooking.

Pan swooped in through an open window mid-breakfast, cutting off the conversation as he landed neatly beside Gwen. She sighed and reluctantly untied the letter and small package strapped to his leg. The letter was from her father—his first message since the night before her entrance exam.

She slipped the unopened gift into her bag and unfolded the letter with more dread than curiosity. She'd half expected him to show up in person, but she knew her mother had strengthened the wards around the house. He couldn't step foot inside, only in the woods surrounding the perimeter. She'd done her best not to go farther than the backyard all break.

"Well, what does it say?" her mother asked, her tone careful.

Gwen cleared her throat and read aloud, "'As I'm sure your mother has told you, I can't interfere with you going to college now that you've been accepted. I've informed Crevan Reid that the arranged marriage will have to wait two years—four, if you're accepted into a coven.'"

Oh, I'm getting into a coven.

"'He's agreed to wait, and my political standing remains. I did not like being out of contact with you last semester, so I'm sending Pan with you to Saint Elias. Write to me. Love, Your Father.'"

The three of them sat there without speaking as the implication that she was still arranged to be married hung in the air.

"Well, that could've been worse," her mother said, breaking the silence.

Gwen rolled her eyes. "It also could've been better."

There wasn't much she could do about her father. She wished, just once, he'd care more about what *she* wanted than about his political alliances. Still, at least she didn't have to worry about the marriage—*yet*. Maybe the fox would get tired of waiting and find someone else to marry in the meantime. A girl could dream.

She was grateful for Pan, at least. No more trekking to the aviary to send letters to her mom. But her father was mistaken if he thought she'd be writing to him.

"Okay," Gwen said, stacking the last of the plates. "I think it's time for us to head back."

Hazel nodded, standing from the table just as Gwen's mother reached across to give Gwen's hand a squeeze.

“I think so too. If you stay any longer, I don’t think I’ll be willing to let you go.” Her mother looked at Hazel. “Either of you.”

Hazel made her way around the table and wrapped Gwen’s mother in a hug. She returned it fully as she winked at Gwen. Gwen went in for a hug once Hazel was done. Her mother’s embrace was home—soft, warm, and safe. Leaving her for SEU had been the hardest thing Gwen had ever done, but it was getting easier. Not because she wanted to leave her, but because she knew her mother would be here waiting for her with open arms when it was time for her to return.

“I love you, Mom,” Gwen said.

“I love you, too, Gwenny.” She ushered them towards the front porch. Once outside, she said, “You two aren’t allowed to get into trouble at the same time, understood? That way, one of you can always bail the other out.”

Gwen and Hazel chuckled.

“That means you have to take turns, Gwendolyn. Let Hazel get into trouble too. You can’t have it all for yourself,” her mother said with a laugh.

Gwen smirked. Her mother knew her too well. She was lucky the chancellor hadn’t told her mom they’d broken curfew; she’d be lecturing them into next semester.

“We’ll do our best, Liana,” Hazel promised.

Gwen nodded in agreement before hoisting her bag over her shoulder and drawing her wand. Pan fluttered from the back of a nearby chair to her shoulder, gripping tightly with his talons.

Hazel waved her wand. “*Advinere.*”

Gwen did the same.

The upending current of space travel swept them along. A moment later, they landed in the clearing just outside of Eagles Ridge.

What a drastic difference from her first arrival.

Back in September, she’d stepped into this clearing full of nerves and desperation, praying the mountain would be enough to hide her from her father's plans. Now, she gazed up at it with quiet awe. It felt less like a fortress and more like an old friend—one she hadn't realized she'd missed. And now, for the first time, she felt like she could breathe. She was safe here—at least for the next four years. She was home.

Other students were also making their path into town, and Hazel and Gwen quickly followed suit. Gwen couldn't help herself—she scanned every person, wondering if she'd see Harland. A second glance told her he wasn't among them, and she was filled with disappointment, which annoyed her.

It's been like twelve hours. Get it together.

The girls took off into town, chatting openly about what they'd missed most about school. The streets were quieter than usual, with some students waiting to return from home until Sunday. As they walked the streets, Gwen noticed several flyers drifting along with the breeze. She snagged one from the air when it drew near.

Missing: Dana Trace.

Below the words was a photo of a young woman in her twenties, smiling and full of life. *Last seen leaving for work.* Gwen's stomach sunk. First the dogs, now people? Gwen had thought they'd found the culprit when they'd killed the bear and nothing else had happened, but then the incident with Mara, and now someone else missing a few weeks later? That couldn't be a coincidence, could it?

"What's that?" Hazel asked, and Gwen lifted the flyer.

Hazel chewed her lip as she read, brows furrowing. She released the paper back into the air for it to move about town. "We assumed the bear was behind the dogs," Hazel said. "But what if it wasn't?"

Gwen nodded, glad she and Hazel were on the same page. "That bear was sick. Maybe it's not the only infected thing out there."

"Yeah, maybe. But where are the bodies?" Hazel asked, as they approached the far edge of town.

"Not all animals kill openly. Some of them like to hide their prey," Gwen explained.

Hazel gave her a wide-eyed stare, but Gwen just shrugged.

"Should we tell someone? About the bear, I mean?" Hazel asked.

Gwen shook her head. "Telling now after all this time would make us look more suspicious than ever."

"I think we need to do some research," Hazel replied. "See if there's even anything to tell—if there are even any known illnesses that could make an animal resistant to magic."

Gwen was sure the answer was no but she knew Hazel wouldn't accept it without looking.

"Let's drop off our bags and head to the library," Hazel said.

Gwen flicked her wand, and their bags vanished into thin air. "Done."

She sent Pan to their dorm room as they started toward the library. But Gwen's mind wasn't on the bear, or the missing woman, or even Mara as they walked. All she could think about was Harland—his face, his touch, the way he looked at her like she was everything to him. If she was going to be any real help to Hazel, she needed to clear her head first. And that meant seeing him. Gwen knew Hazel wouldn't like it—but she didn't want to lie. She already had to lie to everyone else.

When they reached the steps of the library, Gwen hesitated. "I'll meet you inside. I need to see Harland."

Hazel grimaced. "Gwen, it's not even time for your potion."

"I know. I'll be quick. Promise."

Hazel gave a small nod, but Gwen could see the disappointment in her eyes. Hazel didn't say anything else as she headed inside.

Gwen considered knocking. This wasn't her usual time to see him, but after last night, they were past that. She turned the knob slowly and stepped inside. Harland was stretched out on the couch, a book open in his hands. At the sight of her, his eyes widened.

"What are you doing here?" he asked, standing up quickly. He glanced at his watch, confusion and concern flashing across his face.

"I couldn't wait until tonight," she said, smiling as she crossed the room. Her arms moved around his waist like they always did—casual, familiar. But this time, he pulled away from her. His movement stung like a slap. What was he doing?

"Gwendolyn, we need to talk."

His words echoed in her mind. She knew what they usually meant, but there was no way he was saying them after last night.

She swallowed her doubt. "Talk about what?"

Harland ran his hands through his hair as he met her gaze. The cold resolve she saw there stole her breath. She didn't need him to explain, his thoughts were as plain as day. "You can't be serious. Not after last night."

"Gwen, it's not like that." Harland reached for her but she took a step away and he stopped. "I just think we need to slow down."

Tears began to fill her eyes. She stepped back, forcing them not to fall, willing them not to betray how much she felt for him. "So, what you got what you wanted and now you're done with me?"

"Don't do that, you know it's not like that," he tried to reassure her.

She didn't understand how he could do this to her. How could she have been so stupid? She'd trusted him.

"Gwen this last semester with you has been amazing, and last night was better than I ever could have imagined." He paused, his jaw tightening as if he was still deciding how to break her heart. "But being back here today, I realized, I can never give you what you truly deserve. I can't be anything more than a secret, someone hiding in the background of your life."

"Then you should have stopped this before we slept together." A single tear slid down her cheek.

He leaned in to wipe it away and she let him. "I know and I'm sorry. I shouldn't have let things go that far."

She recoiled at his words. How could he say that? The question burned in her throat, but before she could speak, her Wilderness Watch compact buzzed sharply, along with his.

He pulled his compact out of his back pocket to read the message but Gwen didn't bother. Her world was in shambles and she couldn't bring herself to care.

"There's a missing hiker." Harland sighed as he studied Gwen's face. "We have to go, but we can finish this conversation later."

She followed him out without another word. It was over, there was nothing left to say between them. There would be no follow up conversation. There would be no slowing down. Gwen couldn't go back to pining after him, accepting scraps when she knew what really being with him felt like.

I shouldn't have let things go that far. Each time those words played in her mind, they hit her like a blow, over and over until the only thing she felt was battered and bruised.

As they walked to the admin building in silence, Gwen's mind raced with questions. What had happened in the last few hours to change his mind? How could she have read things so wrong?

What did I *do wrong?*

The answer was nothing yet that knowledge didn't touch her tailspinning emotions.

She caught him glancing at her more than once, but she didn't return a single look. Keeping her expression blank, she refused to let him see her fall apart. When his hand grazed hers, she crossed her arms to keep it from happening again.

Energy buzzed in the air as they entered the Wilderness Watch office. It was a stark contrast to the silent walk there. Volunteers and "voluntolds" like herself wedged themselves into their orange jumpsuits. Others had already dressed and were double-checking their emergency packs for the necessary supplies.

She spotted Hazel, who was holding their packs. Thank Terra, she hadn't even thought to go get hers. Hazel approached her, handing her her bag, and Harland headed over towards the other professors.

Good. Get away from me. She couldn't think straight, couldn't breathe with him so close.

"Is everything alright?" Hazel asked.

Great. That meant Gwen was doing a shit job of hiding her feelings.

"Peachy," Gwen said, then whispered, "I should have gone to the library with you."

Hazel squeezed Gwen's hand in silent understanding, and Gwen clung to it like a lifeline.

"You deserve better," Hazel said. "Don't you let him make you think otherwise."

The support of her friend made her tears threaten to come out again. Hazel was right. She *did* deserve better. She shouldn't have to convince anyone to be with her.

Captain Jackson approached them in his signature bomber jacket layered over his own jumpsuit. "You two get dressed. We're heading out in five minutes."

Gwen quickly changed, putting the jumpsuit on like a shield of armor, and brick by brick, she built an ice-cold wall around her heart, steeling her resolve. She was done letting him make her feel unworthy.

She'd never been more grateful for Wilderness Watch. She was ready to do something active, to have something else to focus on other than the end of her relationship with Harland. If she could even call it that—a relationship usually involved two people, and she was pretty sure she'd been in that one alone.

Gwen followed Hazel's lead to two unoccupied lockers. Hazel stashed her bag and pulled on the orange coveralls, nearly losing balance and catching herself on Gwen's shoulder. After lacing up their boots, Hazel and Gwen checked their packs for their essentials—a flask with water, a stretcher, a fire starter, and a bewitched blanket that could be wrapped around a building if needed.

"Gather 'round," Captain Jackson shouted over the excited din of the room. "Time for the briefing!"

He gave them a few moments to shuffle into a broad circle. There were about fifteen members present, meaning a third of them were absent, including Logan and Serena. Like Klaus, they likely hadn't returned from winter break yet.

Gwen caught Harland staring at her from across the room. When their eyes met, his expression turned cold, detached, as if she were nothing more than any other student standing in this room. He didn't nod, didn't acknowledge her. Didn't even let his expression falter.

Her jaw tightened, and she forced herself to look away, chin lifted, expression impassive. She refused to let him see her upset. Whatever had happened over break was done. *They* were done.

"Listen up! Eyes on me, ears on me."

The room immediately drew silent.

"We're looking for Frank Mitchell. He's a thirty-one-year-old male mundane from Canada who has been staying in Eagles Ridge for the last week. He's white, five foot ten, 175 pounds. Blonde hair and blue eyes." Captain Jackson paused, waiting for some of the volunteers to write the information down. "Frank was last seen wearing brown hiking pants and a navy-blue snow coat. He's been missing for twenty-four hours at this point and he was last seen at Kodiak Brew, where he got a coffee and disclosed that he was headed out to hike. The exact trail is unknown." After a few seconds, he continued, "Specs received, understood, and committed?"

The volunteers nodded their heads. "Yes, Captain."

Gwen didn't miss the low tones of Harland's response from the corner of the room. She could pick his smoky voice out of any room, therian hearing or not, and she hated how in tune she'd become to him.

"Now time for quadrant assignments. You have eyes, y'all can see we're short on volunteers tonight. Doesn't change the rules. No less than three to a quadrant, which means the quadrants will have to be bigger."

Captain Jackson split a stack of papers, handing the two halves to the volunteers on his left and right to pass along the circle.

Hazel got the quadrant map first and handed the stack to Gwen.

Gwen barely glanced at it—Hazel probably already had it memorized.

Hazel whispered in Gwen's ear, "If we take the lower right quadrant, it'll take us back to where we saw the bear."

"Why in Salem—" Gwen stopped, a smile taking hold of her face. "Hazel, you're a genius."

If they took that quadrant, they could check to see if there were signs of any other infected animals there. Part of her knew they shouldn't go without her wolf, but she needed to feel like she was making progress with something. She didn't really care if it was by finding the missing hiker or finding answers about the bear.

Gwen's hand flew into the air.

"Yes, Gwen?" Captain Jackson grunted.

"Captain, I'd like to take the lower right with Hazel."

Captain Jackson arched his brow. Yeah, maybe requesting a quadrant was weird, but Gwen didn't let it deter her.

"We go out there a lot. We're familiar with the area and can cover it quickly, sir."

Captain Jackson gave a quick nod. "Fine."

Gwen's heart lifted with the idea that maybe something would go her way today.

"Bellamy, you'll go with them."

Gwen's heart plummeted back into the dirt.

Hazel froze next to her, eyes bulging in their sockets as she whirled to look at Dane. At first, he'd done his best to antagonize Hazel, but she'd gotten good at simply pretending he didn't exist. Gwen was actually proud of her because she'd have busted his nose by now if she was Hazel.

Dane rolled his eyes, clearly irritated at the pairing. "Can't Jon do it?"

"No assignment changes."

"Can this night get any worse?" Gwen asked.

Hazel ignored her and searched the map. She pulled on Gwen's arm and drew a small circle on their quadrant with her finger as she whispered, "I think this is the spot where we first saw the bear. Let's start there."

"This isn't a sightseeing trip," Dane interjected.

Gwen shot him a look. How had he heard them?

"We're looking for a missing person," he continued.

Hazel sniffed, refusing to look at him as she spoke. "It's not out of our way. We have to search there anyway."

Dane started to respond, but Captain Jackson barked, "Grab a broom from the supplies cabinet and let's roll out."

Gwen and Hazel drew their wands, calling their brooms to them. They weren't riding shitty school brooms anymore. Dane did the same, clearly a snob too.

The three of them took flight as soon as they reached the tunnel entrance. Hazel led the way with the map and flew over the quadrant boundary. Thick snow blanketed the landscape, hiding markers and changes in terrain, which made things look very different than the last time Gwen had flown here. She wanted to shout at Hazel to slow down so they didn't miss the spot, but Dane beat her to it.

Hazel didn't slow.

Maybe she didn't hear him.

It was also possible she was ignoring him.

Hazel began to slow when they reached a barren section of the forest where the trees were charred and splintered. This was definitely the spot they had been attacked by the rabid bear. Hazel landed, with Gwen just a moment behind. Dane quickly followed.

"Let's do a quick scan of the area and then head back to the beginning and do it right," Dane said. He only looked at Gwen as he spoke, as if Hazel didn't exist. He didn't wait for a response, he simply moved through the trees, leaving them to figure out their own path.

He sure is a bossy prick.

"I guess we should split up and meet back here in fifteen minutes?" Hazel asked.

"Sounds good. I'll go north, you go south?" Gwen said.

Hazel nodded, but paused before she walked away. "Think we should tell him the last time we were here, we saw a rabid bear and a wolf pack?"

She and Gwen looked at each other and then both laughed.

Hazel moved south with her broom in tow. "Be careful!"

"Back at you."

Gwen took the path next to the tree Hazel had climbed the night they'd encountered the bear. She trudged through the thick snow, but the spell on her boots kept her warm and dry. As she approached the tree, she saw the lightning char marks with new eyes. Hazel had called the lightning that night straight from the sky with her emotions alone. A chill ran down Gwen's spine. Things could've gone much worse.

Gwen hadn't been walking more than five minutes when she heard a bloodcurdling scream. The sound sent a chill down her spine as it echoed around the mountainside. She couldn't make out what direction it came from, so she flew south where Hazel was, shouting her name the whole way. If it was another animal, she hoped Hazel had the sense to get on her broom and take off.

Gwen saw Hazel below and the knot in her stomach loosened.

Gwen quickly landed with a fluid dismount. "I'm guessing that wasn't you?"

"No."

The scream came again, and this time, it was much closer. Gwen and Hazel ran towards it as fast as they could.

The idiot should have made a plan with us.

Gwen strained to listen for any growls or grunts as she ran, afraid there was another rabid animal waiting for them. They arrived at a clearing to find Dane pinned against a tree by a man.

"Who's that, an ex-boyfriend?" Gwen asked.

"I think that's our hiker," Hazel said.

Gwen recalled the specs. He had blonde hair, and was wearing brown pants and a blue snow coat. Hazel was right.

"Wonder what Dane did to piss the him off?"

As soon as she said the words, Frank's head snapped towards them and they gasped.

His face was a ruin of torn flesh and dried blood. One side of his head was scorched black, the skin there blistered like he'd walked through a forest fire. The other half sagged grotesquely, as if it were trying to peel away from the bone entirely. His clouded eyes locked onto her. *Gross.*

Frank shoved Dane—sending him crashing into a nearby tree with a sickening thud. Dane slumped to the ground, unmoving, as the hiker launched himself across the clearing at the girls. There was a good fifty feet between them, but he moved with incredible speed.

On instinct, Gwen stepped backward, away from him, and jolted as her shoulder struck something solid. Her heart leapt in panic before she realized it was only a tree. She let out a shaky breath, feeling a little stupid for scaring herself. Then she spotted Hazel beside her, arms raised, palms out in a soothing motion, and remembered they were in real trouble.

"Frank, we're with the rescue team. We're here to help you get back to town." Hazel's sweet Southern accent was turned all the way up.

But Frank didn't stop. He didn't even blink. He continued to charge as an inhuman screech erupted from his throat.

"Gwen, I think it's time to shift," Hazel pleaded.

"I can't. Harland's potion doesn't wear off for another three hours." Fear spiked through her heart. Gwen had been sure Harland's potion was a miracle drug, but now it had betrayed her, leaving her truly defenseless for the first time in her life.

"What do we do?" Hazel asked.

"Get on your broom."

Hazel didn't hesitate to follow Gwen's lead. They launched into the air, out of Frank's reach. He ran beneath them, snarling, rage brimming in his bloodshot eyes.

"Cast!" Gwen ordered, pulling out her wand.

Hazel and Gwen shot defensive spells at him. Immobilization. Sleep. Shields. Nothing worked. Frank remained unfazed.

What the hell are we going to do?

Before Gwen could think of an answer, Frank turned and ran back towards Dane. The snow was so deep, he moved slowly, but he'd eventually make it there.

Fuck!

Gwen used the leg-breaking spell, hoping to slow him down if nothing else. Frank did fall to the snow-covered ground, unable to stay steady on his broken appendages, but then he began to drag himself toward Dane, his legs twisting uselessly behind him as he left a dark, smeared stain in the snow.

Magic wouldn't work. He was going to be on Dane in seconds. Gwen had no options. They had to regain his attention.

She landed and screamed, "Hey!"

"Gwen, what are you doing?" Hazel yelled.

"Saving that piece of shit's life." Gwen waved her arms in the air as she ran through calf-deep snow towards Frank. "Hey!"

But he never looked back. She continued running and screaming until she was within ten feet of him. Finally, he looked over his shoulder. His milky eyes flashed as he turned to chase Gwen.

She jerked to a stop and began to backpedal. "That's right, Frank. You don't want him. You want me," Gwen taunted, praying he didn't turn around.

She beckoned Frank with her hands as she walked backwards, keeping an eye on him at all times. As she took another step, her foot fell through the snow and caught on something hard beneath it, throwing her off balance. The unstable footing and momentum sent her tumbling. Gwen turned to catch herself, and her boot wedged beneath a tree root. Gwen cried out as her ankle twisted on impact.

"Gwen, are you okay? Hazel asked as she flew directly above her.

"It's my ankle." Gwen immediately took off her bracelet, intending to let her therian abilities heal her, but the pain persisted. Harland's potion was still in effect.

Gwen tried to move, but her boot wouldn't budge.

Frank's snarls grew louder—he was closing in.

Hazel cast spells at him from above. She flew to the right and called to him, trying to gain his attention, but Frank only had eyes for Gwen.

A blanket of snow covered him with Hazel's next spell, but he broke through it in seconds. Gwen used her hands and undamaged foot to push herself forward, but the trapped boot held as pain arced up her leg.

"Hazel, I need you to use your lightning."

Hazel flew in close, shaking her head. "No way. You're too close, I could hit you."

Gwen felt a hard tug on her free leg as Frank sunk his nails into her coveralls and began to pull his way up her body.

"Hazel!" Gwen screamed.

Hazel

Think!

Spells were clearly not the answer. They hadn't worked with the bear and they weren't working now. But Hazel knew what *had* worked.

She landed her broom a dozen feet away and lifted her hands as she pulled the energy in the air to her. It came quickly, as if it had simply been waiting on her to reach for it. As she aimed her hands, she realized she could just as easily hit Gwen as she could Frank. She couldn't risk Gwen, so she sprinted closer.

Gwen screamed as she kept Frank hoisted above her, clawing at her insulated uniform. Hazel reached them in seconds, her heart pounding with exertion and fear. She wrapped her hands around the back of his head. Frank tried to turn, but she pushed the magic into him. The skin beneath her touch sizzled and body fluid bubbled under her hands as she forced all the pent-up energy she held into him.

Just him. Just him, Hazel begged the energy, wanting none of the electricity to seep into Gwen.

Instantly, Frank collapsed onto Gwen, neck turned at an impossible angle, undoubtedly broken. His milky eyes stared, unblinking, into nothing.

"Ew, get him off!" Gwen cried, pushing at the lifeless body.

Hazel rushed to her side, sliding Frank off and placing him next to Gwen as gently as possible. Gwen bolted up and began wiping at her clothing, trying to get the foul-smelling blood off while balancing on one foot.

"Are you okay?" Hazel asked.

"Sprained ankle. I'll heal in a few hours," Gwen reassured her.

Hazel moved her gaze to the man lying beside them, took in his relatively young appearance, and felt her stomach churn.

"Do you think he's alive?" Hazel asked. *Did I kill him?*

She'd shocked Mara and she was still alive. But then again, she'd been trying to restrain herself. Tonight, she'd only been thinking of one thing: saving Gwen.

Gwen nudged Frank with her good foot. "No."

The girls studied him upclose. Jagged tears seeped pus on one half of his face and burned skin wept from the blisters on the other.

The sight of him, mixed with the knowledge that she'd just killed a man, was too much. Hazel turned away, running a few feet before her stomach emptied itself of the acid and bile that had been eating away at her from the inside out. A bright-orange suit caught her eye as she wiped her mouth.

"Oh shit, Dane!" Hazel said. With all the commotion, they'd nearly forgotten about him.

"You go. I can barely walk," Gwen said.

Hazel took off to the other side of the clearing, leaving Gwen with Frank.

Dane laid slumped against the trunk of a pine tree. Black marks in the tree smoked above his head, and the distinct scent of burning pine filled the air.

"I know how Frank got burned," Hazel called loudly.

"How's that?" Gwen asked as she used handfuls of snow to wash away the blood still covering her.

"Looks like Dane used fire manipulation," Hazel answered as she lowered herself to her knees beside him, thankful her bewitched coveralls were impervious to the snow.

Blood covered Dane's mouth, neck, and chest, and his nose was swollen. Hazel drew closer, dropping to her knees to check on him. His warm breath was visible in the air, telling her he was still alive.

"He's out cold, but he'll live. I think he broke his nose. There's blood everywhere," Hazel called out. She breathed easier knowing he hadn't seen her use fulgurkinesis. Hazel shook him gently, not knowing what injuries he might have.

He didn't respond.

"Bellamy, wake up," she said again, shaking slightly harder.

When he still didn't wake, concern filled her. She hated the guy, sure, but she didn't want him to be seriously injured. Not unless she was the one responsible, at least.

Hazel removed one glove, then reached for his face, pausing before making contact. She hadn't touched Dane since their first meeting and it felt weird. Personal. Taboo. But was it weirder she'd known this person for nearly five years and had only touched him once?

Nonsense.

She reached forward and placed her hand against his forehead. "Dane? Can you hear me?"

He groaned, but his eyes remained closed.

"Dane. It's me, Hazel. Can you open your eyes?"

A vibration—a hum—sounded softly from the back of his throat. With something that sounded disturbingly like affection, Dane mumbled, "Hazel..."

Hazel froze and thought about removing her hand, but then

Dane's eyes shot open wide, staring at her. Fear filled them as he practically rolled away from her and threw up an arm as if to block her pursuit.

Hazel blinked. She'd never seen Dane so scared.

"Dane, it's me. You got knocked out. Are you okay?"

When Dane sat up, the fear Hazel had seen there was gone, replaced by rage. "I'm fine."

Hazel stood and leaned forward to help Dane stand.

He recoiled from her. "Don't fucking touch me," he growled. He looked at her as if she were diseased—like Frank or the bear.

Hazel rolled her eyes. "Sorry to see the brain injury didn't change your personality."

She turned her back on him and walked away. She'd made it halfway across the clearing back to Gwen when something caught her eye. A small orange pack laid half buried in the snow. Hazel picked it up and opened it to see the usual Wilderness Watch essentials, including the water flask and fire starter. She looked at Gwen, thinking she'd dropped it during her attack, but she still wore hers on her back. Hazel pulled the straps of her own before wheeling about to inspect Dane.

He wiped his bloody nose as he watched her warily from thirty feet away. Thirty feet away—where he'd done fire magic. Not here, where his fire starter laid, but all the way over there.

Hazel's eyes went wide as she studied him.

Thoughts of her second week of Alchemy lab, the one where she'd been forced to partner with Dane, surfaced in her mind.

"As you all know, the art of conjuring the elements—air, fire, water, and earth—were lost when the fae disappeared..."

He'd done fire magic without a fire starter. Which, like fulgurkinesis, wasn't technically possible—for mages.

Dane must've seen the dots connect in Hazel's brain because he was charging across the clearing before Hazel could even zip the pack up.

He tore it from her hands. "Stay the fuck out of my things."

Hazel backed away, hands up as if calming a wild animal, as her mind spun out of control.

Is Dane another Forsaken?

Dane followed, something dark and sinister in his eyes, his jaw clenched as he pursued her.

Hazel's heart pounded in her chest. If she was right, this secret was life-changing. Life-ending. She reached for her wand.

"Hey guys, you need to come see this," Gwen called from the other side of the clearing, sitting next to Frank on the forest floor.

Dane stopped and blinked, finally breaking eye contact with Hazel. She released a breath as the tension in the air broke. Dane gave her a wide berth as he went to see what Gwen was talking about. Hazel followed from a safe distance.

Dane took a deep inhale of breath a fraction of a second before Hazel saw it. Frank's face, still half-burned and covered in gashes, was now sunken, the edges of his wounds pulling taut around his skull as though his skin had been suctioned tight. Moments ago, during the fight, his face had been plump and full, but now it was hollow, brittle, and dry. Not a single drop of blood or pus wept from his wounds. And his eyes looked disturbingly flat, like there was nothing left behind the lids. It appeared as though the slightest touch would crack him apart. Not that she'd be touching him. A shiver went down her spine at the thought.

Frank stunk of death, and, oddly, something floral. It was familiar to Hazel, and she tried to place it, but her attention drifted when she noticed a strange mark on the side of Frank's neck.

"What the hell did you do to him, Gwen?" Dane asked.

"I didn't do shit!" Gwen responded.

Dane whirled, staring at her as if he could see through her exterior, into her soul. "You?"

Hazel swallowed. What could she say? Someone had to take the credit. "If only you'd managed to stay awake, you would know."

Dane arched a brow, as if he doubted Hazel had actually done it. He probably hated the idea of her being stronger than him. Though if he was a Forsaken, too, maybe she wasn't. She tried not to let him sense where her thoughts wandered, and rolled her eyes for a dramatic effect.

"What I did doesn't explain the hole in his neck." Hazel leaned closer to inspect the mangled hole, his skin jagged around the edges with the sinew exposed beneath.

Did an animal take a bite of him?

"Or the burn marks on his face," Gwen said. "Dane, care to explain?"

It was a fair question. Fire manipulation made sense when a source was readily available, but not when you had to dig out a fire starter. But Gwen didn't know that Dane didn't need one.

Hazel turned to watch Dane, who still hadn't answered yet. She wanted him to deny it, to give a plausible explanation that had nothing to do with him also being a Forsaken. But the warning that met her in his gaze told her there was no such explanation. His secret was as deadly as theirs and he wouldn't be sharing it freely.

A heartbeat passed before he looked away, putting on his pack. "I already had my starter out, trying to score the trees to keep track of the searched areas. He just happened to find me in the middle of that."

That was a perfectly reasonable explanation. While there were other ways to mark a tree, a burn would be one of the clearest.

He's a damn good liar.

Hazel wanted to call him on it, to make him tell the truth, but when his eyes met hers, she saw that same emotion she'd seen when she'd woken him: fear.

Dane was worse than a wild animal, but just as predictable. If she got too close while he was afraid, he'd lash out at her, and they didn't have time to deal with that right now.

"Whatever. Let's load him up and get him back," Gwen said. "My ankle hurts." She'd used a bandage from the pack, but there were no healing potions for her to use and her therian abilities clearly hadn't come back yet. Gwen laid out the stretcher from her pack on the snow next to Frank.

Hazel studied Dane for a moment longer. *Having something over him wouldn't be the worst thing in the world.* She pulled out her wand and levitated Frank to the stretcher.

The pressure of Dane's gaze never left her as she helped Gwen buckle the lifeless body to the board. Hazel pulled a lanyard from the side of the stretcher and slipped it around her neck. It had a small crystal hanging on the end of it with a glyph that matched the one on the stretcher, linking them together. As soon as it settled against her chest, the magic flared. The stretcher was now tethered to her—programmed to follow wherever she went, adjusting for terrain and pace without needing to be pulled or guided.

The girls summoned and mounted their brooms while Dane went to hunt for his in the snow. He must not have had a glyph on his.

Once he'd found it and they'd all taken off into the air, Dane led the flight, casting a bright light from his wand for the girls to follow all the way back to campus.

Hazel sat on the edge of a hospital bed and watched as one of the medics felt for a pulse on Frank's wrist and then his neck before rushing out the door. They'd moved him from the stretcher to a hospital bed upon their arrival. He laid lifeless next to Dane. She was glad she didn't have to lay beside him.

Whispers floated in from the hallway, too low for Hazel to make out. She wondered if it had been long enough since her last elixir for Gwen's hearing to return. Hazel gave her a look, and Gwen shook her head.

Hex the luck.

Captain Jackson walked in, stopping in front of Dane, who sat on the end of a bed. "What happened?"

Hazel kept her mouth shut and her eyes on the medical room floor. She'd been wracking her brain, trying to think of a lie, but nothing sounded believable. Hell, even the truth didn't sound possible. She prayed Gwen had thought of something—she'd been lying about her identity for much longer than Hazel.

The knot in her stomach loosened when Gwen jumped in to answer.

"We all split up and then we heard a scream. Hazel and I ran to Dane, getting there just in time to see Frank throw him against a tree and knock him out."

"You're covered in blood," Captain Jackson barked, as if noticing it for the first time. He tried to inspect Gwen, but she batted him away.

"It's not mine. It's Frank's," she said. "Frank attacked me after he finished with Dane. He was already covered in blood when we arrived. I think it's his, or maybe Dane's." Gwen's breath hitched. "Oh Salem, I don't even know whose blood is on me." She stood from her bed, favoring her good ankle, and began removing her coveralls.

"Can you please find her some sweats?" Captain Jackson asked.

The medic left the room at the request.

Hazel stood and lended Gwen her arm so she didn't fall over as she disrobed. She gave Gwen's arm a squeeze to let her know she wasn't alone. And she wasn't. This was twice they'd been attacked in the forest, twice Gwen had come back covered in blood, but this time, she didn't have her wolf and it was clearly taking its toll.

The medic returned with a hoodie and shorts sporting the university's name and passed it to Gwen. She put them on quietly, sat back down on the bed, and pulled her legs to her chest.

The medic turned to Hazel. "How did he die?"

Hazel's mouth went dry. She had no answer. No explanation. At least, not one that wouldn't end up with a visit from the Brecilian Knights.

"Aren't you going to check on him?" She motioned to Dane.

"I'm fine," Dane said adamantly as he threw Hazel a dirty look.

"I'll set his nose in a minute. I want to know about the dead man in my infirmary and why he looks the way he does."

"He—he was already like that," Hazel said.

"He was already burned?"

Hazel felt Dane's gaze pierce into her, but she didn't look at him. "Yes."

That wasn't technically a lie. Hazel *had* found Frank that way.

"He attacked Dane *and* Gwendolyn?" Captain Jackson asked.

"Yes, he did," Hazel whispered, glancing down at her feet, but then remembered that she needed to be confident if she wanted them to believe her, so she looked right at the medic and Captain Jackson. "What Gwen said was all true. He attacked Dane and we cast, but nothing worked. Then he started running back to Dane, so Gwen drew him away." Hazel took a breath, the fear of the moment filling her as she retold the story. "Gwen fell and twisted her ankle."

"What did you do?"

Hazel's heart sped up, as she knew this would be the part she had to sell. She glanced at Gwen, hoping for some kind of reassurance that it would be okay.

But Gwen didn't reassure her. She just shook her head.

Lie.

The medic and Captain Jackson didn't need to know how she'd done it because they could never replicate it anyway.

"I cast *Nivis Acervus*. That's when he stopped."

"*Nivis Acervus*?" Captain Jackson asked, eyes wide in disbelief. Hazel knew he was asking himself how that spell worked when nothing else had.

"It was the only thing that slowed him down. I guess the weight of the snow crushed him."

Hazel looked at Gwen for assurance again, and this time, she nodded behind the medic's back.

The medic crossed her arms as she leaned in to whisper to Captain Jackson. "That doesn't explain the blood loss, Captain."

Hazel jerked her gaze to Gwen to check that she'd heard the same. Gwen's wide eyes told her she had.

Captain Jackson observed their silent interaction before starting toward the door. "I need to contact the chancellor. Medic Sanderson, could you please set Mr. Bellamy's nose?" With that, he left the room.

Hazel wanted to tell the medic to leave Dane's nose the way it was so his face would finally match how ugly he was on the inside, but she kept the thought to herself.

"This looks quite rough, Dane. How did you damage it so badly?" Medic Sanderson asked as she applied a healing salve to the split skin along the bridge of his nose.

Dane sniffed as if he was above the question and immediately winced. Hazel tried not to laugh.

"I headbutted him, hoping to knock him out. It didn't work."

Hazel mouthed to Gwen, *Idiot.*

Gwen snickered and tried to cover it with a cough.

"Is that how you managed to fight him off?" Medic Sanderson asked as she aimed her wand at Dane's nose.

Dane's gaze met Hazel's. "Yeah."

The medic was too caught up in Dane's injuries to see the challenge in his eyes, but Hazel saw it. He was practically daring her to call him out about not using a fire starter.

But Hazel said nothing.

Conjuring fire was as impossible as conjuring electricity, both abilities were long believed extinct with the Forsaken, yet she knew for sure both had happened tonight. She would keep her secret along with his.

For now.

CHAPTER 30

Hazel

"Please have a seat, Miss Thorne, Miss Bishop."

Chancellor Lucas gestured toward the empty pair of crimson wingback chairs across from her desk. She already sat, bobbing on her floating chair, behind her oak desk. Previously, the desk had been meticulously organized, but tonight, papers were strewn about as if Chancellor Lucas had been in the middle of something before they'd been called in to speak with her.

"I would like to have a discussion about what you both witnessed tonight."

She closed the book before her on the table. It looked old, the pages yellowing and the leather binding cracked along the folds. Hazel tried to make out the title but the lettering was too faded to read in the low light.

"I understand you've both been through a great ordeal and I'm glad to see for myself you've come out on the other side. Now, I want to discuss how you did that. But first, please, ladies, your wands." Chancellor Lucas held out her palm.

Hazel reflexively covered her wand holster with her hand. "What? Why do you need to see our wands?" Her eyes shot to Gwen. They'd stopped Frank from killing them all. What did it matter how they did it?

"I am going to do a thorough investigation on the events of this evening, and that includes understanding how Frank was stopped, in case we need to replicate it." When neither Hazel nor Gwen moved to comply, she continued, "I understand things can happen when emotions are heightened and—"

"Emotions were *heightened*," Gwen interrupted, enunciating the words as she leaned forward in her chair, "because someone was trying to eat Dane Bellamy's face off before we stopped them—and then that someone tried to *eat mine*. No, not someone—the person the school sent us out there to look for! We did what we had to survive."

The chancellor said nothing as she stared between Gwen and Hazel, assessing them as if trying to determine her next move.

Hazel tugged at the pants of her coveralls as the tension grew. She didn't want to be insubordinate, but she also didn't want them to find out she was hiding something.

Chancellor Lucas was a smart woman. She would connect the dots. None of Dane's, Hazel's, or Gwen's defensive or offensive spells had touched Frank. *Will they believe a simple snowbank spell stopped him?*

Her stomach knotted. It was only a matter of time until she figured out Hazel had lied about how she'd really killed Frank. Guilt washed over her as she thought the word "kill." What if there had been another way to save him—to heal him? Had Hazel robbed him of that?

Chancellor Lucas raised a brow. "I will not ask again. Please hand over your wands."

Hazel stood, her knees nearly going out from underneath her as she leaned to place her wand on the chancellor's desk. She snatched her hand back quickly to hide its tremor.

Gwen's jaw clenched as she remained in her seat. Hazel flashed her a look that said not to argue. With a huff, Gwen walked to the desk and half-tossed the wand onto the surface before sitting back down and crossing her arms.

Chancellor Lucas looked at Gwen's wand first, studying it from end to tip, and then held it up in the air, aiming it towards the girls as she cast *itero*, a repetition spell. Hazel had never seen it done before; it was typically only used in disciplinary matters, and Hazel had never been in trouble a day in her life.

The girls both flinched as a solid form shot between their heads. They turned to see a blank canvas within a gold frame in the middle of the far wall. The wand released a stream of color that landed on the canvas like oil. For a moment, it was a stationary splash of vivid puce green, then it began to bubble, and steam rose from the oil. After a few seconds, the page eventually caught fire, going up in a smoke so thick they could no longer see the canvas nor the oil. When it finally dissipated, there was nothing there but a blank white canvas in a gold frame again. Hazel prayed that meant the spell hadn't worked.

"You tried a scalding hex," Chancellor Lucas stated.

Gwen glanced at Hazel and nodded. "I was trying to hurt him, so he'd quit attacking me and maybe run away."

"And you're saying this didn't do the job?" There was something akin to curiosity in the chancellor's voice.

"I'm saying it didn't even faze him. But I already told Captain Jackson that, and I'm pretty sure he already told you," Gwen snapped, rubbing at her temples.

Hazel was thankful Gwen had her back, but she wished she'd quit being so antagonistic to the woman who held their entire futures in her hands.

Chancellor Lucas acted as if Gwen hadn't spoken. She laid Gwen's wand down and picked up Hazel's next to it. She repeated, "*Itero.*"

This time, the wand blasted a muted, blue powder-like residue that splattered against the canvas. Wisps of cold vapor emanated from the canvas and filled the room. After a few seconds, it dissipated without a trace.

"What spell did you use specifically, Miss Thorne?"

Hazel swallowed, afraid she might incriminate herself. It didn't matter that she'd used fulgurkinesis to save Gwen's and Dane's lives. The truth was she had used her abilities and cost someone their life. They were going to send her home. No, they were going to kill her. Gwen made it very clear the Knights wouldn't let a Forsaken live. Her throat filled with bile and she fought to keep the contents in her stomach in place. She would not help Chancellor Lucas draw any conclusions.

"*Nivis Acervus*."

"That is the spell that stopped it?" The chancellor leaned over the desk, propping herself up on her elbows, hands clasped in a fist.

Hazel nodded and resisted the urge to squirm in her seat. She was convinced the chancellor could see into her guilty mind.

"What made you try that spell?"

"Nothing else had worked," Hazel explained truthfully.

"But that—a simple snowbank spell—stopped it." The chancellor waited, her neutral mask of indifference still intact.

She was too close, Hazel could feel it.

"Honestly, I was lucky," Hazel said.

Gwen twisted slightly in her seat at Hazel's lie.

The chancellor crossed her arms and studied Hazel as if weighing the truth in her words. After a stretch of awkward silence, she finally spoke, "Yes, you are quite *something*. First Jude's partner, and now this spell. I'm trying to determine how much of that is luck or if it's something else."

Hazel's eyes widened in surprise. It shouldn't be shocking that the chancellor found out about Mara—she was Jude's partner, after all—but fear that they all suspected she was an elf snaked through her.

"Perhaps resourcefulness. I suppose time will tell," Chancellor

Lucas added. "Did you think it would have this effect? Did you think the spell would kill it?"

"Why do you keep doing that?" Hazel asked.

"Doing what?"

"Calling the missing man an 'it.' He has a name. Frank," Gwen said, pinpointing exactly what had been bothering Hazel.

The chancellor's eyes glinted at the reprimanding tone of Gwen's voice. "His name *was* Frank."

Hazel sucked in a breath, feeling as though she'd slapped her. Yes, the chancellor was right, because Frank was dead. He was dead because of Hazel.

The chancellor uncrossed her arms. "But he stopped being Frank before you found him, about twenty-four hours before he was reported missing."

Hazel's eyes widened. She hadn't killed Frank? He'd already been dead?

Hazel shook her head in denial. "He walked—no, ran—and fought and—"

The chancellor held a hand up. "I understand you've both been through a lot this evening. You've seen unimaginable things. I assure you we have this under control and what we don't need is for the school to end up in a panic over something that is very much in hand. We learned some incredibly valuable information tonight that will help us keep this from happening in the future."

Gwen slapped the desk, the loud pop startling Hazel. "Chancellor, you've got to be kidding. We need answers. What in Salem was that thing?"

"It was undead." Chancellor Lucas's face returned to neutral as she looked back and forth between the girls.

"What?" Hazel and Gwen asked at the same time.

"I can't share any other information with you at this time. You saved Dane's life tonight. You should be very proud of that fact. As I was saying, I know this was an extraordinarily stressful evening for the both of you, but I want you to rest easy tonight knowing you did the right thing and that you granted a kindness to Frank, regardless of the outcome."

Hazel felt the weight in her chest ease. She didn't kill him and they weren't going to call the Knights to charge her with murder. She was able to take a full breath for the first time in hours.

"Chancellor, what did that to him?" Gwen asked.

"I cannot discuss this with you—*either* of you," she added when Hazel opened her mouth to interject. "As I mentioned before, we learned some very important things we needed to know tonight. We're going to be implementing new security measures, and now we are armed with the information we need to protect ourselves should we encounter an undead again."

Hazel stomach clenched. They didn't have the information they needed. She wanted to confess immediately—a snowbank would do nothing to stop an undead. But she couldn't tell the truth without putting her life at risk. Even if she could, they couldn't replicate the magic.

Hazel stayed quiet despite the battle within her.

"Again?" Gwen questioned. "You think whatever did this could do it again?"

The chancellor laid her palms flat on the table. "Not *what*, Miss Bishop, but *who*."

Gwen

"We need to warn people," Gwen urged. She couldn't believe what she was hearing. "We need to tell people how to defend themselves."

Hazel nodded enthusiastically beside her.

"Miss Bishop, what do you think the person who is doing this will do once they learn we are on to them? Do you think they'll simply turn themselves in? No, you can't be that naïve."

Gwen's cheeks burned as she bit back a childish response.

"I'm asking you in all seriousness, Gwendolyn. What would you do if someone found out about your deepest, darkest secret? Would you turn yourself in?"

Your deepest, darkest secret reverberated in Gwen's brain.

She blanched. Was Chancellor Lucas implying what Gwen thought she was implying?

Hazel looked rapidly between the chancellor and Gwen.

"I'm asking you a question, Miss Bishop. You so badly wanted to be in this conversation. I'm letting you join it, but now you hold your tongue?"

Gwen opened her mouth to retort, but a shooting pain from her shin arced up her thigh and down into her foot. Hex that tree root she'd tripped over. Until Harland's potion wore off, she'd have to deal with the pain. Gwen snapped her mouth closed, suppressing a snarl. Had she been in wolf form, her hackles would've been raised. She was an injured wolf and the chancellor was backing her into a corner. She wanted to tell her she should be careful. It would be her fault if she got bit, not Gwen's. Instead, she bit her own tongue and glowered at the chancellor. Gwen met her gaze dead-on, never wavering. She was determined to be thankful for the battle she was winning, which was staying in her chair instead of ripping into the chancellor's throat.

The chancellor continued, eyes never leaving Gwen's, "Part of participating in a mature adult conversation is answering the hard questions, so let me ask you one more time. What would you do if you were the predator and you found out we knew what you were up to?"

Hazel released a breath as she looked at Gwen once more.

Gwen remained alert, back straight, leaning forward in her chair for another moment. Then her shoulders relaxed as she interpreted the chancellor's words. While it no longer seemed she was implying something about Gwen's own secrets, she knew that the woman was trying to intimidate her. She didn't look away, only feigning calm as she answered truthfully, "I'd run. You'd never find me."

"What if you felt backed into the corner with nowhere to turn? Perhaps in a mountain with warded walls and restrictions on materialization?"

Gwen didn't hesitate. "I'd fight my way out."

"Precisely. That is why we cannot tell anyone what we know. While we know what this person is up to, they've been very careful to conceal themselves. Any evidence we had to track them was cleansed by the snow when Hazel cast her spell tonight."

Hazel hung her head.

"So now we must wait and watch to discern who might be doing this."

"Wait until what? Until they take someone again?" Gwen demanded.

"We will be watching closely. Close enough for them to know, for them to become nervous, and for them to slip up." The chancellor's gaze slid to Hazel. "I can see your wheels turning, Miss Thorne. Please tell me what lucky thing they've spun up."

Hazel reached up and tucked her hair behind an ear. "Things are escalating, aren't they?"

Chancellor Lucas steepled her fingers together in front of her face as she contemplated Hazel's question, only to answer it with one of her own. "How did you draw that conclusion?"

"First, the dogs. Mutilated and very much dead, not undead." Hazel paused and flashed a look at Gwen. "Now a mundane, mutilated and very much undead."

Hazel had skipped over the bear. It was clearly a piece of the pattern, but Gwen was glad she hadn't shared it. Both of their secrets could depend on it. They could blame it on luck the first time, but escaping an undead twice? It would raise too many questions they couldn't answer.

"Yes, it does seem the culprit is becoming bolder."

A light bulb went off inside Gwen's pain-clouded mind. "You're going to bait a trap."

The chancellor smiled at Gwen and then Hazel over the tips of her fingers.

Hazel swallowed. "How will you do it?"

Chancellor Lucas arched a brow at Hazel, hard resolve in her eyes.

"She's not going to tell us," Gwen groused. She'd seen her father wear that look many times as he cooked up the very schemes that had made her family cut all ties with him. "I wouldn't." A thought occurred to Gwen. "Is that what we were? Bait?"

The chancellor narrowed her eyes at Gwen. "I'm going to pretend you didn't just ask me that. I'm appreciative of both of you, so I have allowed this conversation to go on longer than it should have. You must keep any mention of the night's events to yourself, for everyone's sake. I am proud of your bravery tonight, as well as the ability you both showed in character and in magical talent." She paused, flashing them a smile that didn't reach her eyes. "As a reward, I'm going to allow you to recuse yourself from all the Wilderness Watch outings moving forward. I've let Captain Jackson know you aren't expected to report in for any further searches, as I imagine it will take you some time to recover from this evening's events."

"A reward? You mean a bribe," Gwen said. "My silence can't be bought. If I feel that people need to know something because you're not prioritizing their safety, nothing is going to keep me from telling them." Gwen stood, her shin searing as she applied weight on it. She needed that damned potion to get out of her system.

The chancellor smiled at Gwen, and instead of addressing her threat, she said, "I really do think that we should consider what's best moving forward. You've been injured tonight, Gwen."

Gwen's eyes went straight to her leg. There was no blood nor damage to give it away. She looked back to see the chancellor's smirk. Hex it. Gwen's immediate reaction to her statement had confirmed her suspicions. The chancellor hadn't been sure, but now she was.

"It may be best if you return home to Britton Place to heal." The glint in the chancellor's eyes told Gwen this wasn't about her injury at all. The implied message was clear—keep your mouth shut or you will be sent home.

How dare she? After all of the hard work she'd put in to be here.

She took a step toward the chancellor at the desk with her uninjured leg.

Hazel shot out of her chair, pulling on Gwen's arm. "We understand your concern, but that's not necessary," Hazel said. "We're very tired and just need to rest. I think we should head back to our room."

It was Hazel's turn to be ignored.

"What do you think, Gwendolyn? Do you feel well enough to stay or do you need to return home?" Chancellor Lucas asked.

The unsaid words hung in the air. *Will you stay quiet or do I have to make you stay quiet?*

Gwen clenched her jaw. If she did so any harder, a tooth would crack.

"I'm not going anywhere," she forced through her teeth.

Chancellor Lucas gave her a slow smile. "In that case, I think Hazel is right. Best to return to your room."

Hazel tugged on Gwen's arm before she could give a retort. Gwen was too tired, too injured, to argue any further, so she let Hazel lead her from the room.

"Gwen, what were you thinking? She's the head of the school. You can't speak to her like that," Hazel said the second Gwen's butt touched the couch.

"And you, Hazel, can't just sit there like a good little puppy while she kicks you!"

Gwen let out a sigh of relief once her leg was propped up. A tingle wrapped around her ankle. Harland's potion seemed to be wearing off and her therian abilities were returning. She'd be healed soon.

Hazel stood across the room, eyes wide. “That’s *not* what I was doing!”

“You sat right there in silence, never objecting to any of the ridiculous things she said!” Gwen grimaced as she worked to pull up her pant leg.

Hazel crossed her arms. “I didn’t need to object. You were doing enough of that for the both of us.”

“Yeah, because if I didn’t, it wouldn’t get done.” Gwen tried to lift her pant leg once again, cursing as the hem caught around her calf. Apparently, the injury was worse than she’d thought if it was taking this long to heal.

“That’s not fair, Gwen, and you know it. If it wasn’t for me, you’d be on your way home to Maine, not sitting here in this room.”

Gwen lowered her leg and leaned back against the couch once more in a frustrated huff. She didn’t argue because she knew at least part of that was true. She’d never dreamed the chancellor would try to send her home. She looked at Hazel, hoping she could see the sincere gratitude she felt there.

“Here, let me help you.” Hazel lifted her wand to cast a stretching spell that allowed Gwen to finally pull the hem up over her shin. They saw a gnarly black and blue bruise that wrapped along Gwen’s shin and down around her ankle. It had already begun to turn green, as her body’s rapid healing took over.

Hazel summoned ice from the fridge and wrapped it in a rag for Gwen to place against her ankle. “I didn’t realize how much pain you were in back there.”

Gwen sighed. The ice felt good against her throbbing tendons. “It’s okay. I was doing my best to hide it, though somehow, that bitch figured it out.”

“I guess she’s the chancellor of the university for a reason. She’s quite smart.”

It was Gwen’s turn to roll her eyes.

Hazel added, “But I don’t think she’s as clever as she thinks she is.”

Gwen pouted when Hazel didn't explain. "I'm in pain here. Don't make me put things together for myself."

"She didn't mean to, but she told us more than she'd intended. She confirmed the person doing all of this is showing a clear pattern of escalation. So after dogs, a bear, and a mundane—" Hazel stopped, her jaw dropping as Gwen watched the wheels turn behind her eyes.

"Spill it, Hazel!"

"I think it's more than one mundane. I think whoever did this tried to get Mara. I also think they're the reason for those mundane men in town forgetting their memories, and the other missing people."

"That's a big jump, Hazel," Gwen said, skeptical.

"You heard the medic! She said Frank had suffered blood loss. You saw that huge hole in his neck," Hazel said, gesturing wildly with her hands as if connecting the invisible strings of the timeline. "Mara and Jude both said that Mara's cardiac arrest was the result of unexplained blood loss!"

Gwen slumped back on the couch, processing it all. "Salem burn us," Gwen said, now sure Hazel was right. There were too many odd things going on for it to be a coincidence.

"And the chancellor said it herself. This is an escalation. The culprit is getting braver. So after all that, what's next?" Hazel asked, clearly coaching Gwen to her conclusion.

Gwen's eyes widened. "They're going to go after a mage."

Hazel nodded grimly. "Which means we know *why* they're doing this."

Gwen thought about it. "Power?"

"It has to be. I mean, that's why we're all here, isn't it? Except this person is on a whole other level. Like desperate. "

"So we wait and we watch for a desperate someone who wouldn't expect us to be watching."

"We wait," Hazel said in agreement.

CHAPTER 31

Hazel

Heat filled the cavern. A peek over the side of the stone bridge revealed a bubbling lake of magma hundreds of meters below. The orange glow mesmerized and enchanted to the point of distraction. It called to Hazel with a promise it wouldn't burn her, but embrace her. She warred with herself about whether to leap from the edge.

Suddenly, a giant scaled mass flew up from under her feet and then overhead so quickly, Hazel barely had enough time to pull back. The force of its wings tossed her hair and clothing, and she shielded her eyes. The bridge shook under its weight as it landed. Hazel lowered her hands to see the amber dragon. He gazed into her eyes, smoke leaking from his nostrils.

"Little bird, you are taking too long. Embrace it. Accept it. Become," the dragon spoke into her mind as he'd done in the entrance exam.

Hazel shook her head. *Embrace what? Being an elf?* She *had* been using fulgurkinesis. And she was even getting better at calling it and expelling it—thanks to Gwen's crystal wolf. *Is that what he means?*

“Or become like me.” The words came from behind her.

She whipped around to see her mother, young and beautiful as she always was in her dreams. Hazel had stopped looking for her altogether, hurt and anger making her doubt her mother. This was the first time she’d seen her since Samhain, even in her dreams.

Hazel opened her mouth to ask a question, but something—someone—on the stone bridge, behind her mother, caught her eye.

A man laid there, still and quiet. Hazel moved past her mother to see closer when she recognized the blue winter coat, but the man was different than she’d last seen him. Frank’s face wasn’t burned, there were no wounds on his cheeks, and his closed eyes were no longer sunken. He looked at peace, as if he were resting rather than lying dead upon the bridge.

Hazel leaned over him, a tear slipping down her cheek from the memory of his brutal death, as she tried to see if the hole in his neck had been healed. As she reached to pull the collar of his coat down, his eyes opened, revealing dark-red orbs of pure hatred.

“You killed me,” Frank snarled, his words rough and harsh as he forced them out.

Hazel shook her head, holding her hands up in defense. “No—no, I didn’t.”

Frank sat up and pointed at her with a single, accusatory finger. “Murderer.”

Hazel backed away and glanced at her mother. What would she think? “You were already dead,” Hazel explained as Frank began to stand.

“Says who?” he growled as he took a step towards her.

Hazel’s breath hitched. “I’m so sorry!”

No sooner did the words leave her lips, did Frank lunge at her, fingers shaped into claws as he grasped her shoulders in a bone-crunching grip.

Hazel cried out as she fought, shoving him in the chest, but he didn’t budge. He pulled her to him, grabbed her head, turned it to the side, and exposed her neck. With a hiss, he bared his teeth and sank his fangs into her neck.

Hazel screamed as she woke in her bed. Her sheets were wet with sweat and stuck to her bare legs. She brought her fingers to her neck to feel for marks. There weren't any.

It wasn't real. It was a nightmare.

But it had felt real.

The cold, sweat-drenched sheets had to go, so Hazel ripped them from the bed and tossed them in her laundry basket before remaking her bed with her spare set. She was too awake now, so Hazel trudged her way to the shower.

The hot water chased away the cold dread, but her thoughts wouldn't release the dream. If that's what it was.

She'd dreamed of the dragon a couple of times since the exam, always bits and pieces of what happened during the tests, until the dream where he'd antagonized her into using fulgurkinesis. Which had turned out to be an ability she had—was that a coincidence?

This dream, though, had been different. He'd said odd things to her, which was now making her consider the possibility it wasn't a dream at all, but rather a vision like those of her mother. Her mother being in the dream made the possibility even more likely, yet it was still highly unlikely, wasn't it?

She let out a deep sigh.

Dragons weren't real and her mother had no reason to be down in that cavern.

Frank being in her dreams was a whole other element that she had no explanation for. He was dead. Like he'd said, she'd killed him. There was no way she could be seeing a vision of him.

No, it must have been a nightmare.

But that thought did nothing to assuage her guilt.

Or to remove the feeling of his teeth in her neck.

Hazel and Gwen settled into their preferred table in the dining hall and began silently eating their comfort breakfast foods.

Gwen ate her homemade Pop Tart in three bites, then waved her wand and created a silencing bubble. "Why the hell would they want their blood?"

Hazel worked on chewing a mouthful of waffle while she considered that very question. She'd come up with a few possibilities last night. "You can do summoning spells with blood," Hazel said, and Gwen shrugged. Hazel agreed it wasn't likely. "It's the primary ingredient in a personalized curse."

"Yeah, but you don't need massive amounts of blood to do those kinds of magic," Gwen said.

She was right. There was no logical reason for anyone to take that much blood. Curses, location spells, and summons all required a single drop. Someone might take extra for insurance purposes or for multiple uses, but not enough to send someone into cardiac arrest.

Gwen twisted her charm bracelet about her wrist. "Why take enough to kill a man? Better yet, if you were trying to kill a man, why would you choose blood loss? There are much more efficient ways. It just doesn't make sense to me."

Hazel chewed her lip and thought it through for the hundredth time. Maybe they were giving this person too much credit. Maybe they weren't an evil mastermind, just an evil mind.

Gwen let out a discontented sigh and Hazel knew it had nothing to do with the talk of blood. Her friend was devastated over Harland. Hazel believed Gwen had made the right call in ending things with him, she just hoped Gwen stood firm in that. She hated seeing her friend so sad, she didn't want her to have to ever go through this again.

"How are you holding up?" Hazel asked.

Gwen hung her head and rubbed her eyes. "I don't want to talk about it."

The quiver in her voice told Hazel she was barely hanging on, so she dropped it.

Several girls hurried past, grabbing both of their attention. Hazel raised a brow as they made a beeline for the next table over.

"What the hell is going on over there?" Gwen asked.

Gwen let the silencing bubble fall and Hazel was immediately hit with the sound of fists pounding the table in rhythm, and voices rising in a chant that made her ears ring. The energy surged like a battle cry. The rushing girls had stopped below a group of guys standing on their table. They were all muscular, with veins corded tight across their arms and necks. They looked like ruzo players, biceps bulging out from under their short sleeves, cuffs cutting into the skin.

The single outlier, a boyish mage with dark-red hair, was impossible to miss, given he was the smallest of the bunch by no less than fifty pounds and didn't look a day over fifteen. He rubbed his hand on a napkin before working the stopper off of a vial of thick gray liquid. His friends cheered as he uncapped it. The boy put the vial to his lips and threw back his head, swallowing all of the contents in one long pull. More cheers erupted as he threw the vial to the table with such force it shattered.

The mage lurched. Hazel thought he might be sick. But instead of throwing up, he burped. The group laughed as someone clapped him on the back. Suddenly, his small frame twisted and contorted as the potion took effect. Gwen and Hazel kept watch as his body was replaced by slabs of muscle and popping veins, like the rest. The guys took turns exchanging fist bumps and high fives with their newest look-alike.

Hazel and Gwen's eyes met, both trying not to laugh at the scene, knowing this amazing accomplishment would wear off in a day or less. No power elixir was permanent.

A light bulb went off in Hazel's mind. The elixir wouldn't last. The dream about Frank biting her. The mark on his neck.

"They're drinking the blood," Hazel said.

Gwen laughed, but Hazel's face remained neutral. "Oh, you're serious."

"Think about it," Hazel urged, leaning in as Gwen's gaze sharpened. "We know the person who turned Frank into an undead and attacked Mara is after power, and now we know that they've taken blood."

A beat of silence hung between them. Hazel almost didn't want to say it out loud.

"We never stopped to ask ourselves *how* they're taking it. Those two things can't be separate, they have to be connected. They have to be taking the blood to absorb the power."

Gwen's brows rose higher and higher as she caught up to Hazel's reasoning. "You're talking about blood magic." Her upper lip curled at the implication and the words hung heavy between them.

Blood magic was illegal. Even further, it was immoral. To steal power through the life force of another living being was truly wicked, and all practice and information on it was strictly forbidden. It wasn't hard to enforce, given how revolting the practice was.

The back of Hazel's neck pricked with the sensation of being watched. She glanced around, and several pairs of eyes snapped away. A group in the far corner sat unnervingly still, all facing their direction. Some students whispered behind cupped hands, others not bothering to hide it.

Hazel leaned in. "What's going on? Why is everyone looking at us?"

Gwen sat up stock straight as her eyes furrowed. "I have no idea."

The dining hall had gone strangely quiet, the usual clatter of plates and buzz of conversation replaced with a heavy hush.

A girl nearby let out a sharp snort, not bothering to hide her glare. She whispered something to her friend, too low to catch, but the word that followed echoed like a crack fracturing the still air. "Murderers."

Hazel stiffened.

"I think last night is officially the hot topic," Gwen murmured, her voice tight.

Salem burn us, they know.

The school had found out what they'd done to Frank. The looks of accusation and judgment were worse than Hazel had imagined. Who had told?

It didn't matter. They knew. Or at least they thought they did. They wouldn't know he was already dead—the chancellor had made it clear that information would remain hidden at all costs.

"I think we should leave," Hazel said quietly, standing and grabbing her tray.

Gwen's jaw clenched as if she wanted to argue, then she stood to leave as well. Hazel's shoulders lightened, thankful that Gwen wasn't going to cause a scene.

As they left quickly and quietly, Hazel kept her eyes down, but caught Gwen flashing challenging looks at anyone stupid enough to make eye contact with her before they exited the building.

They ran into Rafe and Jordan on the front steps of the dining hall. Both of them wore unusually serious expressions.

"We've been looking for you," Jordan said, skipping his usual sarcasm. "We've been hearing stuff."

Hazel looked up at him, her throat tight. What had he heard? Most importantly, did he believe it?

Jordan crossed his arms. "People are saying you two killed a lost hiker."

Gwen and Hazel shared a look.

"Like, on purpose," Jordan added when they didn't deny it.

"We didn't," Gwen said flatly.

"We know," Rafe said. His voice was calm but firm as he laid a hand on Hazel's shoulder. "We just wanted to check in."

The knots in Hazel's stomach eased with his touch. As long as Rafe and Jordan believed them, it was all going to be okay.

Gwen gave them a halfhearted smile. "Thanks. But maybe don't stand too close. Might ruin your reputations."

Jordan rolled his eyes. "Please. If anything, this makes you more interesting."

Hazel bit back a groan. She didn't want to be interesting. After saving Mara and putting herself at risk, she didn't want to draw any extra attention to herself or to Gwen.

"So what's actually going on?" Rafe asked.

A group of students exited behind them, their animated conversations immediately stopping as they saw Hazel and Gwen.

"Not here. Let's go to our room," Hazel said quietly.

The guys nodded without hesitation.

As they walked, Rafe slipped an arm around Hazel's shoulders, and Jordan did the same with Gwen. A simple, wordless act of protection. Together, the four of them headed for the dorms.

They walked in silence at first, until the group behind them turned off for a different part of the campus. Even with the glares gone, the weight of them lingered.

As they approached the dorms, more students emerged. Hazel sighed. It was breakfast time, so they'd surely pass many more on their way to their room.

Gwen nudged Hazel with her elbow. "Should we take the back door?"

Hazel's eyes widened. She hadn't even considered it—largely because she hadn't used it since Gwen had shown her how to open it. The door was for emergencies only, and while Hazel knew it might be a tad dramatic, she felt like this event qualified. She didn't think she could face one more judgmental look.

"Yes, please," Hazel said.

"The what?" Rafe raised an eyebrow as he kept step beside her.

Hazel flashed him a small smile. "You'll see."

Rafe's eyes studied her lips before flicking to her eyes. His one-armed embrace tightened ever so slightly, pulling her side flush with his. Hazel buzzed with contentment.

They moved deeper into the trees, the world growing quieter with each step. Gwen led them with ease down an invisible winding path until the dorms had disappeared behind thick trunks and pine needles. Once they were far enough in, she stopped.

"This is it."

Jordan gave them each a long, skeptical look. "You two have a secret entrance to your room and this is the first time we're hearing about it?"

"We weren't keeping it from you," Gwen said. "We just haven't needed it until now."

Rafe looked around. "There's nothing here."

Hazel smiled faintly and reached for her wand. She stepped forward and whispered a few words under her breath, pressing the tip of her wand to what looked like a solid stretch of bark on a wide, frost-covered tree. The air shimmered as a narrow wooden door materialized in front of them, built seamlessly into the trunk. Hazel turned the handle and pushed open the wooden door. The scent of pine and old stone gave way to the familiar comfort of their dorm.

Rafe stepped through first and came to a dead stop just inside. "Whoa."

Jordan followed and immediately let out a low whistle. "This is your *dorm*?"

"It's huge," Rafe said, turning in a slow circle. "Ours looks like a shoebox compared to this."

Jordan ran a hand through his hair. "Seriously, what the hell? How did you get this extra space? Did you bribe the mountain?"

Gwen dropped her coat on the arm of the couch. "No bribes. Just a little spatial manipulation."

Jordan narrowed his eyes. "*You* did this?"

Gwen flashed him a proud grin.

"This is criminal," Jordan said, dropping dramatically onto the nearest couch cushion. "You have to do this to our room."

"No promises," Gwen replied as she plopped down next to him.

Rafe chuckled and shook his head as he sank into the oversized armchair across from them. "I feel betrayed. Deeply and personally."

Hazel smiled faintly and moved toward the hearth, kneeling in front of it. She lit a match, and flames sprang to life in the fireplace, casting flickering shadows across the room and filling it with gentle warmth. For the first time since breakfast, it felt like she wasn't inside a fish bowl with the world peering in at her.

Jordan sank deeper into the couch, exhaling like the weight of the entire day had finally caught up to him. Gwen leaned into him without hesitation. He wrapped an arm around her shoulders, pulling her close. She tucked into him easily, like she belonged there.

A sudden bang rattled the back door, loud enough to make them all jump.

Gwen groaned. "That's probably Klaus. I should've never told him about the back entrance." She pushed up off the couch and crossed the room, twisting the lock and opening the door.

Klaus stepped inside, windswept and intense, his eyes scanning the room in one sweep. "We need to talk."

Gwen rolled her eyes. "You can drop the dramatics. They already know about the rumors. It's all over school."

He let out a slow breath and ran a hand down his face. "Well then—what the hell is going on?"

Gwen didn't answer as she turned her back on him and went to reclaim her spot beside Jordan, curling into him once again. Klaus hesitated, then sat beside her on the other side.

Hazel felt the moment shift. She glanced at Gwen, and their eyes met. There was no need to speak—they both knew, whatever came next, there was no undoing it.

The chancellor might have been okay with keeping everyone in the dark, but Gwen had been right—people deserved to know so they could protect themselves. While Hazel and Gwen couldn't tell everyone or they would be expelled, they could tell the people they trusted to keep this secret.

"First things first. You all have to promise you're not going to tell *anyone* what we're about to tell you. Our places here depend on it," Hazel said.

Rafe drew an "X" over his heart with his finger. "I promise."

Jordan copied him. "Promise."

Hazel studied Rafe's face, looking for any signs he might be lying, but saw none. Still, she had to address the one thing that scared her the most.

"Not even your father," Hazel added.

Hurt flashed in his eyes, but Rafe nodded. "I swear I will never tell my father any of the things we discuss, especially if they could ever get you or Gwen in trouble."

Sincerity rang true in his words.

Gwen looked pointedly at Klaus. "Say promise."

Klaus rolled his eyes, but said, "I promise."

"Even our moms—scratch that, *especially* our moms," she added.

Klaus nodded.

So Hazel and Gwen told them everything. Well, almost everything. They left out the part about Gwen being a therian and Hazel being an elf. Otherwise, they were an open book about the dogs and the bear, the men in town, Mara, Frank, and the chancellor. Then they told them their suspicions about the how of it all. Hazel felt a weight lifted from her shoulders with each truth they shared, but the lies they told to hide their own secrets coiled deep in her belly, making her feel sick.

She didn't want to lie anymore, but telling the truth meant she was asking her friends to lie *for* her.

"That's disgusting," Jordan said.

"So what's the plan now?" Rafe asked.

"We research and we keep watch," Hazel answered.

"And we prepare," Gwen said.

"You are to do nothing of the sort, Gwendolyn," Klaus scolded. "You need to stay as far away from whatever is happening as possible."

"Well, seeing as how that hasn't worked out for me so far, do you want me to be caught in the crosshairs again, unprepared?"

Klaus crossed his arms.

"We've been lucky so far, but like you and my dad taught me, luck will only get you so far."

"Fine," Klaus agreed. "Do all the research you want, but don't go looking for whatever is out there. I know you think you're strong enough to handle it, but don't."

Gwen reluctantly agreed.

"So what are we searching for?" Jordan asked.

Hazel's head tilted as she considered. "Anything on the undead or blood magic."

"Class starts at 10:30. We need to be heading out soon," Gwen said.

Rafe nodded. "We'll have to pick this up later."

Gwen gave Klaus a hug before he left for Coventry. Then Rafe, Jordan, and Gwen headed to Practical Curses, leaving Hazel to walk alone to Study of the Arcane. She wasn't looking forward to handling the stares and whispers by herself and could only hope the class would go on without incident.

Study of the Arcane had continued this semester. Last semester had focused on the theoretical foundations of foresight and telekinesis—subjects Hazel had absorbed with quiet fascination. She'd learned more in a few months than Elkmont had managed to teach her in years. Despite the tension that clung to campus now, she couldn't help the spark of curiosity stirring in her chest. This semester, they were finally moving on to the remaining two branches of arcane study: shadowsong and astral projection.

Sorcerer Oswald took his spot at the front of the class.

"Today, we will begin the study of shadowsong. Each of these branches are difficult in their own right. This course will not be any easier than last semester's," he explained.

Hazel had managed to demonstrate foresight, but not telekinesis. She was anxious to learn if she had a talent for the remaining arcane magics.

"As with the previous two branches, shadowsong has levels of difficulty. Some mages—not all—can see spirits. Some can hear them."

A chill went down Hazel's spine.

"Even fewer can do both," he continued. "History tells us that the skill of actually communing with spirits is the most rare. Our university is said to be the most haunted place of all time. Many scholars believe it's because the mountain simply keeps more spirits here than ordinary locations, like a magnet for the soul." He paused for a moment as if weighing his next words. "Others suggest it's because SEU was built upon a site that witnessed many distressing deaths."

Hazel sat up straight. *The exam must take more lives than I realized.*

Sorcerer Oswald waved his wand, and two dozen mage outlines appeared in the air. "Raise your wand if you believe you have encountered any spirits since arriving at SEU."

Several wands lifted, and then the corresponding number of mage outlines lit up in the air.

Hazel's eyes swept over the classroom to see if she knew any of the mages, then paused when she spied a familiar figure. Two rows ahead, Nova's wand was raised.

A quiet knot formed in Hazel's chest. They'd sat together all last semester, so when Nova hadn't joined her in their usual spot, she'd assumed Nova had switched courses.

She must have heard the rumors too.

Hazel sank low in her seat.

"Miss Taylor," Sorcerer Oswald said, adjusting his spectacles. "Where did you have your encounter?"

Nova sat straighter. "In the library, sir."

She said it so confidently, and Hazel knew her to be an honest person, so she had no doubts in her answer. After all of her visits last semester, Hazel couldn't say she'd seen one ghost. Perhaps she didn't have the gift of shadowsong after all.

Sorcerer Oswald chuckled, pulling Hazel's attention back to him. He looked directly at her, or so she felt. "Six of twenty-seven of you believe you have seen spirits. I believe that number is actually higher." Hazel sat forward in her seat and Oswald looked away. "Some of those with the gift are so naturally talented, they struggle to tell the difference between the living and the dead, while others are simply in denial, telling themselves their minds are playing tricks on them."

Hazel's head spun with Oswald's implication. Her mind raced back to Samhain, where she could've sworn she'd seen her mother disappear into the Pyre of the Dead. The way Hazel had seen her in the library and then she'd been gone in an instant. She'd been so sure she'd been astral projecting.

A dead weight settled in her stomach.

Was it possible she'd been seeing her mother's *spirit* all this time?

No. Hazel refused to believe that.

CHAPTER 32

Gwen

Gwen sat next to Hazel in the back row of History of the Great War, their last class of the afternoon. They had their pick of seats, like they had the last two weeks—since Frank's death. No one wanted to be near them. Gwen's senses pricked as the prying, judging eyes watched them settle in. She wasn't in the mood for this today. It was bad enough having to see Harland after their breakup. Gwen looked up, eyes shooting daggers at two women who sat on the aisle across from them and they quickly looked away.

Assholes.

But not everyone was brave—or stupid—enough to stare at them. Most were cowardly, whispering behind cupped hands. Little did they know Gwen could still hear the shit they said if she slipped off her bracelet.

She did just that.

"I can't believe they haven't been expelled yet," a guy who lived on the same floor as Rafe and Jordan whispered to another.

"They're probably waiting for the psych—"

Gwen threw her history book to the ground with a bang. The whole room jumped to look about. Even more eyes landed on them, but Gwen wasn't sorry. Today was not the day to mess with her. And they needed to realize that ignoring and gossiping about them wasn't going to make them go away. Especially when they hadn't done anything wrong.

I'm going to give them a reason to be afraid of me when I finally find out who told everyone about Frank.

Before Gwen could retrieve her book, Rafe appeared and scooped it up off the floor. "You good?" He looked around the room, his jaw clenched. He seemed just as pissed as Gwen, though she was sure it had more to do with Hazel than herself. She had a sneaking suspicion that he was definitely falling for her friend hard.

"Yeah, just dealing with some pests," Gwen said, taking the book back from him.

Rafe slid past Gwen to sit next to Hazel, smiling at her in a way that lit up his whole face, his white teeth shining against his handsome warm, brown skin. Yeah, that was how men were supposed to look at the women they liked.

"Hey!" Hazel said to Rafe, a little too loud and happy given their current social standing. Hazel wasn't oblivious to the awkward tension in the room, but she was pretending it didn't exist. Gwen couldn't do that.

Jordan appeared in front of the empty seat next to Gwen, bleary-eyed, with his coffee cup in hand. "How is she so happy to be in class?"

Gwen shrugged. "Learning really gets her going."

Jordan made a gagging sound, and Gwen snorted.

"I heard that!" Hazel said, smacking Gwen on the arm before adding, "And Gwen's right."

A waving hand shot in the air a few rows ahead of them, drawing all their gazes. Gwen leaned forward to see it was Nova, her fingers wiggling and gaze fixed on Jordan, beckoning him forward.

“Aren’t you going to sit with us?” Gwen asked when Jordan still didn’t sit down.

Jordan took a sip of coffee and gave a shy smile. “I sorta promised I’d sit with her and Elodie today. I’ll see you guys later?” He didn’t wait for a response before continuing down the aisle and making his way next to Nova. She stood to greet him with a kiss on the cheek before they both sat.

While they didn’t stare or whisper, Elodie and Nova had been avoiding Hazel and Gwen since the rumors had begun circulating. She didn’t blame them, but now they were going to take her oldest friend? Gwen’s wolf growled within her mind and lunged for control. She slammed her mental doors shut just in time. Her wolf was territorial on the best of days, but with all of the challenging glances being thrown their way, its anger was on a hair trigger today.

Gwen quickly fastened her bracelet back onto her wrist, and the wolf instantly quieted.

The empty seat next to Gwen left a bitter feeling in her stomach that grew into anger with each passing second. She’d put herself on the line by telling him the truth and he was acting like it was nothing. Not to mention, she needed his help right now to figure things out. Surely standing by her was more important than sitting with Nova, who he could see anytime.

Harland walked on stage, pulling Gwen out of that downward spiral and into a different one. He always looked professional, but today, he wore slacks, a button-up shirt, and a vest. Something about his demeanor was solemn, nearly grave. She couldn’t help but wonder if he was hurting too. His words played over in her mind for the thousandth time: *I can’t be anything more than a secret.*

No, *she’d* been the one hiding in the background of his life. Gwen would’ve gladly laid everything on the line for him. She had, with her heart, her body, and worst of all her secret. He was the one who felt she wasn’t worth the risk of exposure. She couldn’t believe she’d trusted him.

But she wouldn’t let it happen again. She’d locked her heart away under the same steel door she trapped her wolf inside and now she was ready to take a page from Hazel's playbook and focus on more important things, like class.

The room quietened as the students watched Harland tip his head back to drink his potion. He cleared his throat softly, and the sound echoed throughout the room like a bass drum. He didn't apologize, even after several students winced.

"Today, we're going to continue our discussion of the Great War escalation. We've been in class for two weeks now and it's time to get to the truly juicy bits."

When Harland spoke, he commanded attention. Each and every student hung on every word, which pissed Gwen off. It was why she purposely tried to ignore him when she couldn't take seeing his smug, respectable-looking face for one more second. But it was hard, because she loved history and this topic was one of her favorites.

And he was still Harland.

"In the 1200s, the fae, therians, and elves—the arguably physically and magically superior species—entered the fight, but very little is understood about *why*."

The silence in his pause was deafening. Gwen could've heard a pin drop.

Harland paced slowly toward the podium at the corner of the stage. "So what changed? Why did the siphoners all of a sudden become a threat to the other demi-humans after 700 years?"

Damn it, he had her attention. She was fully intrigued by the question she'd never thought to ask. Hazel twitched in her seat, and Gwen knew not knowing was eating her up too.

Harland reached into the wooden podium and pulled out a large wooden box. It was faded and old but unblemished by time—preserved. He placed it on top of the podium. "No ideas?" He withdrew his wand from his arm holster and pointed it at the box. With the flick of his wrist, the box popped open.

An uneasy stillness settled over the room, and even Gwen waited with bated breath.

Harland pulled out a cream-colored tome covered in indistinguishable bluish-gray swirls. The book was one of the largest Gwen had ever seen, yet something about it was strangely familiar. It appeared to be handmade, the pages irregularly thick and somewhat misshapen between the covers.

Harland held the book out gingerly as he walked back to the middle of the stage. "Fortunately for you, the answer lies within this tome. You're among the lucky few who will get to experience it firsthand."

A wave of murmurs ripped through the auditorium. There was only one type of book that could be *experienced*: Leabhar Feòla.

"Book of Flesh," Hazel whispered, her voice filled with a mixture of awe and disgust.

Gwen inched forward in her seat as her eyes narrowed on the cover. It was bound with tattooed skin, specifically glyphs that were embedded in the skin's owner while they were still alive.

"Made from the skin of a fae warrior who fought in the Great War, the glyphs inked within allowed the fae to pass on his last memories in an effort to provide intelligence to the cause, even after death."

Gwen swallowed, overcome with grotesque fascination. In all of her searching for ancient therian texts, she'd never once encountered a Leabhar Feòla. Only a few remained in existence, as the practice had slowly died out after the disappearance of the fae. While the fae had mastered the practice, they were incredibly dangerous to make, and mages who attempted it often ended up trapped within their own minds.

"Reading a Leabhar Feòla is an intense experience in all cases, as being transplanted into someone else's memories before they die is disconcerting to say the least, but this book is particularly..." Harland paused before finding the right word, "triggering."

Gwen and Hazel looked at one another, wide-eyed. Gwen couldn't believe this was happening. She was about to experience a Leabhar Feòla and learn about the Great War in one fell swoop. She jolted, realizing there was a very high probability that she would get to see a therian in the vision, if they'd been part of the battle.

"I will provide you with the necessary background, but in an effort to be the best anthropologists and historians you can be, I will say nothing that could bias or sway you beyond the facts."

Gwen's knees bounced in impatience. Knowing that there might be a therian in the memory had her chomping at the bit to read it.

"This fae commander fought using elemental conjuring and manipulation. He was head of his unit, and quite experienced in the art of battle. You will not see him use this magic—you will *experience* him using this magic. You will not see him fight and take lives—you will *experience* him fighting and taking lives."

A few murmurs broke out through the room and Harland stopped. He studied them all closely, still holding the book gently within his hands. When the room quietened again, he continued, "You will not see him die. You will *experience* his death."

"What?" a masculine voice asked from the front, the question edged with worry.

"I assure you that this is perfectly safe. While mentally, it will feel like you are moving about, physically, you will still be right here, sitting safely in your seats."

Gwen chewed her lip. It was a good thing she trusted her bracelet. There was no telling what her wolf would do if it felt that someone was killing them.

"One last thing to note is that when you begin to read, you'll be alone within the memory. No one can hear or speak to you until the memory has unfolded completely. If you feel yourself begin to panic, rest assured, it *will* end."

Hazel's hand shot into the air.

"Yes, Miss Thorne?" Harland asked, not even needing a second to squint to see who'd raised their hand.

"Is there anything we should be looking for specifically?" she asked.

Harland nodded as he began to pace across the stage. "Yes. You should be trying to find the answer about how the Forsaken became such a threat that mages were forced to end the existence of the most powerful beings to ever exist—fae, elves, siphoners, and therians."

His eyes landed on her as he finished speaking, and goosebumps erupted on Gwen's arms. She could only imagine the terrifying amount of power it would take to do what he described. *If we were so powerful, how did they wipe us out?* But they hadn't—not entirely. If they had, Hazel and Gwen wouldn't exist. Maybe today, she'd learn firsthand why they'd been forced into hiding, and why mages hated the Forsaken so much.

Harland's gaze left her as he paced back to the middle of the stage and studied the rest of the class. "If you're too weak to stomach this, leave now and take a zero for the assignment."

A handful of mages stood immediately and walked out. Their feet echoed awkwardly against the floor while the rest of the students waited in silence. When the door finally banged shut behind the last of them, the tension was thick enough to cut.

Harland extended the book in front of him, laying it flat on the palm of his right hand and forearm. With his left hand, he gripped the cover. "The past is more than a story. It's a roadmap. Remember that."

Then he pulled open the pages, and a warm yellow glow burst forth. Harland squinted against the bright light bathing his face and shoulders, but he didn't look down as he turned the book pages towards the room.

There were no words to be seen. It was simply as if they were staring into the sun. Or a soul.

There was nowhere to look but directly at the light. Gwen was positive she couldn't have looked away if she'd wanted to. Every few seconds, the glow would diminish ever so slightly and then flare even brighter than before. Movement in her line of sight caught her attention. One by one, heads dipped forward as bodies went lax in the seats directly in Gwen's field of vision.

The book was pulling them in.

Gwen's heart beat against her ribs.

The light pulsed again, and next to her, she felt more than saw Hazel's head dip.

The air caught in Gwen's lungs as the classroom dissolved around her. There was no sound, no sensation. Just light.

Then darkness.

Tiny, soft orbs appeared in the distance. Lanterns. The world brightened, as a silvery light bathed everything around her. She was outside, standing in the moonlight.

Her body felt heavy. The sensation wasn't painful, but restrictive. She tried to look down, but couldn't. Instead, she could only watch in irritation as a pair of soldiers walked away from her—*him*, the commander. But the irritation wasn't her own, for she knew only fascination in this moment.

It was an odd feeling to be watching from the inside, unable to make any decisions for herself, not even where to look. But she knew something about sharing her mind with her wolf, so it was only awkward, not distressing to have her own thoughts and feelings stuffed in here next to a stranger's.

Once they were out of earshot, Gwen looked down to adjust her crotch. She found herself wearing a combination of thick leather and metal armor. She stood in the mud up to her ankles, yet she was still quite tall.

At her waist, she spied a beautiful golden sword. She wrapped her fingers around the hilt and winced, drawing back. Freshly burst blisters coated her calloused and scarred hands. No, not her hands. *His* hands. This wasn't her pain. It was his.

Separating her identity from his was harder than she'd imagined.

He ignored the pain and wrapped his hands around the hilt of the sword once more. The sting was the same, but his determination was stronger.

"Ullaich!" a bellowing voice rang out. Gwen realized it came from *his* mouth.

Prepare. Gwen didn't know this language, but the fae did.

The fae commander turned abruptly, trudging his way to a long line of soldiers. His legs burned with the effort of moving quickly through the mud. He took a deep breath, and Gwen smelled smoke in the air. A ripple of sadness shot through her that was not her own, but it was there one moment and gone the next. The commander was laser-focused.

Rows upon rows of soldiers lined up in formation. Hundreds, at least. Some of them had tattoos that peeked above their neck armor and even on their faces, while others had pointed ears that Gwen had only seen in illustrations of fae and elves.

In the row next to theirs, cloaks obscured the soldiers beneath. Wind tugged at their cloaks as well as banners held by line leaders, but it was too dark for Gwen to make out the sigils upon them with the fae's eyes.

"Am màrt!" his deep voice boomed. *March.*

In perfect unison, they moved like it was second nature to walk in such a way. The clink of chains drew his—and Gwen's—attention. A handful of soldiers were shackled, hands and ankles, with golden chains. They each walked in sync with a partner, a shiny golden ring glinting in the moonlight on each of their fingers.

The fae commander Gwen inhabited felt gratitude as he looked at them. He thought nothing of the chains, nor rings, but Gwen did. Her stomach clenched. The chains were exactly like the ones sitting on the shelf in Alterion and the rings matched the one she'd taken, the one she was currently wearing. If she was right, she was looking at therian soldiers.

The commander looked away, forcing Gwen to do the same. He studied a rocky ledge a hundred yards away. His gaze did not waver until the regiment was parallel with it, but his mind whirled with a mixture of duty and dread, and Gwen was pretty sure a bit of reverence for what was coming: war.

The fae commander broke formation and climbed up the large stone rock until he reached the flat top.

"Bràithrean...." he called. *Brothers.*

The soldiers below looked up at him with somber faces, all fear of death erased. They knew what awaited them on the battlefield.

The commander began his speech, still speaking in his own language, but Gwen understood every word. "Today, we must fight like our lives depend on it—because they do. The schaden will stop at nothing to take you down. But we will not be stopped!"

The soldiers yelled out in a unified cry and beat their fists against their chests.

What are schaden? She'd never heard the word. But because he didn't think of the answer, Gwen didn't learn it.

"Most of the enemies you'll fight today are already dead, controlled by the schaden."

Gwen's mind whirled. Already dead? She thought of the bear, of Frank. There was no—

"Feel no remorse putting them down, for it is a mercy. Target the schaden and those they control will finally rest."

The soldiers nodded vigorously below. These weren't just warnings or words to them. They were an absolution of guilt before they'd even struck a blow.

Gwen wondered if that was what they'd done for Frank—allowed him to rest.

"May Macha hold you, Babda carry you, and Nemain empower you."

"The Morrígan!" those with inked skin roared back. The names meant nothing to Gwen, but as the fae commander spoke them with honor and praise, she guessed they were gods or goddesses of the fae.

"And may the rest of your gods take pity on your souls," he said as he looked at the other flanks.

War cries erupted. Feet stomped in the mud, and the beat of a drum, slow and steady, filled the air. Behind it all, there was a whooshing sound, loud and powerful, something familiar yet unrecognizable to Gwen.

A shadow fell over the regiment, and Gwen—the fae commander

—looked up in time to see an amethyst dragon fly past overhead. The forced air from its wings sent soldiers staggering as banners and cloaks whipped wildly in the wind. It was followed by an amber dragon, then a sapphire dragon. When the fourth and final dragon soared past, it swiveled its massive garnet head and stared directly into the eyes of the fae commander, giving him a single, deliberate nod. Then it unleashed a stream of fire into the air, in front of the battalion, illuminating the dark plain below and leaving a clear path of destruction in its wake. That was where the battle was to take place.

Internally, Gwen gaped. Even with eyes that weren't her own, she recognized them—all of them, but especially the garnet dragon. It had the same ridges, the same opalescent shimmer within the scales. Most importantly, it had the same scar across its left eyelid. She would never forget it after the exam.

A rock settled in Gwen's stomach. There was no way such a coincidence could exist. Hazel had been right. The dragons were real, not constructs of the exam. But that would mean they were over a thousand years old, which felt impossible.

"Our great weapons have arrived! March!"

The regiment moved forward as the fae commander climbed back down and took his spot in the rear.

A roar rent the air and the commander's eardrums shook with the force of it.

That was the signal. Their enemy had arrived.

Resolve tinged in hatred landed like a weight upon the commander's shoulders. He would kill them all today or die trying.

The metallic clash of swords and grunts of rage rang out all around them. The fae commander panted as he dodged the swing of a broadsword, and then gathered up the wind that swept down the plains. There was no need to conjure wind and waste the magic when the source was so readily available. Gwen extended her hands, heels of her palms together, towards the second line of the encroaching army. An invisible ram punched a hole right through the enemy's ranks, sending bodies flying. That's what they were—bodies. Undead, controlled to fight on behalf of the schaden.

When the first line of defense had broken into hand-to-hand combat, they'd finally gotten close enough for Gwen to truly see. And smell. Their skin was sallow, translucent in bits. Rot had set in for many, their eyes the first to go as they oozed out their sockets. Gwen thought she might be sick, although how she'd throw up in this body, she didn't know.

The smell was inescapable. Each and every one reeked of death and decay; the stench of it hung in the air like overripe fruit gone bad mingled with the sharp, fecal tang of putrefaction. There were just too many of them to block it out. At least a thousand—a few hundred more than what the fae and their reinforcements had brought. The commander's stomach clenched as he took in the overwhelming size of the enemy.

Mindless, vicious shells of what they once were, they attacked with abandon. Like puppets on a string, there was no calculation, no thoughts, other than to kill.

The fae commander sent bursts of wind around him, knocking off undead when they gained advantage on his soldiers. The precision he used to not hit his soldiers was impressive, but Gwen could feel him fatiguing with the effort it required.

Ten feet away, a fae soldier collapsed to the ground under the weight of his attacker. The undead snarled and snapped at his face. Gwen knew exactly what that felt like. She wished she could fight back, help the soldier, but she was stuck as a bystander in this war that had been fought long ago.

The commander channeled a burst of air toward the undead, dislodging him from the soldier, who didn't hesitate. He chased after the undead, pulled back his sword, and beheaded him. It never rose again.

Across the field at the enemy's rear, a dozen dark-cloaked figures stood under torches near an outcropping of rocks below the mountain range looming behind them. Gwen knew in her gut those were the schaden. The puppet masters.

They watched the rear flank, where another regiment attacked from the right. The amount of damage was significant, and the front lines began to progress forward, only a hundred yards now from the schaden themselves. Maybe Gwen would get to see them defeated.

Bursts of magic exploded from beneath the schadens' cloaks and then settled over the battlefield like dust.

Whatever the magic had been, Gwen knew it was bad as dread brewed in the pit of the commander's stomach.

Within seconds, it took hold. Soldiers that lay dead began to twitch in the mud. Panic swelled within the commander, but Gwen felt him squash it down.

He focused on one thought: *Take down the schaden.*

"Unleash the fera!"

Gwen panicked as the commander turned to watch the handlers use their enchanted rings to unlock the shackles. Within moments, the golden chains laid in the dark muck of battle.

As soon as the chains hit the ground, the handlers stepped back, giving the feras a wide berth. In a blink, the five shackled men she'd seen earlier shifted, unable to stay in their human forms without the chains.

The men were now replaced by a bear, a mountain lion, a jaguar, a wolf, and a fox. Primal roars ripped from their throats. Gwen was going to be sick. Those chains were barbaric. Now she understood why her skin had felt so attuned to the ones at Alterion. She vowed to destroy them if she ever made it back into that library.

The feras charged without orders. Some barreled through the enemies' lines, while others dipped and slipped through cracks, too fast to be stopped. Sadness overwhelmed her as she watched her ancestors run into battle.

The fae commander followed. As he ran, magic gathered under

his skin, thrumming in a way that felt similar to the sensation Gwen felt before a shift, but this thrum didn't dissipate; it built upon itself until it felt as though the fae would burst at the seams with it.

Three undead charged him as he approached their lines. With no hesitation, he lifted his hands, and fire erupted.

Hazel

Blood and death surrounded them. Hazel struggled to tell where she ended and the fae commander began. His rage, fear, and desperation coursed through her. Their hearts beat in unison, scraping against his rib cage painfully as he fought off the undead while trying to keep up with the fera.

It would take them all to bring the schaden down.

It was so dark and everything was happening too quickly. Hazel could barely process the scenes before her, but the fae commander pressed on as if he'd been made for this.

An amethyst dragon flew overhead, aimed straight for the platform the schaden stood upon. Its maw opened wide and a stream of ice erupted, only visible thanks to the schadens' lit torches. The ice shattered against a translucent shield. The fragments ricocheted off, raining down into the battle below like knives.

Screams rang out as the shards hit both the living and undead. Soldiers from both sides fell.

Frustration coiled tight in the fae commander's chest. They couldn't bring down the shields without putting their own at risk.

The first dragon was followed by the amber dragon. Hazel held her breath as she watched the beast breathe flames against the shield. She'd recognize him anywhere—the dragon who'd burned her in the exam, the one from her dreams.

I knew it!

The garnet dragon and sapphire dragon fired together, fire and ice, from opposite directions. The ice fragments fell down upon the battle once more, but there was nothing to be done. The shield had to come down.

Despite working in quick succession to overload the shield, it held.

But a thin crack appeared at the top. They had weakened it, at least.

The dragons circled about and came back, blasting the shield once more. The crack grew by a foot, but the shield remained.

The bodies, soldiers and undead alike, became too dense in the chaos as they tried to flee from the falling frozen shards while also fighting for their lives. The fae commander slowed to push his way through the retreating soldiers, the undead hot on their heels.

Power surged under the fae commander's skin as he shot rivers of fire at the approaching undead. With clothes, hair, even skin aflame, they continued to press forward. Burning them wasn't enough. He had to maintain the flames long enough for them to collapse. He pumped more and more magic into the stream of flames until finally, those before him laid upon the ground, charred and twitching.

Each time he did so, Hazel was able to see the carnage obscured by the night. This reality was old, but it was not any less horrific with age.

Hundreds were dead and the battle was not yet over.

Every use of flame depleted his energy. Too much energy. Hazel felt it dwindling to a dangerous low. If he didn't stop, he'd have nothing left to take down the schaden. He needed food or rest, but neither was available.

But he was a seasoned warrior, and nothing as simple as fatigue would keep him from winning this battle, so he shifted tactics.

An undead mage attacked, and the fae commander pulled his broadsword forth at the same time he called the fire once more—but instead of a barrage of flame, he wrapped the flame around the blade. The focus it required was draining, but of will, not magic.

Mere seconds passed from when he drew the massive claymore to then severing the undead's head from her shoulders. It landed in the mud with a splat, milky eyes reflecting the flames that burned her hair. Hazel shuddered, thankful that the fae commander looked away from the carnage and on to the next enemy.

Blow after blow, the commander took out his enemy—although not all lost their heads. Others, he simply cut off their limbs and left them to burn. By the time he reached the outcropping, the dragons had made two more passes and were coming back for another.

As the sapphire dragon approached, the unfathomable happened.

The dragon's massive frame shifted, or perhaps dissolved away, midair until a man remained. He landed past the schadens' shield with a harsh thunk before he rolled into a stop, mere feet from the masters of the undead.

Hazel felt as if the world had been turned on its axis. Dragons were shifters? Nothing Hazel had ever read or heard insinuated such a thing, but she'd just watched it happen.

The commander's relief and hope flooded Hazel's senses despite the utter fear she felt witnessing the heat of the battle. The shield was only designed to keep out the dragons.

The fae commander launched himself upon the platform, using one arm to haul his body over the side while the other kept his blazing weapon ready. He knew this was it—their chance to end them.

The dragon shifter approached the schaden wearing a crown upon the hood of their dark-red cloak.

A glowing halo appeared above the mountain peaks at the schadens' backs. For a moment, Hazel wondered what magical being was on their way to save the day, but then someone yelled out, squashing her hopes.

"Daylight is upon us!"

"Daylight!" another yelled.

The schaden turned to look back at the coming dawn rising behind them.

Elation filled the fae commander once more. Hazel could only feel the same hope he did, despite having no idea what daylight had to do with a damned thing. Still, he did not slow. He would take no chances.

The crowned schaden waved their arm above them, and within seconds, the hope evaporated as quickly as it had come. Dark, ominous storm clouds filled the sky, blocking out the waning light of the moon, as well as the burgeoning daybreak.

Hazel might've once said the moment was miraculous, but she knew those clouds. She'd called those clouds. A pit of dread burned in her stomach as she considered the implications. How had she done anything like these monsters?

Slowly, the schaden lifted its finger, pointing directly at the fae commander. Lightning struck behind him, and Hazel realized she knew absolutely nothing.

The commander spared a look over his shoulder to see one of the therians—feras—laying dead at the edge of the outcropping. Its body smoked and sizzled from the strike, like the bear Hazel had killed in the fall.

What am I?

Horror bloomed in Hazel's heart, while solemn determination steeled the fae commander's spine. He advanced, clearing five, then ten feet. In less than three seconds, he'd cleared the distance, raised his sword, and slashed his blade across the enemy's throat—

As a bolt of lightning slammed into him.

A searing pain tore through him.

And then a blinding light.

CHAPTER 33

Hazel

A shuddering breath wracked Hazel's trembling body as the light from the Leabhar Feòla guttered out. She felt Gwen next to her and heard her release a heavy exhale. They were in class, safe from death and war. She touched her cheek, the sensation of something wet drawing her attention. She'd been crying.

The experience had been more than terrifying; it had been life-changing to see so many lives taken so quickly.

Rafe took her hand, but didn't look at her. He wiped away a tear too.

It's over. The schaden are dead. It's in the past. Hazel took a deep breath as she rubbed at her aching chest.

Except it wasn't.

The truth settled over her, quiet and cold. She was living, breathing proof that not everything was dead and buried. Seeing the abilities she had tapped into used in such a brutal, evil way had her questioning everything. She'd been convinced she was an elf, but the schaden had called the lightning the way Hazel could—and they'd used it for evil. To kill.

Am I a schaden? What even is that?

"We'll end the class here today to allow you to digest what you have witnessed," Thacker said, his voice more somber than usual. She wondered if it was because of his breakup with Gwen. "We will discuss your discoveries next class."

The thought of discussing what she'd witnessed made her stomach churn. She'd take this experience to the grave if she could. She was already an outcast because of Frank, and she'd done nothing but try to save her friend and Dane. No one could ever know that she had anything in common with the schaden.

"You alright?" Rafe asked her, finally releasing her hand. She'd forgotten he was holding it.

Hazel swallowed, missing the warmth of his touch already. "I think I will be."

His eyes searched hers. "I'm here if you need anything."

Rafe waited for Jordan while Hazel and Gwen stood to leave the classroom. They shared a wide-eyed look as they moved to the door. The weight of what they'd experienced hung between them, thick, heavy, and inescapable. Hazel wasn't sure what it all meant.

"Miss Bishop, stay behind a moment," Thacker called out.

Hazel paused, but Gwen didn't slow. Instead, she put her head down and ducked through the heavy door and into the corridor.

Hazel jogged to catch up with her friend. "Fuck him." Gwen deserved better. She still couldn't believe he'd called things off after they'd hooked up. And although Hazel was glad their relationship was over, she felt for Gwen.

Gwen nodded but said nothing.

When they were far enough down the hall, Gwen pulled her wand and cast the silencing spell. "Did you see the dragons and the lightning?"

Of course she had. How could she miss them? Bile rose in Hazel's throat as she prayed to Terra that Gwen hadn't drawn the same conclusions.

"You don't think..." Hazel started, afraid to finish her own question.

"You are *not* a schaden," Gwen said firmly.

Her words hung in the air between them. But how could Gwen know for sure? They didn't even know what a schaden truly was, only that they were bad enough to unite the Forsaken against them. A heavy silence settled between them as they walked across the south oval.

A new thought occurred to Hazel. "How long can therians live?"

Gwen blinked at the sudden change in conversation. "As long as mages," she finally answered. "We have the ability to heal but not live forever."

Hazel nodded, but before she could ask about the dragons, Gwen spoke up again. "I can't explain the dragons. I have no idea how they existed then *and* now. In all my research on therians, I've never come across any mention of them."

"I told you they were real," Hazel said, then gave her friend a playful nudge.

Gwen laughed. "You were due an I-told-you-so by now. Honestly, I'm surprised it didn't happen sooner. But don't expect it to happen again."

"I guess we have more research to do," Gwen added.

"Library?" Hazel asked.

Gwen nodded. "Yes, but I need to write a letter to my dad first. I'll meet you there."

Gwen's dad was a scary man who worked in the underbelly of the magical world and traded in secrets, from what Hazel understood. He definitely might have some information that could be useful, but it would kill Gwen to ask. That's how she knew Gwen was just as worried as her.

"Okay, I can just meet you there."Hazel's shoulders sagged as she remembered that the book Oswald had told her about hadn't been there yesterday when she'd looked. Or the day before. Not once in the last two weeks. She couldn't bear another disappointment.

If she wanted answers she was going to have to go straight to the source.

"Actually, I'm going to talk to Sorcerer Oswald. He's given me information on the Forsaken before."

While the library hadn't always been as forthcoming with information as they'd like, Oswald was the only professor to give her information on the elves. She hoped he'd do the same when she asked about the schaden. Even though Gwen was adamant Hazel was not one, the question still loomed over them both. They couldn't deny that the schaden had used lightning magic. And so did Hazel. They needed answers, and waiting to hear back from Gwen's father could take days.

Before she could rush off to find Oswald, Gwen stepped forward and pulled Hazel into a tight hug.

Hazel stiffened with surprise. Gwen didn't *do* hugs. But when Gwen held on for a moment, Hazel relaxed into it and returned the pressure with a grateful squeeze.

As Gwen pulled away and gave her a solemn nod, Hazel tried to smile but couldn't make her mouth cooperate.

If she's hugging me, this is bad. So very bad.

Gwen released the silencing spell and continued across campus to the dorms. Hazel watched her friend go, fear about what she might find rooting her in place. What if she *was* a schaden? Did that mean she'd become power hungry and evil like them? What would Gwen think of her? What would Rafe do?

The thoughts swirled in her mind well past when Gwen was out of view.

"That's the girl." The loud words snapped Hazel out of her downward spiral. "I heard she killed him."

Hazel looked up to see two coven members in matching green Circen shirts staring back at her as they walked by, not even trying to hide the fact they were talking about her.

Without a word, Hazel took off to the administration building.

Hazel took a deep breath to calm her nerves and then knocked twice on the narrow doorway of Sorcerer Oswald's office.

"Come in," he called through the door.

Oswald looked up from a pile of scrolls, a magnifying glass in hand, as Hazel entered the room and smiled.

"Miss Thorne." He paused, observing her closely. "Is everything okay?"

Oswald was probably the nicest, most sincere man she'd ever met. She knew him to be open and honest. If she could trust anyone to tell her the truth, it was him.

But then why was it so hard for her to ask him about what she'd seen today?

She eyed the chair in front of his desk, but decided against it, too anxious to sit. "What can you tell me about dragons or schaden?" Hazel half-whispered the words, as if speaking them aloud would make her fears come true.

Oswald's brows lifted until they almost touched his hairline. "Dragons and schaden?" Then he nodded. "I take it you've come from Sorcerer Thacker's class on the Leabhar Feòla?"

Hazel nodded, shifting from foot to foot.

"I thought I had prepared you for that." He interlocked his fingers as he set them on his desk. "Have you not checked out the book I recommended, Miss Thorne?"

Hazel flushed. "No, Sorcerer. It's been checked out since last semester. The librarian won't tell me who has it, so I can't even track it down and ask to borrow it."

Oswald shifted back in his chair and laughed softly, shaking his head. "Ah, yes. She does that sometimes—keeps things hidden."

Hazel's brows furrowed. *Why would the librarian keep things hidden?*

"Don't worry, she always puts them back. Go look again. It's probably there by now."

Given that Hazel had looked at least a dozen times, his words did nothing to ease her mind.

"Sorcerer, do you think you could just tell me about the schaden?" Desperation laced her every word. She needed him to confirm she wasn't one. If he could do that, she could research dragons on her own.

Oswald thoughtfully ran his hand over his long white beard. "I know that it's important to Sorcerer Thacker for you to come up with your own conclusions, but I can tell you a couple of things to make your research a bit easier. *Schaden* is a term that faded away due to society's erroneous preference for the unifying classification of siphoners."

"So you're saying that schaden are a subgroup of siphoners?" She'd considered the possibility that schaden was another name for siphoners, but the idea of a subgroup was new altogether. "So in order to be a schaden, one must be a siphoner?"

"Yes, that's correct," Oswald said. "But it's important to make the distinction that not all siphoners are schaden."

Is he saying not all siphoners are evil? Hazel clung to the lifeline he'd tossed her, praying that was true. *If* she was a siphoner, she needed to believe she was good and not doomed for evil.

Hazel's head spun from the truths they danced around. She wanted to come out and ask him, *Am I an elf or am I a schaden?* But that question would also be an admission that Hazel wasn't prepared to make nor ask Oswald to keep secret.

Hazel bit back what she truly wanted to say and simply murmured, "Thank you."

She left his office quickly, heart pounding against her ribs. For months, she'd been trying to figure out her new abilities based on the assumption that she was an elf. She'd only begun to accept it, to settle into the idea. And now, everything she thought she knew about herself was unraveling again.

The library greeted Hazel with its usual hush, but today, it felt heavier, like the building itself was holding its breath. As she walked to their usual table, her footsteps echoed across the polished stone floor. Hazel found Gwen wearing a deep frown on her face as she read from a book Hazel didn't recognize.

"Are you upset about Thacker?" she asked as she sat across from Gwen. She wondered what he wanted after class, what he intended to say to her and if Gwen was dwelling on that too.

"No, not everything is about him." Gwen rolled her eyes. "We have bigger things to worry about than my doomed love life. Right now I'm just dreading the fallout from asking my dad for information."

Hazel chewed her lip, unsure of what to say. She wasn't sure she could bring herself to write to her own father, even in the most dire of circumstances. Gwen was braver than her.

"I understand. I'm sorry you had to," Hazel said.

Gwen ran a hand through her white waves. "I just hope the price of his insight isn't too high."

"Whatever it is, I'm here to help." Hazel reached over to squeeze Gwen's hand. "What did you end up asking about?"

"I asked if he knew anything about dragon shifters and if there are any physical traits that might identify a schaden or a siphoner," Gwen said without looking up.

Schaden. Siphoner.

The words landed with a thud in Hazel's chest.

Please don't let the answer be raven-black hair and hazel eyes. Please don't let it be me.

Hazel wondered if Gwen was scared of her. But she was still here. Hazel exhaled, letting that truth steady her. Gwen hadn't turned her back on her. Whatever they were about to find out, they were going to face it together.

Gwen closed the book in front of her and added it to the discard pile before pulling another from the stack next to her. "Did Oswald help at all?"

Hazel explained the difference he'd given between schaden and siphoners.

"Well, that wasn't much," Gwen said. "But at least it gives us hope you might not turn out to be a complete psycho."

"Who's a psycho?" Rafe asked, rounding the bookshelf that secluded their favorite table.

Hazel and Gwen shared a quick glance. They were both in agreement that all talk of their identities was off the table. Hazel couldn't bear to think of how Rafe would react to finding out she possessed the same abilities the schaden did. Would he be afraid of her? Would he tell his father?

"The schaden," Hazel said quickly. "After what we've figured out about the blood magic, and now what we saw in class, we need answers."

Rafe's expression turned serious. "Can I help?"

The thought of telling him no crossed her mind. She wanted him to stay as far away from the truth about the Forsaken—about her—as possible. But the weight of his eager eyes, and the memory of the way he'd held her hand in class today, made it impossible to say no.

Hazel nodded. "Yeah. Of course."

"Where's Jordan?" Gwen asked as Rafe sat next to Hazel.

"With Elodie and Nova," Rafe said, rubbing the back of his neck. "They're studying in our room."

Gwen rolled her eyes. Hazel found herself doing the same.

Of the five people who actually *knew* what was going on with the attacks, only three of them seemed to care. Though she couldn't be sure Klaus wasn't doing his own research at Alterion. Hazel clenched her jaw against the spike of frustration. She didn't expect Jordan to understand the full weight of what they were dealing with—not yet—but it still stung. They could've used him. Gwen had said this was how he was when he started dating someone; Hazel understood now.

"What's the plan?" Rafe asked, glancing between them.

"Find anything on siphoners or schaden," Gwen instructed. "Then meet back at our table."

Hazel nodded, relieved Gwen hadn't mentioned the dragons. There was no way to explain why they needed that information without telling him about the exam. Their secrets were starting to stack up. Hopefully Gwen's dad would be able to shed some light on the dragons, since they wouldn't be able to research them tonight.

They each claimed a floor and split off without further discussion. Hazel's stomach twisted as she headed towards the fourth floor to find Oswald's book. She wasn't sure if she wanted to find something or nothing at all. The higher she climbed, the quieter it got. Not only were there fewer students, but the lighting was dimmer and the air was dustier.

The floor was empty. The only sounds were her own footsteps and the soft rustle of her coat. Dusk filtered in through the windows along the back wall, painting the room in fractured gem tones.

She made her way to the aisle where Oswald's recommended text was supposed to live.

Please be here. Just this once.

The rows on the fourth floor felt endless, but Hazel knew exactly where she was going. She'd walked this path more times than she could count since she'd seen her mother last semester. She didn't hold her breath, hoping for a glimpse of her mother. The woman had never returned to the library. Not once. And Hazel's visions always took place in daylight. With dusk seeping through the stained-glass windows, she doubted there was any chance of a sighting.

The deep, rich scent of old paper filled Hazel's nose as she turned down the right row and read the spines. A part of her hoped it would be there. Another small part hoped it wasn't. She bent down to look at the low shelf, and shock zinged through her as she took in the book. It was nondescript, wrapped in green cloth with faded gold lettering. The book was average-sized, and there was a ribbon down the center, like a diary, or a religious text.

Her hands shook as she plucked it from the shelf and ran her finger down the title. *Spellcraft and Scholarship*. Her breath hitched as a thrill shot through her, battling the dread pooling in her stomach.

She couldn't wait long enough to get back to Gwen and Rafe. They might ask questions. She needed to look first, to prepare herself. Hazel lit the end of her wand and held it over her head to see the text within the room's dim lighting.

Dust fluttered from the pages as she opened it, particles floating in the light from her wand. She turned the cover back with the utmost caution for fear of damaging the spine. The pages were thick and yellowed, which was highly unusual for a text at SEU. Most were enchanted to protect them from aging in such ways. On the second page, there was a handwritten date on the inside from twenty-five years ago.

That's when Mom was here.

She turned to the next page. It had only one line.

To those who seek the truth regardless of how hard it might be to learn. May your eyes be forever opened.

A chill ran down Hazel's back. She knew what it was to want to dig your head in the sand.

Footsteps echoed through the empty floor. Hazel leaned to her left to glance down the aisle, but no one was there. She leaned to the right and she caught a glimpse of a tall, thick silhouette darting between the shelves.

Hazel shifted quickly to the other side, but there was no one there either. "Rafe?"

No answer.

The dim chandeliers that hung in the center of the room flickered, then went out. The floor was plunged into darkness, leaving only the dusky-hued colors of the stained-glass window and the light of Hazel's wand.

The footsteps moved closer.

This wasn't the first time she'd felt like someone was with her on this floor, but this time, her gut screamed at her to move.

She quickly extinguished her wand to hide in the darkness and forced air through her nose to quiet her breathing. She tucked the book to her chest and moved to the far wall, opposite of where the silhouette had headed. Keeping her back to the wall, Hazel tried to observe from all directions as she made her way toward the staircase. She made it to the darkest part of the room, the epicenter between the dusk light filtering through the stained-glass window and the light from the lower floors weakly reaching up the stairs.

Her heart pounded against her ribs as she approached the shelf that bisected the room in two. While the path was clear, the shelf was solid, meaning anyone could be standing on the other side and she wouldn't know. She took a deep breath to steel herself. Her nerves buzzed with adrenaline, and it reminded her that she had a weapon no one could expect. Hopefully it wouldn't come to that.

She pulled the electricity in the air tightly around her like a blanket, and then bolted.

As she passed the shelf, a hand wrapped around her arm, the one that held the book.

It *burned.* It felt as though her skin was melting away.

She screamed and released all the power she'd built up into her attacker before yanking her arm away. The book fell from her hands as her attacker hit the ground with a groan.

Hazel ran toward the stairs. She dared only the briefest of glances over her shoulder. The tall silhouette was moving backwards, dissolving into the darkness of the room.

She panted as she reached the top stair, turning to see if she was being pursued. The faint outline of the book in the center of the floor tempted her to go back, but it was a risk she couldn't take. She could be on this floor with the person responsible for Frank.

Hazel stumbled on the staircase more than once on her descent due to looking back over her shoulder to see if her attacker had changed their mind about following her. She thought she saw a shadow at the top of the stairs for a moment but didn't allow herself to stop to confirm. Once back on the second floor, she ran through the aisles to reach the study table. Rafe and Gwen lifted their heads as Hazel rushed toward them, huffing for air.

Rafe pulled out the chair next to him and Hazel sat down. Brows drawn together, Rafe asked, "Are you okay?"

"There was someone up on the fourth floor with me. The lights went out and they came after me," Hazel whispered as she looked around. It could have been anyone.

Gwen immediately stood to study the direction she'd come from.

"I never saw who it was, but I thought it was you at first, " Hazel added, glancing at Rafe.

Rafe studied Hazel's arm where she held it gingerly. "What happened?"

Hazel rolled up her sleeve to find red, angry flesh in the shape of a handprint on her arm.

Gwen gasped, pulling herself from the chair to come closer to inspect it. "You look like you've been burned!"

"I feel like it too." Hazel touched it gently and winced.

Rafe pulled out his wand and cast a soothing spell Hazel had never heard before. The burning subsided immediately. After a few moments, the red faded to pink, though the shape remained.

"How did you get away?" Rafe asked, his face full of concern. His hand rested on Hazel's as he waited for her answer. His thumb made little circles on her wrist. He made her feel safe, and it felt good, so Hazel didn't pull away. She should have. She knew better than to toe this line with all the secrets she was keeping from him, but she leaned into it.

"I'm not sure. I screamed when they touched me and I think it scared them." She paused. Hazel's eyes went directly to Gwen, communicating without words what she didn't want to say. "Maybe they were worried someone would hear me? Whatever it was, they backed off."

Rafe looked puzzled, but Gwen didn't push. Hazel wanted to change the subject.

"Should we leave?" Rafe asked. He didn't look scared. His set jaw made him look angry as he looked around the floor.

Gwen sat back down. "No. Whoever is behind this is a coward, and they only try to come after people they think they can overpower. They're not brave enough to take on all three of us."

Rafe looked at Hazel, and she nodded her agreement.

"Did you find anything?" she asked as she helped Rafe and Gwen stack their books.

"Actually, yeah," Rafe said, pulling a book out of one of his stacks. "This one's saying blood can boost spell power and accuracy."

Hazel glanced up.

"According to the book, siphoners started using it to amplify spells they were too weak to cast on their own."

"That makes sense," Hazel said. Siphoners were like mages, who used earth magic, except they possessed the powers of telepathy and manipulation. "We use blood to claim enchantments. It binds the magic to you. Makes it personal."

"Exactly," Rafe said. "But—" he paused, tapping the page, "what actually *makes* a siphoner a schaden isn't using blood in spells. It's *drinking* it."

A breath of air escaped Hazel's lungs. Her shoulders slumped slightly as tension left her. She hadn't crossed that line. Not yet, not ever.

There was no way she was a schaden. Siphoner or elf—that was the question.

Rafe continued, "Siphoners can go their whole lives enhancing spells. But once they start drinking blood—feeding off it directly—they begin to change. That's when they evolve into something else."

Not all siphoners are schaden.

Oswald's reasoning for the distinction became abundantly clear to Hazel. Schaden made a dark, twisted choice to steal blood for power, while siphoners rejected the temptation.

Schaden is a term that faded away due to society's erroneous preference for the unifying classification of siphoners.

Yet history painted siphoners like monsters anyway. But why? Hazel felt as though they'd been handed a puzzle without all the pieces.

"Did it mention anything about siphoners and lightning?" she asked, unable to stop herself.

Rafe shook his head, flipping a few pages. "No. There's nothing about any powers aside from unparalleled mind control."

It was known that siphoners could perform emotional manipulation, even compulsion. Hazel had shown none of those abilities. Maybe she wasn't a siphoner either.

Damn it, if I hadn't dropped that book, I would know for sure!

She thought about asking Rafe and Gwen to go back with her to get it, but was unwilling to put her friends at risk. They had no idea how to fight a siphoner, or a schaden.

Hazel leaned in closer, resisting the urge to take the book from him and see the information for herself. "So what, schaden just got better at it after drinking blood?"

Rafe nodded, his finger trailing the lines of text as he read. "Their powers became so strong that they were able to control their victims even after death."

"Just like Frank," Gwen said.

The three of them shared a look, then Rafe turned the page.

"When feeding from magical victims, they were able to claim any magical abilities as their own until the undead connection deteriorated."

Hazel's gaze locked on to Gwen's and a silent understanding passed between them. The pieces of the puzzle, unsettling as they might be, were now snapping into place with terrifying clarity. The resurrected slain soldiers they'd seen in the Leabhar Feòla. The lightning the schaden had possessed only after raising them from the dead.

The schaden had controlled an undead elf who possessed lightning powers.

An immense weight lifted from Hazel's shoulders. She wasn't a siphoner. She was an elf.

"So are we actually saying we think a living, breathing schaden is responsible for Frank?" Rafe asked, incredulous. He didn't know what they knew: that the Forsaken weren't all gone like history claimed, at least not therians and elves. And if therians and elves were real—if *dragons* were—then what else was?

"And Mara," Gwen added.

Rafe ran a hand through his hair as he processed the information. After a moment, he said, "We have to be mistaken. If any of the Forsaken were still alive, the Brecilian Knights would know. My dad would've told me."

"I wouldn't count on that," Gwen said, crossing her arms.

Rafe looked like she'd slapped him. This conversation was dangerously close to information Hazel—and Gwen—didn't want Rafe to know yet.

"Okay, let's back up here. Are you saying that only schaden would drink blood and could control the dead?" Hazel asked, brows furrowed in thought.

"Well, the book is saying that," Rafe clarified. "Which makes the person behind these attacks either really dumb or really..." he trailed off.

"Really what?" Hazel asked.

"Really intentional," he finished.

"What do you mean?" Gwen asked.

"The whole world thinks the Forsaken are extinct. If they *do* exist—and I'm not saying they do—but if they do..." Rafe took a deep breath like he was bracing himself for what he was about to say next, "then maybe the attacker wants the rest of the world to know. Maybe they're tired of living in the shadows."

His words sent a dagger of fear into Hazel's heart—fear for Gwen and fear for herself. If schaden were discovered, how long would it be before their secrets were revealed too?

CHAPTER 34

Gwen

The scent of herbs and simmering tinctures hung heavy in the dorm kitchen, clinging to Gwen's sleeves and hair as she stirred a thick green liquid clockwise for the required fifth rotation. Potion-making was soothing for her—tedious, yes, but controlled. Predictable.

She and Hazel had been brewing off and on since their trip to the library after Harland's class last month. They'd found nothing in the books about how to fight off a schaden or siphoner, but they weren't planning to be caught off guard again. With two new reports of missing mundanes, they needed to be more prepared than ever.

The continuous attacks weren't doing anything to help their reputation, but on the plus side, hiding from her classmates also made it easy for her to avoid seeing Harland outside of class.

Unfortunately it also meant they couldn't afford to slack off. They'd gotten lucky with Frank, thanks to Hazel, but they couldn't solely rely on her. She was only one person, and she couldn't be everywhere at once.

If only they could figure out how to bottle lightning.

Potion duty fell to Gwen today, and she didn't mind. She'd roped Klaus into helping while Hazel scoured the library for anything they could use against this deranged psycho—that's what they were to Gwen. If Rafe was right, and they wanted to be caught, then they had a death wish, because that's what was waiting for them when the Brecilian Knights discovered their existence.

"The rumors shouldn't still be circulating. It's March. The gossip should've died out by now," Klaus said.

Gwen sighed as she double-checked the measurements for the next ingredient. "We've been over this, Klaus. Every time someone goes missing, the accusations pick back up. There's literally no one else to blame in their minds. Hazel and I are the easiest ones to point a finger at."

"But that's my point!" Klaus slapped the countertop. "I think someone out there is stirring the pot, trying to make you two the scapegoats."

Gwen stirred the elixir with a copper spoon and took a deep breath. "I have enough conspiracies to deal with right now." If Klaus was right, and she ever found out who was behind it, they would pay. But until they had evidence, she couldn't worry about it or it would drive her crazy. "Let's focus on the things we can actually do something about."

She shoved an empty vial at Klaus to give him something to do. They were extracting the elixir from the pewter cauldron when a sharp tap echoed from the window. Pan.

Gwen crossed the room and unlatched the pane, letting the hawk hop inside with a rustle of feathers. He extended one leg, and she quickly untied the tiny scroll fastened to it. She recognized her father's handwriting immediately.

As for your first question, there have long been rumors about dragons, but no evidence since the end of the Great War. For the second question, there are no clear physical traits until the transition has fully taken place. After enough blood is consumed, retractable canines are acquired.

If you suspect someone, stay far away from them. Tell me immediately.

Be careful, Gwen.

She rolled her eyes at the last line. Her father's protectiveness wasn't new, but it always came with the creeping assumption that she *wouldn't* be careful unless reminded.

Of course they don't have any major physical characteristics.

She'd been hoping for a wart on their nose, or something equally overt. Still, the part about the canines was useful. It might come in handy if they ever got close enough to see while they were protracted.

Fat chance.

What stood out to Gwen the most was that her father didn't deny their existence, siphoners *or* schaden. He knew they existed and had never told her. Gwen didn't know whether to be angry or thankful she hadn't spent her life being suspicious of everyone she ever met. For the first time in her life, Gwen understood a secret her father had kept.

"What does dear old Dolphus have to say?" Klaus asked.

Gwen shoved the letter at him as he finished corking the last vial. "Take a look for yourself. I need to go update Hazel—she's been anxious waiting for the letter."

Klaus nodded as he began to read her father's message. Gwen grabbed her jacket, checked that the burners were off, and headed out the door.

The hall outside the dorm was quiet, only the faint hum of distant conversation echoing down the stone corridor. Gwen moved quickly out of Poe Hall and into the north oval, weaving around a cluster of freshmen without a word. She had no patience for distractions.

Of course, that was exactly when one found her. A shadow swooped overhead with a shrill cry that made her duck instinctively.

"Oh shit," she muttered, realizing a second too late what was happening. The bald eagle dive-bombed her like she was prey, talons extended. She didn't get her arm up fast enough. Pain slashed across her shoulder and upper back as its claws sunk in. She hissed through her teeth and stumbled forward, finally thrusting her arm out in frustration.

"Here! Damn it!"

The eagle moved down to her forearm with perfect grace, like she was the one who'd ruined the landing. A letter was tied tightly around its leg, which Gwen removed. With a soft flutter of its wings, the eagle pushed off and took to the sky again, talons missing her face by inches this time.

"I hate eagles," she mumbled darkly, watching it disappear across the rooftop of the building.

With no one around to see, Gwen slipped off her bracelet long enough to heal the fresh scratches on her back. Warmth spread along her skin as the ache eased. She rolled her shoulder, satisfied, and slipped the bracelet back on as quickly as she'd removed it.

Gwen looked down at the letter, and narrowed her eyes as she recognized the handwriting written on the envelope.

What now, Harland?

After momentarily considering tossing it into the trash, Gwen's curiosity won out and she conceded to reading it. She'd been successfully avoiding him for nearly two months now. She sat in the back of each class and never raised her hand or even answered when he called on her. He'd tried to make her stay after each class, but she always ignored his request. She'd managed to go without a single interaction with him. Cutting him out cold turkey had been hard at first, but she knew it was the only way.

So she'd leaned into hating him, because pining after him wasn't going to help stop the ache.

Gwen pulled the letter from the envelope.

Miss Bishop,

Your delinquency from your first two advisor meetings of the semester has been noted. Check in during my office hours today to avoid probationary action.

Gwen didn't read any further.

The fucking audacity of this guy!

The door clanged shut behind Gwen as she stepped into the history building. The lack of student chatter made the echo feel intrusive, like a loud noise in the middle of a church service. Gwen wound her way through the halls, working herself up into a frenzy as she mentally practiced putting Harland in his place.

The wind in her sails deflated slightly at seeing a student waiting outside of his office. Abigail wasn't in History of the Great War, but Gwen remembered her from Glyph Decryption last semester. She was a quiet, thin girl with mousy brown hair and porcelain skin who wasn't one for confrontation.

"Hey Abigail, I have to speak with Sorcerer Thacker. It's urgent and will only take a second. Can I go first?"

Abigail gave Gwen a wide-eyed look. "Sure, I'm not in a rush."

Gwen rolled her eyes. Great. She believed the rumors too. She resisted the urge to play into Abigail's fears, knowing it would make things worse, but she was getting tired of everyone being afraid of her. She needed to do something to make them stop talking about her. If something didn't break her way soon, she would. If it weren't for her friends, she already would have.

She muttered her thanks as the door opened and a student she didn't know emerged. She pushed past them and slammed the door behind her.

Harland sat at his desk, wearing a white button-up rolled up at the sleeves and his bewitched spectacles. He looked up at her, and Gwen stopped short.

Salem, she hated how attractive he looked. His mahogany desk was littered with papers and Gwen was overcome with a memory of him pushing everything to the floor, setting her on it, and kissing her deeply.

She swallowed, pushing the thought away.

"Miss Bishop, I'm glad to see you today."

"I can't say the same." Gwen threw his letter at him. The balled-up paper hit him in the chest.

He didn't blink, his attention never leaving Gwen. "I'm sorry you're upset. I think we can be—"

"You've made it clear there's no 'we.' Consider this my formal request for an advisor reassignment," Gwen said as she crossed her arms.

Harland leaned back in his chair, mirroring her posture, but his face remained neutral. "It's too late in the year for a reassignment request. We'll be done the first week of May. Surely you can be mature enough about this to last until then."

Gwen narrowed her eyes at him. *Fuck you.*

"Let me make this clear." She leaned in toward him and tried not to let his scent smother her anger. "Whether I get a reassignment or not, this is the last time I'm coming to see you. Here or anywhere. I don't care whether you reassign me or excuse me from our visits for the rest of the year, but unless you want me to go to Chancellor Lucas, you'll pretend you don't know me."

Harland stood from his chair and leaned over, placing his hands on his desk. His eyes searched Gwen's intently as the muscles in his forearms flexed under his weight. The taut muscles brought back memories of their night together on his kitchen counter, his lean body on top of hers, making her tingle from the inside out. She wanted to feel it again.

"We both know that isn't really what you want, Gwendolyn."

His words broke the spell his close proximity had been weaving. He'd used her name, and while she'd loved it every time he'd ever said it before, she saw it for what it was in that moment.

A manipulation.

"You're right, it's not. But you've already proven you can't give me what I want."

With that, Gwen stormed out of the office without a look back. She put her head down to hide the tears she fought back as she walked down the hall, praying she didn't run into anyone. She'd been so stupid about him. About trusting him.

She wished she never had to see him again.

Then she remembered—she still had his key. She dug it out from the bottom of her bag, fingers closing around the familiar shape. Turning around, she headed back towards his office. Realizing it would probably hit with a much more satisfying *oomph* than throwing that stupid letter had, she picked up her pace.

She flung open his door without a knock, forgetting all etiquette. As the door swung wide, she saw Harland hovering over Abigail, who sat unmoving in a chair, her back against the wall. He was close enough to kiss her.

What the fuck?

His key slipped from her fingers, dropping to the floor with a loud clank as shock coursed through her. Harland froze and made eye contact with her as he lifted his hands.

"What are you doing?" Gwen's voice shook with fear. She didn't know what she'd walked in on, but she knew it wasn't good.

"Gwen, this isn't what it looks like."

"I'm not even sure *what* it looks like." Gwen's voice shook as she asked, "Abigail, are you alright?"

Abigail didn't answer. She simply stared at Harland, a vacant expression on her face, as if she hadn't heard Gwen. As if Gwen wasn't even there.

"What are you doing to her?"

"She's in a trance. She can't hear you, but I assure you, she is perfectly fine."

She wanted to believe him, but it looked so off. Gwen's hand flicked to her bracelet as she studied the scene. Her gut told her something was wrong.

Her fingers touched the clasp—and she was thrown against the wall. A second later, Harland's hands were around her throat and her feet no longer touched the floor. Pain seared up through her neck and into her head from the strain. He looked down where Gwen fought to unclasp the hook of her bracelet.

"I wouldn't do that if I were you," Harland warned. His voice was deep and commanding, unlike anything she'd heard from him before.

Her hand dropped to her side, and he lowered her enough that she wasn't dangling, but he was still very much in control. His breath warmed her skin and he smelled like oak and leather. His scent alone made her quiver. She could feel her knees weakening with such close contact and cursed her body for betraying her. He moved closer to her until their lips were nearly touching. His hand moved from her throat to her jaw and then his thumb was on her mouth, gliding over her bottom lip. When he moved it back to her jaw, his lips were on hers.

The kiss was soft at first, then, both of them hungry for one another, it became rougher.

He moaned her name. "Gwendolyn."

A warmth spread in her chest at the sound of her name emitted from his lips while her instincts screamed at her to run. Her arm hairs stood on end as the heat from his touch ran up her throat. A burst of electricity bolted from her lips, shocking them both.

"Ow!"

Harland touched his lip as if checking for injury where she'd shocked him. A look of betrayal covered his face when he saw her bracelet dangling from her fingertips. She'd managed to get it off during their kiss.

Gwen had no clue how she'd shocked him, but she was thankful. It jolted her back to reality like an ice bath. To Abigail who hadn't moved or said a word.

"This isn't what it looks like," Harland said, reaching for her again.

Gwen dropped into a low crouch, hands braced against the floor, weight coiled in her limbs. She didn't look like a wolf—she looked like a predator. Lupine. Fluid. Ready to strike. If he wanted to touch her again, he'd have to come down to *her* level, and down here, he'd be at a disadvantage. This was her territory.

Harland hesitated, blinking as he registered the shift in her posture. Slowly, he lowered his arm and straightened, masking a flicker of unease behind a smirk.

"Well played. You're better on all fours than I am."

She ignored the innuendo and let out a low warning growl. "I'm leaving here with Abigail." Her voice was steady, but the threat beneath it was unmistakable as she moved closer to her classmate.

Harland moved with her, placing himself squarely between them. His voice hardened. "You most certainly are not." He eyed her warily, as if she might bite. She would. "I think we can come up with a better outcome than that, Miss Bishop."

Gwen considered her options. If she shifted and was able to attack him, she could become a danger to Abigail, which would potentially leave them all worse off than they were now. Her best choice was to escape and get help.

She remained crouched in an attack position but began to change footing, never looking at the door, as to not give her intentions away. She trained her eyes on him until her back was nearly touching the door. All at once, she leapt to a standing position. Thacker threw his arms up to protect himself, but Gwen fled. She skirted sideways across the threshold as his eyes widened in realization. Then she turned her back and ran. She didn't risk a glance back. Just a tiny distraction could cost her precious seconds in speed and balance, so she kept looking forward and ran as fast as her legs would carry her.

She took the stairs two at a time until she was out of the history building. The open landscape of the oval gave her some sense of security. People turned and stared at her as she flew across the grass, legs and arms pumping like the trained runner she was. When she finally made it to the library doors, she threw them open and ran straight towards the table she knew her friends would be at. As she passed the other students, they turned to look at her and whisper. She didn't have time for that right now. She was getting sick of all the rumors. With the wide berth the other students gave her, she quickly made it to Hazel, who luckily sat alone. Rafe was nowhere in sight.

Hazel turned to her as she approached, eyes wide in confusion and then alarm as she took in Gwen's fear.

She slid on her bracelet as her wolf clawed at her mind, trying to protect her. The library was not the place to shift. As soon as it settled, Gwen cast the silencing spell.

"What's going on?" Hazel asked, grabbing on to Gwen's arm.

"I saw Sorcerer Thacker doing something to Abigail from our Glyph Decryption course."

Hazel began to blush. "By something, do you mean—"

"No," Gwen began. Was that what she meant? "Well, actually, I don't know what I saw, to be honest. She didn't seem to be able to hear me, though. He said she was in a trance."

"What the—" Hazel's eyes widened as she looked over Gwen's shoulder. "Oh shit, he's here."

"You know nothing," Gwen instructed as she hastily dropped the spell.

She spun, resting her arms behind her back. On the outside, she looked nonchalant, but in reality, she was readying her wand. Her fingers kneaded the onyx stone of her wand as he approached.

"Miss Bishop, I need to speak with you for a moment." He

sounded as if it were any other day. As if she hadn't caught him with Abigail. As if he hadn't held her by her throat. As if he hadn't kissed her against the wall.

How had she not seen it? How good he was at pretending.

"You can speak with me right here," Gwen retorted.

"In private."

"No."

He looked at her as if he was dealing with a petulant child. His tone was soft and patient as he said, "It will only be a minute. We can stay in the library, if you prefer." He gestured to the left side of the stacks behind their table. "There appears to be an empty aisle." He cast a spell, sending students running from the bookshelves.

Gwen studied the section he'd cleared. It was in Hazel's line of sight. The library was full of students. The problem was, he was a sorcerer with years on her. As talented as she was in combat, she'd never fought this man. He could be her match, and she couldn't rely on her wolf in such a public place where people could see, let alone get hurt. She could say no, she could refuse, but then that would push him to escalate the situation. What if he detained her on some trumped-up charge and she was left alone at his mercy once more? No, remaining in the library was the best choice.

She looked back at him with narrowed eyes. "Fine, but that's as far as I go."

"I'll come with—" Hazel started.

Harland looked at Gwen, cutting his chin to the side.

Gwen shook her head. "No, Hazel. You stay. If I'm not back in five minutes, go get help."

She prayed it didn't come to that.

Harland gestured to the aisle next to them, a flick of his finger indicating Gwen should lead the way. Typically, that would've been fine with her—she preferred to lead—but after what she'd witnessed today, the thought of having Harland at her back made the hairs on her neck stand up. Absolutely not happening.

"You first," Gwen insisted, her voice tight.

Without a word, he moved towards the towering shelves, the dim light of the library casting long shadows that flickered with his every step. Gwen followed reluctantly, the faint scent of aging parchment and ink thickening the deeper they went. He didn't stop at the first row, or the second, weaving through the labyrinth of books until they reached the farthest wall, a secluded alcove where prying eyes couldn't spy on them.

Gwen crossed her arms as he cast a silencing spell. She wanted to be annoyed with him for removing them so far from Hazel, but she knew it was to her advantage too. She had her own secrets to protect, after all.

As much as she wanted to unleash the raw words of fury trapped in her throat, she thought of her training and worked hard on squashing her reactionary tendencies. Control—always control.

"I know it looked bad—" Harland began.

"You think!" Gwen snapped, her words sharper than broken glass. It had looked illicit, immoral, yet Gwen still had no idea what had actually occurred.

"I'm only doing what's necessary to keep everyone safe. I need you to trust me." *The last time I trusted you, you broke my heart.* She wasn't about to make that same mistake twice. She crossed her arms tighter and kept her face cold.

"I'm working on interrogating students per Chancellor Lucas's orders. If you tell anyone, it will jeopardize everything."

"You expect me to believe that the chancellor gave you permission to put students under a spell without their knowledge?"

The skepticism sat heavy on her tongue, but inside, a small, stubborn flicker of hope clung to the excuse, desperate to believe he wasn't the predator she feared he might be. Maybe, he really was trying to find the person responsible for all the deaths.

Harland raised a brow at her. She gritted her teeth. Okay, so it was true that Gwen had learned Chancellor Lucas didn't play by the rules. But withholding information and actually bewitching students were two totally different levels of rule-bending.

Harland sighed, pinching the bridge of his nose. "Gwen, if you tell, the chancellor will punish you. She already wants to send you home after Frank. Don't push her hand."

Surprise rippled through her, making her stomach lurch. "I had nothing to do with Frank!"

"I know." His gaze was steady. "But she thinks you're easy enough to blame. It might make the true culprit feel complacent enough to slip up, which Lucas would love to happen." It was like he was saying the words from memory, from a real conversation he'd had.

Her nails bit into her palms as she worked to hide her fury. "That bitch," Gwen muttered. Was she the one responsible for leaking Frank's death to the university too? The thought made her chest tighten.

"I know you don't want to leave." He paused, his eyes softening as he said the next words. "I don't want you to leave either."

"Yeah, you made that real clear." Sarcasm dripped from every word.

"That's not fair and you know it. I only said we needed to slow down. You're the one who ended us."

"You said it was a mistake." She couldn't believe she was having this conversation with him here but it needed to be said. Or that he was defending himself and blaming her. Her eyes started to water at the memory and he reached for her but then dropped his arm as he looked around realizing he couldn't be seen consoling her.

"That's not what I said and you know it. You are not a mistake, we were not a mistake. I just think we moved faster than we should have. Being back here after spending the holidays with you in my house where we could exist freely..." He paused, searching gaze and sighing at what he saw there. "It was harder than you realize."

Gwen wondered if he meant it or if he just thought that's what she wanted to hear. *No! I won't let him suck me back in.* She strengthened her resolve to continue hating him. She wouldn't let him break her again.

"I can't do this with you here, now."

He nodded in understanding and she saw a flicker of hurt flash across his face. But she couldn't worry about that right now. She had more pressing things to concern herself with, like her place at SEU.

"What do you suggest I do about the chancellor? Because I can't go out there and lie to everyone. I don't have it in me, like you do, apparently."

"I can help you, if you'll let me."

Could she let him? She searched his face for some hint of deceit, but all she found was raw intensity.

"What did you have in mind?"

"A simple spell. It won't remove the memory. It will only make it where you can't talk about it."

Gwen's stomach twisted. "How do I know you won't just erase my memory anyway?"

"Because I could accidentally erase us." He looked briefly down at her lips and then back to her eyes again. "And that's not a chance I'm willing to take."

Gwen chewed her bottom lip, her heart pounding in her chest. Maybe if he did erase her memories of him, it would make things easier, but she knew he wouldn't because she could see the sincerity in his eyes. The risk was low and she needed to stay at SEU to watch over her friends.

Finally, she swallowed hard. "Okay, do it."

Harland gave a relieved smile, pulled out his wand, and aimed it at her. "*Verba Flectere.*"

A faint shimmer passed between them like heat off pavement. The air rippled, then stilled, but everything else remained the same.

"Tell me about what you saw today," Harland instructed.

Gwen narrowed her eyes as she thought about her wording. "I walked in on you being a huge creep to Abigail."

Except that wasn't what came out of her lips. "I saw you tutoring Abigail in your office."

Her breath hitched. *What the actual fuck?*

Gwen tried again. "You're a creep—"

But she said, "You're a great—"

Gwen stopped, shocked by the effects of the spell.

"If you try to speak of what you saw today," Harland said quietly, "the truth will elude you each time. You'll tell a lie in its place."

Gwen's stomach churned as the weight of it settled over her like a net, invisible but unyielding.

Then she decided to say something about him that didn't happen today.

"We had sex," she said matter of factly, the words coming out just like she'd intended. So the spell *did* only work if she tried to talk about Abigail.

A bright and wide smile lit up his face. "We had great sex."

"We had mediocre sex," she lied and then stormed off back to Hazel, breaking the silencing bubble.

Hazel

Hazel grew restless as she waited for Gwen. She split her attention between the clock on the library wall to keep track of the time and the aisle where she could see the outline of Harland and Gwen through the shelves. One minute passed, then two. She'd give them five minutes and then she would go after them. Something was off. She'd never seen Gwen so worked up—and that was saying something, given all the shit they'd been through this year.

Hazel had issues with Thacker's abuse of power over Gwen, but she'd always kept her mouth shut. She didn't want to lose Gwen, and besides, she understood the need to make your own choices, even if they were wrong. But maybe it wasn't just Gwen. Maybe there were others Hazel should have been looking out for this whole time.

Guilt swelled in her chest as the seconds ticked by like hours. Hazel waited exactly five minutes and then drew her wand.

But before she could even stand up, Gwen emerged from the aisle, Harland nowhere in sight. Hazel sighed, her heartbeat slowing as she took in Gwen's calm demeanor.

Gwen approached the table and flashed a tight smile. "I'm exhausted. I'll see you back at the dorms."

She's joking if she thinks I'm waiting for these details. Perhaps she didn't want to speak about it in the library. Not that it had stopped her before.

"Okay, I'll come with you."

Gwen nodded and waited for Hazel to pack up her books. Hazel studied Gwen's face, looking for any sign of anger or distress, but Gwen looked perfectly neutral. Calm, even, which was not how she typically looked after an encounter with Thacker.

As the girls walked across the oval toward the dorms, Hazel finally asked, "So what happened?"

Gwen blinked at her. "What do you mean?"

Nothing about Gwen's face said she was playing dumb, but there was absolutely no way she didn't know what Hazel was talking about.

"What did Thacker say?"

"Hazel, that's really none of your business."

Gwen had always been an open book, this was not like her. Thacker must have blackmailed her or worse.

"Did he threaten you?" Hazel whispered.

Gwen laughed manically. "As if anyone could threaten me. I promise you I can take care of myself. I just don't have to tell you everything, so drop it."

She felt like Gwen had slapped her.

They'd shared everything, every tiny little detail of their lives since Gwen had shifted in front of her. Hazel's throat tightened. Her steps slowed half a beat before she matched pace again, gaze fixed firmly on the ground. She didn't say another word. Her fingers tugged at the hem of her sleeve, over and over again, and she nodded in the right places as Gwen talked about her dad's letter all the way back to the dorm.

Gwen set her bag down and took a seat on the couch before covering up with a blanket and reaching for a book. All seemed right in Gwen's world.

It didn't make any sense.

Gwen had been scared when she'd found Hazel in the library today. If everything was okay, then great, but there had to be an explanation, a resolution. Why was Gwen dodging?

Is she pretending? Is she worried that if she tells me, something bad will happen?

Hazel played it over and over in her mind as worry gnawed at her. She needed to know what happened in the stacks. With so much going on around them lately, she couldn't risk brushing this off.

She thought about how to broach the subject again. While Gwen hadn't wanted to share her conversation with Thacker in the stacks, she *had* wanted to share what she'd seen at his office. If Gwen had brought it up with her before, it was safe—and only fair—for Hazel to bring it up now.

"Did you find out why Abigail was in Thacker's office?" Hazel asked. She braced herself for the backlash.

Gwen's brows drew together. "Abigail?"

"From Glyph Decryption."

"Oh, yeah. She was there for some tutoring."

"Since when do professors tutor?" Hazel asked.

Gwen stood, shaking her head. "Hazel, not everyone is as smart as you. A lot of students need tutoring," she bit out, taking Hazel aback.

Hazel didn't understand why Gwen was getting upset. *She* was the one who'd come to Hazel freaking out about it only minutes ago.

"You thought something weird was going on when you found them," Hazel explained in her defense.

Gwen shrugged. "I was overreacting, being dramatic because I was jealous," she said playfully, all frustration absent from her tone.

Hazel's mouth popped open. Never in her wildest dream would she have seen Gwen take ownership of a flaw or mistake—not even jokingly. The words were so unlike Gwen, Hazel almost laughed.

"I just need to let it go."

Hazel felt like she was living in a parallel universe. Since when had Gwen *ever* let anything go?

With that, Gwen went to her room and shut the door, cutting off any further communication on the matter.

Hazel sat in stunned silence, unsure of what the hell had just happened, but positive that Thacker was behind it.

CHAPTER 35

Gwen

"Chug, chug, chug!" Jordan chanted, banging his hand on the table as Gwen downed her elixir in one go. They'd arrived at the Incantor party a few minutes ago to find the music pulsing through the floorboards and laughter spilling from every direction. The ruzo finals had taken place that afternoon between Alterion and Incantor. Alterion had come out on top, but Incantor had played them the closest game in school history, only losing by one point in overtime. Despite losing, Incantor celebrated the accomplishment happily.

Hazel had left her a note saying she'd meet them here, but Gwen hadn't seen her yet.

To be honest, Gwen wasn't sure she wanted to see Hazel. She needed to enjoy herself, let loose, and quit dwelling on stupid mistakes, but Hazel had taken every opportunity over the last month to bring up Harland and Abigail, which left Gwen feeling guilty from the lies Harland's spell spouted from her lips.

Gwen slammed down her empty glass with a dramatic flourish, harder than intended, nearly shattering it. Jordan whooped and threw an arm around her shoulders, pulling her in. She let herself lean into him, nuzzling her temple against his shoulder with an unbothered grin. She'd missed him.

Jordan had been absent most of the semester and Gwen hadn't realized how much she'd felt that gap until now. Between the entire university still giving them the cold shoulder, hiding a secret from Hazel, and Klaus's busy coven schedule, Gwen had begun to feel incredibly lonely. Even tonight, the partygoers gave her a wide berth and the whispers continued. But she didn't care.

While part of her was frustrated with Jordan, the comfort of having him back, wrapped around her like old times, pushed away any negative thoughts. Things felt right for the first time in over three months.

"Apparently, you two have to be drunk to be nice to each other," Rafe commented dryly, raising his drink.

Gwen threw a napkin at Rafe but missed.

Ignoring Rafe, Jordan finished the rest of his drink. "Do you want another?"

Gwen shook her head. Her blood hummed in her veins, all of her troubles melting away.

Jordan headed toward the bar, leaving her with Rafe.

Two girls from class walked up and started flirting with him, taking every opportunity to glare at Gwen. *Oh good, more haters.*

They whispered something in Rafe's ear and he blushed.

"Sorry, I can't. I'm hanging out with a friend."

"Aw, I'm sure she can spare you for a couple minutes," the blonde one pouted.

"No—"

"Sure I can," Gwen said.

Rafe cut her a glare, clearly not wanting to go with the girls.

"You go have fun! Jordan will be right back."

Rafe rolled his eyes, and Gwen winked at him as she waved him off. There would be hell to pay for that later, but she couldn't bring herself to care as her favorite song came on. Gwen danced to the music, letting her eyes drift close and her other senses take the lead.

"Where'd Rafe go?" Jordan asked, slipping his arms around her waist like it was the most natural thing in the world. After ending things with Harland, it was nice to be wrapped in someone's arms. Someone safe and familiar.

Gwen leaned back into him slightly, resting against his chest as she nodded toward the far side of the room. "Over there."

Rafe was seated at a low table, deep in a round of tarot, surrounded by a group of girls. She heard a collective giggle come from them at a card he'd drawn. By the sad look on Rafe's face, he'd not had nearly enough to drink yet.

"What's up with Rafe tonight?" Gwen asked.

Jordan's chin brushed the top of her hair as he gestured toward the front door. "Why don't you ask Hazel?"

Gwen looked to find Hazel entering the Incantor house. She started to hang her coat on the rack but stopped, keeping it draped over her arm. Hazel scanned the room and Gwen gave her a little wave. Hazel rushed over, cheeks flushed and breath short.

As she walked toward them, the conversations in the room didn't stop, but thinned, fracturing into uneven whispers. All night, Gwen had felt the way eyes slid over her like she wasn't really there. But now they stuck, landing on Hazel with sharp scrutiny. Gwen clenched her jaw. It had been easier to ignore her classmates when it was just her. She could pretend it didn't bother her, that she didn't notice the way they talked about her. But watching it happen to Hazel—seeing her best friend walk straight into the storm—was different. It was infuriating.

"I'm so sick of everyone staring," Hazel muttered under her breath when she reached Gwen and Jordan. "They did it my entire walk over here."

Gwen smirked as she locked eyes with one of the offenders across the room, holding their gaze until they looked away. "Cowards."

"When are they going to stop blaming us for Frank's death and the missing people?" Hazel's voice was tight. "This secret is getting harder and harder to keep."

"Yeah, well, short of me ripping out all their throats, there's not much we can do about it," Gwen said.

Hazel huffed out a humorless laugh.

Gwen looped her arm through Hazel's. "Come on. You need a drink." She tugged Hazel toward the bar, her tone light but her grip steady. "Let them stare." Gwen had learned a long time ago that people would think what they wanted. She'd never been the type to care what these people thought.

"You've had enough," the Incantor bartender told her. "Limit's two drinks."

Gwen rolled her eyes. "It's not for me."

The mage handed Hazel an elixir, then they headed back to Jordan, who was no longer alone. Nova and Elodie stood on either side of him, laughing at something she couldn't hear.

Great. Her perfect night was ruined. Nova and Elodie hadn't spoken to Gwen or Hazel in months and it stung more than she cared to admit. Now, they would steal Jordan away for the rest of the night.

"Here, I don't want this." Hazel gave Gwen her drink.

Gwen finished it in one gulp as she strolled up to Elodie and Nova. She was sick of being ignored—by everyone. She was going to put an end to it right now. She wrapped her arms around Jordan, and he took a step away from her.

"Seriously? You were fine to have your arms around me before she showed up," Gwen said.

"Gwen, stop." Jordan glanced at Nova.

"No. I'm tired of the dynamics of our friendship changing every time you find a pretty girl. I don't do that to you, because at the end of the day, you have always come first."

"You've never had a boyfriend!" Jordan yelled a little too loudly, making heads turn. His voice lowered as he continued. "It's not the same, and maybe one day, you'll allow a guy to be more than just a fuck boy. Until then, I don't want to hear your criticism on how I'm a shitty friend to you when I'm trying to be a respectful boyfriend."

"Maybe I think you're a shitty friend because you never even told me you two were together."

"You're right," Nova finally spoke up. She laid her hand on Jordan's shoulder. "We should have told you."

"Oh!" Gwen said, throwing her arms wide, not caring that the entire room was watching. "So now you're speaking to me? No thanks." Gwen started to back away. "I don't need friends who abandon me at the first sign of trouble."

Gwen stormed off toward the bathroom, and Hazel tried to follow.

"I need a minute," Gwen said, barely able to get the words out.

Hazel looked like she wanted to hug her, but instead, nodded in understanding before she headed back toward the group.

Luckily, there was no line, so she was able to run in and slam the door before her tears fell. She wasn't trying to come between him and Nova. Maybe she was being unfair in how she'd finally stuck up for herself, but she wasn't wrong that he was being inconsistent in their friendship, and with someone who had dropped her like a bad habit. No, she, Hazel, Nova, and Elodie hadn't been the best of friends, but she'd thought they were close enough that they would have bothered to ask her or Hazel if the rumors were true. Both Jordan and Nova's actions felt like betrayals, each causing their own festering wounds that Gwen was done ignoring.

Beep beep beep. The familiar sound of the Wilderness Watch compact alert sounded, but Gwen didn't have her compact on her. It had to be someone else's.

"Great, what is it now?" a shrill voice asked outside the bathroom door.

Gwen listened closely as worry spiked through her. *Please don't be a missing hiker.*

A moment passed, and a resonant voice answered, "They called off the search for the hiker that went missing in February."

"Is she alive?" the shrill voice asked.

Gwen knew the answer in her gut, but she held her breath and hoped for a different outcome anyway.

"Dead."

Gwen closed her eyes as memories of Frank's corpse flashed in her mind. She felt sorry for whoever had found her. Seeing something like that would keep anyone up at night.

"Great. They're definitely going to close down the town for tourism after this," a third voice spoke, their tone laced with annoyance. "There goes our free tuition and board."

Yeah, worry about your precious tuition while people are dying, you piece of shit. Gwen knew it wasn't fair to be angry at them—they didn't know the truth like she did—but she was sick of making excuses for people when no one allowed her or Hazel any.

"If they could figure out what's happening to these people, we could try to prevent it," the resonant voice said.

Someone scoffed. "Have they tried asking Hazel Thorne or Gwen Bishop?"

The people listening laughed in agreement.

Gwen clenched her fists at her sides, fury tightening her muscles as she stood by the door. She'd been pissed off by one too many things tonight, but this was the final straw. It was time to leave.

Hazel

Hazel didn't want to drink, not when she was in enemy territory. Alcohol was not the smart choice right now, nor some mysterious party elixir.

Jordan was on the dance floor with Nova. He didn't seem that upset about the fight he'd had with Gwen. She suspected Gwen wouldn't be getting over it that quickly. Elodie joined the dance floor with a cute guy from their history class. Hazel scanned the room for

Amelia and saw her talking to another girl across the room. *I wonder what happened between them.*

As Hazel stood off in the corner of the room, she felt the sensation of being watched. Several groups whispered around the edges of the room and she caught more than one person staring at her.

She finally spotted Rafe in the kitchen. He leaned against the counter, bobbing his head to the music that filtered through the coven house. He seemed lost in the song, completely unaware of the world around him. Hazel was drawn to him like a moth to a flame, wanting just an ounce of his carefree attitude.

"Hey," Hazel said.

Rafe opened his eyes and bestowed her with a megawatt smile that made her heart flutter. She'd never seen him smile so big. "Hey, Hazzzel," Rafe slurred. His eyes were relaxed, sleepy, even as he stared deeply into her eyes.

"I thought the cut off was two drinks?" Hazel asked teasingly.

Rafe lifted his finger to her mouth, pressing gently. "Shhhhhh."

His skin was warm against her lips and she liked it. Before he could break contact, Hazel grabbed his finger, lowering it but still holding on. She grinned in response to this silly, intoxicated side of him she'd never seen before.

The scent of nostalgia in the form of a honeysuckle flower washed over her.

"What have you been drinking?" Hazel reached for his cup. Whatever it was had him acting quite out of character.

He brought it to his lips and finished it before she could take it from him. "It's a secret." He leaned in a little more, his breath now smelling like strawberries. *I wonder if he tastes like it too.* "Incantor's specialty."

Hazel's curiosity withered. *Great. No telling what's in that drink.*

"How about I get you some water?" Hazel asked.

She began to move around the counter, but Rafe's strong arm snaked around her waist.

"No," Rafe leaned down and whispered. "Wait."

Butterflies took flight in her stomach as he pulled her softly against his hard, large frame.

"For what?" Hazel murmured back, lost in the sensation of his lips grazing her ear.

"I have a secret." The warmth of his breath on her skin made her shiver in anticipation.

"Do you want to share it with me?" she whispered back, swallowing down the want that filled her.

"Mmhmm." His lips were blue from the drink. He looked like a kid who'd just finished their popsicle. "But I shouldn't."

"Tell me the secret, Rafe." Hazel knew it was unfair to try to get information out of an intoxicated person, but she couldn't stand not knowing.

"I love you, Hazel." The words sounded like a promise and a revelation all at once. He giggled slightly after saying them, then sighed contentedly, as if relieved to have them off his chest.

Hazel went stiff in his arms. While the words sent a thrill through her, she also knew they couldn't be true. He'd never made a move—not really—and never asked her out. He wouldn't have said that to her if he was sober.

"I love you too, Rafe." She patted him on the shoulder and took a step back.

He hadn't meant to hurt her, but he had. Those words were so precious to her and yet they weren't real.

"No, not like that!" He grabbed her hands.

Their gazes met, and all Hazel could see was earnest devotion in them. Her breath hitched. He looked at her as if she was the sun itself.

"I'm *in* love with you, Hazel." His words were so adamant, they put a crack in her doubt.

The declaration sent warmth coursing through her while shock settled deep in her belly. She desperately wanted it to be true.

"You," he said, sliding his hands down her arms and linking their fingers, "are perfect."

The words hit her like a bucket of cold water, waking her from the fantasy she'd been lost in.

He doesn't even know me. Not really.

She'd been hiding the truth—lying to him—for months. That wasn't perfect. That wasn't deserving of love.

Rafe deserved so much better. Someone who was honest about who they were.

The thought of him with another woman landed like a knife to the heart and she flinched.

Rafe lifted her hand to his lips, but Hazel pulled back out of his grasp. He looked as though she'd slapped him.

"What are you so scared of, Hazel?" His question was followed by a hiccup, but it didn't take away the sadness in his eyes.

The hurt on his face filled her with guilt, but Hazel knew that closing this door now was better for him in the long run, no matter how much it was killing her. She couldn't tell him the truth, and so she said nothing at all.

Hazel bolted into the living room, running straight into Gwen.

"What's wrong?" Gwen asked, eyes scanning the room, body tensed like she was ready to fight.

"Nothing," Hazel said quickly as tears filled her eyes. "We need to go."

Gwen nodded in agreement, but as they approached the door, almost in the clear, someone said, "Good riddance."

Hazel spun around to grab Gwen by the wrist. "Ignore it."

Gwen shook off Hazel's grip and approached the girl who'd spoken. "You seem to always have so much to say unless it's to my face. Please, feel free. Speak up."

The girl looked away this time, saying nothing else.

Gwen smirked. "That's what I thought." She breezed past Hazel and left the house.

The girls walked in silence for several minutes. Hazel was lost in the events of the evening, buried under a mountain of emotions that made her miss Gwen's turmoil.

“Thanks for nothing back there,” Gwen bit out.

Hazel was taken aback. This wasn’t on her. “What did you want me to do, Gwen? As always, you were making a big enough scene for the both of us.”

“I won’t apologize for being brave enough to stand up to them. One of us has to.”

After Rafe and now Gwen, Hazel had had her fill of everyone saying whatever they felt like to her. She wasn’t scared. She wasn’t afraid. She was careful and intentional. And there was nothing wrong with that. If anything, they each needed to take a page from her book.

“You say brave, I say reckless. Making stupid mistakes doesn’t make you brave, Gwen. It makes you irresponsible.”

Gwen recoiled. “Is this about Harland?”

Hazel laughed bitterly. “Well, it would definitely be easier taking life advice from someone who hadn’t slept with our professor.”

“Keep your voice down!” Gwen hissed.

“Why, Gwen? I thought you were sick of secrets?” Hazel bit out sarcastically.

Gwen’s face hardened. “Fine. How about I tell yours?”

Hazel stilled. She knew Gwen wouldn’t, but the casual way she threatened to pissed her off. “Go ahead,” she said quietly, then added, “You haven’t exactly kept your own very well. Why would I expect you to be any better at keeping mine?

Gwen’s eyes went wide and hurt flashed across her face. Hazel’s blow had landed right where she wanted it to. But the second it did, she regretted it. Before she could take it back, Gwen straightened, and whatever hurt had flickered in her eyes vanished. Her expression hardened into a mask of fury.

“Well,” Gwen said coldly, “maybe I wouldn’t have had to blow my cover if I wasn’t so busy saving *your* life, while *you* were off chasing after a mom who clearly doesn’t want you.”

Hazel stood frozen in place, blinking against the sudden sting in her eyes. She wanted to scream, to throw something, to rewind the entire night and walk away before any of this had ever happened. Instead, Gwen turned on her heel and walked off, leaving Hazel trembling on the sidewalk, her whole world collapsing around her.

When Hazel reached the dorm room, Gwen's door was closed with no light shining underneath.

Fine with me.

She didn't have the energy or the strength to try and patch things up. Not tonight. Maybe not ever.

Her hands trembled as she changed clothes, every movement slow and numb. Crawling into bed, she pulled the blankets up to her chin like they might shield her from the weight pressing down on her chest. She stared at the ceiling, but all she could see was Gwen's face, twisted with rage. All she could hear were the words they'd hurled at each other like weapons, words that cut deeper than anything their classmates had said. Gwen had been her anchor. Her best friend. The one person she could turn to when everything went wrong. Now Hazel wasn't sure if there was anything left between them but ash.

She turned on her side, curling in on herself. The ache in her chest wasn't from the fight—it was from the realization that she truly had no one now.

CHAPTER 36

Gwen

Gwen stepped into History of the Great War alone, the soft murmur of conversation and rustling parchment filling the room. Her gaze swept across the lecture hall and landed on Hazel, already seated in the back on the opposite side of where they usually sat.

So this is how it's going to be.

Clearly, Hazel was still mad. Which, honestly, was fine. Gwen was still pissed too. She took her usual seat, shoulders stiff, and dropped her bag beside her chair. A moment later, Jordan walked in and made a beeline for Elodie and Nova, laughing at something one of them said as he slid into the open seat between them. Rafe trailed in behind him, hesitating for a second, then joined their group without a word. Gwen blinked, then gave a dry, bitter laugh.

Hazel might be giving Gwen the silent treatment, but it looked like she wasn't the only one Hazel had managed to alienate last night. Rafe wasn't sitting with her either. Well. At least they were alone together. Gwen leaned back in her chair, arms crossed as she stared daggers at the back of Jordan's head from across the room.

"Alright, today, we'll be talking about the treaty. As you all know by now from reading your textbooks, the signing of the treaty for the Great War was held right inside this very mountain."

A few students gasped, as they clearly hadn't done the reading assignment. Harland ignored them and continued with the lesson.

"During the signing, the leaders of each faction gathered here in an effort to create peace. But when the mages got here, the Schaden refused to give up blood magic. In turn, the fae, elves, and therians refused to relinquish the dragons under their control. The mages were forced to do the unthinkable to protect themselves against such powerful, untrustworthy beings. They cast a spell wiping out all non-mage demi-humans—the Forsaken." His eyes landed on Gwen. Tension rolled off of her.

She'd grown up hearing it over and over at Bathurst—the Forsaken were the worst of the worst. Dangerous. Twisted. Corruptible. Mages were taught to look down on them, to fear them, and feel righteous in the choice that had been made long ago. But at home, her mother's voice had always offered a softer truth. *"You're good, Gwen. No matter what your heritage is."*

Still, those warnings from Bathurst had sunk deep. And now, sitting in this classroom, listening to the same old narrative play out—mages as heroes, the Forsaken as threats—it all rang hollow, given everything she knew now about the role the fae, elves, and therians had played in the war to take down the schaden. For the first time, Gwen heard the story for what it really was: revisionist history. The mages weren't the only good guys, no matter how hard they tried to paint themselves that way.

For a moment, Gwen was glad the other students were ignoring her. *Fine. Let them.* But then she thought of her family, and her mom's quiet reassurances, and she realized just like not all Forsaken were evil, not all mages were either.

"And that concludes today's lesson. Please review your syllabus and be ready for the exam next week," Harland reminded them.

Gwen must have zoned out, because somehow, class was over.

She stood and stormed out of the classroom, boots pounding against the floor loud enough to make people turn. A few students gawked as she passed, but she didn't care. She stared them down, eyes sharp.

Say something. I dare you.

Harland didn't stop her. He hadn't asked her to stay behind since she got that letter from him. And for some reason, that bothered her more than it should've.

She paused as she reached the oval. She didn't want to go back to the dorm. Not with Hazel there. Not after everything that had passed unsaid between them. So she went to the library.

All the tables filled up throughout the day except hers. Even with all the other tables now full, her classmates chose to sit on the floor rather than join her.

That's fine. I don't want them sitting with me anyway.

She'd gathered every book she could find on schaden. She'd put her boots on the table and crossed her legs, in an attempt to show how unbothered she was. Someone knocked them off, and she looked up, ready to unleash her irritation as Logan sat down across from her. They hadn't spoken since that day in the secret Alterion library.

She hadn't missed him. He was the reason she was no further in her search for fera information.

"What are you doing?" Gwen asked, glaring at him. His sandy-blond hair was longer than the last time she'd seen him, and it hung down into his warm green eyes.

"Studying, and I don't want your boots in my face."

"Then sit somewhere else."

Ignoring her, he started rifling through the books on the table until he found one he was interested in. His strong hands flipped through the delicate pages with ease.

"Hey, those are mine."

His eyebrows rose in challenge, a clear invite to try and stop him. While she could, the last thing she needed was another enemy.

Gwen cleared her throat. "You can borrow it."

He laughed, a low rumble moving through the library. The sound gave Gwen goosebumps.

"Why are you sitting here?"

"I told you, I'm studying." His biceps flexed as he swapped his book out for another from her pile.

Gwen's jaw clenched. She didn't like him touching her stuff.

"Didn't you hear I'm shunned?" Gwen asked.

"I don't listen to rumors," Logan said with a shrug.

Gwen looked up from her book and studied him. He seemed serious. "Even before rumors, I didn't think you liked me."

He said nothing, and made no movements to indicate he was leaving.

The silence frustrated her, so she dug in.

"Well I don't like you either."

Gwen noticed the room had fallen silent, unnaturally so. There was no rustling of papers, nor squeak of chairs. He must have cast a silencing bubble around them to keep out prying ears.

Gwen felt his gaze on her, the weight of its dominance challenging her. She returned it, and was surprised to see a flash of hurt fill his eyes. There and gone in an instant.

Maybe he wasn't as unaffected by her as he wanted to seem.

"I don't like being vulnerable or relying on others. You knowing my secret puts me at great risk," Logan said.

"You know mine," Gwen countered, also hating being vulnerable or relying on someone she barely knew to keep her secret.

He grunted in reply, indicating tit for tat didn't bring him much satisfaction. Gwen knew he preferred the upper hand, simply because she did.

It occurred to her that now might be the perfect opportunity to warn him about the blood magic users. After all, she wasn't the only one in danger. And, maybe, sharing this big moment would show him that she was trustworthy.

"I have something I need to tell you. Can you keep the spell going a bit longer?"

He nodded, leaning into the table.

"This is going to make me sound crazy, but I think you have the right to decide for yourself."

She told him the truth about what had happened with Frank. When Harland's spell didn't impact her ability to tell the truth, she told him about the chancellor and the promises she'd been forced to make to keep her spot at SEU. The words came out as she intended, true and direct, so she kept going. When she explained what they'd concluded about schaden, Logan studied her with furrowed brows. When she was done, she was sure Harland had kept his word, that only her discoveries about Abigail were off limits.

"You're right, it does sound crazy," Logan said, leaning back in his chair.

Gwen picked her book back up and scanned to find her spot. "Fine, don't believe me. I just thought you ought to know the truth."

Regardless if he believed or not, a weight had been lifted from Gwen's chest.

"I didn't say I didn't believe you."

Gwen met his gaze. "So you do?"

"I didn't say that either."

Gwen rolled her eyes. He was infuriating. *Why did I even bother?*

Logan crossed his arms. "You've had months to process this information and you're giving me minutes."

Gwen hated that he was right.

"Give me time," Logan said.

With that, the sounds of ruffling pages and students murmuring all came rushing back to her. He was done discussing the subject.

After several hours of working in silence, Logan finally got up to leave. "Watch your back," he said, the only indication that he might actually believe what she'd said earlier.

She nodded. "You too."

He'd almost made it to the library's exit when Gwen noticed Serena approaching him.

"You're awfully brave," Serena said, perfectly loud enough for Gwen to hear. Maybe she wanted her to. "Haven't you heard the rumors? She killed someone."

He didn't defend Gwen, not that she'd expected him to. "I think you need to be worrying about your own *affairs*, Serena. I've heard the rumors about you too."

Serena's jaw dropped and then he was gone.

Gwen had to stifle a laugh. Telling Serena off was as close to defending Gwen's honor as Logan was going to get. She could use all the allies she could get right now so she'd take it.

She'd been there for hours and needed to stretch her legs. Walking down the history aisle, Gwen searched for any other books on schaden with no luck. A few aisles over, Gwen heard Hazel's voice.

"Wait! Come back."

Who could Hazel possibly be talking to?

Gwen moved closer to find out. But no one was there; it was only Hazel, talking to herself.

She must be losing it.

"No, don't leave," Hazel said to the air in front of her, and then she took off running through the library.

Gwen followed, but froze when she saw a figure appear that looked eerily like Hazel from behind—tall with onyx hair, in a purple cloak. Hazel stopped, too, but when the figure disappeared into thin air, she started running again.

Merlin's balls! We're both losing it. Shaking her head, Gwen took off after her.

Someone stepped out from an aisle and Hazel smacked straight into them. The man, sporting dark-green paisley robes and a long white beard, stumbled a few steps backward, eyes wide in bewilderment.

A noise down the aisle on Gwen's right drew her attention. Was it the disappearing woman? Momentarily torn between announcing herself or answering to her natural instinct to hunt, Gwen ducked into the row of books to investigate.

Hazel

"Sorcerer Oswald, I'm so sorry!"

Hazel glanced around for her mother, but there was no sign of her. She sucked in a deep breath as the facts hit her—here one moment and gone the next. Refusing to answer her calls or pleas, as if she didn't even know Hazel was there.

What if her mother wasn't ignoring her? What if she couldn't even hear her? She didn't want to believe it—she'd rejected the idea the first time it had crossed her mind and hadn't allowed herself to consider it again since Oswald's initial class on shadowsong—but now the possibility overwhelmed her as the evidence stacked up. Had her mother been a ghost all this time?

"Miss Thorne, are you okay?" Oswald studied her closely.

Hazel nodded, numb and only half listening as she processed the idea of mother being dead.

"As awkward as the timing is, I'm glad I ran into you," he said. He pulled out his wand and cast a silencing bubble.

"You—" Her understanding of words was delayed, her mind bogged down in a battle between disbelief and logic. "You are?" she asked finally, confused. Technically, she'd been the one to run into him.

"Yes, I wanted to see if you've had a chance to read that book I suggested."

Hazel looked down, ashamed that she'd still failed to read the book. She cursed herself for the millionth time for dropping it. Every time she'd returned to look for it, it was gone. Whoever had attacked her had probably taken it. She wished to Terra she could figure out why.

"I haven't gotten a chance yet, Sorcerer. The book is still missing."

"Hmm." He thought for a moment. "So you haven't been able to deduce what you are yet?"

Hazel froze. Was he actually going to confirm that he knew what she was?

She didn't respond, keeping silent to not give away anything. Plausible deniability.

He chuckled. "You're just like her."

"My mother?" Hazel's lips quivered as she asked, his question bringing back thoughts of her mother and whether she was alive or not.

"No, I'm speaking of your aunt, Evelyn."

Hazel furrowed her brows, his words snapping her out of her inner turmoil. Her mother had never mentioned any resemblance, but it made sense; they were family.

"While your mother was an excellent student, she didn't have half of the power Evelyn did. You remind me so much of her, it's like seeing a ghost." Oswald laughed.

Hazel balked. "I've always been told I look like my mother."

Sorcerer Oswald chucked. "Well, they were twins, after all."

Twins? Hazel sucked in a breath. Her mother had spoken many times of her youth and how much she'd missed her sister, but she'd never mentioned she was her twin.

Why had she kept that from us?

Hazel felt lightheaded as she considered how little she actually knew about her mother. She'd thought it had just been her magic that had been kept a secret, but there was so much more.

Did I even really know her?

"It's the way you carry yourself, though, that is the true similarity, and why I say you remind me of Evelyn." Oswald stroked his long white beard. "Her death was truly a tragedy."

"Yes," Hazel said absently. Her mind was still buzzing with the new secrets Oswald had revealed and the idea that her mother's spirit might be around the corner. "My mother always told us the cancer took her quickly."

Oswald stilled and angled his head as he narrowed his eyes at her. He clearly had an issue with what she'd said.

"What is it, Sorcerer?" Hazel held her breath, completely unsure of what to expect.

"I think you need to ask Evelyn about her death."

Hazel nearly choked on the answer. "Excuse me?"

"Haven't you seen her?"

"Seen her? She's—" Hazel stopped abruptly. Her eyes widened as the implication of his words sunk in. She turned to look behind the sorcerer, then back the way she'd come, finding no one and nothing but books and shelves in sight.

"I'm sure you have. She's the most popular ghost on campus, and the most mischievous." Sorcerer Oswald gave her a wicked grin. "I'm pretty confident she's the one who keeps hiding the book I sent you after."

Her mother wasn't dead. Her breath hitched as relief filled her. It was Evelyn she'd been seeing, not her mother

"Why would she hide the book, Sorcerer?" Hazel asked.

"Precisely! Why?" He waved his wand, breaking the silencing spell. "I have a class I have to get to, but if you have any questions, please come find me."

He left her with more questions than answers.

She finally understood Gwen's love of history and her obsession with her ancestors. Because now she wanted it too—the truth buried in old texts, the stories etched into bloodlines, the names and faces of those who came before. Her ancestors. Her people. Who she was.

She'd been so worried about her mother, she'd never yearned for a connection with anyone else until now.

She had to tell Gwen.

But then she remembered they were fighting and the horrible words they'd said to each other. Hazel had played on Gwen's fears of being an out-of-control fera and Gwen had attacked her by saying the one thing that would cut her the worst. She didn't know how they would forgive each other, and Hazel's heart ached.

It was hard enough being hated by her best friend, but to top it off, Rafe hadn't spoken to her since he'd confessed his feelings. Jordan hadn't looked at her since he and Gwen blew up at each other. She wasn't just not talking to Gwen—she wasn't talking to *any* of their friends. There was no one to tell. Thinking about it now, their issues seemed so small compared to everything else going on right now.

I want my friends back.

She'd find a way to fix their friendship, all of them.

CHAPTER 37

Hazel

Hazel glanced at the clock hanging next to the fireplace in their dorm living room. It was getting late. It had been hours since she'd seen Gwen studying in the library. She had no idea when she'd be back —*if* she'd be back—and the silence was starting to press in on all sides. Thick. Suffocating. Hazel had hoped to talk to her tonight. To fix things. To undo the rift they'd created the night of the party. It had been days since they'd spoken, and with every minute that passed, Hazel felt more alone. But more than that, she missed her friend.

The waiting and anticipation made it impossible to sit, so Hazel started to pace around the living room. If Gwen was not home in five minutes, she'd move on to plan B.

When the long hand moved from three to four, Hazel grabbed her coat and slipped out the door. Gwen wasn't the only friendship that needed repairing. So she made her way through Poe Hall until she found herself in front of a familiar front door. She took a deep breath to steel her resolve and then knocked.

A few moments passed before Hazel heard the deadbolt turn and the door opened wide enough for Jordan to stick his head out. With a wary expression, he glanced up and down the hall—looking for Gwen. As far as Hazel knew, they hadn't made up either.

"It's just me," Hazel promised. "Can I talk to Rafe?"

Jordan's face softened. "I don't think he's ready yet, Hazel."

"I need—" Hazel began, but Rafe's deep timbre sounded from the other side of the door and she stopped.

Jordan stepped back with a nod. Rafe took his place and stepped through the door, pulling it closed behind him.

He rubbed the back of his neck as he avoided her gaze. The welcoming smile that would have typically greeted her was nowhere to be seen, and it dug the empty, dark hole growing in Hazel's heart a little deeper.

"Hi," Hazel said softly.

The warm brown eyes she'd missed so much finally met hers. She didn't see the coldness, or even anger, she'd been expecting. What she saw could only be described as shyness.

"Wanna go for a walk?" Rafe asked.

Her heart soared with the request. Hazel nodded, not wanting to word-vomit her happiness all over him.

As they walked through the halls of the dorms, the usual easy rhythm between them was replaced by a heavy, unspoken tension. Rafe's hands were shoved deep into his pockets, and he stared straight ahead. Hazel realized it might not be that easy to go back to how things used to be. She opened her mouth to speak, but the words caught in her throat. The silence stretched, each passing second feeling like an eternity as they walked the rest of the way through the building. She'd never been so uncomfortable in his presence before, and she hated it.

As they exited Poe Hall, she followed Rafe down the steps.

"Rafe, I can't take this anymore," she blurted out before they made it to the sidewalk. "Tell me how to fix it."

Rafe spun to stare into her eyes, his own wide with confusion. "Fix it? Hazel, you haven't done anything wrong. I did."

Hazel shook her head. "You'd been drinking. I'm not going to hold that against you."

"It was a bit more than that." Rafe closed his eyes, taking a deep breath before continuing. "I was on gossamer serum."

Hazel's brows drew together as she considered the truth of his words. He'd been so giddy, so silly. The symptoms of gossamer serum fit perfectly. The freeing feeling of having all doubts removed was reportedly exhilarating. That was, until reality set in and lives were ruined. Anxiety served a purpose. It kept your mouth shut and your body intact and on the ground.

"How did you even get that?" It wasn't something anyone should be handing out recreationally.

Rafe squeezed the bridge of his nose as if it hurt him to even recall it. "Dane Bellamy offered it to me."

Hazel gaped. "You took a potion from Dane Bellamy? Rafe!"

Rafe sighed. "I know. I thought it was harmless, but I didn't realize that serum also has a truth-telling component."

She was going to kill Dane.

"Are you sure it wasn't—"

"Everything I said that night was true." Rafe looked into her eyes intensely, a raw vulnerability visible as he studied her expression for a reaction. Hazel wanted to look away, to make a joke and play it off, but knew that wouldn't work. Not this time.

"Can we just wipe the slate clean? Pretend you never said any of it?" Hazel asked, nearly pleading.

Sadness flashed across Rafe's face, and she looked away. She understood his pain because she felt it too. She didn't want to be asking this of him. Not only was Rafe the kindest, sweetest man she'd ever known, but she also felt the same about him. Their time apart these last few days had made her realize she wanted to be with Rafe, every second of every day, to feel his lips against hers and his hands on her skin.

But Hazel's conscience told her that it was wrong to move forward with Rafe in that way while lying to—or keeping secrets from—him. And so she endured the pain she was causing them both in hopes of keeping him in her life in some capacity.

"Can I show you something?" he asked, his voice full of hope.

Hazel nodded. While they walked, she tried to block off her heart from the feelings that could go nowhere. Selfish hope bloomed in her chest that maybe they could move past what happened and let things go back to the way they'd been. She'd spent days without him and couldn't bear it a second longer.

She resisted the urge to fill the silence as they walked. Rafe led her toward the back of the Poe Hall and onto the grass between the dorms and Coventry. They continued on toward a cluster of trees that lined the cavern walls.

"Where are we headed?" Hazel asked. Her curiosity outshone any tension she felt. For a moment, it was almost like old times—them together, off on an adventure. They were just missing Jordan and Gwen.

Rafe smiled mischievously, taking Hazel by surprise and filling her with warmth. "I don't believe it," he said. "I actually know something that Hazel Thorne, smartest mage of our class, doesn't know."

Hazel gave him a playful push. "Yeah, yeah. Tell me."

"No, I think I'll let it be a surprise."

Hazel rolled her eyes, although she delighted in seeing his playfulness emerge.

Rafe wound a path between the trees, leading them to the cavern wall. The area was coated in moss and ivy, unlike the bare walls near the administration building.

Rafe stopped and turned to Hazel. His smile was wide now, like a little boy on Christmas morning. It was endearing and beyond charming. Hazel couldn't resist matching it.

"What are we doing here?"

Rafe reached an arm out toward the lichen, never taking his eyes off Hazel. He dipped his hand within the growth and then pulled the whole section back like a curtain.

She stepped forward, her chest brushing against Rafe's as she peered into the opening. It was so dark she couldn't see anything.

"What is this place?"

"Do you trust me?" Rafe asked, a wicked gleam in his eyes. He was really enjoying this.

Hazel swallowed and nodded.

He offered her his upturned palm, and Hazel slid her hand into his without hesitation because she *did* trust Rafe. He linked their fingers, and she silently reveled in how much bigger his hands were than her own. They were rough, and the thought of what they'd feel like against the rest of her body came unbidden to her mind, but she tried to push it out immediately, even though heat curled low in her belly.

Rafe stepped into the dark opening, holding the curtain of greenery back to pull Hazel into the small tunnel with him. Once she was inside, he allowed the curtain to close and they were enveloped in complete darkness.

Hazel reached for her holstered wand, but Rafe stilled her with his free hand.

"We don't need the light," he explained.

"It's pitch black in here."

"Not for long." He guided her forward.

Hazel pressed into Rafe's side as they followed a bend in the tunnel. Her cheeks warmed in response to his firm muscles moving against her, and she was thankful he couldn't see her face.

As her eyes adjusted to the dark, she realized there was a dull, blue light emanating from the path before them that grew faintly brighter as they progressed.

They reached another curtain of greenery, but this one was backlit by the soft blue light.

Rafe pulled the curtain back, and Hazel's jaw dropped as she took in the scene. A huge cavern lay before them, filled with three large pools of water, each glowing an iridescent blue. The space was warm and humid. Steam wafted from the pools and drifted lazily about the cavern.

She'd never seen anything so beautiful.

Rafe led her to the left pool, which looked to be the smallest, but Hazel found it was actually the largest, half hidden behind the encroaching cavern wall. Rafe slipped around the edge of it, pulling Hazel with him.

Hazel gasped. Above the pool was a ceiling of the bioluminescent mushrooms they'd seen during the mine cart trip into the exam and also all over the closed Mutari coven.

"I thought movement lit them?" Hazel asked, amazed.

"It's the steam from the hot springs. It keeps them activated."

"Incredible," Hazel said.

Rafe released Hazel's hand and moved to climb up the small boulders that lined the edge of the pool. He stood at the top and offered his hand to Hazel again. His smooth skin and dark hair were illuminated by the bluish-green brilliance of the mushrooms, making him look stunningly ethereal.

Yes, Rafe was a catch. He deserved someone who could be with him without hiding anything.

Despite knowing better, Hazel found herself desperate to take his hand back. She bit her lip when the warmth of his skin enveloped her once more. As she stepped up onto the rock, her feet seemed to sink into the surface, and she realized it was covered in a soft moss.

"How have I never heard of this place?" Hazel asked.

Rafe chuckled. "It's an upperclassmen secret."

"Then how do you know about it?"

"Alterion is pretty set on having me," he said, flashing her a smile that practically twinkled in the glow.

His words, *having me*, echoed in her ears, and she understood why they wanted him. Rafe was tough, magically talented, and smart. But more than that, he was loyal, and Alterion valued a pack mentality above all the other covens.

"Will you get in trouble for showing me?"

Rafe shrugged. "Worth it."

Hazel laughed. They were so alike but so very different. Rafe fought none of the anxiety Hazel carried around daily.

Rafe's face changed as he listened to her laughter. His eyes became desperate, like a sober man who had a drink set before him. He swallowed, his gaze fixed on her lips. "I missed that."

"Missed what?" Hazel breathed the words, filled with a sudden, fierce hunger to know his every thought, feeling. Her heart raced, and her conscience demanded that she retreat, to safeguard their friendship. They were in dangerous territory, and if Hazel didn't resist, they might do something they couldn't take back—but right now, she was finding it harder and harder to care.

He stepped forward, the space between them shrinking until his breath ghosted over her cheek. His free hand lifted a strand for her long onyx hair, sending a jolt of awareness through her. She registered the subtle pressure of his other hand still holding hers. Logic screamed at her to break the connection, to reestablish the boundaries that were now blurring, but the pull of his presence after days of absence was softening her resolve entirely.

"You," Rafe said.

His rough voice sent a delicious tingle down Hazel's spine.

But his words pushed her from scared to overwhelmed, and she felt the world tilt, like she was losing control. Her conscience screamed at her to let go of his hand, but she couldn't bring herself to do it.

"Then why did you shut me out?" The question tumbled out, laced with a hurt she hadn't realized was still so raw.

Rafe sighed and said nothing for several seconds. His jaw clenched and unclenched, clearly working through his next words. Then he laid the truth bare. "I was ashamed, Hazel."

A sharp lance of pain pierced her heart. Hazel blinked rapidly, forcing herself to look down at their intertwined hands so he wouldn't see the hurt there.

"Ashamed that you told me you loved me?" Her words were barely a whisper.

Stop being so selfish. You can't want him to love you while saying you can't be together.

"Salem, no." His grip tightened on her hand as he leaned in to gaze into her eyes, allowing her to see the truth there. "Ashamed that I made such a mess of it."

"Oh," Hazel breathed. A wave of relief washed over her that she had no business feeling from his reassurance.

"Truth or dare?" Rafe asked, taking her by surprise. His gaze held a flicker of something playful amidst the lingering tension.

Hazel let out a shaky laugh. "Where did that come from?"

"Come on," Rafe pressed, his eyes holding a curious intensity that Hazel couldn't resist. "Truth or dare?"

Both options terrified her. "Truth."

Rafe grinned like he'd won the lottery. "What do you want from us, Hazel?"

She paused, chewing her lip as she weighed her words. "I want us to keep being friends, like we have all year."

Rafe arched his brow, a hint of disbelief in his gaze. "And that's *all* you want?"

"It's what I want *most*," she insisted, though her voice remained small with the knowledge that she was hiding from him. "More than anything else." Her voice strengthened as she added, "You're important to me. I don't want to jeopardize us on other wishes that might not work out."

Rafe closed his eyes, a flicker of pain crossing his features. Slowly, deliberately, he released her hands, as if it physically pained him to do it. When he looked at her again, determination painted his features. "Your turn," Rafe said.

"Truth or dare?"

"Truth," he said immediately.

Hazel considered the weight of the question, and how a delicate balance was needed to help them get past what they felt for each other and find their way back to the easy friendship they'd shared before.

"Can we go back to the way things were?" she asked.

Rafe shook his head. "I don't want to be your friend. I want to be more than your friend, and I can't shove these feelings down anymore." He took a deep breath. "I can't, because they're making me sick. When I'm awake, I think of you, and when I'm asleep, I dream of you, and when I'm away from you, I want to be near you, and when I'm with you I want to be touching you."

She looked at him, unsure of what to say, of how to fix this. His words were a thrilling revelation, yet an impossible prospect. He didn't know what she was keeping from him. He might look at her differently, love her less if he knew what she really was.

"I'd be lying to you every day, pretending that I didn't want more from you in every way possible, and that's not me, Hazel. Lying to you would break me. So no, I can't go back. I know that's not what you want to hear, but it's the truth."

Hazel's mind raced as she said nothing, frozen within an internal battle of desire and fear. He didn't want to lie. Hazel understood that more than she could say. But she also wanted him. Right now, she wasn't sure which desire would win out. She'd tried not to let it get this far, for her feelings to get this deep, but somehow, she'd ended up here anyway.

"I don't know why you're scared, but I promise that I can be brave enough for the both of us," Rafe said. "Whatever comes at us or for us, I will fight for you, because you're worth it." He squeezed her hand gently. "Just give us a chance, Hazel."

Maybe I can tell him. Maybe he won't care. He'd been so supportive all year, through the rumors and learning the truth about the attacks. But those truths were one thing—her secret was on an entirely other level. Even if he wanted to keep her secret—which she felt more and more confident he would—telling him would be putting him at risk while asking him to keep it from his father. It was a position that Hazel didn't want to put him in.

He'd left her two options—let him go and lose him now, or hide the truth and *possibly* lose him later. Either way, she was going to hurt him in the end. The question was, which end could she live with?

When Hazel had still not spoken after his confession, Rafe turned, his shoulders slumped in defeat, and he began to go back the way they'd come. The real possibility of him leaving, of a future without him in her life after everyone else she'd lost, hit like a shot to the heart. She couldn't do it. Just the thought made her heart ache.

How is this any better than it aching in the future?

She reached out, her fingers closing around his wrist. He stopped instantly, his warm brown eyes shifting to devour her. Beneath her thumb, Hazel felt his pulse race, a frantic rhythm that echoed hers.

Please forgive me, Rafe. I'm not strong enough to let you go.

"So what does forward look like?" Hazel asked, swallowing.

A smile bloomed on Rafe's face. He didn't hesitate. His wrist twisted in her grip and he tugged, pulling her to him until she was flush against his chest. He reached a hand up, his knuckles brushing her cheek as he tucked a stray strand of hair behind her ear. His gaze dropped to her mouth, a silent question in his eyes before he leaned forward.

"Let me show you?"

Hazel's heart galloped in her chest. Every nerve ending in her body flared to life, acutely aware of the hard planes of his chest beneath her fingertips, the heat radiating from his skin. Her nipples tightened against his shirt. A shaky breath escaped her lips, and she could only manage a small, eager nod.

Rafe pulled back slowly, his palms framing her cheeks as the pad of his thumb slid over her lower lip. The feather-light whisper of contact sent a jolt through her. A palpable hunger Hazel had never felt before simmered beneath the surface of her skin, and when Hazel thought she couldn't wait any longer, his fingers traced the delicate curve of her ear with a tenderness that made her shiver. A tingle started in her earlobe and spiraled down to her core.

She'd never been touched like this before. The intimacy was terrifying yet thrilling. She wanted more.

"Truth or dare?" she whispered, her voice a husky timbre she barely recognized.

"Dare," Rafe said, without hesitation.

"Kiss me," Hazel breathed, the words slipping out soft and raw and needy.

Rafe didn't hesitate. His lips sealed over hers, and in that instant, all worry and what-ifs evaporated from her thoughts, kissed away by the heat of his mouth.

A well opened up inside of her, unleashing all the want and desire she'd been pushing down for months. Hazel fisted the front of his shirt, pulling him as close as she could get him, his hard body causing the storm raging within her.

Rafe cupped the back of her head with one hand, his fingers tangling in her hair, tilting her neck to offer him better access. His other arm wound around her waist while his lips trailed a burning path down the sensitive curve of her throat.

Hazel nearly objected, instantly missing his lips against hers. Then he kissed the delicate skin below her earlobe, and a sigh escaped her. She stood on her tiptoes, every cell of her body screaming for more. She wanted—*needed*—in a desperate, aching way that only he could satisfy.

As if he could read her mind, Rafe slid his hand down her lower back to rest on her ass. He paused a moment before he hoisted her up with his strong arms. Hazel didn't have to think about it as her body responded instinctively to him. That's how it had always been with her and Rafe—perfectly natural.

She wrapped her legs around his waist, instantly registering the hard ridge beneath his jeans, pressing against her deliciously. A low moan escaped her as she tangled her fingers in Rafe's thick strands of hair, pulling his mouth against hers once more, in a hungry kiss. It was everything. But not enough. Hazel wanted more. She arched her hips, desperate to fill the need inside her.

It was his turn to moan. The sound made her core tighten with anticipation, and she rolled her hips once more, the friction igniting a firestorm within her.

Her back met the yielding softness of moss on the large boulder beneath them as Rafe gently lowered her down. His body settled between her outstretched legs, his arms bracing his weight above her.

Their lips found each other again. His tongue tasted her as Hazel's hands roamed down his back, feeling the taut muscles flexing beneath his shirt. Her fingers slipped beneath the hem, seeking the bare heat of his skin.

Rafe broke the kiss, propping himself up enough to reach back with one hand and pull his shirt off in one swift, fluid motion. The sudden sight of his bare chest and flexing muscles was a punch to Hazel's senses. She reached for him greedily, her hands splaying across his warm skin, her mouth finding his once more, her tongue tangling with him in a possessive dance.

A wildfire raged within Hazel that consumed her and demanded quenching. She thought she might explode if she didn't.

Rafe's hand slid to the sensitive skin at her waist and lifted her shirt until her breasts were exposed to the warm, damp air. Hazel's breath froze in her chest, a sudden wave of vulnerability washing over her. What if he didn't find her attractive?

"Terra take me," he sighed.

"Rafe," Hazel breathed, all her fears melting away.

And then his mouth was on her nipple, the wet of his lips and the teasing twirl of his tongue stoking the fire within her. A moan escaped her as she writhed beneath him, her hips instinctively arching, seeking.

Hazel slid her hands between their bodies, her fingers finding the hard length of him through the rough denim of his jeans. She felt the insistent throb beneath her touch.

Rafe froze. "Hazel." Her name was both a warning and a question.

She looked down to see his eyes watching her intently, full of heat.

"Please," she said.

Rafe slid off her, and her body went cold.

Then his hands found her thighs and began unbuttoning her jeans. His gaze never left her face as he pulled them slowly off her body along with her shoes.

He then reached for her panties, but paused. Hazel sighed in frustration, and he laughed before hooking his thumbs around the sides. This time, his gaze dropped, no longer meeting hers. His dark eyes devoured her, his eyes going from brown to black with desire.

Completely bare and fully vulnerable, Hazel squirmed as she waited for him to make a move. She'd never done this before but she trusted him to guide her.

He spread her thighs wider as he lowered himself between her legs. Then his tongue traced her delicately, making her gasp. He pressed his tongue inside her. The shocking, intimate invasion sent a jolt of pure pleasure through her, and Hazel's back arched off the moss with a gasp.

"Rafe!"

"Trust me?" he asked.

"You know I do," she half-panted.

A confident smile played on Rafe's lips before he dipped his head again, this time tracing a deliberate path upwards to the sensitive circle between her legs. Hazel threw herself back on the ground as a helpless whimper escaped her lips. Blood roared in her ears as tingles surged outward from where his tongue worshipped her.

It was unlike anything she'd ever felt. She reached for him, her hands sinking into his silky hair as she lifted her hips. Rafe's answering low chuckle vibrated against her, sending a delectable, new sensation dancing along her nerves.

Then, agonizingly, he pulled back. Hazel bit her lip, barely suppressing a frustrated whine of protest.

"Everything about you is so fucking soft," Rafe said. "I never want to let you go."

His words stoked the fire within her.

"Rafe, please," she gasped, her body arching beneath him.

Hazel's head rolled to the side when she felt him insert a finger inside her. A moan escaped her as he stroked. This was the more she needed, yet it still wasn't enough.

Rafe added a second finger, the gentle strokes against her inner wall making her feel exquisitely full. Hazel thought she might scream from the pressure, yet it felt too good to be called pain.

Pressing her head into the soft moss, Hazel felt the delicious sensation build and build until she thought she might combust. He swirled his free thumb over her, and a shockwave went through her. Stars exploded behind her eyelids as her inner muscles squeezed around Rafe's fingers, legs trembling uncontrollably with the euphoria that racked her body.

Rafe settled over the top of her once again, covering her in his warmth. He kissed her mouth, her cheeks, her nose. She'd always imagined feeling raw and exposed in such a moment, but instead, a profound sense of safety enveloped her as Rafe held her in his arms.

Their gazes met once more. Rafe grinned as he tucked her messy hair behind her ear, and Hazel returned his grin, completely content.

"I have been wanting to do that all year," Rafe said, and Hazel almost swore he blushed, but the blue illumination on his face made it hard to tell for sure.

A loud splash echoed from across the cavern. Hazel froze, her eyes widening as Rafe shifted, his larger frame covering nearly all of her exposed skin.

Hazel peered over his shoulder, a knot of unease tightening in her chest, but saw nothing.

Rafe reached back quickly to grab Hazel's discarded clothes. "You get dressed. I'll go stall whoever it is," Rafe whispered.

Hazel nodded, not wanting to alert anyone to their presence by speaking.

He gave her a long look, full of all the things they'd just said with their bodies, then he pressed his lips quickly against hers before standing. After grabbing his shirt and tugging it over his broad shoulders and chest, he hopped off the boulder and slipped around the jagged cavern wall.

Not wasting a second, Hazel scrambled to put on her panties and then her jeans, wiggling them over her sensitive hips and buttoning them quickly with trembling fingers. As she slipped on her shoes, low murmurs drifted through the cavern, but Hazel had no indication of who was speaking or what was being said.

Then nothing. Complete silence.

She waited for what felt like eternity—though it was probably only a few minutes. But as the seconds dragged on, doubt snaked its way into her thoughts.

Why isn't he back yet? Did he get what he wanted, then leave me here?

Stop that, she told herself. *Rafe's not like that.*

Besides, if anyone had gotten what they wanted, it was her.

When another stretch of unnerving silence passed and he didn't return, the safety of the cave began to feel less like comfort and more like confinement. The need to know, to see him, eclipsed her caution. Unable to wait any longer, she followed Rafe.

She gingerly stepped down from the moss-covered rocks. "Rafe?"

Silence answered. She strained to hear the faintest sound of voices or even footsteps. Nothing.

Hazel approached the end of the cave wall that kept her hidden from the entrance. Cautiously, she peeked around the edge. There was only darkness.

From the heart of the darkness, a whisper of crimson light shimmered into being—quiet, deliberate, and impossibly close. It drifted toward her like an uncoiling serpent, mesmerizing her.

"What—"

It struck her right between the eyes. Hazel cried out as she clutched her face, pain blooming sharp and blinding. Then she felt nothing.

CHAPTER 38

Gwen

Gwen stretched out on the sofa, her gaze fixed on the fireplace across from her. The flames danced lazily until she lifted her wand and gave them something to do. With a flick of her wrist, the fire shifted—curling into shapes, scenes from her favorite childhood story. A wolf padded through a forest, followed by a knight with a shining sword. A castle rose behind them in glowing orange light, its towers swaying slightly in the flicker of heat. The last time she'd read the book was with Hazel over Christmas break, because Hazel had never heard of it. They'd curled up on Gwen's bed with cocoa, Hazel laughing at the cheesy dialogue, while Gwen pretended not to smile. The memory stung now.

It had been days since they'd spoken. The dorm was quiet. The rest of the students were most likely asleep; it was pretty late on a Sunday night. Gwen wished she could hear them talking or running down the halls—even with them all hating her, it made her feel less alone. The silence scraped against her skin.

She sighed and let the fire collapse. Nothing held her attention these days. Everything felt dull and muted without her friends around, especially Hazel. Not that she could blame her. Gwen had pushed her too far. She should have never brought up Hazel's mom.

Her eyes flicked to the doorway, half hoping she'd see Hazel standing there, arms crossed, still annoyed—but there. The space remained empty, like it had every night since their fight. When Gwen was home, Hazel would be in her room with the door shut. The past two nights, she hadn't bothered coming home at all. Gwen had a good hunch she was hiding out with Rafe.

She hated how much she missed her friend.

The silence pressed in, thick and heavy, until a voice—Victoria's—shattered it from the hallway.

The RA's amplified voice blared into the room as she walked by. "The dorm is on lockdown. Do not leave your rooms. Repeat: students have gone missing. You are not to leave your rooms."

Gwen sat up straight, every muscle tensing as the warning repeated itself once more.

She blinked, confused, as the words sank in. Missing?

Click. The sound of the lock sent Gwen bounding across the room in a few strides. She twisted the knob, but it didn't budge.

They'd locked them in? This had to be serious. Gwen's mind raced.

Students are missing?

For a flicker of a second, she thought of Hazel—but shook the thought away. Hazel was probably locked in the library or in Rafe's dorm. *She's fine.* Still, a tight knot of unease curled in her chest.

The melancholy that had weighed her down moments ago shifted into something sharper, tighter. Anxiety curled in her gut as she pressed her ear against the door, straining to catch another announcement or even footsteps, but the hallway had gone silent again. She backed away from the door and laid back onto the couch.

A few moments later, the back door slammed open. She twisted over the arm of the couch expecting to see Hazel. Instead, she saw

Jordan bursting through the doorway, wide-eyed and panting, one hand braced against the wall to steady himself.

"What do you want?" Gwen asked, more out of habit than hostility. Her tone came out flat, less bite to it than usual. If she was being honest, she was relieved it wasn't just her in here anymore.

"It's Rafe and Hazel," he managed between breaths.

Gwen sat up straight. "What?"

"They're missing. They have been since Friday."

A cold wash of dread slid down Gwen's spine.

"You're sure?" she asked.

"Yes," Jordan said, still catching his breath. "When I told the chancellor that I hadn't seen them all weekend, they sent out a preliminary search. Once they confirmed they weren't in the mountain or Eagles Ridge, they sent out an alert. They're locking down the dorms and Coventry."

No one had been by to check their room, although Gwen had spent a good deal of her day on the quad. Maybe they had and she hadn't been home. She should have been here. Even a few more hours' notice would have been a leg up.

Two days. Two days, and I didn't notice.

She'd been too wrapped up in her own self-pity and anger to realize her best friend had been taken. Gwen wanted to scream out her frustration, but instead followed the training her dad had given her and pushed all emotion aside. Now was not the time to feel; it was the time to be logical and strategic.

Gwen crossed the room before Jordan could say another word. She grabbed a piece of paper and scribbled a note.

I need help. Come quick, and bring the Sons.

She couldn't risk telling her mother and inadvertently putting her in danger. Her father had talents her mother did not possess, not to mention an army that would rally behind him. It didn't matter if he drove her crazy; he was the most capable of helping her. If she ran into danger, he'd find her. No matter what happened between them, he was always there for her. She'd get Hazel, and everything would be fine. But if it wasn't, she knew he'd come for her—for them.

She tied the letter to Pan's leg and then opened the window. "Hurry," she ordered the bird. With a screech, the hawk took flight.

Next, she grabbed the canvas pack she kept stashed behind the couch, suddenly thankful she and Hazel had never turned in their official Wilderness Watch gear. She pulled out her hiking pants, boots, long-sleeve shirt, and jacket. Raising her wand, she aimed it at her clothes and cast, "*Redire Para.*" This would magic them back to her backpack when she shifted.

Next, she grabbed the potions she and Hazel had been brewing all semester. Mostly minor healing, energy boosters—nothing game-changing, but better than going in blind. She also grabbed the equipment from Hazel's pack, including a second stretcher, and shoved it into hers. She prayed to Terra she wouldn't need either of them.

Gwen pulled out the compact in the front pocket of her pack and opened it.

Rafael Emilo De La Vega and Catherine Hazel Thorne are missing. Professors only report to the admin building.

How had she missed the alert? Then she remembered she'd silenced hers when they were excused from Wilderness Watch, while Hazel had kept carrying hers.

Bile rose in Gwen's throat as the weight of everything sunk in. Hazel and Rafe were missing. If the person behind all the attacks hadn't drained their blood already, they would soon. They were running out of time.

"Is the tunnel sealed?" Gwen asked. She zipped the pack shut and shoved it into Jordan's unsuspecting hands.

"Not yet," he said. "But once they finish here, it's next. We need to go. Now."

Gwen nodded in agreement. The fear that Hazel was dead sat like a cold weight in her chest, but moving gave it somewhere to go.

They stepped out the back door, into the cool evening air. The woods beyond the dorm stretched out like a shadowed maze, familiar and protective, shielding them from anyone wandering the grounds.

She paused just long enough to turn to Jordan. "Okay, listen. We don't have time for a long explanation, so you're getting the abbreviated version."

He blinked at her, still clutching the pack. "Okay..."

Please stay calm and collected. She needed him not to freak out. She could not do this without him.

"I'm a therian," she said flatly. "But I can't shift back on my own."

"What?"

"I said abbreviated." She unclasped the bracelet wrapped around her wrist, the small charms shimmering faintly under the moonlight, and she pressed it into his hand. "Guard this with your life. You lose it, I'll kill you."

Jordan stared at the bracelet like it might bite him. "What does it—"

"When the time comes for me to shift back into human form, put it around my paw. It's the only way I can shift back. Got it?"

He opened his mouth, clearly full of questions, but Gwen gave him a look that brooked no room for argument. His mouth snapped closed. "Got it."

Gwen breathed a sigh of relief at his quick acceptance and cursed that this was the way she had to tell him.

Stepping back, she exhaled once, then let the shift take her. Her bones cracked, reshaping. Muscles flexed, and fur spread across her skin like wildfire, although it never hurt. Her clothes tore away as her body grew, stretched, and became something else entirely.

Jordan stumbled back a step, mouth fully open. "Merlin's balls! I think we had enough time for you to mention you were a giant white wolf before shifting."

Gwen crouched low, massive shoulders flexing, and gave him a look paired with the toss of her head—*Get on.*

Jordan seemed to understand, and he moved toward her but then paused, stooping low to scoop something off the ground.

"I think you dropped this." He held out the golden ring Gwen had pilfered from Alterion during Samhain. She'd forgotten to spell it before shifting. Gwen let out a whine and Jordan slipped the ring into the same pocket he'd stored the bracelet, then he climbed onto her back with more hesitation than grace, arms looping tightly around her neck. The moment he settled, she ran.

The forest blurred around them as Gwen sprinted through the trees, her paws pounding the earth in a steady rhythm. Branches whipped past. Moonlight fractured across her white coat, turning her into a streak of silver between the shadows. Jordan clung to her back, hunched low, trying not to bounce with every powerful stride.

She knew the path by heart—the way the roots dipped and curled, the shortcut behind the history building, the slope that led straight to the tunnel entrance. Her ears twitched as she listened for anyone nearby. So far, the coast was clear.

Then she heard them—voices, far away but moving swiftly towards them. Up ahead, through the trees, the administration building glowed with light. Figures moved through the entranceway. They were heading straight for the tunnel.

Shit.

Gwen pushed harder, claws digging into the soil for traction as she veered wide, circling around the building. Jordan tensed against her back but didn't speak.

The tunnel entrance came into view. Gwen didn't slow. She barreled straight through, and Jordan ducked instinctively. Behind them, voices shouted at them to stop. But she didn't slow or turn back as the tunnel swallowed them whole.

Heavy footsteps padded the ground far behind them. They were being chased. She pushed herself harder than she ever had before, making it to the tunnel exit in record time. Before anyone could catch up to them, Gwen darted into the woods outside Eagles Ridge, and the darkness of the forest surrounded them.

She listened closely, but heard nothing. Whoever was chasing them was now gone.

Hazel

Hazel's back ached from leaning against the cold, rough stone wall of the cave. Her left arm was stretched awkwardly above her head, where a glyph-covered cuff wrapped around her wrist, securing her to the wall by a short, golden chain. Each small movement rattled the chain, but there was no give.

The only light in the cave came from a small fire in the center of the room, its flickering glow casting long shadows that danced across the damp walls. It wasn't the same cave she'd been in with Rafe—that much she was sure of.

Here, the walls seemed to close in, the frigid air chilled her to the bones, and the silence pressed against her ears. There were no pools of warm water, no softly glowing mushrooms. But for all she knew, it could still be part of the same underground system.

Hazel wasn't sure how she had gotten here. She remembered going to look for Rafe, and then magic had struck her, fast and hard. When she'd woken, she'd been chained to this wall, her body sore and her mouth dry. Rafe had been there beside her, confined by the same chain, slumped over and silent, with bruises blooming across his jaw and temple. He hadn't woken right away, and for several terrifying hours, she'd thought he never would.

When Rafe finally did stir, he'd been as confused as Hazel. He didn't remember what happened either—just a sharp pain and then darkness.

That had been… she wasn't even sure. A day ago? Two? He'd drifted in and out of consciousness ever since, his body too battered to stay awake for long. Right now, he was asleep again, slouching against the wall beside her, a deep bruise stretching from his jaw to his temple and dried blood crusted near his hairline. His lower lip was split, and he winced even in sleep.

He needed rest more than she did, and Hazel tried to give it to him. They'd been taking shifts to keep watch, but Hazel didn't trust him to stay awake, so she hadn't gotten any more than a few moments of sleep. Not that there was much either of them could do chained like this, but still. She hated the idea of them both unconscious, defenseless, when their captor came back.

Their captor was a woman, though Hazel couldn't have picked her out of a lineup if she tried. Her face blurred unnaturally, like the ruzo players—a blank slate impossible to focus on. She moved with an unsettling grace, her frame short and thin, her footsteps so soft and measured. The woman barely spoke, and when she did, her voice was distorted with a spell.

She'd appeared a few hours after Rafe had woken the first time, but no matter how much Hazel and Rafe had pleaded, she'd never acknowledged them. Hazel had been so frustrated, so desperate, she'd tried to shoot her lightning at her, but the lightning didn't obey. Hazel felt it along her skin, in her bones, but it was as if it couldn't *hear* her commands.

So the woman continued to ignore them, but brought them water and bland food every now and then, enough to keep them alive. Barely.

On the far side of the cave, almost swallowed by the shadows, another figure sat slumped against the wall. Hazel hadn't noticed him at first—he barely ever moved, and the firelight didn't reach far enough. But every once in a while, she'd heard a shallow breath or the faintest rustle of chains. When her eyes had finally adjusted to the darkness, recognition struck like a punch to the gut. *Tristan.* The bartender from Kodiak Brew.

His skin was pale and sickly, stretched too thin over his bones. His head lolled forward, chin resting limply against his chest as if he was barely hanging on.

He hadn't spoken once since they'd been here. She'd tried to ask him questions, but he'd never answered, too far gone. Several times, she'd watched as the woman had crouched beside him in the dark. He'd scream out in pain, and after a few minutes, he'd go quiet and still again.

Hazel didn't know exactly what the woman was doing to him, but her instincts whispered the answer. Draining his blood. For days. He couldn't last much longer.

And when he was gone, she and Rafe would be next.

On the other side of Rafe sat a small iron box. Her wand was inside it, along with Rafe's. She'd seen them both during one of the woman's rare visits, when she'd opened the box to take something out. Hazel was almost certain the box was locked, but she'd still tried to reach it with her free hand more than once, bruising her wrist in the process.

Useless. She felt useless.

Hazel clenched her hand around the crystal wolf in her pocket for the millionth time, but felt nothing. She prayed to Terra to give her an ounce of her power back, but it remained quiet, out of her reach. She suspected the glyphs on the cuff around her wrist kept the magic at bay.

She stared at the iron box with her wand in it, wondering if it was as useless as the crystal wolf, but still willing it to slide a few inches closer, desperate for any chance to break free.

A noise echoed faintly from beyond the cave entrance.

She stopped moving, quieting the chains as she strained to listen.

A man's voice—sharp, angry. "You only got one of them."

Hazel froze, heart thudding. She couldn't see anything beyond the bend in the cave, but the voices carried.

I know that voice. The familiarity scratched at Hazel's tired brain but it was too quiet, too far away. She couldn't place it. Her eyes closed as she tried to push away the distractions of Tristan's ragged breath and the crackle of the small fire and focus on the new voice.

The woman answered, her tone cool and unbothered but distorted as always. "They haven't been seen together in days. I saw the opportunity to take one of them, so I did."

"You've botched the entire operation," the man said, irate. "This was supposed to be clean. Precise. Not sloppy."

Botched. As the word rolled off his tongue, it sounded a lot like the way her least favorite professor said "Bishop."

Hazel was hit with a wave of recognition.

Thacker.

His tone was harsh, meaner than she'd ever heard him, but the cadence, the resonance and timbre? They were all in sync with Hazel's auditory memory.

Memories surfaced of overhearing Thacker speaking with Jude in their office last semester. His inappropriate infatuation with Gwen. The worrying encounter with Abigail that Gwen had refused to give her answers about once she'd spoken with Harland.

What if *he* was the one behind these attacks?

That would mean he's a schaden. Hazel sat up straight.

Maybe this woman was doing his bidding, completely under his manipulation.

Hazel's stomach clenched. *I probably know her.*

Tristan started coughing, deep and wet.

There was a pause—too long. Hazel held her breath as she prepared for them to come check on him. Then, footsteps. Heavy ones faded away. Hazel guessed the man walked off, his footwear scraping the stone floor. A few moments later, lighter steps followed—the woman's, she was sure of it.

Silence returned, thick and absolute. They were alone again. Hazel's hand trembled as she clenched the edge of her sweater.

If she was right, and it *was* Thacker, then they were up against someone more powerful and more organized than they'd ever imagined. And despite being their professor, he hadn't sounded like he cared whether she or Rafe survived this.

Hazel swallowed hard and forced herself to breathe slowly. Panic wouldn't help. She'd held it together this long, but exhaustion clawed at her, her limbs heavy, her thoughts hazy. She was running on scraps of sleep and constant adrenaline, terrified to rest for more than a minute. She leaned her head back against the wall and stared at the flickering firelight.

Gwen would've noticed by now, she told herself.

Even if they weren't speaking. Even if Hazel had needed space. Gwen would notice and send help. At least, she hoped.

If Harland hasn't gotten control of her completely.

The sound of footsteps made Hazel's blood run cold. She stiffened. Her eyes locked on the narrow passage, chain clinking softly as she shifted her weight.

Rafe remained still beside her. Tristan didn't move.

A familiar figure stepped into the firelight. Hazel's breath caught in her throat—it was Alec, the owner of Kodiak Brew, who'd helped her save Mara.

She'd thought the voice was familiar—she felt sure it was Thacker, but what if she was wrong? She was sleep-deprived and under incredible stress. What if it was actually Alec's? Her heart thudded violently against her ribs. He wasn't cloaked or masked, which meant he didn't care if Hazel knew who he was.

Without a word, Alec rushed to Tristan's side, dropping to his knees beside the unconscious man, his hands hovering over him.

"Get away from him," Hazel snapped, her voice sharper than she intended yet still trembling with fear. "If you come any closer, I swear—"

Alec froze, then slowly turned to face her, hands lifted in surrender. "Calm down," he said quickly. "I'm here to rescue you."

His gravelly voice was nothing like the man she'd heard minutes ago. Still, she couldn't trust it—anyone—right now. Not until she knew for sure. If there was one helper, there could be more. Her heart pounded in her chest, and even as her mind fought to weigh the truth of his words, her body refused to relax. Every muscle stayed coiled, ready for the worst.

After a moment, Alec gestured over his shoulder and added, "Tristan works for me at Kodiak Brew."

Hazel nodded slowly. She remembered the first night at Kodiak Brew when Alec had paid for their elixirs. Tristan had told her it would be rude to refuse the owner's offer.

"He's been missing for a week. I've been searching for him ever since," Alec continued. "When I stumbled upon this cave, I thought I'd better check it out in case he came in here for shelter. Finding you was a surprise."

A burst of hope shot through her. "Do they know we're missing?"

Alec shook his head slowly, and the dream that Gwen would find them was snatched from her. Gwen and Hazel hadn't spoken in days. Maybe Gwen hadn't even realized Hazel was missing. She pushed the thought from her mind, clinging to hope, because without it, she had nothing. Gwen would find them and bring help.

The idea reminded Hazel of the day she'd helped save Mara—when they'd found her unconscious in the alleyway with Alec.

Hazel narrowed her eyes but didn't move. Her gaze locked onto his amber eyes. "How can I be sure I can trust you?"

"You can't," Alec said simply with the shrug of his shoulders. "But I'm the only chance you've got."

"Hazel, we don't have much of a choice," Rafe said, voice thick with pain and exhaustion, surprising her. She'd thought he was asleep.

Hazel's chest tightened. She didn't trust Alec—not fully. But the chain bit into her wrist, and Rafe could barely keep his eyes open. If

Alec could get her out, even if it was a trick, she had to take the risk. She'd run. She'd find help. She'd use her fulgurkinesis. Even if it meant leaving Rafe behind to do it. The thought gutted her, but staying here would kill them both.

"Fine," she said, barely above a whisper. "If you can break the chain, do it."

Alec nodded and stepped forward, pulling his wand from his belt. He crouched beside her, inspecting the cuff. "Hold still," he ordered.

Hazel did—until a sound, sharp and distinct, broke the quiet behind him. Her breath caught. That wasn't the wind.

A gasp escaped her as a figure emerged from the shadows.

"Alec! Behind you!"

He turned.

A blast of magic cracked through the cave, and Alec's body went rigid, limbs locking before he collapsed hard beside the fire. Hazel screamed, twisting against her chain, the metal digging into her skin. The blurry-faced woman stood behind him, her wand glowing faintly in her hand.

Just like that, hope was gone.

The woman took Alec's wand, placing it in the box with hers, and chained his limp body next to Hazel before vanishing back into the dark. His head lolled forward, hair damp with sweat, his breathing slow and uneven.

After that, time blurred. Hazel didn't sleep, but her mind fogged under the weight of sleep deprivation. She stared at the fire until it became little more than color and movement, and imagined what she'd do to the woman once she was free and had her lightning back. The woman would pay for what she'd done to Tristan, to Rafe, and now to Alec. To Mara and Frank. Yes, she'd regret the day she'd made the mistake of hurting people Hazel cared about.

A groan pulled her back. Alec shifted against the wall, head lifting slightly.

"You're awake," she rasped, her voice rough with dryness and tension. "Are you alright?"

"Barely," Alec muttered, squinting at the firelight. "That spell felt like getting hit by a truck."

Rafe stirred at the sound of their voices, blinking groggily. Hazel reached for him with her unchained hand, gently brushing his shoulder. Together, they began explaining to Alec what little they knew—the chains, Tristan and the woman who fed on him. Alec listened without interrupting, his expression growing darker with every word.

After a long silence, he shifted, wincing as pain flickered across his face from where he'd landed on it. His nose was most certainly broken. "I'll take the first watch," he said, settling into a straighter position. "You two need rest."

Hazel didn't argue. Her body was screaming for sleep, her mind thick with fog. Plus, he was chained—what could he do to them? She let her eyes close as she leaned back against the wall. Rafe's shoulder brushed hers, providing her the only modicum of comfort she'd had since they'd been taken.

If Alec found them, maybe someone else would too.

For the first time in what felt like forever, she didn't fight the pull of unconsciousness.

CHAPTER 39

Gwen

Snow fell in thick, silent sheets outside the mountain, blanketing the forest in white and swallowing all sound. Gwen's paws tore across the icy ground, her breath huffing out in clouds as she ran, the cold biting through her thick white fur. Jordan clung to her back, arms wrapped tightly around her neck. He kept adjusting, shifting, pulling at her fur with every bump and jolt as he tried not to fall off. It was driving her *mad*.

The wolf in her was already on edge, and every time he tugged a little too hard, her body tensed with the urge to shake him off and spin, fangs bared. It would take nothing, *nothing,* to throw him and tear into him for riding her like some domesticated pet. She shook her head sharply, forcing herself to focus. She could be furious *after* they got to Hazel.

She skidded to a halt near a snowbank, head swiveling to check for pursuers. Behind them, their tracks trailed clearly through the snow—easy for anyone to follow. But then Jordan lifted his wand

and cast a spell behind them, the snow smoothing over in their wake like no one had ever passed.

Smart.

Guilt slammed into her chest harder than the cold ever could.

She'd gotten so mad at him for keeping a secret when she'd had her own, much bigger one. Yet here he was, taking it in stride without any apprehension. Jordan was her oldest friend. He'd been with her since they were kids, long before Saint Elias or Elkmont. And still, he hadn't been the first person she'd told about her shift. Not that she'd told anyone on purpose, but... still. *He should have known first.* He deserved that.

Realizing she hadn't been a very good friend this semester, she let out a low whine. Jordan wasn't the only person she'd let down. Gwen hadn't even noticed that Hazel and Rafe were missing. She'd been too lost in her own head, too angry, too distracted. The people she cared about had been taken—were possibly dying—and she hadn't done a damn thing.

The thought burned like fire under her skin. She wouldn't let that happen. She lowered her head and ran harder, snow flinging up around her as she surged forward again. She'd find them and she would make things right.

Gwen slowed as they reached the clearing where she and Hazel had been attacked by the bear. Given that they'd found Frank nearby, too, Gwen felt like this area was the best place to start. The snow was undisturbed now, but the trees hit by lightning that day were still splintered and short. She sniffed deeply at the ground, trying to catch even a whisper of Hazel's scent beneath the cold. Nothing. Just ice and earth.

She growled, frustration flaring in her chest as she turned and moved toward the place where they'd fought Frank. Gwen paced along the tree line, nose to the snow, but again found nothing. Jordan's breath, his clothes rubbing against her fur, and the howling wind from the encroaching snowstorm were the only distinguishable sounds in the air. There was no trail for her to follow and she was out of leads. She snarled under her breath, fur bristling. Every second wasted felt like another second too late. Hazel could be *anywhere*—hurt, scared, worse.

Gwen pushed deeper into the woods than she'd ever dared to go, Jordan clinging on with every step. Her paws hit the frozen ground with growing urgency, breath burning in her lungs. Then she heard a sound, faint and distant—something that did not belong to the forest. Voices.

Her ears perked up and every part of her snapped to attention as she followed the sound. The strong scent of honey drifted towards her—*Hazel.* Gwen bolted, and Jordan squeezed her tightly with his knees. Hazel's scent grew stronger with every step, driving Gwen forward as her heart beat against her ribs and adrenaline surged through her legs. Hazel was close.

So close.

The cave entrance loomed ahead, carved low into the side of a ridge, half buried in snow. Hazel's scent poured from within and Gwen knew she was inside. As they drew closer, new scents stood out. Rafe's signature woody pine and a third, familiar scent that Gwen couldn't place. Her wolf had no objection to it, which was a good sign.

Gwen didn't wait. She lunged for the cave opening, and a shock-wave of power threw her and Jordan backward mid-stride.

Jordan yelped as he was flung off her back, landing with a crunch somewhere behind her. Gwen landed on her side. Pain lanced through her body as she scrambled to her feet, lips curled as she fought to catch her breath. Whoever had taken Hazel and Rafe had put a force field around the entrance.

Shit.

She needed to shift so she could cast. She growled at Jordan, who was groaning and dusting snow from his coat a few feet away. He blinked at her, dazed for half a second, as she held out her paw. He fumbled for the golden charm bracelet, then ran over and carefully placed it on her.

The shift hit instantly. Bones snapped, muscles tightened, fur shrank back into skin. Gwen collapsed and let out a squeal as her naked ass hit the snow.

Jordan averted his eyes the second she shifted and tossed her the backpack.

Gwen took the bag and pulled out her clothes. Once she was dressed, she marched straight to the barrier with her wand in hand.

"So you're a wolf."

"Now isn't the time," she bit out.

"Right." Jordan nodded, solemn. "But if it *were* the time and the circumstances were different, I want you to know I think it's pretty cool."

Gwen let her mouth slide into a small smile of relief. "You'll keep my secret?" she asked, already knowing the answer.

"Obviously." He grinned at her and nudged her with his arm. "Oh, and here's your ring." He pulled it out of his pocket. Gwen grabbed it and placed it on her finger.

There was so much unspoken between them—like how shitty they'd been to each other this semester, mostly her—but she knew their friendship would endure it. She could apologize once their friends were safe.

"You're sure they're here?" Jordan asked. He placed his hands on the invisible barrier, and it shimmered faintly.

"I heard voices earlier. I picked up Hazel's scent and then Rafe's when we got closer. There's a third, but I can't place it." Gwen peered into the cave, but the narrow entrance curved a few feet in and she could see nothing beyond it. "We need to find a way to take this force field down before whoever took them comes back."

Jordan nodded in agreement as they raised their wands and began casting. She gave the barrier every spell she knew for disruption, breach, dismantling. Nothing worked, not even as Jordan's spells combined with hers. The barrier held firm, humming with quiet defiance.

Gwen's pulse pounded in her ears. They were *right there* and she couldn't get to them. She wanted to scream for them, but didn't, in case whoever took them was nearby, though she sensed no one. Her hands trembled as she lowered her wand. The barrier showed no signs of dropping. It might as well have been a wall of stone.

She backed away, pacing in a tight circle, her boots crunching in the snow. Her mind scrambled through possibilities.

If Hazel was here, she'd know exactly what to try. Or she could at least blast it with her lightning.

"What about the potions?" Jordan asked. "Maybe something in the bag could help?"

Gwen shook her head as he ruffled through the vials. There was nothing in there but healing, energy, and anti-venom potions. None of it would get them through a magical barrier. He dropped the bag, and Gwen growled in frustration.

"We have to go back to campus and get help." It killed Gwen to say it, but they couldn't waste time.

She slipped her bracelet off and tossed it back to Jordan, who caught it easily and stuck it back in his coat pocket.

A moan came from the cave, a sound of agony and terror.

"Hazel!" Gwen screamed.

Gwen slammed her fists into the invisible wall and Jordan joined her. Helplessness threatened to drown her as the barrier held.

"*Fuck!*" she screamed, voice raw and furious, echoing through the trees. Gwen's wolf howled within her, threatening to shift if she didn't get a hold on her emotions.

Gwen slammed her palms against the barrier again, then again, the pain vibrating up through her arms. She pressed her forehead to the shimmering field, teeth clenching as her canines elongated. Her friends were in there and needed her, but she was letting them down. She released a guttural snarl and punched the barrier with everything she had left—all her therian strength, her anger, her fear.

A bolt of blue and white lightning arced from her hand into the barrier. It cracked across the field in a web of energy, rippling outward like shattered glass. The barrier pulsed once, then collapsed. Gwen stumbled back a step, eyes wide. Even her wolf had gone quiet with shock.

The barrier was gone. She stared at her hands, still crackling faintly with residual static.

How in Salem did I do that?

"Here," Jordan said as he stared at her in awe, handing Gwen her bracelet.

She took the bracelet and pocketed it. She still needed her therian senses.

Another moan escaped the cave, and Gwen bolted through the entrance, Jordan right behind her. They rushed down a narrow tunnel that twisted through the rock until it finally opened into a smaller cave off to the right. The heat hit Gwen like a wave after the snow, the air thick and stifling.

She skidded to a halt as she rounded the bend in the cave. For a heartbeat, her world froze. Rafe leaned against the wall, eyes shut, his skin pale and clammy. Bruises darkened the side of his neck and bloomed down his arm, dried blood crusted at the corner of his mouth. Hazel was beside him, whispering quietly to someone seated on her other side.

Gwen's chest tightened. *Hazel.* Relief flooded her so fast it nearly knocked her off balance.

"Hazel," she breathed, her voice breaking. Her friend looked ashen and her eyes were bloodshot. She looked like she hadn't slept in days. Hazel's clothes were filthy, but bloodless, and Gwen was thankful there appeared to be no physical damage.

Hazel looked up, her eyes going wide. "Gwen?" Her voice cracked as tears spilled down her cheeks. "Gwen! Jordan! Thank Terra—" Hazel cried out, starting to move before the chain yanked her back. She fell against the wall with a shaky breath, her whole body trembling.

Gwen and Jordan ran to them. Jordan knelt in front of Rafe and tried to rouse him as Gwen dropped to her knees and pulled Hazel into a tight hug. Hazel stunk of fear and dirt as she clung to Gwen like she wasn't sure she was real.

"You're okay," Gwen murmured, holding her tighter. "You're okay."

Hazel nodded against her. "You have to go—you and Jordan. Hurry, before she comes back. Please, Gwen. Please." Her voice trembled with panic.

Gwen pulled back enough to meet her eyes, brushing Hazel's hair gently behind her ear. "I'm not leaving without you."

She inhaled deeply, letting her senses unfurl beyond the firelight, beyond the stone walls. The woods were still. The only scents on the wind were snow, pine, and animals—not a single sign of magic or danger closing in.

"There's no one nearby," she said, firm but calm. "We have time."

Within the cave, that third familiar scent was stronger, along with Hazel and Rafe's. And the pungent scent of blood.

Gwen turned to investigate and her gaze snapped to the figure next to Hazel—Alec. The owner of Kodiak Brew.

What the hell is he doing here?

She inhaled to determine if he was the familiar third scent, but no scent trail emanated from him. The hair on the back of her neck rose with alarm.

Hazel noticed the change in her expression and quickly said, "You can trust him. I think. He tried to help us."

Gwen didn't respond. She just narrowed her eyes at Alec, who offered her a slow smile. Anyone who could smile like that at a time like this was either unhinged or used to danger, and that only made her distrust him more.

"It's good to see you again, Gwendolyn," he said.

Her lip curled with contempt. How did he know her proper name?

"He came to find Tristan," Hazel explained before Gwen could snap at him.

Ah, yes. The cute bartender. That's the third scent.

“Wher—” Gwen began, but Jordan’s voice broke through—quiet, strained, and cracked with emotion.

“Gwen, what do I do?”

He knelt beside Rafe, his hands hovering uselessly over him, eyes wide and filled with panic. With good reason—Rafe was still unconscious.

Gwen shoved everything else aside and went straight into triage mode. “There are two healing potions in the side pocket,” she instructed Jordan. “The vials are red. Give one to Hazel, the other to Rafe.”

Hazel shook her head. “I don’t—”

“It’s nonnegotiable,” Gwen said, cutting her off.

Hazel hesitated for only a moment before uncorking it and drinking. The color began to return to her face almost instantly. “What about Alec?” she asked, voice still hoarse.

Gwen shrugged without looking at him. “Sorry. I only had two.”

Alec’s nose was clearly broken, but she didn’t see any other injuries—he’d live.

Jordan uncorked the other one for Rafe and coaxed the liquid between his cracked lips. For a moment, nothing happened. Gwen worried that they were too late. Then Rafe twitched, blinked, and let out a hoarse groan. Color slowly returned to his face and the purply-green contusions on his face began to yellow.

“Thanks,” he rasped, voice barely audible.

Gwen exhaled, the knot in her chest loosening a little. Rafe still looked like hell.

“The blue vial in the other side pocket is for energy.”

Jordan nodded and pulled out two more vials, handing one to Hazel before carefully tipping the other between Rafe’s lips. A few seconds later, his eyes flew open. He blinked rapidly, the energy hitting him like a jolt.

His gaze darted around the cave, trying to piece things together. “What are you two doing here?”

Relief rushed through Gwen. He was going to be okay.

"Saving your ass," she said with a half-smile. "Good to have you back."

Rafe grinned weakly. "About time the cavalry showed up. Where's everyone else?"

"It's just us," Jordan answered.

"Great. We're screwed," Rafe groaned.

Jordan laughed in response, giving his friend a gentle squeeze that made Rafe wince.

Not if I have anything to say about it.

As soon as Gwen got those chains off her friends, they'd be walking out of this cave—and Rafe could eat those words.

Gwen turned back to Jordan. "There's water in the bag and a few granola bars. Give them to him and Hazel."

Jordan nodded and moved to follow her instructions, already digging into the pack. While he tended to their friends, Gwen switched her focus to the chains. Her relief was already morphing into determination.

We need to get out of here, fast.

There was still no sign of anyone coming—but their luck wouldn't hold out forever.

"Do you know where the key is?" Gwen asked, her voice low as she crouched beside Hazel and examined the intricate locking mechanism.

Hazel shook her head. "She never used one."

Behind them, a voice spoke quietly—measured, deliberate. "The key is a ring."

Gwen's head snapped toward Alec. The steadiness of his voice sent a ripple of unease down her spine. *How could he be so sure if he just got here?*

"What?" she asked, her tone sharp.

Alec nodded toward her hand. "Where did you get the one on your finger?"

She didn't answer his question. It was none of his business. But she thought back to when she'd taken it from Alterion on Samhain.

She realized then that these chains looked eerily similar to the ones she'd seen in the hidden library. The same ones from the class with the Leabhar Feòla when the fae commander watched the feras be released.

Gwen mimicked what she'd seen in class. The jewel on the ring fit perfectly in the diamond cut out on the chains. With a soft *click*, the cuff popped open and dropped to the stone floor.

Gwen cut her eyes to Alec. *How did he know about these chains?*

Hazel sucked in a breath, clutching her wrist and rubbing the sore skin. She stood slowly and wrapped her arms around Gwen's neck. "Thank you." Releasing her after a moment, Hazel rushed to the other side of the room. "Can one of you unlock this box? Our wands are in it."

Gwen moved to help her, but Jordan stopped her. "I'll do it. You get Rafe out of those chains."

She nodded and moved back to Rafe.

His bruises were nearly gone and she hoped the potion would fully heal them. Rafe watched as she unlocked his chains.

"Thank you for coming," he told her solemnly. Then he looked at Hazel and his eyes filled with moisture. "I couldn't—"

"Don't mention it," Gwen muttered.

The last shackle hit the ground with a metallic clank and she helped him to his feet. Rafe hugged her shakily before limping over to Hazel, who was across the cave with Jordan, retrieving their wands from the box.

As Gwen moved to follow him, Alec's voice cut through the silence. "Aren't you going to unchain me?" His tone was maddeningly calm, like he wasn't currently shackled to a cave wall.

"No," Gwen said flatly.

Hazel turned to her with a frown. "Gwen, I told you, he tried to help us."

Gwen's eyes never left Alec. "I don't care. I don't trust him."

"Why?" Hazel asked, caught off guard.

"Because he doesn't smell like *anything,*" Gwen snapped, her voice edged with frustration.

That got his attention. His smile didn't falter, but there was a flicker of something sharper behind his eyes. "Just a simple cloaking spell," he said smoothly, almost too casually. "To keep the trackers off me while I searched for Tristan."

"Then drop it."

A beat passed. Alec held her gaze, but didn't move. Finally, he sighed. "I can't with these chains on."

Gwen's shoulders tightened. Her instincts screamed at her not to trust him.

Hazel stepped forward, eyes pleading. "We can't leave him here."

"Fine, but don't give him his wand back."

Alec glared at her, and Gwen felt a sliver of satisfaction.

When he didn't protest about the wand, she stalked over to him, yanked the ring from her finger, and shoved it into Alec's shackle. The cuff fell open like the others.

"Don't make me regret this," she muttered.

Alec rubbed his wrist with a slight wince, then his smile returned like he hadn't been seconds from being abandoned.

Gwen didn't smile back.

"Okay, now Tristan," Hazel said, crouched beside his still form in the shadows.

Gwen joined Hazel and froze. She barely recognized Tristan. He was gaunt, hollow-cheeked, his skin pale as ash, wrists raw and bloody from the shackles. His appearance hit her like a punch, such a stark contrast from the filled-out, handsome young man she'd flirted with at the bar last fall.

He didn't stir as she slipped the ring into the lock and released the cuff. Jordan caught his limp body as it slumped forward. Rafe stepped in, wobbling slightly but steady enough to help while Hazel prepped the Wilderness Watch stretcher. Together, they lifted him onto it. The moment Tristan's weight settled, the canvas frame floated off the ground with a soft hum of magic. It hovered steadily at knee height, easily supporting Tristan's weight. Gwen thanked Terra again that she'd never returned her Wilderness Watch pack.

"Leave him," Alec said, brushing dirt from his pants like he had all the time in the world. "He's basically dead. He'll slow us down."

Gwen spun on him, eyes blazing. "If we're leaving anyone, it's *you.*"

Alec didn't reply, only arching a brow.

Hazel stepped forward, her voice rising. "You came for him and now you want to leave him? He works for you!"

Alec didn't meet Hazel's eyes.

Beside them, Jordan pulled the lanyard from the side of the stretcher and slipped it around his neck, ensuring it would follow him. It was one less thing they'd have to carry. And right now, Gwen was grateful for anything that made getting out easier.

"Let's move," Gwen said, her voice low but firm.

Hazel walked past Alec, who stood in the back, and stepped up beside Gwen. Hazel's posture was steadier since imbibing the potions. There was strength in her stride again. Jordan and Rafe fell in behind her, the stretcher gliding smoothly between them.

Together, they led the group to the exit.

CHAPTER 40

Hazel

When they finally reached the mouth of the cave, Hazel stopped in her tracks. The cold slapped her in the face like a fist of ice as she stared at the snow before them; at least three feet of it had filled the entrance, piled high and untouched.

"Shit," she murmured.

That was going to slow them down. But they weren't staying in the cave another second.

"I'm going to cast a water barrier charm on everyone to keep us from getting soaked through," Hazel said.

No one objected.

Starting with Rafe, Hazel moved one by one through the group, murmuring the spell as she passed. A faint shimmer rippled across their clothes as the enchantment took hold. When she finished, she added a heating charm for good measure, layering it on top of the barrier like a second skin. Gwen was the only one built for this kind of cold, thanks to her therian metabolism.

The rest of us need every bit of help we can get.

The cold still bit at her cheeks, but now it was manageable. They pressed forward into the snow, the fresh powder nearly reaching Hazel's knees. It slowed their pace, turned every step into a slog, but no one complained. Not out loud, anyway. They were finally out, and no matter what came next, it beat being held captive.

"It's a decent distance to Eagles Ridge," Gwen said with a glance over her shoulder. "We'll have to pace ourselves."

Hazel nodded. "We've got this."

She felt sharper than she had in days. The healing potion had done its job, along with the energy potion, granola bars, and water. Her limbs still ached, but she didn't let that stop her. She wasn't just ready to keep up—she was ready to fight.

She moved to Gwen's side, matching her stride. Behind them, Rafe and Jordan followed closely, keeping pace while flanking the stretcher. Tristan lay eerily still on it, and Alec walked beside him, both of them unarmed, stripped of their wands.

Hazel didn't miss the way Rafe's hand never strayed far from his wand at his belt or the tightness in Jordan's jaw as they kept guard over Alec and Tristan. They weren't out of danger yet.

The trees thickened ahead, branches sagging under the weight of the snow. They slowed as they approached the edge of the clearing, where the path narrowed between towering pines. Gwen held up a hand and came to a stop.

"I'm going to scout ahead," she said. "Stay here. Keep quiet."

Hazel wanted to protest splitting up, but Gwen took off, not making a sound as she moved—a silent reminder that she had abilities the rest of them didn't. Gwen would be okay on her own. She was faster, quieter, and more capable of this task than any of them out here. Without shifting, she moved quickly, vanishing into the trees. The silence that followed wrapped around them like a weighted cloak.

Hazel rubbed her arms, even though the heating charm kept the worst of the cold at bay. Her eyes stayed fixed on the tree line until

Gwen emerged again, moving fast. She slid the bracelet back onto her wrist as she reached them.

"There's an undead animal out there," Gwen said, breath visible in the cold. "I can smell it, but the rot's masking what kind of animal it is. It's close."

Hazel's stomach twisted. Her mind flashed to the undead bear from last semester—how massive it had been, how fast, how relentless. It had taken a pack of wolves and lightning to take it down, and even then, they'd barely survived.

"Let's get out of here before it finds us," Jordan said.

The group agreed, and moved forward in silence, every step sinking into the snow. The tree line loomed ahead, skeletal branches casting long shadows across the clearing. Hazel kept close to Gwen, wand in hand, her ears straining for any sign of movement. The forest felt too still, like it was holding its breath.

Then, the undead stepped into their path.

A lynx—at least, what used to be one—emerged from the trees, its fur mottled with ice and decay. One ear was torn clean through, and strips of flesh hung loose from its front leg, exposing slick muscle and bone beneath. Its eyes glowed faintly in the moonlight, dull and unnatural. It didn't snarl. It didn't growl. It just stood there, watching. The group froze, and the lynx did too.

It's not attacking. Why?

Gwen motioned to her left and they all shifted slightly, testing its intent. The lynx moved with them, silent and exact, adjusting its stance to keep its body directly in their path. It was guarding them. They weren't getting past it without a fight.

A low crack sounded from deeper in the woods. Branches snapped as snow crunched under something massive. Hazel's heart skipped as an undead bear lumbered out from between the trees, its movements slow but deliberate. Patches of fur were gone, revealing raw, mangled skin stretched over emaciated limbs. Its eyes were sunken and milky, its muzzle soaked in something dark. The stink of decay hit them a second later, thick and cloying.

Hazel took an instinctive step back.

The lynx remained in front of them, unmoving. The bear blocked the path to their left. And suddenly, it was obvious.

"They're going to try to herd us back to the cave," Hazel practically shouted as the weight of what was happening hit her.

The lynx crept forward a step. The bear mirrored the movement, and together, they began pressing the group back—inch by inch—toward the cave, confirming her suspicions.

She caught Gwen's eye. No words passed between them, but the look said everything.

No more running.

Hazel shifted her stance, wand steady in her hand. Alec stood to her left, still wandless, his coat pulled tight around him. Tristan's body hovered between them, drifting slightly as the wind picked up. Jordan stepped forward and removed the enchanted lanyard from his neck—the one tethered to the stretcher. Without hesitation, he leaned over and looped it around Alec's neck.

Alec blinked in surprise, immediately annoyed. "You've got to be joking," he said, eyes narrowing at Jordan.

"You're not doing anything else," Jordan muttered. "Just keep him from sliding into the snow."

Alec huffed, clearly insulted, but didn't argue further. The stretcher drifted obediently toward him, falling into step at his side. Behind Hazel, Jordan and Rafe moved into position, wands raised and expressions grim.

Jordan planted himself in front of the bear. Rafe turned his focus toward the lynx. They outnumbered the animals, but that meant nothing. These beasts were powerful alive, but as undead, they were nearly unstoppable. Hazel squared her shoulders, heart thudding in her chest.

They weren't going back into that cave. The air was brittle with cold and rising fear, every breath shallow and white. The undead hadn't moved yet, but Hazel could feel the pressure building, the inevitability of the moment just before the chaos.

Alec shifted beside her, his voice low and urgent. "Give me my wand."

Gwen's head snapped toward him and she let out a deep, threatening growl from the back of her throat. It was enough. Alec took a half-step back. It was clear Gwen wouldn't be giving him his wand back anytime soon. Hazel wished she would; they could use all the help they could get. But she understood why Gwen didn't trust him. She had her own doubts. Their captor had clearly been talking to a man, and while Hazel was almost certain it wasn't Alec, she wasn't one hundred percent. So she didn't press the issue.

The silence stretched like a wire pulled too tight.

Hazel fired the first spell, and the others followed. Spells flew from every direction. Jordan's incantation echoed off the trees, Rafe's wand flashed with blue light, and Gwen launched a curse that would've torn through anything living. The lynx staggered under the impact, but didn't fall. The bear didn't even flinch.

Hazel's stomach sank. These creatures didn't bleed. Didn't react. Didn't stop. She cast again. Nothing. Hazel's hand trembled, her wand useless. She glanced at her friends, and watched as each of their spells did nothing against the undead. Panic scratched at the edge of her throat, but she swallowed it down. Magic wasn't enough, at least not mage magic.

Fulgurkinesis was the answer. Thoughts of how Rafe and Jordan might view her, of who they might tell, passed through her mind, but she buried them. None of that mattered if they didn't survive.

You have to do it.

Hazel reached into her pocket, where she kept the small crystal wolf. Electricity surged through her, hot and wild. *Too much.* She forced some of it back inside the wolf until only her palms glowed with the energy.

With a sharp breath, she aimed straight at the lynx and let go. The bolt hit with a crack, the flash quicker than the blink of an eye. The lynx convulsed, then collapsed into the snow, twitching once before going still. Smoke curled up from its fur, the scent of sulfur and burnt hair thick in the air.

Hazel's chest rose and fell in quick bursts. It had worked.

"Yeah!" Rafe and Jordan yelled together.

Her secret was out now, but she didn't care as long as it saved her friends.

As Hazel turned her focus toward the advancing bear, the lynx convulsed unnervingly and stood back up. In one swift, brutal motion, it leaped onto Gwen, claws lashing out. Hazel's hand shot upward, ready to strike again.

"Not while it's on me! You'll kill us both!" Gwen yelled.

The words cut through the chaos, stopping Hazel just in time as Gwen wrestled with the weight of the undead animal clinging to her. Jordan screamed—sharp, panicked, and too close. Hazel pivoted at the sound and saw the blur of movement as the bear reared back and swung. Its massive paw collided with Jordan's chest, lifting him off his feet and flinging him into a tree with a sickening crack. He hit the trunk hard, then crumpled, sliding down into the snow without a sound.

"Jordan!" Rafe shouted as he ran to his side, but Jordan didn't move.

Hazel's breath caught. He was out cold and the bear was still coming.

Rage surged up through Hazel, eclipsing fear in a blinding wave. Jordan was down. Gwen was trapped. Her friends could die if she didn't act fast.

She turned back to the bear, raised both hands, and this time, she didn't hold back. Instead, she let the power tear through her.

Electricity exploded from her fingertips—white-hot, violent, and wild. The blast struck the bear square in the chest, lighting up its decaying body in a flicker of blinding arcs. The bear staggered, limbs locking as the charge ripped through it. Hazel didn't stop. She poured as much lightning as she could into the strike, pushing past the pain, past the shaking in her arms.

Finally, the bear collapsed, steam rising from its motionless form.

One down.

The moment the bear hit the ground, the lynx launched. It sprang from Gwen's shoulder, claws outstretched, and crashed into Hazel with full force, knocking her backward into the snow. She hit hard, breath leaving her in a sharp gasp.

But her hands were already glowing with the residual charge. Without hesitation, she thrust her palm into the lynx's chest and released the last of her magic. The electricity hit point-blank, slamming into its rib cage with a crack of thunder. The creature convulsed once as foam formed at its lips. Then it went limp, its body falling across hers in a heavy, smoking heap.

Hazel rolled the lynx's body off her chest, muscles trembling, lungs dragging in sharp, cold air. Her hands were numb, her magic drained.

For a brief moment, the world was silent, except for the hiss of cooling snow and the crackle of scorched fur. She'd done it—she'd stopped them. Her friends were safe because of her. Then her mind raced to Jordan and she sat up. She needed to make sure he was alright.

Before she could stand, Gwen shouted, "Hazel—look out!"

Hazel turned, heart lurching. Tristan was sliding off the stretcher a few feet away. His limbs moved with that same unnatural stiffness she'd seen in the lynx. His eyes opened, revealing milky irises. Empty.

No.

Hazel's stomach dropped. He must have died on the stretcher during the fight. Tristan was undead and headed straight for her.

Gwen

"They know you're the one who can take them out," Gwen breathed, every muscle locking tight. "You've got to recharge."

Hazel's glow was gone. The crackling light that had lit her up like a live wire moments ago had faded completely, leaving only the raw exhaustion on her face.

"I can't." She held up the crystal wolf and added, "I'm completely tapped out. When I reach for more, I feel it but I can't call it."

Gwen's stomach dropped. Spirit magic—the magic she used to call the lightning—was like a muscle and Hazel wasn't in fighting shape.

Tristan lunged, crashing into Hazel with terrifying speed. She barely got her hands up before he slammed her to the ground.

"Get off her!" Gwen shouted, firing a spell that struck him in the shoulder.

He didn't even flinch.

Another spell. Then another—but they didn't stop him. If she didn't do something fast, Tristan was going to tear her apart.

"Gwen, call the lightning and take him down!" Alec shouted at her from a dozen yards away, where he'd joined Rafe and Jordan.

"It doesn't work that way! That's Hazel's power not mine," she snarled at him.

"Yes, it does!" he shouted back, his jaw clenching.

"You do it then!" Gwen threw him his wand and waited for him to attack.

"It's not mine to call," Alec said as he aimed at Tristan, but cast nothing.

Great, I have to do it myself. Alec and Rafe will know my secret too. Gwen's stomach knotted but she pushed the worry down. *What's two more in the grand scheme of things?*

The only thing that truly mattered was saving Hazel, who was still struggling to fight Tristan off.

With a growl of frustration, Gwen shifted—skin to fur, fingers to claws.

Her wolf form hit the snow running.

Behind them, Rafe stood protectively over Jordan's unconscious form, casting again and again at Tristan, forcing him back by inches.

"By Terra, you've both been holding out on us!" Rafe whooped.

Gwen collided into Tristan with a bone-jarring crunch, but Gwen didn't stop, didn't let herself think. She sank her teeth into his neck and ripped a chunk of flesh off. His head was still attached to his body and she pushed through the foul taste, tearing pieces of him off one at a time. He continued to claw at her, but even as his nails cut into her sides, she didn't stop.

Alec stood just beyond the edge of the fight, his wand clutched tightly in his hand. His expression was focused, grim, but still he did nothing.

Coward.

Tristan ripped from her grip, and Gwen lunged at him to get him back under her control. At the same moment, Alec finally raised his wand and cast. The spell struck Tristan's chest in a burst of raw magic. It surged through his body—and into Gwen, still latched on to him with bared fangs and a mouthful of muscle.

Magic whipped through the connection, and Gwen barely had time to register the danger before her legs buckled, her jaw went slack, and everything blurred into darkness as the ground rushed up to meet her.

CHAPTER 41

Gwen

Gwen stirred to the sound of distant voices and the low rumble of carts rolling over cobblestone. The air smelled faintly of damp earth and hearth smoke. They were close to town. She blinked, disoriented, and then realized she was lying on a stretcher, bundled in an emergency blanket.

Hazel walked with quiet determination beside her, her hand steady on the lanyard, controlling the stretcher's movement. To her surprise, she was fully clothed. Hazel must have found her clothes that she'd spelled to return to the backpack when she shifted. *Shit my ring.* She hadn't had time to spell it to her backpack at the cave, it was probably buried beneath a foot of snow. At least Hazel had managed to find her bracelet. She felt the metal beneath her wrist but it was unclasped. With it off, her body must have healed itself. Good thinking on Hazel's part.

On the other side of her, Alec strolled like he had all the time in the world, his expression unreadable. When he caught her eye, he smiled, then winked. Gwen furrowed her brow as she frowned back at him. He was the reason she was on this thing, and she didn't trust him.

She glanced forward to find Jordan laid out on a second stretcher a few feet ahead of her. Rafe walked beside him, his hand on Jordan's shoulder.

She pushed herself upright on the stretcher to see if Jordan was awake, and Hazel startled beside her.

"Oh, thank Terra," Hazel breathed, relief flooding her face.

Gwen swung her legs over the side of the stretcher.

"Hey—no, stay down," Hazel said quickly, reaching for her arm. "You took a pretty gnarly spell."

"Yeah," Gwen snapped, brushing Hazel's hand off. Her eyes locked onto Alec. "Thanks to him." She didn't shout, but her voice was sharp.

"I was aiming for Tristan," Alec said, his voice maddeningly calm. "You'd released him from your grip when I shot the spell. If you hadn't latched back on to him, it never would have hit you."

Gwen rolled her eyes so hard it almost hurt. "Right. Because blasting me unconscious is just a technical error?"

He was right; she *had* let go of Tristan when he aimed the spell, but it didn't make her any less pissed.

"Can you please lie back down? You're still recovering," Hazel said, her voice gentle, pleading.

"I'm fine." Gwen shook her head. "Fully healed."

Before Hazel could argue again, Gwen shoved the blanket aside and jumped down from the stretcher. Her boots hit the dirt with a solid thud. She straightened up, steady on her feet. She wouldn't be going back into town on a stretcher.

"Perks of being a therian," she added, as she reattached her bracelet.

"About that," Rafe muttered.

She turned to him, already tensing.

This was going to be difficult to cover up. She'd gotten lucky with Harland. Logan had a mutual reason to keep her secret. Hazel and

Jordan were her best friends. And while she was close with Rafe and wanted to trust him, she couldn't negate that his father was a Brecilian Knight.

Alec, she didn't trust at all.

"When all this is over, we're talking about these secrets," Rafe said. He looked at Hazel. "*All* of them."

Not only had Gwen shifted, but Hazel had used lightning.

Hazel flashed him an apologetic grimace. "Any chance you could keep both of those things a secret until we do?"

"Obviously," Rafe said, though the tension in his jaw betrayed the edge beneath the joke. She hoped it was because he was left out of the secret, not that he was mad about who they truly were.

Both of them turned to look at Alec.

He sighed, then made an exaggerated X over his heart. "Secret's safe with me."

That's not going to be good enough for me.

"Swear it?" Gwen said, drawing her wand slowly from her belt.

Rafe raised a brow. "You think I'd actually tell someone?"

"No. I trust you," Gwen said, and she meant it for the most part. "But I can't risk it, not when our lives are on the line. People slip. I don't think you'd do it on purpose."

Rafe nodded in understanding.

"Do you trust *me*?" Alec asked with an arched brow.

"No," Gwen said grimly.

He let out a low laugh, sending a chill down her spine.

Hazel eyed him strangely, but said nothing.

"What about Jordan?" Rafe asked.

Her amusement faded as her gaze shifted to the stretcher a few feet ahead. Jordan still hadn't stirred. His face was pale, his brow creased even while unconscious. Guilt coiled low in her stomach.

I should've grabbed more potions.

"I'll have to wait until he's awake," she said. And he *would* wake up. She couldn't let herself believe anything else.

Gwen tightened her grip on her wand, its familiar weight

grounding her. She thought back to Harland—the way he'd locked her words down in the library, sealing away the truth about Abigail with nothing more than a whispered phrase. Whenever she tried to speak of it, the words bent around the truth like water around a stone. It had been suffocating at first, until Hazel had dropped the subject, but now she understood the usefulness of the spell.

She lifted her wand and pointed it at Rafe. "I need you to say, 'I swear I won't tell anyone about you being a therian and Hazel being an elf.'"

Rafe's eyes widened as she said the last words, finally understanding the full picture. He gazed at Hazel, his heart in his eyes, as he nodded and repeated the words back to Gwen before she cast, "*Verba Flectere*."

Then it was Alec's turn. A faint shimmer passed between them as the air rippled and stilled.

"That's it?" Rafe asked when she was finished with both of them.

"That's it," she confirmed. "If you try to talk about it," Gwen added, "your words will shift. Twist. You'll end up saying something else. Something that sounds normal—but isn't the truth."

Rafe blinked. "That's mildly unnerving."

Alec said nothing, and she wondered if he'd used the spell before.

"You'll be able to think about it," she added, "but not speak it. Not to anyone."

Hazel looked at Gwen, wide-eyed. "You've got a spell for everything, don't you?"

Gwen met her gaze, and smiled. "Just the things that matter."

The group fell into a rhythm as they continued forward, making their way out of the forest. Worry about how they were going to explain this without revealing themselves gnawed at Gwen as they walked. Would they be able to sell a story about a rescue mission in which Gwen and Hazel saved them all with a spell—again?

As they exited the safety of the trees, they were greeted by the sight of Eagles Ridge. Snow-dusted rooftops glinted under the winter sun. Figures moved briskly between buildings, spells flaring briefly as people cast protections, carried supplies, and gave orders. A massive canvas tent dominated the town square, its flaps snapping in the wind.

A moment passed before someone noticed them.

"There they are!" a woman shouted, her voice echoing across the town square.

Heads turned, one by one, in a ripple effect. People began running toward them from every direction and shouting their names or crying out, "They're back!" and "Over here. Get the medics!"

The fragile calm that had carried them through the woods shattered like glass as hands reached for them—checking for injuries, pulling them into stunned embraces, and leading them toward the large tent in the center of town with a mix of panic and celebration.

As she entered the medical tent, the familiar smell of cigars hit Gwen—her father. There were so many feelings triggered by his scent, including frustration, fear, and hope. In this moment, relief won out. If he was here, then nothing could get to her.

He was at the other end of the tent. His gray hair was shorter than the last time she'd seen him, but the white stripe framing his face still remained. He was wearing his patented leather jacket, with a Sons of Chaos patch that matched Pan's, jeans, and boots. He turned as her eyes landed on him, and he opened his arms, beckoning her. She felt like a little girl again—happy to have a dad that showed up, even if she knew he was flawed in countless ways.

Gwen rushed towards him, and he caught her in a hug. He held her tightly, for a heartbeat. Then he pulled back, gripping her shoulders hard.

"What were you thinking?" he snapped, eyes sharp with worry. "You could've been killed."

"I'm sorry, Dad."

He hugged her once more before letting go, allowing the medic to guide her toward one of the cots that lined both sides of the tent. Jordan was at the far end next to Alec, and a few beds down sat Rafe and Hazel. Gwen settled onto the edge of a cot a few feet away as a medic checked her pulse, her eyes, her reflexes, before moving on.

This is pointless. I'm fine.

Her dad never left her side. He didn't speak, didn't sit. He paced, back and forth, like a wolf barely tolerating the leash.

Gwen was the first to be cleared. The healer gave her a quick nod and moved on. She stood and began moving towards Hazel, who was bruised but sitting upright.

Her father caught her arm. "You're done here," he said. It wasn't harsh, but it wasn't a request either.

"I want to check on—" she started, but he was already steering her toward the tent flap.

"They'll be fine," he said, eyes scanning the perimeter.

She hesitated, glancing back at her friends—at *her pack*—but followed. She didn't have the strength to argue. Outside, the cold slapped her back to attention. Gwen didn't get far before a man approached, wearing a leather jacket with a Sons of Chaos patch embroidered on it. She stalled as her eyes locked on him. Her uncle. She hadn't seen him in years, had barely spoken to him even when she had. But she'd recognize his face anywhere.

He looked eerily like her father, except for the hair. While her father's was silver-grey—a blend of her grandfather's jet black and her grandmother's snow white—Rendall, his younger brother, had inherited her grandfather's coloring entirely. If she had to guess, her Uncle Rendall was a black wolf when he shifted since hair color often mirrored a therian's fur.

He gave her a polite, quick nod like she was someone he vaguely remembered before returning his attention to her father. "The Knights have a lead. They're investigating someone directly tied to the incident."

Gwen's stomach twisted at the mention of the Knights.

Of course they're here.

If that fact bothered her father, he didn't make it known.

"They haven't released a name yet," Rendall added.

Beside her, her father went rigid. His jaw clenched. "We'll conduct our own investigation." Rendall was her father's Beta, his second-in-command, so he would do whatever he told him. Her father turned to her. "Tell me everything. Now."

His tone didn't leave room for argument, but Gwen had no plans to tell him everything. She was going to leave out the fact that Hazel was an elf with fulgurkinesis and the part where Gwen had shifted in front of witnesses. If he found out, she didn't know what he'd do—but it wouldn't be good.

She kept her voice steady as she recounted the cave, the undead creatures, and Tristan. She told him about the fight, the injuries, and how they'd made it back. Her father listened in neutral silence. When she finished, he gave a short nod, then turned to Rendall.

"Round up the others and do a perimeter search. Make sure nothing followed them back."

Rendall gave a crisp nod and strode off without a word.

"Gwen!" Nova yelled from a couple yards away. Klaus towered next to her, his giant form impossible to miss.

It was clear they had come from the direction of Saint Elias, led by Maduro, Harland, Jude, and Oswald. At the sight of her, they broke away from the faculty and ran straight for her.

Gwen blinked, stunned. She hadn't expected them to be allowed out of the mountain. She wondered who had pulled those strings and if it might have been Harland. When she caught his eye, he gave her a concerned look. He moved to follow Klaus when Jude grabbed his arm and herded him towards the Knights outside of Kodiak Brew. He gave her a small nod and she returned it to let him know she was alright. It was the only thing they could do in such a crowded space.

Nova reached her first, eyes wide and brimming with tears. She threw her arms around Gwen, holding her tight. "Thank Terra you're alright," she whispered against her shoulder.

Gwen stood frozen for half a beat before returning the hug, guilt already rising in her throat. She'd caused such a scene the last time they'd been together that she wasn't sure she deserved this reaction.

Nova pulled back enough to look her in the eye. "Jordan?" she asked, her voice shaky.

Gwen nodded. "He's going to be okay." She hoped she wasn't lying. "He's still inside the medical tent."

Nova gave her a grateful look before sprinting toward the medical tent.

Klaus moved beside Gwen, hands in his coat pockets, trying to look casual despite the bags under his eyes and the tension in his jaw. "Your mom's going to kill you," he muttered, just loud enough for her to hear.

Gwen ignored him and pulled him into a hug.

"She should be more concerned with her father right now," said a voice behind him.

Klaus went rigid, and Gwen released him. He turned slowly, eyes widening slightly as he registered who was standing there.

"Sir," he said quickly, giving a curt nod.

Her father didn't return the greeting. They'd never gotten along; her mom's side pretty much hated him and he knew it. He studied Klaus for a moment, then said, "There's a tent two rows over short on hands. Go."

His Alpha voice hit the air like a low pulse, subtle but undeniable. Klaus's posture straightened, his expression neutralizing. He nodded again, eyes dropping, and without a word, turned and headed toward the other tent.

"You didn't have to do that!" Gwen said as she watched him go.

Her father ignored her. She hated when he used his Alpha voice. She knew what it felt like to have your will bend without permission.

Footsteps crunched behind them as Rendall returned.

"The Sons are assembled," he said quietly. "They're waiting outside town. There was nothing in the perimeter."

Her father gave a single nod. "We'll check the cave." His eyes flicked briefly to Gwen, unreadable. "I'll meet them at the tree line in a moment."

Rendall hesitated for half a breath, then turned and disappeared back into the bustle, leaving them alone again.

"I'm leaving Pan with you again," her father said, finally. "I don't trust your judgment."

Gwen bristled, jaw tightening. *Of course you don't.*

Then his tone dropped—deep, firm, laced with that unmistakable Alpha command he'd used on Klaus. "Pack your things and head home."

The air shifted, thick with expectation. The words were meant to force obedience. To leave no room for argument. But Gwen didn't flinch, didn't move.

Oh shit! Her heart kicked hard against her ribs. *It didn't work.*

Her father was an Alpha and she was not. Could never be. It should have worked. The only other time she'd seen that voice fail was with Logan—and she'd told herself he must not be an Alpha. Only men were Alphas, but not all men. She was a woman—women therians weren't born with the Alpha gene. And only other Alphas could resist the Alpha voice.

Her breath caught in her throat, but she forced a nod and turned on her heel. As soon as she moved away, her father disappeared into the trees and Gwen let out a breath. She waited just long enough to be sure he was truly gone before heading straight for the medical tent.

Gwen nearly collided with Rafe and Hazel as she lifted the tent flap to enter. She threw her arms around Hazel first, then Rafe, pulling both of them in tight. She looked around, hopeful for Jordan, but he wasn't with them.

"Is he...?"

"Still out," Rafe said gently, "but the medics say he'll wake soon. They're sure of it."

Hazel nodded, her expression tired but steady. "He's going to be okay."

Relief poured through Gwen. *He's going to be okay.*

Maduro stepped into their path, followed by Miggins, Oswald,

Jude, Harland, and two Knights, their silver-etched badges glinting beneath their cloaks.

"We need to speak with you," Maduro said.

Gwen tensed. *Of course they did.*

Hazel

Hazel stepped through the doors of Kodiak Brew, followed by Gwen and Rafe. The scent of roasted beans had been replaced by wax polish, wet wool, and tension so thick it stuck to the back of her throat.

The tables were pushed aside, and the chairs made a semi-circle around the room, filled with a few Knights and a group of familiar Sorcerers from Saint Elias. Rafe's father sat in the center of the circle. Two Knights took the empty seats to the right of Estaban De La Vega, while Maduro took the seat on his left, with Miggins, Oswald, Jude, and finally Thacker filling in the empty seats on that side of the circle. Hazel froze as she watched Thacker closely for any signs of guilt, but he looked as he always did—put together and at ease. If he was behind the attacks, he was hiding it flawlessly. Except for one little problem—he'd slipped up and let Hazel hear his voice.

Looking at him now, with her mind and energy restored from the potions Gwen had brought, she was more sure than ever. It had been him.

Three empty chairs sat in the middle of the semi-circle, clearly for them.

Why in Salem aren't there four? Where is Alec?

It looked like a courtroom, and she didn't think it was fair he got to skip the hot seat.

Knight De La Vega gestured with a hand for them to sit.

Hazel's palms were slick with sweat, and her pulse thudded in her throat as she waited for someone to say something. Beside her,

Gwen radiated tension, shoulders rigid and jaw clenched. Hazel swallowed hard and tried to slow her breathing. She kept her face neutral, her voice ready—but her chest felt tight, like the whole room was pressing in on her.

She glanced sideways at Rafe, steady and silent beside her. She trusted him. But still, she was glad Gwen had cast the spell in the woods, binding his words from revealing what they were. No matter how messy things got in here, it would ensure the truth wasn't let out.

Knight De La Vega looked toward Sorcerer Maduro. "Where is the chancellor?" he asked, his tone flat but expectant.

Maduro exhaled. "She's currently indisposed, handling communications with parents and senior coven leaders. She's asked me to sit in."

Hazel wasn't sure if the chancellor's absence was in their favor or not.

"Fine. We'll begin with you." He looked down at his clipboard as if looking for her name, then said, "Catherine Hazel Thorne."

Rafe stiffened beside her.

Hazel swallowed. *He used my legal name. This can't be good.*

Gwen opened her mouth to speak, but he held up a hand without even glancing her way.

"You'll have your turn. Now Miss Thorne, please tell us in your own words what happened."

Hazel shifted in her seat, trying to stay grounded under the weight of a dozen eyes.

"The night we disappeared," she began, glancing quickly at Rafe, "we were in the woods on the outskirts of campus." She left out that they were in the hot spring caves reserved for upperclassmen in case it would get Rafe in trouble. Besides, she didn't think it mattered where on campus they'd been taken, just that they were. "We heard a sound and Rafe went to check it out. When he didn't come back, I followed him, then everything went black."

She walked them through what happened after—waking up in

chains, seeing Tristan barely conscious, Rafe drifting in and out. She told them about the box their wands were locked inside. About the woman's blurred face, how she barely spoke, and when she did, it was distorted.

At the mention of the woman, Knight De La Vega stiffened.

Another Knight leaned toward him. "That tracks with what we found." The Knight made a subtle glance—quick, almost indistinguishable—toward where Jude sat before returning his gaze to the three of them.

Hazel's skin prickled.

Knight De La Vega looked at his son. "Rafael De La Vega, can you please recount your memories?" He was so formal. Clearly Rafe wouldn't be getting any preferential treatment.

Rafe cleared his throat. "I'm sorry, I'm not much help," he admitted quietly. "I was out unconscious for most of it." His cheeks flushed as he looked down. Hazel caught the way his jaw tightened and thought—not unkindly—that he was probably embarrassed to say it in front of his father.

Another Knight addressed Hazel. "Do you know who the woman was, Miss Thorne?"

Hazel shook her head. "No. But there was a man too."

"Did you know him?" the Knight asked.

"I—" The words lodged in her throat as she glanced at Gwen. She hadn't warned her, or even shared her suspicions. There hadn't been time. "I think I know who it was."

The room seemed to constrict, and Gwen jolted beside her. She and Rafe both turned to look at Hazel, wide-eyed. Hazel avoided Gwen's gaze as she weighed the option of really saying it out loud, and how much it might hurt Gwen, or anger her. But it was too late. She'd already said she had a suspicion. She couldn't back down now.

Hazel's eyes landed on Thacker.

"I think it was him."

Thacker's brows shot to his hairline, showing perfect surprise. If

Hazel didn't know in her gut she was right, she'd be questioning herself on his reaction alone.

The room went dead silent with the implication. Even the low murmurs between the Knights and faculty died off. All eyes shifted toward Sorcerer Thacker.

One of the Knights stepped forward, his blonde brows furrowed as he kept one hand on the wand holstered at his hip. "What do you mean 'think?' You actually saw him? In the cave?"

"No," Hazel admitted. "I heard him speaking to her outside the cave."

Murmurs erupted once more.

"Didn't you say their voices were distorted?" a redheaded Knight cut in sharply.

"The woman's was," Hazel explained. The Knight was already shaking his head before she finished, "but not his."

Knight De La Vega rubbed his chin. "Sorcerer Thacker has been helping us look for you. His absence surely would have been noticed."

Hazel had no argument for that other than mages could advinere, but everyone knew that.

"You were in a cave where the acoustics were already distorted," the redheaded Knight said. "Add that on top of the fact that you were sleep-deprived and under incredible duress." He crossed his arms as he sat back in his chair. "There's no evidence of a second suspect. Is there a chance you could be wrong?" He quirked a brow. "Or could have been dreaming?"

Several Knights nodded in agreement.

Hazel opened her mouth, closed it. *Could I be wrong?* She knew she'd been nearly delirious from lack of sleep. Maybe she *had* drifted off and had a nightmare. Maybe her subconscious had wanted to blame Thacker because she already knew shady things about him.

Her stomach twisted in knots as she looked back at Maduro and Jude, both studying her with curiosity, but not encouragement. Thacker's eyes landed on her, but she refused to return his gaze or

Gwen's, who was practically staring a hole through the side of her face.

"I don't know."

Rafe reached over and squeezed her hand. Hazel immediately exhaled, her chest loosening a tiny bit.

At least one person isn't upset with me.

"Do you have anything else that supports your suspicions of Sorcerer Thacker, Miss Thorne?" Knight De La Vega asked.

Hazel swallowed. Yes, there were plenty of things that made her suspicious of him. She couldn't tell them about the conversation with Jude. That was hearsay, and there was nothing illegal about the conversation. While Thacker's relationship with Gwen had been wrong, it didn't make him a murderer. That left her with one piece of information to share.

She drew a deep breath, trying to gather herself, and then flashed Gwen a sympathetic look. "Earlier this semester, Gwen came to tell me that she caught Thacker doing something inappropriate with a student in his office. He chased her down in the library and insisted they have a private conversation. When she returned, she wouldn't tell me what happened."

That earned a pause.

"Or *couldn't*," Hazel added.

Gwen frowned at Hazel, sadness filling her eyes. Guilt bubbled in Hazel's stomach for bringing Gwen into it and betraying a secret between them.

"Sorcerer Thacker has been assisting the chancellor," Sorcerer Maduro said, and all eyes landed on her. "Along with several other faculty members. We've been working privately to investigate certain students. To rule out any potential connections to the attacks."

Hazel blinked. "Then why did he spell Gwen?"

There was a beat of silence.

"I used a secrecy spell to keep her from speaking about the investigation. It was confidential. We couldn't risk panic," Thacker said, his voice gentle yet slightly condescending.

Hazel's heart thudded hard. She looked at Gwen instinctively, and in that moment, it clicked—the way Gwen had used the same spell in the woods on Rafe and Alec. That's how she'd known it. Thacker had taught her.

Hazel felt her cheeks flush, heat crawling up her neck—not from embarrassment, but anger. If she'd had all the facts, she might not have accused him. But there was no taking it back now. Hopefully Gwen would forgive her.

The Knights shifted their attention to Gwen. Before the next question could leave their lips, the door to Kodiak Brew slammed open, a gust of wind cutting through the warmth of the fire from the hearth.

A young mage burst in, breathless. "Mara's in the wind."

Every head in the room turned.

"She's gone," the runner continued. "Left before anyone could question her."

Hazel felt the words ripple through the room like a detonation—quiet but devastating. Jude went pale, hands clenching at their sides. They looked like someone had knocked the air out of them.

"We searched her home and found maps, blood markers, and books on siphoning. It's enough to move her to the top of the list."

"That makes no sense," Hazel blurted out. "Mara is mundane."

Knight De La Vega studied Hazel with pity in his eyes. "That's what she wanted us to believe."

Hazel's heart sank.

No.

The room broke into speculation, some convinced, others less so.

Hazel's voice broke through before she could second-guess it. "It wasn't her. She was drained," she said, her voice firm.

"We believe it was a way to throw off suspicion," Knight De La Vega said. "And it almost worked."

The following silence was suffocating.

This was absurd. Hazel looked to Jude, waiting for them to defend their partner. Their shoulders tensed and their hands trembled slightly at their sides. Then came the sound. Soft. Shaky. A choked breath that turned into a whimper. And then they broke. Jude's face crumpled as the tears came in earnest, their body folding in on itself as if they could somehow disappear inside their own grief. Hazel stood and took a step toward them, but stopped when Sorcerer Maduro reached them first.

"We'll need to question them," Knight De La Vega said to the Knight at his side. "Usher Jude to the holding tent."

Hazel watched them go while her stomach churned with everything she couldn't say, couldn't fix. The door closed behind them, and somehow, the room felt colder. All eyes turned back to her and her friends.

Rafe's father spoke, clinical and detached. "I think we're done here."

Another Knight nodded. "We've gotten all we need from the three of you."

Hazel swallowed hard and looked over at Gwen, whose face was carved from stone. Rafe's expression was also unreadable, but she could see it in his eyes—he was ready to get out of this place. So was she.

CHAPTER 42

Hazel

Hazel sat on the cold floor of the cave, her wrist shackled to the wall by a familiar length of gold chain.

No. No, not again.

Panic surged through her chest, stealing the air from her lungs. Her heart thundered as she yanked at the chain, willing it to break, to give, to do something—but it didn't budge. The metal bit into her skin, cruel and unrelenting.

The cave was dark and damp, the air thick with the scent of mildew and old blood. Firelight flickered weakly in the center of the space, casting shadows that twisted and crawled across the floor like living things. She pulled her legs into herself, and the shadows fell back. She rocked herself back and forth to help slow her breathing, but then she heard a slow, shallow breath coming from the other side of the room. Hazel whipped her head toward the sound, her pulse spiking again. Was it Rafe?

Terror clamped down on her lungs as she tried to make out the figure in the darkness. Not him too.

Please, this can't be happening again.

The chains rattled as she pulled against them, trying to reach him—but the shadows danced towards her again and she pressed herself back against the wall.

"Rafe?" she whispered, but there was no reply.

A jolt shot through her body and Hazel gasped as she snapped awake. She blinked up at the dim ceiling of the dorm room, heart still racing, and found Gwen kneeling beside her, one hand on her shoulder.

"Ouch," Gwen muttered, shaking out her hand. "You shocked me."

"Sorry," Hazel breathed, still trying to catch up to the present.

Gwen gave a tired half-smile. "It's okay. You were having another nightmare."

She'd been having nightmares ever since they returned from the cave three weeks ago. Each one was different from the next, making it impossible for her to tell what was real, what was a vision, and what wasn't. It made her long for the dreams of her mother—or aunt, rather—but those had vanished when these began.

Hazel sat up slowly, the warm blanket slipping from her shoulders as the morning light filtered through the dorm window. She must have fallen asleep on the couch last night when they'd returned from Kodiak Brew. They'd been out celebrating passing their finals and Hazel had had a lot to drink. The new bartender didn't seem to care as much about serving underaged students as Tristan. Her heart ached for him; he'd died so young and deserved better than the hand he'd been dealt. That was one of the reasons she'd drank as much as she did.

Once Mara had been declared public enemy number one, the student body had stopped hating them. No one whispered when they walked in a room anymore, unless it was to call them heroes. Rafe and Hazel had finished out the semester as a couple, along with Nova and Jordan. Elodie and Gwen were still single but Gwen didn't seem quite as jealous of Nova anymore. They'd even sung karaoke together last night, their voices half mocking, half sincere as they belted out an old mage-rock anthem. Everything was right in her world.

And yet the weight in her chest hadn't lifted.

Tristan was dead, Mara was missing, and Jude—well they'd never returned to campus after Mara was accused. Hazel was having a harder time adjusting back to normal life than her friends. She was still convinced of Mara's innocence, which meant whoever took them was still out there lurking.

She wanted to warn her friends of her fears, but after being wrong about Thacker, she'd kept it to herself. Which left her alone with her feelings. She wanted to talk to Jude about all of it, but Sorcerer Maduro had warned against it. She'd told her that Jude needed time, and Hazel was trying to respect that.

"You should start packing," Gwen said. "I've got to re-spell the room before we leave."

Hazel let out a dramatic groan and flopped back on the couch. "I don't want to leave. I'm not ready to go back to Arkansas, and I have nowhere else to go."

The last thing she wanted was to go home to her brother, who'd just tell her to forgive their father and pretend everything was fine. While she felt a twinge of sadness knowing it had been a whole school year since she'd seen her father, the reality that she hadn't heard from either of them since she'd left erased any bit of guilt she carried for leaving.

"Aren't you coming back with me?" Gwen asked, blinking like it should've been obvious.

Hazel sat up straighter. "What?"

Hope soared within her. She hadn't dared ask Gwen, refusing to intrude on her family or wear out her welcome, but spending the holidays in Britton Place with Gwen's family had been one of the best times of her life. It would be a dream to spend a summer there.

Gwen shrugged casually. "I assumed you'd stay with me and my mom this summer."

Hazel stared at her for a moment, overwhelmed by the offer—by how natural Gwen made it sound, like it hadn't even been a question when it was what Hazel had hoped for all semester.

She stood and pulled Gwen into a hug before she could stop herself. "Thank you," she murmured into Gwen's hair.

Gwen stepped back and grinned. "I signed us up to be counselors at Camp Camelot. Jordan and Rafe are going to do it too."

"Seriously?" Hazel had never been to summer camp, and the idea thrilled her.

"Seriously." Gwen tossed her a duffel bag from the bed. "Now pack. If you make me spell around your stuff, I'm going to 'accidentally' charm all your clothes pink."

Hazel laughed but packed quickly, not sure if Gwen was joking. Gwen muttered to herself and waved her wand at Hazel's bedroom ceiling.

Nothing happened.

Hazel glanced up. "You okay over there?"

Gwen frowned dramatically. "It's not working. I think the room's stuck like this forever."

Hazel's eyes widened. "What do you mean stuck?! You said—"

Gwen cracked a grin, wand twirling between her fingers. "Relax. I'm messing with you."

Hazel groaned, tossing a rolled-up pair of socks at her head. "You're the worst."

"And yet, I'm your best friend." Gwen winked and finally cast the proper charm. The room immediately began to shimmer and shift as it returned to its natural state.

Hazel shook her head, smiling despite herself. Gwen seemed like her normal self again. Which meant maybe Hazel would soon too.

"Hey, I've got to run something back to the library." Hazel slung her backpack over her shoulder. "Want to come with me?"

Gwen grabbed her jacket from the hook by the door. "I've got my own detour to make."

Hazel didn't ask where, but part of her wondered if it was to see

Thacker. The guilt edged back in, sharp and familiar, with the thought of him. She'd accused him. Publicly. Loudly. Finals had been awkward enough, but he hadn't seemed angry—just detached. Still, she hated how that hung between her and Gwen, although her friend had never held it against her.

"Meet at the admin building?" Hazel asked.

"Sounds good."

Before leaving Hazel cast at their bags, making them disappear. When they arrived at the admin building later their luggage would be there waiting on them. Then they stepped into the hallway together and the door swung shut behind them.

Hazel entered the library to find it utterly silent, which wasn't unexpected, given the semester was over. The librarian wasn't at her station, so Hazel placed her books in the return stack and then headed deeper into the library. A faint, familiar giggle stopped her in her tracks.

"Evelyn?" Hazel whispered as her heart sped up.

No one answered.

A shimmering flutter of purple on the stairs caught her eye. A soft, lilting giggle echoed down again. It was Evelyn. She stood just outside her line of sight, only the edge of her cloak visible. A moment passed, and when she didn't move, didn't run, Hazel knew Evelyn was inviting her to follow.

Hazel walked behind her as she proceeded up the stairs. They climbed up, passing the second floor, then the third, but only Hazel's steps sounded on the mahogany staircase. When Hazel reached the fourth floor, Evelyn was nowhere to be seen. But Hazel knew where to go. She could navigate to this row of books blindfolded by now, with how many times she'd visited.

The last time she'd come here, she had been afraid, chased off. This time, she felt emboldened by her new powers, her newfound identity. An elf. A friend that would stop at nothing to save those she loved. Hazel was a lot more than she'd ever expected.

The book sat neatly on the shelf, as if it hadn't evaded her all semester. Hazel took a deep breath as she reached for it, a tremor of anticipation coursed through her. As soon as she held the book in her hands, she clutched it to her chest and scanned her surroundings, straining to hear any sign of another. Evelyn still wasn't here. No one was.

She breathed a sigh of relief before cracking open the book and skipping straight to the first page. Black ink was scrawled in the margins. Someone had left notes.

"Finally," an airy voice said from behind her.

Hazel whirled, her breath catching at the sight of the iridescent image of her aunt staring back at her with the same black hair and hazel eyes as her own. A pang of longing twisted in Hazel's chest at Evelyn's striking resemblance to her mother—the same light dusting of freckles across the bridge of her nose, the delicate curve of a cupid's bow on her upper lip. Yet, there were differences too—Evelyn's face was rounder, like Hazel's, while Cora's was more oval.

"It's you," Hazel breathed in disbelief.

"You have gotten quicker." Evelyn winked.

Her words, so similar to the ones from Hazel's dreams, struck her to the core. This whole time, she was supposed to be here with Evelyn. It wasn't her mother who'd brought her to SEU. It was Evelyn who'd haunted her visions and egged her on to come to Saint Elias.

And now she was fulfilling her vision.

"Why have you been hiding from me?"

"I haven't been hiding," Evelyn said. "I've been waiting for you to catch up."

Hazel suppressed an eye roll at her double speak. The last thing she wanted to do was make Evelyn leave again by disrespecting her.

"But then why make it so hard? Why hide the book from me?"

Hazel's voice trembled as she asked two of the questions that had plagued her since learning of Evelyn's ghost.

Evelyn laughed, an eerie, twinkling sound that sent shivers down Hazel's spine. "You weren't ready, little bird."

Hazel tilted her head as her brows rose. "So you burned me to keep from getting it?"

"I have burned many things, but never you," Evelyn promised, putting her translucent hand over her chest.

Hazel blinked rapidly as she digested the words. *Never you.*

"Then who burn—" Hazel stopped. There was only one other person on campus with the ability to conjure an element—that she knew of. He also happened to hate her.

Dane Bellamy.

That fucking asshole.

"See! You've gotten so quick," Evelyn said, reading the realization on Hazel's face. "Now read the book—all of it." Evelyn arched a brow. "Then we can speak again."

Hazel sucked in a breath. Surely, she couldn't be leaving so soon. Hazel had so many more questions. "Wait! Please! Do you know where my mother is?"

Evelyn reached for Hazel's shoulder, but did not touch her, letting her hand hover as she gazed at Hazel with sadness. "Cora shut herself off to me years ago."

Hazel's throat tightened as disappointment filled her. She'd come to SEU in hopes of finding answers about her mother. And while she had some, none of them were the one that mattered to her most: was her mother okay?

"But I can teach you how to reach for her," Evelyn said.

Hope flooded Hazel.

"As soon as you finish the book." Evelyn flashed a dimpled smile at her, then vanished as abruptly as she'd appeared.

A giddy, uncontrollable laugh bubbled up from Hazel's chest; adrenaline pumped in her veins from seeing her aunt's ghost, finally having the book safely in her hands, and the promise of learning how to reach her mother—whatever that meant. Relief wasn't a good enough word. She laughed until her sides hurt.

What a year!

After wiping the tears of delirious relief from her eyes, Hazel took a deep breath. She finally focused on the first note in the margin. A single word leapt out to her: *Dragon*.

She settled in, eager to finally unlock the answers held within the book's pages.

Gwen

Gwen took a deep breath as she raised her fist to knock on Harland's door—for the third time. Maybe this time, she'd actually knock instead of turning around and walking off. She wasn't sure what she was expecting from this interaction. She was still angry with him for how he treated her after Christmas, but now that so much time had passed, the anger had dulled to annoyance. He'd basically been a ghost since Hazel's accusation, but Gwen needed to speak to him. To get closure.

This would be her last chance to see him until the fall. The campus was mostly emptied out for the summer, but she hoped to catch him before he left.

Her nerves hummed with anticipation as she finally knocked.

No answer.

She knocked again.

Still nothing.

Heart pounding, Gwen tried the handle. It turned easily. The door creaked open, revealing an empty room.

Stepping inside the familiar quiet of his professor's quarters, Gwen moved through the vacant space that held so many moments for them—Harland's hand covering hers as they stirred her elixir, the shared laughter echoing in the small living room during late-night study sessions while they waited for the elixir to finish. A sharp pang of longing filled her chest, and she hated herself for it. She missed the effortless comfort she found in his presence, the easy banter that had flowed between them, just as much as the physical fireworks. For the millionth time, she wished for a reality where he was not her professor, leaving him free to be completely hers.

As she drifted towards the small kitchen, a white envelope lying on the counter caught her eye. Her name was scrawled across the front in his unmistakable handwriting. She snatched it up and tore it open.

Dear Miss Bishop,

This letter is spelled for your eyes only. I guess it's presumptuous of me to assume you will stop by here on your way home for the summer, especially after how things ended. I suppose if I come back next year and it's still sitting here, I'll know where things stand between us. I hope for my sake, it's not.

I know I don't deserve it, but I'm hoping you'll give me a second chance. This last semester has been unbearable without you. I know it's my fault for pulling away, but my feelings for you were becoming so intense that I grew scared. It's not an excuse, just an absurd fact, but after I almost lost you my need for you is bigger than my fear. Please come back to me.

Always yours,

Harland

A subtle weight shifted inside the envelope. Gwen tipped the contents into her palm—his key.

She scanned the letter once more, searching for clues, and then flipped it over. On the back, he'd added a few more words.

PS Visit me.

She stared at the two words for a long moment, a smile tugging at her lips despite the tangled web of their situation. He'd given her an open invitation to his place. Whether she was ready to use it or not, she knew he wouldn't be seeing anyone else this summer. A thrill shot through her at the thought that he'd be waiting on her for a change.

She slid the note and key into her pocket, then left the cottage. Her heart was lighter as she headed toward the admin building. Gwen had barely made it out of the professors' quarters when Logan jogged out from the Coventry archway.

"Wait up!" he called.

Gwen looked around to see who he was talking to, but with no one else nearby, she realized he was talking to her.

"Klaus said you needed this," he said, holding out a package. It was shaped like a book, wrapped in plain brown paper and tied loosely with twine. She raised a brow as she accepted it.

"What you did for your friends was brave," he explained, his voice flat. A beat passed before he added, "And stupid."

Gwen opened her mouth to fire something back, but he cut her off.

"Consider this a peace offering." His tone made it clear he didn't give them out often. Gwen smiled at the compliment. "But don't expect any more favors. If you want Alterion resources, you'll have to fight your way in like the rest of your classmates." He gave her a sharp wink, then walked away.

Gwen tore the paper off right there on the sidewalk, her heart hammering against her ribs. It was the book—*Malsano de la Animo*. The one she'd tried to smuggle out of Alterion. The one every thread of research about feras had pointed toward.

The title stared up at her, printed in inky black. The night she'd found it, she thought it was written in Latin, but now looking at it more closely, it most certainly was not Latin, although similar. She flipped it open. Nothing on the pages made sense. It wasn't even any language she knew of.

"Great," she muttered, snapping it closed with a frustrated huff.

This is completely useless unless I can figure out how to read it.

She shoved the book and wrapping paper into her backpack and took off down the path toward the admin building.

Hazel was waiting for her when she arrived, her face pale and eyes wide as she wrung her hands.

"Salem, you look like you've seen a ghost."

"I did!" Hazel said. "I saw my Aunt Evelyn. I talked to her." She pulled a green book with gold lettering from her bag.

Gwen didn't know what was so special about it. "Hazel, the semester is over."

Hazel pointed at a note in the margin. "Look."

"'Dragons are made by being burned and bound,'" Gwen read aloud. She scrunched up her brows. "I thought that dragons were hatched —born—whatever."

"I know. Me too. Keep reading."

"'Only the strongest Geminae Animarum will survive.'" Gwen paused, letting the unfamiliar Latin words roll around in her thoughts as she dissected their roots. Gemini meant twins. Anima meant soul. A flicker of recognition sparked as the Latin translation clicked into place. "Geminae Animarum? Twin Souls?"

Hazel nodded, confirming Gwen's translation to Latin was correct, then she frantically flipped the page and pointed at another note.

"'The therian and their partner must accept the bond to become.'" Gwen's brain hurt. None of this made any sense. "To become what? What do they mean 'partner'?"

"I don't know." Hazel chewed on her lip.

"Who wrote these notes?" Gwen asked.

"My aunt I think," Hazel said.

"Why in Salem was she concerned about dragons?"

"I don't know—yet. I need time to go over it properly," Hazel said, storing the book in her bag.

Gwen nodded. "Let's go home."

They made their way through the tunnel to Eagles Ridge, talking about dragons and their year at Saint Elias, though they skirted around the last month. Gwen knew that Hazel still harbored guilt about mistakenly accusing Harland. But Gwen wasn't angry. She'd have done the same if their roles were reversed. Hopefully the summer would allow them to overcome the awkwardness that still reared its ugly head anytime they spoke of him. Or the kidnapping. Or history.

As they reached the ward lines that would allow them to *advinere* to Maine, a breeze picked up. It carried a familiar scent that tickled Gwen's nose. It wasn't an overtly foul smell, but uncommon and somewhat unpleasant—like boiled eggs.

Where do I know that from?

Her instincts nagged at her, so Gwen stretched her senses, but with her bracelet on, she couldn't place it.

Gwen grabbed Hazel's arm and pulled her to a stop. "Wait."

Hazel looked around. "What's wrong?"

Gwen unlatched her bracelet and inhaled deeply, taking in the scents around her. The odors of sulfur and fire permeated the air. She *knew* that smell.

A gust of wind carried the scent in from behind them.

Gwen turned, with every intention of hunting it down, but she stopped short when saw who watched them.

Alec.

He stood against the back of a building, arms crossed as his amber eyes studied them both.

Her wolf snarled inside her mind. Its instincts insisted that the smell came from him. But she needed to confirm it. She closed her eyes and shut off her other senses. Sight, sound, touch, even the subtle shifts in the air all faded into the muted background until the world went utterly dark. Then she inhaled deeply and sifted through the scented layers of the world around her. She found it beneath the clean scent of mountain air and salty tang of the sea. It was a scent that belied power and chaos. She'd smelled it during the exam, and then again while experiencing the Leabhar Feòla.

Her heart pounded a frantic rhythm against her ribs as her eyes shot open, wide with a mixture of fear and fury. "He's been masking his scent this whole time—since we got to Alaska," she whispered to Hazel, her voice trembling with the shock of the revelation. "I knew no one smelled like nothing."

Hazel swallowed. "Schaden?"

Gwen shook her head. "Dragon."

The End

THANK YOU FOR READING

We know TBRs are limitless and there is not enough time in our short lives to read all the books on our wishlists. We are sincerely honored that you have spent precious time and energy on our book. It was a joy to write and we hope that it was a joy for you to read. If it was, we would appreciate a short review on your preferred bookish platform. As debut indie authors, reviews are crucial and even a line or two would mean the world to us.

ALSO BY NADIA TATE

Coming Soon

THE CULLING OF COVENS

Book two of the Saint Elias University Series will continue Gwen and Hazel's journey at SEU as they enter the Culling to find a coven to call their own.

Sign up at https://www.authornadiatate.com/newsletter for Nadia Tate's newsletter and be the first to see book two's cover.

ACKNOWLEDGMENTS

At our hearts, we are storytellers. We love a good yap, sharing the tea, and making people laugh, so it should have been no surprise to our friends and families when we said we wanted to write a book. It probably wasn't. But then we did it. For three and half years (with a few hiatuses for mental health) we dreamed, world built, plotted, scene blocked, wrote, re-wrote, edited, edited again (and again), and then finally proofed. And we truly believe we shocked everyone—but most of all ourselves.

Our list of people to be thankful for is long and we know how lucky we are for that. First, to our parents, Mark, Debbie, and Linda. Somewhere along the way, you raised two perfect children into two perfect readers who then became two perfect writers... Just kidding! We know we are flawed, but more importantly we have been raised in such a way that we believe we can accomplish anything we set our minds to. What a testament to your love.

To our significant others, Dan and Jonathan, your patience is unmatched. Thank you for loving us the way best friend co-authors need to be loved—there was no roadmap for this journey, but you have both been wonderful navigators.

To those who never let us sleep on our dreams, even when it would have been easier to throw in the towel. Jon, you have been our biggest cheerleader. Thank you for believing in us even when we didn't believe in ourselves. Bo, Trish, and Austyn, thank you for helping us put the final touches on our book baby, but even more, thank you for all of your unwavering support and kind words.

Mandy, thank you for our personalized author signature, it was the best gift for an author duo who had no idea how to sign their names.

To our friends and family that constantly asked about the book, checked in on us, and encouraged us, we can never thank you enough. You kept us motivated more than you will ever know. Anita, Steve, Aaron, Mitch, Kyle, Katie, Kevin, Linda, Bethany, Alan and Vonda thank you for being such an integral part of our lives. We know we would not be who we are today without growing up a part of your family.

To our critique group, we will never forget how you helped shape us as writers, dreamers, and readers. We met by happenstance, but now it surely feels like fate because our debut book is out in the world and it's in large part to your support, guidance, critiques, and feedback. Our skin is thicker, our hearts are fuller, and our words are tighter for having met you. Thank you, Cynthia, Jamie, Bethany, Coda, Haley, and Danielle.

To the Oklahoma Romance Writers Guild, thank you for the hard work from your leadership, the opportunities to gain invaluable insight from your members, and the priceless workshops/panels you have hosted that helped teach us about the many facets of being authors. We look forward to our lifelong membership.

To our editors, thank you for helping us shape this into the book we wanted it to be. As we hold our dream-come-to-life in our hands, we hope you remember that you specialize in helping dreams come true and that is a beautiful, precious thing.

Last but not least, thank you to the haters. To the ones who believed we wouldn't do it, or listened with judgment as we talked about our dreams. Nothing motivates two aries women more than someone thinking they can't do something. Looking forward to chatting about book two.

ABOUT THE AUTHOR

Best friends and co-authors, Nadia and Tate do everything together—from playing board games to camping to finishing each other's sentences. What began as a fun story for their friends has grown into a shared adventure: writing.

While they write together now, both Nadia and Tate each have over a decade of writing experience. Nadia has been crafting stories since 2006. Her love for storytelling began at a young age, inspired by her aunt's romance novels. As an avid reader, she found escape from small town life through books, whether contemporary or fantasy, and now she hopes to help others do the same.

Tate began writing in 2014, using it as a way to cope with the loss of her mother. Though her mother had tried to spark a love of reading in her as a child, it wasn't until adulthood that Tate truly fell in love with books. Now, she can't stop reading or writing, and she enjoys a wide range of genres from urban fantasy to thrillers. She knows her mother would be proud of how far she's come.

Together, Nadia and Tate bring unique perspectives to their stories. The Summoning of Mages is the first book in their Saint Elias series, perfect for magic-loving fans seeking an escape from reality.

instagram.com/authornadiatate

facebook.com/authornadiatate

tiktok.com/@authornadiatate

www.ingramcontent.com/pod-product-compliance
Lightning Source LLC
Chambersburg PA
CBHW020931310726
48980CB00007B/719/J

9798999847263